Rise of the Cinder Fae

Undying Raven Press

Retailer Paperback ISBN: 979-8-9898388-0-6

Retailer Hardcover ISBN: 979-8-9898388-1-3

Instagram:

authorwhitneydean

Dustjacket by bookishaveril

Paperback and eBook by procastle_studios

Interior art by coconutsnow.art

for my fictional, feisty, and bloodthirsty little witch.
you aren't even real yet it's because of you my dreams came true.

Preface

This is a Dark Fantasy Romance.
It contains mature, violent, and graphic situations.
While it is a Slow Burn Romance, it does ignite multiple times
with on-page, open door detail.
Content warnings can be found on
whitneydean.com

Playlist

- Sand by Dove Cameron
- I Remember Everything by Zach Bryan feat. Kacey Musgraves
- What Was I Made For? by Billie Eilish
- My Love Mine All Mine by Mitski
- Lose Control by Teddy Swims
- Bad Things by Nation Haven
- God's Game by Dove Cameron
- FRAGILE THINGS by Dove Cameron
- Make Me (Cry) by Noah Cyrus, Labrinth
- Don't Blame Me by Taylor Swift

Prologue

Elora

An icy breeze swept my dark blonde locks over my shoulders as it tried to push through the thick and hazy heat pouring over Ashbury from the mountains. Beaded dew clung to every inch of my exposed skin like drops of sweat, causing every movement to be accompanied by discomfort when I tried to shake it off my hands.

I fidgeted with loose threads in the pockets of my knit shawl while looking out over the vast, outstretched dips of the dry and ashy valleys. The once plentiful, once erect kingdom of Ashbury was shrouded in a permanent red—a dark maroon that resembled the color of dried blood, but the dreary shade held memories of bloodshed. But now, the painted sky comes from the insurmountable heat that molded the rocky mountainsides within the valleys into coal.

A process that took hundreds of millions of years was reduced to weeks because of the Cinder Faeries—a powerful species unlike any other and spread throughout lands far beyond. From stories I had heard from the gossipers in our small town, the faeries hold majority authority in other kingdoms but not ours.

Enslaved to a neighboring kingdom, the faeries exchanged coal once a month for the bare minimum in return. Upon the condition of providing warmth for the Kingdom of Pumpkin Hollow, Ashbury received protection from its standing army and not much else.

Keeping the faeries pleased included keeping the inhabitants of Ashbury alive, but that was a generous description. Breathing would be a more proper term if someone were to ask precisely how we benefitted from the bargain sworn many moons ago.

Our forced gratefulness to the King of Pumpkin Hollow while my people lived in rags on the street, begging for coins to purchase a stale loaf of bread, was laughable. My shawl was barely more than threads over a moth-eaten, ripped smock. I couldn't remember the last time I had fresh garments, the laundered scent of a happier home gone and buried long ago.

The daily comfort of standing on my terrace every morning while listening to the sounds of my forlorn kingdom ironically fulfilled me. From where I stood, distant chatter in town was drowned by the grunts and shouts of the faeries littered amongst the mountains.

From my terrace, I watched the faeries reach the peaks of the mountains to perch on ledges, spirals of smoke coming from their hands as they molded and shaped rock fragments. The crisp air thickened with the smell of fire, drying the chilly air and surrounding me with staunch humidity.

I could not spot the men who guarded them, but I knew they lingered close by, armed with arrows in case a faerie tried to escape. A quarter of a century had passed since the winged creatures arrived in Ashbury, and six had died from attempting to flee. Only forty remained.

Stationed along the inner wall—a stone casing built not long after their arrival—men watched and waited with instructions to pierce the wings of any faerie brave enough to leave, but years had passed since the last male tried. Since that day, the faeries had accepted Ashbury as their home.

The heat radiating from their powers was potent enough to warm Ashbury and keep it in a constant haze of boiling-hot temperatures, combating nature's elements. Sometimes, it became nearly suffocating to be near the mountains, but it had become a warmth I relied on. With full meals a rarity, I constantly shivered and barely had enough skin to cover my bones. But when the sun rose, their heat became a blanket.

Without the faeries, Ashbury would be useless. The protection given to us by the king would be snatched away, leaving what remained of our town defenseless against attacks—of which there would be.

Tiny and barely a speak on maps, Ashbury wouldn't be given any attention if it wasn't for a rumor that left us vulnerable. Somehow, word had spread that within our mountains, a spring awaited, but not just any typical spring.

An enchanted spring.

Only it wasn't a rumor.

The stigma surrounding Ashbury as a desolate, fallen kingdom eventually stopped wanderers from seeking it out.... Well, anyone who stumbled upon our faeries was shot with arrows and burned. When travelers stopped returning home after visiting, it prevented others from trying.

But I had located the spring.

While exploring the caves within the smallest mountain, I stumbled upon it and nearly into it. Azrea, one of the female faeries and my closest friend, confirmed the water was spelled with vast and ancient magic and needed to be consumed for the spell to work. But when I tried to take a drink, she stopped me. Fae magic was potent and deadly for humans to consume, and while I had plenty to long for, no amount of power seemed worth dying for.

Shielding my eyes with one hand, I used the other to wave at Cedric as he settled on a ledge near the peak of the tallest mountain. But beside him, shoving Cedric behind him and out of my sight, was Dolfe—the unofficial leader of the Cinder Faeries and his brother.

He barely tolerated me on his best day.

My lack of wisdom at twenty-one compared to their hundreds of years of knowledge irritated him. Distracting Azrea from her duties enraged him the most, and he never hesitated to scold me. And perhaps his brother trying to court me since I turned eighteen three years ago didn't help.

Dolfe reprimanded him each time he found us together, but it didn't stop Cedric from seeking me out each time I visited. Since Cedric was considered a winged warrior, the idea of courting a mortal woman was blasphemous. Faeries could bond with humans through the exchange of blood, something I found to be disgusting and an archaic tradition, according to Azrea.

But fate could also *gift* bonds.

Only two males weren't bonded, and Cedric was one of them. He made no secret of his interest in me, though the idea of giving blood and taking him to mate did not sound appealing. But knowing I would never be deserving of a warrior did not prevent me from genuinely enjoying gawking at Cedric.

Their graceful movements, the strain of their corded muscles, and the sweat glistening on their skin were undoubtedly beautiful and mesmerizing. And since I was one of the only humans allowed near them, I benefitted daily from their unfathomable allure. But much to my dismay, they weren't allowed to touch me because of my father—the fallen Prince of Ashbury.

Before my birth, King Jasper brought war to Ashbury and overpowered our legion quickly. After disassembling our monarchy, which included my grandfather, he tore down cottages and manors, only leaving ours while the rest of our people were forced to start over. My father remained in the king's good graces because he betrayed my grandfather. Yes, he was a traitor to his home—his birthright—for reasons that remained unknown, even to me.

Because of his loyalty to the wretched king, my stepsisters and I were invited to the royal ball in Pumpkin Hollow the following evening. I dreaded it immensely and continued to search for a reason not to attend.

No one else in Ashbury was invited—something I wasn't looking forward to explaining when inquiries inevitably came. Questions would arise when others learned that my stepmother was fitting us for new gowns. I hadn't asked how she planned to pay for new dresses, aware of our financial state since my father's death six months ago, and she wasted no time at all spending what remained of our fortune.

I had worn the same dresses for months.

Sometimes, I dreamed of freeing the faeries and escaping with Cedric to find more and live our remaining days amongst them. Cinder Faeries were only a fraction of the others that existed—supposedly. I hadn't received solid confirmation from Azrea, nor had I ever left Ashbury to learn for myself.

The faeries were annoyingly tight-lipped about their species.

My closeness with Azrea was my only saving grace to being allowed near them. No one else was allowed to cross the valleys, but I had grown up around them as the Keeper's daughter. And it was nearing time for my daily visit, but first....

PART ONE

the pauper

One

I tense upon entering the palace manor's dusty, once-lavish library. My stepmother and stepsisters lounge on the chaise, spaced perfectly enough to not leave a spare inch for me. I roll my eyes and clear my throat, drawing the attention of the more obnoxious stepsister, Dolly, who blanches at the sight of me breathing the same air. "Ellie finally decided to come down from her ivory tower!" she goads, dramatically throwing an arm over her forehead while dangling her head from the worn armrest.

I wonder what would happen if I stomp on it. A swift kick to Dolly's forehead might make me feel better. I am not at all bitter that if it wasn't for my traitorous father, I might've indeed spent my morning in an ivory tower. Our manor is large and belonged to my grandfather. He didn't want to erect a castle because he wanted to appear equal to the people he reigned over, but the empty space mocks us now.

As fraternal twins, the stepsisters are foul in personalities and physicalities. Unblessed by Aphrodite, their noses slope downward and are uncentered between their squinted eyes and misshapen brows. And their lips resemble their mother's—thin and venomous.

"Elora, run along and brew some tea." My stepmother flicks her wrist toward the kitchen adjacent to the library.

Biting my tongue, I drag my feet from the library to the kitchen. Since my father's death, I've become the wench of the household, performing all the chores needed to keep the manor from crumbling into the dust we breathe.

After my mother's death fifteen years ago, my father, Harry, wed Regina. I still struggle to understand what he ever saw in her. While my mother was kind and beloved amongst our people, Regina is *not*.

Newly widowed with two young daughters, Regina wasted no time saddling my father. His proposal sealed my unfortunate fate of being bound to such deplorable women for the rest of my life. To my credit, I did try to get along with them. It wasn't until my father's death that I realized my efforts were all for nothing.

Regina loathes me.

I tidy the kitchen while waiting for the tea to brew on the cast iron stove. Teabags aren't rare in our market, but *flavored* tea is. Tiny drops of honey suffice well enough to add sweetness to the bland tea, even though it's nearly gone.

Since I'm the one to cook each meal, I often wait to wash dishes until the pile grows too large. Exhaustion often partnered with my obsessive need to clean the manor to maintain the reputation we no longer have, leaving me to rarely fall asleep before the midnight hour. It doesn't leave much time for market shopping to replenish simple pleasures like honey for our tea.

"Ellie!" Regina calls.

The snap of her fingers was muffled from the other room but clear enough for me to mutter obscenities at the beckoning. Ellie, the nickname my mother gave me, sounds like poison from the three of them.

After pouring four mugs to the brim and sacrificing honey in my tea, I balance a tray on my hip and return to the library, taking great care not to spill a drop. Regina and the twins haven't moved, but Regina scowls after noticing the tray.

"Instead of filling our cups to the top and leaving extra, you selfishly poured a mug for yourself." The worst quality about

Regina is she always believes every word that comes out of her mouth. "Dolly and Daffodil spent their morning in the freezing library while you remained in your room. You should think about someone other than yourself."

My *room* is the attic, which remains wide open to the elements all year. Regina promptly moved me upstairs upon my father's passing and gave my former room to Daffodil. And while the attic remains heated from the faeries, it is not immune to the brisk autumn winds in the early mornings and late nights. I consider myself lucky not to have expired from the heat this past summer.

Autumn is the most tolerable of our seasons, but if I continue each day without food, it will be the one to kill me—not that it matters.

I extend the tray to Regina and lower my gaze as she retrieves the three fullest mugs, then place the tray on a nearby table to retrieve the last mug. I would have been satisfied with a quarter's mug worth. Having a full one is a gift.

I inhale the tea while ignoring the growls of my empty stomach and pretend the cup is filled with nothing but the nectar of bees instead.

"It would be nice if Ellie baked biscuits," Dolly sighs.

"She can, my sweet." Regina holds Dolly's mug while she rises from lying across Daffodil's stomach. "Ellie—"

"We do not have the ingredients," I interrupt before Regina can demand I *run along* again. "Since you dismissed our maids and servants, I haven't found time to restock our pantries."

I should have mentioned aloud that it would have been helpful if we had the funds to do so. Our pantries have never overflowed with food, but we always had what was needed. Both pantries remain bare now.

"Perhaps if you spent less time relaxing...." Daffodil takes a sip from her mug and gags. "I detest strong tea!"

Wasting the little honey we had left on Daffodil was a mistake. "I sweetened it with honey, Daffodil."

"Horrid lies you tell," Daffodil replies, sticking out her tongue after another sip. "You purposely tried to poison me!"

If only I could.

"Why have you come here, Ellie?" Dolly stands and extends her arms above her head—as if she's exhausted from being able to sleep in my warm bed every night. Drops of tea spill over the mug's rim and splash on her worn yet recently shined shoes. "I doubt you know how to read."

Dolly knows I learned to read as a young girl. All three women understand that I could outwit them if quizzed about essential things, so they often insult me instead. I would readily challenge them if I could be sure Regina wouldn't toss me in the cold from overstepping.

I bite my tongue so hard I taste copper. "I need to speak with Reg—" I catch myself. "Stepmother."

Insistent that I refer to her as that, not mother, and not by her name, Regina always chooses every demand maliciously. Regina's favorite way to keep me controlled is to remind me of her position in the household as sole executor over my future and the possessions my father left us.

Harry left us shockingly little compared to what I believed we had, but I wasn't one to take a roof over my head for granted.

Regina dismisses her daughters to bathe. Unfortunately for me, we will be fitted for dresses for the impending royal ball this afternoon. As Regina's least favorite daughter, I don't understand why I'm being forced to attend unless it's purely to remain in the king's good graces since he supposedly respected my father.

Waiting until the twins slowly leave the library, taking their time to annoy me further, I place her mug on the empty tray. "Stepmother, I would again like to plead that you do not force me to attend the ball tomorrow evening."

Regina's replying, unamused scowl is the only answer needed, but I continue despite it, "It is most likely to allow us to meet the man the king has chosen to take the permanent position of Keeper of the Faeries. I do not want to meet him."

Regina places her mug beside mine on the tray and clasps her hands on her lap. "Ellie—"

"I must insist," I interrupt bravely. "The king didn't even bother to attend father's life celebration. The invitation is his pathetic attempt at an apology, though I don't honestly believe he cares in the slightest that he missed it—"

"*Elora*," Regina emphasizes.

"He has no interest in our well-being!"

"Enough!" she shouts. "What you are saying is treasonous. The king cares greatly for the inhabitants of Ashbury."

I extend an arm toward the library doors. "Go outside! Viable businesses no longer exist. Our bakery with stale croissants, a vendor to sell and distribute the leftovers he provides from Pumpkin Hollow, and the hobbyists selling knickknacks they've made hardly prove he cares at all!"

I drop my arm and ball my hand into a fist. "I have traded croissants for buttons with hungry children in town. And since none of us are allowed to cross the bridge to search for work in Pumpkin Hollow unless we dare to brave the miles of rocky valleys without food or water, I have a difficult time believing he is not just *waiting* for all of us to die."

I pant, the outburst surprising even me. Regina drums two polished nails against her lips—another luxury she refuses to live without—and studies me with slightly narrowed eyes.

Dull, yellowing, hazel eyes.

My mother's eyes were bronze, matched her favorite season, and never glared at me.

Regina has a perpetual glower.

"What do you suggest we do?" she asks. "With your father's death, our own power is slipping from our grasp. I do not wish to carry the burden of every person in Ashbury while mourning your father."

I resist the urge to laugh. Regina was dressed in black for three days before returning to her distastefully bright dresses, ready to trap another man into marriage. But with Regina nearing sixty years old with two grown daughters, her prospects are nonexistent. At twenty-eight years old, Dolly and Daffodil have passed what our realm considers a marriageable age for women, leaving me as our only hope for a decent bloodline.

"I don't know," I sigh.

The grin on her thin lips gives me pause. "Perhaps...."—she trails off as her grin widens—"....There is something to be considered."

I shudder when Regina stands and tilts her head slightly. Unlike the twins, Regina is polished. She might have been beautiful when young, but not anymore. My mother believed that if a woman was beautiful within, the outer shell would reflect it.

Staring at Regina, I agree.

Winding her hair so tightly on her head every morning has receded her hairline and stretched her skin thin, angling her sharp cheekbones into triangular blades. "If you wish all to be well with our family and Ashbury, there is a solution, Elora."

At the mention of my full name, my eyes widened. I should walk away and never return until the idea brewing in Regina's mind drowns. Nothing but evil lives within the sharp corners of her grin.

I try to keep her voice steady as I ask, "And which solution is that?"

Regina tucks a curl behind my ear. The tender touch does the opposite of what she intended—it does not calm me but tightens my insides. Unblessed by the gods, my height is quickly swallowed by most, but I rarely notice anymore. With Regina, the way she swallows me is comparable to a fisherman and his catch.

It never ends well for me, but Regina always leaves satisfied.

I pick up my mug of tea, hoping the warmth will calm the trembling Regina's unwavering stare is causing.

"The prince is returning to Pumpkin Hollow for the ball," Regina says.

I would like to know what that has to do with me or finding a way to help everyone else. I hardly know anything about the prince, uninterested in listening to the stories of his grand adventures and trysts like all the others.

And your point is?

"You will make him fall madly in love with you."

Two

I nearly choke on a sip of tea, coughing through an almost unsuccessful swallow—embarrassingly close to drooling liquid on the scuffed wood floor. I misheard her, surely. But Regina's expression conveys no sign of humor as she waits for me to try and breathe again. If I die, she will have no one else to shock with her outlandish ideas.

I rasp, "I'm sorry?"

Regina takes my mug from my hands and returns it to the tray, leaving me to again stand awkwardly. "It is quite simple, Ellie. You aren't fond of someone else taking your father's place as Keeper, correct?"

"Well, I—"

"And the prince is not promised to anyone and hasn't been for some time. Living like this is exhausting." She waves her hand through the dusty air, gesturing toward the bare library shelves and rundown furniture. "Our fortune is gone. The men in this kingdom are...."—her nose slightly wrinkled—"not suitable for someone of my stature."

"Stepmother, I hardly doubt the king will want me—"

"You are a princess, are you not?" she interrupts again. "You have royal blood. You will provide a strong heir."

I can't stop twisting my fingers, and my hands grow slippery from rising moisture. "I am no more royal than Daffodil," I argue. "My grandfather's reign was short. He founded Ashbury. One generation does not a royal make."

Regina clicks her tongue in disagreement. "We still reside in the palace manor. Whether you admit to it or not, you would be in line to be queen if not for the invasion of Ashbury. It would reflect well on the king's graciousness to betroth his heir to the fallen princess. And it would return power to our hands."

"I do not care for power—"

"You care for food, for warmth, for your *people*."

I pinch my lips. I could argue more, but a faint knock on the manor's front door halts the conversation entirely. We haven't received visitors since my father's death. Our elaborate front porch collects as much dust as the air inside the manor.

I ask, "Perhaps the seamstress is early?"

She sighs deeply and gestures for me to exit the library. "You won't find out by standing there. I certainly cannot answer." She smoothes her tight bun to tuck in stray hairs. "It would be inappropriate."

I roll my eyes as I spin on my heel to leave the library and hastily walk through the dark hallways. The once-colorful walls are bare from having sold all the collected artwork for enough coins to purchase groceries. Without any portraits on the walls to absorb noise, each step of my worn boots against the wood floors echoes behind me.

My heart thunders when I pause just before the front door. The last time I opened this door to a visitor, I learned my father had died. A courier delivered the news the afternoon of his death to inform us—with no sympathy, mind you—that Harry had a heart attack on his way home after spending the morning in Pumpkin Hollow with the king.

It would have been treasonous to inquire about the suspicious timing, but my father was healthy for his age. As if anticipating our curiosity, the courier had also delivered a handwritten note from the king's physician confirming the cause of death. His ashes in an intricate box accompanied the letter, along with the verbal condolences of the king, spoken by the young courier. The last time I ever talked to my father was the morning of, and I wasn't given a chance to say goodbye to his physical self.

He lives wherever souls go at the end now.

I jump at the sound of another knock and blink away the memory to open the windowless door. The same courier stands on the other side. He immediately studies my ripped smock and scuffed boots before clearing his throat and readjusting his stance to look me in the eyes.

"You have been summoned by the faeries," he says.

I snort. "I've been *summoned*? I'm there every day."

"If you'll follow me," he continues, extending his arm toward the mountains, "I will escort you."

I cross my arms. "I don't need to be escorted. As I said, I am there daily. I don't need permission as the Keeper's daughter—"

"*Former* Keeper," he emphasizes. *Prick*. "One faerie, in particular, has fallen ill and claims only you know how to properly mix the tonic required for their healing."

I do not know what he means, but I play along. In all the years I've known the faeries, none of them have shown signs of weakness. "Ah," I say, rocking on my heels. "Right, of course. I have what's needed just inside. If you allow me a moment, I will collect it and follow you."

I wait for no confirmation before closing the door and scurrying to the kitchen. I open pantry doors and scour cabinets for anything auspicious enough to pass as a healing tonic for creatures so powerful that they could squish me with their fist before I stand and laugh to myself. It seems juvenile that anyone would believe I could heal them, but someone must need me direly enough to create that lie.

Placing my hands on my hips, I lick my lips as I spin slowly around the kitchen. The honey jar sits on the counter, mocking me with its nearly empty bottle, with the lid off. It's better than arriving empty-handed. I secure the cap and slip the jar into the pocket of my waist-apron.

❧

Despite his apparent curiosity, the courier doesn't inquire about the contents of the jar bulging awkwardly from my pocket. If he requests I pull it out, he will know I'm a fraud, but we arrive silently at the guarded entry of the mountains. Like the stone casing keeping the faeries inside, the iron gate keeps the people of Ashbury out. Two of the king's men stand at the barred fence morning and night, armed with swords.

"I take my leave from you," the courier says with a slight dip of his chin in the way of goodbye.

I ignore him. I'm displeased with his haughty demeanor. Couriers in Pumpkin Hollow are a dime a dozen. I've met many throughout the years. Carrying a satchel and wearing colors of the crest does not make him any more special than the crossing-sweepers. In fact, I prefer them to him.

The screeching hinges send chills barreling down my spine as I wait for one of the guards to unlock the iron gate. Unbeknownst to any man here, I keep a key to the lock hidden in the bottom of my boot—just in case a day ever comes when I'm prohibited from entering.

I curtsy and paint a grateful smile on my face while he holds the gate open. "Thank you," I say sweetly. I wish to maintain a decent acquaintance with as many of the king's men as possible in case it proves in my favor someday.

I'm welcomed through the gate without a word or a smile, but I've become used to that. The guards weren't particularly kind to my father, either, and most likely expected me never to return after his death, but the faeries are the only family I have left. Unless I am forcibly removed, I will continue visiting.

Most faeries hover above me as they mine the rocky mountain

peaks, but I beeline toward the cave belonging to the only faerie who would *summon* me.

Sweat gathers on my forehead from the heat radiating off the faeries above me. On days like this, when I'm covered in perspiration and can hardly breathe from falling ash and stifling heat, I wish the guards *would* send me home. It's hard enough not to feel physically inadequate around the faeries on a good day. As I am at this moment, I feel downright ghastly.

Comparing any human to the faeries is laughable, whether that person is attractive or not. My mother was considered beautiful, and I inherited the bulk of her genetics, but I still possess some of my father's characteristics, like his hair color.

Matted to my scalp from sweat, my dark blonde curls have clumped together. My hair is always unmanageable, but adding the smothering humidity has spiraled the ringlets and knotted the ends. I broke my years-old hairbrush weeks ago and haven't been able to replace it yet, so I walk around looking unkempt most days.

Since Ashbury lives under a constant cloud of haze and smoke, my skin remains pale and flushed cherry-red when experiencing emotion of any sort. The starvation has eliminated most of my curves, which further prohibits my ability to gain the attention of any prospective spouse, leaving me rather scrawny and frail.

But I do have my mother's almond-shaped eyes. The irises aren't bronze as hers were, but the color of melted chocolate. Hidden within and only visible in sunlight lived golden flecks—freckled and splattered. My father used to pretend I had treasure within the irises and would chase me around the manor while pretending to be a pirate searching for gold.

The game he used to play with me died when my mother did.

❧

I enter the dwelling where Azrea and Dolfe reside, smirking and crossing my arms. Azrea lounges on a thin cot with a lazy smile. I retrieve the nearly empty jar of honey from my pocket and toss it to her. "Your healing tonic, m'lady."

Azrea tips the jar upside down with an amused grin. "It's nearly empty, Ellie. How will this save me?"

"It's a gamble you'll need to take, I suppose."

While she opened the lid and scooped out the remaining honey drop with her finger, I plopped down on the cot beside hers. As vital as the faeries are in our realm, they needed to be given proper accommodations after arriving. Instead, they were placed in dwellings within the mountains.

"You saved me from a rather uncomfortable conversation," I say, slipping the jar back into my pocket after she finished. I will eventually refill it when I have the coins to do so. "I would have been here soon. You didn't need to send a courier for me."

She dismisses me with a wave of her hand. "I like to be reminded of the control I have left, even if it's only for a drop of honey. Tell me about the conversation."

"Regina," I sigh. "Isn't that enough?"

"Hardly," she replies, leaning back to rest on her palm.

I'm not ready to repeat it aloud that my stepmother wants me to seduce and wed the prince. "Are you ill, Azrea?"

She rolls her eyes but does not immediately deny my inquiry. "I am under the weather today, but I'm well. Dolfe is annoyingly cautious with my health."

I scowl in jest. "How could he care so much for his mate?"

Sitting up, Azrea takes hold of my shoulders and shakes me—gently to her, aggressively to me, but she often forgets the potency of her strength against my feebleness. She apologizes when I wince from the pressure and releases me but urges me to resume the subject I want to change.

I cover my face with my hands, my voice muffled when I say, "She wants me to wed the prince." I drop my hand, the distaste for the idea clearly written in my expression. "We're attending the royal ball tomorrow night. She thinks it's as simple as him seeing me and solving all my problems."

Her eyebrow lifts slightly. "What problems?"

I gesture dramatically over my body. "Aside from the apparent starvation, you mean? The health of my people, the longevity of Ashbury.... I'm assuming the reason for her idea is fortune restoration, though she didn't mention it. I would not put it past her to place her needs before the needs of others."

Azrea is not a warrior, which leaves her without wings to block eavesdroppers from listening to our conversations, but her power does supply the ability to build invisible barriers of air around us, allowing temporary invisibility. Each time she encloses us, the air tightens into a heated cocoon of torture.

"There must be another way to keep our conversations private," I groan, pressing my cheek against the cool inner wall of the dwelling. It is my only reprieve during visits.

"We don't need one of the king's men to hear of this, Ellie. I fear you would be forcibly removed and taken to the castle for punishment."

"I do not interest them enough to care about what I say," I mutter.

She glances outside. "But I am cautious of them, Elora. I have to be."

Them—the guards on patrol, armed with bows and arrows, willing to maim any of the faeries if needed.

I remember the day a male tried to escape years ago. I had visited the faeries with my father the day coal was scheduled to be delivered to Pumpkin Hollow when a male attempted to flee. He reached the mountain's peak before arrows pierced his wings. He tumbled down the mountain, and the fall killed him.

My father sent me home and didn't return until late that evening. It was the first time I had ever witnessed him weeping.

Azrea rests her hand gently on my knee, drawing me away from the tainted memory. "I must be honest with you. I do not see the negative connotations of her suggestion. If we explore Regina's suggestion and the prince does fall in love with you, it would guarantee the longevity of Ashbury."

I blink, then pinch my arm.

She slaps my hand away. "What are you doing?"

"I must be dreaming!" I exclaimed dramatically, pressing the back of my hand against my forehead. "The starvation must've taken me away because surely you are not implying that I should consider this foolish suggestion."

"Elora," she sighs with an eye roll. "It would reflect poorly on the king if you became princess again and he left your home impoverished. And it would guarantee your role as Keeper, would it not?"

I slide from the wall to the cot, melting into the airless warmth and convinced I'm hallucinating. "The king only tolerated my father because he helped destroy the monarchy. You know, the one his father built? Why would the king reinstate my title as *his* princess now?"

"For his son? I believe a father would want to bring his son happiness." She takes my hand. "I am simply helping you see both sides, Ellie."

I frown. "It's risky, Azrea. Rumors surrounding the king heavily detail his intolerance of those who commit treason...."

She grins slyly. "What's treasonous about a girl wanting to fall in love with a prince? He would never know."

"Gods," I mutter. "It seems so juvenile. Trusting Regina with anything of this significance is dangerous."

She scoffs. "Do you believe she'd risk her chance of living lavishly once more? Her reasoning might be selfish, but I think it might be beneficial."

The idea of marrying the prince is vile, but the reasoning does make sense—as much as I hate to admit it to myself. "I suppose it would be a sweet irony to become their princess, but it's *me*. I wouldn't have the slightest idea of how to ensnare him. And he doesn't have the best reputation."

Her eyes light with amusement. "And you're inexperienced, I know. But you are beautiful, Ellie, even without a hairbrush."

Compliments of any kind make me fidget. My mother poured

affirmations on me daily, but my father rarely continued after her death unless something I did reminded him of her.

He *tried* to be a good father to me for a short time.

Since he worked for the king, he was awarded substantial wages. A tutor from Pumpkin Hollow visited our palace manor twice a week when I was a girl to give me proper education and etiquette lessons. He hoped to bring me to the castle one day, but that day never came, and I stopped wishing for it.

I squeeze Azrea's hand. "Meeting the prince wouldn't bring any harm. If I succeed, the marriage wouldn't need to be forever. And I certainly do *not* have to like him."

Before saying anything else, she places a finger against her lips just as a shadow invades the cave. Outstretched wings and a tall silhouette fill the entrance and block any light from entering, infiltrating Azrea's barrier and dwindling the tight cocoon of magic into nothing.

She can separate us from everyone *except* her mate.

With his arm propped against the arched opening and his glare pinned to me, Azrea stands to face him. The tension between them is often suffocating and *always* apparent.

"I was just leaving," I lied.

Beautiful and mouthwatering, Dolfe stands nearly seven feet tall with red hair to his shoulders, corded muscles against ivory skin, and hooded eyes of red and gold.

But that isn't why he intimidates me.

It's the mammoth-size wings, blacker than a raven's feathers, stretching taller than him and wide enough to fill a cave. His wings are the largest set of all the warriors, giving him the most power over the rest. And the bastard knows it.

If anyone is more arrogant than the prince, it's Dolfe.

All Cinder Fae have distinct similarities—red hair as bright as cherries or dark maroon and gold or red eyes with flames illuminating the irises. Their skin colors are all beautifully cohesive and vary between ivory, bronze, and ebony.

Imprisoning them was a mistake.

Bragging about their beauty and magic and giving them rooms in the castle would have been more fitting, but the king did not want anything to outshine *him*.

Azrea pulls me up and winks before turning away from me to goad her mate. "Couldn't live without me longer than a few moments, brute?"

His neck strains from tension, revealing the excruciatingly sharp structure of his jaw.

"I'll leave you to it," I mumble, slapping Dolfe's hard chest with my palm and instantly regretting it when a string reverberates through my wrist.

The barrier returns behind me as I exit.

The little information I've pried about mates from Azrea included the intensity of their bonds. The guards learned it when they tried to prevent Dolfe from touching Azrea long ago.

One of the king's men lost his hand and never returned. My father somehow managed to save Dolfe from paying with his life for his crime, and the incident created an unspoken rule between the faeries and the men who guard them: allow any bonded pair to *reconnect* when needed.

Desiring someone enough to crave their touch multiple times a day is not something I ever imagined myself finding. And if I decide to agree to this plan of marrying the prince, I doubt I ever will.

Three

Stalling before returning to the manor to discuss Regina's unsettling idea in length placed me in a field of dying daisies—fitting for the only eternal resting place in Ashbury. Upon death, people in Ashbury are burned by the faeries, and the ashes are spread amongst soil that smells of ash and bleeds red when the sky opens for rainfall.

Bunching my aged skirt in my hands—a hand-me-down from Dolly—I sit on the dry, cracked field and pluck a brown stem from the ground. The soil in our valleys isn't potent enough to grow crops or plants, and the ash littering the air quickly suffocates any plant or flower trying to spout.

Before Ashbury fell to the king, our resources came from Hogsfeet, the kingdom across the river, far below a cliffside. King Jasper took their lives, ransacked their merchant tents, and left the castle to rot. It has decayed from neglect over the years.

On the rare occasions when the sky clears, turrets can be seen from the cliff's edge, but searching the castle is forbidden. If caught by one of the king's guards, the perpetrator would be cited and dragged back. Like the faeries, we are never allowed to leave our crumbling kingdom.

If someone does somehow manage to flee, the elements would handle them. In my twenty-one years, no successful story of someone finding life outside of Ashbury has graced my ears. King Jasper would go to murderous lengths to prevent anyone from discovering the faeries.

After my father's passing, fear spread quickly throughout our town. Without his protection and closeness to the king, we waited for the day the king would cross the bridge to finish what he started a quarter of a century ago. He doesn't need any of us.

Why keep us alive?

Revenge could lead to the warping of my soul, but marrying the prince might be worth the sacrifice of my independence if it will offset the betrayal of my grandfather, our once reigning king, by his own heir.

Our people suffered while we continued to benefit from my father's traitorous actions. I did not understand as a child how wrong it was for us to live lavishly while others struggled to feed their families. But Nemesis enacted her justice against us as we faced the consequences of his decisions shortly after his death.

The marriage would only need to last until an annulment or until Ashbury could be restored. After living through years with Regina, how much worse could a prince be?

I sigh aloud at my own naivety.

Aside from his age of twenty-eight, my knowledge of the prince doesn't extend past the rumors. He has been nicknamed a womanizer since women never last more than a night by his side, though many have tried. His travels are always assumed to find a princess, but his standards must be unreachable for him never to return with one by his side.

Aside from my loyalty—if only for my time spent bettering Ashbury during the proposed schemed marriage—I have nothing to offer him.

"Ellie?"

The deliciously warm voice pours over me. Shirtless and antagonizing with his blatant beauty, Cedric stands beside me, his cropped hair swaying in the sticky, humid breeze. The heat, combined with the muggy air from incoming storms on the horizon, melts off him and onto me.

I shrug off my shawl. "Cedric!" I beam. "Does Dolfe know—"

"No," he interrupts with a sheepish grin, lowering to sit. "He is still tending to his mate."

I wrinkle my nose. "Right, sure," I say as if I don't have questions about what *'tending to'* entails. "How long have they been bonded?"

He flicks his gaze up toward the sky in pause. "Ah.... For as long as I can remember."

"The *obsession* never fades?"

He chuckles warmly. "Not with bonds."

"And you've never.... Felt that way?"

"Not with another faerie," he replies in a low murmur, giving me nothing else, though I wouldn't know how to respond if he had.

Even as a male of few words, I never dislike his company. Dolfe works hard to keep us apart, so shared moments between us are few and far between. And flirting with him is a guilty vice. The distraction it gives us makes our reality slightly less dreary.

With Cedric nearly as tall as his brother, I remain as mismatched against him as I am with the rest. His muscular frame would swallow me whole if we ever did more than graze *accidentally*.

And that description doesn't include his wings.

Tucked in and brushing the soil, the tips of hundreds of black feathers shift with the wind. I've spent many evenings studying them when close enough to watch Cedric work, but Dolfe always prevents me from touching them.

That never stops the *longing*.

Membranes spread throughout each wing like tangled webs of color and beauty—violet and red interweaving to create magenta netting.

I bite my lip, expecting Dolfe to pop out and scold me for even considering asking, "May I?"

With a grin, Cedric nods. "I wondered when you'd ask, Ellie."

Smiling and trembling with excitement, I move to my knees. I brush the muscles shaped like steel bars that connect his wings to his back, molding perfectly to his skin, almost as if sewn to his spine. He stills but does not stop me.

I ask, "Do they hurt?"

He shrugs. "The wings are heavy but never painful."

"They're beautiful," I sigh.

He spreads his wings. Their length easily outstretches my height and more, and he laughs when I extend my arms to compare our size. Lunging for the left wing, I lift the feathers to trace over a thick, membranous vein. Corded and delicate to the eye, the sturdiness beneath my fingers surprises me. I itch to take a needle to the thick strings of yarn his veins resemble and weave a portrait of the beauty I find in them.

He twists to remove the wing from my touch. "They're sensitive," he snarls painfully but lightens when he notices my fear. "You didn't hurt me, Ellie. It's a different kind of sensitivity."

The desperation to explore what *that* means is always squashed by trepidation. Instead, I touch the tip of his slanted ear. "Are these? Azrea never allows me to touch hers."

He gently lowers my hand with his. "Yes."

I sink to my shins with a dissatisfied sigh. He flips my hand over and traces the lines in my palm. I ache for more serene moments between us that aren't tainted with the unknown. "Tell me how I can help my people, Cedric. Tell me what to do. I'll give you a kiss if you do."

He throws his head back in laughter. The melodic sound is joyous and soothing. "Will you?"

I hum my approval. "Please?"

He applies pressure to my palm with his thumb. "Ah, Ellie, I'm not a leader. I'm a fighter."

I tilt my head. "Can you tell me where you came from? Do you have stories of wars before you came here?"

Someone could find us and reprimand him for being with me.

We aren't far from the mountains, but the faeries can only stray a certain distance when they need a break. I have no doubt that one of the king's men is watching us closely, armed to harm Cedric if needed.

The faeries are considered predators, and assumptions would be made about us if they haven't been already. Aside from their pride and frightening powers, the faeries are gentle creatures. If either of us would prey on the other, I would jump on him. He has centuries of practiced self-control, whereas I am growing desperate to experience pleasure. And gods, he makes me sore to even look at. Touching him....

I stop all my thoughts there.

"I have stories, Ellie." His tone becomes distant and sorrowful. "But they're not memories I want to relive."

I squeeze his hand instinctively from the pain in his voice. "But you made it," I say, though I doubt it will take away the torment of the moments he has lived through. "There's a reason Dolfe reminds me you're a warrior as often as possible."

Cedric huffs a laugh through his nose. "Dolfe's beliefs are traditional, but they're not mine." His bright eyes stare into my dark ones. "You're not less than me, Ellie. Don't let him make you believe otherwise."

Heat creeps up my neck, and I can't hold his intense gaze. Instead, I look down at our locked hands. "I can't live hundreds of years, Cedric. Our story would only be a moment in your lifespan. I am just a lowly human."

He flattens his palm against mine. His hand is nearly twice the size of mine. "I've been around many species in my years, Ellie. I would take a lowly human over them any day."

Prying never seems to get me anywhere with any of the faeries, but I silently wonder about the other species. I read many books before selling them and often doubted how fictional they were.

"Ellie?"

I wait with a smile, lifting my eyes to his once more.

"Watch the clouds with me?"

We lay on the rocky soil, our hands still touching but our fingers never interlocking, and watch the blood-red clouds inch across the sky until they disappear into clear blue across the bridge.

My heart chips away at the realization that this peaceful moment between us could be the last if I decide to sacrifice my freedom for the prince.

❧

I delayed as long as I could.

Cedric wasn't called back, but we knew Dolfe would seek him out soon. I said goodbye with a hug, not realizing how my cheek would be pressed against his bare chest, and his amusement was teasing me about how my red cheeks matched the color of the sky.

Even if what I feel for him isn't the all-consuming love between mates, I will at least leave this world one day having felt *something*.

It is late afternoon before I return to the manor, having stopped by the market on the way home to purchase a stale loaf of bread and refill the honey jar halfway. Upon my arrival, Regina was waiting for me in my father's study, further souring my mood.

He used to spend every morning here, pouring over personal and Ashbury's finances. Though he wasn't the prince anymore, he was still given the responsibilities of one, which is why I constantly have to remind myself that the king wouldn't have had a reason to have him killed. Harry was in charge of estimating the costs of pails to deliver across the bridge into Pumpkin Hollow. They are costly to acquire for residents, and the king is constantly adjusting the price of each one based on pounds per pail. My people always receive whatever is left—usually no more than fragments.

Sometimes, Azrea sneaks a few into the pockets of my waist-apron, but I can't carry too many without drawing suspicion. Regina caught me giving one to loiters in town once, then promptly scolded me for not thinking of how cold Daffodil and Dolly must be.

One day after Harry's death, our manor was raided by a

handful of the king's men to obtain the financial statements. It was unnecessary since I would've gladly handed them over.

The study contained portraits of my mother until his death, and then Regina quickly tore them up or shoved them inside his desk drawers. After she retired to bed one evening, I tried to reclaim one of them, but she discovered it the following day. Hardly anything in the manor remains of my parents.

And now, the smell of his cigars has been replaced by her stench—corpse lilies.

"Stepmother," I greet plainly, holding up the tote of groceries. "Bread and honey."

She dismisses me with a flick of her wrist. "If you agree to my plan, we will have the luxury of food and drink once more."

Despite her trying to paint it differently, I knew this scheme had everything to do with her. I will only agree to it once I hear precisely what her plan entails.

"Close the door, Ellie. As much as I love my daughters, they do not keep secrets well."

Fighting the urge to agree aloud, I spin on my heel and close the door. I learned firsthand how inept at secret-keeping the twins were during my twelfth year when I tasted a piece of my yearling cake before a gathering.

Regina had thrown such a fit that evening that she tossed the entire cake into the garbage and sent my friends home early as punishment. My father had saved for months to put together a decent soiree for me—had even invited the prince and princess, not that they bothered to show up—only for it to be ripped from my hands.

I blamed myself for years.

My father hid a piece of cake and split it with me in the dark long after Regina retired to bed. It was a secret we kept for years.

And now, here I stand, plotting with her.

Sitting on the edge of a worn leather chair, I gesture for her to speak first. My legs bounce with anxious jitters. Partnering with Regina is not something I ever imagined doing, but going to irrational lengths to save those who deserve to be freed from the king is a risk I must take.

Clasping her hands together with elbows propped on the desk, her gaze turns serious. "The prince is unattached," she begins. "He has been for quite some time...."

I interrupt with, "Was he once attached?"

"There are only rumors," she replies, annoyed by my interference. "The king is anxious for a grandson to ensure a long line of succession. Like your grandfather, he was and is the first king of Pumpkin Hollow."

"He's doing a wonderful job," I mutter.

"*Elora*," she emphasizes, "enough."

I purse my lips, refraining from informing her that childbearing is out of the question. Children are the furthest thing from my mind, nor do I anticipate being with the prince.... *Physically*.

Her face twists into a sneer. "You resemble your mother." Her way of saying, *'you're not hideous to look at.'* "And you were raised properly by a respected man. King Jasper hasn't seen you. I believe he will find you as"—she pauses to clear her throat—"enchanting as your father did."

I don't smile, but I do warm from the compliment, as backhanded as it might've been. "If I do this, do you believe it'll help Ashbury? Help our people?"

"If you do this correctly," she answers, "and restore our fortune, keep us in the king's good graces, and remain the prince's beloved by providing an heir, then yes."

An heir will not happen, but the rest could be possible. "And what happens if I'm caught? How would he punish me? Father spoke of beheadings, and I have heard something about the King's Collection—"

"All gossip," she replies with a tight smile, though part of me believes she wants him to take my head. "He will simply banish you back to Ashbury, perhaps take our manor and everything we have left. It will certainly ruin your father's reputation...."

I stop her from continuing with, "I understand."

"If required to make further appearances after the ball, you will choose a dress from Dolly's wardrobe. You cannot arrive...." She dramatically waves across the length of my body with her hand.

I roll my eyes. The prospect of wearing dresses brighter than the sun nauseates me, but I have to take what I can get. "Very well. I will attempt to finagle the prince into marriage or a courtship—"

"You will do much more than attempt, Elora." As she leaned forward, the room suddenly became chillier, even with the solitary window raised to allow warm air. "The survival of your precious Ashbury depends on your success."

❧

The seamstress writing my measurements in chalk across her arm has sewn my dresses since I was young. She always speaks loudly about how my mother was her muse when Regina is nearby. As evidenced by her snippy tone when addressing the three other women, she cares nothing for Regina or her daughters.

Their measurements are hurriedly jotted down, so her focus can shift to me. Daffodil and Dolly stomp out of the sitting room from the snub, but Regina remains.

Her trust in me is nonexistent.

"I have the most beautiful fabric for this occasion!" Susannah, the seamstress, exclaims.

Short and plump, she reminds me of a mouse with her pointed nose set between eyes too close together, especially when her nose always wrinkles when writing numbers. But she is the only one left in Ashbury still interested in my well-being.

"Our darling Elora is attending a royal ball!" She pats my backside, unashamedly comfortable with me from knowing me my entire life. "Your mother would be so proud."

I genuinely smile. My mother loved grand things, even if no balls or banquets were held in Ashbury after the war. She would sometimes speak of attending them as a young girl and detail how my father courted her by following her around the banquet halls. I used to lay in her closet—it was a luxury to have one at all—and stare at the bright tulle skirts above me, hoping to one day attend a ball of my own. Now, I wish to be excused from one.

But Susannah is right: my mother would be proud. She would have been the one to dress me, brush my hair, and perhaps allow me to dab a bit of color on my cheeks despite the risk of toxins and being referred to as *controversial*. My mother was a natural beauty, but even she could not stop her curiosity when cosmetics were smuggled across the bridge.

"We need the dresses by late afternoon tomorrow," Regina says, turning her nose up at the mention of my mother. "I do not pay for tardiness."

Sighing, I mouth silent apologies to Susannah. A professional seamstress for so long will likely spend all night preparing the gowns. No threat is needed.

"They'll be here," Susannah responds with a bite. "Please tell me you have soap, Elora! You can't arrive at the castle with unwashed hair!"

I wince when trying to brush through the knotted ends with my fingers. "I have to use it sparsely, Susannah. I haven't enough—"

Regina clears her throat. I snap my mouth shut. Of course, she doesn't want me babbling about our lack of funds. No one is aware that Regina spent our fortune on frivolous things. "Elora will be washed and ready for the ball," Regina replies. "I will style her hair myself."

Oh, *gods*. My chances of snagging the prince's attention are slim to none already.

Susannah sympathizes with me, her faltering grin a replica of mine. "All will be well," she promises, rolling the aged measuring tape. "Your dress will make up for it."

I bury a laugh and guide Susannah out of the sitting room and front door, falling against it with a sigh after her departure. I am not looking forward to this and cover my ears when Dolly and Daffodil squeal their excitement.

Absolute imbeciles.

Spending the last evening before possibly changing my life will not be wasted on them.

I climb the spiral staircase to the attic and fall to my bed, coughing from the dust that follows. Mountainside ash floats in the breeze and always lands in my attic. I often remind myself to close the balcony door every night, but the taste of the fiery air gives me hope that while I might be trapped, I'm not entirely alone. Azrea and Cedric aren't far.

And freedom is always a wish away.

But the dreams that followed me in sleep weren't as light-hearted as my last thought before drifting. Morose and dark, fire and war cries filled my chest with terror. But the screams of warriors as their wings snapped and tore drenched me in sweat.

Four

Stretching my arms over my head, I pull and tug at the ache in my bones from a restless night's sleep. Nightmares never plague me, yet the more I fear for our future, the more deeply entrenched the fears become in my mind. And I can't say I care for the visions that accompany them.

A pail of stagnant water, dark from the residue left by coal, is grimy against my skin when I splash my face. The bucket is large enough to stand inside when I need to bathe, but I rarely have time or resources to scrub my body.

What I wouldn't give for a warm bath. And *soap*.

I stare into the black water on edge, frazzled and second-guessing the entire scheme.

Me? Seduce a prince?

I've never even been *kissed*—not in a way that matters. Every boy in town fears my father and his connection to the king. The possible repercussions of fooling around with the daughter of a man in the king's favor didn't give me many options.

How can I convince a womanizing prince to marry me *and* keep me around long enough to gain what I need *without* having his children?

I pick up the pail to pour the mucky water over my entire body when the water ripples. Confused, I set it down and kneeled to press my ear to the floor, listening for movement downstairs. A figure landing on the balcony causes me to jump and kick the pail of water sideways. My chance of bathing later has evaporated quicker than a breath unless I find enough coins to purchase a new bucket of clean water.

"Azrea," I breathe, confused. "How are you here? *Why* are you here? Did anyone see you?"

I stand when she points to the sky, watching Dolfe shoot across and hide behind the clouds until he gracefully lands on a ridge. "He could have been *seen*, Az. He could've been shot—"

She smooths my knotted curls. "Dolfe knows when he can cloak himself with the clouds. I don't have long, but I wanted to see you." She wraps her arms around me. "I imagine you're fretting about meeting the prince this evening."

"*Fretting*," I scoff. "Fretting is one word to describe my absolute panic, sure." My attention splits between her and finding something to soak up the spilled water. "He might not even show up this evening. And I'm hoping he doesn't. Because I can't. This could risk everything. If he finds out? Gods. It might do more harm than good!"

She gently shushes me. "Elora, you can't be forced into this. I am not asking this of you." Before assisting me with the spill, she closes my balcony door. If anyone sees her, her absence will be reported. "I haven't been entirely honest with you."

"Shocking," I mutter, dropping the rag. "None of you ever are. I don't even know where you come from—"

"Everywhere," she states bluntly. "We come from all over, Ellie. We move every quarter of a century to somewhere new—"

Every quarter of a century.

I shake my head, quickly interrupting, "No, Azrea, you did not come here to tell me you're leaving."

Her expression softens. "Sit with me, please."

Her long legs stretch across the floor as we sit on the damp wood, but I am too panicked to care. "You can't leave," I reiterate. "I can't lose you. Ashbury can't lose you."

She takes my hand with hers. "Ellie, I am with child."

My mouth dries.

"I was not ill yesterday," she continues softly, "I am taking great care of my body. Fae children are rare, and we've wanted this for a century. It has finally happened."

As my gaze lowers to her stomach, my eyes fill with water. Different emotions flow through me like a wild river, and all I can think to ask is, "But why?"

She laughs breathily in return. "I imagine you're inquiring why Fae children are rare, but I don't have a satisfying answer. It is how it's always been. I believe it has something to do with the powers we're gifted by fate. Immeasurable powers and centuries-long lives wouldn't be as enticing if given to every creature."

"Sure," I whisper, blinking, unsure what to say.

She places a hand on her stomach. "Ellie, there are reasons we move so often, but I need to be near Fae healers for this child. When a Fae child is born, faeries feel a shift—not just Cinders, but all. There are faeries, Ellie...."

When she pauses, I lift my eyes to her face, struck by the lingering fear in how her gaze drifts toward my balcony. And her voice lowers when she adds, "Not all are kind. My child will be sought. And I cannot risk you or anyone else in Ashbury when that happens."

Tension in my neck from holding the weight of my town's survival causes my shoulders to sag. "I don't understand, Azrea. Are you saying that someone will come for you if you stay here? Who? If you leave, we will remain just as vulnerable. The king only has use for us if you're here to provide coal...."

She winces slightly, and then it dawns on me.

"That's why you're encouraging me to follow Regina's plan," I say slowly. "You believe if I wed the prince, you'll be able to leave Ashbury without consequence to those left behind."

"Yes," she admits.

I stand and pace, trying to shove a hand through my hair. I can't shuffle through every thought, let alone imagine my life without Azrea. The faeries are the only family I have left—all that remains of my childhood. If they leave, I will have to bear each burden alone.

I ask, "Why can't you bring a healer here? Why can't you burn whoever seeks out your child? You have powers; the king would gladly help you eliminate—"

"It is not as simple as that, Ellie." She stands, only to sit on the edge of my bed to watch my pace across the attic. "More faeries arriving at Ashbury would only mean more are forced to work for the king. Your father tried for years to give us more of a voice, to allow us the freedom to live amongst you, but he was unsuccessful. It would risk too many lives for us to stay."

"You are risking lives by leaving!" I shout.

Her gaze falls to the floor, and I sigh. "Azrea, I am overjoyed for you and Dolfe. Truly, I am, but I do not believe for a moment that you expected me to accept this."

"I meant to inform you yesterday," she replies, "but when you arrived upset and told me of what Regina said, I thought...." She trails off with a shake of her head. "I thought it might aid both of us."

"There is nothing either of us could do to soothe your absence in my life, Azrea." I desperately wish I had cold water to wash away the burning, rising cry in my throat. "But I do understand that leaving is what you feel is necessary. I would like to request time, though."

"Of course," she replies, confusion evident in how her eyebrows draw together. "Ellie, we wouldn't leave you in a lurch."

I nod because, logically, I know that. But it doesn't make their plan easier to swallow. I know she didn't come here to inform me of a betrayal, but that is what it feels like.

"I suppose I really must try my hardest to impress the prince this evening," I sigh, looking down at my dirty nightgown and soot-covered feet.

Azrea stands seconds before the balcony door opens, revealing

Dolfe waiting on the other side. After all this time, their ability to sense one another nearby still baffles me.

Azrea places her hands gently on either side of my face and mesmerizes me with her fiery eyes. "You will be the best aunt," she whispers with a heartfelt smile.

I murmur in a sad reply, "From afar."

"You'll never be without me, Ellie." She tugs me closer. "My soul will collide with yours again, whether we stay or go."

With each second that passes, the risk of them being here and away from the mountains increases. So, I watch them depart from my balcony, finally allowing tears to slide down my cheeks as they disappear behind the clouds and land on a ridge on the tallest mountain, their hands alighting with fire to mine as if they never left.

My determination to come out of this scheme victorious was admittedly torn between helping Azrea and my village, but I selfishly want her to always stay by my side. I need to try to understand their fears.

Tonight has to be for the survival of Ashbury.

If only I had the confidence to succeed.

My gaze moves to the smaller mountain nestled in the center of the larger two and barely visible from where I stand on my balcony, and a dangerous, impulsive idea blossoms.

And I decided to follow it.

I'm panting by the time I reach the smallest mountain, having worked entirely too hard to avoid being seen by any of the faeries. The men at the gate allowed me to pass without question, but the difficulty was ensuring Azrea didn't spot me before entering the hollow tunnel that hid the spring within.

Luckily, the faeries moved on from this mountain long ago. After they arrived, their strength nearly collapsed the smallest mountain. The ground shook and rumbled so loudly throughout

Ashbury that the king sent an entire brigade of soldiers in fear of an attack occurring. According to Azrea, that wasn't even a drop of what their magic indeed was. All three mountains would come tumbling down if they used the full scope of their cinder magic.

Sometimes, I wonder why they didn't. They could easily wipe us off the map, erase King Jasper from history, and prevent any faerie from being under his control again, but they haven't. They haven't burnt us to a crisp or fought back, and it baffles me. They've been forced to work until sundown for over twenty-five years, and for *what*?

Faeries are revered in other kingdoms—so much so that stories have even reached the town gossipers in Ashbury. Why stay in a place where so much neglect has been forced upon them?

I could ask myself the same question.

Wiping the sweat off my forehead with my sleeve, I silently remind myself that I'm out of clean water at the manor and will need to try and find a way to bathe. Otherwise, I will meet the prince covered in ashy residue and smelling like sweat and disappointment.

After we located the spring a year ago, we surrounded it with tall rocks to prevent others from finding it. And now, I groan and curse as all my strength goes into rolling the stones away to reveal the glistening water that lives behind them.

I nearly collapse on the ground after the last rock is shoved far enough to the side to allow me to see the spring. And I gasped, just as I did the first time we discovered it. I expected it to have dried up, but the water remained bright blue and glowing. The air above the clear-blue water glitters with old magic, the softest bells ringing from the depths. It isn't large, situated in the shape of a crescent moon against the inner wall of the cave, and can hardly be considered a body of water by its size alone. But something about it was enough to bring in travelers seeking it out.

Admittedly, after finding it with Azrea, my curiosity wasn't potent enough to inquire about it. A well-known clump of gossiping ninnies loitered in town and often discussed the rumors associated with it, but I didn't have the interest or energy to engage them in conversation. I wish I had now.

Azrea was blunt about the risks of human consumption. Even the tiniest sip could kill me. But my task of ensnaring the most eligible bachelor in surrounding lands would be much easier if I had faerie magic flowing through me.

"You can do this," I encourage myself, ignoring my clammy palms as unease takes over. "It's just a little magic."

Retrieving a small cup from the pocket of my waist-apron, I kneel and shakily scoop water into it. The chiming of the invisible bells increases, filling the cave with echoing rings of enchantment and decorating the dark walls with ripples of a twinkling blue glow. I consider that a sign of incentive.

Placing the rim against my lips, I squeeze my eyes shut and tip it back, but the sharp call of my name from the entrance causes me to drop the cup back into the spring.

Sighing, I look over my shoulder at Azrea. With her eyes narrowed on me, the red irises look harsh against the gentle blue on the walls. "What are you doing here?" she asks.

"Well, I—"

"I should've known you wouldn't take the news well," she mutters as she approaches. "But I never would've imagined you would do this. Ellie, I told you what could happen if you tried to drink from this spring!"

I drag my fingers across my forehead. "How did you even know I was here?"

"Please," she huffs with an eye roll. "I picked up on your scent when I came down for a drink of water. I followed it to find you here. Not only are you risking your life by trying to drink this, you could get trapped in this cave. Rocks fall from the peaks constantly, and you *know* that."

Grabbing the collar of my smock, I dip my head to smell it. "I have a scent? What does it smell like?"

She pulls me up by my elbow. "Go home, Ellie."

I step back after tearing myself free and shake my head. "No. If the outcome of tonight leads to the beginning of freedom for my people, I cannot go...." Trailing off from my thoughts, I look down at my soot-covered body. "As this. I need help. I need assurance that I can be who the prince needs me to be, at least long enough for a betrothal."

"Faerie magic is not something that fades with him," Azrea explains. "This spell is ancient. Not even I can break through the wards guarding it to learn where it came from."

I wrinkle my nose. "Wards? It's guarded?"

She carefully places her hands on her hips and combs through her words before replying, "Long ago, faeries cast spells. Enchantments, if you will. And each spell had to be warded to prevent the power within from falling into the wrong hands."

I raise an eyebrow. "I feel like there's more to *that* story."

"I am not giving you a history lesson, Ellie."

"Do *you* cast spells?"

She releases a deep sigh, chock-full of irritation and impatience. "Not for a long time, and I can't read this one."

We peer into the illuminated spring, unable to see the bottom. It seems endless, and the pull I have toward it is indescribable. "I don't think it'll harm me," I say.

"Just...." she trails off and runs a hand through her impeccably perfect locks of hair, hardly damp at all from the mist that permanently lives on her skin.

The cinders appear perfect even when they're not.

As if my life isn't already unfair.

She crouches and stares into the water, her eyes moving perfectly with the ripples as if speaking with the water. And I am just as mesmerized with her as with whatever lurks beneath the surface. It isn't any wonder why Dolfe is so protective of her. Though every cinder female is undoubtedly attractive, there's an allure about Azrea that isn't replicated in any of the others—an elegance that seems too good for this place. I cannot fathom how beautiful her child will be between her and Dolfe's undeniable beauty.

Azrea shivers. "The wards are too strong, Ellie. I cannot learn when it was created or what rules were set forth."

"*Rules*? You never mentioned rules last time!"

She skims the surface with her fingertips. The glow brightens and chases her hand, the bells chiming in a soothing flow. "I didn't realize we would return to discuss you drinking this. Magic requires balance, Elora."

She dips her finger into the water, but nothing changes. "Wishing magic spans hundreds of years—older than me. I haven't seen an enchantment spell in many lifetimes, but the caster of a spell always leaves an order."

I pinch the bridge of my nose. "An order?"

She nods, peering up at me. "You'll need to give it something in exchange."

Five

I curse under my breath. The idea seemed brilliant before I knew I would have to give something back. I didn't have anything *to* give. And besides, what would it want from me? For gods' sake, it's an enchanted spring full of faerie magic.

"Can you tell if it's safe?"

Azrea flicks her eyes toward the cave ceiling, blowing a strand of hair from her face. She is exasperated with me, but I'm running low on options. "Your body wasn't created for power, Ellie. It will never be *safe*."

"Azrea!" A daunting and deep voice roars.

The water ripples in response.

Grimacing, she turns to face an enraged Dolfe and mutters, "I should've put the fucking shield up."

"It's my fault!" I shout, stepping forward. And honestly, he won't be surprised by that. "I came here alone."

Dolfe keeps his glare pinned to Azrea—a refreshing change from the one usually cast on me. "Azrea knows better than to tamper with ancient magic." The cave seems ten times smaller with him inside, his fists clenched at his sides and his wings tucked in tight. If he extends his wings, they'll brush the ceiling. "Especially a spell so potent that her powers can't penetrate it."

"I need it," I say. "I have something.... some*one*.... that must fall in love with me. And as you would agree, I am not the most charming person."

Dolfe growls. I flinch at the reveal of his sharp fangs and briefly wonder if he's ever actually experienced eating humans. "Enchantment spells ward against using them for emotions like love, Elora. You can't use them against the will of others."

Well, *fuck*.

"I wasn't going to allow her to use it at all," Azrea argues, her top row of sharp teeth bared in response.

I take a small step away from them.

"She is human," he needlessly reminds us. "If you want to kill her, there are much easier ways. I have a few."

I hold my hands up defensively. "We don't need to take it that far, though I appreciate the kind offer."

"I do not feel threatened by this magic," Azrea continues. "I would've dragged her out of here if I did!"

"Enchantment spells are disguised as friendly, Azrea. That is the entire point of them. They lure you in. You, of all faeries, should understand that."

Her eyes narrow. My eyebrow raises in curiosity.

Dolfe's intimidating glower shifts to me. "Whatever you need cannot be important enough to bind yourself to magic, Elora. It is unforgiving."

"Aw," I coo. "Do you care about me, Dolfe?"

When he answers with a snarl, I sigh. "I won't ingest too much, and I won't ask for anything drastic."

"There isn't need to ask for anything at all," he volleys, stepping closer to peer into the glittering spring.

I don't know Dolfe's history—I don't know *any* of their histories—but the soft blue water reflects beautifully against his red eyes as he searches for the depths. "It is deep," he murmurs, "Strong."

"Yes," Azrea replies softly.

"It is spoken in the old language," he continues.

"Yes," she whispers, "Can you—"

"Yes," he replies.

I look between them. “The old language? Is that the bells?”

I am ignored.

He asks, “How can this be?”

The look shared between them makes me envious of the silent information passed.

After a moment, he finally says, “It can only be broken by consumption. If you drink this, the spell will live within you until your request comes true.”

“That is quite the change of heart, Dolfe.” Logically, I should be more suspicious but am too anxious to dwell upon it.

I lower to my knees and lean over the water, grasping the mug that had floated away. But before I could fill it, Dolfe crouched and prevented me from it. “I do not know what it will ask for in return, Elora. Like Azrea, I do not feel threatened by this magic, but that does not mean it isn’t powerful.”

“I have nothing left to lose,” I whisper, looking from him to Azrea lingering behind him. “Ashbury will be invaded once you leave, and we will lose. The king will search for the spring. If they don’t find it, Ashbury will be forgotten. If they do, I would hate to be here when he makes his wish.”

Dolfe ponders silently before closing his eyes, his ears perking as the bells strengthen and bounce off the cave walls. I remain silent while he deciphers the sounds, worried he might toss me in if I push too hard.

“It was not born from darkness nor cast by evil. Something is there, but I do not believe a sip will harm you. But I must caution you—”

“Please don’t,” I interrupt. “I do not want to be warned. I know you find me naive, but I don’t want to overthink this.”

“What will you ask for?” he inquires.

Blinking, I touch the shimmering haze above the water but feel nothing. “I want to wish for time reversal or the king’s death, but that won’t be allowed, will it?”

“No,” he sighs.

“And I cannot wish for love,” I reiterated, partially annoyed. “I can't wish for you to stay. Then what *can* I use this bloody spell for, hm?"

Azrea snorts.

If I can't wish for something against the will of others, it needs to be something for me.

"Confidence," I whisper.

He runs a hand down his face. "You're risking your life for self-assurance?"

I can't help but smile at his annoyance. "We were not all born with Fae beauty, Dolfe. I am rather plain and have nothing to offer him. I must believe in myself if I stand a chance at drawing and keeping his attention. And it's better than wishing for a frilly dress."

"A spring hundreds of years old filled with a powerful enchantment spell is dwindling down to the confidence of a twenty-one-year-old human," he mutters.

"Dolfe," Azrea scolds. "If she wishes for anything greater, the spell could kill her. It needs to be small."

I shove Dolfe's hand away. "If you'll excuse me, I have a spell to drink." Dipping the mug in the water, I fill it to the brim and pause. "Do I need to say something? Chant?"

"No," Dolfe replies impatiently. "Close your eyes, think of what you want, and drink. And hurry. The guards will notice us missing soon."

I want so many things that I don't entirely trust myself to do this. The temptation to wish Regina and her vile daughters out of my life is strong. And buying food and soap without guilt would be swell.

But I'm not doing this because of what I want.

I close my eyes, place Azrea and Cedric in the center of my mind, hold the happier memories of my childhood running through the streets of Ashbury, and wish for enough confidence to beguile the prince.

Or it could take my heart in return.

Can I wish to *not* fall in love with him?

I'm considering too many things at once.

He asks, "Who is this man?"

"The prince," Azrea replies.

"The *who*? Azrea, no, she can't."

Dolfe reaches for me and says my name twice, but it's too late. The water touches my lips and tickles when gliding down my throat. When I swallow the last drop, the light in the spring vanishes. Glitter no longer hovers above the dark water.

Because of me, something rare and beautiful no longer exists. But then, I think of my wish with slight regret. Can confidence *break*? Or did I doom myself to arrogance for all eternity?

"I didn't attach a condition," I mutter with a sigh. "It has no reason to break."

Dolfe looks absolutely *stressed*.

I glance at Azrea. Should I feel different? Nothing outwardly has changed. I remain in my shawl and ripped smock, my cheeks and eyes still hollow, but I *feel* different.

"I think it worked," I whisper.

Tingling in my toes and fingers spread across my arms and legs. But I startle when something cold floods my mind. Closing my eyes, I watch rippling water soak through a stone wall and drip into a dread-filled room. Cold—everything is so cold.

I drop the mug into the water as my eyes flutter open. Azrea steps toward me when I sway, but Dolfe catches me first with his hand on the small of my back.

I try to shake my mind free of the liquid and blink rapidly to steady myself.

"Take a deep breath," Dolfe instructs. "There is magic living inside you, Elora."

"I'm fine," I assured him, even as the corner of my eyes began to blur.

"You shouldn't have done this," he whispers, frowning.

"You knew," I murmur, but when my eyes fall closed, I hear him curse before darkness swallows me whole.

Black eyes chase me from a dream.

I awaken alone in a dwelling, sweaty and woozy. Covering my forehead with my palm, I slowly rise and look around. I smell *fantastic*, with a body's worth of sweat drenching my clothes and hair. "Gods," I mutter, peeling strands of hair from my face and neck and *out* of my mouth.

From the sunlight pouring in, I'm disappointed that I didn't sleep through the ball. And judging by the grunts outside, I'm still with the faeries. "Az!" I whisper-shout, groaning as I crawl to the opening to peek out.

Raul, the most intolerable-of-all-humans winged male, glances down from a low ridge with a disappointed sigh. "You fucking lived."

I *loathe* him. And partially blame him for the fatigue in my muscles. It's his blasted magic that caused me to lose consciousness.

Chunks of coal land next to my hands and graze the tip of my pinky finger. I hiss and duck into the cave just as a more significant ember lands right where my head just was.

"You did that on purpose!" I shout, thrusting my hand out with a crude gesture.

Azrea appears and crouches, taking my face in her hands to study my eyes.

"I'm fine," I say with squished cheeks. "It was Raul's hatred for me that nearly killed me."

She leans back and looks up, hurling obscenities at Raul. He doubles them in reply.

"Ignore him," she says, tugging my hands to pull me out of the cave. "That's what I do."

"Gladly," I reply, removing my shawl to wrap around my waist. "Gods, Dolfe was serious about the warning. That was... potent."

And I only consumed a few drops of magic. The idea that whatever lived within me wasn't even a taste of their ocean's worth is an overwhelming thought.

She places her hands on my shoulders. "How do you feel?"

Ah, right, the whole reason I consumed the spell—confidence in my ability to see this through. "Um, I feel..." I wrinkle my nose and try to gauge if it even worked. "Capable?"

She breathes a sigh of relief and pulls me into a tight embrace. I ignore the threat of my ribs cracking and try to keep breathing until she releases me, then stretch my arms above my head to straighten my ribcage. "If I die, it might be because of you, Az."

A chunk of coal smacks the back of my head. With narrowed eyes, I slowly look over my shoulder to see Raul hanging from jutting rocks with one hand, tossing another ember in the air with his other.

Azrea shouts at him to leave me alone, but I lean down to grab the piece that hit me and give him no warning before throwing it. It hits him in the jaw hard enough that his smug smirk falls right off.

Azrea shoves me behind her just as he drops to the ground and stalks toward us.

"Raul," she warns.

His palms light with flame. I roll my eyes.

He's one step away from tossing her to get to me when Cedric lands between us and spreads his wings to block me. Raul growls, Cedric snarls, and I try to climb Cedric's back to give Raul a piece of my mind when Azrea claws me off.

"Go home, Elora." She bites back a laugh. "Raul is not the one you want to test your newfound confidence on."

"Oh, I think he is!" I shout, trying to shove past her. "Asshole!"

"Fucking human," he retorts, shoving Cedric's chest before shooting off from the ground to return to his ridge.

Cedric nods toward the guards watching us. "You better go, Ellie." He palms my head in his hand. "I'd miss you too much if you were banished."

"Cedric!" Dolfe shouts from a shelf near the peak. "Off!"

I'm tempted to channel my bravery into kissing Cedric, but

Dolfe *really* isn't the one I want to battle. Cedric steps closer when Dolfe lands before us, looking at me.

"Do you remember anything?" Dolfe asks with the slightest hint of concern in his tone.

I shake my head, bewildered. "Aside from drinking it? No. Am I supposed to?"

Dolfe doesn't reply. "Go home, Elora."

I step away from Cedric with a sigh. "I'll check in when I can. Wish me luck!"

Azrea cleans a smudge of soot from my cheek. "You don't need luck, Ellie. Not anymore."

"Gods," I mutter, wincing from the pain radiating across my skull. Regina pulls strands of my hair so tightly that I'm positive she's ripping hair off my head.

After bathing twice and using the remaining soap, I smelled like vanilla and rose petals. My skin shows no sign of ash or dirt. It's already an improvement. But now, Dolly is insistent I owe her *double* the amount of water for allowing me to use hers.

And if Regina doesn't ease up on my hair, I will arrive at the ball completely bald. "Have you met the prince before?" I ask her, trying to fill the complete silence with something.

I met him once when I was a child. It was only momentarily before he ran off, utterly uninterested in my existence. I doubt he'll remember me this evening.

"Yes," Regina answers sharply. "Prince Finnian is handsome, stringent, and loyal to his father and the crown."

Great. We will have nothing in common.

"I've heard rumors of his womanizing—"

"Elora!" Regina hisses, dropping my hair to run to the door and peeking into the hall. Every servant and maid was dismissed long ago, so the only ears she could protect us from were her own daughters'.

She closes the door before whirling to face me. "If we are going to do this successfully, there can be no doubts about your infatuation with him."

"Sorry," I grumbled, reaching up to salvage what she had made of my hair so far. "I just wanted advice on how to set myself apart from the others. And there *have* been others."

"Of course, there have been others!" She slaps my hands away. "You won't impress him with looks alone. He has traveled often. He's had relations with many women, most of them royals. It doesn't matter if he's a womanizer. You should be grateful if he even looks at you, Elora. If you wed, you need to give him freedom."

I scowl. "I allow him to have affairs?"

"He is the *prince*," she repeats--as if that should automatically give him permission to be scum. "Be on your best behavior, Elora. Do not embarrass me."

"I am not uneasy about this evening," I assure her, even as she wraps my hair in a tight enough bun to guarantee a long-lasting headache. "I know what's at risk if I do not succeed."

"Our entire future," she needlessly reminds me, as if not hearing me at all, "and the lives of your people."

Their lives are already jeopardized, whether I found a way to help them or not. It's purely a result of the spell that the thought doesn't strike fear into me as it usually would. But if my plan fails and the prince hates me, I will remain unnecessarily cocky forever. My usual, anxiety-ridden self is submerged under a pool of certainty, and I'm at war within.

And I have decided I do not care for magic.

I will never touch it again.

Six

"You are ravishing, Elora!"

I spin around, my eyes twinkling from the dress wrapped around me in flowing layers of silvery-blue tulle.

When Susannah arrived at the manor, I was slightly disappointed at the bright, simple dresses in her arms, though I had no reason to be disappointed. Weeks had turned into months since I owned anything new, and I was ashamed when discontentment arose. But when she caught my half-smile, half-frown, she laughed.

Behind her, pulling a large box from the back of her wagon, was her tailor, a boy I had met a few times. Ashbury was small enough to know everyone, but since my father's passing, I had become reclusive unless scrounging enough coins to run errands. Neither of us exchanged pleasantries when he carried the box inside.

He waited in the wagon for Susannah to dress me and fawn over me, much like my mother used to do when we could afford matching dresses. And now, I wore a dress so divine that I wondered if maybe the enchantment had something to do with the way it molded perfectly to my body, pushing up my breasts and giving me the curves I longed for.

Regina left us alone while she tended to Dolly and Daffodil, slipping them into the hideous gowns Susannah was underpaid for. Their choice of colors was so bright that even Susannah muttered something about the obnoxiousness of the designs.

Sleeveless, I shiver without my shawl, but Susannah slaps the back of my hand when I reach for it. "Don't you dare cover up!" she scolds, spinning me around to face a broken mirror. "And for the love of the gods, take down this ridiculous hair."

I bite my bottom lip to stifle a grin as she barely avoids ripping my scalp off while battling with bands and pins placed around my head. My hair is simply too thick to hold anything decent in place. Curls have already fallen over my shoulder, leaving the bun lopsided. "Regina will be upset...."

"Regina can take it up with me," she snaps. She grabs a brush from the vanity and combs the remainder of the knots and tangles, apologizing for every snag.

I shrug it off. My mother used to brush and braid my hair every night after my bath. Having someone who genuinely wants to brush my hair is enough for the twinkle in my eyes to turn into a shimmer. "My dress is beautiful, Susannah. Why did you wait so long to use this fabric?"

It is unlike anything I have ever seen. The skirt is full, the bodice tight, and the straps so thin that you can hardly notice them against my pale skin. Azrea would throw a fit if she saw me.

Susannah sighs deeply while parting my hair in sections. "Before... well, before everything, the war, the dependence on Pumpkin Hollow, we had lavish balls."

I listen intently. I rarely hear stories about life before the invasion, living only on the few stories my mother used to tell.

"I was busy, Elora. Swamped! And I loved every second!" She places the brush on the vanity and strokes the curls with her fingers. "Soldiers ransacked our village. They stole my supplies and most of my earnings. I wasn't left with enough to start over, but a cabinet was left untouched in the back corner of my shoppe."

"With this fabric?"

She gently spins me around to face her. "I never thought I'd have a reason to use it, but I couldn't bring myself to sell it." Touching the tip of my nose with her finger, she smiles. "You look just like her, Elora. She would be proud of you."

I want to tell her how wrong she is—that there isn't anything I've done recently that my mother should be proud of. I'm failing to keep our family name from being dragged through the dirt. And one of my greatest fears is being known as Regina's stepdaughter instead of my mother's daughter.

But instead, I give her a small smile. "I'll find a way to pay you back, Susannah."

She takes my hands. "Nonsense, Elora. I want you to have fun this evening. Dance, eat, and meet someone who will take you away from this place."

I frown.

"You deserve more than this, Elora. More than this place, more than carrying your father's past, more than Regina."

"This is my home," I whisper.

"Elora." Her tone is soft, but her expression is one I've grown to recognize from everyone who looks at me—one of pity and remorse. "It stopped being home the moment the light left your eyes."

Once upon a time, we had a carriage.

It would be convenient if we still had it, but I sold it for coins weeks ago. The king graciously offered one of his carriages for this evening, but only *after* we crossed the bridge into Pumpkin Hollow by foot. And typically, that wouldn't be different from how I usually travel. But holding up a heavy ball gown to not sully the bottom only adds to my hatred for the king.

If the prince is anything like his father, I won't hold my breath for a happy marriage.

Much to Susannah's dismay, I pulled my shawl on before Regina rushed us out the door, but not without remarks about my loose curls. Being short on time meant she couldn't fix my hair, though I didn't doubt she would make me pay for undoing her handiwork somehow.

Looking toward the mountains, I resist the urge to wave. Azrea and Dolfe sit on one of the highest ledges, watching as we near the bridge.

Az waves, but Dolfe *shockingly* doesn't.

"Are the faeries aware of your scheming?"

My smile leaves my face, and I drop my chin. Trusting Regina is risky. And even with Dolly and Daffodil lagging behind us and voicing their complaints, I'm still uncomfortable discussing the faeries with her.

"They know," I reply softly.

A placated smile is her only response.

Silence accompanies us the rest of the way to the bridge. It doesn't matter how often I visited growing up; the sight always elicits the same response: complete and utter awe.

The history of the bridge has yet to be discovered. The king demanded the Cinder Faeries study it after they arrived, but even they needed help deciphering the history of it or what kind of magic lurked within.

Gods'-honest truth, Azrea told me once.

Connecting Ashbury to Pumpkin Hollow is a thick and shimmering glass bridge. It spans a mile long and is only wide enough for a carriage to cross. And thousands of pumpkins lay beneath the bridge, stacked high and boasting different sizes and colors.

The pumpkins never rot or grow but live trapped underneath the glass. Overgrown vines and stems snake around the glass to create a railing while preventing anyone from finding a way beneath it.

On either side of the bridge are tall, steep cliffs. One cliff stretches far enough to reach the mountains, while the other side leads into one of the bordering forests. Every inch of possibility has been explored multiple times, but there isn't a way for anyone to squeeze through and study the giant pumpkins.

Pure, untouched magic lives beneath the glass.

The bridge is King Jasper's most prized possession and one of the reasons why Pumpkin Hollow's army is so substantial.

Dolly pinches her nose. "Gods, I forgot how horrible the smell of pumpkin is!" Her nasal voice is nearly as awful as she is.

"*Almost* as unbearable as Ellie's unsweetened tea," Daffodil agrees.

I grit my teeth and hope the prince will fall so deeply in love with me that he banishes the three of them for all eternity.

Dolly pulls a thread loose from my shawl. "Are you going to wear this gods-awful thing to the ball? Mother, you can't let her! We will already be judged for arriving with the Fae's pet. They already think she's strange!"

There are worse things to be considered.

And I doubt anyone knows I even exist.

I yank my arm free and bite my lip as the thread pulls another loose. It will be no more than a ball of yarn soon. "If we are judged for anything, Dolly, it will be for your—"

Regina claps her hands together to prevent me from finishing the first insult I've hurled toward one of them in months. "Girls, this evening is about family unity."

"What family?" I mutter under my breath.

Regina wraps her hand around my elbow with a tight squeeze. "Our family," she replies dryly. "I do hope you remember that, Elora. You are nothing without me. And I have ways of reminding you if it drops out of your unsightly little head."

I don't miss the threat. "I apologize, stepmother. I am just... anxious." And that isn't a lie. I am very concerned about arriving with this group of tasteless women.

"Tonight will be splendid," she assures, but not for my benefit. Her reassurance is to promise her daughters that *I* won't embarrass them this evening. "I will fill the king's ear with memories of your father while you dance the night away with a man of your choosing!"

She takes the arms of her daughters. "And he loved you so

dearly, girls. He would compliment how divine you look in your dresses."

I frown, brushing my bodice gently. Did my father compliment them? My father stopped assuring me of my beauty completely. Maybe he was pouring his love onto them instead.

Hooves trotting at the opposite end draws our attention, and my breath catches in my chest. An ivory carriage in the shape of a pumpkin awaits us. Unlike the hand wagons in Ashbury, the dome-shaped carriage was hitched to two broad-muscled horses whiter than snow.

"How darling!" Regina exclaims before lowering her voice to add, "A bit much."

It's a *bit* much, but charming.

"Big smiles, girls! And keep them on your faces all night long," Regina demands.

Regina leads Dolly and Daffodil across the bridge while I trail behind with a forced smile. Maybe if I stomp hard enough, the bridge will shatter and swallow them whole.

Being too dense, Daffodil keeps her eyes closed while crossing, tripping over her feet, and lands in a heap on the glass. Dolly doubles over in laughter, earning a glare from Regina as she assists in pulling Daffodil up.

My cheeks heat from embarrassment. The coachman watches from his bench, unamused. His gaze flickers to me, and his expression softens into recognition. The genuine warmth in his eyes makes my smile ease.

Though I'm not proud of my father, I am grateful for the respect he gained from the inhabitants of Pumpkin Hollow. Hopefully, it will earn me some generosity this evening.

"Hello," I greeted him.

"Miss Elora," he replies. "I have not seen you since you were a youngling."

I hum. "I apologize for my daft memory, but I do not remember you."

"You shouldn't." He steps down from his iron-clad casing to

reveal a gold velvet seat. "I was removed from deliveries years ago to begin work on this."

I take in the carefully crafted detail of the carriage. Not only is it shaped like a pumpkin, but it has the same ridges of the shell. Stepping back, I shake my head in slight awe that even the top of the carriage boasts a golden stem.

"The roof can come off," he explains, "to allow sun and air to come through on warm days." His hand taps one of the wheels nearly as tall as me. "And these were imported from a kingdom far away."

"A kingdom that has golden steel?"

He lowers his voice into a whisper, "Well, we painted them gold."

I wink. "Your secret is safe with me."

I brush my fingers across the oval door's smooth ivory and gold hinges. "Did you paint these, too? These materials are unique. I've never seen anything like this."

He beams, clearly proud of his hard work. I imagine building a carriage this large wasn't a simple task. "These are real. Bars of gold were sawed and shaped for all the rest. The king favors uniqueness. We have three in total."

Building a carriage based on a bridge doesn't seem very unique, but I need to keep those opinions to myself. "I wonder where our king drew such distinctive inspiration. I am honored that he sent for us. I will express my gratitude." I slap my smile back on. "My family will accompany me this evening. This is my stepmother, Regina, and her daughters, Dolly and Daffodil."

He does not acknowledge them. "We best get moving, Miss Elora. The ball is about to begin."

Unlike the doors in our manor, the one he pulls open to escort us inside the carriage does not squeak. And the gold, velvety plush benches are more luxurious than any of our beds. The drawn curtains over the small window within the door are made of gold velvet and tied together by a thick, ivory rope.

I would take the inside of this carriage over my ashy attic any day. And that irritates me.

A bridge separates two vastly different kingdoms under *one* ruler. His kingdom has the luxury of pumpkin carriages that surely cost more than a year's worth of food for a family in Ashbury. And when I peek through the curtains as the carriage rolls over a rocky pathway toward the castle, I'm disgusted that even their root vegetables were plentiful, yet *we* provide them with the warmth they crave.

"Elora," Regina warns after noticing my disgust. "It's how it's always been. It will remain so."

"It's awful," I whisper, leaning against the comfortable plush backing of my seat. "We can barely afford bread, and they have gardens all the way to the bridge! That is why we're not allowed to cross!" My whisper grows to breathy shouting, but I can't find the strength to care if I'm heard.

"*Elora*," Regina sighs. "Enough."

Her calm tone only furthers my irritation.

I throw my arms up and face the window, watching in anger as roots and stalks grow in size. My people are starving while my possible future husband lives lavishly without care. The vegetables look overgrown and rotten. His people do not even *need* them, yet we could be cited for crossing to take some.

Protection from other kingdoms seems useless when the one protecting us makes us live in squalor while they benefit from the little magic we have. And gods, flirting with the realm's future king and pretending he's worth more than the soap I can't afford makes my skin prickle with fiery nerves.

"Her face is horrible," Dolly whispers to her mother. "Why did we bring her?"

"Dolly," I snap, eyes narrowing. "Do us all a favor and *shut up.*"

I listen to her shocked protests and pleas for Regina to do something, but all I focus on is the sound of the bell tower chiming in the distance, warning me of my proximity to the arrogant and thoughtless prince.

And I silently vow to never fall in love with him.

❧

I drew the curtains shut for the rest of the ride, unable to stomach any more of their riches. When we come to a stop, Dolly and Daffodil nearly fall out of the carriage from excitement while Regina trails behind them and attempts to calm their theatrics.

I give them a head start, staying hidden inside to distance myself. Regina only takes a minute to glance over her shoulder and snap at me to follow them. Because without me, she stands no chance at making it through the door with their incoherent squeals.

The coachman extends his hand to me—an offer he does not make with the others.

Understandably.

Adjusting my shawl over my shoulders, the one comfort I still have from home, I scoot forward. "I never asked your name, sir."

"Octavius," he replies with a slight bow.

"Pleasure to meet you officially, Octavius." I take his hand, surprised to not be trembling, and almost ask if he will be the one to take us home, but then, words just cease to exist.

I stand frozen, mouth agape, jaw slack, and eyes adjusting to the castle's diamond-encrusted towers, gates, and turrets.

Now, I understand.

The pumpkin carriages match the ones beneath the bridge because the castle looks entirely made of *glass*.

It is breathtaking.

I can't fathom how something so exquisite exists just a bridge away. The glittering turrets on the twin towers blend into the night sky and reflect the stars. The lowered drawbridge is lined with gray, blue, and black pumpkins to match the ambiance of the nearing midnight hour.

And I am the only one noticing such magnificence. The residents crossing the bridge are more interested in the stranger gawking at the castle than the decor, but this is a regular occurrence for them.

To me, it is something I had longed for since I was a child, breathlessly listening to my father while he detailed his visits to this kingdom, but never once did he describe the very magic that mirrored the sky surrounding us.

I itch to explore.

"Are those painted?" I whisper to Octavius, referencing the multi-colored pumpkins.

He chuckles. "Enjoy your evening, Miss Elora."

I should allow myself *one* evening to play my favorite childhood game of make-believe. I could pretend I won't spend only an evening here before returning to a cold, empty manor haunted by memories.

"Ellie!" Regina yells.

I tear my eyes away from the castle. The silver heels Susannah lent me echo off the marble bridge as I try to catch up but pause at each distraction like a toddler in the wild.

Above us, scattered windows boast exaggerated balconies with glass doors and terraces, rounded iron railings encasing them. And stacks of pumpkins are visible from the ground.

Each terrace has them, except one.

On one of the highest balconies, out of the moonlight and hidden in darkness, a man stares down at the crowd filtering inside. The whites of his knuckles show while grasping the railing, his chest and arms bare and ridged from muscles. And for a split second, he looks directly at me. Even from where I stand, I notice the bright blue of his eyes.

Any further details of his face or hair are hidden in the dark, but his gaze holds annoyance.

I don't know if it's for me or the event about to unfold within these glass walls.

But I can't linger.

I glance over my shoulder as Ashbury is shrouded in maroon from the dwindling sun rays, longing for one last look at Azrea and

Dolfe on the ridge. Compared to the liveliness surrounding me, our fallen kingdom, indeed, does seem forgotten.

I can't forget the reason I came.

Despite how much I might want to pretend to be the princess from the wooden castle my father gifted me as a girl, aside from the enchantment within me to make it appear like I could live this life, this disguise won't last.

It will fade just as I have.

I will always be nothing more than an outsider looking in.

Seven

Standing on the terrace and hidden from the gaggle of familiar faces below, I watch the abundance of fluffy dresses cross the drawbridge. The invitees have become so used to these events that the exciting chatter has ceased altogether, and something bordering boredom and entitlement lives in their expressions and haughty stares.

How inconvenient would it be if the bridge came up and all of them tumbled into the water below? My suggestion of keeping it stocked with savage beasts is never taken seriously, so the worst that could happen is their dresses would be ruined.

Another grand ball thrown in my honor—specifically for me to find a bride—is not how I want to spend my evening.

Unfortunately, my father's captain thwarted my attempt to leave Pumpkin Hollow beforehand. He was waiting for me on the outskirts of our land, listening in amusement when I listed off every reason why I should not be subjected to another night of poking and prodding, yet escorted me back like a child.

Now, I stand here, ignoring the person shouting my name from the hallway. I'm not dressed yet, though it's my responsibility to welcome guests into the castle. I've already met all of them, and none ever hold my interest, so wasting my time on useless chatter is pointless.

"Honestly, Finnian."

I sigh.

My sister, Irina, always finds a way into my private quarters. The amount of times my locks have changed never matters. Irina always manages to get what she wants—a luxury awarded to the younger sibling of an heir.

Responsibility and Irina don't mix.

"Mother will insist you wear a shirt, as do I."

I ignore her. "Why are you *here*, Irina?"

She leans over the iron railing of my balcony, following my annoyed glower to the crowd filtering inside. "You didn't tell me you were home, Finn."

My knuckles whiten around the iron. "Arrived this morning, learned of the ball, and tried to leave again." Staying away from Pumpkin Hollow as often as possible is a habit of mine. "Jasper anticipated my escape and had men waiting for me on the outskirts."

"That wasn't an apology."

I fight off a grin. "Sorry."

She huffs a breathy laugh at the insincerity. "It's one night. One more night to add to the dozens, and then you can return here to your cave and drink to forget."

My mother decorated my cave and boasted far too many trinkets and mementos from childhood. I rarely spent time here, but that never stops her from adding more each time I leave. All I need is a bed and an alcohol cart, but sharing that with her once managed to double the jackets in my wardrobe.

"Until the next one," I mumble. "These won't stop until I've wed, Irina."

She frowns at the truth. And as we watch women hurriedly shove through the doors to spend another night trying to snag my attention, the silence between us says enough.

I must choose someone to stop the madness.

"It doesn't have to be for love, Finn." She places a hand over mine. "We witnessed that growing up around Jasper and our mother. They tolerate one another."

"Maybe I don't want to be the same as our father, Irina." I slide my hand from underneath hers and cross my arms over my chest. "Maybe I don't want to only welcome my wife into my quarters at night to give him a grandson to torture with traditions and...." I trail off with a hollow sigh.

"Everything else," she finishes. "I know, but I don't believe you have a choice."

It's a needless reminder. I've never had a choice. As the first-born son, the crown prince, the one standing to inherit and lead this kingdom one day, and the man to continue keeping the faeries controlled, my fate was decided the day my mother became pregnant with me.

But that isn't what keeps me up at night.

I was born to rule, given the best tutors, trained in the king's guard, became a ranking officer, and could lead in my sleep. Having to provide an heir stops me from wanting to move forward.

"I could abdicate." I glance at her with a grin. "I could give everything to you."

She breaks into a laugh. "You would never see me again."

I offer my position to her constantly as a running gag between us, but I would never place this pressure on my little sister. She faces enough of that with Jasper's daily reminders to find a prince to wed. One has tried to visit her multiple times, but she conveniently disappears for the length of his stay.

If she ever leaves, my only ally will be gone.

Irina, though maddening, as all younger sisters must be, is the only one who has been with me through everything. She vets the women I might consider but always ends up frightening them. She isn't threatening at first glance, but her eyes—feline, topaz eyes under long eyelashes—chip away at the falsehood each woman has built.

No one can lie to Irina. One conversation with her and every woman is suddenly unsure if they want a future with me.

Being twenty-four, she's nearing the age to be considered too old to wed, but being the sister of an eligible bachelor keeps her viable. It's not a law for women to marry before twenty-two, but my father highly encourages it. And if Jasper tells you to do something, you risk your head if you don't.

Loud squealing from the courtyard grabs our attention. In a blend of headache-inducing bright dresses, two grown women skip across the bridge, their nasal voices carrying through the crisp autumn air. Behind them, dramatizing each wave as if she were the queen, an older woman trails in an equally distasteful dress.

I lean forward. "Who the fuck are they?"

Irina squints. "I don't recognize them."

Behind them, a woman with dark blonde curls bouncing over her shoulders has her head tilted up, her lips parted from what I assume is an admiration of the castle.

It isn't until her wide eyes meet mine that I pause and hold her stare. I've never seen her, nor does she appear to belong in Pumpkin Hollow. And when she turned her head toward Ashbury, I sighed when Irina burst into laughter.

"He invited bumpkins from Ashbury!" she exclaims.

"Fuck me," I mutter, shoving a hand through my hair. "Does he believe me to be *that* desperate?"

Irina gleefully skips into my quarters, throws a silk shirt at me, and chooses a jacket. "This should liven up our evening, indeed! Who knows, Finn? The one in the bright teal dress looks just your type."

Ignoring her, I fasten the buttons of my shirt and catch the jacket before it whacks me in the face. Though the silk shirt is plain, the coat she chose is not. It's my least favorite—a fact she knows—and embroidered heavily across the lapels. And with the interior lined with thick velvet, being in a crowded ballroom is unbearable.

"I don't want this—"

She clicks her tongue and wags her finger. "If you arrive in anything less, Mother will demand you return and change. I am saving you a trip."

Shrugging the jacket on, I curse under my breath. "The trip back is what I look forward to, Irina."

Rising on her toes, she adjusts the collar and fastens the bottom two buttons of my waistcoat. "Come on, Finnian! I'll stay right beside you, but this evening will be different. I *feel* it."

I arch a brow. "You spend too much time with Bohemians."

She shrugs. "We never know which ones might have known my mother, so I'm nice to all of them."

She often tries to liven up the rumors surrounding her. Irina looks nothing like our mother or me. She's petite with golden skin and black hair, compared to my beige skin and dark brown hair. With her topaz eyes against my bright blue, the validity of her title has been questioned many times.

And because of the rumors, Irina stays hidden—not by choice. Jasper often voices how unique she is, and he loves nothing more than having something others don't, but he also cares far too much about what others think of him. Because of that, Irina's life remains barren unless she's asked to travel or attend formal gatherings.

She's become skilled at disguising herself and wandering off into the night.

But Irina is my sister—simple as that.

"He keeps his affairs short for that reason, Irina. Less risk. You belong to our mother."

She points to her nose with disgust. "At least I know Jasper is my father."

"You're my sister, Irina. Stop speaking." I point to an unopened bottle of whiskey on the alcohol cart near my bed. "You drink half. I'll take the other. Only then will I accompany you to this ball."

Gasps and quiet claps, all the regular, dull grandeur, followed my entrance into the ballroom, decorated far too obnoxiously for such a common occurrence. Portraits painted of our family hang between each window, the smiles Irina and I had as children disappearing as we grew older, but the top of each picture is draped with colorful materials to match whatever outfit we were forced into that day. Beneath the windows are stacks of faux-black and silver pumpkins, occasionally mixed with the legitimate blue.

My father has women specifically employed to walk around the room and ensure none of the black or silver paint is chipping to reveal the orange or white pumpkin shells. Sometimes, when boredom overcomes her, Irina peels the paint off and draws attention to them—only so Jasper will end the entire night from embarrassment.

Servants walk around with trays full of undoubtedly pumpkin-flavored treats, but guests most only want the liquor accompanying them. We all need to be immune to the inability to deny someone if they ask for a dance. Men are more willing to ignore the stares of women, but it would be inappropriate for a woman to refuse a man's invitation.

At least, according to my father, which is why Irina lingers close by me the majority of the evening. Men do not dare ask for her hand when I am near; the women who arrive with them do not allow them to try without fuss.

I acknowledge no one while searching for the obnoxious peasant foursome, expecting to find them in the crowd waiting for a dance, but instead, I see them bowing to my parents on their thrones.

Irina nudges me. "Brave little bumpkins."

She takes my arm and pulls me through gawking women, none of them approaching me with Irina at my side. Why pay bodyguards when everyone fears my sister?

As we near the women, I notice the loudest ones are twins—both brunette, squawking their introductions like rabid geese and drawing the attention of everyone nearby.

Behind them, the older woman thrusts her hand out to my father as if expecting him to kiss it. But it isn't the twins she's bragging about—it's the timid blonde toying with the bottom of a raggedy shawl and gnawing on her bottom lip.

Well, she isn't awful to look at. She matches Irina in height, but it seems like food is a stranger to her. Frail and petite, the shawl that swallows her is mismatched against the elegance of her dress. I would believe she came from money if not for how small and uncomfortable she seems. I trace the sharp cut of her jaw with my eyes, drawing downward to her throat that bobs from a hard swallow.

Unlike the other women in the room, her interest isn't zeroed in on me. She doesn't seem to notice me standing here at all. Her eyes continuously dart between Jasper and the twins, but each time they speak, her eyes roll.

She releases her plump bottom lip, the skin red from irritation. She slides her tongue across it to presumably lessen the sting. And I am still staring at her.

Irina clears her throat.

I blink away from the inspection of the timid woman as all heads whip toward me. Uninterested, I don't acknowledge the twins and the older woman when they dip into a curtsy. No, my focus returns to the blonde. Her anxiety has completely melted away and been replaced by a glare.

She is downright *glowering* at me.

Her dark brown eyes shine with disdain, her pout pursed. And is that... is she looking at me with *disgust*?

"Finnian!" My father booms, standing from his throne. His belly falls over his waistband, his stature nearly as wide as the twins. "This is Harry's daughter."

I raise an eyebrow. "Am I supposed to know who that is?"

Irina pinches my arm hard enough for me to shove her hand away. "Fuck, Irina."

But the blonde... she laughs. A mocking, glaringly obvious fake laugh that boils my blood. "I am not surprised you don't recall our meeting as children," she says.

My manners disappear and join the grateful attitude she clearly left behind in Ashbury. "It is disrespectful to speak to a member of the royal family without a proper introduction and dropping a curtsy."

My mother, Honora, still on her throne, squeezes her eyes shut and sighs.

The blonde dips into a dramatic bow from the corner of my eye, but my smug grin falters when it isn't me she addresses. "Princess Irina," she drawls, "you are even lovelier in person."

I scowl at my sister when she loosens a laugh and covers her mouth. And when the blonde raises, she curls a challenging brow at me. Something about her sets my teeth on edge.

I want to bite her bottom lip to show her how harrowing it could be. I sneer at her disrespect, unsure of why it makes me so fucking angry. "You are in the presence of the prince!"

A flicker of amusement lights her eyes. "Where?"

My fists clench at my sides.

"Elora!" the woman scolds.

Elora. *Elora*. Ah, yes.

We met long ago when my father forced me to accompany him to the bridge to meet the Keeper. I haven't returned since that day, but I did meet her father. Harry was the only man Jasper wanted to speak with regarding the Cinder Faeries. From my understanding, they are tricky beasts to work with, but that doesn't explain why his daughter loathes me.

We didn't speak that day. She wasn't allowed to climb beneath the bridge with me. I wanted to find ways to pop the pumpkins so my father would stop obsessing over them.

My mother stands and squeezes my arm. "Please excuse my son. He travels often and seems to have forgotten how to properly behave in front of guests."

The warning in her voice awakens the young boy in me, and I

sigh. I need to show kindness to this group of primarily unsightly women.

"Elora is mourning her father," the woman says.

I rack my brain for what his wife's name is, but memorizing Harry's personal life hasn't ever been on my list of priorities.

"She is normally much kinder."

With the way Elora continues to bait me with her boredom, I doubt that greatly.

Irina claps her hands. "I know what will lessen the tension! A dance." She pinches my arm *again*. "Ask her to dance, Finnian."

"If you like your fingers, you will stop."

My father quickly agrees to Irina's sickening idea. "What a splendid idea! Go ahead, Finnian."

My mother steps forward before either of us can interject. "Elora, would you like me to take the..."—she struggles to find a word—"Shrug?"

My mother, the *Queen* of Pumpkin Hollow, just offered to hold the ball of yarn around Elora's shoulders.

What the fuck is happening?

This has to be a prank Irina set up.

My father would never force me into a relationship with a lowly from Ashbury. We haven't reached that point of desperation yet, but my father is staring at her like she hung the fucking moon. And no matter how hard I try, I can't remember anything about her other than who her father was.

Why was she invited? And why did she agree to attend if she dislikes me so greatly?

Elora hesitates before slowly uncovering her ivory skin.

Porcelain—fragile and breakable like pristine porcelain.

Swallowing, I roll my shoulders back and extend a hand to her. *Also* swallowing my pride, I ask, "Elora, will you honor me with a dance?" And fuck, if she says no, I'm leaving.

And she's considering it.

She repulsively stares at my hand before a hint of resolve crosses her face. Taking my hand, she dips into a pathetic curtsy—it's offensive at this point—and tightly nods.

I note her soft skin.

And Irina smiles victoriously.

'Traitor,' I silently mouthed at her before leading Elora to the center of the room. The crowd parts for us with envious looks of intrigue. Yes, that's how every woman stares at her, but the men are leering for entirely *different* reasons.

And she doesn't seem to notice. Or care.

If I disregard her bold audacity and consider allowing her to keep her head, I can admit Elora is attractive. I would flirt into her bed if I didn't find her so irritating.

But I want nothing more than to get this over with and return to my quarters while she slinks back to Ashbury and far away from me.

The quartet ends their song abruptly to begin anew for us. I sigh, disappointed to be subjected to an entire piece with her. The rarity of me dancing with anyone keeps everyone off the floor to watch us in bewilderment.

Placing a hand around her waist, I pull her close enough to provide easier access for her to reach my shoulder, though she has to be a foot shorter than me. But she smells like vanilla and honey, and it's not a horrid combination.

She *barely* touches me in return.

"I can't imagine you've danced properly, so I will lead."

"I can't imagine you've ever led, so color me curious," she snaps.

I have half a mind to abandon this idea altogether, particularly annoyed by how my hand molds perfectly around her waist. "Are you pleasant with every man you meet, or am I just lucky?" I grin in satisfaction at the glare that earns me.

She avoids eye contact with me while we dance, but I don't believe it's from inferiority. She genuinely does not like me. But I am surprised at how well she keeps up with me, our steps perfectly in sync. "You've had lessons," I say.

"Is that a question?"

I wonder how far she would fly if I tossed her. "I am astonished, that's all."

"Yes, I can hardly believe it either!" She gasps dramatically. "I can move my feet just as the prince can. Gods, what a blessing!"

I suck in a tight breath, unable to recall the last time I wanted to wrap my hands around a throat this terribly. "Why were you invited here?"

Her expression softens when her gaze shifts to our families, watching us closely. "Because of my father. Harry was respected in your circle."

Jasper's faithful fucks are not in my circle, but I nod. "And your mother?"

"She is not my mother," she says quickly, locking eyes with me. "Regina is my stepmother. *Those* women are *her* daughters."

I'm not the only one Elora dislikes. Her tone is evidence enough that she can't stand them. I can't blame her.

"My mother died many years ago." She returns to looking anywhere else but at me. "She never visited Pumpkin Hollow."

I nearly offer my condolences, but they never bring peace to anyone, no matter the intentions. "And Regina brought you here to find someone to wed?"

"Something like that," she mutters.

"Has anyone drawn your attention?"

She snorts, looks at me, then rolls her eyes. "Absolutely not."

Fuck, this woman is a stone wall. Soft and warm to the touch, but spews icy venom. Yet, she intrigues me. "No? Let's look around, shall we?" I spin her quickly. "The man behind me is a duke—a cousin of some woman on my mother's side. I've never met her, and he's unbearable. It might be a perfect match."

She *almost* curses at me but visibly holds back. Instead, she glances behind me with a smirk. "Attractive, yet sour. It must be a family trait. Maybe I'll dance with him next and compare which of you I dislike more."

I grind my jaw. She just compared me to my vile... third or

fourth cousin. We give titles away to family members in bulk so they'll remain away from the castle and on their own acre. "So, you find me attractive?"

She beams a bright, faux smile. "Until you speak."

The song ends, but I do not let her pull away. I hold her still until the second song begins. "You are just,"—I roll my neck and exhale—"*Lovely*."

My disguised insult does not hit the way I wished it would as she replies, "Likewise."

I am growing desperate to unravel her reasoning for being here. "My father wouldn't have invited you solely because he liked your father."

She sighs deeply. "I have remained close to the faeries. I would guess that has something to do with it. I assume the man who took my father's position can't handle them."

Ah. This is the woman the faeries idolize, the one the guards complain about to my father for her frequent visits. She once became trapped in a dwelling, and Jasper was furious about the faeries losing a day's work to retrieve her—not that a child had nearly died.

"You're their distraction."

Again, she's unbothered. "Then, I am their distraction. If I worked long days in the heat without breaks and hardly any food, I would be glad for distractions, too. We don't all have the luxury of hopping into as many beds as possible."

"*Wow*," I emphasize. Admittedly, I never paid much mind to the faeries and their daily schedules nor inquired if they were well taken care of. Why should I when this ray of sunshine does it for me? "Are you accusing our king of not supplying the faeries with what they need?" I will skip the remark about the many beds.

Because she isn't wrong.

Unease tenses her shoulders, but her eyebrow raises in a challenge. "Visit, then ask."

"Maybe I will," I reply, tightening my grip on her waist when her eyes roll in disbelief. Bringing her close enough for her body to press against mine, I delight in the way her eyes widen in surprise. "Is there a reason you dislike me, Elora? I apologize for not noticing you many years ago if you're upset about that."

"Gods, I am not that desperate for your attention." Her scowl could be seen from the heavens. "I doubt your fragile, egotistical complex handles the truth very well, Prince Finnian."

She tears away from me entirely as the final note rings through the room. "But if I were you, I would pay a little more attention to what's happening in your realm before you pepper me with questions about how someone like *me* ended up in *your* castle."

She spins on her heel and leaves me standing alone before I have time to follow up with what in Hades' name *that* meant.

And I want to fucking follow her.

I step forward to chase her but am soon surrounded by women begging for their chance to dance with me. And I watch Elora storm out of the room with all her tulle and anger.

Eight

Banished from the ball after Elora's grand exit, I pace my father's study. I've never been the one left standing, humiliated by such a dreadful and infuriating woman.

She left *me*.

I hold her entire future in the palm of my hand and could demand Ashbury be exiled from Pumpkin Hollow if I choose, yet she believes *she* could walk away from *me*.

Upon returning to his private quarters, my father leaves me to my frustration while he disrobes out of his ballroom attire and into a long, exuberant velvet robe that looks quite ridiculous.

And now, he watches in amusement as I glare, annoyed that any part of my evening brings him joy.

"I want her banished," I growl.

Whether or not I'm behaving like a petulant child makes no difference when that.... That *woman* brings such a deep-rooted anger to the surface.

And I can't stop thinking about how her golden-brown eyes glared at me.

"I want her out of this castle. I want her gone," I continue, fuming as he calmly pours two mugfuls of whiskey. "I don't understand why you brought her here."

He offers a mug. Drops splash to the ground as I rip it from his hand and chug until it's emptied. The smooth liquor slides down my throat and fuels my anger.

I need a bite—a distraction.

Not something as soft as her skin.

"She is close to the faeries." He sips from his mug slowly. "Her mother—"

"Stepmother," I interrupt. "That's not her biological mother."

I'm not sure why I'm defending that wily little...

"I don't care who she is," he replies. "We spoke while the two of you danced. Elora was raised properly. Harry ensured she was tutored by one of us. She lives in the palace manor in Ashbury. And she remains respected by their people."

"She is *maddening*," I argue.

He brushes me off with a lazy wave of his hand. "Find me a woman who isn't. She is the one, Finnian."

My legs nearly give out. I wish I hadn't swigged so quickly because I'll need more. "The one for *whom*?"

His deep-throated chuckle causes my knuckles to whiten around my mug. "The one for *you*."

Gut *punch*. Speechless.

"Unless you'd like me to bring her to my bed instead."

I count backward from ten. My father is nothing short of despicable. He's the reason I stay away for such long periods. I loathe when he speaks of other women when he has someone like my mother as his queen, but I must choose my battles wisely.

"I would rather she leave."

His wrinkled, bloated face hardens.

When multiple chins sprouted, he grew a long beard to cover them, but it didn't cover his swollen stomach. And despite what Irina believes, no part of her resembles him.

"I need a Keeper the faeries won't argue with. The man in Harry's place is afraid of them." He taps a finger against his mug. "Elora isn't. They listen to her."

My jaw pops, still unconvinced.

"Elora is beloved in Ashbury. Murmurs of displeased residents have reached my men at the mountain gates. Do you know what follows those murmurs, boy?"

I place the mug on the table hard enough to rattle the bottle of whiskey. I hate being referred to as '*boy.*'

"Revolts," he says. "And if the faeries want to protect that young woman, we're in for a fight. I need the pails doubled. If Elora is our princess, they won't fight the order."

"Doubled? Why?"

He bangs a fist against the table. "I don't need a reason! I can raise taxes on pails. Because the faeries need to be reminded who is in control." He points a finger at me. "You will watch her interactions with them."

"Free them," I say. "Kill them. We don't need them."

He finishes his first mugful. "I will never free them. They are too unique to be killed. And who's to say that other faeries won't hear of it and come for us? No one knows they're here. If an entire species of faeries is gone, someone will know."

I raise an eyebrow. "How? It seems eliminating them would solve some of our problems. You have the glass bridge. Why do you need more than that?"

"You have a lot to learn about being king. The power lies within the quantity, Finnian. The faeries promised themselves to me long ago. And I will never forget a bargain. And why eliminate cheap labor?"

To provide jobs for your people, imbecile.

But Jasper doesn't use logic when making decisions—his thoughts are driven by what he owns that others never will.

It is an incurable disease.

Exhaustion wraps tightly around me. I've been home for one day and already wish to leave. "Elora alluded to Ashbury not being taken care of. Could that be why they're displeased?"

"I let them *live*," he rattles. "We deliver weekly shipments of food. They've become spoiled by what we provide."

Ashbury once thrived as a kingdom. I do not doubt the

remaining elders wish they had fought harder against my father's forces. And it all happened because he wanted the damn bridge.

I contemplate knocking him unconscious with the bottle of whiskey. "Having Elora as my bride won't silence the murmurs."

Eliminating my weapon, he pours the remainder of the whiskey into his mug. "Marry Elora, secure her allegiance to the crown, and study her relationship with the faeries." He takes a sip and coughs, dribbling whiskey down his beard. "She is not like her father. She is feisty and cares more about Ashbury than the kingdom that protects it. I've been watching her, Finnian."

"She loathes me," I argue weakly, but that's all I have left.

"Change her mind."

I don't want a wife, but I would gladly take anyone over her. Being shackled to anyone is a nightmare, but Elora will poison me the first chance she gets. "And if your plan doesn't work? If she continues to hate me, favor the faeries, start a revolt?"

He motions toward the balcony with his mug. "She'll make a fine addition to my collection."

The gallows rest right beneath his window. And his rumored collection isn't a rumor at all.

"And once you get a son out of her, you'll never have to speak to her again. I'll send her away." He stands and slaps my shoulder. "At least you'll get a decent fuck out of her."

I scowl at the crude remark. "What if someone spoke of Irina in that way?"

His belly shakes from a laugh. "Find me a man willing."

I clench my fists at my sides. I want to strangle him, but it wouldn't change a damn thing. "Give me more time."

"Time is up," he responds as someone knocks on the door. "It is your duty to follow the orders of your king. Being my son awards you no favors."

Aside from a horse of my own, I've never asked him for anything. The first time I requested to decide my own future, he denied it.

Shock and disgust ricocheted through my chest and into my

stomach. Elora's stepsisters giggle on the other side of the door, wearing extravagant nightgowns—much nicer than anything they could own. With our own in-house seamstresses, they sewed dresses and garments specifically for guests, which meant these two were welcomed in the castle for a night.

Ghastly—they are ghastly.

"Why are they here?" I garnered a reputation long ago for being rude. There is no reason to change for their sake.

Jasper plasters a smile on his face and winks at the women, even as they flutter their eyelashes at me. "I offered Elora's family the guest wing for the evening."

"Of course," I mutter.

Even if my mother wasn't beautiful, she was his *wife* and right down the hallway. Instead of seeking pleasure with her, he invites women who blatantly wish to sleep with me instead.

My disapproval lives in the glare I give him. "Do you want to know why marriage has never been my priority?" I tilt my head in their direction. "You've never given me a great example."

"You listen here, boy..."

"You will be discarded quicker than leftovers. And he has gout," I inform the women before I shove past them and leave.

"Dear, you must stop pacing."

My chest rumbles in disapproval. My pacing has resumed; I've only since moved to my mother's terrace. Aside from breakfast and formal events, my memory lacks recent encounters between my parents.

"Why haven't you left him?" Frustration building suffocates me slowly. "You know what he's doing down the hall, right?"

Her elegant nightgown pools at her feet when she sits. "Finnian—"

I stop and face her from the terrace. Jasper's balcony doors are closed, but I can hear them giggling together. My mother, being subjected to his affairs in this way, curls my stomach into knots.

Pensively, her eyes lowering to her clasped hands in her lap, she ponders in silence. The years of degradation and disrespect are in her hunched shoulders, the black under her eyes from restless nights, and her anxious sighs.

I was eight when I saw him bring a woman to his quarters. I was fourteen when I caught him pressed against the wall with another. I went through three tutors growing up because he would grow bored after a few weeks. The taste of luxury was an addiction, and each woman wanted a taste of our life, but he wasn't a giver.

He takes.

At events when needed, my mother shines as the beloved queen, but behind closed doors, when it's just us, I'm given the rare glimpse of what his choices have done to her.

He has completely broken her down.

But he's the king, the leader of thousands, the owner of faeries and trapped pumpkins, and more than willing to take the heads of those who dared question him. My mother lives in a loveless marriage to keep her son on the throne, and that realization doesn't require an answer.

I know why she's stayed.

My mother rubs her hands together but doesn't look up. And I can barely hear her when she says, "He is my heart's keeper, Finnian. I was once his, but he took it back and kept mine."

I lean against the doorframe, unsure of what to say. My mother was a princess in a kingdom far away with a substantial dowry and was only seventeen when sold to my grandfather for Jasper to marry.

I have the faintest memories of moments of laughter and stolen kisses between them, but then my mother went away for months and returned with Irina.

I was only four but soon thrown into training for kingship—a requirement given to most princes when reaching fourteen, but not me. I was trained for loyalty before I could read.

The disagreements between them that followed stemmed from that. My mother wanted a childhood for me, and my father wanted an heir. I would hide in the nursery and play with Irina to avoid their shouting. It was why it enraged me when rumors were spread about Irina's legitimacy as the princess. We both suffered at the hands of Jasper's strenuous tasks and only found reprieve at night when we'd escaped the guards to explore the kingdom.

But then, I reached fourteen.

He sent me away and forced me to train with our army. My nights of leisure with my sister slowly turned into sleeping in tents with the troops and having alcohol at my fingertips.

I did not return to my mother as her boy.

And that was the day the light left her eyes.

I haven't been able to bring it back since.

"He wants me to marry Elora."

The corners of her mouth tilt upward—I've learned secrets are held in those slight upturns. "He does."

I move inside and close the balcony doors. "And you agree with him?"

"Your father wants leverage," she says softly. "Elora will be a mediator between kingdoms."

"Ashbury is not a kingdom," I correct. "It is a domain we own. Elora isn't needed. We can force the faeries to do as we please. It should not require me to marry someone so... so..."

"Like you?"

I narrow my eyes. "So *difficult*."

She motions to the drink cart. I pour her favorite Moscato into a cup and place it before her. "The faeries are stubborn." She takes a sip. "And angry. The man who replaced Harry is fearful of them. Elora isn't."

"But—"

"You believe you're up to the challenge, I know. But they will not respond well to you." She stands and carries her drink to the bed. "They view her as one of them. You've been away for a long time, Finnian. This is what's transpired since you left."

"You know why I leave, Mother."

She lowers to the edge of her bed. "Our kingdom benefits from the faeries, Finnian. With Elora as your bride, they will learn to trust you."

"Even after we double the pails?"

She finishes her wine and places the cup on her bedside table. "One step at a time, son."

Sighing, I drop my head, defeated, and only then do I notice Elora's raggedy shawl on the chair next to my mother. "Give it back to her at breakfast," she says. "Her family will be there."

My chest tightens. My horse could be saddled quickly. I could leave and never return, but that would leave Irina and my mother alone with Jasper's anger.

For them, I need to do this.

"Irina will help her adjust," she assures me.

Marrying Elora would eliminate my excuse for not providing a son to carry our name. Questions would arise when months pass with no proof of consummation. I need to figure that out, too.

"And she is already aware," she adds.

A sliver of amusement pushes past the despair. "Of course, she is. I bet you ten gold coins she waits for me in my quarters."

My mother laughs. "Make it twenty."

Upon closing the door to my quarters, it takes me less than a minute to locate Irina. As always, she is leaning over my balcony, looking down below into the empty courtyard. The guests have already left for the evening, except for Elora and her accompanying triple headaches. Irina would've stayed here all night until I returned to talk about them.

She looks at me over her shoulder. "A smile wasn't what I expected to see."

Chuckling, I shrug off my jacket and consider tossing it over the balcony so I'll never have to wear it again. "Mother owes me twenty gold coins."

I drop Elora's cardigan on the table as Irina comes inside to throw herself backward across my bed dramatically. It reminds me of when she'd topple over and knock down my blocks just so I would pay attention to her.

"I take it they did not inform you—"

"Of my saddling?" I kick off my boots. "Indeed, they did."

With a raised brow, she twists and balances on her elbow. "You're rather calm. I thought you'd be halfway to the neighboring realm by now."

"It crossed my mind," I mumble. "But Jasper undoubtedly prepared for that, I'm sure." I grab my last full bottle of whiskey from my liquor cart. "I can't escape this one, Irina."

I don't bother with a glass, flicking the cap off and chugging. It takes her only seconds to stand, grab it from me, and do the same.

Irina used to disguise herself to leave the castle in the evenings when I went to train with the army. I was sixteen the first time she popped into my tent, flirted her way into my bunkmate's liquor stash, and had her first drink of whiskey under my supervision.

Now, we use it to drown our responsibilities and ignore the nagging reminder that we are the children of an unjust king.

Irina keeps the bottle out of my reach. "She's not so bad, is she?"

I scoff. "She's beneath us, Irina. Jasper only welcomed her into the castle because of her closeness to the faeries. He wants to double their load, and without her, they'll refuse."

Irina rolls her eyes. "Beneath us? Honestly, Finnian, could you be more of a snob?" She thrusts the bottle toward me. "You sound bitter."

My rotten sister has drunk more than half already. "I'm not bitter," I argue, taking a few steps back to prevent her from stealing the bottle again. "Why would I be bitter?"

She blows short pieces of hair from her eyes. She had stormed out of the castle one night after fighting with Jasper and managed to talk someone into cutting parts of her long hair to her chin. I believe she regrets it now.

"You're bitter because Jasper needs a woman for this, and you think it's something you can handle on your own."

"It is," I say bluntly. "We own the faeries."

She crosses her arms. "I'm disappointed in you, Finn." She lunges for the bottle. "They are living, breathing creatures. We shouldn't *own* anyone."

I sink into a chair with a sigh. I'm disappointed in myself, too. "What would you have me do, Irina? Free them?"

She climbs on the table and sits crisscrossed, balancing the nearly empty bottle in her lap. The bracelets on her wrists clink together— gifts from the Bohemians. Irina is given an allowance, but only when guarded and watched carefully and *only* in the daylight.

When Irina manages to flee the castle, she trades whatever she bought with her allowance for jewelry from wagons. Jasper has yet to find out how she's always able to escape, but seeing her at breakfast every morning with evidence of her victories is promptly followed by a fight between them.

Since Irina is convinced she doesn't belong here, I believe she wants to feel part of *something*. And she looks remarkably similar to the free-spirited travelers that linger on the outskirts of our lands.

Jasper never allows them into Pumpkin Hollow and rarely lets Irina out. If it wasn't for me being here, Irina would flee.

And her remark about not owning anyone suddenly holds weight. Irina is trapped, too.

"If you freed them, he would put your head on a stake. I do believe Elora is a peaceful resolution. Maybe he'll treat them kinder if she's as close to them as he thinks she is. If they're difficult, it's because of him."

Peaceful isn't in Jasper's vocabulary. "So, you think I should do this?"

"Not for Jasper," she says. "But I do believe it's time for a change. And Elora will be a challenge for him."

I grin. "He already has enough of a challenge with you, Irina." I tip my head back and stare at the ceiling. "Fine. I will talk to her tomorrow, but I'm annulling the marriage once I've established a working relationship with the faeries."

A breathy laugh escapes her. "A marriage of convenience. How romantic."

I curse. "Believe me, Irina. The only one this is convenient for is her." I recall Elora's glares and venomous insults, my jaw clicking as a fresh wave of annoyance rises and nearly drowns me. "Romance is out of the question."

Nine

I've always heard the heavens belong in the clouds, hidden high enough for the gods to watch us from above and judge our sins. But that is untrue.

The bed I slept in is the heavens.

The pillows, soft as clouds and thick, eliminated every sore muscle in my neck from the months of cleaning the wood floors of our manor on my knees. The velvety soft quilts partner well with the open balcony doors, allowing the chilly breeze to flow through —*not* followed by ashy flakes.

And I slept free of dreams or nightmares.

My eyes flutter open. A gray canopy hangs from the tall bedposts, preventing any light from seeping through, masking me in darkness. If not for the two slivers of sunlight peeking through and painting the bedspread, I could easily trick myself into falling back asleep. I wouldn't have to bathe and join the royal family for breakfast—not that bathing is necessary since my skin is still free of soot and smudges.

After my grand departure from the ball last night, Regina caught up to me and reminded me why I came here. The reasoning did not include insulting the prince and leaving him to stand alone.

Most unfortunate for me.

He deserved it.

But then, King Jasper and his overzealous, belly-bouncing laughter and beard strokes followed us out and offered the guest wing for the evening, referencing my father as if he is my only saving grace to being allowed in this precious kingdom of pumpkins and despicable behavior.

"Oh, how wonderful of you!" I shouted in mockery of Regina's reply to his offer, my following groan muffled when I buried my face into the pillow.

Staying came with a condition, of course—I wonder if the king ever makes an offer without one—*Breakfast.*

It could be worse. My display of hatred for the prince could've led to my banishment from the castle, yet it somehow worked in my favor instead. Maintaining my disgust for him will be simple, but it will accomplish nothing.

Ignorant prick.

Reducing my feelings last night to those of a scorned woman simply because he doesn't remember meeting me as a child is precisely why I know it will never work between us.

He thinks far too highly of himself.

My thoughts of him are interrupted by a soft click of the door. I scramble to my knees and slowly pull one of the canopy flaps to the side. The quarters I was given are more significant than my entire attic and split into multiple rooms, most of which I'd never use, even if I lived here.

From where I hide, I watch a maid scurry through the hallway with a steaming bucket of water. Not to pour on me—no, that would be too convenient—but to fill the tub. The water boilers in the castle must be specific for the wings of the royal family. I can't imagine the king wouldn't have been one of the first to install the turn-of-the-century experiments, though I am in no position to turn down a steaming hot bath.

The maid tiptoes out and closes the door.

I appreciate the effort not to disturb my slumber, but I've slept alone in the attic so long that a mouse's footsteps could wake me.

And now, I need to drag myself away from the safety and comfort of this bed to flirt with a rat *politely*.

I crawl off the bed, drag my feet into the bathroom, and discard my silk nightgown to slip into the cast iron tub, my skin reddening instantly from the warmth. I take advantage of the multiple bars of soap, delighting in each scent and covering my body in sudsy bubbles. I resemble froth in a warm cup of coffee—a drink I've tasted only once.

Years ago, the king gifted my father a small bag of roast in gratitude for a vast delivery of coal. He mixed milk and sugar into his mug, drank the entirety one evening, and didn't sleep for two days, looking wild with darting eyes.

The scalding iron of the tub is undoubtedly leaving burn marks across my back, but I am in no rush to leave. Stepping foot into the hallway will make this entire scheme real. And though my father was close to the king, it does not mean my life will be spared if our plan is discovered.

The nerves and the hot water are causing me to sweat, and I can't arrive at breakfast smelling awful.

I wash the bubbles off my body and wring the water out of my hair. The provided robe hanging on the door is as soft as the quilts on the bed, making me want to crawl back in and never leave.

Wrapping it tightly around me, I contemplate arriving to breakfast in only this but open the doors of the finely crafted wardrobe to find something decent to wear.

I expected Regina to use the connecting door to burst inside and dress me, but she is most likely preoccupied with choosing something for Dolly and Daffodil—perhaps painting them with horrendously bright oils.

Garments of every size are stacked in neat piles on perfectly spaced shelves. Of course, assuming that King Jasper doesn't often house starved guests, even the most petite dress swallows me.

If anything, breakfast will provide a decent meal.

I twist the corset's laces tightly around my waist and lower back, leaving indentations on my fingers, and sigh when the gauzy fabric slips from my shoulders and settles around my upper arms.

I can make this work.

If the rumors surrounding the prince are true, the slight exposure of my skin will work in my favor—not that I'll know how to react if it does. His abundance of experience against my lack *of* could be what botches this entire ordeal.

But the dress is elegant.

And for a moment, just one solitary moment, I wonder if I'll be given dresses like this one if I become Finnian's wife—if every skirt will *swoosh* and sway in the warm breeze. It would be refreshing to look at my reflection daily and not wish it away. Because in the stillness of this moment, my mother's words don't seem entirely untrue.

As lovely as a caterpillar getting its wings, she would always say to me.

The alluring blush-pink, delicate, and nearly sheer gauze softens the harsh lines around my eyes. My cheeks hold a pinch of color from the warm bath, and the whole night's sleep has lightened the purple spots beneath my eyes.

The triple-layered sleeves fall down my arms and completely cover my hands. The ribbon around the waist leaves spare inches, but not enough to hide the *tiniest* hint of curves. And my curls seem brighter against the pastel—properly washed and combed for once.

And even under the unusual circumstances, my reflection doesn't show an ash-covered, impoverished girl. I stare at what could've been if Ashbury hadn't been ransacked and destroyed and if Pumpkin Hollow had offered a partnership instead of complete destruction.

I stare at the woman who would've been the princess if my father hadn't betrayed our entire future.

The pressure to rectify his wrongdoings makes the pulsing knots in my neck return in full.

I admit I'm lost after passing two libraries, jiggling doorknobs on multiple locked doors, and breathlessly climbing up and down too many staircases. The glass castle might be beautiful outside, but it is a never-ending maze within.

Why do they need so much space with only four royal family members? I never imagined a day I would miss my attic, but as I spin in a circle, convinced I'm right back where I started, I do.

Choking on ash seems preferable over the gnawing feeling in my gut that missing breakfast will conjure Regina's wrath.

I whip around at the sound of light laughter. The mysterious Princess of Pumpkin Hollow leans against a wall with a wide smile. Her existence has always been well-established, but no stories are ever told of her, only hearsay.

We also met once as children when she surprised her father by coming out from underneath the carriage on one of his excursions to the bridge. We played together for less than ten minutes before he forced her to return to the castle with two guards.

Looking at her in a simple red dress, her raven hair curled at the ends, and her honeyed skin makes my breath catch the way it always does when I see Azrea. Irina is *breathtaking*.

And she looks nothing like her mother and even less like Finnian, which makes me like her more. "Have you been following me, Princess Irina?" I grin coyly. "It would be cruel for you to watch me wander and not offer help."

Irina doesn't change her leisurely stance, but amusement alights her eyes. "I wanted to see how long it took you to notice me." She clicks her tongue with a sigh. "*Too* long, Elora. You'll need to be more observant if you plan to stay."

"And why would I stay?" I challenge her. "If it was not evident last night, I don't care for the grandness of Pumpkin Hollow when coming from somewhere much less..." *Pleasant*, I silently snap, be *pleasant*. "...prosperous."

Her eyes speak for her—she knows exactly what I'm insinuating. If this spell ever wears off, my embarrassment from reliving the moments of bravado and arrogance will cause me to lose years of sleep.

She straightens from the wall and gestures behind me with a flick of her wrist. "Come. If we're late, the vein in Jasper's forehead will pop."

I stifle a laugh and follow a step behind her as she effortlessly leads me through the maze.

As the doors of the grand hall come into view, gold and nearly reaching the ceiling, I shiver and pause.

Irina glances at me over her shoulder, noting my frazzled expression and darting eyes. King Jasper's voice booms through the closed doors, Regina's gods-awful laughter following.

I loathe the whole lot of them.

"It's all a game, Elora." Her confident tone softens into understanding. "All of this? It's all a game. It always has been. Plaster on a smile and play your cards."

"Are you playing, too?" I whisper, stalling.

She looks behind me in the empty hallway with a sorrowful half-smile before settling on me again. "I've been playing my entire life, Elora." From her corset, she brandishes a card from between her breasts and hands it to me.

The thin paper has faded in color from age, but I've seen cards like this one from street peddlers in Ashbury.

"I had an entire deck once," she explains, "One day, I spread them across the floor to admire the colors. The artist had drawn each deck differently, which meant I had something no one else did." She nods to the card in my hand. "Jasper saw them, called me a spoiled crook, and burned them."

My lips part. "Why are you telling me this?"

She flips the card over. I stare at a portrait of the king with a lopsided crown and crooked nose. "This is the one he missed. And I kept it to remind myself who the real crook is, Elora."

My gaze slowly lifts to hers.

"I don't know why you're here, Elora, but I recognize something in you that resembles me." She doesn't convey what that might be, but it does bring another smile to her face. "Finnian tried to find me a new deck, but Jasper banished the peddlers to the outskirts. The artist moved on. And being the prince can limit one's reach when his father is a dreadful king."

I return the card to her, stealing one last look at the crooked king drawn on the back. "That's when a prince should become a man." I understand the love she holds for her brother, but it doesn't excuse him from a lifetime of turning his nose to the neglect of my people. "My father was a weak prince. I won't be impressed with another."

Irina opened one of the heavy doors, revealing a peek of the dining table full of food, and left me with parting words, "Don't mistake survival for weakness, Elora. It doesn't all look the same."

Ten

We're the last ones to join breakfast.

Irina blames my tardiness on herself, creating a story about introducing me to a servant she enjoys flirting with. And she speaks so boldly and paints such a vivid tale that I nearly believe her. While she speaks in grand tones, I take advantage of how easily her storytelling ensnares everyone and study the dining room. Towers of blue, silver, and orange pumpkins are again stacked in every corner, similar to how the ballroom was decorated. But, even I can admit that they liven the gray-checkered tile floor.

A cathedral ceiling boasts six stained glass windows for sun rays to gloss the walls in colorful shapes. And in the center of the room, a table set for sixteen with intricately painted porcelain dishes and platters full of food awaits.

King Jasper and Queen Honora are sitting on each end of the table with Finnian directly in the center—who I am actively avoiding. Regina, Dolly, and Daffodil have surrounded the king. And the more Irina speaks, the angrier he becomes.

I flinch when he bangs his fist on the tabletop, rattling glasses, and orders her to sit down. She takes my hand and drags me toward two empty chairs across from Finnian.

Finally, my examining stare lands on him.

He shakes his head at his sister, but pride lingers in how he looks at her. It doesn't make me like him, but I can appreciate his excellent personality choice.

Irina's remark about survival remains nestled in my mind. Nothing about Finnian screams neglected, down to the embellished garb he's wearing with no thread out of place. Both times I've been around him, he always looks so.... Pristine.

Dolly and Daffodil's incessant giggling behind a napkin interrupts my inspection of him. I scowl at them but mask my hatred when Finnian taps a finger against the table to grab my attention. Judging by the way his jaw pops when my narrowed eyes meet his unenthusiastic stare, I realize that being civil toward me is no easier for him than pretending to like him will be for me. "Hungry?" he asks me.

Before I reply, he lowers his gaze to my exposed shoulders, drifting over the hollow collarbone. Discomfort from the dress barely clinging to me heats my cheeks. "Starved," I reply dryly.

I avert my attention from him and instead focus on the selection of meats and fruits. Even at Ashbury's best, we've never had this many selections.

"Girls!" Regina snaps as the giggling grows louder. '*You are both grown women*' is what she should have said, but settled with, "Enough."

They immediately silence but continue to look at the king with brazen smiles. I want to promise that I am not as immature as them, but I keep my snarky remarks tucked away.

"Eat, Elora." Queen Honora smiles at me. "I recommend the pumpkin casserole."

I wrinkle my nose.

Pumpkins might be quaint for decor, but pumpkin-flavored food turns my stomach. "Pumpkin foods in Pumpkin Hollow," I say, "How fitting. Is it only during autumn?"

We tried sowing pumpkins in the valleys last spring, but our dry soil killed them.

"Of course not!" King Jasper exclaims. "Why would it be?"

Gods, a direct question, and one he expects me to answer.

His reasoning for staring at me so intensely is because of *pumpkins*. Regina purses her lips in anticipation.

"Well," I begin, clearing my throat. "Pumpkins are typically planted in spring for autumn celebration."

His chest rumbles with a haughty chortle. "I employ gardeners year-round, girl. We are excluded from the *typical*."

I didn't realize nature had favorites; how foolish of me. "Of course," I reply sweetly. "I'm not sure why I would imply otherwise. The castle gardens boast plenty of *a*typical foods and flowers."

Queen Honora breaks the tension with polite laughter. "King Jasper has his favorites."

Irina snorts while filling her plate with bacon and eggs. "I'll say." She drops two pieces of bacon on my plate. "These did not come from pumpkin-flavored pigs."

"Thank gods," I whisper before gnawing off the end of a strip, my eyes nearly rolling back from the warm, flavorful taste. Bacon was my favorite as a child, but it has since become a luxury, and I haven't had any since before my father's passing.

Since no one in Ashbury was allowed land ownership, we kept one cow, two pigs, two chickens, and a goat in separate pens outside the village. King Jasper seized them years ago, making us entirely dependent on meat deliveries from Pumpkin Hollow. The shrewd bastard only sends leftovers.

Dangle a bone in front of a rabid animal, and they will stay loyal to you. Whether we've grown tired of it or not, the idea of losing our food source keeps us in line. And since wagons full of bodies are delivered to the faeries once a month for burning, it serves as a reminder of what will happen if we fight back each time smoke from the valleys rises.

"Harry dined with us on occasion," King Jasper says. "Your father," he adds, like I don't fucking know that already.

He chews with his mouth open and belly cradling the table edge. "Did he tell you about when he dined with his king?"

I try to control my disgust, forcing myself to not look anywhere but his eyes. "Of course, he did." If I plan to survive here, I'll need a solid gut and better gag reflex. "He always reflected on his time with you positively."

King Jasper drops his fist to the table again to ensure he remains the center of attention. I don't flinch this time, but Irina mutters obscenities under her breath. "Of course! I was good to your father.' Twas sad to hear of his death."

I suppose I missed the condolence letters or offers to keep my family afloat after his passing. "Thank you."

"Elora is just like him," Regina pops in.

Her fake smile nearly makes me roll my eyes. She loathes me, so if she believes I'm similar to my father, she must've really hated him.

"The faeries respect her like they respected him," she continues. "They are foul creatures and hard to handle, but they listen to my daughter."

I drop the strip of bacon onto my plate and curl my fingers into loose fists. Not once has she ever referred to me as *her daughter.* I try to blink away tears from the blatant lies.

Even Dolly stares at her mother in surprise.

My mug of orange juice scoots closer. I lift my eyes to meet Finnian's as he subtly inches it toward me. He says nothing but must remember my reaction when he referred to her as my mother last night while we danced.

His kind gesture surprised me, and I sipped the freshly squeezed juice. The tangy aroma wafting into my nostrils decreases my heart rate until King Jasper speaks again. "Foul creatures, indeed." He stuffs a piece of bacon in his mouth. "They've given me trouble since Harry's death. They're disrespectful toward his replacement."

The only foul creature is him.

Finnian asks, "Is that true, Elora?"

"No," I whisper, then roll my shoulders back. "No, they are not foul; they're misunderstood. The faeries are useful and loyal, maybe a little hot-tempered, but they can't help that."

When no one seems to understand the insinuation, I add, "because of their *fire*."

Finnian cracks the tiniest grin, though it is quickly masked by indifference. He must've remembered how much he despises me.

"Have you witnessed their fire, Elora?" Queen Honora inquires. "I haven't had the pleasure of meeting the faeries, but I am curious how their magic works."

"It doesn't seem magical when we're choking on ash," Daffodil pipes in.

"The queen did not address you," Irina calmly states, but the lethal way her eyes narrow makes Daffodil cower.

Regina looks ready to climb across the table but is smart enough to stay in her chair. Gobsmacked, I exchange a look with Finnian. He doesn't seem surprised and gestures for me to answer.

"I see their fire daily," I reply. "But only once have I witnessed their true power. Fire can spread across their entire bodies, but that is unnecessary for mining."

Queen Honora leans forward, intrigued.

I tug on the end of a curl. I've never needed to explain the faeries' powers to anyone, nor have I ever been questioned on how they came to be. It never mattered to me. Their existence is magical enough without explanation. "Their palms resemble embers," I continue, "with only their hands, they turn solid, centuries-old rock into coal."

I close my eyes and pull out one of my many memories of watching them work. "The winged males work from the peaks of the mountains to the bottom, while the non-winged mine the surface. The mountainside remains warm, but so do they. Their bodies produce endless heat. Being near them makes humans sweat, but the faeries remain physically flawless."

Opening my eyes, I'm surprised to find everyone staring at me silently. "They are mesmerizing to watch and beautiful." I smile broadly. “It is easy for humans to feel inferior around them, but I could watch them work all day.”

“Perhaps you could introduce me to them,” Queen Honora says.

My smile falters. Selfishly, I don’t want anyone near them, but the man sitting at the head of the table believes they belong to him, and I need to maintain that notion. “I would love that.”

“I would like to meet them, too.” Finnian places his elbows on the table, again staring at me far too vigorously. “Properly. I believe my only encounters with them were as a boy.”

“Sure,” I reply with a tight grin. “I would be pleased to introduce all of you to the faeries, but you do not need my permission.”

“I believe we do,” King Jasper interjects. “I think they only listen to you, even though I am their king.”

My tongue dries from his threatening tone. “The faeries will always perform to your pleasure, King Jasper.” I tuck my trembling hands in my lap. “They are grateful for your protection, as we all are.”

I want to ask Azrea to burn him into ash so desperately that I can taste it on my tongue.

“It is true,” Regina adds, touching where her heart should be. Gods, the theatrics. “We are forever indebted to Pumpkin Hollow.”

Irina sighs deeply. “As if his ego isn’t large enough.”

“Irina,” Finnian warns through clenched teeth, either out of protection for his sister or allegiance to the king.

Irina seems capable of handling herself.

King Jasper ignores Irina’s insult, too focused on the bestowal of compliments.

“Enough politics,” Queen Honora says. “You are our guests, and we owe your family just as much for assisting with the faeries. I do hope you’ve left room for pumpkin pastries.”

I don’t miss Irina’s throaty murmur when she adds, “And kiss Jasper’s pumpkin-flavored ass,” making me bite my bottom lip to cover a laugh at Finnian’s exasperated glare.

"Ellie!" Daffodil squawks, snapping her fingers in my direction. "My plate needs to be taken away."

I shrink in my chair.

Irina snaps her head toward her, confused. "What the fuck is she supposed to do about that?"

Dolly crows. "She always cleans up after us. Don't you, Ellie?"

Every inch of me tingles with shame.

Regina forces a nervous laugh. "Oh, you know how sisters can be! They are always playing with one another."

I refuse to look anywhere but my plate. Perhaps if I slide underneath the table, no one will notice. I could disappear somewhere in the castle maze, never to be found again.

Irina calls for one of the servants posted around the table specifically to jump in when needed. "The floral one wants to play a game. Would you please stack used plates for her to carry to the kitchens? And go ahead and include her sister."

My head snaps up at the request. Regina stares at Irina in a combination of anger and shock. "I don't believe that's necessary...." she says but is quickly interrupted.

"The princess asked you to do something," Finnian says, speaking to the servant.

I watch in awe-shocked silence as the servant stacks ten plates in two piles and instructs Dolly and Daffodil on where to take them. Their cheeks redden, their heads shaking, but Irina claps her hands together twice. "You are not allowed to refuse my requests, *guests*."

The king does not argue to the contrary, looking rather amused instead. Watching people perform minimal tasks is most likely one of his favorite games.

Dolly and Daffodil stand, looking at Regina for help, but she can't argue with Irina. The stacks of plates shake in their hands, their steps toward the door sloppy from continuously looking backward, hoping Irina will allow them to return to the table.

A plate from Dolly's stack falls and shatters, her gasp carrying loudly through the room. The king laughs, only furthering their embarrassment as they run from the room, dropping more plates and shrieking through loud, fake cries.

Irina exchanges a mischievous grin with her brother before glaring at Regina. “We like to play, too,” is all she says.

But I recognize the look on Regina’s face.

And I will be the one to pay for the games played.

Eleven

Daffodil and Dolly have yet to return to the table. Regina requested to be excused moments earlier to try and find them, and I stayed silent while the remaining four idly chattered, keeping the conversation light. I imagine anything important won't be discussed around me, especially since I am from Ashbury. The king rarely speaks, instead focusing on me —*studying* me.

For some reason, he doesn't seem to trust me, which won't bode well for my plan of trying to marry his heir.

I take a bite of pumpkin pastry before Irina snatches it from my hand to feed the dogs lounging at her feet, unbeknownst to me until one licked my ankle and nearly caused my heart to leap out of my chest. They were gifts from a princess, she explained, one that desperately wants Finnian.

Gifting giant Mastiffs who lurk underneath tablecloths didn't work in her favor. Though, I find them rather adorable for their size. "What are their names?" I ask, reaching down to pet the one who favors my ankles.

Though the dogs belong to Finnian, Irina responds, "The brown one is Zeb, and he is the most loving if you couldn't tell." A black dog appears when she slips a piece of bacon beneath the table, his canines chomping on the strip. "The shark is called George, but I call him Georgie."

Georgie is terrifying and only visible by the dull whites of his eyes and the faintest sound of chewing. Zeb, however, has laid his head down in my lap and is staring at me with big eyes.

"I believe he wants me to feed him," I say with a slight grin.

"Don't," Irina instructs. "He has the foulest stench when he's fed food from the table, quite like my brother."

I pinch my lips together to try and prevent a smile from forming, sneaking a peek at Finnian, who is staring at Irina, unamused. "The princess was intolerable," he mutters.

"Perhaps your standards are too high," Irina replies.

The king huffs his agreement, and that's when Finnian stands and deposits his napkin on his plate full of leftovers. And my annoyance with him only grows when a servant comes to collect it. Five residents of Ashbury would gladly split what remained on his plate, but he has the luxury of walking away from the table without wondering where his next meal will come from or even *when* he'll be able to eat again.

This will never work between us.

I left the great hall to lose my way in the winding corridors again. Truthfully, I want to find a way outside to admire the diamond-encrusted towers in the daylight before returning to Ashbury, but I have been unable to locate the front entrance.

I nearly jump out of my skin when Finnian calls my name from a doorway. Irina was right; I need to be more observant.

"Elora," he says again when I don't acknowledge him. My pulse is drumming so loudly in my ears that it would not surprise me if he could hear it. "I have something of yours."

He dangles my shawl between two fingers as if holding a rat by its tail. I snatch it from him with a scowl. "I am surprised you deigned to touch it, Your Highness."

He leans against the doorframe with his arms crossed. I ignore how attractive I find him, just as I did at the ball and breakfast. I *refuse* to study him. His arrogance equally matches his good looks, but that isn't why I came here. I can't focus on how the whites of his eyes resemble clouds against the sky-blue irises.

Marrying him would undoubtedly include ignoring his wandering eye. As the princely playboy, it must be an active one.

"You may call me Lord or Sir," he gloats.

"I can think of a few other ones."

Godsdamnit, even his smirk is attractive.

"You don't like me, do you?"

"I don't know you," I reply flatly.

"You don't want to know me," he adds, his smile stretching into a grin. "You've formed opinions about me. I doubt I can change them."

If only I had learned to think before speaking. "Why does what I think matter, hm? Have you grown bored of seducing royals? Decided to slum it?"

And if looks could kill, I would be in more pieces than the cardigan draped over my arm.

He straightens, rolls his shoulders back, and towers over me. He has to be *at least* a foot taller than me, but I don't shrivel or slink away. I should, but my feet remain planted.

I expect insults or orders to leave the castle, but instead, he says, "I would like to give you a tour of our gardens."

I blink. "What?"

He nearly repeats it when he pauses and rolls his head to the left. "My sister is eavesdropping."

Irina saunters out of the shadows with a pout, followed closely by Zeb and Georgie. "Finn is always ruining my fun. She'll need this if you insist on giving her a tour."

I gasped when Irina hiked up her skirt and slid a tube of rouge from her stocking. Not once have I ever worn stockings, and certainly not lacy ones. I ask, "Where did you get those?"

Irina dropped her skirt and popped the lid off to smear the color across my lips. "I have friends." She sucks in her lips and releases them with a harsh breath, a *smack* following.

Feeling completely ridiculous, I replicate her, though my *pop* isn't nearly as flawless.

She wipes the corner of my mouth, utterly unaware of personal space, and laughs at my shock. "Honestly, Elora, are you scandalized?"

"Um," I squeak.

She disappears behind me and tightens the laces of my corset. "Wenches and horrible gossipers wander outside, Elora." She drags her fingers through my curls. "You are fresh blood."

Finnian sighs. "Fuck, Irina. I'm just taking her to the gardens."

Grabbing my shoulders, she spins me around so quickly that I stumble. "Maids talk, too. I'll leave this in your room." And with a wink and my shawl, she turns and leaves me dizzy.

I touch my bottom lip. "What color is this?"

With an amused grin, Finnian replies, "Red."

"Oh, gods." I rub my lips together in an attempt to fade the color. "She's quite—"

"Obnoxious?"

I can't help but smile. "*Colorful.* She must never bore you."

"Me or anyone else." He looks at my shoulders, then my lips, before settling on my eyes. "Accompany me?"

This would be the time to change my mind, take it all back, spend time with Azrea before she leaves, and survive with a faerie spell within my veins. But instead, I take a steadying breath, avoid his too-blue eyes, and nod.

Arches of white daisies are placed along long pathways in gardens landscaped like a dream. Nothing could've prepared me for what lies behind the castle in colorful, gentle chaos. Multi-colored flowers line each side of dirt paths, leaving only spots of green grass. Masking my wonderment would be pointless—my breathless gasps make it clear as we wander farther from the castle.

I crouch to brush my fingertips across the petals of a blue flower. The bright and bold hues contrast beautifully with the glassy exterior of the castle. I barely hear Finnian dismiss lingering gardeners and don't spare them a glance as they scurry away from us.

"Forget-Me-Not."

I hum my approval. "I've read about these but have never...." I pause, tilting my head. "I've never seen flowers so lively and.... Well, alive. Sometimes, my father would bring me a bouquet after spending the day here—" I stop myself from continuing. Memories with my father are tainted with gray.

"We have a flower shoppe in town, but these,"—he kneels beside me—"are rare and short-lived. These are my mother's favorites and are unavailable in the flower shoppe."

I tuck my fingers into my lap to stop touching something so uncommon. "If they're rare, how do they grow here?"

He shrugs. "They are as perplexing as the pumpkins beneath the bridge. There's something else I'd like to show you."

As content as I would be to remain with the flowers, my curiosity is more prominent.

I dust my palms off on my skirt as I stand—a habit I've picked up from spending days in the mountains.

When he holds his arm out for me, I blink. My hesitation seems to amuse him. "The pathway ends before we reach where I want to take you," he explains.

I curl an eyebrow. "I am familiar with uneven terrain, Prince Finnian."

My rejection irritates him. He lowers his arm and replaces his relaxed grin with a tight nod. "Very well."

Several moments of silence pass as we walk side-by-side down the path and deeper into the gardens. Finally, he glances down at me. "Are you always so...."

I brace. Insulting? Stubborn?

"*Tense*?"

I whip my head around, curls bouncing. Aches in my neck prove I am often tense, but his question twists my insides into knots. "Unlike you, I do not have luxurious gardens and idle days to wander them. Some of us have daily responsibilities."

"And you don't believe I do?"

Dumbfounded, I shake my head. "Everything you could ever need is at your fingertips. I doubt you would last a day in Ashbury." It would be a lie to say I didn't want to offend him. Everything about his ignorance flares my fury. And despite how cordial he's acting toward me, it can't erase the years of neglect my people have suffered while he's spent years traveling the countryside, seemingly uninterested in what's happening in his realm. "And to answer your rude inquiry, yes. I am often tense, but I do not expect you to understand why."

"I have responsibilities, Elora." He rolls his neck with a tight exhale. "And I wouldn't expect you to understand mine, either. But you've made assumptions about me—"

"Assumptions?" I interject with a breathy laugh. "Tell me the rumors are wrong, and I will gladly apologize."

"Depends on what you've heard," he mutters.

I'm not sure where we're going, but I've managed to get two steps ahead of him. "You know *precisely* what they say about you."

"And instead of deciding what you think of me, you're letting others do it for you?" He chuckles. "That would make you tense, overcritical, *and* gullible."

I gasp and spin, nearly causing him to stumble into me. "And I guess that would make you haughty and careless. Not to mention *amoral*."

"Amoral?" He throws his head back in laughter. "Does that mean you're a prude, Elora?"

I gape. I have half a mind to slap the grin off his face, but I'm too flabbergasted to finish a thought, let alone form a retort. "Thank you for this enlightening tour."

I pass by him, but he doesn't let me get far before he's at my side again. "This is twice you've walked away from me," he snaps, his tone laden with irritation.

"I'm shocked you can count."

A low growl rumbles in his chest as he wraps a hand around my wrist and tugs me backward. I nearly trip over my own feet when he twists me around to face him. "You've forgotten your place, Elora."

I attempt to yank free. "My *place*?"

"I am your prince, Elora. Whether you like me or not, that does require your respect."

I bark an annoyed laugh. "That is exactly your problem, *Lord* Finnian. You believe your title *deserves* my respect. What have you done to earn it, hm?" I step closer. "I might not have much, but I have the decency to not lie to you." I press a finger against his chest. "You do *not* have my respect."

Gods, I am failing miserably, but pretending to like him is much more complicated than I thought it would be. He could call for guards and have my wrists bound quicker than a breath.

Instead, a deep crease forms between his brows. His warm breath fans my face. An irritatingly divine hint of whiskey lingers, with the pleasant orchid aroma wafting off him.

His eyes search mine. I hold his stare through uneven breaths, the height difference between us shooting discomfort down my spine from the upward tilt of my chin.

I will not be the one to back down from this.

Finally, he releases my wrist and looks down at my finger against his chest instead. Then, he removes my hand from his chest, slides the tip of his thumb across my palm, and applies pressure to a point that nearly causes my breath to catch. It doesn't hurt, but it certainly holds my attention.

And I don't pull my hand away.

"Come with me," he says.

To the gallows? The dungeon?

"Come with you *where*?"

He looks ready to eat me alive, but his reply intrigues me.

"To smash pumpkins."

Twelve

Somehow, I allowed him to keep my hand in his while he pulled me away from the path, past greenery and shrubs, and through trees until we stood in front of a greenhouse. The warmth of his fingers fades when he releases me to stiffly stride to the double doors. If I didn't know any better, I would say I've managed to get under his skin. He hasn't said anything since I agreed to follow him.

When he disappears inside, I bend my arm back and fiddle with the laces of my corset, nervously looking around. He is free to be anywhere he pleases in Pumpkin Hollow, but I could be escorted off the premises.

When he reappears without his jacket and sleeves rolled up to his elbows, he beckons me forward by hooking his finger.

He is making it irritatingly tricky not to study every physical aspect of him. There's a reason women want him. Imagining myself swallowed by his solid frame has *even* me grateful that he isn't entirely hideous physically.

His personality could use some work.

I stay completely still until he takes a step forward. Fearing he'll chase and drag me back, I sigh and obey. His pleased grin nearly makes me turn around, but he reaches forward and places his hand on the small of my back as if already anticipating that.

Pushing me forward gently, he grandly gestures inside. Maintaining a stoic expression, I slowly step through the doorway.

The facade quickly drops.

Stretching back farther than I can see are rows and rows of pumpkins, every size imaginable, on moist, rich soil.

Leafy green vines weave through the pumpkins and snake up windows, allowing only streaks of sunshine to come through. And all I can say is, "These pumpkins are not painted."

The silvers, whites, blues, and orange pumpkins mix and mingle in a sporadic pattern. "How? The ones at the ball—"

"Those were painted," he interrupts. "He keeps these hidden from the public due to their unique color."

"But... But how?"

He points to the farthest edge of the greenhouse. "Those thick roots are buried underground. Can you guess where they end?"

"The bridge," I breathe.

"The bridge," he confirms. "But try as he might, he can't get underneath the bridge. He buried the vines long ago so no one above ground could see them." He shakes his head slightly. "A lot of manpower went into protecting pumpkins."

I steal a glance at him. "You sound bitter."

"These are his prized possessions." He nudges a pumpkin with his boot. "Fucking pumpkins, Elora. He went to war to protect the bridge and would do it again."

"For pumpkins," I reiterate with condescending laughter. "He warred with Ashbury for pumpkins."

It might be dangerous to speak freely in front of Finnian, but I find the notion as ridiculous as he mentioned.

"Not just for pumpkins, Elora." He doesn't seem to be defending Jasper's motives but educating me. "For the bridge, for the land, for control and power. And he's kept it for the faeries."

I turn to fully face him. Like Irina, he's being surprisingly open with me. "Why did you bring me here? Why are you telling me this?"

"Because you're angry," he replies. "You're angry with me. I disagree with your opinion of me, but I understand you might feel you're owed something for how Ashbury has been treated."

I scoff. "And you think smashing pumpkins will earn my forgiveness? It will atone for our neglect?"

"I care nothing for your forgiveness, Elora."

I can't say I admire his honesty.

"But if we are to be friends, you deserve the opportunity to destroy something he holds dear."

"Friends," I repeat, raising an eyebrow in disbelief. "Why would you want to be my friend? I can't imagine you need more friends."

He doesn't flounder for an answer. "Irina likes you. And if she wants you around, we will see one another again." With a smirk, he adds, "Believe me, I won't come searching for you to walk the castle gardens or leisurely read in the library."

I roll my eyes. "You can read?"

He ignores me, backing away to grab the handle of a wooden mallet. "It'll feel really fucking good, Elora. Let me help you feel good."

Well, that does something to me.

I run my tongue along the roof of my mouth with a slight corner grin. He drags two fingers across his bottom lip as if hiding a smile at my cautiousness. But then, he takes the lead.

He coolly passes by me to settle in front of a giant orange pumpkin in the middle of the rest after stepping over dozens of vines to reach it. I pull in the corner of my bottom lip when he rears back, veins in his hands straining from the mallet's weight above his head, and watch as he brings it down forcefully.

Years spent watching the faeries work with their toned, half-naked bodies and corded muscles didn't prepare me to see the prince's sleeves rolled up, back muscles stretching taut beneath his shirt, with his broad stance and confident posture. The memory of him from breakfast as a pristine, untouchable, always-in-impeccable-clothing-and-freshly-bathed has wholly shattered.

And I'm studying him so intensely that the second pounding of the mallet against the pumpkin's hard shell makes me flinch.

A jagged crack splits the shell.

And one more hit breaks it in half.

His chest rises and falls with tight breaths as he kicks the halves apart. Seedy guts stick to the soil and disgustingly cover his boots as he comes over and extends the mallet.

It would be unfair to walk away, but if someone catches us....

"You won't have another chance, Elora."

I exhale a deep breath and grab the handle. Despite the lack of food in Ashbury, I've built *some* strength from scrubbing the floors of our manor, but definitely not enough to swing at a pumpkin.

I drag the mallet across the ground to a much smaller pumpkin —almost embarrassingly small compared to the one he just broke —but I chose it for a reason.

White as snow without a speck of soil, it encompasses everything wrong about Pumpkin Hollow. Untouched, well taken care of, and about to be destroyed by the fallen princess.

Even my anger toward the king doesn't stop my arms from shaking as I raise the mallet above my head. I should've asked the enchantment for strength because the first swing didn't even dent the shell.

Finnian *tsks*. "I expected more from you, Elora. Is your only weapon that mouth of yours?"

My lower stomach tightens. "The one you keep staring at?"

I don't turn to gauge his reaction. Instead, I lift and swing again and again. The shell splits wide enough to spit pulpy strands and seeds across my skirt. Panting, I wipe beaded sweat from my brow with the back of my hand.

And then, I smile.

Because Finnian was right. This frivolous and somewhat immature idea of his feels *good*.

When I turn, he has another mallet and notes my satisfied smile with a slight nod. Then asks, "Again?"

❧

Morning turned into afternoon in a blur.

I didn't work nearly as quickly as Finnian, but we damaged fifteen pumpkins before I dropped my mallet to the ground to double over. My frizzy curls are sticking to my neck and shoulders, and the dress is attached to my body from sweat. My heart might explode if I don't catch my breath.

But breaking pumpkins apart has been oddly freeing. All my frustration was put into every swing, and the sound of shells splitting apart was cathartic.

Finnian tosses his mallet to the ground and tips his head back, closing his eyes as he inhales and exhales deeply through his nostrils. His brown-nearly-black hair glistens in a ray of sunlight, and his dampened ivory shirt has become sheer, revealing patches of skin across his chest and ribcage. And when I scoop a handful of stringy seeds off the ground to throw at him, it's purely to force myself to stop staring at him.

He lifts a hand to scrape the seeds from his stomach. I suck in my top lip to keep from laughing at the disgust on his face despite the guts from destroyed pumpkins already caked all over his clothing.

He bends over slowly, never looking at me, not moving quickly enough to frighten me, but the second I step away, he grabs a handful of seeds and hurls them at me.

I cry out when the lukewarm clump of strings strikes my chest, further ruining my defaced dress.

We exchange mischievous glances.

Then, lunge.

He throws seeds at me in fistfuls while I dodge them to return his hits with my own. He covers my dress, shoulders, and even the lower half of my face, bathing me in pumpkin seeds. I manage to douse his hair, the roots sticking to the sweat. But when my untouched hair becomes his next challenge, I dart toward the door with my hands over my head.

"Don't!" I shout. "Truce, truce!"

Laughing, he wraps an arm around my waist and tugs me backward. I squirm in his grip, twisting to get away and trying to dodge the fist hovering over my head.

"Truce?" I offer again, shoving his arm away. "Truce!"

I lower my arms just enough to peek at him when he stills. His broad smile fills me with a false sense of security, but he takes the distraction to cup my head in his palm and *smush* the seeds into my hair. Squeezing my eyes shut, I whine.

He erupts into laughter.

"Gods, you fiend!" I try to shove away from him, but he keeps an arm around my waist. "Do you know how long it will take me to get this out?"

"You?" He shakes his head wildly, emphasizing his tousled locks covered in seeds. "I have a meeting tomorrow morning!"

I snort. "Oh, in that case..."—I grab clumpy strings from my chest and spread them across his cheek. "Pumpkin delight."

He leans down and rubs his cheek against my forehead, growling when I try to shove him away again.

"Truce," I beg.

Chuckling, he straightens and peels a string from my shoulder. "Okay, okay. Truce."

As he keeps me pressed against him, our proximity is suddenly chest-tightening. And when I raise my gaze, his stare lowers to my mouth, further proving my earlier point. His finger twists a strand of my hair, but he flexes his hand as he releases it before it lowers to my ribs.

My skirt tightens around my waist when he bunches it between his fingers, pulling me half an inch closer. My heart pounds, my breath quickening. But then, voices in the distance made his head snap toward the door.

"Fuck," he whispers, releasing me to run to the door and peering through a crack.

I suck in a breath, blinking away the confusing disappointment. *You don't like him*, I remind myself. I am purely reacting to the endearing way he looks covered in pumpkin pieces. We bonded over smashing shells—that's it.

He curses again, grabs his jacket from the ground, and jogs to me. I don't have a chance to ask who's outside before he takes my hand and drags me to the back of the greenhouse.

I take one last look at the damage we inflicted on the rare pumpkins, somewhat prideful that we managed to smash so many, and wishing I could be here to see the look on the king's face when he realizes that it's not enjoyable seeing something you love destroyed.

Finnian opens a back door, looks around, pulls me outside, and closes the door quietly behind us. "Gardeners must've returned and heard us. Once they see what we did, they'll report it to Jasper."

Fear steals my breath.

He notices my wide eyes. "Elora, you'll be fine. I just need to return you to the castle."

"*You'll* be fine. If the king learns it was me—"

Finnian stops fidgeting to lock gazes with me. "I need you to trust me."

I don't have another choice.

Instead of jogging back the way we came, he tugs me deeper into the woods, shushing me each time I ask where he's taking me. But tucked far back into the forest—far enough where I can hear water somewhere nearby—is a stone staircase leading down to a latched door in the ground.

The wooden door is brown, chipped, and cracked, and it almost looks as if it was created specifically to blend into the ground. But it can't be disguised with the conspicuous staircase in the middle of a forest, drawing more attention toward it.

I tilt my head curiously. "Why would someone build a staircase? The door—"

"It made it easier to escape," he mutters, searching the ground for something.

I blink, looking from the door to him. "You built this?"

Silence follows my question, but it doesn't quiet my interest. Why would he need to escape? And how often did it happen for him to need a staircase for easier access?

Finally, he sighs, retrieves a large rock, jumps down into the narrow space containing the door, and slams the rock against an iron padlock. I recoil, wincing at each clang.

When the lock breaks and rolls off, he drops the rock and places his foot on one of the stairs, extending a hand to me.

I don't hesitate to take it.

Thirteen

Crisp and cool air blankets us, combatting the sweat we built from smashing pumpkins. Our shoes splash in residual puddles from rainwater dripping out of cracks overhead; the tunnel is so narrow that the rippling water bounces off the stone walls.

Elora's hand trembles in mine, either from fear or the cold air, and doesn't utter a word, not even an audible breath.

Irina uses this passageway often to escape the castle but has yet to inform me that a padlock was added to the door.

We remain underground for only a short time before the tunnel splits left and brings us into the castle basements. Light funnels through the small, foggy windows at surface level, allowing anyone below to see infiltrators—the entire reason the corridor was built.

Jasper never takes chances.

And Elora isn't releasing my hand.

I understand her frayed nerves from nearly getting caught, and while she's correct in assuming Jasper would punish her, no one will learn it was us in the greenhouse. It wasn't even my original plan to take her there, but when she admitted to not respecting me, I recognized the anger in her eyes. It replicates how helpless I often feel in matters regarding my father.

The idea of Elora being tossed in the dungeon for smashing pumpkins is ridiculous, but that doesn't matter. Jasper prides himself on owning rarities and has taken too many lives to change his stance. And whether or not he believes he needs Elora for the faeries, he would take it all away quicker than a blink if it meant proving a point.

No one touches what he believes he's earned.

I need to get the pumpkin seeds off her before anyone finds us. The guest wing is placed on one of the highest floors, mine only one above hers. The hallways will be full of maids who would tattle on us in exchange for a favor.

A soft pattering of footsteps around the corner gives me pause, and then I open the first door I find and shove Elora inside. She snorts while looking around the tiny linen closet, barely big enough for her, let alone both of us.

I smile but whisper for her to *hush*.

She nods against my chest, her hand squeezing mine, when a door beside ours opens. I recognize the voice as that of one of my mother's maids, talking to herself while retrieving blankets. Elora's shoulders shake from silent laughter, and it takes considerable effort for me not to follow in the hysterics from the absurdity of being stuffed in a closet in fear of retribution for breaking pumpkins.

She shifts a step, eliminating another inch between us. My breath catches when I look down at her. Her body is nothing more than a silhouette in the dark, but it's evident that her chin is tipped up.

Twice, I've considered kissing her.

In the dark, we could pretend to be strangers. I wouldn't be the son of a king she loathes, and I could act as if I don't need to marry her for his gain, that she hasn't irritated me to the point of wanting her out of this kingdom.

I *could* pretend that she doesn't set my teeth on edge—I could convince myself that wanting to kiss her has nothing to do with genuinely wanting to shut her up each time she opens her mouth, but lying would take far greater energy than how simple it would be just to lean down and see if her lips are as soft as her skin.

It hasn't been long enough since my last drunken escapade in a tavern from my travels that I could be desperate for someone as ... *brutal* as her... but I still somehow feel a draw.

Maybe that *is* the draw—how much she hates me.

Maybe I'm drawn to how much I despise her.

In the dark, one kiss could be a secret shared.

But twice, we've been interrupted.

When the door next to ours slams shut, she jumps. I loosen a tight breath. As footsteps fade, I push the door open with my back and lean out to ensure the maid is gone.

I drag Elora out of the linen closet. A strand from my shirt has connected to her shoulder, and she wrinkles her nose when peeling it off her to rub on my shirt.

Never mind that she is completely covered in them—this one grosses her out.

"Thanks," I mutter with a chuckle.

She gestures to her ruined dress. "How are we getting to the main floor like this?"

I grin. "We're not."

Curiosity crosses her expression, but she doesn't prod further. As short-lived as it might be, I've gained her trust. One wrong move will put us right back where we started.

Traipsing down dark corridors and committing pumpkin treason is one thing—proposing marriage to someone who has spent years hearing wretched stories about me is an entirely different challenge.

And if I could describe Elora in one word, that would be it.

Challenging.

Pulling her into a room, I drop her hand to remove my jacket and toss it on a small table that wobbles from the added weight. Stacks of small, circular basins emit the scent of mint and lavender, leftover from the soap used for laundering clothing during fall and winter when it becomes too cold for the maids to sit by the creek within the forest.

I grab a basin from the top of a stack and flip the valve on the wall. "It takes a minute," I say. "And it'll be cold as fuck. We used this passageway during thunderstorms after playing in the rain as kids."

"And you would wash off the mud in here," she finishes with a nod, hooking her thumb behind her to an old wardrobe. "Clothes?"

I lift my shoulder in a slight shrug. "It's been a long time since I've been here. You can check."

She doesn't; instead, she rocks on her heels. Water spurts in drops before free-flowing into the basin.

Clearing my throat, I keep my eyes down. "If you step out of your dress, I'll pour this over you."

She sucks in a breath and gnaws on her bottom lip. My remark about her being a prude was meant to insult her, but her nervous fidgeting now confirms I was correct.

I give her my best attempt at a kind half-grin. "We can try to make it to the guest wing as we are, but I can't guarantee we won't be seen."

She weighs the options, looking from me to the basin and back again. But fear can outweigh almost anything.

Her hands disappear behind her to untie the laces of her corset. My fingers tighten around the basin's rim, averting my gaze again. I know of the rumors she continues to remind me of—my reputation with women.

I can't deny them, but I won't take advantage of her. I need her trust in me to extend beyond hiding her from Jasper's wrath.

But I swallow when her dress drops, leaving her in a nearly sheer ivory slip. Her breasts and stomach remain covered, but the hem stops at her upper thighs, and I have to force myself to only look at her face instead of searching for where the slip ends.

She tugs on the bottom before crossing her arms over her stomach, her eyes lowering to the floor. A hint of red pools in her cheeks, but how her matted curls fall over her shoulders, strands of pumpkin all over her skin, and goosebumps on her arms make me ache. I itch to touch her, but I fear she will flee.

Like a doe caught in the forest, she freezes when I stand before her. With hooded eyes, the gold in her irises brightening each time a sliver of sun hits them, she peers up at me when I lift the basin over her head. “It’s cold,” I reminded her.

She squeezes her eyes shut to brace for impact, but I barely tip it over. The water dribbles on her head, allowing her a few seconds to adjust to the temperature.

She visibly shivers and sputters, bouncing on her toes when I gradually increase the amount. Continuously moving to stay warm, she lifts her hands to detangle the seeds from her hair.

It takes three refills before seeing more skin than strands.

Her head tips backward, her lips part as she drags her hands through the curls with the falling water. I reach around her with one hand to gather the ends of her hair in my palm, squeezing the drops of water out.

But my gaze.... It lowers from her lips to her shoulders, to the peaks of her nipples hardened from the chilly water. I have the damnedest feeling she doesn’t realize how alluring she is.

Soft as silk, her skin reminds me of a first sip of tea, the smooth liquid gliding across your tongue. Even wet, her curls are the color of champagne, And with her chocolate eyes..... wanting to taste the combination of chocolate and champagne makes my mouth water.

Before my thoughts overpower logic, I release her hair and step back. With one hand in her hair, she lowers her chin and uses the other to reach for the basin. “My turn?” she asks.

How can I convey to her that what’s unraveling between us is the most intimate I’ve been with a woman? Yes, I’ve sought pleasure and given it twice over, but I’ve never confused the two. Intimacy does not always equate to satisfaction, but I don’t try to explain that. I just nod, trying to convey nothing but disinterest.

But her evident inexperience and how ravishing she looks when drenched hardens my cock.

Taking the basin from me, she disappears behind me to refill it. I unbutton my shirt and add it to her discarded dress, leaving my pants and boots on. My desire to touch her would be quickly discovered if I removed anything else.

I pick the strands off my pants while waiting for the basin to fill, throwing the seeds on the pile of hers. "We could fill another greenhouse with these," I say, attempting to fill the tension-soaked air.

Her breathy laugh makes me grin. "And what would your father do if he wasn't the only one with pumpkins so rare?"

I click my tongue. "Banish us. Perhaps we should try?"

She pops up before me with the basin filled to the rim, water splashing onto my bare stomach. I hiss from the bite, and she giggles her apologies.

"I am already technically banished unless invited," she says.

She raises onto her toes to reach my shoulders, hyper-focused on clearing my neck. The tip of her tongue flips up to partially cover her top lip from intensely concentrating.

"I am extending a permanent invitation," I say, leaning forward to make it simpler for her.

Her fingers brush through the hair on my neck.

I swallow a groan.

"I don't think that's necessary. I will write my insults in a letter and send them across the bridge." Her tone carries a mixture of snark and amusement. "You never answered me earlier. *Can* you read?"

I pinch her side, resulting in her nearly dropping the basin. The remaining water floods my hair and rushes down my neck. I cry out from the sudden pricking of freezing water.

And she *snickers*. "Serves you right."

I lift my chin with a glare. "Is that so?"

With a defiant nod, she steps away to refill, but I wrap an arm around her waist, pull her back, and shake the water from my hair. She squeals from the droplets that coat her face and shoulders and shoves my head away. "You are such a child!" she scolds with a smile she tries to bury. "Let me wash you before your father assumes I stole you away for ransom."

I release her with a lazy grin. Her condescending eye roll earns another pinch as she steps around me, swatting my hand away. "They wouldn't believe you took me," I reply. "I leave as often as I can."

"Why?"

I turn my head to find her after her blunt inquiry. Her back is turned, her shoulder against the wall, and her feet are crossed while waiting. The slip barely reaches her mid-thigh.

I wonder how she tastes.

I consider running my head under the cold flow of water to freeze all thoughts of her. "I'm not needed here," I say. "When he needs something from me, he prevents me from leaving, so I try to stay away as often as possible."

She turns around and presses her back against the wall. Her fingers dance against the stone, drumming an uneven beat. "Is that why you're unaware of what's happened in Ashbury?"

I sigh and drop my head, shoving a hand through my hair and chucking seeds to the ground. "I take responsibility for my choices, Elora. I don't have a satisfactory answer to that."

She nods with a frown. The progress we've made is so fragile and could shatter so easily.

"I'm here now, though." I want her to know that I won't leave any time soon, even if the reason isn't honorable. "It might take time, but I am meeting with my father and his advisers tomorrow morning to catch up on what I've missed."

Overflowing water splashes on her feet, and she curses, switching the valve off. "Will you discuss the faeries?"

I lift an eyebrow. "Maybe. Why?"

She returns to me with a slight shrug. "Because they're my friends." She waits for me to bend over before washing my skin off. "I would like to know what the plan is for them."

"The plan won't differ," I say, partially lying and excluding their upcoming requirement to provide more, and decided to quickly change the subject. Something about Elora makes hiding the truth uncomfortable. "I would like it if you'd eat with us tomorrow. It's Midsetting. Do you know what that is?"

She slightly shakes her head.

"My mother's favorite time of day is when the afternoon sun meets evening." I smile softly. "Every autumn, she chooses a day when the sky will have the softest golden glow."

"And that's tomorrow?"

I shrug. "She always seems to know."

Her pensive expression softens. "I planned to return home this evening."

I could exercise my control and position to demand she stay, but forcing her would anger her. "It's already evening. I'll take you home tomorrow after we dine. Okay?"

She squeezes one eye shut and wrinkles her nose. "On one condition?"

My cheeks sting from smiling so often today. "And what is that, Elora?"

"No more pumpkins."

I tuck a curl behind her ear with a laugh. "Consider it done."

Elora's dress drags across the floor.

The rickety wardrobe in the basement held no clothing for me, leaving me bare-chested in the castle hallways with my boots and jacket in my left hand while keeping the other one free to catch her in case she trips.

Elora continues referring to it as a *smock*, but to me, it's a very long, antique dress with pockets. She's nearly tripped twice already, keeping her hands in her pockets to hold up the skirt while we climb the stairs to the guest wing.

Every time I laugh, she glares and mutters something crude, only furthering my enjoyment in seeing her so... unkempt. She can't be cruel to me when she looks so ludicrous, and I'm taking advantage of it.

When we approach the door to her guest quarters, she calls my name when I continue. Wordlessly, I motion for her to follow me. Her bare feet thump against the floor as she jogs to catch up, nearly tumbling forward *again*.

I caught her by the elbow. "That's three."

She yanks her elbow away with a frustrated sigh. "If you insist I stay another night, you could've offered to carry me. We would've gotten here quicker, and it would give me more time to tame these."

My lopsided grin results from her waving a clump of curls around. I prefer their wild bounce compared to the subdued knots. They soften her perpetual glare.

"Would you like me to carry you up these stairs, Elora?"

She scowls. "No."

"You brought it up."

"I was being facetious. Where are we going? I know you're not here often—"

I stop her from another insult. "Irina's wing. She'll loan you a dress for tomorrow and ensure you eat something this evening."

She frowns. "Was something wrong with what I chose to wear at breakfast?"

How can I phrase this delicately?

"The guest quarters are stocked with attire for every invitation one receives. Your chosen dress was fine for dining, but I believe Irina will have something more.... Your taste."

And more her *size*.

From Elora's remark this morning about being starved and how her dress nearly fell off each time she moved, I presumed her hatred for us has something to do with Ashbury not receiving enough food.

I plan to find out.

In her silence, I gently touch her arm. "Elora, it was only an idea. If you'd like, we can return to the guest wing."

"It's not that," she murmurs, then sighs. "I arrived here believing I would be treated...." she pauses when we level out on Irina's floor. "I wasn't expecting kindness. From you, especially."

I can't bury the deep frown that follows her words, disappointed that she has been mistreated and believes the worst in all of us. "Elora, what have you heard about me?"

She blows out a deep breath and shifts awkwardly. "Does it matter?"

I would bet pounds of gold that I know precisely which rumors she's heard. They are always the same.

"It matters to me."

She lifts her gaze. "Well—"

"I heard he kicks kittens and steals from the poor," a voice from the shadows replies. Irina appears with a feline grin. "And that he wets the bed, but wait...." Her grin widens. "That's not a rumor, is it?"

Elora smiles wide, but I narrow my eyes at my sister. "Stalking the prince is a treasonable offense, Irina."

"What *isn't* treasonable in Pumpkin Hollow, Finn?" She slips a hand behind Elora to open the door to her private quarters. "I'll be right in to scandalize you more, doe. Help yourself to my liquor."

Elora takes one step inside before glancing at me over her shoulder. "I'll see you tomorrow?"

She has taken my stories of frequent absences seriously, so I nod my acknowledgment. "Tomorrow," I confirm.

Irina dramatically waves her hand over my body after Elora closes the door. "Half-naked with the visiting fallen princess. I am not the only one to scandalize the innocent today."

I lean against the wall, ignoring her. "The fallen princess," I repeat. "Is that what you've named her?"

Irina blows the short wisps of hair out of her eyes. "It's what she's referred to here. I've snooped and lurked. She's caused quite the stir through town. No one can believe you danced with her at the ball. Envy is running rampant."

I shrug a shoulder, as uninterested in townie chatter as I've always been. "Always happy to provide useless entertainment to the masses, I guess."

She relaxes against her door. "You'll send her scurrying too soon, Finn."

"What are you babbling about?"

"The rumors she's heard will either result in you lying or admitting to their truth." She lowers her voice. "She's smart, Finn. She won't agree to marriage if she believes she's just a challenge to be won."

I close my eyes and throw my head back against the wall, hard enough for a dull sting to shoot through my skull. "I know, but I've thought about it more since last night, too. She's.... *bearable* to be around. We don't have to like one another. We simply need to tolerate one another for events."

Irina casts a look of disapproval. "You want to use her."

"Not necessarily," I grumble. "But it would alleviate the pressure of finding a bride."

"Yes, because we must make this easier for *you*." She rolls her eyes as she searches her hallway for eavesdroppers. "Remain charming. Jasper gave you a particular task. If he needs to step in, this won't be simple for either of you."

I lower my chin to stare at Irina's door intensely enough to burn a hole through it if I could. "She shouldn't learn the truth when it's too late. A betrothal might make Jasper back off, but it would make me no better than him."

She places a gentle touch on my arm. "I talked to her this morning. She's as displeased with Jasper as we are." She holds up one finger before I can pry. "She didn't reveal why she came here, but I believe we can enact change with her. We need to work together. But first, you need to secure an engagement."

Irina is right. Jasper will intervene if Elora leaves too soon and I push her away. His ways of controlling people.... I can't finish the thought. If Elora is harmed, the faeries might retaliate, and he'll have an excuse to wipe Ashbury off the map.

I hardly know any residents, but I don't believe they need to receive Jasper's wrath simply for being born in a kingdom across the bridge. Elora isn't my first choice for a bride, but if marrying her would prevent the deaths of an entire domain, the guilt of resisting an engagement isn't something I could drown in liquor.

"Treat her well," I say. "I will escort both of you to Midsetting tomorrow. And make sure she eats something." I pull the padlock from my pocket and drop it in her palm. "No leaving tonight, please. Let her stay with you. And you owe me a bottle of whiskey when you escape."

Her eyes light up while spinning the lock around her finger. "I don't know what you're talking about, Finn."

Fourteen

I fidget in the borrowed dress, smoothing the fabric while staring at myself in the floor-length mirror, searching for imperfections. The color of bubbling champagne, the dress boasts low straps that wrap snugly around my arms, even when I move. Shiny and small diamonds pin the waist to the tulle skirt—a magnificent work of art in itself. The tulle lengthens into a short train that effortlessly flows behind me with each step.

Instead of complicated laces, a line of buttons begins in the middle of my back and ends at the base of my spine. And somehow, I managed to secure myself in—no thanks to the always disappearing Irina. She left shortly after finishing my hair, promising to return in time for Midsetting, but that is *very* soon.

Most of my hair is pinned up—stragglers curling around my shoulders—and she clipped a gold butterfly into my hair. She used a rounded hairbrush after I bathed, which tightly coiled the natural spirals. Again, I'm staring at a stranger.

I look nothing like myself.

I may be victorious if Irina continues to dress me.

I stopped wishing for anything long ago, but hope has indeed made a home in my chest. My fingertips tingle with excitement at attending Midsetting, a tradition I've never heard of, even from my father's multiple visits to Pumpkin Hollow. And Finnian might be more tolerable than I gave him credit for.

He might even be charming.

Azrea would love this dress. It reminds me of her eyes—bold and unyielding, but not orange and full of fire.

No, the gold is enchanting and elegant.

A knock on the door draws my attention away from admiring the dress, instead adjusting the train behind me as I shuffle toward it, careful not to rip any of the delicate fabric.

Finnian is standing on the other side, and I'm more pleased to see him than I want to be. And I find myself smiling.

He swallows in greeting as he takes me in, his gaze lingering on my bare shoulders. Cedric has stared at me similarly several times, but never with such unyielding *focus*.

I spin once to distract myself from dissecting why Finnian is staring at me in a way that warms my cheeks. "Well?" I ask, readjusting the straps around my arms. They haven't moved, but it gives me something to do with my hands. "Irina chose it," I add quickly, "And she did my hair—"

"You look beautiful, Elora."

There is no condescending jest to be found.

"It's missing something, though."

"Oh?" I run my hands down my stomach and look behind me at the train before touching the pin in my hair. "I doubt anything else will fit. Do you see how tight this is? And she didn't leave anything else...." Trailing off, I peek up as he pulls something from his pocket.

"Turn," he says.

"Finnian—"

"*Turn*," he repeats.

As much joy as arguing with him brings me, his deepened tone warns me that trying would be pointless. With bated breath, I turn slowly. And in a motion that tells me he's done this before, he places a strand of pearls around my neck.

I can't form words.

Pearls are rare to acquire, usually requiring travel since our realm isn't near large bodies of water. I've heard the shoppe here has a small stock, but the cost is unfathomable. I didn't believe I would ever touch a pearl or wear a strand of them.

My mother had an imitation necklace once—a gift from my father, who apologized for being swindled by a vagrant—but my mother acted as if he'd given her treasure. I fell asleep on the steps that evening while watching them dance in the sitting room, my mother's soft voice the only melody to gracefully carry them.

The strand Finnian clasped around my neck is heavier than the imitation strand and cold against my skin, but when his fingers brush over the top of my spine, I'm not entirely convinced the goosebumps on my arms aren't from his touch.

He rests his hands on my shoulders. His warm breath tickles my neck and causes the loose strands of hair to flutter. "This is my mother's." He speaks so profoundly that I close my eyes to focus on his calming tremor. "She rarely wears them."

"Oh," is all I respond.

He removes his hands, but the feeling lingers. Being near him is single-handedly shoving past the gifted confidence of the wishing spell.

Turning to face him, the suffocating tension between us builds sweat at the base of my spine. He slides his hands into his pockets, and my gaze drops to his chest. I remember every inch of his bare chest, the grooves of his abdomen, the curves of his muscles because even when I was trying not to look at him yesterday, I did.

And suddenly, my mouth is as parched as the valleys in Ashbury. Even as often as I've gawked at the faeries, standing here with him makes me wish for a splash of water on my face.

Gods, I barely know him.

I'm not even supposed to *like* him.

I try to think of Ashbury, of the withered stalks in the fields, of Azrea and her nearing departure, but when Finnian breathes my name, it calls to a deep, dark pebble of longing within.

He takes a step closer.

Permission, I realize. He's testing how close I'll allow him to be. And I will myself to move away; I silently beg myself to remember logic and poetry about heartache, but his lingering stare on my mouth nearly causes me to shout for him to *hurry*.

But then, a flurry of black hair shoves past him. "Gods, Finnian, must you take up the entire doorway?"

Irina breezes past me and into her bedroom, explaining in a garble of shouts why she's late, where she's been, and how she successfully avoided the guards.

Finnian simply sighs.

I swallow my disappointment by sliding my hands across my waist and pretending to be interested in Irina's rambling.

"What did the two of you do after I left?" he asks.

I blink. "Hm? Oh." I'm unsure what to do with my hands, but they won't stop moving. "She had platters of food brought here, and we fell asleep on the terrace."

He rocks on the balls of his feet. "You weren't cold?"

Idle, awkward chatter to pretend we aren't drawn together like moths to a flame would be more amusing if I wasn't dumbfounded by it. Pointless tension, I keep reminding myself. It can't go further. I didn't come here to fall for him, and I refuse to allow how attractive I find him to divert me from my task. The constant interruptions must be happening for a reason.

"Ah, uh, no. Blankets."

Hades, Elora, honestly. I was speaking in complete sentences my second yearling, and that's how I chose to reply?

I have never been so grateful for someone than when Irina pops up beside me and drops a pair of gold slippers at my feet. I take Finnian's extended hand and scrunch my skirt in the other to slide into the shoes, but before I can drop my hand from his, he moves it to rest in the soft crook of his arm.

He looks from me to Irina, and his entire face hardens.

Irina's eyes widened before she shoved his arm. "*What*?"

I point to the corner of my mouth where a smudge of rouge

has painted hers. Instead of the shame I would feel if the roles were reversed, her feline eyes light up with delight. "I guess you know where I've truly been."

"Fix it, Irina. Now."

Finnian's demand isn't princely but brotherly. His tone held distinctive frustration, and his jaw popped when Irina rolled her eyes and disappeared again.

I ask, "Is she seeing someone?"

From the few interactions I've witnessed between them, it's apparent that both are very cautious with what information they give about one another. "Yes," he clips. "A man and a woman."

I haven't even properly kissed yet, and Irina has the affection of two people. "Is that why there was a padlock on the tunnel door?"

He nods once but offers no further insight.

I don't pry. "How unfortunate that she's withheld from the ones who cause her smile to never leave her face like that."

Finnian casts a sorrowful gaze. "Yes, well. The responsibility of her title doesn't allow for frivolous, clandestine meetings."

I hum my disapproval, the unjust response spinning spirals of anger in my stomach. "All of yours are rather public, yet the tales are followed with praise for the handsome prince. Why are hers hidden and paired with disapproval?"

His body tenses against mine.

"It seems unfair," I continue. "I haven't heard of you being locked in the castle."

His comforting sky-blue eyes morph into icy tundras. "Do not speak of which you do not understand, Elora."

The warning brings a scowl to my face. "Have I forgotten my *place* again, Lord Finnian?"

His deep-throated chuckle is closer to a growl. Using our connected arms, he pulls me an inch closer and fingers the strand of pearls around my neck. My breathing shallows.

"This makes a divine collar around your pretty little neck, Elora." He wraps a finger around the strand and tugs me close enough that his breath blankets my face. "What a shame it would be if you lost it."

I jerk my head away just as Irina reappears. Fear coils tightly around my gut.

"Do not frighten our doe, Finn." Irina shoves his chest. "He doesn't bite, Elora."

Finnian keeps his unapologetically dark stare on me even as Irina walks into the hallway. "Are you frightened, little doe?"

I don't reply, nor do I believe Irina.

Finnian's bite would be undoubtedly paralyzing.

The four-columned pavilion's glass roof beautifully reflects the setting sun's glow. This is where Finnian originally planned to take me yesterday before changing his mind to the greenhouse instead—a fact he shared with me while he followed behind Irina.

I refuse to acknowledge him and still successfully ignore his existence while studying our surroundings.

Towers of *un*smashed pumpkins encompass each column of the glass box we are crammed into. Sweat is glistening on our foreheads, but no one has dared to complain about the heat. I understand wanting to admire the beauty of the autumn sky, but we have no shade or cover while trapped under a roof that might as well be a mirror.

King Jasper has said nothing about the criminal act on his precious pumpkins but blames the queen for the temperature—as if she invented the sun herself. Dolly and Daffodil, who were also invited to stay another night after their embarrassing display at breakfast yesterday morning, fan themselves with both hands while agreeing with him.

When the king deigns to speak to me, it's always the same—faeries and my father. He seems to have trouble understanding that my personality involves characteristics outside those subjects. For example, I hold a revitalized disgust for his son. That would be a topic I could speak endlessly about. I would gladly detail my regret for believing he could be a trustworthy adversary.

Regina glares at me, studies Finnian, and glares at me again. Each of my interactions during Midsetting has become entirely redundant. I doubt the three of them will leave the castle until I do since we're *family*.

"Do you hunt, Elora?"

Digging myself out of my hole of hatred means tearing my eyes away from the bunnies, sniffing for food in the gardens, and pretending my joy of being here is solely because of the king's company. It has become a little easier masking my scowl, though he certainly doesn't make it easy when questioning me with his mouth full of another pumpkin concoction.

"I do not," I reply, forcing a smile. "My father did, as you might know, but he never taught me how to use a bow." And since Ashbury has no food *for* animals, wildlife is nonexistent.

His mouth is stained with red wine when he takes a draw for a goblet made of gold and bright jewels. "Where do you find your meat?"

This is a test, I realize.

"From the weekly deliveries from Pumpkin Hollow, Your Majesty." Of expired, rotting carcass.

He hums with a nod. "Is it enough?"

Everything *stops*.

Nothing but complete silence fills the heated chamber, except for my heart, when it plummets into my stomach. *Lie*, I plead silently, lie until you're confident you won't *die*.

Regina speaks first. "Ashbury is grateful for anything—"

But that king doesn't want to hear from her, looking nowhere but at me. "I did not address you. I would like to hear Elora's response."

Every set of eyes falls on me. Dolly and Daffodil's twisted grins tell me they won't miss me when I will undoubtedly *not* answer how he wants.

The only comfort I find is in Irina's encouraging nod.

This is why I came here. To help my people.

This is why I risked drinking faerie-tainted water.

But that didn't include speaking to the king about this directly. If he locks his own daughter away for disagreeing with him about her own life, what leverage do *I* have?

I pray a bolt of lightning will spread the clouds and strike him down, but until that happens, I need to grasp the remnants of bravery. "I think progress for any realm is constantly changing. My stepmother is correct about our gratitude, however…." I clear my throat. "Ashbury would benefit from additional deliveries of food and water." My ears rang, and every organ in my body flew in an effort not to be chopped up and used as fertilizer in the gardens, but I did it. I said what needed to be said.

Finnian notices my trembling hands when I tuck them under the table, and his hand covers both of mine without appearing to move. I want to pull away; I want to shove him off, but the touch does remind me to breathe.

King Jasper ponders and stares in silence. Then, the deep laugh in his chest causes me to grip Finnian's hand tightly—as if that will stop retaliation for my honesty. It's not Finnian's responsibility to save me, nor do I believe he would.

"An extra wagon a week it is," he says.

I blink.

It can't be that simple. If any valuable lesson came from my father, nothing comes without strings.

"Thank you," I breathe, the uneven tremor of my voice the very least of my problems.

Queen Honora clasps her hands together with a soft smile. "Shall we retire? It is warm."

"You're a bright girl," the king interjects. "You remind me of your father."

I have the damnedest feeling that it isn't a compliment.

"I have a proposition for you," the king continues.

Irina glances at Finninan.

Finnian removes his hand from mine. Whatever the proposition is, he knows. Queen Honora's fading smile warns me that I won't be able to deny it.

"I am willing to discuss improvements for Ashbury," he begins, but he only would have known my reason for coming here by speaking with....

Regina.

Gods, what agreement did she make on my behalf?

A servant clears the plates from the table before Jasper speaks again. "I need you to take your father's place as Keeper of the Faeries."

"Of course," I accepted quickly. "I would be delighted to remain close to the faeries, and as you can imagine, I did learn quite a bit from shadowing my father."

Regina's scowl flips into a triumphant grin, stretching her thin skin taut.

My relief is short-lived.

"After speaking with your mother—"

"Stepmother," Irina corrects.

Regina's scowl snaps to Irina, only to be met with an icy glower from the queen.

Jasper ignores Irina. "We have come to an agreement. I know your hardship since your father's passing and that a dowry does not accompany you."

A dowry. Those are only needed when....

"But you are well-bred. Good breeding leads to strong lines."

Did he truly just compare me to a fucking horse?

Finnian inches away from me, guilt enveloping his profile. I start to shake my head, but I can't move. My fate has been decided, my freedom stripped away. This was supposed to be my choice, my decision. I needed to be able to walk away—that was our agreement. If I'm to be the Keeper, marriage isn't required. I can earn wages until the faeries leave, be given the power to do something, and *not* be tied to such an arrogant prince.

But riches will always outweigh me.

"The union between the Prince of Pumpkin Hollow and the fallen Princess of Ashbury will reflect well on our realm when a son is born."

The fallen princess.

That *name.*

He wants to twist his invasion of my kingdom into a story of unity. 'A union' is precisely what I wanted. It's what I need for my home to thrive, but the condition, the removal of *choice.* "A son," I repeat slowly, as if it's multiple syllables. "A son...."

Dolly barks a heinous laugh. "You want Ellie to be your princess? She is nothing but a servant! She scrubs floors!"

Daffodil joins in. "All hail Ellie! The princess of ash and dirty rags!"

They break into a fit of laughter. Regina says nothing to calm them, to stop them, only broadening her smile at the blooming pink of my cheeks. "What have you done?" I whisper to her.

"Oh, Ellie," Regina says, "It's what your father wanted."

My lips part. What *my* father wanted?

"Enough!" Finnian shouts over their incessant mockery. "Leave this castle. You are no longer welcome here."

Regina's victorious smirk drops. "But the agreement...."

"We have restored your fortune," Finnian interrupts. "That was the extent of what you'd get in return for your cooperation."

Am I breathing? I can't be.

Everything around me is spinning too quickly.

"Her cooperation?" I ask breathily. "You knew about this?"

It is Irina who replies for him, "Arranged marriages are by contract, Elora. It is signed by each party when negotiating a betrothal."

"But there isn't a betrothal—"

"There is," Finnian mutters. "I signed."

The heat and shock have made me dizzy and cold, and I am unable to reconcile any of this. I should feel ecstatic that my efforts aren't needed, but instead, I feel.... Betrayed.

His kindness was all a lie. Nothing between us was real. Every touch and stolen look was fabricated to gain my trust.

Not allowing me to leave, begging for me to stay for Midsetting. Gods, his meeting this morning was for this moment.

"But my father is dead," is all I can argue.

"He came to me long ago," the king says, rubbing his bloated belly. "I wanted to meet you first, but not during your bereavement. He signed his name before his death."

The heat has dried my eyes to the point where tears won't fall, but they've certainly impeded my vision; everyone surrounding me is nothing more than blurs.

My own father signed away my future.

Freedom was *never* a wish. It never even existed.

King Jasper leans forward despite the lack of room between his stomach and the table. "We will discuss timeframes for providing an heir another day. Until then, you will assist with the faeries, and I will listen to your requests."

He will *listen*, not honor.

I can't fight this. I didn't emancipate from the household after my father died. I stayed for the memories and proximity to Azrea, and that choice sealed my life to Regina's decisions. As sole executor, she could've prevented this. She didn't have to agree with my father's decision, but she did.

She signed me away.

I blurt, "What if I don't want this?"

Finnian stills. Irina lowers her eyes.

But the king lazily waves his hand around the empty air. "Use your imagination."

I read too much as a child because my vast imagination can create the worst horror stories. The gallows, the deaths of everyone I hold dear, the final destruction of Ashbury. He could take his pick.

I push my chair out and stand. Fatigue nearly overcomes me when backing away from the table on shaky legs. "I need a moment."

Ancient fae magic within the spell prevents me from wishing against the will of others, but humans.... People like the king and Regina will stop at nothing to benefit from imprisoning others. The second I crossed that bridge, my life was decided.

I fell right into their trap.

Such a foolish doe to graze where lions play.

PART TWO

the princess

Fifteen

Irina stands to run after Elora, calling her name, but Elora doesn't turn back. I move to follow Irina, but Jasper hits his fist against the table. "Irina!" Jasper rumbles, "Sit down! We do not chase lowly girls." He calls for one of the men hidden in the gardens to fetch *the girl* and bring her back to the table.

But, I stand. "Leave her be. You bombarded her with this information. It was unnecessary."

Irina, whose strength derives from defiance, lingers in the doorway of the glass summerhouse. "She is not part of this family yet. You will allow her to grieve her freedom."

"I am her king!" he bellows in response.

"And *wretched*. I know that stealing power from women is your favorite pastime, but she does not *belong* to you," Irina adds, her disgusted glare moving to *me*. "She is apparently *yours* now. How fucking disappointing." Gripping her skirt in her hands, she flares it as she spins and leaves, leaving me no time to form a reply.

"Irina!" Jasper shouts, grunting as he stands.

I lean on the table with his fists. "Leave them be," I repeat, pointing to the man awaiting instruction while looking nowhere but at my despicable father. "Call him off."

Jasper's chest heaves, his fists clenching. Irina's disobedience is typical behavior, but mine shocks him. I was born and bred to agree with every decision and am partially the reason Elora's freedom was stripped away from her, but I will not allow him to torment her before she has time to accept it.

The remaining guests remain silent. Jasper reluctantly motions for the guard to return to his post while my mother breathes a sigh of relief—not for Elora's sake. Jasper has often clarified that being his son will not prevent any punishment he deems fit.

"Ellie always has to be the center of attention," one of the step-sisters says with a sigh. I haven't cared enough to learn their names. One of them is a hideous flower, I think.

The vile creature continues, "If I looked like her, I would try to draw *less* attention to myself."

My nostrils flare from the sharp air intake at her remark—the insulting way she speaks about my future *wife*. "Leave," I demand. "Your invitation across the bridge has expired."

Regina dares to look offended. "But the wedding! Elora is my—"

My entire body tenses. "Do not say daughter. You are not her mother. You gave her up without a thought."

Regina rears back. I silently dare her to test me, but my mother speaks before she can rile me further, "The wedding will be small. It is happening quickly, per our king's request. It will be blessed by a presiding bishop for the gods to bestow goodwill upon them." My mother stands and clasps her hands, resting them against her waist. "My son is correct. Your presence is no longer needed."

The floral sister wraps her hand around Jasper's wrist. "Your Majesty—"

He yanks his arm from her and stands so quickly that his chair topples backward. "You should lose your hand for touching your king so freely!" Again, he calls for his men, desperate to order someone around. "Escort them from Pumpkin Hollow immediately."

The twins shriek in protest, but Regina calmly stands and bows to Jasper. "Girls, it is time to return to the palace manor. Thank the king for his generosity."

Each woman dips into pathetic curtsies with trembling bottom lips. How is Elora years younger than them, yet they behave like scorned children?

But Regina gazes upon me with an unsettling curve of her mouth. It is an unspoken challenge that I cannot prepare for. "Send Elora to collect her things," she says.

My only response is to gesture for them to leave. And it isn't until they are out of earshot that I turn to Jasper with fantasies of the sun burning him alive that I say, "It was not part of our agreement to inform Elora of this tonight. She barely knows me."

He grunts. "I do not require your permission, boy."

I open my mouth to spew everything he needs to hear—why his people fear him, why none of his family respects him—but my mother gently touches my arm.

"Go, son."

I contemplate speaking anyway. The need to break free from him grows by the day, but my mother would be the one to receive the brunt of his anger. And the maddening urge to find Elora outweighs the desire to kill him where he stands.

For now.

❧

"She's not in there."

"Hades," I snap, flinching. Knocking relentlessly on Elora's door has proved pointless. "Where is she, Irina?"

Irina lifts a shoulder in a shrug, avoiding my gaze.

"Irina," I growled. "I didn't know—"

"That you signed away her freedom? I find that hard to believe." She crosses her arms. "After everything he's put us through, you did the same to her."

I drag a hand down my face. "It's not as simple as that, Irina. And you said to secure an engagement!"

She shoves my chest with both hands. *Twice*. "By honorable means, Finnian! Excuse me for assuming you would know that!"

I fight the urge to hang my head like a scorned dog.

"You could've gotten to know her and gained her trust, but instead, you took away her choices." She threads both hands in her hair. "We had a chance with her. She'll never trust you now."

I sink against the wall.

"What happened this morning, hm?" Her lips pinch, waiting for me to respond. "When you left, you asked me to treat her well. What changed between then and now? Did you fuck someone last night? Did you find someone else and forget about her?"

"No, Irina. I didn't go anywhere last night." Honestly, it crossed my mind after I left her yesterday evening. After seeing Elora soaked and wondering how sweet she might taste, I wondered if sinking my cock into someone else would soothe the ache of not touching her, but I couldn't.... Stomach the idea.

"We met with the advisers this morning," I murmured, closing my eyes. "We didn't speak of Elora, but then..."—my hand curls into a fist—"Regina came in and approached Jasper with a proposition. She informed us that a male warrior has been trying to court Elora for years."

Jealousy from that moment resurfaces. "The male is the brother of their leader. And the leader's mate is her closest friend. Because of those two faeries, they will do anything to ensure her safety. Jasper already feared their closeness, but they're *loyal* to her, Irina. Loyalty is dangerous in the wrong hands."

She gestures for me to continue. "*And*?"

"*And*," I sigh, "with the rumors of displeased residents in Ashbury, Jasper agreed with Regina. Forcing Elora to wed instead of giving me time to entice her would be more beneficial."

"For *whom*?" She wags a finger when my exasperation turns to annoyance from her probing. "No, Finnian. You didn't have to agree with him."

"I did it for her," I say quietly. "Regina agreed to abide by Harry's wish of a betrothal *only* if their fortune was restored. I just... blacked out. Elora was being traded like livestock, and I wanted her away from Regina. I didn't want her to return with them."

"He'll *kill* her," she reminds me, her teeth clenched and fists balled. "If she doesn't follow exactly what you laid out in the arrangement, he will kill her. He doesn't give second chances."

"I'll protect her—"

"How?"

I haven't found time to detail a plan.

"Keeping me from having to wed is not the same as protecting Elora when she doesn't provide an heir, Finnian."

Nothing I could say would satisfy her because she was right. Nausea hasn't left me since I signed my name underneath his. "I just want to find her, Irina."

She turned and walked away, but I chased her. "Irina, please. I need you to trust me. Be upset with me, but trust that I will protect her. I don't know how yet, but I'm your brother. Hasn't that earned me a little faith?"

The topaz color of her eyes always darkens each time she cries, which is rare. Irina is unbreakable, yet when she looks at me over her shoulder, the disappointment in her tearful gaze makes my chest tighten. "You are my brother, Finn. And my best friend." She entirely turns to place a gentle hand on my chest. "And I love you. But I swear to the gods, Finnian, if you fail, if that girl loses her life because of you, you will never see me again."

"Irina," I breathe, eyes widening in surprise.

"I will not stand by and let another man control the fate of women, Finnian."

My throat constricts as I try to swallow her heavy words. The thought of never seeing my sister again brings an entirely new level of regret to my mistake. A dagger would've hurt less than being compared to our father.

"I can protect both of you," I promise.

She stares at her hand on my chest, contemplating divulging Elora's whereabouts.

"Irina, *please*."

She squeezes her eyes shut. "I told her to use the underground tunnel to leave the castle undetected. She wants to go home."

❧

I stumble down the steps just as Elora opens the tunnel door. Out of breath and red-faced from running around the castle to beat her here, I lunge when she tries to slip back inside.

I take her wrist. "Elora—"

She tries to pull herself free. "Go away!"

"Elora," I try again, dragging her closer. "Elora, I was going to tell you privately. I didn't know he planned on telling you...."

"You think that's why I'm upset?!" She stabs her finger against my sternum repeatedly. "You *tricked* me."

Wincing, I rub my chest. As small as they might be, Irina and Elora hold a surprising amount of pain-inducing strength. "I didn't trick you, Elora, and this wasn't to be cruel."

"Let me go," she snaps, trying to peel my fingers from around her wrist.

"No," I growl, "Not until you listen."

She reaches into the pocket of a gray hooded cloak. I recognize it from Irina's wardrobe. She has multiple coverings available for disguising herself to leave the castle. Seeing Elora in one to escape *me* enrages me.

I wait for her to produce a small weapon to drive through my chest, but she opens her fist for the strand of pearls to dangle from her fingers. "My *collar*, Lord Finnian."

Sighing, I let her drop it in my palm. Rattling off my list of things to apologize for in my mind, I'm not prepared for the elbow she drives into my stomach. I release her on impact and double over to groan. She breaks into a run, heading the complete *opposite* way of Ashbury.

This girl really needs a sense of direction.

"Elora," I rasp, straightening to inhale deeply and cursing from the ache in my stomach. And the farther away from me she gets, the angrier I become. My years in the army did not prepare me for the elbow of a scorned woman.

When she disappears behind the tree line without so much as a glance to be sure she hasn't left me permanently maimed, my resolve to speak to her changes into a determined *need*.

I sprint after her. Her breathless pants aren't far ahead, but I stumble back when she steps out from behind a tree. I don't manage to dodge the first two apples she forcefully throws against my chest. They don't hurt nearly as bad as her elbow, but my patience with her dwindles.

I catch the third apple with one hand and bite, staring at the cunning little doe. She notes the change in my eyes, the rolling of my neck, and widens her eyes when I mouth,

Run.

❧

Our forest isn't deep.

At least, not in the direction she's headed. It spans for miles, but she's not doing more than running in a giant half-circle.

Despite the jerky zigzags she's making to lose me, we'll reach the stables soon. She's quicker than I thought she would be, but her comfort of walking away from me is growing tiresome.

Her hood has fallen, revealing the tight braid tucked underneath, untamed curls trying to escape. I have the briefest need to wrap it around my wrist, but that can't happen. I can't have her in the ways I fantasize about.

When she cuts left, I grin.

The forest layout lives within my mind, so I stay straight, pouncing the second she reappears. With my arm around her waist, I pin her against a trunk.

Her cries of frustration broaden my grin.

Her arms flail, trying to hit any piece of me she can. I grab her wrists with one hand and lock them above her head.

"Is this how you should treat your future husband, Elora?"

She seethes. Puckering her lips, she rears back, but before she can spit on me, I squish her cheeks. "*Swallow*, Elora."

I watch the soft bob of her throat as she listens for once and swallows. "Good girl," I say, releasing her face but not her wrists. "Will you listen to me now?"

Her chest heaves, her cheeks flushed in the sweetest pink, reminding me of the sky in Ashbury when the sun sets. "There is nothing you could possibly say—"

I pull her braid from underneath the cloak and toy with the end. "Tell me you didn't come here to marry me."

She goes completely still.

After Irina mentioned Elora's displeasure with Jasper, her acceptance of his invitation to the ball made sense. I was too annoyed by the mysterious draw to her to figure out the undeniable reason just yet.

I do not require her verbal confirmation. "That's what I thought. What did you need from me, Elora?"

"I don't know what you're talking about."

"If we're going to make this marriage work,"—I chuckle when she loosens a curse under her breath—"There needs to be honesty between us." I place the tip of my finger under her chin to drag her gaze to me. "Tell me."

She searches my eyes, unaware of the obscene effort it is taking for me not to lower my eyes to her pout. Her rigid body against mine, our hips connected, and being alone with her feels like an elephant sitting on my chest.

She frees a defeated sigh. "Ashbury."

My knowing nod earns me another glare. "And you thought if you could... what? Seduce me? That I would give you what you crave? All you had to do was ask, little doe."

A pleasing, deeper red fills her cheeks. I bring that color out of her frequently. She becomes embarrassed quickly, or I make her nervous, but I selfishly hope for the latter.

I don't wait for an answer. "This partnership can benefit both of us, Elora. What does Ashbury need?"

Her breathy laugh accompanies an eye roll. "You think it's as simple as giving you a list?" She shakes her head. "Everything."

I raise an eyebrow in disbelief. Meeting with the advisers this morning conveyed some of their neglect, but it can't be as bad as she leads me to believe. "He agreed to another wagon a week...."

"Your ignorance leaves much to be desired."

I increase the pressure against her body with mine and tighten my hold around her wrists. I am straddling dangerous territory with her here, away from the castle and other lifeforms. "*Enough*. I am willing to help you, Elora, but your short-sighted remarks won't do you any favors. Specifics, little doe."

"I can't give you specifics—"

"Are you always this stubborn?"

"You have no idea what you're asking of me! You haven't cared enough to visit!" The desperation in her tone gives me pause. "I can't give you specifics because I'm serious. Everything, Finnian. Ashbury needs everything."

It's nearing nightfall, but the plea in how she said my name causes me to question my skepticism. "Show me."

"Can we not take the carriage?"

Strapping the saddle to my horse, I shake my head. "This will be faster, and my whereabouts won't be questioned. Coachmen are required to inform Jasper of my movements. Whisking away my hesitant bride-to-be would raise the alarm." I point in the direction of the bell tower. The very top of the steeple is visible above the trees. "The bell rings for three reasons, Elora."

Resting my elbows on my horse's back, I use my fingers to count. "One, a royal wedding, and I have a lot of cousins. Two, Jasper's yearling." I roll my eyes along with her. A grown man still requiring bells to be rung as he ages is over-the-top and befitting for my father. "And the third is when I leave this realm. It's to alert him that I've left again and allow him plenty of time to send someone after me."

She wrinkles her nose. "He does that?"

"Yes, Elora," I sigh. "He does that."

"Irina mentioned surviving..." She raises onto her toes to meet my eyes over the height of my horse. "Is that what you've been doing?"

I weigh her question with cautiousness. Furthering her hatred for my father would risk us all, but especially her. Instead, I slip on my mask of arrogance. "Worried about me, little doe?"

I worry she can see through me, but a scowl soon replaces her curiosity. "Let's get this over with."

I pat my horse's flank. "This is Major."

White as snow, Major might seem similar to our other horses, except he sports a thick black line from his forehead to his nostrils. Bred to travel, he is also the largest. He intimidates most, but his personality resembles falling asleep in a blanket of fresh powder.

Gentle giant.

"When he was born, my father wanted him for the stripe. He has a knack for collecting rarities."

The quirk of her eyebrow means she's already figured that out.

"Major was supposed to be for me. I begged my mother to speak with him. He gave in, but only if I took the responsibility of breaking him."

"He's magnificent." She trails her finger down his stripe. "Hello, Major."

I smile when he greets her with a low neigh. "Have you ridden a horse?"

She sheepishly shakes her head.

I brush off the swelling in my chest, mistakenly prideful that I will be the first man she rides with. "He's gentle," I assure her. "Horses sense what their rider feels. If you're nervous, he'll adjust to your needs."

She hums while smiling, still affectionately petting him. "Horses sound more caring than humans."

"They are," I confirm. "Horses are empathic. Come. I'll help you."

I mount Major first but plant my hands on my thighs instead of extending one to her. From the few days I've known her, she seems to be the type who would rather be taught than given.

Her lack of height isn't helpful.

"One hand on the horn." I point to it. "One foot in the stirrup. Swing one leg over, but try not to kick me, as tempting as it might be."

I wait patiently while she follows my instructions, and I keep my hands to myself, even when she struggles to lift high enough to place her foot in the stirrup.

Major shuffles closer to help, but it throws her off-balance enough for me to grab her elbow. "Steady," I command Major.

She blows a loose curl from her eyes and jumps but remains balanced on one leg while she gauges how to swing her other leg over without kicking me. Grinning, I lean back a few inches and lightly pat her hip.

Licking her lips, she bends and swings. I cradle her legs between mine and grab her waist to pull her back until she's pressed against my chest, delighting in her gasp.

"Now what?" she whispers.

I place my hand over hers on the horn. "Now, Elora, you show me why you so desperately wanted to marry me."

Sixteen

She might not realize it, but her entire body perfectly molds to mine, her head tilted against my shoulder. From a stolen glance at her face, she appears lost in thought. I want to inquire what distracts her, but I don't want her to move.

Earning her trust back won't come quickly, but allowing her to feel safe in my embrace moves me one step closer.

The lowering sun provides a last lick of the warm, golden glow of the sky. Against the nearing red clouds of Ashbury, autumn is depicted flawlessly when the colors clash.

I risk losing her warmth when I ask, "The clouds are from the faeries' heat?"

"Yes," she breathes.

Even from our proximity to Ashbury, the red sky reminds me of tales of the empyrean heaven, occupied by flame and spiraling ash clouds. The cool breeze of the autumn air grows distinctly muggier and sticks to my skin. I didn't prepare for travel as she had, and my bulky dinner jacket now mocks me as sweat beads across my brow.

"How will I cross?" she asks softly.

Her voice no longer holds the typical bravado. Instead, it seems to be sharing a border with sorrow. And though my life has always been decided for me, I imagine that hearing that her father made the decision for her future without consulting her was hard for her. She cannot question him or even ask if it's true. She's taking the word of a king she loathes, a stepmother who despises her, and a prince she doesn't trust.

I glance down at her again. A single tear slides down her cheek and twists my insides. Even though she came to Pumpkin Hollow to procure a betrothal on her own, she still had the choice to return home if she changed her mind.

Now, it has been forced upon her.

"Elora, I promise to make this transition as smooth as possible. No one will prevent you from returning any time you please." I risk a hand slap when I gently graze her thigh with my palm. "You're free to borrow Major whenever you want. Or, I can provide you with your own horse."

Her silence edges me to desperation. We might not be friends, but we can't be enemies. "Major has sired colts. You can choose one. I will even train him myself."

"I did not see colts," she whispers, her tone distant.

"The stable Major resides in is only one of many," I explain. "Our army is large, and we have enough horses for half of them. Pumpkin Hollow expands across many acres."

She stares ahead. "Do you know Ashbury's history?"

"I do," I reply.

"My father was a traitor."

I nod with a slight frown. "And you believe you're betraying Ashbury by becoming my wife?"

She toys with the end of her braid. "When it was my decision, I didn't. It was a sacrifice I would make for my people—for their survival."

I don't utter a word, even slowing my breathing. Complete sentences not riddled with insults are far and few between, and I don't want to interrupt.

She wipes the tear from her cheek. "I worry I'll forget. I'll be so consumed with having everything I could ever want, and I'll forget."

"You won't forget," I assure. "You will still be involved, Elora. You will build a plan to present to Jasper when not with the faeries. It may not have happened as you planned, but it's still happening. It's still a victory."

"Did you know?" she murmured.

I want to pretend I didn't hear her—avoid it altogether and hope she forgets she asked.

"Was it always the plan? Did you know what my father did?" She closes her eyes. "Did you know what he signed?"

I loosened a deep sigh. "I didn't know who you were until the ball. Afterward, I asked Jasper to remove you from Pumpkin Hollow completely. I wanted you banished entirely."

Her cheek *barely* pulls up into a grin.

"But, he revealed why he invited you after you stormed out. He required me to secure an engagement, but a forced arrangement wasn't discussed. He didn't inform me of your father's decision until this morning's meeting."

Her grin disappears. "What changed?"

I contemplate telling her the truth—that Regina traded her without hesitancy. "Your stepmother interrupted our meeting with a proposal. If we restored Harry's fortune, she would agree to your father's betrothal proposal. Since your father signed his name before his death, we didn't require her permission, but the exchange simplifies it. She could have fought to keep you in her household as the executor."

"She wouldn't have," she replies. "My mother was the only person who never would've...." She trails off and rises from my chest, tugging on her cloak. "It doesn't matter now. I will be the Keeper."

I pull her back, hoping to calm her agitation, but she can't sit still. "And you will do well as the Keeper. The faeries are loyal to you, from my understanding."

I don't mention the male who has tried courting her, nor do I inquire about her friend. She's protective of them. And I don't particularly want to learn if her feelings are reciprocated.

"And," I continue, "since the faeries haven't been simple to work with lately, restoring your family's fortune was a small price for acquiring you."

"He could've just asked me," she snaps.

"He doesn't ask when he can take it."

She rolls her hips to reposition. I suppress a groan when I notice the lack of space between our lower halves. The friction she's causing against my inner thighs is painful from the inability to touch her in the ways I know how.

She's only here because she has to be. Repeating that reminder will be our only saving grace for keeping the lines between us crystalline. Elora is the type to make me beg.

And I would. On my knees.

No. *Stop.*

I didn't realize how much younger she was than me. And her doe-eyed nature, the way her lips part each time she's scandalized by my sister, means there are so many things I could teach her—so many ways to show her why pleasure is addictive. I could satisfy her in ways she has probably never even thought about.

My curiosity about if she's ever been touched is nearly as prominent as how much energy is going into not touching her thighs again. And her long, svelte throat would fit nicely in the palm of my hand. I can imagine the sound she'd make if my teeth gently scraped where her pulse pounds against her skin.

Another readjustment of her hips equates to nearly brushing against my cock. My thoughts spiral. "Stop moving," I rasp with pathetically masked strain.

"Sorry," she mumbles. "I'm not used to sitting like this. I don't believe I could ride for as long as you must when traveling."

I flick my gaze up at the blood-marked sky, willing myself not to give any attention to her thighs spread between mine. "You get used to it," I reply.

"You get used to having something this large between your legs? I can't imagine—"

"Elora, stop *talking*."

She twists to glare at me. I return it tenfold—glowering because I want to negotiate touching between us.

"Why did you agree to it? I am not your favorite person."

"Far from it," I mutter. "I wanted Regina and her daughters out of the castle. And because it's my duty as the prince to accept the king's orders, no matter how *disagreeable* I find them." Maintaining the facade of only tolerating her because I have to will lessen the risk of genuine feelings sprouting. With her life already at stake, I can't imagine what I would do to protect her if I fell in love with her.

"*Did* they leave? Why do *you* dislike them?"

"They were collecting their things when I came to find you," I say. "And I dislike them because your stepsisters fucked Jasper. The night you arrived, he invited them to partake in post-ball activities."

Her lips parted in surprise. "Your mother—"

"Knows." My jaw pops. "She always knows. Has always known. That tryst wasn't his first. He's had many affairs."

Her expression softens into shame. "I'm sorry, Finnian. They are horrid women."

"We'll collect your things from the palace manor before we leave." I nod ahead. "We're almost to the bridge."

"Stop, we have to stop." She tugs on my hand that is resting on the horn. "Major can't go into Ashbury."

I shake my head. "It'll be quicker—"

She cuts in with, "Finnian, he'll be stolen and traded. Some of them haven't even seen a horse. We'll be surrounded. My people aren't cruel, but they are desperate. We need to hide him."

"Elora, I can handle it."

"Finnian, please—"

I peel her hands off the saddle and pin them against her stomach to stop her incessant need to take control. "Elora, no one will touch him. You need to trust that I can keep you safe—"

"It's not about me!" she shouts. "I need *you* to trust *me*. Major cannot cross the bridge. I care for him, Finnian. Please."

My horse has gained her favor in the length of a ride while I still struggle to draw any emotion from her that isn't tinged with hatred. But my fondness for Major and the desperation in her voice makes me believe her.

I click my tongue and spout Major's command to halt. "We won't need to hide him," I say, pushing her forward a couple of inches for me to slide off.

Whistling through my teeth, I wait as a pair of soldiers pop up from behind tall wheat crops and rush over.

Elora's eyes go wide.

Since residents of Ashbury aren't allowed to cross the bridge, Jasper takes precautions in case one of them tries. "You didn't know they were here," I state knowingly. "That was done purposely."

Her plump pout thins. "They have weapons."

Each soldier is strapped with a sword and daggers in their boots. And without a doubt, I know bows and quivers of arrows remain hidden in their lookout spots for any escaping faerie.

"Their orders are to restrain, not harm." I grab her waist and lower her to the ground. "If someone tries to escape, they will bring them to Pumpkin Hollow."

She steps away from me. "For your father to behead them? I've heard the rumors, you know. About his collection."

My gaze darts to the approaching men. I'll need to discuss with her privately how candid she is about her hatred for my father. Every person employed by him has strict orders to inform him of every word spoken about him.

And Elora will be watched extra carefully.

"Every captive is treated fairly, little doe."

Collection or not, I'm not going to overwhelm her yet with every horror story involving Jasper.

I whisper in her ear, "Thank them for their service, Elora." When she shakes her head, I trap her chin between my fingers, eliminating even more inches between us. To the men behind me, it will look as if I'm kissing my bride. "If you wish to live, you stubborn creature, do it."

She yanks her chin free from my grasp but forces a sweet smile. "Thank you for your loyalty to our king."

I nearly laugh from the heavy disdain in her voice, but the men dip their chins and supply me with a dagger to carry.

"Do you need an escort, Sir Finnian?" one inquires. I recognize the voice underneath his helmet as that of one of my comrades from my nights of sleeping in tents with the lot of them.

I slide the dagger into my waistband. "No, I believe the spitfire beside me is defense enough."

As she walks away, she mutters her dislike for me, leaving me to lead Major to the dead crops he'll still try to graze. Weekly deliveries of grains, vegetables, and the healthiest hay in all the nearby realms account for his diet, yet Major would settle for dirt if given the choice.

I jog after her. "Will we see the faeries?"

She looks toward the mountains, searching the peaks. "They're finished for the day. I'm not allowed in until morning."

"You have me," I remind her. "I'm free to see them whenever I want. And you will be once we wed."

"They need their rest."

I inhale deeply through my nose and try to calm the rage inside my chest. I want to be patient with her, but I'm still the second in command of this realm and do not need her permission. "I want to meet them, Elora. Is there a reason why I shouldn't?"

She whips her head toward me. "No. Why would there be?"

I turn to walk backward in front of her. "I've heard of their beauty." I watch her expression, selfishly hoping to ignite envy within her so I won't feel pathetic alone. "Are you afraid I'll prefer a female over you?"

The gold specks in her eyes darken into the color of saffron the closer we get to the path. I can't look away.

"Believe me, once you see the males, you won't ask that again." Her exasperation with me changes into a rotten smirk. "Still want to see them?"

No. "Yes."

"Fine," she replies haughtily. "It would be my *pleasure*."

I can't control the way my eyes narrow.

But she grins. "We'll go there first."

❧

Elora snickers each time I cough.

The air is *littered* with flakes, and they stick to *everything*. I wish I hadn't left my jacket on Major. I could've permanently ruined it and would never have to wear it again.

But the mountains?

A fucking lair of Hades.

Elora is sweating, but I'm dripping. One cough away from stripping naked to breathe easier.

The guards at the entrance are in a different uniform, but I understand why. They would fucking pass out from heat exhaustion if sporting their full armor. And I will never again question why they only work six-hour shifts instead of the twelve required for all other duties.

The fresh pair of men look surprised to see me, immediately offering a canteen of water. Taking it would defeat Elora's point—I need to know how the people of Ashbury lived.

I refuse the canteen.

Elora looks impressed, but it's fleeting. I wouldn't be impressed with me, either. This is her daily life while I live under clear skies and drink fluids whenever possible.

Grabbing Elora's wrist, I drag her back to the iron gate when she tries to pass by the guards. "Elora will soon be the Keeper. She has my permission to come and go as she pleases. After we wed, relinquish daily logs to her, and she will present them to our king."

"Long live our king," they chant in unison.

Gods, that fucking phrase. It isn't a requirement, and some never use it, but the ones who do are the men who would readily follow my father into the underworld if he asked.

Elora will have to be very careful.

Elora's nose scrunches. "I have to see him?"

I clamp a hand over her mouth and draw her to my chest in a seemingly loving embrace. "Since she is my bride, treat her like you treat me."

She pries my hand off. "Lucky me."

Sighing, I move my hand to her neck and squeeze. She yelps and tries to step away, but I hold her against my chest. "Understood?"

They bow, nod, and recite the exact phrase again, all while Elora tries to free herself like a wild animal that's been chained. I dismiss them and pull her into a corner once we pass the gate. "You have to stop," I snapped. "You will be the princess, Elora. And yes, if you want this position, you must show him the logs *daily*."

She rolls her eyes. I grip her chin *again* since it is the only way to hold her attention. "I'm serious, Elora. Being my wife will not save your life if enough people report your displeasure. I will help you with this, but it requires effort from both of us."

"*Fine*," she mutters.

I raise an eyebrow.

Sighing, she wraps a hand around my wrist. "Fine," she says softer, "I understand."

I release her, but she squeezes my wrist to prevent me from stepping away. "Does it not bother you?" she inquires, continuing at my bewilderment, "That being your wife isn't important if he's upset? Shouldn't your happiness outweigh his anger?"

I frown. "Elora, he made me watch my best mate's beheading. I was sixteen when my friend stood up for me after my lashings." I blink away the stained memory. "His beheading was a warning to anyone else in my life that defending me comes at a cost."

Her hand slides into mine. "Finnian, that's awful."

"Believe me, little doe, my happiness doesn't matter to him. He will always remind me of my place. I am the prince first, son second." I need to change the subject. "Your stepsister referred to you as Ellie."

She removes her hand from mine. "Please don't call me that."

I give her a half-hearted smile. "I shared something very personal with you."

She kicks at the dirt on the ground. "It's what my parents called me. Regina and her daughters use it as an insult. It's tainted."

Just another reason to loathe them.

I don't pry further. "After you, wife."

She scowled, but nerves seemed to overcome her when she twisted her hands together while leading me. Something about being here, or me being with her, makes her nervous.

We pass multiple caves without a faerie in sight. I look up, down, and sideways but find no one. While searching the peaks, I bump into Elora, who has stopped in front of a deep, empty dwelling. I move to step inside, but she grabs my arm to prevent it. "Wait," she says.

"For *what*? There's no one here."

A shadow forms at the entrance. I take a small step back. Elora grins, the tension in her shoulders slipping away.

And then, from the darkness, comes a set of faeries. The female is tall with golden skin, her hair and eyes the color of fire, but I can't form an opinion of her beauty before a low growl interrupts my inspection.

I thought I was tall, but the male was at least a foot taller than me. His hair is strapped back, flames blaring in his eyes, and he has nothing but a pair of charred trousers on.

But their ears draw the most intrigue. Slanted and pointed, the enduring uniqueness lessens their intimidation a sliver.

He steps closer to me. I fight the urge to duck behind Elora, instead rolling my shoulders back and ignoring the black wings spreading behind him to hide the female.

Elora rolls her eyes. "Dolfe, he won't touch Azrea."

"Azrea," I repeat, risking a glance at the female peeking out from behind a wing. "I assume you're the one Elora speaks fondly of."

Dolfe crosses his arms. "Who is he, Elora?"

"The prince," she replies, clearly annoyed by my presence on her sacred ground. "He insisted he meet you."

She shoves past Dolfe's wing, ignoring his snarl of protest, and throws her arms around the female. Elora is petite next to me. These creatures could snap her neck with a breath.

I instinctively move to pull her away, but Dolfe flares a wing to prohibit me. I bare my teeth at the rejection, but the shock of the feral need to protect her soon slackens my jaw.

I swallow.

But he smirks.

I clear my throat to regain composure. "I am Prince Finnian. The king has given Elora the position of Keeper."

Dolfe sighs deeply. "Fuck."

"Ignore him," Elora says. I can no longer see her behind the wing he refuses to lower. "He often pretends to hate me."

"Move, brute." Azrea's voice is airy and melodic. And when she steps out from behind him, I stare at her legs—purely because I haven't ever seen a being move as gracefully as she does.

Even the male, who again growls at me in warning, is smooth with his sharp reflexes.

Azrea blocks Dolfe from ripping me to shreds by standing between us. Our height differences aren't as noticeable, but she still has a few inches on me. Her hair is down but pinned with a silver relic shaped like a snowflake.

I ask, "Where did you get that?"

She touches the pin in her hair, sudden fear in her eyes as she tries to unclasp it.

I hold my palms up toward her. "I'm not going to take it. I travel often, and it reminds me of a story I was once told."

She tilts her head. "What story?"

"Ah." I run a hand through my hair and try to recall the details of a drunken night out. "Years ago, maybe... eight? My travels took me to a kingdom very far from here. One evening, the scholar joined me for dinner and spoke of faeries that control snow, much like you control fire. Do you know them?"

Azrea looks over her shoulder at Dolfe. One look exchanged between them holds an entire conversation.

"Many varieties of Fae exist," Dolfe says.

That doesn't answer my question. Even though I've never been interested in the Fae, standing before two faeries has changed that. Before tonight, they were more of a tale to be told—an unspoken secret. But now, I'm curious about the stories I've heard. I want to know their history, where they came from, and why they've insisted on staying here when it's evident they're meant for much more than mining mountainsides.

Elora pops up beside Azrea. "Finnian came to meet you and visit Ashbury. He's going to help me restore it."

I will *try*. "I am unaware if you were made privy to Elora's scheme of marrying me, but my father arranged our union today."

Azrea and Elora trade a look. I am growing jealous of being the only one who doesn't understand the secret language between them. In Pumpkin Hollow, control is given to me. It seems Elora holds the power here, which means my father is correct.

He, indeed, has been watching her.

Dolfe doesn't look pleased, but Azrea smiles. "That's wonderful," she says. "Elora will be a beautiful bride."

Simultaneously, they glance behind me. I turn to find another male similar to Dolfe, with short hair and glowing eyes fixed on Elora. He isn't as tall, but he is still taller than me, and the way he stares at Elora is unsettling.

I've yet to figure out where these faeries were coming from. Every cave looks empty and dark.

"Bride?" the male asks quietly.

"Cedric," Elora greets with a guilty smile.

Ah.

The longing in his eyes while he stares at her feels like a threat. No, she doesn't like me, nor is she mine in a conventional sense, but that doesn't stop me from shuffling to the side to block her from his view. "Yes," I answered his question.

My bride.

His eyes narrow, his wings slowly spread, and his hands curl into fists.

Elora grabs my arm and pulls me toward her just as Dolfe replaces me to press a hand against Cedric's chest. "Return to your dwelling," he demands, "Now."

I recognize the tone immediately as one I use when protecting my sister.

They're brothers.

Cedric shoves Dolfe's hand off and steps toward us, but I thrust an arm to my side to stop Elora from moving forward. "Stay behind me, Elora," I say.

"Cedric," she pleads. "Cedric, we're just friends. I can't explain it right now, but—"

"Elora!" Dolfe shouts. "Enough."

Azrea pulls Elora to her, but I remain still. My breathing quickens, irritation swelling at the classification of being her *friend*, causing me to act irrationally, and I say, "But I will be her husband. And I am your prince. I would heed your brother's advice and return unscathed."

"Is this true, Ellie?" Cedric's voice raises. "Are you marrying him?"

Ellie. *He* called her Ellie.

I stop the guards from approaching by raising my hand to the side. "Yes," I answered again, "She is."

"Cedric," Azrea warns. "Go. Prince Finnian, please take Elora and leave."

I shouldn't be dismissed, but I've been trained to choose my battles wisely and am severely outnumbered. Taking on a species I know nothing of seems like a quick way to die.

"I'm sorry," Elora whispers tearfully.

Azrea brushes a hand down Elora's hair before nodding at me. I grab Elora's hand and pull her behind me, muttering to the guards as we pass them, "Don't punish him. I am torturing him enough by marrying the woman he loves."

Seventeen

"Slow down!" I shout, tripping over the dips of the valleys as Finnian leads us away from the mountains but not closer to town. The rising moon has eliminated some of our light, and his anger isn't a reliable guide.

"Finnian," I tried again, looking ahead. "Finnian!" I scream, putting every ounce of strength I have into yanking him back.

Pebbles tumble down the steep cliff ahead. I pant from the rush of adrenaline and double over. He places his hands on his waist and stares into the dark abyss below. Except for the black, spiraled castle turrets of the abandoned castle below, only trees can be seen from our vantage point.

And the soft flow of the river just beneath is soothing against my harsh breaths. "Hogsfeet," I say, breathless and annoyed.

"I know," he mutters.

Of course, he does. If I can be sure of anything, Finnian has studied his realm, even with his apparent disinterest in its wellbeing.

Slowly, deeply, I inhale to prevent my heart from exploding. "Why are you so upset?"

"I'm not," he replies dryly.

I straighten and point to the near-death experience we just had of almost falling down the cliffside. "You could've killed us!"

He says nothing, keeping his back to me as he stares below. The river cannot be seen, but the sound of the stream calms my heart enough for me to try again. "Finnian."

He doesn't turn, but he does speak. "He'll kill him."

My heart plummets. "What?"

"If Jasper learns of your relationship with Cedric, he'll kill him." He lowers his chin slightly. "Regina informed him of the male trying to court you but left out that you.... have been courted."

I shook my head. "Finnian—"

"It's fine, Elora." He shrugs a shoulder. "Keep your affairs hidden. I'll do the same."

It's as if he drove a dagger through my stomach.

I wasn't planning on having affairs, but it doesn't surprise me that he is already planning for his. He has a reputation for a reason. So, instead of a denial, I blink back tears and nod.

He turns to face me. "It's getting late. We'll walk through town and stop by your manor before we return to Pumpkin Hollow."

Speechless, I trail behind him when he leads us away from the cliffside and toward town. I would be more surprised that he knows where it is if I didn't assume he was forced to study maps of the realm. It's been evident since meeting him that Finnian is brilliant and cunning, which has only added to the frustration of his constant absence.

The smog has cleared enough for stars to twinkle above us, the crescent moon shining brightly enough to lend us visibility.

Finnian stares straight ahead, and only when he's covered in shadows from the mountains as we pass them do I allow myself to take in what I haven't yet. Him.

I study him while he avoids me.

Past the rumors and blatant arrogance, he harbors a certain darkness. Coming home to learn that his realm isn't all he thought seemed to upset him more than he wanted me to see. Fatigued by his father, he's made more effort to behave decently toward me. But the more I learn about his childhood, the more I wonder if he's only impenetrable because he's protecting his heart—the one others claim he doesn't have.

Looking at him, even when he's brooding and back to being an ass, I can admit to myself that Finnian is....

Well, handsome.

The time spent outside has added a hint of red to his sandy skin. His hair remains disheveled at all times, even when he attempts to fix it with an idle swipe of his hand, and the color of the strands resembles coffee grounds—dark brown, but the right amount of sun brings out gold. But tonight, soaked with sweat and blanketed by night, it's nearly black.

He always has a broad and confident smile—not only when discovering new ways to annoy me.

But even that's missing tonight.

He might not be as broad as the faeries in stature, but he's solid. Protective. And he packs just as many muscles beneath his attire. I can still vividly recall the grooves of his abdomen from seeing him shirtless after we smashed pumpkins.

And I feel.... safe when he's near me.

His voice deepens when stern or severe, but he doesn't question himself. Everything about him screams polished and primed to someday rule. And the thought of him having affairs bothers me. Gnaws at me.

Irritates me.

Angers me.

He glances at me when the heat of my stare becomes too warm. I swallow my words instead of asking him, *how fucking dare you?* But why would he change for me? He's being forced into this arrangement, too. Pleasure matters to him, so why should he give that up for his inexperienced wife?

"Have you ever been there?" I blurt out, attempting to squash the silence.

He refocuses his gaze elsewhere. "Where?"

"Hogsfeet."

He shakes his head. "The only way to get there is through the mountains. That was my first time visiting those, so...."

"Right," I interrupt, "Of course."

"Have you?"

"We're not allowed, and the cliffside is too steep."

We step over bits of broken rock from our dismantled road. If one of the carriages from Pumpkin Hollow ever crosses the bridge, a wheel will surely pop off from the uneven terrain.

"No one ever leaves?" he asks.

I fill the empty air with a detailed reply. "Attempting to travel to Hogsfeet would likely result in death. There's a vertical pathway that leads down the cliffside, but only a skilled rider would be able to take it unscathed. I wasn't alive when your father overtook it, but I can't imagine soldiers did it by foot."

"Some did," he replies. "But the bulk of destruction came from weapons that can launch rocks, lead, steel, anything needed to maim. We still have them, but weapons have advanced greatly since then."

I shove the imagery out of my mind. "Have you ever fought?"

"In battle? I haven't needed to. If another kingdom ever tries to seize our land, I will. And if word ever spreads that we have faeries or fucking magical pumpkins, that might happen." He nods to the mountains. "Are the rumors true?"

I avoid eye contact. "Of magic within? No." Not anymore. It lives within me now.

He points ahead. "No one escapes through the unoccupied side of Ashbury?"

"Rarely," I sigh. "It's desolate. The last man who tried returned to convey that escaping would lead to dehydration. Troops are sent every two weeks to scour the outskirts for bodies or to arrest trespassers." Talking about it floods me with outrage all over again. "The king doesn't want to take care of us, but he doesn't want us to leave."

"He will never risk someone coming to claim what he believes is his."

I hated the incessant situation of me belonging to someone so vile, ready to be used at any given moment, but taking that out on Finnian would be unfair.

I thrust my arm out toward what lies ahead. "Welcome to Ashbury, Prince Finnian."

Even at nightfall, the ruin of Ashbury is apparent.

He steps forward, and his face contorts into a combination of shock, disgust, and disbelief.

I wasn't born long after the war, but it didn't always look like this—bare, filthy, and permanently in a state of haze. It held life even after the castle was torn apart and manors erected.

Having a kingdom of such promise over the bridge brought hope to our people that we would be treated the same. But hope died once broken things stopped being repaired and food deliveries lessened. And once hope is gone, the resurrection of it is nearly impossible.

A person can only live on faith for so long.

We pass by multiple boarded shoppes. He tries to peek inside each one, only to ask what it once was. With each answer, more sorrow clings to him. He only brightens when we come upon a water well, but his face falls when he sees only stones within.

"Two men were killed for trying to dig up the stones," I explained. "He has made us completely dependent on what he provides."

Lunging forward, he grabs stones and tosses them aside, growing more frantic by the second.

"Finnian." I dodge a rock. "Finnian, stop."

But he doesn't stop. He digs until his fingers and palms bleed, dripping onto the rocks he grabs.

Only then do I take one of his arms. "Finnian, this was filled years ago. The water has dried."

A growl of frustration passes through his lips as he backs away from the water well and crouches. I wrap a hand around my throat as a dry sob burns from the raw emotions he's experiencing right in front of me.

He honestly didn't understand until now.

"I didn't know," he rasps. "I didn't know about any of this."

While I've known my father was a traitor my entire life, he is only now learning the depths of his father's neglect.

"I know," I whisper.

And I do. I believe him.

"I have been so concerned with my own..."—he pauses and lowers his head— "I understand why you hate us. Hate me."

I place a hand on his shoulder. "I don't hate you—"

He shakes me off and stands. "Show me more."

I showed him everything.

I take him to the general store and wait while he picks through the leftovers. I show him the pails of water delivered by wagons weekly and explain the cost of bottles residents must buy to bring any water home.

I walk him down a row of manors, sharing that each one houses two to three families since some were burned after a tried-and-failed revolt soon after the war.

I point out two more water wells. He ducks into any place not boarded or still open. We walk down rows of cottages that haven't been repaired in years. He notices the Bohemians dancing by a fire with wagons around them and asks how they can get into Ashbury, explaining that the king banished them to the outskirts.

"They've memorized the guards' shift changes and routes to move between kingdoms undetected." Divulging every secret seems risky, but it's the point I've reached to save my people. "They trade goods with us." I smile while watching them dance. "Sometimes, they stay in one of the cottages but mostly remain outside when it's cool."

He gestures toward a man in the center of the group. "That's Irina's lover. He is why she leaves the castle." He points to a woman dancing gracefully in front of the man. "And that's her other lover."

My smile falls.

The man locks gazes with me before noticing Finnian at my side. Excitement soon lights his eyes, only for his expression to fill with disappointment when Finnian shakes his head.

"She's not here," Finnian says aloud with a frown.

He can't hear us from this distance, but he nods.

I ask, "They aren't frightened of you, are they?"

"No," he confirms. "I cover for Irina when she leaves. She was supposed to visit them tonight but went this afternoon instead. He must've told her they planned to be here tonight. Irina is daring, but she won't risk coming here."

He holds out his hands to study the cuts. Most of the blood has dried, but some still drips down his palms. I nudge his arm with the only grin I can conjure. "Let's get you cleaned up."

We're almost to the palace manor when a young boy no older than four runs out from between crumbling villas and tugs on Finnian's shirt. Finnian looks down with a raised eyebrow, but his expression softens when he notices the tot gazing up at him.

The boy proudly extends his palm to show us a brown button. I smile, familiar with this game. But Finnian's confusion is written clearly on his face, clearing his throat. "Ah, um..." He side-eyes me and whispers, "Is it a gift?"

"He wants to trade," I explained.

"Oh, of course." Finnian lowers and takes the button from the boy's palm after wiping the blood from his hands on his pants and inspects every detail by holding it under the moonlight. Gas-lit street lamps are readily spread throughout Pumpkin Hollow, but we aren't provided the resources, nor do we have the funds to pay lamplighters even if we did.

Finnian spins the button between his fingers. "I've been looking for one of these. Are you positive you'd like to trade?"

Beaming, the boy nods.

Reaching into his boot, Finnian soon pulls out a leather pouch and instructs him to hold out *both* hands this time. The tot excitedly stomps his feet while trying to keep his hands still. Finnian places one hand beneath the boy's hands to steady them while he dumps the contents of the pouch into his palms.

Gold coins slip from his hands and fall to the ground. The boy stares at the few left in his palms in shock.

Most of our people haven't ever seen gold or silver.

I kneel to assist Finnian in picking up the rogue coins and slip the ones from the boy's hands into a pocket on his pants that doesn't have a hole. But Finnian stops me, retrieves the coins, and pours them back into the pouch.

He secures it with a leather strap and gifts it to the boy.

"Only show your mama, okay?" I say, wrapping my hands around his small ones. "Don't show this to anyone else."

"*Treasure*," he whispers.

"Treasure," I confirm. "And everyone wants treasure. I know your mama, but I don't remember where you live."

Before I realize what he's doing, Finnian wraps an arm around the boy's waist and lifts him up. "We better escort him home before the pirates find him."

"Finnian, you'll be recognized—"

With a frown, Finnian slightly shakes his head. "Why would I be? I've never been here. And they've never left."

❧

Though smog has cleared enough to allow moonlight to illuminate the cobblestone streets, lingering fog hangs overhead as we follow where Baxter, the young boy, points. Finnian admires the older styles of architecture of the villas that my people rebuilt not long after the war. Never having visited the town of Pumpkin Hollow before the ball, I imagine its buildings receive facelifts often.

I might be displeased with Ashbury's neglect, but even I can admit that our town holds a certain charm of days past. Men used brick and stones from the demolished manors, meaning each villa or shoppe is made of contrasting blacks and grays. Windows were accented by hand and trimmed with intricate terra cotta paneling.

Even in disarray, slowing down and genuinely admiring my town under fog and moonlight helps me remember why I'm fighting so hard to ensure its survival. But Finnian was correct—no one seemed to recognize him. We've passed by many townsfolk, most waving or greeting me, but no one pays any mind to the handsome stranger beside me.

Baxter wiggles free from Finnian's grip and takes his hand instead, tugging him toward the sound of a recorder and an airy voice. Under a crumbling awning, candles burning nearly down to the wick, Baxter's mother sings and spins another little boy around while her husband sits on the porch steps. Upon seeing Baxter, his father waves him over.

But Baxter drops Finnian's hand to take mine instead, pulling me over to his mother. She welcomes me with a smile but doesn't stray from her song, encouraging me to mimic her soft, gentle footsteps.

The dance isn't one I should know—it's apparent that it was created by her—but I'm still determined to learn it anyway. Every misstep I make is met with a giggle by Baxter and his brother, and I find myself laughing with them.

It's not until Baxter tries to spin me, causing me to bend much lower, that Finnian taps on his shoulder. Baxter pouts but begrudgingly transfers my hand to Finnian's.

Unlike the night of the ball, I don't hesitate to place my hand on his shoulder, but instead of extending our arms, he puts his hands on my waist. We exchange no pleasantries—not that we ever would—but every mismatched step is followed by broad smiles or awkward laughter.

Finally, we move in harmony.

He spins me out, twirls me back, then dips me down, eliciting squeals and clapping from the boys. Baxter's father abandons his recorder to steal his wife away from their son, and soon, we're joined by a few others who must've heard the commotion. Finnian spins me out again, but I'm caught by an older man I recognize from childhood.

With a mischievous grin, Finnian steals my partner's wife and dances with her while I'm spun and traded by my partners, my stomach sore from laughing and gasping each time I'm given away. Someone else has grabbed the recorder, but two others have joined him, and a trio has soon formed to lead us in a dance made of awkward footsteps and laughter so loud that it fills the streets.

And it quickly becomes a game—how long they can keep me away from Finnian. And though I hate to admit it to myself, the frustration building in his eyes each time I'm moved further away is oddly satisfying.

Nothing but deafening joyous laughter and words of songs fill the air, and I'm filled with bittersweet regret. I've spent so many days in the manor or with the faeries that I've long forgotten how resilient my people are. They're hungry and don't have much to their names, but they find hope in each other.

I envy their uninhibited cheer but am grateful for their enduring optimism. And I desperately want to be the one to prolong it for them—to provide them with endless, carefree nights like these. I don't want them to worry about feeding their children or having enough coins to purchase fresh water.

An arm sliding around my waist from behind distracts me from my determined thoughts. I tip my chin up to find Finnian pulling me away from my partner, placating him with a friendly smile but giving him no doubt that I'm finished being passed around. Finnian resumes our dance, his hands wrapped around my waist and holding me close enough to make it not such a strain on my neck to peer up at him.

He has picked up on the offbeat song much quicker than me,

and I allow him to lead me—shocking to even me. The unwavering way his blue eyes stare into my eyes, even as he spins me out and back in, catching me against his chest, his arm sliding around my waist, causes an oddly unsettling flutter in my chest.

He tucks a curl behind my ear, brushes his thumb down my cheek slowly, and whispers barely loud enough for me to hear over the continuous laughter around us, "Why did it have to be you?"

His question surprises me, but then.... I laugh.

I laugh so fully and genuinely that a broad smile stretches across his mouth as he gently dips me and knocks his forehead against mine. "Show me where you came from, little doe."

He raises me to my feet, takes my hand, and tugs me away from the crowd. We wave goodbye to Baxter, who quickly falls asleep on the porch steps.

The silence is easy and comfortable between us while we walk toward the palace manor, the distance dwindling the crowd's laughter into nearly nothing. Finally, he retrieves Baxter's button from his pocket and pinches it between his fingers. "What was he wanting to trade for, Elora?"

Suddenly, the lighthearted evening becomes heavy once more as I'm reminded why I brought him here.

"Food," I say softly, "he wanted food."

Eighteen

We enter the manor with sighs of relief. Since we rode to Ashbury on Major, we arrived quicker than the carriage carrying Regina, Dolly, and Daffodil, but I do not doubt they're not far behind.

Lighting candles as I lead him inside, Finnian finally inquires about the lack of lighting in town and our manor, pointing out the oil lamp in the entryway. It was another trinket my father brought back after one of his afternoons in Pumpkin Hollow when I was just a girl.

"Well," I begin with a slight shrug, "Even though it's possible to create coal gas, we don't have enough leftovers. Any remaining pails keep the manors heated, especially during autumn and winter."

"Surely oil is affordable—"

"Finnian, oil hasn't been provided to us in over a decade."

Flames flicker across his face from the candlelight, and a fresh wave of confusion is evident in his eyes. "Elora—"

"I know," I interrupted again. "You weren't aware."

"It's not an excuse, Elora."

Wordlessly, I nod and lead him toward the kitchen, but his unyielding curiosity causes him to reverse and duck his head into the library. He inspects the room with a frown.

"We had more books," I say with a sigh. "I had to sell some but traded most of them."

"For what?"

"Whatever I could." I drag one of the small footstools over to the bookshelves. "Soap, bottles, rags, stale biscuits." I stand on the stool and rise to my toes, sliding my hand behind a row of books on the highest shelf.

He appears beside me after watching me flounder with searching and keeps his eyes locked on mine when he reaches up, pushes past my hand, and retrieves the bottle I was searching for.

My heart *skips*.

He reads the ripped label with a grin. "This is hard liquor, Elora. I didn't take you for a drinker."

I remember to breathe. "I'm not. I've never tasted a drop of liquor. I thought it might help clean the cuts on your hands." I've kept two bottles hidden from Regina that my father kept in his study for instances like these.

"There are better ways to numb the pain." As he says it, his gaze lowers to my mouth while he unscrews the cap. He flicks it off with his finger and tilts his head back to nearly empty the bottle in a single gulp.

Judging by the tension in his jaw, it isn't the pain from the cuts he is referencing.

Only a quarter of the liquor remained when he offered the bottle to me. Hesitantly, I bring the bottle to my nose and cough from the smell alone. His throaty chuckle sends a shiver down my spine. "It tastes sweeter than it smells," he says.

Having my first drop of liquor with him is better than trying it alone. Or with Irina. I can't imagine the trouble we'd get into.

Holding my breath, I tip the bottle back slowly, unprepared for how quickly it pours freely. My cheeks puff as I try to swallow, my nose scrunching from the bitter bite pushing through the faintest hint of honey.

He drags the tip of his thumb across my bottom lip to catch

the drops dribbling out and slides it into his mouth, sucking the liquor off.

What is this unfamiliar *ache*?

My breath is cool and honeyed as I release a tight breath. He leans forward to seemingly steal it for himself. And I'm wholly convinced I understand now why so many women have been drawn to him in the past. He oozes a brassy confidence, and it's disarming.

It doesn't matter how much we dislike one another or how often we are reminded why it can never be more than this; we always end up suffocated by smoldering heat.

He retrieves a second bottle from the shelf with a wink. "For the ride home."

He casually strolls out of the room, leaving me lightheaded—either from lack of oxygen or alcohol.

When I move my feet, he's already found the kitchen. He slides the unopened liquor bottle into his pocket and leans against a table while I light a handful of candles, lower to my knees, and shuffle through a cabinet.

"Are you always this secretive?" he inquires.

"When I have to survive." My voice is muffled from nearly submerging myself into the cabinet. After locating a small jug of water, I bump my head when coming out.

"And this uncoordinated?"

I loosen an exasperated breath. "Do you want my help or not?"

He nods with a smirk.

I bury my smile and grab a rag from behind him, pouring the leftover liquor over his hands. He hisses when I drag the cloth across the cuts to clean the dried blood from his palms.

"Sorry," I whisper, cleaning the liquor off with water.

"Such a doting wife already."

I snort. "I'm not your wife yet."

"Five days." He sinks against the table and spreads his knees, touching my waist lightly and inching me closer. His moist palm dampens my cloak, but he doesn't seem to notice. "You will be my wife in five days."

Gods, that's fast.

I remove his hand from my waist to dry the water from his palms. "I am surprised it isn't tomorrow."

He chuckles. "Jasper would prefer that, but traditions need to be followed." He tucks a curl behind my ear. "Do you want to know what they are?"

The bright blue of his eyes doesn't dull, even with only flickering candlelight. And when he stares at me like this, I forget how to function like a grown woman. I lose myself in the icy glaciers that combat the heat I've known my entire life. Being with him satisfies the longing for a cold sip of water.

How he looks at me must be how he's looked at dozens of others, but he makes me feel like I'm the only one.

I haven't yearned for many things in my life, but I learned long ago to not be envious. Yet, I am. Being jealous of any woman he's breathed near or laughed with is unnerving. Would it be too much to ask that he never do that again? Just so I won't have to think about it.

I don't know, Elora, are you willing to satisfy him? Learn what he likes? What he craves?

My internal questions cause me to blush, and he *grins*. I toss the rag onto the table, mortified by how long I've stared at him without speaking. "Not yet. Don't tell me yet. Let me be just Elora for one more night. I'll go collect my things."

Nothing in the attic is important enough to bring to the castle. I just needed a few moments away from him—away from all of it. And I want one last look at my former life.

Breezing out to my terrace is an awakening.

Something so small once seemed so big until I stepped into the castle, where the balconies are more expansive than the entire attic, with immaculate, expressive detailing on the rail guards.

I swallow the sight of my shattered town with a breath of reprieve. The mindset I had going into this has completely flipped. The struggle, I fear, has nothing to do with Finnian but with how to handle King Jasper going forward.

I look over the crumbling villa roofs barely visible, past the mountains separating such contrasting places, and into the black sky. So much of my life has been focused on Ashbury that I've never considered what could exist outside this realm.

Resting my arms on the decaying railing, I lean forward and try to count the stars above Hogsfeet and wonder, just for a moment, if after we help Ashbury, Finnian might take me with him. He has seen so much, visited many places, and heard many stories. Perhaps, if we stay friendly, he wouldn't mind showing me some of the wonderment outside this place.

I blink the weariness away, my eyes falling out of focus and blurring, and a fleeting piece from one of my nightmares covers the possibility of a future with him like a weighted blanket.

And suddenly, I'm transported. It's as if I've been plucked from my world and dropped into another, but the edges of the vision are blurry. A dark shadow encompasses a beautiful yet broken Fae male, half his face covered by overcast gloom.

I see only his profile as he stares out a tall archway at the moon, and it's only then that I realize that his world *is* mine. His moon is mine. Yet, he doesn't seem to notice me behind him until I gasp from the terror spiraling around my spine.

Because when he turns his head to the side, one side of his face is only bone. I am staring at a haunting, skeletal Fae male.

I tried to speak—I want to ask *how*, but I don't exist here.

But still, even though I don't think he can see me, he slowly turns to search, staring directly at me.... *through* me.

I jump from the hand touching the small of my back, pulling me from wherever I was back to where I *am*.

Clasping my forehead, I pant as the male twists into nothing but my own mind, leaving me again underneath the starry sky.

"Elora," Finnian says, curling his fingers around my hip.

I search for the male again in my mind.

Finnian tugs on my cloak. "Are you all right?"

I cover my eyes with my hand. "I'm fine. I have vivid dreams, and maybe I fell asleep." I laugh at the absurdity of how drastically everything has changed so quickly. "I'm exhausted."

"I know." He tugs my wrist away from my face. "What are you doing up here?"

"Oh." I gesture toward the barely visible town beneath us. "This is my favorite place to come and admire the mountains."

He leans against the railing. I wince when a crack shoots through the crumbling clay shell encasing the iron, but he doesn't seem to mind, crossing his arms with a grin. "I do the same from my balcony. It's how I first saw you."

It was him I saw the night of the ball. Of course. I noticed his eyes then, just as I stare at them now. "Do you often stalk guests from your terrace, Lord Finnian?"

He ducks his head, and is that.... blushing?

"I didn't want to attend the ball that evening, but Irina noticed you and forced me downstairs." His grin twists into a smirk. "I wish I had fought harder."

I throw my head back in laughter, but it fades when I catch Finnian's frown as he stares into the attic. And I sigh when he leaves me to return inside. "Finnian—"

"What is this, Elora?"

I play nervously with the end of my braid, watching as he takes in the small bed, the cracked wardrobe, and the pail of stagnant water.

"What *is* this place?" He turns in a circle, noticing the stack of relics and mementos in the corner. "She stuck you up here, didn't she? She placed you up here with forgotten things. They weren't lying, were they? You were their maid."

My eyes fill with tears.

He tours the room angrily and rips the loose door on the wardrobe from its hinges, tossing it against the wall. "Did your father leave you with nothing?" he shouts, picking up the broken hairbrush from my makeshift bedside table and tossing it on the bed. "Answer me!"

"He did," I reply, my voice shaking, "but he left it in her name. He left me to her. When he died, she spent what remained and sold most of my things to try and recover some of the funds, but then gave my room to Daffodil—"

"And she sent you to me," he finishes. "And you agreed. You agreed to help her."

"No," I argue, "No, I agreed because it was in the best interest of Ashbury, or I thought it would be, but I made a mistake in going to her for help. I wasn't aware of what my father did, I didn't know you'd be *forced* into marriage—"

"Fuck, and we gave everything back to her!" He storms out of the attic, continuing to shout as he descends the stairs to the second level. "We gave everything back to her! We gave everything back to the woman who stuck you in an attic and made you clean up after her and her fucking daughters!"

I call his name as he ducks into Dolly's room. "This wasn't mine—"

He's not listening to me anymore.

He holds up a bright dress from her wardrobe. "This looks new."

He doesn't wait for me to confirm before he's back in the hallway, crossing into Regina's room. It's evident by the size that this room didn't once belong to me, either. He stands in the doorway and takes in the large bed, towering wardrobe, vanity, and the luxury my father left behind for her, muttering strings of obscenities as he shoves past me to step into my former room.

He pauses at the dollhouse that's covered in nightgowns and discarded dresses. "This was yours, wasn't it?"

I press a palm against each eye to push tears away. "My father built it for me when I was young—before my mother died—but Regina wouldn't let me take it to the attic."

He rips the clothes off the dollhouse and tosses them behind him, ignoring the roof caving in while he lifts it off the floor. "Do you have a wagon?"

"Finnian, the dollhouse is broken."

He snaps his head toward me with a glare. "Wagon, Elora. If not, I'll fucking carry it all the way back."

I point a finger into the hallway. "Downstairs, out the back. But we have Major waiting—"

"Get what you need and meet me out front."

He leaves me standing alone, choked and ashamed of how horribly I've allowed Regina to treat me.

I drag my feet to the back of the room and drop to my knees in front of Daffodil's wardrobe, reaching behind piles of clothing to fetch the small velvet sack of wooden dolls.

I stuff it into the front pocket of my cloak and close the door to my former life for the last time.

Nineteen

I stand in my father's study to reclaim the last piece of my childhood worth taking. Tearfully, I gently pull the painted portrait of my mother from my father's desk—the one remaining part of her that Regina never destroyed.

I had hidden this under a pile of tax forms my father kept when organizing shipments. The corners of the picture are bent, and the paint is faded, but it's the only way I can still see my mother and her kind, mischievous smile.

Susannah was right—this place hasn't been my home in a long time. It holds memories, but even those have dimmed. Strangely, the castle is the first place I've felt welcomed in a long time—even if it also came with strings.

I will always be on strings.

After my mother died, I didn't speak for weeks. My father remarried so quickly that I wasn't given a chance to wade through my grief, let alone try to accept someone taking her place. Months after Regina and her daughters moved in, my father returned from a day trip to Pumpkin Hollow. He sat with me on the floor, pulled me into his lap, and surprised me with a small marionette.

She was broken, he had explained, about to be tossed out for her faded smile and limbs held together by splintered wood and string, but he saved her from a burn pile.

He made her dance and talk, cursed when her strings tangled, and made me laugh from his frustration when the bottom half of her arm fell to the floor. And by the end, I was singing.

He instructed me on how to move her and gave me a small semblance of control. I spent every afternoon with my marionette. She listened to all my secrets, she helped me channel my confusion and heartache into song, and she would dance.

Her limbs were broken, but *I* was mending.

Until the day Regina heard me singing about my mother.

The next afternoon, my marionette was in pieces on the floor with her strings wrapped around her neck. Regina shouted at me for crying over something so small and insignificant. And my father said nothing.

So, I became the marionette.

I moved when told, spoke when spoken to, and harbored guilt any time I needed to cry. Over time, I learned to be grateful for my strings because they meant I was still valuable. And if I was helpful, I had a reason to survive.

Remorse and sorrow veiled the memories of my mother and buried them deep within me. When Azrea befriended me when I came of age, I started moving independently but felt the tension of my strings with each step.

Candlelight flares, and I go cold.

"Hello, Ellie." Regina steps inside with a malicious grin.

I look behind her in hopes of Finnian surprising her with a dagger to her back, but we're all alone.

Tucking the picture in my pocket with the velvet pouch of dolls, I step out from behind the desk. "Finnian is waiting for me outside."

She blocks me from leaving. "Yes, with my wagon. Daffodil was so upset when she noticed her dollhouse that we used the back door so we wouldn't have to face the thief."

I narrow my eyes. "*He* is not the thief."

She *tsks*. "My, my. Such crassness after what I did for you. You are allowed to return to the castle while we have been banished to live in this,"—she waves her hand around—"Dump."

"You changed the plan!" I shout. "You didn't give me time to try it my way. You didn't tell me about...." I trail off, unable to say it aloud. I haven't been allowed to try and reconcile why my father wanted me to marry Finnian—what the reason could possibly be. He could've warned me even if it was for the same reason that I set out to try.

She scowls. "Look at yourself, Elora. Did you honestly believe he would've fallen for someone like you? The king wanted to meet you. If I had told you before the ball that you were arranged to wed, you would've tried escaping with one of your beasts."

The doubt she has worked tirelessly to place in me over the years left me unable to deny her cruelty. "You have my father's fortune," I whisper. "We can part ways peacefully."

Malice has stretched her skin so tight across her cheekbones that she looks skeletal in the flickering flames of the dying candles. "Part ways?" She slowly prowls closer. "Ellie, we are family. You will never leave me."

I step away. "You are not my family. You have never been my family. Just because my father took pity on you does not mean I owe you anything."

Her brows nearly reach her hairline, her lips twist into a sneer, and her long nose points down at me. And for a second, I am the small girl again, listening to her lecture me about something I'd done to upset her.

"You stupid, weak girl." She drags a cold finger across my jaw. "Did you think it would be so simple?"

I become dizzy from the uptick of my heartbeat. "Why are you doing this?"

"Because he stuck me with you!" Her eyes bulge with hatred. "Because I spent years lying beside your father while he cried your mother's name in his sleep!" Her spiteful tone makes me shrink. "I hoped you would freeze in the attic, but your survival gave me hope that your constant existence meant I would be rewarded for my patience."

I feel so, so small. "How did you know about Cedric?"

She grabs my wrist and drags me back to the desk, opening the bottom drawer. And underneath a stack of paper, she pulls out a yellowed journal I believed I'd lost months ago.

She waves it in my face with a condescending laugh. "You wrote in great detail about how you wondered what it would be like to.... oh, what's the phrase you used?"

A tear rolls down my cheek.

"Make love," she mocks. "Tell me, Ellie, did you find out? I wonder how your prince would feel if I showed this to him?"

I clench my teeth. "What do you *want*?"

Her fingers tighten around my wrist—not enough to bruise, but to warn. "You've forgotten your place, Ellie. Did you believe you'd be the only one to live in the castle?"

"They won't welcome you back," I whisper. "Dolly and Daffodil spent the night with the king."

"They spent two nights, you fool!" A sharp pain shoots through my shoulder when she tugs my wrist. "I needed a backup plan in case you failed! You will marry Prince Finnian and demand a wing for us. The only reason you were allowed inside is because of your father."

The study has gone deathly cold. I shiver from pain and fear, from icy tears falling down my cheeks and neck, from the breath I can't seem to inhale. And I can't remember exactly when I started sobbing, but I couldn't control it anymore.

"Without him tolerating you following him around and without me allowing you to remain here when you brought absolutely nothing of value to me, you are *nothing*."

The heart in my throat isn't because of the pain pulsing through my frail wrist; it's not even because of another reminder that I don't belong in this family; it's that she believes I owe her something for being allowed to stay.

With our arms locked between us, I can't go anywhere when

she dissolves more space until her face is only inches from mine. "I am not staying in this manor while your mother's memories haunt these halls."

The weight of her words is drowning me in despair.

Her hand slips into my pocket to pull out the portrait of my mother. "I wouldn't get too close to your prince, Elora." She crumbles the picture into a ball. "We wouldn't want your fragile heart to break when he learns your secret. You should warn your precious faerie about how thin these walls are."

Oh, gods. Azrea. She heard Azrea in the attic.

She knows.

And to further detail the lengths she'd go to retain control over me, she adds, "I think wings would look lovely above our mantle, don't you?" She releases me with a look of disgust and turns away. "Run along now, Ellie. You are easy to forget, and the prince's eye is not easily kept."

She prevents me from recovering the portrait of my mother by stepping on it. The sound of the thin canvas tearing into pieces causes what's left of my heart to chip away.

I run outside and fall against the front door with sobs so deep in my chest that I don't make a sound. No spell or magic could ever outweigh cruelty. The spell might fade.

But the truth never will.

Finnian finds me slumped against the door with tears streaking my cheeks and eyes hollow. I haven't moved or searched for him since stepping outside, nor can I get a grip on my fear. Regina knows of Azrea being with child—she heard about their plan to escape. It was brilliant of her not to play that card until now—after I've been trapped into marriage.

Finnian lowers to try and catch my gaze, but my empty stare remains on the broken rubble of our drive. "I heard the back door and thought it was you, but no one was back there when I checked."

"It was Regina," I whisper.

He slowly stands. "What did she say to you?"

"Nothing I didn't already know." My words leave in a garbled mixture of choked defeat and shame. With the faeries asleep, the breeze is free to break the heated barrier and brushes the back of my neck, sending a fresh wave of discomforting chills. "I want to leave, Finnian."

I grab his arm when he steps toward the front door. "Finnian, please don't."

He places his hand on the doorknob, but I wedge between him and the door. "Finnian, she's not worth it."

"Why do you allow her to treat you this way?" He places a hand on my shoulder. "Her venom is treasonous against the crown. Any insult toward you is against me. This can end."

"My father's name attached to hers is still worth something here, Finnian. My people would not take kindly to the prince sending someone to the gallows for hurting my feelings." I force a grin. "I'm not worth an uprising."

"But it's a precedent I can set—"

Everything aches. "Please, Finnian."

He contemplates for a moment while staring at the door. Finally, he lowers his hand from the handle. "If this continues—"

"I understand. Let's return to Major."

He tucks a curl behind my ear—a simple gesture that's happening more frequently. I can't help but wonder if it's a bridge he's building to thaw the ice between us.

"Termane is your family name, yes?" he asks while leading us into a leisurely stroll, pulling the small wagon containing my dollhouse behind him.

"Termane," I confirm. "When a position was given to my father, I heard him tell my mother that he had hoped he'd retain the title of Lord Termane since he was paid wages by the king."

He tips his head back to stare at the stars. "That would've given Ashbury too much power and hope."

"You know what's ironic?" I wait until he lowers his chin before a genuine smile crosses my face. "If I had become Princess of Ashbury, we most likely would've been arranged to marry anyway."

His resounding laughter fills the empty air. "I could've sent you love letters across the bridge, courted you properly. Perhaps you wouldn't dislike me so much."

I snort. "If that's what you need to believe. I can't imagine you writing a love letter."

He mockingly gasps. "I could've copied a poem. I've heard those are romantic."

I slap my forehead. "Of course! Women swoon over men who use the work of others."

He playfully shoves his elbow into my ribs. "Even an alternate me can't impress you."

I pretend to be insulted. "Try *harder*."

The last thing I want to admit is that I'm beginning to tolerate him. The two days I've spent with him are comparable to our valleys' ups and downs. I can never prepare for what he's bound to say or do, leaving me in constant caution and intrigue.

I slide the bottle of liquor from his pocket and take a sip. The bitter honey doesn't taste better than my last swig, but I need the courage. "What happens now?"

He needs no further clarification. "The engagement will be announced in the morning. I will accompany you to breakfast in the town square for a casual introduction into society, and then you won't see me for a while."

I frown. "Why?"

He sighs. "We'll attend separate events. You will spend most days with Irina or my mother." His tone becomes distant. "My mother told Regina it would be an intimate wedding, but she lied. I will be tasked with entertaining visiting royals."

"Why won't I?"

"Because you're not royalty." He drags a hand down his face.

"You'll hear things about where you came from, Elora. Jasper is going to spin this in a favorable way to make us look..."

"Charitable?"

"Irina will protect you."

His forced grin of assurance only makes me take a longer sip.

He continues, "The visiting royals aren't.... just stay by Irina."

I refuse to look at him. "Where will I sleep after we wed?"

He clears his throat. "My quarters span the length of an entire floor. There is a guestroom that adjoins my bedroom. It has a bed and everything you need."

I scowl. "Have other women slept there? Will I have to listen to other women in your bed during your *affairs*?"

"Elora," he sighs, shoving a hand through his hair. "I won't question you if you don't question me."

When I trip over my feet, I shake the bottle after realizing I've already drunk half. Even with my brain as thin as a stew, I can't ask about the son I will be expected to provide.

"This union is absurd," I slur.

His eyes flicker with amusement as he takes the bottle from me. "Because you find me so handsome that I intimidate you?"

I try to laugh but only shake my head as my already sour mood twists into remorse. "Because we're enemies, Finnian. Your father killed my grandfather. No betrothal, grand wedding, or town square stroll can change that. Your father took away my birthright. I could've been a princess without needing to marry you. I could've fallen in love with someone else."

Silently, he nods and drains the remaining liquor, much to my dismay, but I don't miss the way his fingers whiten around the bottle. "I don't think Cedric would've liked that."

My sight blurs. "There is only one way this can end."

I barely feel his hand on my lower back as the stars above us start to spin. "And which way is that, little doe?"

"Ruin," emerges in a breath as the starry sky envelopes me.

Twenty

R*uin.*

So much heavy truth lives in that word. It repeats endlessly in my mind while riding back to Pumpkin Hollow with Elora asleep in my arms. I want her to open her eyes and go into deep detail about what she meant by that. But, since she just consumed hard liquor for the first time, I'll have to accept that I can't accidentally pinch her in hopes she'll wake up and instead need to be honorable.

Plus, it has started to rain.

After leaving the wagon containing the dollhouse with the lookouts and leaving strict instructions to bring it to the castle, I hoisted Elora on Major for us to return.

Raindrops pelt against the stable while I removed Major's saddle. Elora doesn't stir on the bed of hay where I laid her. This storm is the first of many to come. Autumn always holds the most downpour for our realm, causing the already-brisk temperatures to carry more of a bite.

I will need to drop the gate of Major's stall before we leave to keep him warm and dry, meaning I will have to carry Elora back to the castle in heavy rainfall if she doesn't wake.

Her eyelids flutter when thunder rolls.

I crouch and gently squeeze her shoulder. "Elora," I murmur, "we need to return. Morning is upon us."

And it will be a painful one if her body has the same reaction to alcohol as mine does. I've built a tolerance, but too much still causes my head to pound.

She pouts her bottom lip when I nudge her again, lifting her hand to lazily try and swat me away. Sighing, I run a hand through my hair as it drops onto my forehead from the muggy condensation building. The howling wind torpedoes the raindrops, whipping icy beads into the stall. Major neighs in protest.

Elora's eyes pop open, and she blinks to focus on me.

"Hello, little drunk. Can you stand?"

Something inaudible passed her lips as she sloppily twisted to all fours and held out a hand. I try not to chuckle when I take her hand and pull her up. "You truly are a doe," I remark as I note her trembling legs.

She mocks me with slurs.

"So, you're a mean drunk."

Her airy and light laughter makes me smile while dragging her out of the stall with me. I balance her against a wall before tossing in two blankets and lowering the wall gate of Major's stall. Elora waves to Major before the door closes.

Peeking outside, I grimace. Rain is pouring in so many directions from the shifting winds, disguising the pathway back to the castle. "If this doesn't sober you up, nothing will." I pull the hood of the cloak over her head. "Want to run?"

The liquored glaze of her eyes lightens the brown and reveals uneven splotches of gold—as if an artist shook a paintbrush over them to add color to his canvas.

She locks her gaze with me before completely falling against my chest. I wrap an arm around her waist and woefully accept the hefty droplets of rain against my face and neck while we trudge through the storm.

"Fuck!" she shouts, barely audible over thunder.

I can't stop laughing at her reactions, trying to hold her steady when she tries to haphazardly increase our speed. Mud splashes on our boots and pants, the moist ground becoming increasingly treacherous by the second.

Breathless, we pause under an old tree with substantial branches and leaves, giving us a quick reprieve. "Why can't we stay in the stables until it passes?" she yells.

"It'll be morning before it does!" I shrug. "We can, but we'll be going to breakfast smelling like a horse and covered in hay."

She rolls her eyes. "Is that different from how you normally smell?"

Even wasted, she still finds a way to insult me. "I am more than willing to roll around in the hay with you, Elora."

She scowls. "Oh, I bet you are. Need that son, don't you?"

She's a mean *and* brave drunk.

No one else would ever be allowed to speak to me in the way she does and live, yet I continue giving her chances.

"You won't have to worry about that," I say.

She tries to blink water from her eyes. "Why not?"

I turn from her and point toward the castle. "The storm will get worse before it lightens. We need to continue."

She shoves my chest. "What did you mean by that, Finnian?"

I forge ahead and ignore her. She remains close enough to shove me forward a step. Reaching behind me, I grab her wrist and yank her forward. "Put your hands on me again, Elora."

She does, using her free hand to push my shoulder. "He made it clear that I will lose my life if I don't obey the guidelines you set!"

"I didn't set them," I growled.

We are completely drenched. My hair covers my eyes from rainfall, and her cloak has become so heavy that she shoves the hood off. Her unruly curls are sopping wet against her chest. And I will not discuss the matter of an heir with her in the middle of a rainstorm while she looks deliciously divine when soaked.

I release her and turn, but she follows me. "Oh, I see! You'll send me away, won't you?" She nearly slips in the mud, but why would that stop her from speaking? "You'll have your little affairs"

—she makes weird gestures with her fingers as if squishing the very idea—"And compensate whoever ends up pregnant with your child."

"Elora," I warn.

"And you'll send me away to pretend it's me."

I remain silent, but my anger is pooling.

"You claim to loathe your father...."

"I don't loathe him," I mutter, lying out of habit.

"But you behave like him."

I freeze. "You say a lot for not knowing what the fuck you're talking about, Elora."

She mocks me by dipping in a drunken, dramatic bow. "Forgive me, oh great one. I didn't realize I am your wife for appearances only."

She leaves me with a parting glare before stalking off. I watch her for a solid minute while contemplating returning to the stables alone and leaving her to figure out her way back. But instead, I find myself chasing her. *Again*.

"It's unsurprising how a man hasn't snatched you up yet!" I shout. "Because you would drive them fucking mad!"

She whirls on me and bends quickly, gathering a fistful of mud to hurl at me. It lands on my cheek and neck, dripping down my shirt. "You took away any chance of that, too!" she yells.

"I'll return you to Cedric soon enough!" I argue, bitter jealousy rebuilding.

She exerts a cry of frustration. "I do not belong to Cedric, you idiot!" Running a muddy hand through her fallen braid, she leaves her fingers weaved through her tangled strands. "But don't let me stand in the way of your affairs, you godsdamn...."

She doesn't finish before she's gone again, leaving me panting and bewildered. Was her reaction to his anger earlier purely from guilt?

She stomps through the gardens, attempting to step over the rare flowers. I plow right through them, bringing plenty of dirt and leaves. "What do you mean, Elora?"

She glances at me over her shoulder. "It doesn't matter," is what I think she says.

Water has lodged in my ears.

"Fuck, Elora. Stop and talk to me!"

I reach for her, but the slick water works favorably for her, and she effortlessly slips from my grasp.

She approaches the steps to the basement door, but I stop her before she can disappear inside by grabbing her arms and spinning her around. "Why are you so fucking difficult?"

She crosses her arms. "Forgive me for not wanting to wake up every morning to your face staring back at me."

I bend, eating the distance between us. "And you think I want to live day in and day out dodging your insults?"

"You've had plenty of practice dodging responsibilities, so it should be simple!"

I curse at her. At the unforgiving rainfall. "You didn't seem to mind when you came here to weasel your way into my bed."

She scoffs. "At no point did I ever want to be in your bed where so many others have been."

No one but me has ever been in my bed.

But when would I tell her that?

Fucking never.

She nearly whacks me in the face when she tosses her arms up. "This is never going to work between us! We're too different!"

I knocked her hand out of the way. "You're absolutely right, Elora. I am a logical—"

"Completely devoid of emotion—"

"Resourceful and willing participant in this while you are just.... you're just...." I point behind us toward the greenhouse. "A little gourd!"

Raindrops fill her mouth when her jaw falls slack. Visibly irritated and shivering, she tries to shove me away, but I don't move an inch.

"Playboy prince," she goads.

I tip my head back in shocked laughter. "Playboy prince? Jealous, Elora? Envious of everyone I've touched?" I place my hands on either side of her head. "Upset about my affairs?"

"But not shocked."

Our reason for arguing washes away in the falling rain when warmth spreads through me at the idea of her being envious.

"Have you been kissed, Elora?"

Her eyes flare. "That doesn't concern you."

I should move back, lessen the tension, gouge my own eyes for staring at her lips— her venomous pout that loves to insult me.

But instead, I grin and drag my eyes up to hers. "I thought we agreed to be honest with each other, Elora. You're aware of my.... Conquests."

"Gods," she mutters. "You're disgusting."

"Tell me you're not jealous." My voice drops an octave. "Tell me it doesn't bother you that I've touched someone else."

Teasing the idea of it becoming physical between us is frivolous and unsustainable, but I itch to hear her lies—that it doesn't ignite a fire in her like it did to me when I thought Cedric had already claimed her as his.

"I'm not jealous," she says. "Because you are not mine, just as I am not yours."

I dangerously inch closer. "Aren't you?" Slowly, I drag my knuckles across her jaw. "Answer my question, Elora."

"Which one?" Her voice has lost the edge and gained a nervous rattle.

The heat between our bodies swallows the falling rain. "Have you been kissed by someone?"

"Yes," she whispers.

I grin almost manically. "Liar."

Her silent reply is a gift. And the logic I bragged about dissipates when I cup her neck and bring her to me in a sky-splintering kiss. Suffocating tension between us since the night we met breathes life into the mold of her lips against mine. For never being kissed, the softly confident way she moves with me makes me groan.

I can't form a thought.

All I do is taste.

Honeyed liquor has coated her lips and the tip of her tongue as I tease her with mine by sweeping it across her bottom lip. Her fingers claw at my chest with every ounce of hatred she feels toward me, yet she returns the fervor tenfold. Unapologetically and so fucking good.

Forbidden tastes so much sweeter than if this was allowable between us. And when my fingers tear through her hair, it's only to bring her closer, kiss her harder, *breathe* her in.

The temptation to take her to the highest peak of pleasure is right at my fingertips, knowing I could quickly shove her inside to hear her breathy whimpers as I fall to my knees for her.

Tasting her—I'm dying for a taste.

My body is rigid against hers.

Fuck, I want her.

But I pull away from her because I can't *have* her. Her chest heaves, her tongue darts out to gather what lingers of our kiss from her lips, and I can't move.

Want keeps me frozen to the ground.

She moves like she wants to kiss me again, but I wrap my fingers around her wrists to stop her. Rejection causes her hands to drop.

I nearly apologize, but I won't. Not for this.

I will never apologize for kissing her.

She frowns and climbs out of her lustful daze. So much filters through her eyes: doubt, confusion, shame, and longing.

But I can't coddle her.

I can't assure her that I want her.

Instead, I allow her to open the door, slip inside, and do not chase her. I sink to sit on the steps, tilting my head up to drown in the rain. I've just stolen her first kiss, and I'd readily become a thief to take so much fucking more from her.

I pass Elora's door without stopping, not even pausing to check in on Irina. But I should know my sister better than that and am not surprised to find her sitting against my door. "What'd you do?"

"Greetings have taken a turn around here," I mutter, sliding down the wall opposite her.

She rests her hands on her lap. "I found Elora wandering the halls, drunk. I helped her get in the bathtub, and she started rambling about you and a kiss and asked me about.... Oh, what did you call them?"

I clear the water from my face and avoid answering her question.

"Conquests," she finishes.

I bravely looked at her to find her scowling at me. Irate, I stand and search my pockets for the key to my door. "I don't like how you look at me lately, Irina."

"I don't like *you* lately." Standing, she wiggles a key in front of my face but jerks her hand away and unlocks the door.

I can't even lock her out when she always finds a fucking key to steal. "Please come in, I fucking guess."

She lingers in the doorway. "You kissed Elora. *Elora*."

I track mud inside and kick off my boots, uncaring where they land. The taste of Elora is still fresh, and my chest aches from wanting more—from the throbbing I'm still experiencing at the mention of her name.

"What were you thinking, Finn?"

I pop the top button of my shirt to steady my breathing, but it doesn't calm the uneven beats of frustrated inhales. "I don't know, Irina. Why don't we sit down and fucking dissect it?"

"Finnian!" she yells.

I throw my arms up. "I don't fucking know! What do you want me to say? I kissed her because I wanted to kiss her, because she makes me..."—I tug my hair—"Fucking enraged!"

I begin pacing. "Because I go mad when she yells at me. I want to wrap my hands around her throat, but I can't. She's uncontrollable and mean. So fucking callous and bold."

"Hades," she whispers, "you're falling."

"No," I deny. "No, I'm not."

"Finnian—"

"I'm not," I reiterated, clenching *everything* and facing her. "I can't."

She leans her head against the doorframe. "Would it be awful to want your wife, Finn?"

I grip the back of a chair. I can't stand still and might seek out trouble at a tavern just to have a place for this bottled energy to go. "Yes, Irina. It would."

Anyone close to me, anything I value, is a way for him to control me. Irina and my mother are the only ones I ever allow close anymore. If Elora becomes to me what she could be, he will use that to his advantage. Threaten her.

I refuse to let it get that far.

And.... I'm his son. I've spent years watching the way he's slowly torn apart my mother, dangled us in front of her to keep her here. I refuse to be that... be him.

"I am going to say this once, Finnian. And I promise to never speak of it again."

Her serious tone nearly compelled me to change the subject, detour, and pretend I didn't hear her. But I nod.

"I know what you've been trained for." Her deep breath is strained. "I know what you believe must be done for this kingdom. I understand where your loyalty is, and I know *why* you're loyal."

Her voice cracks, and I frown.

She couldn't know.

"I saw it happen—the lashings."

I stop breathing.

"I know you defied your commander. And I saw what they did to you."

I barely get the words out when I ask, "You were there?"

Her eyes shimmered, and she swallowed her raspy cry. "I understand the fear you have."

I hang my head with a shuddering breath. The lashings

preceded my mate's beheading. His screaming pleas to be spared have never left me. They never will. And I promised myself to never put someone else at risk like that again.

"It's why I stayed away," I whisper. "If I'm not here, he can't hurt you. He leaves mother alone."

She comes to me with tears running down her cheeks. "I know," she assures me, "but you're here now." She squeezes my arm gently. "You have to learn how to *live*, Finnian. You can't spend your life fighting him by not being here."

I have to look away from her. Seeing my little sister upset, the one person I've spent my life protecting is a path I can never come back from if I start down it. I've built defenses around her for so long that I can't accept them crumbling.

"I can't... let him hurt her, Irina."

"Then... she needs to know everything." She wipes the tears from her cheeks. "If you can't let yourself get close to her, she needs to know. Because..."—she pinches the bridge of her nose with a sigh—"he invited *her* to the wedding."

My head snaps up. I search her face for the lie—I wait for her to laugh and tell me she's joking, but her apologetic grin screams the truth.

"It's why I was strolling at midnight," she explains. "I broke into his study when he went to bed and saw the list of invitees."

I shake my head in disbelief. "Why?"

"Because he's sick," she states bluntly. "Everything is a game to him. Elora needs to hear the truth from you, or she'll hear it from someone else."

"My task is to keep the guests entertained. I can keep *her* away from Elora."

Exasperated, Irina brushes me off. Moments of heaviness are rare between us, and we always do our best to dwindle them quickly into nothing. If we think too heavily about our lives, liquor becomes the only way to numb.

"I'm going to check on Elora." She walks to the door. "It would be rather dull if she drowns in the bathtub."

"I'm sure she'll appreciate the sentiment." Before she leaves, I call her name once. "After breakfast tomorrow, I won't be around much."

"Don't fret, brother." She doesn't bother to turn. "I've got her."

I grab the bottle of whiskey that Irina replaced after her afternoon tryst with her lovers. From my balcony, I hear Elora's laugh below through Irina's open balcony doors.

Irina found her alive.

I sink to the floor, flick the lid off, and drink until I can no longer taste her.

Twenty-One

A deep, husky call rattles until my eyes open. I immediately raise my arm to block the sun pouring over my balcony wall. Groaning, I roll my neck side-to-side, wincing from the dull ache on the right. I squint an eye and brave the sunlight at the sound of ruffling feathers, greeting the forest raven perched on the ledge with a glare.

Its head bobs as it looks from me to the empty bottle of whiskey knocked on its side. My last memory includes the bottle and emptying the contents on my tongue. The high tolerance I like to brag about mocks me with a pounding headache, and every other part of my body screams and curses every time I move—punishment for sleeping on the cold stone floor.

"Irina would say you're a bad omen," I say to the bird, licking my dry lips. My sister has spent way too much time with self-proclaimed philosophers, in my opinion.

The raven spread its wings and dove toward me, nearly brushing my cheeks with its feathers before shooting into the air. I swat at it as I stand, growling. "Fucking birds," I grumble while walking inside and slamming the balcony doors shut.

Every sluggish move I make is followed by another ounce of regret from drinking. It's a habit I've always struggled to break.

The sun is battling gray, looming clouds. Rain won't be far

behind. Getting caught in another storm with Elora will only further my inability to stop wanting her—if only to fuck the venom right out of her.

I pour a mugful of rum. It isn't my favorite liquor, but I keep draining every bottle of whiskey. The memories I've perfected burying needed to stay that way, yet they continue resurfacing, and I don't have the energy to face today while being angry with Jasper all over again.

It serves no one.

The sour rum goes down quickly. I suck in cold air through clenched teeth to chase it, shaking my head to clear the fogginess from drinking. Another moment passed before I refilled the mug and chugged the liquor.

"Stop," I say aloud, but memories plague me anyway.

Irina was there the day I received lashings.

The lashings weren't given with enough force to leave scars. Jasper didn't want my mother to find out; we had an image to maintain. If anyone saw me shirtless, questions about how I received them would arise, and if anyone learned that it was my father's orders the commander followed that day, the truth about how horrible he treats us would come out.

If they learned it was he who ordered my friend's beheading because he didn't believe the blood pouring down my back was painful enough, people might doubt the love he has for his beloved heir—the nonexistent fatherly love.

My wrists were still bound to the wooden stake when the sword was raised, and my hair was pulled when I tried to duck my head. He wanted me to watch my friend's head roll.

And Irina saw everything.

The person I've spent years protecting for that reason, the woman I didn't want to be subjected to the depths of his evil, witnessed all of it.

After the beheading, his family departed from the realm under threat of Jasper adding them to his collection next if they ever told the truth about who ordered the execution. I used to visit them when I could, but their hollow eyes haunted my dreams. My visits have been replaced with yearly allowances, but they never accept them.

No, Elora can't mean anything to me.

She can't.

So, I drink some more.

❧

I take a cold bath and splash my face with icy water to soothe the broken vessels in my eyes, but they remain. I comb my hair back, stare into the wardrobe with a sigh, then venture into the *very* rarely used closet adjacent to the guest room and dress in all black instead of the ungodly amount of blue and silver I have.

The idea of dressing in the colors of the family crest doesn't appeal to me for this outing. If Jasper inquires why, I'll tell him I want to remain neutral for the visiting royals.

Unable to continue stalling, I leave my wing, prepared for Irina to jump out from behind a wall at any moment, but only servants pass by. Maybe she stayed with Elora overnight and could dwindle the impending awkwardness between us. I could escort them to breakfast since being near Elora always causes me to nearly die of thirst and choke.

But it only takes one knock on Elora's door for her to breathlessly open it and curse under her breath. "It's just you," she says without remorse.

Well, at least her hatred is consistent.

Before I can rattle off apologies, she twists and flails her arms behind her. Her champagne curls bounce and get caught between her fingers and dress.

"May I inquire—"

"I thought you were Irina," she interrupts before sighing. "She popped in this morning, shoved this dress in my arms, and disappeared without helping me into it. I suppose she only does things when it's convenient for her."

I lean against the doorframe with an amused grin. "You're learning quickly," I reply. "Do you need assistance?"

"Not from you," she snaps. Her resistance only lasts a heartbeat before she squeezes her eyes shut. "Yes."

I join her at the mirror and motion for her to spin. Mumbling what I'm positive are mostly insults, she turns. I regret offering to help her as soon as I notice her spine exposed by the parted fabric of her dress.

And I imagine what it would look like arched off the bed. Or a table. Or the fucking floor; I wouldn't be picky.

"Please tell me you know how to tie," she says after a moment, sighing impatiently.

I had gone still and quiet while staring at the curve of her spine under the nearly sheer backing. Silently, I take the untied laces on her lower back and pull them so tightly that she gasps and clutches her stomach. "I do," I say.

Her glare reflecting back at me makes me chuckle.

"My mother put in an order for more dresses."

"I know," she mumbles. "Three seamstresses were here before the sun was even awake to take measurements."

When I didn't convey surprise, she repeated, "*Three*."

"And? You'll be required to wear dresses daily, Elora. We have an entire staff dedicated to our clothing."

She wrinkles her nose. "I have never owned dresses so.... complicated." She tilts her head. "I am content in my smock and shawl."

"You will be princess consort," I remind her, dropping my hands from where they had absentmindedly landed on her waist. "You will have responsibilities and appearances to make. A raggedy cardigan—"

She whirls and crosses her arms. "Us being married will not give you the right to make every decision for me."

I lift an eyebrow at the challenge. "I might know a thing or two more than you do about royal life. We don't all have the luxury of watching faeries all day."

Her lips part, but then her expression changes into determination. "When will I see them again?"

I try to control the jealousy from rebuilding. Why does she want to see them so soon? Will she kiss Cedric just to anger me? Punish me? Fucking *torture* me? "This afternoon, if you want."

She hums her approval and leaves me standing in the entryway to disappear into her bedroom.

I try to remain still but somehow end up following her. "Elora, we need to talk about what happened last night."

She slips the raggedy shawl on. "Last night?"

She's going to make me say it.

I clear my throat. "Me kissing you."

She asks, "We kissed?" without missing a beat, gathering her hair to lift from underneath her collar. "I don't remember."

"You don't *remember*?"

She shrugs. "I guess it wasn't memorable."

I inch closer. "Oh, believe me. You enjoyed it."

Walk away, Finn.

She taps her chin. "Did I?" Walking backward, she maintains eye contact with me while wrapping a hand around the bedpost to slide her shoes on. "Maybe you've been lied to about how well you kiss."

I slide my hands into my pockets to prevent pushing her down on the bed. "I give pleasure as well as I take it, little doe."

She pulls in her bottom lip with her teeth while she hums, narrowing her eyes and gazing at me curiously. She has to be fucking with me. That kiss is seared into my mind. She's brushing it off to lighten the tension between us.

But fuck, she's convincing.

She approaches me with the tiniest grin underneath smug, hooded eyes. "As long as it doesn't happen again, Finnian." And slides past me without looking back.

And I forget how to breathe.

As determined as she is to feign boredom with this lifestyle, Elora can't hide her awe during our stroll through town. Her eyes widened, and her breath hitched at every corner. Nothing about Pumpkin Hollow impresses me, but after visiting Ashbury with her, I understand why it appeals to her.

Comfort and luxury exist here—something she isn't privy to. Even though her palace manor is the largest in Ashbury, the inside reflects her father's wages. Since Regina has already blown through their fortune once, it's only a matter of time before she does it again. Luckily, we only agreed to give back what she lost *once*. A wiser woman would've negotiated for a lifetime of care and comfort.

Elora stops at every shoppe to smush her face against the window, significantly delaying our breakfast at the bakery. It's a scheduled appearance, but I'm also fucking starving.

Couriers announced our engagement this morning, which keeps us surrounded by gawkers and gossipers, but she doesn't notice them. I need her to spend more than a minute with me before running off again to give them something to discuss.

"Elora, *darling*."

She whips her head around so fast that I'm surprised her neck doesn't snap. "Don't call me that."

I force a tight smile. "Little doe?"

She rolls her eyes. "What?"

"Leaving me while you take off like an overexcited child isn't part of our agreement."

"*Our* agreement?" She fans herself with her hand but still refuses to remove the cardigan she insists on wearing everywhere. The incoming rain has made the air muggy and warm, but she's too stubborn to admit that. "Fine," she sighs. "Where to, Lord Finnian?"

Reaching, I grab her wrist and tug her closer. "Back to name-calling, are we?"

She resists as much as she can. "Is that not your title?"

To prevent her from fleeing, I curl an arm around her waist and press her against my chest. "My title isn't normally masked with insults."

"That you know of," she mutters.

She's limp in my hold, perturbed and ornery, and maybe still slightly bitter about my rejection last night. Sighing, I tip her chin up with my finger. The gold in her irises snags me when she turns doe-eyed with a hint of longing.

"Put your hand on my chest, Elora."

Her pout thins. Our audience circles us like starved vultures. Feeding them is the entire point of this outing, and she needs to improve her acting dramatically.

"*Now*, Elora."

Her heartbeat against my chest leaps. And slowly, very slowly, her palm gradually lifts and hovers over my chest. I cover her hand with mine and press it against me, away from *my* hammering heartbeat.

She tilts her head up and gives herself away.

She remembers our kiss *very* well.

"Good girl," I whisper.

She watches my gaze instinctively fall to her mouth. I can't help how my body reacts to hers, nor how I can remember the honeyed taste of her lips. It's all instinctual and embedded in my memories, heated and.... Hades, I want her.

She baits me further, licking her lips as if priming them for a kiss. Conflicted, I don't know how to talk myself into something while also talking myself out of it.

"Tell me what you're thinking," I say.

This could be dangerous.

Tell me you hate me.

Tell me to let you go.

But she doesn't say either of those things.

"I'm thinking you might kiss me," she whispers, her voice wavering from nerves.

"Do you want me to kiss you?"

I've never wanted to hear yes and no simultaneously, but I'm leaning more toward wanting her to assure me that kissing her would be fine—that it won't lead to Jasper using her against me, that it'll only lead to her in my bed.

Fuck, the things I could teach her.

She isn't telling me to fuck off, which is already an improvement from when we met. "I don't want to scandalize our crowd," she murmurs.

I drag my knuckles across her jaw with a mischievous grin. "Oh, little doe, you don't know the meaning of the word." Leaning in, I whisper in her ear, "I know ways to make even the gods turn crimson."

I doubt she meant for her fingers to clutch my shirt, leaving no space between our bodies. My cock has grown rigid while holding her and imagining all the ways I could show her just how genuinely scandalous we could be together.

I continue against my better judgment, lowering my voice to say, "Instead of my shirt, you could be grasping bedsheets. Imagine the soft silk against your skin while my lips explore your neck, your shoulders.... imagine my teeth grazing your ribcage, Elora, the pain bringing you pleasure."

Her hand slides up my chest, and she barely presses her fingertips into the base of my throat. And I don't know why I risk such a public display of anything more than tolerance, but I backed her into the stone wall of a shoppe. "Look at me, Elora."

Her breathing quickens, but she doesn't move to obey. I force her chin up by wrapping a clump of curls around my fist and tugging. The most delicate shade of pink has colored her cheeks, conveying what I've always known but desperately want to hear. "Has anyone touched you, little doe?"

Her stubbornness and need to drive me mad gives her pause, but she shakes her head. I have to balance my free hand against the brick behind her to stop myself from unraveling her right here, in front of onlookers.

"Our kiss was your first?"

Lie to me, Elora. I need anything but confirmation from her. I need to know she's been kissed by someone else—otherwise, she'll feel too much like *mine*.

"Yes," she breathes.

I search her face, desperately wanting to find the lie, but I know one doesn't exist. "Fuck, Elora, you should've lied."

"I know," she murmurs.

As tempting as the idea is, I can't take her *here*.

Instead, I use my grip on her hair to stretch her neck taut and lean down, leaving a kiss on the corner of her mouth.

Her hands don't leave me, but a slight frown appears. "Have you been drinking?"

If I wasn't laden with lust, the concern in her voice would puncture my chest more than it does, but then I realize her disappointment stems from believing my behavior is solely because of that—that teasing her, wanting her, is a result of not being able to think clearly.

I want to assure her that the only thing I'm drunk on is her presence, but I don't. And my silence is confirmation enough.

She drops her hand from my chest.

And just like that, I lost her.

The baker's call for fresh pumpkin scones earns me a glare from Elora. "You promised no more pumpkins," she mutters.

"They offer other things, Elora."

I glance around and notice two undercover guards dressed casually and watching our every move. I suspected that Jasper would send them to keep him informed on how his investment is behaving.

I reach for her hand and hold it tightly, squeezing when she tries to yank it away. "Don't look," I say, "but we're being watched."

She stops fighting me.

I keep my voice low when I add, "This is your life now, Elora.

When we're in public, every behavior will be analyzed and reported."

Her inhales quicken. "Is it because I stormed out of dinner?"

I chuckle from frustrated amusement—not from her reacting to her freedom being stripped away, but because Jasper will still try to find reasons to dispose of her once satisfied.

"No. Well, that didn't help, but no. It's because you're you. And because you're friendly with Irina." My forced smile turns sorrowful. "She's watched constantly, too."

Moving my hand to the small of her back, I guide her inside the large bakery. Mouthwatering smells and delights waft into my nose. Typically busy and sold out of everything, I'm pleased to find the shelves fully stocked. That can only mean they were alerted to our upcoming arrival.

A worker closes the door behind us to prevent anyone from following us inside, allowing a moment of reprieve.

She looks back and forth until I bring her in front of me and press her back against my chest, wrapping an arm around her waist from behind. "They're outside, Elora. It's just us, but they can see inside."

Her shoulders relax. "What can I do?"

"Everything you're told," I reply woefully. "Pretend you're grateful. I'll protect you, but I'd rather not need a reason to have to."

She turns her head sideways and tilts it back to gaze at me. "Thank you for telling me. I am grateful for that."

It's the first time she's ever genuinely thanked me for something. I'm not fond of the way my chest swells. "Who else would I smash pumpkins with if you're not around?"

Her broad smile stretches from ear to ear.

We share a peaceful moment until I say, "Order anything you like. Choose something for me. I'll wait for you outside."

Her fear returns. "Finnian, I can't afford any of this."

I gently spin her around to face me, cup my hands around her throat, and lean in until I'm positive I have her undivided attention. "That is not something you ever have to worry about again, little doe. As the princess consort, you'll never pay for anything. You will always have food and water."

Her eyes fill with tears, but grief prevents her from relief. "But my people—"

I interrupt her by calling for the baker, a short fellow with white hair and kind eyes. He's been in my life since I was a tot, and because of it, we've cut all formalities when alone, but he bows to me upon seeing Elora.

"Prince Finnian," he greets.

"Elora, this is Rhoadie. Rhoadie, Elora is my betrothed."

Elora shifts uncomfortably when Rhoadie grabs her hand and bows with a smile—a courtesy she will never become content with receiving. I don't plan on letting anyone skimp on treating her with the respect she deserves.

"Hello," she says softly, placing her hands behind her back once freed.

I slide my hands up and down her arms. "Rhoadie, what do you do with your leftovers? On rare occasions, you have any left."

His deep belly laugh causes Elora to smile. "Throw them out, I 'spose."

"Can you start saving them for me? Load them into a wagon, and I'll send someone for them every evening. And perhaps, if you have ingredients with upcoming expiration dates, use them to ensure leftovers?"

He bows with a wink before throwing a soiled rag over his shoulder to return to his pastries. I tug on one of Elora's curls until she looks at me with genuine fondness.

"I'm willing to help you, Elora. Whatever he's able to provide will be delivered to Ashbury. Change won't happen overnight, but we have an agreement, right? If you'll keep pretending, I'll assist when I can."

I swallow from the emotion that sweeps across her face, but I can't allow myself to take credit for the gesture. While I care about helping the people in Ashbury recover from the neglect bestowed upon them by my father, the determination-edged desperation is due to the wall Elora has built around herself. I want to be the one to tear it down.

I don't deserve her trust or her forced dedication to my heinous father, but I want it.

I break our prolonged stare by clearing my throat, refusing to dissect why it feels like she can see right through me—why it feels like she just met me for the first time. I've worked too long and hard for my reputation of being aloof and callous to be torn apart by a maddening, irritatingly beautiful woman with just a look.

"As I said before, order for us."

I step outside and gulp fresh air like I haven't breathed since meeting her, yet I can't stop myself from turning to watch her timidly approach the counter.

And I regret ever returning to this godsforsaken kingdom.

Twenty-Two

Rhoadie is far too patient with me.

I can't decide which pastry I want. I haven't heard of half of what the bakery offers—the majority containing pumpkin. With my father's wages, we always had food, but our choices were limited in Ashbury. And when deliveries slowly started to slim down, we were left with a rotating selection of stale breads and nearly rotted vegetables for stew.

I imagine King Jasper looked at the number Regina requested be restored and laughed. A fortune to us is a drop in the bucket for him, even if I only base it on how much each pastry costs.

"Do you mind if I ask you why the royal family doesn't need to pay?" I don't have to feign innocence—I am curious why the wealthiest family in the realm doesn't have to pay for food when their subjects do.

He gestures to the shelves filled with bags of flour and ingredients lined across the wall behind him. "I restock monthly by submitting order forms to the...."—he pauses and flicks his wrist toward the door—"... it's a very complicated process, but my longstanding relationship with the royal family allows me to pay wholesale pricing for ingredients. Because of it, I save money, and they eat here at no cost."

I nod but raise an eyebrow. "Finnian alluded to me not needing to pay for anything *ever*. Do all merchants have the same relationship with them as you do?"

Rhoadie slides the towel between his fingers, contemplatively nodding from side to side. I could ask Finnian these questions, but I remain cautious around him and hesitant to believe everything he says.

"Different people do different things for many reasons," he says, and I realize he's being discreet, too. "Sometimes respect, sometimes relationships, sometimes...."

I know the words he doesn't want to say.

Fear.

And on the off-chance that the king has ears everywhere, I don't allow him to say it. "I understand."

I gnaw on my lower lip while returning my focus on selecting pastries. Rhoadie smiles warmly. The deep smokiness of his voice comforts me like a crackling fire as he reminds me of the names of each pastry again. And he smells like sugar.

If I'm not allowed to spend time with Finnian while he entertains visitors, perhaps I can spend it here with Rhoadie. "Can you, um, suggest something?" I try to maintain a polite smile. "Maybe something *not* with pumpkin?"

Laughing, he grabs a wooden slate. "I have been asked to bake the cake for your wedding." He places a crisp pastry on the slate and waves an arm around in grand gestures above his head. "Very, very, tall and made with spiced pumpkin buns."

I blow out an annoyed breath. "Of course. The king should have what he wants."

He adds a crescent bun. "But then, I received an adjustment from a courier."

I tilt my head. "Oh?"

"Unsigned," he continued, passing the slate to me, "but with the royal seal. Honestly, I was surprised to be asked to bake the cake when the royal pastry chef in the castle could."

I nod, following his pointed look to Finnian waiting by the door. "He requested you?"

"I recognized the handwriting," he replies. "The change order stated that the three top layers of the cake be vanilla cream with gingerbread and chocolate."

I dip my chin, smiling at the floor. After our kiss and his rejection, I began questioning why he even kissed me. The tension between us needed to be dispelled, but he's always up, down, and never easy to read. It's why I pretended not to remember.

I didn't want to hear his reasoning, an apology, or why he let me walk away. But now... now, I'm back to not knowing how to react to anything he does.

He has the oddest way of showing he cares and seems determined to pretend he doesn't.

"Thank you for telling me." Refocusing on Rhoadie, I squint one eye with a sly grin. "What's his *least* favorite pastry?"

I join Finnian at an iron patio table several moments later with two mugs of steaming cinnamon cider and a slate full of treats.

"It's warm for cider," I say, "but he insisted."

He shakes his head with a laugh. "He makes too much cider at the start of the season. He'll still be selling it mid-winter and will have to throw it out to brew a fresh batch, but I'm sure you made an old man happy." He studies the slate. "And which is mine?"

I pick up the doughy vanilla pastry, leaving him with a wheat muffin top. "I wasn't sure what you like, so I chose the safest option."

He forces a smile. "You chose correctly. I love wheat."

I watch with hidden delight as he sinks his teeth into the muffin top while I tear a piece of my warm pastry. "Great! I'll remember that for next time."

He seems to have trouble chewing. "Were you friendly?" He takes a long sip from his mug after swallowing the first bite.

I roll my eyes. "Contrary to belief, I can get along with people.

It's you I find difficult to interact with. Is something wrong with your pastry?"

He hides his mouth with his mug. "No, no, just more thirsty than hungry."

I take a bite from mine, licking the smeared cream from my lips. "Too bad I don't share."

"No need," he replies, staring at the muffin top. "Wheat.... wheat is my favorite."

"Oh?" I pull a paper sack containing his *actual* favorite from behind me. "I guess you wouldn't want this warm gingerbread bun? More for me."

He narrows his eyes, looks from me to the bakery, then settles on me again. "Did you... did Rhoadie tell you I dislike wheat?"

I shrug and take a bite from the corner of the gingerbread bun. "I thought we were supposed to be *honest* with one another."

His jaw drops. "You little...." Reaching under the table, he hooks a finger around the back of my chair and drags me closer.

I lean back, squealing when he grabs my wrist and tries to force my hand to his mouth. "Finnian!" I shout, raising my other hand to wipe some vanilla cream from my pastry across his cheek. "Leave me alone!"

He laughs while pinching my side farthest from him, so I have no choice but to lean toward him. I drop my pastry on the table to shove his head away, but he turns and wipes the icing from his cheek onto my palm.

"Gods, you child." I swipe the frosty palm against his neck and curse when he manages to steal a massive chunk of the gingerbread bun.

He raises his head to grin at me. He's even perfected how to smugly *chew*. "I fucking hate wheat," he says after swallowing.

I tip my head back in genuine laughter.

He brings my wrist to his mouth for another bite instead of just taking it from me. "I was force-fed wheat as a child to supposedly grow strong. Rhoadie would hide a gingerbread bun or cookie in each delivery."

I mock him with a puckered bottom lip. "Poor little prince."

He coils an arm around my waist and pinches me again until I yelp. "And now, he's helping my wife poison me."

"Gods, and you're dramatic." I shove another bite into his mouth. "Poison is too quick. I would much rather slowly torture you."

He prevents me from dusting the crumbs from my hand by inserting the tips of two fingers just past his lips. And when he gently sucks, my stomach tightens and fills with a twisting, spiraling ache—identical to the one I had when he kissed me.

I stare at his mouth when he pushes my fingers an inch further. Everything around us fades into a blur when my eyes lift to his. And for a moment, it's only us in the busy town square, everyone else ceasing to exist.

He removes my fingers and kisses the tip of each one. "You torture me very well, little doe."

I am genuinely doubting the validity of the spell I drank because every time he looks at me like this, I can't remember my own name. Even more so when I ask, "Do I?" like I'm short of breath.

With a grin, he laces our fingers together and rests our hands against his thigh. "We have company."

I jump when Irina plops into another chair and grabs my unfinished pastry. It takes a wholehearted effort to look away from Finnian to smile at Irina. "It's impressive how you always know where to find us," I say.

"It might seem large, but Pumpkin Hollow is really fucking small," she replies, bored as usual but as beautiful as always.

Her deep-red dress and thigh-hugging boots aren't what makes me lean forward and reach for her. It's the revelation of a large hoop in her ear when she tucks her hair to the side.

"Gifts from my friends." She winks. "I nearly gave my mother a heart attack."

Putting holes in your body is a relatively new concept in our realm, though I've heard about the practice from gossipers in Ashbury.

Finnian sighs. "She breezed into breakfast one morning without warning any of us. It's typical in other places I've visited, but Jasper hoped to avoid it here."

Irina pins a flat gaze on her brother. "Perhaps it shouldn't be up to a man to decide what we do with our bodies. It's not like I walked in with ink."

I wrinkle my nose. "Ink?"

Irina motions for Finnian to explain since her mouth is full of *my* pastry. He squeezes my hand for my attention. "Other countries and realms partake in rituals of marking their bodies with ink by burning it onto their skin."

I shudder. "That sounds painful."

Finnian takes a sip of cider from my mug since Irina commandeered his. "One of the kings in a neighboring kingdom has one on his chest of his family crest. I told Jasper about it, and he outlawed the practice."

"He needs everything taintless and untouched." Irina blanches. "Except his marriage vows, of course."

"Irina," Finnian warns.

"Let them fucking report that back to him, Finn." Irina boldly waves at one of the lurking undercover guards. "He knows we're aware."

I admire Irina for her candidness.

Finnian, however, groans. "Why are you here?"

"Mm," she hums while sipping. "I have been asked to escort Elora to Ashbury to inform her faeries that she will be occupied until the wedding."

"I'll take her," Finnian says.

I frown. "Why can't I see them before the wedding?"

"Because we have events all week." She picks up a leather tote from the ground and drops it on the table. "I have their orders for next week. We'll deliver them today. The next delivery isn't scheduled until—"

"The end of the month," I cut in. "Two weeks. Can I see them before then?"

"Yes," Finnian replies dryly.

Irina smirks at him. "I've heard the faeries are delicious to look at. I can't wait for you to introduce me to them, Elora."

Finnian tenses. Is he.... jealous?

For reasons I don't want to admit to myself just yet, I'm not keen on leaving him alone, either. "What will you do?"

His jaw pops. "Escort you."

Irina wags a finger. "Finnian is leaving us for two nights to partake in a hunting trip with visiting royals. You won't see him until the evening he returns." Her expression turns pensive. "We will host tea for the women that morning."

His fingers loosen from mine, his cocky and relaxed demeanor turning restless. "Have they arrived yet?"

Irina shakes her head. "Not yet, but soon."

"I should return." The warmth of his hand leaves mine as he stands. He seems nervous, his movements sharp yet fidgety as he grabs the slate to return to Rhoadie.

I look at Irina with a raised brow.

"He doesn't like visitors," is the only unconvincing explanation she gives me.

Finnian reappears with fists balling and loosening repeatedly. "Do I need to escort the two of you back to the castle?"

Irina pops the last piece of pastry into her mouth. "Do I need your guidance to return to where I've lived my entire life?" She points to the glaringly obvious castle in the distance. "How will I ever find it? No, Finnian. I think we can manage."

He curses under his breath before leaning down to me, placing his arms on either side of me, and locking me in. "Heed my warning, Elora. You will be watched, especially during your visit today." His lazy and charming half-grin returns. "You're spoken for in case a certain male tries to convince you otherwise."

"On paper, at least." I flash a rotten smile when his eyes flare. "As long as it stays hidden, right? That was the agreement?"

He rolls his neck. "You said...."

I told him I don't belong to Cedric, but reassuring him of that isn't as entertaining as watching him struggle to swallow. "Gods, you're easy to rile up." I wipe his neck clean of frosting with my finger. "I was drunk. I could've said anything." I lick my fingertip. "But I'll behave for now."

"Finnian," Irina interrupts, "go before he sends in a troop."

But Finnian stays right where he is, zeroed in on me, and twists one of my curls around his finger. "Do you even know how to misbehave, little doe?"

I take the challenge he extends to me and eliminate more space between us. "I guess you'll have to wait and see."

I'm pleased when he stops twisting my hair, freezing as he stares at me in surprise. I seal my victory by standing and brushing against him to stand by Irina. But he stops me before I can get too far by placing his lips against my ear and whispering, "Don't let him touch you."

Our proximity draws more onlookers.

I turn my head toward him enough to make it appear like we're nuzzling. "Didn't you hear your sister? Men shouldn't tell women what to do."

"Men shouldn't," he agrees. "But I am your prince, and you are *my* wife."

"Not yet," I taunt. "And if I remember correctly, Lord Finnian, you are not only mine." I tip my head back so my breath can brush his ear when I add, "Unless you spewed an empty threat, I will not harbor guilt for attention I receive from others, *darling*."

His hand drops to my waist and squeezes before I move out of his reach. "We should end the outing with a kiss to please the crowd," he says, desperation coating the masked plea.

I have him exactly where I want him.

Irina takes my hand, her teeth grabbing her top lip to keep from smiling. She, too, has noticed how fiercely he wants my attention.

I look around at the gossiping ninnies, watching our every move, and hook a finger for him to come to me.

His entirely too cocky demeanor is lowered when I deny him after he leans in, placing my hand against his cheek to leave a featherlight kiss beneath his ear instead. “Enjoy hunting,” I say, grinning at the feral tethering in his eyes from holding himself back. “I can attest to the thrill of being chased and bound by you.”

Irina loops her arm through mine and takes my cue to walk away without looking back.

Heat rises on my neck from his stare.

Irina says, “Touché, doe,” only when we’re out of earshot.

Twenty-Three

Octavius slowly trails us in a carriage toward Ashbury. Hovering rain clouds with rolling thunder linger just close enough to make me nervous. The pumpkin carriage was waiting for us outside the town square when we left Finnian, but Irina ignored it and continued pulling me forward. With the muggy air causing hair to stick to my face and neck, it won't be long before I remove my shawl and tie it around my waist. "Irina, remind me again why we aren't in the carriage?"

My uncomfortable shoes will not withstand mud if it starts to pour.

A shiny sheen of sweat has covered Irina's face. "Because I get a rise from making Jasper's men work for their wages."

I glance over my shoulder and wave at Octavius. "It's only Octavius. I like him. He's been kind to me."

"My darling Elora." She sighs. "If you look to your left, two men hunched in the crops are trying to remain unnoticed." She doesn't bat an eyelash when I lean forward to search. "And on your right, you might notice another man trying to remain inconspicuous as he darts behind tree trunks."

I whip around to stare into the trees. I can't see anyone, but I believe her.

"If we had taken the carriage, they would've hitched a wagon, which would've been far too easy for them." Her leisurely pace doesn't match her spiteful grin. "My mission is to not make anything about Jasper's life simple, Elora, and neither should you."

"He already despises me," I say.

She blows a short piece of hair off her forehead. "He hates everyone but himself, but he won't harm you if he still has use for you."

"Great," I mutter. The ticking dial of the faeries' departure has also become mine. "Finnian said...." I pause, unsure if I should divulge his strange declaration before our kiss.

"Go on," she encourages. "We have no secrets."

The words tumble out quickly, "He said I won't have to worry about giving him a son."

When she doesn't reply, I press further. "When I asked if he'd send me away to pretend I am the one carrying his child, he became very—"

"Upset?" She doesn't wait for me to confirm his complete agitation from the accusation. "That's for two reasons. Finnian was very young when he learned about Jasper's affairs. He loves and respects our mother very much, as he should. She is gentle and kind and loves us entirely too much for the trouble we've caused her. It tears him apart from what Jasper has done to her."

I frown. "Then.... Why did he tell me he would keep his own affairs private?"

She grabs my elbow to spin me around to face her. Octavius calls for his horses to halt. Their hooves skid against the pavement to avoid coming upon us too quickly.

Irina looks *irate*. "Finn told you he'd have affairs?"

I remain as bitter as I did when hearing it the first time, nodding at her question with pursed lips. She looks toward the castle in disgust as if staring directly at him. And as domineering as she is, I do not doubt he can feel her glare from here.

"I love my brother." Her hoop earrings bounce when she twists to drag me into another leisurely stroll. "But, he lacks empathy when he's upset. Were you fighting when he said this?"

"That's all we do." And torturing him with his own threat this morning was gratifying. "But yes, sort of. We had just returned from meeting the faeries, and there's a male who has flirted with me—"

"That was it," she interrupts. "Everything Finnian holds dear is taken from him. I am surprised he hasn't lost Major yet. Jasper leaves me alone because I am bait if he needs something from Finnian."

I've formed so many judgments about the royal family that I never considered the possibility that the king is cruel to everyone—including his own children.

But something she said snagged me. "Are you implying that I'm dear to him?"

She huffs a breathy laugh. "Do you *want* to be dear to him?"

I roll my eyes. Despite how open she's being with me, their loyalty to one another isn't something to be trifled with. She won't reveal anything to me he wouldn't want her to share, no matter how curious I might be. "What's the second reason?"

I don't receive an answer.

We step onto the bridge just as a light drizzle sprinkles my skin. I will beg Irina to allow us to ride back to Pumpkin Hollow with Octavius after we visit with the faeries.

The man hiding in the trees grunts as he slips from the steep cliff, attempting to avoid crossing the bridge with us. Sighing in annoyance, Irina doesn't look at him when she calls, "I know you're there, you idiot. Tell the other two to stay behind, and I'll allow you to follow us without giving you the slip."

"Honestly," she mutters, motioning to the surrounding dips and jagged rocks of the short, steep bluffs. "Men who haven't spent time here believe they can climb treacherous heights. Just once, I want to see a woman ruling a kingdom."

"I doubt such a place exists."

"How disappointing that would be."

After sliding off the cliff, the man lands on his feet and calls for the other two to wait for our return. They can make conversation with the two men undoubtedly hiding in the crops.

"Stay far away from us," she demands. "Wait until we make it to the other side of the bridge before you follow. Otherwise, I will gladly inform the king of how inept you are at remaining unseen."

He glares but obeys. He isn't unattractive from afar and looks to be Finnian's age, but he stares at Irina with such hatred that it makes me uncomfortable.

Irina spins on her heel and takes my hand. "They all want to fuck me," she says bluntly. "And it irritates them to take orders from a woman. I doubt Jasper would take their heads if one of them succeeded in touching me, but Finnian would, and it only goads them further. He was a runt when he was forced to train in the army, but he's equal in strength now."

The man lingering at the end of the bridge watches Irina like a rabid wolf on the hunt.

"Can Finnian order beheadings?"

"No, doe. He'd do it himself."

To my dismay, Irina never shared the second reason why Finnian became so irate with me. Instead, she has spent each moment peppering me with questions about Ashbury—mainly the color-changing sky. Red clouds have intercepted the gray to give the sky a pinkish-hue. Combined with the bluish-gray atmosphere of Pumpkin Hollow as they intersect over the bridge, it is admittedly beautiful.

The trailing bodyguard shouts for us to stay on the pathway leading to the mountains, which has only enabled Irina to do the complete opposite and take the long way around, which leads us closer to town.

Her mysterious existence prevents anyone from approaching us since, like Finnian, no one recognizes her. The satchel containing the order amounts for the weeks ahead is strapped across her chest, but from the bottom, she subtly continues pulling velvet pouches out to leave in various places around town. I don't need to ask to know that each bag contains gold coins, and I can't help but wonder if Finnian informed her of his findings from our visit.

Her need to rebel against her father will work out splendidly for Ashbury.

When she distributes the last pouch to a child, she looks at me with the same bored and unimpressed expression that she frequently has and says, "Penance for never allowing me to visit. I have tried, just so you're aware."

I nudge her ribs with my elbow and smile. "I do know. We played together the day you hid underneath the carriage many years ago. I was the young girl you tried convincing to assist you in finding a way underneath. Finnian was the same when he visited, only he didn't offer to let me play with him."

She kicks a rock with the toe of her boot. "I remember the day I came. When Jasper returned that evening, he nearly whipped me. Finnian offered to take it instead, so he did."

I frown. "And you let him?"

She shakes her head. "I didn't have a choice. Making me watch was more punishment than receiving the whipping myself. I love my brother, Elora." She conveyed that earlier, but this admission wasn't a prelude to her irritation with him. Her reasoning for telling me this time is far more heartbreaking. "I love my brother, and Jasper uses it against me. Finnian loves me, and Jasper uses it against him."

With our arms linked, we couldn't be any closer, but I tried tugging her to me anyway to comfort her. "Please help me understand why he does that," I say softly.

"Having someone to love means having more to lose." Her stare becomes vacant like Finnian's often does, and I wonder if it's a defense mechanism they've built. "Control and fear work splendidly together."

Nausea nestles within. "Irina, why haven't you left? Finnian told me about your lovers. He would help you leave."

"I know he would."

She takes her time with her words. I am pleased to speak with her about this and speak the truth with anyone, so I remain patient with her.

"I know he would," she repeats softly after a moment, "which is why I can't leave. People assume the worst about him." She pointedly raises an eyebrow at me. "He is not nearly as selfish as he's believed to be."

Guilt embraces the nausea.

"Finnian would help me leave this place, but I will not allow my brother to face the consequences for my freedom."

This is the most vulnerability I've seen from Irina. We barely know one another, but she doesn't hold back on how she feels; it is always accompanied by a bite. But when she speaks of her brother, there is a tenderness that I envy. Their love for one another is genuine and loyal. It is not a love I've ever experienced for myself. I do not doubt that my mother might've loved me like this, but I was too young when she passed to learn how it could feel.

"I stayed because Finnian was away often," she continues, "If I had left, Jasper would've beat our mother or sent her to the gallows. The only reason she breathes is because of Finnian. Jasper knows there are *very* few lines he cannot cross with Finn, so he settles for mental torment instead."

I lower my voice into a barely audible whisper, "Why hasn't Finnian—"

"Do not finish that," she snaps, glancing at our trailing escort. "Our army is wholly dedicated to Jasper, Elora. He holds their livelihoods in his hands—he dangles the lives of their families on a string. He is a grand puppet master. Each man is indoctrinated to never question him or disobey."

She lowers her voice even further, causing me to tilt my head to the side to hear her. "If Finnian ever tried.... he might be the heir, but Jasper wouldn't hesitate to have him killed and fuck someone else to start all over. Finnian is a prize to him, Elora. He is handsome, loyal, and trained. And as long as Finnian has something to lose, he will do as Jasper commands."

I am trying to figure out how to respond.

My future has become crystal clear. I only have until the faeries depart from Ashbury to restore my kingdom. After that, Finnian cannot protect me when choosing between his family and me. Deep down, coiling around my spine and threatening to snap it into two, is the realization that I would never put him in the position of having to choose.

When the day comes, my hope lies in whether he's grown to care about me enough to convince Jasper not to wipe Ashbury off the map. Saving my people will be worth the sacrifice. It's the same risk Dolfe took when agreeing to work for the king if the lives of the faeries were spared.

"I won't bring it up again," I assure her.

I point ahead to the iron gate, looming above us from this distance as we climb a steep valley toward the mountains. "We're nearly there. Can the bodyguard stay behind at the gate? The faeries are hesitant around the king's men."

"I'll handle him," she mutters.

Twenty-Four

After a fresh threat, the overbearing man agreed to stay behind while I guided Irina past the faeries who would refuse to speak to us and toward the ones who would. Irina switches between fanning herself with both hands and gathering her long hair to sweep up, resting it atop her head. "Gods, you could've warned me!" she exclaims.

Upon hearing Irina's shriek, Azrea whips her head toward us from the mountain's base and beams. I throw my arms around her, thankful she isn't upset with me because of how our previous visit ended. "What are you doing here, Ellie?" she asks.

I peel away from her to motion for Irina to join us. She stares at Azrea in awe, slowly approaching while simultaneously extending her hand. "I'm Irina," she breathes, "Finnian's sister."

Azrea looks at Irina's hand with an amused grin. The faeries never shake hands with humans—especially with a native of Pumpkin Hollow—but she humors Irina and shakes it once. "Hello, Irina."

Dolfe lands behind her within seconds. Irina's eyes widened at his protective stance and expanded wings, but she didn't back away as most would. As her *brother* nearly did.

Instead, she steps closer and inspects his wings. "May I?"

Azrea isn't half as obnoxious as her mate when blocking him

from gawkers. She finds his discomfort comical instead, never doubting his loyalty to her. And today isn't any different as she nods to Irina's request, much to Dolfe's apparent annoyance as he glares at Azrea.

I've never braved asking to touch Dolfe's wings, always far too fearful of him tossing me into the valleys, but Irina doesn't hesitate to lunge for them. She brushes her fingers across the black feathers and lifts each one to peek at what lies underneath. Exasperated, Dolfe crosses his arms over his chest and tilts his head toward the sky.

Azrea allows Irina a full two minutes to explore before she says, "That's enough."

Irina respectfully steps away and looks between them. "Mates?"

I blink. "How do you know about mates?"

Irina sighed deeply and resumed her disinterested demeanor. "When someone is always heavily guarded, they find things to do. I read. We only had one book about faeries, but it disappeared long ago."

I ask, "Disappeared? To where?"

"I don't know. We had a few books on magic, but then...."—she snaps her fingers—"They vanished into the night."

I raise an eyebrow at Azrea while asking Irina, "Do you remember anything *else* about faeries?"

Dolfe waits for Irina to respond while Azrea shoves a hand through her hair. Irina starts counting on her fingers as she lists far more than I know, "The mates, the scents...."

I interrupt with, "the *scents*?"

"Something about mates smelling the same? And detecting arousal?" She coyly grins at Azrea. "Any truth to that?"

"Perhaps," Azrea replies.

I wrinkle my nose. "Gods, Dolfe must smell all the time."

Azrea nods her confirmation while Dolfe leans in and takes her earlobe between his teeth. He might be secretive about everything else, but he's never one to hide his affection for his mate. It's the only tolerable quality about him.

"All of you sprouted from one place." Irina waves one hand as if trying to pull the name out of thin air. "I can't remember where, but there are different types of faeries."

I ask, "Ones with shadows?" before even realizing it.

Dolfe immediately focuses on me. Azrea lays a hand on my arm. "Ellie," she says gently as if speaking to a toddler. "What made you ask that?"

I swallow. The intensity of Dolfe's stare makes me wish to shrink into a worm and slither away from this conversation. "Um, well." I spin a curl around my finger. "I've had vivid dreams lately. Since that day...." I close my mouth before confessing our secret to Irina.

Azrea nods knowingly. "Every night?"

I step closer to Azrea and farther away from Dolfe. "Not every night. Mostly when I'm distressed or irritated."

Dolfe sighs impatiently. "What did you see, Elora?"

I narrow my eyes at him, then frown. "It was short, but....dark." I shiver while chasing the memory of the hauntingly beautiful male in pain. "One shadow encompassed him, but another was wrapped around a guardrail while he stared at the moon. I couldn't see his whole face...." I trail off, unable to vocalize the skeletal form I saw before me that night.

"He lived long ago." Dolfe's heavy tone sounds more like a warning. "He was Fae, but he became something different. Dangerous. Do not feed into these dreams, Elora."

"I am not feeding into anything, Dolfe."

Irina snorts. "If he's dead, why would her dreams matter?"

A growl erupts from Dolfe's throat. Azrea moves to stand between him and Irina. "We believe in reincarnation, Irina," Azrea explains, "A soul's ability to rebirth. I do not wish to risk Elora's mind against a powerful being. His shadows brought death when he lived."

My blood swims with fear. Every fiber of me is tangled with a fae spell that causes these dreams, connecting me to either the past or present of a powerful being. And I remain unsure if the enchantment is breakable—if it will fade with time or if Finnian will ever do more than only tolerate my existence.

I tremble as panic rises, regretting ever drinking from the spring, wishing I hadn't come up with the idea.

Azrea takes my face between her hands. "Look at me, Ellie. You will be fine."

Even Dolfe attempts a soothing tone. "It is doubtful that his shadows would return to him even if he's returned. It could be your imagination and ongoing obsession with learning more about us."

Azrea hisses at him. "He wouldn't concern himself with you, Elora."

Irina takes my hand. "If he ever shows up here, we'll bribe him with another soul to take."

I laugh lightly, aware of who she would offer up in exchange. My glee is short-lived when a familiar voice approaches behind me. "Did the little mortal bring fresh meat?"

"Fuck off, Raul." Azrea releases me. "Elora works for the king now. If you're not on your best behavior, she can request that your head be used as a meal centerpiece."

"Azrea," Dolfe sighs. "He's one of us."

"So is Elora," she defends.

I turn to face Raul. "You won't see me for a week, but then you'll see me *daily*. And you'll have to obey me." My laugh is a borderline cackle at the look he gives me. "I might just increase your workload because I can."

I won't, but I want him to believe I might.

Brig, another Fae male, falls from the sky to land beside Raul and slaps him on the shoulder. "I'd like to see you touch Ellie just so Azrea can fuck you up."

Dolfe rubs his forehead. Just imagining the possibility of Azrea fighting sends him on the defense. Fighting one of his own wouldn't be ideal, but he would do it for her, especially now.

Brig circles us until he stands before Irina, looking her over with a grin. "And who do we have here?"

I groan. "Leave Irina alone, Brig."

His uncovered chest and trousers revealing his hip bones draw Irina's attention. Brig is one of the most arrogant males in the pack, but he has reason to be. Not only is he beautiful, but he's mated and untouchable. He can flaunt himself without fear of attracting inferiors like me because his mate would happily snap our necks.

"Irina," I warn. "He's mated."

Irina ignores me. "Bow."

All of us drop our jaws or widen our eyes. The faeries never bow to *anyone*—it's one of the reasons the king detests them. Even with their current predicament of working for him, they will never believe themselves to be beneath any of us.

"Did she just demand a warrior to fucking *bow* to her?" Raul snarls.

Irina isn't shaken. Brig towers over her and can rip her into two pieces, but he seems *almost* impressed with her confidence.

So am I, but it doesn't stop me from searching the skies and ground for his mate.

Brig spreads his wings and flaps. The breeze lifts Irina's hair, but her only response is a bemused grin. Feathers have been plucked to reveal a scarred wound on his wing. The thick membrane shows a separation through the middle, and my curiosity about where it came from nearly makes me ask him, but Irina remains my main concern.

Finnian will have my head if anything happens to her, but Irina doesn't look away from Brig when I step forward. "Irina..."

The tension between them isn't sexual—it's strangling with the power struggle between the princess of the realm that keeps him fed and the warrior who possesses a strength we never will. Bowing to her would be admitting that a lesser species controls him, but not listening to her could result in losing his life.

Not that Irina would ever do that, but the guards watching us would.

So, Brig finds a middle ground.

And extends his hand.

Azrea smiles. I breathe a sigh of relief, and Irina nearly takes his peace offering when Raul loosens a growl and shoves her hand away before getting in Brig's face. "The fuck, Brig," he growls.

Dolfe moves, Azrea sighs, but that isn't why I start shouting. It's the bodyguard sent to watch our every move as he runs over with a nocked bow and points it at Raul.

"Don't!" I yell. "Do not shoot him!"

"Otto, stop!" Irina shouts.

I spread my arms wide to try and prevent Dolfe from protecting one of his own, but it won't stop him if I don't handle this quickly. "He's fine! Lower your bow!" I shout.

"He touched the princess," Otto snaps, drawing his elbow back. "He isn't allowed to touch one of our people."

"I'm fine, Otto." Irina steps forward, but it only causes Otto to move a step closer to Raul. "You do not have the authority to harm any of the faeries."

My heart thundered in my chest. I didn't have a chance to get a good look at him before, but he is definitely built like a soldier. His shaggy blond hair partially covers a scar above his eye, and his hardened posture looks ready for a fight.

I hold up my hands. "Otto, please."

Otto shakes his head. "I have the authority to subdue any creature from touching the princess." He slowly inches the bow to the left to angle toward Raul's wing.

Dolfe lunges for Otto, but Azrea grabs him quickly and tries to reason with him. Brig attempts to keep other warriors from circling Otto, Irina shouts at him to lower his weapon, and I am living my worst nightmare.

Verbal reasoning rarely shoves through rage, so I react physically, jumping in front of Otto's arrow to block Raul's wing. "If you want to shoot him, you'll have to shoot me first." My voice shakes from the arrow aimed at my forehead. "You will not touch any of them."

"Elora," Azrea pleads.

"I do not take orders from you," Otto growls.

"She has the king's authority to protect them," Irina says with much more authority than me. "You *do* have to listen to her. Disobeying her is a direct offense against your king."

The two men on shift slowly approach. "The princess is right, Otto. And Elora will be the princess soon."

Otto's eyes narrow at me. "She is not the princess *yet*."

"But I will be." I step forward until the arrowhead touches my skin. "Loosen your arrow, Otto. Irina will ensure Prince Finnian drags you back here and removes your head right where you stand."

"I can't wait to tell him you've threatened his bride." Irina takes my hand. "Lower your weapon, Otto. Now."

A strong hand snatches the arrow from the bow and snaps it in half with his fingers. I release a deep sigh of relief, but my anxiety sharpens when I watch Cedric drop the pieces to the ground. Otto fixes his anger on him, but Cedric bares his teeth.

"You are relieved from duty," Irina says. "Return to Pumpkin Hollow. After I inform my father of your impulsivity, you will be lucky if he even allows you to work in the stables."

I snort. "You think Finnian will allow him near Major? We'll let the prince handle this."

Otto points his finger at me and opens his mouth to say something, but Brig's hand shoves him back. "You've been instructed to leave," he says, his voice dangerously low.

Otto drops the bow to the ground, thrusting his arms out to the side with a grin. Chills cross every inch of my body at his slightly upturned cheeks. "I'm going," he says but zeroes in on me. "I'll be seeing you, princess."

I tip my chin up. "Good."

He mockingly bows to me before being escorted away by the other two guards. Cedric approaches me, touches my chin with his finger, and asks, "Are you okay?"

How quickly I pulled away from him wasn't because of Finnian's warning. It has everything to do with how another male's hands on me feel *wrong*.

He doesn't hide his hurt when his hand falls, but I force a

smile. "I'm fine. Thank you for risking yourself like that for my head."

Irina squishes my chin between her fingers. "It's a very pretty head," she coos and turns to address the surrounding faeries. "My apologies for... whatever that was. We will not let it happen again. I'll let you say goodbye, Elora."

Irina leaves me in the center of the faeries. Azrea embraces me, whispering gratitude against my hair. Patting her hips until her grip loosens enough to let me breathe, I wiggle free. "It was nothing. You're my family." I look at each of them, even Raul. "All of you. I'm not going to let them harm you."

Dolfe doesn't glare *or* sigh at me. Instead, he looks concerned. "You'll be safe walking back to Pumpkin Hollow?"

Brig adds, "He could be hiding, Elora."

I dismiss them with a shrug. "If anything happens to us, Finnian will ensure justice is served. Give me a week, and then I'll work on lessening what's required of you until we devise a plan for you to leave."

"Ellie," Azrea says, but Dolfe takes her hand.

"I'll tell her," he says.

Dolfe motions for me to follow him, waiting until we're in his dwelling before he speaks freely. "We want you to stop this, Elora."

I tilt my head. "Stop? Stop what?"

"The betrothal," Dolfe replies, crossing his arms. "It's unsafe for you to be with those people, Elora."

I jerk my head back. "I'm sorry, what? You're *leaving*. What would you have me do, Dolfe? I can't just.... abandon Ashbury. What would my people do with all of us gone?"

The way he stares at me conveys *pity*. "I admire your tenacity, Elora, but do you honestly believe that you can change the way Jasper has neglected Ashbury for twenty-five years?"

I blink, too shocked to say anything or argue *why* I believe I could help. I've never been Dolfe's favorite person, but I at least thought he would understand the need to keep my people safe more than anyone else. "But you let me drink from the spring, Dolfe. You encouraged it...."

He secures a leather band around his hair, accentuating his prominent jawline even further. "I made a mistake. You don't need to be in Pumpkin Hollow, Elora. Before we leave, we can try and save as many as we can—"

As he speaks, my mind wanders to the group of people I danced with just last night. Seeing the joy on their faces and the hope in their eyes, even under dire circumstances, renewed my purpose. And now, someone who was supposed to believe in me is demanding I walk away from all of it—from the children trading buttons for food on street corners.

Finnian *cares*. He cares for me, and he cares for Baxter. He wants to help—he promised to help.

"No," I whisper, interrupting his list of reasoning. "No, I will not leave. I will not desert them."

"The king is dangerous, Ellie." Cedric steps inside, and I feel suffocated from the size of these Fae brothers against me. "Ashbury won't survive once we're gone."

"Stop," I whisper. "There's still time—"

"There's not!" Cedric shouts. "You need to spend your days in peace, Ellie. Not being the doting bride of the prince."

I whirl around to face him. "Is *that* what this is about? Your jealousy?"

"Leave, Cedric," Dolfe demands.

"He'll let us be together." Cedric grabs my hands. "He won't stand in our way anymore. We talked about it after you left..."

I yank my hands away. "I can't believe this." I shove past Cedric, fuming. "You're welcome, by the way!" I shout to Raul as I stomp past him, ignoring Azrea's calls to stop.

She catches up to me quickly. "Ellie, this is coming from a place of concern. I wanted to believe your plan could work, but it's too late."

"I am not just doing this for you!" I yell, shoving my hands into my hair. "I have people who need me, Azrea! I have the chance to fix my father's mistake!" My voice rattles as emotion builds. "You might be fine accepting the end for my people, but guess what? I'm dead, anyway. The day you leave is the day I will return to being useless. He doesn't..."

I can't even say the words. Finnian doesn't want me to carry his child. Even if he did, there wasn't a guarantee that the king would keep me alive once the faeries were gone.

I will lose everything either way.

I drop my hands, tears fall down my cheeks, and I cough a broken laugh. "You encouraged me to do this, you let me consume the spell, one of you is *living* in my mind, and now you want me to stop?" I shake my head. "It's too fucking late for that, Azrea. I will marry Finnian, accept his help as long as possible, and protect you because I promised."

"Elora," Azrea whispers in desperation, reaching for my hands.

I hold both hands up and step away from her. "I can accept your fate, Azrea; I am overjoyed for your future, but I will not allow you to decide for my people. I will not leave them in the hands of the king while I live a peaceful life with Cedric until I die as a purposeless human while the rest of you continue living your immortal lives. I will not be just a page in your stories!"

Her lips part. "Ellie, I am trying to protect you—"

I can't listen to any more of this. "You were the one person, Az...."—I pause to shove down a rising sob—"...You were supposed to believe in me."

Her voice cracks on my name as I pick up the crumbling pieces of my heart and leave.

Twenty-Five

Irina wasn't waiting for me when I exited the iron gate, allowing me a moment to dry my eyes and press my forehead against the cool outer wall. Azrea's request surprised me. After witnessing their warriors get shot out of the sky for trying to flee, what did they think would happen to me if I decided to leave? It has to be evident to her now that Jasper cares nothing to ensure his son's happiness.

I can't waste more of my life scrubbing floors, living off food scraps, and choking on soot in the attic while waiting for something to happen. I can't leave with them and live with the guilt of abandoning Ashbury. I can't disappoint Irina.

I can't leave Finnian after learning what he's endured from his father all these years. I promised him I would follow through with this. If I break his trust, I will be no better than my father—*his* father. Betrayal isn't an option.

After wiping my cheeks, I tighten the shawl around my waist and ascend the rocky slope in the valley. Dust from my ungraceful climb settles to reveal Irina sitting on the cliff's edge, staring below. Something about this place has drawn both her and Finnian to cradle imminent death. One wrong step and our lives will be added to the death toll of Hogsfeet.

Yet, I sit beside her and dust my hands off on my skirt.

The abandoned castle beneath is more visible than usual today and is eerie underneath dark thunderclouds. I wonder if it's haunted by the wandering souls of the former royal family—if their spirits float through the empty hallways.

What a morbid thing to see right beneath us.

History gone; wiped. It's as if blood wasn't poured to defend their throne—their honor. As if decisions weren't made to protect their people. I can only imagine the screams and cries of women and children as they begged for their lives to be spared while King Jasper stood where we're currently sitting, prideful and victorious.

Ashbury could soon face the same fate—surviving the first war only to die in the next. Someone could stumble upon our kingdom someday and wonder what happened to all of us.

We would be nothing more than a tale.

Irina doesn't rehash what happened with the faeries. After only knowing her briefly, I've learned that she never makes excuses or apologizes twice. Finnian, though cocky, always carries doubt when I shock him or when he can't seem to stop touching me. Irina lives confidently, refined, yet wild, and addicting with her beauty and free-spirited tenacity.

I pity her.

Someone as fearless as her shouldn't be held back from the greatness she could achieve away from here.

"He attacked Hogsfeet the year I was born," Irina says after moments have passed. "My mother wasn't in Pumpkin Hollow. He sent her away and chose that time to render two kingdoms useless. He brought Finnian with him."

Unsure of how to react, I say nothing but feel everything. Finnian was only a boy during the war.

Irina's vacant stare is as somber as the overcast, gloomy clouds hovering above. "He doesn't remember. When Jasper speaks of the war, Finnian's gaze turns gray. Men died in front of him in horrid ways, but he's blocked all of it."

I want to run to him—I don't care where he is or how long it'll take me. I want to ask why he's stayed and hasn't fought back, but he could ask me the same questions.

Loyalty from fear of retaliation.

"He used to have nightmares," she continues. "He would wake up with bloodshot eyes and sweating." She doesn't flinch when soft raindrops fall from the sky. "I would sleep at the foot of his bed every night. Mother begged Jasper to let her fetch a physician. She desperately wanted to find a way to help him."

"But he didn't let her," I guessed.

Her voice deepens when she repeats Jasper's response, "Pain will make him stronger." She rolls her eyes. "It didn't make him stronger. It made him resilient. Finnian doesn't know how to *feel* anything without experiencing guilt. He can't grasp the severity of what happened because he was taught to pretend it didn't exist."

"He smelled like liquor this morning."

Irina's eyes lower. "He's coping. I try to fight with him and get him worked up, but he won't let himself get angry with me. But you... you're chipping away at him."

I frown. "I'm the reason Finnian is drinking?"

"No," she breathes. "You're giving him a reason to stop. He won't allow that. He's been able to control it for a few years and never lets it get too far. It's when he returns home that he struggles. He can't seem to put the bottle down."

I don't press further—I can't.

I wish the raindrops would wash away my curiosity about him and Irina, their life under the pretense of perfection, but it stays.

"The handsome male," she says. "He looked at you like he never wanted to stop. I thought he might break Otto's neck for threatening you."

"Cedric," I whisper.

She doesn't look at me when she asks, "What are your feelings for Cedric?"

I shove curls away from my face and blink away the rain, only for more to flood my vision and blur the castle turrets. "I love Cedric as I love all of them." Whatever I admit to her will return to Finnian, but she shared painful memories with me. It's only fair that I'm honest with her. "Dolfe never allowed us to explore our feelings for one another. Cedric is a warrior, and I'm nothing. I would sometimes imagine something happening between us, but I think..." I pause to trudge through my muddled feelings—a rarity since I've always been told how to feel. "I wanted to pretend I could have something greater than this—that someone could see me as more than just Harry's daughter, more than the fallen princess."

"Do you want to know why they don't?"

I shake my head, but it doesn't stop her. "Because it's how you see yourself. *You* believe you're nothing."

I can't decipher between raindrops and tears.

"Trust me, Elora, blaming yourself for your father's choices will not change them. It won't turn back time." She places a steady hand over my trembling one. "I see you, but it doesn't matter what I think. You need to see you."

I've been invisible my entire life. I've merely existed to those around me. How can I see past what I've been told I am?

Whether out of pity or trust, Irina finally tells me Finnian's second reason for reacting angrily to my accusation. "Our mother was sent away when he was a child only to return with me. Rumors have plagued my legitimacy as the queen's daughter my entire life."

I had heard something about that in town, but I never had an interest in gossiping about the secretive princess, nor does hearing it now make me question her rightful title. "And what does Finnian believe?"

She smiles broadly. "He believes that I am his sister."

"And what do *you* believe?"

"I believe that Honora is my mother. She has loved me and clothed me. Nothing else matters to me." She squeezes my hand. "I don't know his plan or why he lied to you, Elora, but Finnian will not have affairs. Finnian is not our father. He wouldn't do that to you. And he would never subject a child to constant questions of who they really are."

"My feelings for Cedric aren't romantic," I whisper, unsure why I feel the need to reassure her. "I won't hurt Finnian, either."

"I know." She laughs then, pulling me to my feet. "But you can make him wonder about it until you are even. Gods, he truly is insufferable sometimes."

Our hands stay woven together as we kick through the mud to find our way back to the bridge unscathed. Filthy, but safe. But the knot in my stomach isn't from Finnian being insufferable—it's coiled tightly because spending time with him keeps the suffering tolerable.

We made it halfway to the castle before our dresses became too heavy from rainfall. Only then did Irina concede to riding in the carriage. Her annoyed expression was the same as Finnian's when I did something irksome, and sharing that with her brought a rare, carefree smile to her face.

After she insisted I stay with her overnight, I relented, falling asleep after warm baths and sweets for dinner underneath a generous pile of silk blankets. When morning came, she left to fetch us something for breakfast, explaining how rare it was to eat breakfast in her chambers since King Jasper always insisted they dine as a family in the great hall. A performance, she said, for the gossiping wenches who work in the castle.

I've learned nothing positive about the king since arriving days ago. His children despise him, while the queen avoids him. Surviving in this family is looking slimmer by the day.

Before I could undress from the borrowed nightshirt to choose another one of Irina's dresses, I was startled by a knock on her door. Irina refuses to inform me of our plans, but her coy grin has contributed to every jitter.

Unsure of who to expect, my gasp resembles a squeak when I open the door to Queen Honora. Rather horrible at it, I hastily curtsy. We haven't spent a second alone together yet, and I'm unsure how to behave around her.

"Queen Honora, I wasn't expecting you." I glance over my shoulder, grateful Irina's small entryway blocks the view of the unmade bed and goose feathers from our impromptu need to clobber one another with pillows last night.

A very tart wine was involved in our decision to behave like children.

Amused, she gestures inside. Every movement she makes is polished and tight, the complete opposite of my wobbly-at-best attempts to appear like I won't make a fool of the crown.

"May I come in, Elora?"

"Oh, gods!" I hurriedly back away and nod. "Of course, you may. This isn't even where I'm staying. Well, you know that already. Irina invited me to stay with her..." I trailed off when I realized she remained in the hallway to not appear impolite while listening to me babble.

I loosen a breath. "Please come in."

"I assume my daughter isn't here?" She steps inside, unsurprised by silent confirmation. "I have something for you."

I look from her empty hands to the bare hallway behind her, unsure how to convey gratefulness for invisible things.

She follows my confused stare and sighs, calling someone's name. Exasperated, she lowers her voice to say, "I've never bitten anyone, yet they are all timid around me."

A young servant girl enters, filling the small entryway. I wish to avoid entering the bedroom, but with multiple dresses draped over the girl's arm, I can't leave her standing here with nowhere to put them.

"Hello," I greet her, wrinkling my nose when she curtsies.

My thoughts swirl like a flurry of snowflakes. With all my recent unwise decisions at the forefront of my mind, I haven't given much thought to being the princess. Finnian has given vague instructions on how I should behave, but nothing about this will ever seem normal. I will be bowed to, given gifts in exchange for good favor, and respected.

It is oddly unsettling.

The girl doesn't rise from her curtsy until I ask what she brought.

"The dresses you were measured for," Queen Honora replies. "There will be more, but these will do until the wedding." She notes my frazzled expression. "I hope it's all right that I brought these to you."

"Yes, of course. Honestly, I am relieved it's not pumpkins in her arms." I mentally curse at the slip. I should be grateful for any gift. "That was rude—"

But the queen laughs. It isn't a forced or polite laugh; she covers her mouth like I've said the funniest thing she's ever heard. And instead of fearing the repercussions, I smile.

Just days ago, I wouldn't have believed my days would soon consist of laughing with the Queen of Pumpkin Hollow, but how much I enjoy it amazes me. After so many months of grief and loneliness, sharing her light for a moment brings warmth to parts of me that have shriveled away.

She places a hand over her heart as she calms. "I suppose we do give out plenty of pumpkins!"

I half-shrug. "Perhaps. Please come in."

I realize too late that the more appropriate place to welcome guests would be the sitting room, but I am hardly a typical guest, and Irina's quarters contain way too many doors. With Irina as the owner, I wouldn't know what to expect from each one.

Gathering a pile of worn dresses in my arms, I instruct the girl to place the new ones on the table while discarding the bundle in a heap of tulle and gauze. Queen Honora studies the feathers strewn about, a few lifting from the light breeze filtering through the open balcony doors, and smiles.

I join them at the table, trying to keep my eyes from bulging out of my head. Pops of colors and floral embellishments, spiraling trim, draped and layered sleeves with fabric so rich that if they were made of chocolate, I would be comatose after consumption, are waiting neatly for my inspection.

Purples, pinks, blues, pastels galore.

"So bright," I say sweetly, but also somewhat bewildered by how well they coordinate.

She explains with a knowing grin, "Each royal family member is assigned colors to wear at events and during leisurely strolls through the kingdom. These are yours."

"Oh," is honestly the best I can come up with.

Finnian always wears some shade of blue, whereas Irina stays in red and gold. The queen rarely has any color but silver, sometimes getting away with a touch of white. And the king always has the color orange somewhere.

The colors of his pumpkins.

The only one who stands out... is Irina. His cruelty knows no bounds. The rumors of her illegitimacy already make her a target, but he chose loud colors to further segregate her.

Finnian always wears the colors of the crest. It should stand to reason that the princess should, too.

But no, Jasper would instead ensure Irina feels isolated.

"Is everything all right, dear?"

I blink, realizing I have traveled down a deep tunnel of thoughts and forgetting who stands beside me. "Yes, fine. Overwhelmed."

"It will become easier," she says, but her inability to look at me when she says it proves the opposite. She lifts every skirt except the one on the bottom. "This is what you'll wear the evening before your wedding."

The dress she referenced is adorned with gold cuffs on the

sleeves and neckline, but the top layer of the skirt glitters with gold atop ivory. “Champagne,” she says, “Finn’s request.”

Dizziness always finds me so quickly at the mention of his name. “Finnian’s request?”

She instructs the girl to take the dresses to allow me to see his choice clearly. I *shoo* the fluttering butterflies in my stomach and pull at my bottom lip with my fingers, pinching to keep my feet on the floor instead of floating away from the airy way my thoughts drift toward him.

“But why?” I breathe.

The shimmering gold isn’t the only breathtaking feature. Ivory sleeves end at the wrist, but floor-length casing in the same champagne color drapes down and off the table.

Taking the delicate shoulders in my hands, I lift the top of the dress off the table and gasp at the intricately detailed back made of nothing but lace, undoubtedly sewn to reveal the length of my spine.

“I can’t accept this,” I whisper, but it hardly sounds convincing. I *want* to accept this dress from him. “There is nothing I can provide in return—”

“Elora,” she scolds gently. “This is a gift. It doesn’t have strings attached and doesn’t require reciprocation. You will be expected to dress in the others daily. Perhaps Finnian wanted you to have something you’d enjoy.”

“I love all of them,” I partially lie, though they are beautiful. But Finnian’s divine gift is my favorite. “I will thank him when he returns from the hunting trip.”

The kindness didn’t leave her eyes, but she studied me cautiously and dismissed the girl. She waits until we’re alone before leaning a hip against the table’s edge. “I know you’ve heard many stories of your father’s time here, but he truly was admired by many of us.”

I tilt my head. Not once did he ever mention the queen. “I wasn’t aware you were friendly with my father.”

“Oh, yes.” A soft smile appears. “He loved the gardens. He

gifted me with a book once on the history of flowers. You remind me of him. Maybe more guarded but gentle. You're passionate about those you care for, as was he."

I wait for her to reveal that she has discovered my entire plan, that she's aware I only agreed to the marriage to use Finnian's resources for Ashbury, but the confession never comes, and I search for a hidden meaning in her comforting words.

"I am," I confirm. Like Irina, maybe she wants assurance that I will be kind to Finnian. "I do care about Finnian. And Irina."

I might not love him like I would want my children to be loved, but I won't be cruel to him.

Her long silences prove she carefully considers every word she says. "I never met your mother." She grabs my shawl from the back of a chair, tightening a loose thread around the tip of her finger. "I heard tales of her beauty. He would speak of her often. And you."

The draft from the terrace adds to the cold sweep through my veins each time my father is conveyed as loving toward us. Leaving me in Regina's care spoke otherwise.

"Was this hers?" she asks, referencing the shawl.

"Yes. After her death..." I struggle to continue, blinking back tears. "My stepmother insisted he sell everything of hers. I managed to save that before he burned the rest."

"Something I've learned over the years is all of this,"—she waves a hand above our heads—"won't leave with us. These are things. If I part from this world tomorrow, I hope my children won't keep anything of mine for memory's sake." She inches closer to me. "Memories do not live in things."

She places a featherlight touch on my shoulder. "They live within you. Your father must've understood that. If you believe as your stepmother does, you will never move on. I must disagree if you believe the dress I'm wearing now will make any difference to Irina when I'm gone. It might smell like me, but it'll fade as I have."

I wipe away a tear with the back of my hand. "I was six when she died. I have no other way of remembering her."

She hums. "Your memories with her may be few, but her influence on you has lasted. If that isn't the best way to honor her memory, I am unsure another way exists."

Irina calls my name from the entryway. The queen retreats a step and smiles. "I will send this down to be washed. Perhaps mended," she offers, "if that is all right with you."

I want to argue, but I nod. The faded and nearly black shawl would benefit from a scrubbing if only to stop smelling like my sweat. "That would be wonderful. I appreciate your kindness."

Irina carries a silver platter of eggs, bacon, and fruits. She acknowledges her mother quickly before diving into her story about lingering beside the cook while he remade the eggs correctly and *not* runny.

Her mother listens with wrinkles around her eyes from a broad smile, staring at her daughter with nothing short of admiration. I want to apologize to her for my stepsisters and assure her I'm not a reflection of them, but it wouldn't change what they did. And Queen Honora carries herself in a way that doesn't need an apology. She is classier than them, and she knows it.

It is a trait she has passed on to her daughter.

Irina snaps her fingers in my face. "We must eat quickly before your lessons."

I climb out of another hole and jerk my head back. "*Lessons*? What lessons?"

Irina bites the tip of a strawberry with a rotten grin. "Your etiquette lessons, doe."

I shake my head. "I took those as a young girl. My father paid for a tutor…"

"Jasper believes you need a refresher," Irina says. "I will escort you to the great hall for lessons on manners and breathing correctly."

I scowl, not even attempting to hide my annoyance. "*I* need lessons on *my* manners?" I sink into a chair. "How many?"

"We'll be occupied all morning." She tosses me a strawberry. "We will spend all afternoon baking treats for the visiting royals for tea tomorrow morning. Another tradition."

"This evening will be a stroll through town in one of your dresses," the queen adds. "It will be the three of us. You will be given gold to purchase goods from the merchants."

A day full of pretending.

Finnian would be so proud.

I pop the strawberry into my mouth and purposely concede with my mouth full, mimicking the cruel king. "*Fine.*"

Twenty-Six

I've successfully avoided two full days of mindless chatter with visiting royals. I'm not the youngest man here, yet I seem to be the only skilled hunter. My time has been spent catching our meals and roasting them over the coals while the rest drink their way through the trip—not once asking about my bride-to-be, not that I'm complaining. The less I have to hear about Elora's position in life, the more content I'll remain.

The land we've settled on Jasper bought from a dying farmer years ago. He paid him poorly for it, but everyone is always too afraid of him to argue. The land was supposed to be neutral between neighboring kingdoms, but my father has never been one to play by the rules.

I left the rain in Pumpkin Hollow with Elora, but the muggy air finally reached us, adding to my displeasure of having to be here. Twelve in total came, including my father, and there isn't one person I would regret leaving. I've contemplated trying frequently—even shared the plan in secret with Major—and have convinced myself I will return to Pumpkin Hollow to find Elora reconsidering everything after she visited with Cedric.

I inhale deeply to settle the tightness in my chest.

Elora isn't the type of person to negate an agreement. She wants to be trustworthy, convinced if she slips, she'll be no better than her father. Mine is trying to convince one of the visiting queen's maids to enter his tent.

If I suffocate him while everyone sleeps, I wouldn't be the only suspect. I could break the betrothal with Elora, return freedom to her, and maintain a friendship.

But one nagging, irritating feeling twists my gut at the idea of saying goodbye to her. I wouldn't want her freedom extending to marrying someone else. I don't want Cedric touching her or being the one to learn if she *does* know the meaning of misbehaving.

Fuck, I need to stop.

She tolerates me because she's required to do so. I'm putting a solid effort into making this arrangement as endurable for her as possible, but I've spent the entire trip wondering if Irina has completely corrupted her. I didn't give Irina instructions to keep Elora out of trouble; if there's something Irina will always seek, it's trouble.

Purely physical—the longing has to be physical.

Her golden-brown eyes, wild curls, and how her lips pinch when she scowls at me are challenging. The way she tastes like honeyed venom has nothing to do with my inability to focus on anything else.

I need to take a fucking walk.

No one notices when I grab my bow and back away from the rowdy crowd of intoxicated aristocrats, each one feasting on more meats and cheeses than Ashbury has likely ever seen. With any luck, they'll be passed out upon my return, and I can leave at first light before they wake.

Or, I thought no one noticed me.

"Mind if I join you?"

I silently curse. The Prince of Reeve trails behind me like a hyena. If I have to be followed by someone, he's the most tolerable. At twenty-six, Beau is unmarried and has joined me on several outings during my travels. We have nothing in common aside from our addiction to pleasure and liquor. He's satisfied in his position as the Prince of Reeve, whereas I wish to abdicate and never look back, which doesn't leave much conversation between us. But we have an understanding—stay mute about the privileges handed to us.

My distaste for the crown doesn't clash well with his pride for fame and riches.

"Depends," I jest. "Will you leave my sister alone?"

Chuckling, he adjusts the bow strap over his chest. "I try not to make promises I have no intention of keeping." His tone might be light, but his following statement sends flaming-hot heat through my ribcage, "Perhaps I'll focus on your bride tomorrow instead."

It's typical to volley crudely with men—it seems to be a favored ritual of many royals—but the idea of him speaking to Elora curls my fist tightly around my bow. Irina can handle him and has, but Elora is kind. She might be cruel to me, but I've seen her interact with others. She'll entertain him to be polite.

Before embarking on this trip, Jasper informed me that no one could know our marriage was arranged. According to him, it would make us appear weak and further contribute to the rumors circulating about me—that I'm a womanizer and careless. After my tour of Ashbury with Elora, I can admit to one of those. I've been unintentionally careless and only concerned with the well-being of my mother and Irina. I might've bedded too many women in the past, but those days are behind me.

"Her name is Elora, ya?" he asks.

I roll my neck. Would anyone notice if I shot an arrow through his throat? Manipulation is a genetic trait of mine. I could easily convince everyone that I believed he was a bear.

"Yes," I mutter in reply.

"You left Reeve only weeks ago and never mentioned her before disappearing into the back room of a brothel with two duchesses." He knocks my shoulder with his fist like we're fucking bonding. "Does she know you weren't thinking about her?"

There would be too much blood if I shot him through the throat. The head would be an instant kill and cleaner. His body could rot underground while I claim to be innocent. No one will question me because of Jasper's wrath.

"I hadn't met her yet," I explain, "and would prefer if those stories remain between us."

His arrogant laughter nearly sends me back to the others. Elora didn't seem pleased when she smelled whiskey on my breath, but remaining sober was becoming difficult.

"I understand," he says. "You have to keep her convinced of your loyalty until you've sunk your seed in her; then, you'll be a free man." His self-righteous smirk follows. "After your son is born, consider sharing her. I'll be first in line."

One second, he was speaking; the next, I had him pinned against a tree with my arm across his chest. Even in the dark, the whites of his eyes grow larger. I pant like a beast, uncaged, unsure when I tossed my bow to the ground to subdue him.

"Do not speak of her that way." Deathly calm, my voice never wavers. "Elora will not be shared with anyone, and you will show her respect when you address her tomorrow."

He raises his hands. "It wasn't my intention to offend you. I apologize, but it's what everyone is thinking."

I am one breath away from making him a permanent extension of this tree. "Everyone is thinking I'll share my wife?"

"No, Finn," a smooth voice croons behind me. "They believe you'll leave her the way you left me."

Sighing, I release Beau and retrieve my bow to hang idly at my side. Beau readjusts his tunic, but his pride won't come so quickly. He leaves me with a mumbled string of obscenities, sliding a comb from his pocket to fix his tousled hair.

"Prick," I grumble.

"He won't let that go." Agnes strolls out from between trees, her confident sway still the same from years ago. "Still ignoring me? How would your mother feel about that?"

I curl my lip, displeased by the truth. My mother wouldn't want me to treat anyone rudely, but I still hesitate to stop staring at a rock on the ground and lift my gaze.

"Agnes," I greet dryly.

"Oh, you remember!" She claps her hands together. "I wondered if I had become invisible since you've refused to speak to me."

I strap the bow across my chest. "There's nothing to say."

I couldn't breathe long ago when she was near me, but that time has passed. With her long auburn hair and light-blue eyes, her nose splattered with freckles against tanned skin, tales of what our children would look like spanned kingdoms.

Hers is only a day's ride from Pumpkin Hollow. The Fracas Kingdom boasts lush green grass and bountiful supplies of fresh fruits and vegetables. We grow our own but outsource when hosting events, which is why her family received an invitation to my wedding. I refuse to consider that Jasper extended the invite for twisted entertainment.

Our betrothal ended years ago.

It was one of the rare times I pleaded with Jasper not to inquire why I ended it so abruptly and convinced him it wasn't anyone's fault when the threat of war loomed from the dissolution. Six years have passed, but he still reminds me of his generosity in sparing their lives. And I anticipate the day he comes to collect. It doesn't matter that his relationship with her parents has been repaired; I let him down.

The *why* makes no difference.

My union with Agnes was not as quick as meeting Elora and agreeing to marry her within three days, but I was young when I met Agnes. Our meeting was arranged, but the feelings we developed were real. I wasn't ready for marriage at twenty-two, but I didn't want to lose her. Unfortunately, I was unable to comprehend the differences between love and lust.

I did desire her. We spent many evenings on the hillsides. When I proposed, the obligation dampened the joy, but she accepted.

And I believed I had found the person to make accepting my future as the future king bearable.

But the love between us wasn't genuine. It was a match made under pressure: two young royals attempting to make the best out of a forced match. But fuck, it hurt the day I walked away from her.

But now, my desire has been replaced by annoyance. And I wish for Elora's simplicity. Agnes, though beautiful, values title above all else. She wears her riches boldly. Aside from the gold rings on her fingers, her heavy overcoat is embellished with gold flakes. The staunch, steamy air has pooled sweat across her brow, but she would rather display her wealth than remove it. Elora barely accepted the pearl necklace from me. I had to lie to her about where it came from, anticipating her attempts to deny the gift. If she knew I had picked it up from town beforehand, it never would've made it on her neck.

I didn't need to pretend with Elora. And it enables my need to want to impress her. With Agnes, she has everything she could ever want. Her position in life isn't her fault, but Elora remains humble and gracious. Even with how horribly Ashbury has been treated by my father, she's letting me in.

That gift is worth more.

Agnes softens her expression, but I ignore her. Elora might dislike me, but I won't dishonor her by opening old wounds with another woman. "We have plenty to talk about, Finnian. Irina isn't here to protect you."

I grit my teeth. I never asked Irina to get involved, but when Agnes tried to see me after I left her, Irina told her never to return or everyone would learn what she did. "How's Darius, Agnes?"

Her tone is coated with ice. "That's unfair."

I chuckle condescendingly. "How would he feel if he knew you're slinking into the woods to seek me out? I can't imagine I'm a topic he's comfortable with. Does he know you're here?"

Her silence replies for her.

I nod knowingly. "Still keeping secrets."

She brushes her fingers through her hair, balancing her other hand on her hip. All her nervous spasms are still the same. "He's away on business in another country. He wasn't in Fracas when we received the invitation, and I thought this would be a good time—"

"To *what*?" My voice raises. "What can you say to me to change what happened? There is nothing to say, Agnes. Did you think that by coming here, I would leave Elora? Beg for you?"

She blows out a breath. "I just wanted to talk to you, Finnian! You don't need to be so cruel!"

"You fucked my best mate!" I shout, chest heaving, buried betrayal resurfacing. "I didn't invite you here, Agnes. This was not an olive branch. I have no doubts about marrying Elora. This is inappropriate."

"He proposed to me," she whispers.

I expect jealousy, but there's only hollowness. I've wholly moved on from her. Letting Darius handle her constantly lying is a fitting retribution for what they did.

My lack of response narrows her eyes. "Did you hear me? He proposed to me, Finnian. I am marrying someone else."

I move toward her slowly, my back straight, my prowl purposeful. The longing and hope in her eyes that I will lower her to the ground is as satisfying as saying, "My condolences, Agnes, but I will be unable to attend your wedding. I will be too busy pleasuring my wife."

Her eyes flare with envy. But then, a wretched grin replaces it. "I can't wait to meet her, Finnian." She drags a finger down my chest. "We'll have so much to talk about."

I grab her wrist to remove her touch. "If you think Irina protected me, then I fucking challenge you to hurt Elora. I won't touch you, but I can't say the same for my sister."

She rips her arm away. "You will answer to Darius if I'm harmed."

I smirk. "Good. I let him live once. But as you mentioned earlier, cruelty has been bred into me. I look forward to adding another head to my father's collection."

Her breath catches from fear.

For Elora, I'm not sure what I wouldn't do for her if someone harmed her. Trust between us is already delicate. Hiding my past with Agnes from her would demolish any progress we've made. I need to find her before they meet for High Tea.

I leave Agnes in the cold for the second time to saddle my horse and return home.

To Elora.

❧

Except for Beau, everyone had passed out when I returned to camp. The maid my father tried to coerce was asleep outside her queen's tent. I wouldn't have to lie to my mother about whether or not he behaved himself. He wouldn't be pleased to wake and find me missing, but I had more pressing matters to attend to first.

After leaving Major's stall, I jog through the woods toward the castle. Sunlight streamed through the trees from the waking sun, and the others wouldn't be far behind me. High Tea will begin mid-morning, which didn't leave me much time to find and speak with Elora before she meets Agnes. Irina will protect her, but she deserves to hear it from me.

But I don't need to search for Elora.

Flowers in the garden nearly swallow her whole as she sleeps on a soft bed of grass. Her hair is fanned out, her hands partially on her stomach while her legs are twisted and tucked beneath her. Crouching, I pluck the solitary Forget-Me-Not flower from between her fingers and spin it between mine.

Her chest rises and falls steadily, her lips barely parted, and the rising sun emits a soft, golden glow across her creamy skin. If I had the time, I would commission a painter to solidify this moment on canvas. Her mauve dress is wrapped around her legs like a blanket, while the short, puffy sleeves leave goosebumps on her arms. My gaze lingers on her collarbone, imagining how smooth it would feel against my lips.

I brush my fingers down her jaw.

She stirs but doesn't wake. I want to leave her here to doze peacefully while I read a book in the pavilion behind her, but our guests would not find her sleeping in the gardens as charming as I do. There is something about her I do not wish to like, yet I'm drawn to the soft allure of how she looks amongst the gentle pastels of our castle garden.

Cupping her cheek, I drag my thumb over the delicate skin beneath her eye. "Elora," I whisper, "Open your eyes."

A breathy sigh precedes a mulish whimper. Grinning, I whisper her name again, applying the lightest pressure to my touch. Her eyes flutter open, her sleepy gaze focusing on me before she startles and rises. I almost encourage her to slow down, but she lifts to her knees quicker than a breath and loses her balance, toppling forward against my chest.

I embrace her immediately, wrapping my arms around her. "It's just me, little doe."

She doesn't push me away as I expected. Instead, she slides her hands in between my chest and her face, her nerves causing her to tremble. Frowning, I cup her head. "Did you have another nightmare?"

Still crouching, I lower onto my knees but refuse to let her move away. I keep her tucked against me, safe within my arms. "Elora," I encourage, "talk to me, please."

"Yes," she murmurs against her hands.

Lifting her head after a moment, she sighs. Her brown eyes are darkened under the watery enamel from sleep. "I've been sleeping with Irina, but I awoke with a headache and needed fresh air."

I brush my fingers through her curls, repeating each stroke after reaching the ends. "What did you see?"

A distant confusion causes a crease in her forehead as her eyebrows meet. "I don't know. It's as if... it's almost like I'm seeing something from someone else's visions." She rests her forehead against my chest again. "I'm exhausted."

I tug the end of a curl, desperate to see her eyes again. "Should I expect to find you here every morning? The least you could do is water the flowers if you insist on sleeping with them."

Her rare laughter brings a smile to my face.

She lazily lifts a shoulder, but her head stays buried against me. "Show me the watering pail."

I pinch her sides. Yelping, she places her hands over mine and tries to shove them away, but I hold firm with her dress knitted between my fingers.

"Must you do that every time?" she asks.

I win when she tips her chin up.

"There are better ways to get my attention."

Liquid heat floods me from all the ways I would love to test that. "Tell me how, Elora."

Play with me, I plead silently.

She hums, scrunching her nose in faux thought. "Breakfast in bed. Was that negotiated in the contract?"

I click my tongue. "Unfortunately not. I believe it conveys pumpkin porridge every morning. It was my idea, of course."

"Of course," she mocks. "Because your need to irritate me is boundless." A playful grin catches the light. "I hope it's okay that I changed our cake to wheat muffin tops."

Glaring, I snake my hand up her back to squeeze her neck. I can control her easily this way. One light squeeze and her chin lifts inches higher. It's intoxicating the way her curves mold to mine, my hands touching every part she allows.

"You promised to behave," I say.

She nods the best she can with my hand wrapped around her neck.

"And did you?"

She swallows, but I don't believe it's from nerves. She's debating how to answer—weighing my reaction to a snarky remark versus the truth. As long as Cedric didn't touch her, I'll take either. "And what if I didn't?"

I wasn't expecting that one.

Is she.... *flirting* with me?

How far can I take this?

"Well," I begin huskily, loosening the grip on her dress to slowly drag a finger up her spine.

She fucking *shivers*, and I nearly lose all self-control.

"I would be very disappointed."

I apply pressure to the soft indentation between her spine and neck. The tiniest gasp slips through her lips, and she responds by arching her back and pressing her hips against mine. Prude or not, there is no way she can mistake how desperately I want her.

With my other hand, I pry her bottom lip from between her teeth and brush my thumb across it. "If he touched you, Elora, I have the right to defend what's mine."

Her tenacity returns. "*Yours*?"

My hand around her neck shoves into her hair and pulls until her throat stretches. She claws at my ribs to keep from falling backward. I frighten her, but I like it.

"Whether you accept it or not, you are mine."

My smug smirk causes her glare to return, but her eyes have brightened. Hatred isn't the only emotion reflecting back at me. It drives her mad that she might want me.

I taunt her further. "You belong to me, Elora. No one else is allowed to touch you."

Suddenly, her determination drowns everything else. She knows something. Fuck, what did Irina tell her?

"And is anyone allowed to touch *you*?" she asks.

Ah. She's circling back to my remark about having affairs. She must've told Irina, and Irina would've told her I'd never do something like that. I knew it was a mistake to leave them alone together. And Irina most likely wants to kick my ass now.

But I can't make this too easy for her. "That depends on how you answer my next question."

Her pulse is drumming so quickly in her throat that if I touch her the way I want, she might pass out.

Her teeth clench. "*What* question?"

I trace the outline of her jaw with my finger. "Do you want anyone else to touch me?"

She tenses. That reaction makes me grin, but I must hear her say it aloud. "It wouldn't be fair," she whispers.

I shake my head. "I don't give a fuck about what's fair, Elora. Tell me the truth."

Her breathing quickens. A million thoughts seem to filter through her while she searches my eyes. She harbors so much doubt about my loyalty to her that I nearly confess that no woman has ever made me want to choke her and fall to my knees to worship her at the same time as she has.

Elora has awakened a thirst in me that I can't seem to quench unless I'm touching her. Longing—I long for her. I've never yearned for anyone, but I search for her when she isn't near.

I look forward to our encounters, even if only to taste the bane she spews.

The flowers beneath us blur into chaotic color as I wait patiently for a *seed* of truth from her.

And finally, painfully, she admits to something she's spent so much energy trying to deny. "No. I don't want anyone else touching you, Finnian."

The frustration in her voice almost makes me laugh, but I resist for her sake. Instead, I lean in and stare at her mouth with obvious intent, bypassing it to place my lips against her ear and whisper, "Then, I'm yours, Elora."

She slides her hands from my ribs to my chest and nuzzles her cheek against mine. And I decide to brave a proposition.

"There are ways to make this union more tolerable for us, little doe." I gently graze her ear with my teeth. "To use our hatred for one another pleasurably."

Her fucking *hands*.

One slides into my hair and *caresses*.

Dozens of locations race through my mind of where I could take her, though I'm not opposed to welcoming our forthcoming guests with a show.

She breathes my name and the tether snaps.

I turn to kiss her but freeze when a timid voice calls my name. "Fucking Hades," I growl, using my grip on her hair to return her head to my chest.

One of my mother's ladies lowers into a curtsy.

"*What*?" I snap.

All these fucking interruptions.

"The queen sent for Elora." Her voice cracks from nerves. "It is time to dress for High Tea, Lord Finnian."

Fuck.

Elora's breathy laughter as she tries to pull away brings me back to reality. I sought her out to warn her about Agnes, but her presence ensnared me once again.

"I better go," Elora says, her hands leaving my hair and chest to untangle my fingers from her curls. "I'll see you later."

"Elora," I start, but what can I share with her quickly that won't contribute to her doubts about me? "There will be someone there—"

"I know," she interrupts, but she couldn't. Irina wouldn't have told her about Agnes without my permission. "Irina warned me of the queen from.... Oh, I can't remember. The one who insists you should marry her granddaughter?"

The lady-in-waiting clears her throat, urging Elora to leave me *faster*. Elora can't stop fidgeting and stuttering through how Irina advised her to handle High Tea, explaining how her entire morning yesterday was spent with a haughty instructor to relearn manners, laughing when explaining how Irina purposely kept distracting her.

I stand and nearly cut her off when she adds, "Thank you for the dress. I'm unsure if you wanted your mother to tell me it was from you, but.... thank you."

Her genuine and soft gratefulness catches me off-guard.

I kiss her hand. "It was my pleasure."

I nearly kiss her, but her name is called. I'm going to fire every person who dares to interrupt us again.

She flashes an apologetic grin before pulling away from me. "I am interested..."—she bites the corner of her lip with a coy grin—"...in all the ways to hate you pleasurably."

I pull her lip free again. "I can't wait to show you."

She backs away from me, then snaps her fingers as if remembering something. "I left something for you in your quarters."

And then, she's gone.

I smile without restraint until I remember who she's about to meet and what she will endure by being my wife.

And decide I need a drink.

Twenty-Seven

My cheeks hurt from smiling.

Constant repetition from my last encounter with Finnian has made the room unbearably warm. Every day with him becomes more challenging but different from how I expected. I'm struggling to stay away from him.

Would it be so horrible to more-than-tolerate my husband?

Gods, the way he looks at me sometimes sets me aflame. He continues to grow braver each time he touches me, and I never want to stop him. I want to encourage his exploration.

I want him to tell me how he turns the gods crimson when only his voice turns *me* red.

"Elora? *Elora*."

I startle at the sound of the queen's voice. "I apologize. What did you say?"

She pats my shoulder with a knowing smile. "My son is home?"

"Yes," I squeak, then clear my throat. "Yes, Finnian arrived at dawn." *To find me sleeping in the gardens*, I neglect to add.

She sighs in a way only a mother could. "I doubt he slept while he was away. I hope he naps before evening dinner."

Irina idly flips through the pages of a book while lounging on her mother's bed. "I'll stop by his quarters after High Tea."

Stunning per usual, Irina has wrinkled her quaint and airy

swirling gold and red dress. A tiara with a single red ruby sits atop her head—a challenge after she argued that donning tiaras is childish at her age before eventually accepting that she doesn't have a choice.

"It is rather childish," I say long after the conversation has ended. "Dressing up in,"—I lift the skirt of my dress—"gowns and tiaras for Tea. I had a dollhouse as a child and often pretended my dolls were doing the same."

Irina loudly hums her agreement while Queen Honora brushes her fingers through my hair. She dismissed everyone except us, but Irina reminded me that speaking freely is impossible with gossiping wenches.

Her mother scolded her but agreed.

Even if every maid and servant knows the arrangement between Finnian and me, the less information they collect to spread, the happier the king will remain. And that is everyone's highest priority all the time.

Honora begins to braid my hair. "Tell me something, Elora. Why did you play those games?"

She's much gentler than Regina. It doesn't feel as if my skull is about to be torn into pieces. "Um..." I haven't ever given much thought to the reason why. "I guess I wanted to pretend it was me instead."

Irina snickers. "If you only knew."

"Irina, come hold this braid," Honora demands.

Irina dramatically tosses the book onto the bed and stands beside her mother to hold the braid. Honora separates the bottom half of the strands while Zeb rests his head on my lap. Georgie remains spread across the bed, even after Irina has come to stand behind me.

"It does seem frivolous to outsiders, but to us, this is all we've ever known." Honora tilts her head toward her daughter. "While *some* believe the ones outside the castle walls have it better than we do, the life you imagine is seldom what you wished for."

I laugh when Irina sticks out her tongue, even more so when

Honora lightly taps Irina's backside. Being near her mother has brought out an endearing youthfulness in Irina.

"It's ironic, no?" Honora looks between us. "You've each wished for one another's life, yet here we stand together, and we're not so different after all."

After taking the braid from Irina, Honora begins combining the two while we listen in complete silence. "Class differences are archaic and unfortunate, but without them, no one would have anything to wish for. It's natural for humans to need the belief that something better exists because it makes the realization sweeter when it dawns on us that our life isn't about what we have, but the satisfaction we find within."

She loops and tugs my hair, but I'm too focused on what she's saying to mind.

"You are strong, beautiful young women with bright futures. While I agree that our realm hasn't been handled as well as it should've been, I trust that the three of you can enact change. Maybe you won't have to continue wishing for a way out of the life you were given if you can discover ways to find a satisfying middle ground."

Neither of us speaks, but the words sink in like a submerged ship in the sea. I always longed for a life like Irina's, while she wished to be freed from hers. All of us have suffered from neglect, but we assumed it was better elsewhere to stay hopeful.

To strive for more.

Honora retrieves a gold headband and places it atop my head. "No tiara yet, but it doesn't detract from your charm."

"I love it," I breathe, running a hand down the thick braid. I remain in the mauve dress from my slumber in the gardens, and the simplicity of the design pays homage to where I came from, while the company I keep represents the prospective changes we could bring to the monarchy.

"Mother," Irina says softly, removing her tiara. "Do we have time for you to fix my hair?"

I catch the hope in Honora's eyes when she cups Irina's cheek and nods. "Always, my darling. Elora can help me."

Blinking back tears, I switch places with Irina and tenderly squeeze her arm. "It would be an honor."

We follow the queen, hurrying to be the first ones at High Tea to welcome the guests. If my heart doesn't stop beating so quickly, it might erupt before I'm subjected to *dull* royals, as Irina called them.

The guests from the hunting trip were not the only ones invited to the wedding, but they arrived the quickest. I would meet over a hundred royals before the wedding, with more scheduled to attend events over the next few days.

High Tea will consist of thirty women—one of which is the queen, who set on procuring Finnian for her granddaughter. Irina promised to handle that one. Truthfully, she assured me she would take care of everything and remain at my side. I expected to be more nervous, but an unsettling feeling in the pit of my stomach was more akin to dread.

Even the enchantment in my veins can't cure it.

I gasped when we turned the corner. Unseen from town or the gardens, a glass bridge similar to the one between kingdoms leads to a large and open social lounge. The bridge sits above a stream filled with bright orange and blue fish swimming in tandem with the calm waters.

"Remind me to give you a proper tour," Irina says, grinning at my awe. "The lounge was added during our most recent renovation, but it's disguised." She gestures to the stone walls on either side of us. "From the outside, it appears like a normal corridor. It's not until you stand beneath it that you can see the glass. We are hidden between trees."

"But I've been in the forest behind—"

"There's a smaller forest on the far left of the castle," she interjects. "The tea room is situated in a clearing next to an arboretum, directly behind the lounge. Jasper utilizes the lounge most often for the men to smoke tobacco."

I wrinkle my nose. "Finnian smokes tobacco?"

"No, doe. That is not Finn's vice." She points ahead to the lounge. "The walls inside are all glass, and we've hung bird feeders in every tree outside. You might see deers grazing if Finn didn't manage to shoot all of them."

"This is where he went?"

"Kind of. There's land beyond the forest. It is only a morning's ride away from here. It is one of the places Finnian used to take me when I needed to be away from the castle. Now, Jasper uses the land for entertainment."

I absentmindedly nod, trying to commit every piece of information to memory. The more places I know of near the castle, the more locations I can suggest the faeries avoid when they leave. "High Tea.... isn't that normally—"

"For the working class?"

How does she anticipate everything I'm going to say?

"Jasper can't let anyone have anything to themselves. He ordered high-back chairs and tables because he believed we deserved everything the working class had. So, now we must drink our tea and eat finger foods while standing."

I frown deeply. We can hardly afford teabags in Ashbury, and he's adopted an event specifically for the working class just because he can. It's entirely unnecessary, especially when the teabags could be put to better use in Ashbury.

"It's all right if you despise him, Elora."

I glance at Irina.

"I do, too."

We reach the end of the bridge to enter the lounge when Irina reaches for her mother's hand and tilts her head to the side. I follow

Honora's gaze to find Finnian leaning against the wall, nearly blending into the stone casing. His head is tipped back, his eyes closed, and it appears he's fallen asleep.

"Finnian," Honora calls softly.

Upon hearing his name, his eyes flutter open. The clear blue irises have changed into bloodshot and misty.

Irina sighs. "Oh, Finn."

My excitement to see him dwindles into concern. "I don't understand. He was fine this morning."

"My darling boy." His mother greets him with a hand on his cheek. "You should be resting. You cannot join us."

The broken vessels in his eyes have not sprouted from exhaustion. Finnian has been drinking.

Shadowy scruff covers his cheeks, and deep purple circles paint the hollow skin beneath his eyes—details I haven't noticed before because I've been too consumed by his touch to care. But now, he's a shell of the man I spent my morning with. His amorous exterior and charisma have melted away.

"I won't stay long." Heavy, slurred words. "I need to wish my bride luck."

"She doesn't need luck," Irina responds dryly, her annoyance with him unmistakable. "She has me. You need to go before anyone else sees you like this."

A servant from the lounge catches the queen's attention, and she excuses herself, but not without stroking Finnian's cheek first. "Please, son, get some rest."

"Jasper will expect you in the arena," Irina continues, "you can't joust drunk."

My eyes widened. "Jousting? Like *this*?"

"It is one of Finnian's responsibilities to entertain the men when the women are occupied. "If he shows up like this,"—she drags her hand in a dramatic, exasperated wave toward him—"his consequences will be severe."

"Irina, he can't arrive like this!" I shout in a whisper.

"He is a *grown man*," Irina emphasizes.

Finnian ignores her and focuses solely on me. "You look beautiful, Elora."

The compliment would mean more if I could be positive it isn't the liquor talking.

"Can you leave us?" he asks Irina.

Irina looks at me for permission, but I shrug. Briefly closing her eyes, she releases a tight breath through her nose but zeroes in on him. "This is beneath you, Finnian."

His gaze lowers as she steps away to allow us privacy.

I tentatively approach him, unsure how to behave when he's like this. "Is it me?" I twist my hands together. "Is it the wedding? What's making you drink like this?"

He hooks a finger to beckon me over, huskily demanding, "Come here, Elora."

I hesitate but obey, lingering a foot away from him. Reaching forward, he wraps an arm around my waist and drags me closer until my body is flush against his. "Finn—"

He places a finger against my lips. "I can help you leave this place, Elora."

My eyebrows pinch.

"He can't touch you if you're not here."

I pull his hand away from my face. "I can't leave. I have a responsibility to my people, to the faeries. I won't abandon them."

He twists us and pins me against the wall. "Why did you come here, Elora? You shouldn't have come here."

I shove his chest. "Irina was right. You need to leave. I don't like this version of you."

Removing my hands from his chest, he presses them against the wall. "You don't know me, little doe."

"No," I whisper. "You don't want me to know you because I make you feel something."

"Anger? Yes, I suppose you're right."

I roll my eyes with a huff. "*Please.*"

Despite the women arriving behind him, he leans down to rest his forehead against mine. His warm breath reeks of whiskey. I wish

I knew how to console him, but Finnian possesses more demons than I realized.

"You shouldn't be here," he repeats in a broken whisper. "This place is dangerous. He'll suck the life out of you."

"Then breathe it back into me, Finnian."

He moves one hand to cup my throat. "I can't when I'm barely surviving on my own."

Moist silver lines my eyes. "Do you truly wish for me to leave?"

"Hate me, Elora. I need you to hate me."

His lack of an answer angers me enough to reply, "I hate you."

The tip of his tongue sweeps across my bottom lip. "Your lies taste so sweet, little doe."

I lick my lips. "And your misery tastes bitter. Go pity yourself elsewhere, Finnian."

Hungry anger permeates his misplaced desperation for me to abandon him. "You were right." His voice changes into a gravelly tremor. "This can only end one way. Will you forgive me, Elora?"

"For what?"

He applies pressure to my throat, his mouth hovering only inches away from mine. "Ruining you."

I grab his hand to try and pry it away. "I guess that depends on how *you* answer *my* next question."

He drags his nose up my jawline, drawing in a deep breath as if taking what's left of my oxygen for himself. "Ask me."

"Do you want to ruin me?"

He settles his lips right against my ear, his teeth grazing my earlobe before he whispers, "In so many ways."

Everything within me *burns*.

Irina calls his name with a threatening bite from behind him, but Finnian doesn't move. He only growls *in my ear.*

"Finnian," I whisper, "you should go."

"Come with me," he replies, lifting his head.

Logically, I know I can't.

Illogically, I want nothing more.

Irina appears beside him and touches his arm. "Finnian, you must leave before he finds out what you're doing."

He turns his head toward her with a glare. "I don't want her in there with those fucking vipers, Irina."

Irina wrangles my wrist from his tight grip and tugs until he releases me. "You being here is going to make it worse for her. They're already babbling about the two of you out here. It's embarrassing Mother."

"I can give them something to talk about," he responds, cupping my neck.

I feel like I am the rope in a childish game of tug-of-war.

"Finnian," Irina snaps.

He's strung out on nerves and liquor, his glowering lingering on someone inside the lounge. I turn my head to search, but he shifts his hand from my neck to my chin and turns me away. "Let me kiss her," he says to Irina.

"Godsdamnit, Finnian!" Irina bellows. "I highly doubt she wants to kiss you like this. Leave her alone and go!"

He says nothing—no other assurances, no further pleas to follow him toward freedom. Instead, he releases me and backs away without a goodbye, and Irina prevents me from following him. "He'll be okay, Elora. And so will you."

"What is he so afraid of in there?"

Irina pinches the bridge of her nose. "That is a story I don't have time to tell you right now. Just stay beside me, okay?"

But her final words cause me to turn my head to watch as Finnian disappears, "Gods, as if this family didn't have enough problems already."

High Tea was.... well, drab.

The ambiance was an elegant tea, but Irina staying by my side kept everyone young far away from me. Irina would speak for me if they dared to approach or pose a statement that only left me with one answer.

But mostly, they just circled like vultures.

We stood at a table with older women who wore bitter scowls and upturned noses at the simple fact that Finnian was spoken for.

It bothered me, but Irina sought revenge by passively picking apart the daughters or granddaughters they have continuously shoved toward Finnian over the recent years while building me up as someone who understands the needs of our people. And all I was allowed to do was drink tea—none of the selections included the honey tea I loved.

By the time it was over, I was exhausted from boredom. And Irina dragged me out before anyone else could leave, keeping me far away from two women in particular—a gorgeous redhead and a woman with blonde hair so bright it looked white, and both seemed distinctly interested in me.

Irina pulls me into an arboretum between the stream and lounge, collapsing on an extended velvet window seat hidden behind rows of plants and flowers.

I ask, "Am I allowed to speak now?"

A breathy laugh comes from her nose. "Be my guest."

I shift awkwardly on my feet. I could dart out any second with all this pent-up energy. I haven't been able to stop worrying about my soon-to-be husband and his addiction to whiskey. "Shouldn't we check on Finnian?"

"No." She lifts and twists her hand to point out a window above us. "He's in the arena. Or should be."

Grabbing the windowsill, I lift on my toes and search for him but can only see the open enclosure of the arena. "Do you think he's okay?"

She tugs on my skirt, waiting to answer me until I lay beside her. "He will be. Being home this long is an adjustment."

"Has he always drunk like this?"

"Comes and goes."

I roll over onto my stomach. "Once we wed, will you let me in on all these secrets?"

She touches the tip of my nose with her fingertip. "You will be his problem then."

I roll my eyes. "I see. You're only taking care of me out of sisterly duty?"

"Partially." Her stare hollows. "And because you need protection. These people are horrid, Elora. And bored. They pick apart the lives they want, which is pathetic since they have everything. And Finnian marrying someone like you is unheard of."

I huff. "Someone like me."

She pinches my arm. "You know exactly what I mean. Don't get mighty on me now."

I rub the red mark she created with a scowl. "Is this the only way the two of you can communicate with others? Between you and him, I'll always have bruises."

Hearing voices make me sit up, but she yanks me back down and covers my mouth with her hand. "Maids have the best gossip. Stay quiet."

I don't know any of the maids well enough yet to recognize their voices, but Irina's excited smile flips into a frown as we listen.

"She's rather plain," one woman says.

"*Plain*?" Another squawks. "She's unseemly and dull. The pup followed Irina around like an orphaned hound."

The women break into laughter while my cheeks bloom red from embarrassment. They don't need to say my name for me to realize I am the topic of their conversation.

"It doesn't matter," the first voice adds. "Finnian is obviously still in love with you. Why would he be so obvious with her beforehand? He wanted you to see him."

"Fuck," Irina mutters.

I pull Irina's hand away from my mouth. "*Still* in love with her?" I squeak.

The second woman sighs. "He nearly admitted it last night

before he left. He almost kissed me, but I couldn't do that to Darius."

My heart sinks into my stomach, deflated.

Irina raises and leans closer to better hear them, but I wish to find a way out the window and disappear. It was foolish of me to fall into a trap he laid for many others before me.

I'm nothing more than a challenge for him.

"Well, would you? If Finnian truly wanted to be with you again, would you leave Darius?"

"Maybe." I could hear the smugness in her voice. "We were good together in *every* way. I can't imagine that peasant girl could satisfy him like I did. Gods, the way he used to beg for me."

I'm utterly nauseous and devastated, yet not wholly surprised. I've been told my entire life I won't be enough for anyone, and I'm already aware of his experiences with women compared to my experiences with no one at all.

It was daft of me to believe otherwise.

Irina moved to stand, but I grabbed her arm and shook my head. With a stern look, she pinches my chin between her fingers. "Listen to me, doe. *You* decide how people treat you. If you take this from them now, you set a standard for the rest."

She releases me and takes my hand to pull me up, but my eagerness to find them is a drop in her overfilled bucket.

I trail behind her with my spine straight but seconds away from cracking.

Irina locates them quickly. "You sniveling little weasels."

"Irina!" One of them gasps.

Holding her chin high, Irina steps forward. I linger behind her, exchanging looks with the redhead from Tea, who doesn't look the least guilty about what she said.

"Spread all the lies you need, Agnes." Irina focuses on the same woman as me, so Agnes must be the one from Finnian's past—the one he might still love. "We both know Finnian wouldn't touch you again, even if under the threat of death."

Agnes glowers at Irina.

"As for you,"—Irina whips her head toward the other—"Don't pretend I'm unaware of what the two of you do behind closed doors. Curiosity can only be claimed so many times before it becomes redundant."

"Irina, please," the blonde pleads. "Agnes is engaged to be married, and I'm being courted by a prince."

Irina flips her hair over her shoulder. "You should try both at the same time. It's what I do. If you need someone to talk about, brag about my scandalous affairs. Frankly, your shame is disgusting. And your envy is laughable."

Irina prowls closer to Agnes.

Agnes recoils.

"Do you want to know how he feels about you, Agnes? He says you are his biggest regret. He requested your pretentious ass never be allowed in this castle again, so don't be shocked if you're removed. However, I encourage you to stay and watch him marry Elora. I want you to witness the way he looks at her like he never looked at you."

Agnes takes me in from bottom to top with a bored sigh. "Doubtful."

Irina pats her cheek twice to tear her gaze away from me. Agnes' eyes widened. "In two days, you will address Elora as the Princess of Pumpkin Hollow. And one day, the *queen*. And that's if I allow you to keep your tongue. Neither of your lovers will have use for you then, though I can't imagine you know what you're doing anyway."

The color of Agnes' cheeks matches her red hair. "You little—"

Irina *tsks*. "Careful, Agnes." She calls out the word '*peaches*', and a hidden guard steps out from behind a row of tall plants. "I have men in place for wenches like you."

I stare at him in surprise.

Will I always be followed around?

Irina takes my hand. "If you'll excuse us, Finnian requested to see his bride before dinner. We'll see the two of you there."

We leave them gaping and fearful of the man following behind us with a scowl. Irina doesn't seem to mind him as much as Otto, but when I open my mouth to plow her with questions, she stops me and says, "Not until we're behind closed doors."

❧

The second Irina closes the door behind us, I lunge. "Who is she?"

"Elora—"

"No!" I begin untying the laces to the corset, unable to draw in deep breaths since hearing Finnian has been in love before. "I am tired of questions being evaded. That's who he didn't want me to meet, right?"

She cups her forehead in her hand as if a headache is brewing. "Yes."

"Who *is* she?"

"It's complicated." She removed the hoop earrings and tossed them on the entryway table. "They have a history, but it ended years ago. I guarantee everything she said was a lie. He wouldn't have kissed her."

My sweaty hands have made loosening the corset difficult, and Irina comes behind me to assist. "Breathe, Elora."

"Did he love her?"

She leads me into her bedroom, fetches a silk nightgown from the wardrobe, and hands it to me. "They were engaged for six months, but something happened between them, and Finnian called it off."

I slip out of the dress and replace it with the gown. It's still daylight, but I'm tempted to sleep through dinner to avoid seeing Finnian and Agnes in the same room. "What happened between them?"

She takes my hands. "You have every right to know, but he's my brother. I can't tell you what you want to hear. This needs to come from him."

"He didn't even...." I pause and try to suffocate the rising jealousy. "He could have warned me instead of being vague and drunk.

I don't understand him!" Envy is soon replaced by anger. "He likes me, tells me to leave, and teases me. I can't stand him."

Irina looks as defeated as I feel. "It sounds like I'm making excuses for him, but I'm not. He's not always this maddening. Would you like to see him?"

"No. I need space away from him." And I need to stop getting distracted by how my lungs constrict whenever he's near. I didn't come here to fall for him, nor did I ingest a deadly spell that makes me miserable just for him to double my melancholy. "He's too complicated, Irina. I don't know if I can do this."

She squeezes my hand. "You should rest. I need to visit with my mother, but I will return and help you dress for dinner."

"I have too much to fix already. I can't fix him, too." I barely speak above a whisper, my voice betraying me from how badly I wanted to trust him. "I can't compete with her."

Irina pulls the blanket back for me. "No woman should ever have to fix a man, Elora, but Finnian isn't broken. You'll see. Until then, we'll seek revenge by making everyone salivate over you this evening."

I try to smile but am reminded of Regina's final insult. His attention isn't easily kept by someone like me. And if he could leave someone as breathtaking as Agnes, then his parting words of ruining me do not seem like just a threat.

They were a warning.

Twenty-Eight

Dehydration will be what kills me.

With a pounding headache, I slam the door to my private quarters closed. Sweat is pouring off me from alcohol consumption and jousting. Being sober for dinner this evening is unlikely, but when I enter my bedroom, Irina is standing in the middle of a pile of glass shards.

In a pool of my liquor.

Seething, I throw my crumpled shirt at her feet. "What the fuck have you done, Irina?"

"You'll need something larger to wipe this up," she responds dryly.

"I am changing the fucking locks!" I shout, searching my room for the bottles hidden in drawers.

"There's none left, Finn."

I pound a tight fist against my forehead.

Don't kill your sister; don't kill your sister.

Every muscle aches. Nursing them with a cold bath and a bottle of whiskey is needed. "Is there something I can help you with? No? Then get the fuck out, Irina."

"Good. Get fucking angry at me, Finn." She brings out a bottle full of whiskey from behind her back. "Is this what you need, Finnian? Will this solve everything? Hm? Will it help numb you?"

I hold out my hand. "Let me have it, Irina."

"Drinking will not lessen the pain." She kicks the glass at her feet, sending a piece skidding across the floor toward my boots. "It won't erase what he's done. It won't *protect* Elora from him."

"Stop," I growl.

"It won't lessen your feelings for her."

I shake my head, knocking the trinkets off my dresser to let them shatter on the floor. "I don't have any fucking feelings for her!"

"She knows."

The raging heat inside me turns to ice.

"Not everything, but she knows what Agnes meant to you. We overheard a conversation between her and Joan. She claimed you tried to kiss her last night."

I bare my teeth and suck in cold air to soothe the burning in my throat. "I didn't fucking touch her. Does Elora believe her?"

"Does it fucking matter?" She shrugs a shoulder. "You don't care about her, right? Elora doesn't know what to believe, Finn, because you're having a fucking meltdown."

"Give me the fucking bottle, Irina."

"She said you were fine this morning. Why did you show up like that to High Tea?"

"Give me the bottle!" I shout.

"You are hurting both of us!"

I narrow my eyes. "I don't answer to either of you."

"Gods," she mutters, "you prick."

I turn away from the disappointment in her eyes, unable to stomach it.

"We moved past this, Finn."

I don't have an excuse. I can't defend any of my behaviors. Every fiber of my being knows drinking won't change anything—it won't undo signing my name to a betrothal, but the thought of harm coming to Elora because of me is too much to bear.

Irina extends the bottle to me. "Elora doesn't trust you, Finn. I can't keep trying to convince her of something that no longer exists. Take it. If she's going to survive here, I don't have the energy to steer you off this path again. I need to be there for her."

She shoves the bottle against my chest. "I love you, Finn, but you're ruining your chance of finding happiness with her." Her voice shakes. "I'm sorry for what he's done to us, but drowning the memories is only a temporary solution."

I should speak. I need to promise my little sister that I'll protect her and crawl out of this hole again, but no words form.

"Do you like my hair?" she asks.

I arch an eyebrow, bewildered.

"Mother did it."

Slowly, my gaze locks onto hers. She hasn't allowed our mother to touch her hair since she was young. As often as she pretends to not be bothered by the rumors surrounding her, shame has prevented her from becoming too close to Honora. Fearing the truth has kept a solid wall between them.

"You have two options, Finn. You can take this bottle and numb your feelings for Elora."

I turn my head away.

"Or you can move forward. If you don't,"—she places the bottle on the dresser behind me—"then Jasper will continue to win every time. This is what he wanted, Finn. You are a chess piece."

"Elora isn't a game," I say. "I'm not gambling her."

Irina steps away from me. "She's worth the risk, but if you're going to continue being a man unworthy of realizing that, I will protect her from you." Then, she leaves me.

My mouth dries from the threat.

Irina has always been my ally.

I've always protected her, but now she wants to protect someone from *me*. If she believes I'm the monster, arriving at dinner in complete form won't surprise her.

Grabbing the bottle, I twist the cap off and down half while undressing, nearly spitting some out when I slice my foot on a piece of broken glass. Drops of blood trail behind me as I limp out of my bedroom to curse my way to the tub.

But something small catches my eye in the entryway, and I amble over. A small wooden box with a painted red bow sits alone on the entryway table, and I continue drinking while flipping the lid off. A small note sits atop a gingerbread cookie topped with vanilla cream.

Scrawled in dainty penmanship, the ink blotchy from a trembling hand, a message with Elora's name signed to it makes me lower the bottle. I blink to clear the glaze from my eyes and lift the note to read it.

> *Rhoadie told me a secret. A mysterious change order for our wedding cake was unsigned. I wondered who it was, but the stranger wanted gingerbread.*
>
> *I baked this for High Tea but snuck an extra. (No poison, I promise) Enjoy xx Elora*

Grinning, I drop the paper to the table and place the bottle beside it. The heavy buzz from consuming nearly all of the liquor frustrates me when the first bite of the cookie tastes more like whiskey than gingerbread. She baked this for me, and I can't even fucking taste it.

A mirror hanging above the table reflects a stranger staring back —a man I released years ago when Irina approached me, upset about how drinking was changing me.

I drag a hand down the stubble on my chin and try to rub the red from my bloodshot eyes.

Elora came here to risk everything. The least I could do in return is to be a solid partner for her to lean on. And a brother Irina can rely on and trust.

Grabbing the bottle, I jog to the spill on the floor and pour the remaining contents out. I drop the bottle and release a deep breath when it shatters at my feet.

I ended up cutting my finger on the glass while cleaning the liquor, which seemed a fitting punishment for my behavior. Knowing Irina, she purposely planned for that, hoping it would sober me, or she hoped I'd arrive at dinner limping and handless.

Either way, the little rat was right.

It took two baths to clean the sweat from my body and smell decent. I ran out of time to shave, but a quick nap calmed my inflamed eyes. With a clearer mind, I will walk into the Great Hall as the man my family needs to be. I won't be able to speak with Elora until after dinner, but she'll hear an apology from me before the night's end.

Since wedding traditions are heavily followed, the entire table will be set with name cards. With my parents at each end of the table, the importance of titles will start on either side of them and dwindle to the middle, leaving Elora in the very center while I sit beside my father. Irina will be with our mother, which means Elora will be with....

Fuck, Beau and Gabriel.

Gabriel is fine, but I'm not looking forward to watching her interact with him all night. He's a prince in another kingdom—one adopting democracy and leaning away from a reigning monarchy, much to Jasper's disapproval—younger than me and known widely for his charm. Protecting her means keeping my feelings for her hidden from Jasper, but I don't know how well I'll do if another man touches her.

It has become evident that Elora doesn't know how genuinely, naturally lovely she is, and men stare at her each time I take her anywhere, which makes me *irate*.

Adjusting my navy dinner jacket sleeves, I roll my neck and steel my spine before strolling inside the Great Hall. Nearly everyone waits behind their chairs, quietly conversing amongst one another while I search for Elora.

Irina catches my gaze.

I wink.

Her shoulders loosen from the weight I've placed upon her,

but her relaxed smile turns into a mischievous grin when she tilts her head toward Elora's empty chair.

I'm unsure how to dissect that, but she's the only one missing from the table. I mouthed, '*Where is she?*' to Irina, but she shrugged her lie.

I shift my gaze to find the heated stare on my neck, landing squarely on Agnes. Her lips curl into a seductive smile while my eyes narrow into pure hatred. If I lose Elora because of her, I will find a reason for Jasper to invade their kingdom—a battle I will readily partake in.

Beau's father lifts his mug from the table to take a sip of ale. "Where's your blushing bride, Prince Finnian? The smell of duck is a cruel form of torture."

Chuckling, I'm about to spew an excuse for her when gasps and audible murmurs fill the expansive hall. I turn my head to find what has grabbed their attention.

Not what. *Who*.

I stop breathing. My chest tightens from the lack of oxygen, but my only currently working function, *sight*, is zeroed in on the doorway, my knuckles white around the back of my chair.

Elora stands at the front of the room, her chin high and lacking her typical nervous fidgeting. And she allows us to take her in, remaining still until every set of eyes locates her. She wants their attention. And she has mine undivided.

Curls fall in soft waves down her shoulders and back, golden in the soft glow of the hall. The natural blush of her cheeks matches her stained, creamy pink lips. Her velvety porcelain skin is entirely on display beneath a dress much too short—a popular style that has made its way into our kingdom and somehow onto my bride in front of salivating princes.

She is as delicate as a dancer on stage, a luxury banned from our realm, but events I've seen in other places. She reminds me of the gentle and elegant women in pink tulle and oddly-shaped shoes. And painstakingly beautiful.

Her untouchable rarity suffocates me.

And she won't fucking look at me. I silently beg for just one glance. Just one second. If she'll just look at me, she won't question my devotion to this—to her.

Barely reaching her knees, the soft blue dress emphasizes her graceful steps to the table. Every inch of her is poised. My chest swells with pride, but I struggle to swallow from her bare shoulders. She's commanding the entire room.

Not one person speaks; not one man looks away from her, giving me time to create a list of which to hurt later. Women can't seem to decipher between their envy and intrigue. And I stand amongst others who now want what's mine.

I shouldn't break protocol, but I move away from my chair and ignore my father's sharp whisper of protest to meet Elora before she reaches her chair.

I clear my throat. "Elora."

Her expression doesn't change, but I've been around her enough to recognize the change in her eyes from tenderness to fury. "Lord Finnian," she greets with a bite.

I can't help but grin at her anger.

This is my favorite way to play with her.

I step closer, but she doesn't flinch or change her posture. Her breathing doesn't hitch. Fuck, is the damage between us irreparable?

With the tip of my finger, I lift her chin.

Her lips purse.

"Thank you for my treat," I say.

She doesn't soften. "I heard bread is great for soaking up alcohol."

Irina snorts from where she's eavesdropping while I bite back a laugh. "May I escort you to your seat, little doe?"

As addicted as I am to liquor, her craving to be stubborn might be stronger. Her throat bobs from undoubtedly swallowing an insult, but she nods and clasps her hands at her waist to prevent me from taking her hand.

I find the small of her back instead, stealing a look at the feel of bare skin against my palm.

Her entire lower back is exposed.

I pin a glare on Irina. She *smirks.*

I form a tight smile, speaking through clenched teeth when I ask Elora, "Did you know I can request you change your dress?"

Unfazed, she replies, "I am only required to follow orders given by the king. And last I checked, men who control their wives are chauvinist, but as the trunk so the branch...."

My determination to earn her forgiveness is tinged with annoyance. I have half a mind to throw her over my shoulder and carry her out since I can't fight with her in front of Jasper. "Take my jacket then, you little gourd."

"No."

I roll my neck. "We'll speak about this after dinner."

"No, we won't." Steadfast, she twists the dagger lodged in my chest. "I refuse to be alone with you ever again."

My smile falls.

Pulling out her chair for her to sit is simply me going through the motions; her introductions to Beau and Gabriel are nothing more than noise as I circle the table to sit.

I've broken her trust too many times. And I watch in agony as the woman I'm falling for smiles at another man.

Dining is slow torture.

My attention continuously shifts between Elora and the men surrounding me. Spite sickens me each time she laughs at something Beau says, and I nearly stand when Gabriel retrieves a crumb from her hair. And she never looks my way—not once. I've been interrupted twice by her laughter so far, needing to clench my fists under the table to keep from lodging a knife in Beau's windpipe.

And since I can't drink, each feeling is heightened. The self-control I'm exhibiting should make me a god amongst men. Fucking statues should be erected in my honor.

My mother has taken notice of my displeasure, but her only way of consoling me is subtly nodding toward my father to remind me that if I do kill our guests, Jasper might realize I more than tolerate his investment.

Gabriel's father, Richmond, tilts his mug in Elora's direction, allowing me to stare at her for another moment. "She's adjusting well," he says.

"She is," I respond, though my tone is clipped.

"Remind me who her father is?"

"Was," I correct. "The Prince of Ashbury before we took it. Harry Termane."

"May he Rest in Peace," my father quips, raising his empty mug to knock against my full one. "Harry worked for me. He spoke very highly of his daughter."

Elora has gone silent, pretending to listen to Beau while slightly tipping her head toward us. Gabriel's father inquires what Harry did for Jasper, and Elora's gaze shifts to him. With the faeries remaining a secret, I'm also curious about which lie he'll tell. Jasper switches our mugs and takes a long draw from mine, delaying.

"Distribution," I say. "He delivered pails of coal to our residents."

Jasper coughs from inhaling ale too quickly.

Beau's father leans forward. "You mine your own coal?"

I nod. "We do. We have line workers in Ashbury."

"I wasn't aware, either." Richmond points a finger at my father. "Perhaps we can discuss trades. Our coal is delivered on trade routes in bulk shipments and costs a fortune."

Panic crossed Elora's face, and the involuntary shaking of her head had me leaning forward to try to grab her attention.

Jasper acknowledges Richmond with a raised mug. "It is something to discuss after the wedding."

Jasper would never share the easy access to coal, but Elora's reaction has sparked my curiosity. Why wouldn't she want the faeries to provide coal for another kingdom?

Unless it simply stems from possessiveness.

She believes the faeries belong to her, but undoubtedly, if we offer to increase their benefits, she wouldn't deny them the opportunity. Approaching that idea could work if I cannot get back into her good graces naturally.

Annoyed that her attention has drifted away, Beau holds a piece of pumpkin pie in front of her nose. She jerks back and politely declines, but he inches closer, encouraging her to bite. She waves a hand in front of her face to signal him to stop, but he doesn't.

"She declined, Beau."

My words left my mouth sharper than intended and gathered the attention of every man, so I doubled down. "When my bride refuses you, you listen and obey."

Beau drops the pie to his plate and dusts his fingers off with a smug grin. "You gave her to me for the night. Go back to your conversations of trading while I entertain your bride."

Elora scowls at him.

"Women aren't given, Beau. They're earned. Only men understand that, but you've yet to leave the nursery." I glance at Elora. "Darling, Beau is used to taking what he wants, which is why his father has been unable to secure a bride for him."

Beau's father begins to argue in defense, but I don't look at him when I ask, "Am I wrong?" *Silence.* "I didn't think so."

Jasper chuckles. Bastard or not, he understands pride. And whether she forgives me or not, Elora will be my wife, and I will prevent boys like Beau from bothering her.

Elora finally looks at me.

But this is the second time I've embarrassed Beau—now in front of a beautiful woman. "Interesting opinion, Finnian." His grin holds a challenge. "Does that mean Elora knows all the women you've *earned*?"

And I lost her.

Twenty-Nine

Satisfied by Elora's refusal to acknowledge I exist after calling her name, Beau leans back in his chair and chugs the remainder of his ale. And when the women stand to retire to their quarters for the evening, Elora is at Irina's side instantly, back to ignoring me, even when I nearly beg for her to stay despite my father being beside me.

The men usually stay behind to drink until sunrise, but I've already worked out my excuse for leaving early. "As much as I'd like to stay, I must prepare the horses for the daylight ride tomorrow morning," I say, pretending to be dreadfully upset.

I stand slowly to give weight to my reluctance to depart while the men encourage me to stay and drink. "Someone has to be responsible," I jest, slapping Jasper's shoulder. "I expect all of you there in the morning, or you forfeit your bets."

The slow ride through the countryside always ends with a race, and bets are collected afterward, whether they show up or not. Most of them won't wake up after a night of drinking, so I look forward to taking their gold.

"I'll be there," Beau says.

"Hear that, boys? Beau volunteered to be the ass." I round the table, grinning when their exuberant, drunken bellows strengthen from fresh refills. "I'll let you debate which one will ride him."

Leaving them on a high note will please my father and excuse my absence.

Most women remain huddled together to chat, but Irina and Elora have disappeared. Luckily, I know Irina's patterns like the back of my hand. Knowing Jasper won't notice if she leaves tonight, she'll show Elora where she keeps extra clothing sets for nights she escapes undetected.

I dip into the hallway.

When we were young, we would choose a room on the opposite side of the castle and separate to see who could get there first. We played it so often that we started blindfolding each other after learning each corridor. Irina favored the darkest passageways, but the one I discovered to the smallest library was the fastest. If I've assumed correctly about their plans, I'll beat them there.

Irina chose the library on the lowest level of the castle to hide her stash. The door in the back of the room leads to a staircase into the basement, giving her a smooth exit. Bright beams of moonlight cut through the small library windows, assuring I don't trip on strewn books.

I haven't stepped foot in this library for a long time, but remember that Irina always hides her things in the very last row of bookcases, on the bottom shelf, in the back corner.

I grunt when crouching but find her traveling clothes folded neatly and untouched.

Lurking in a dark corner while waiting for them isn't a level of desperation I've reached yet, so I choose a table in the middle of the room to sit and ignite a gas lamp.

I spend a few moments flipping idly through a book, not paying attention to the words, and fidgeting nervously. Knowing Irina, she is most likely forcing Elora to try and find the library to better learn the layout of the castle, but waiting for them is akin to a starved dog waiting for meat. I want to devour the lost, directionless little doe.

A familiar voice attached to a silhouette moves inside the library, drawing my attention from the book I'm not reading. "I remember when you brought me in here. Do you?"

I drag a hand down my face. "You followed me here? What the fuck, Agnes?"

She brushes the spines of books while creeping closer. "I thought that's what you wanted. You're sitting at the same table—"

"Stop," I grumble, unwilling to relive tainted memories of me and her together. "I haven't said a word to you all evening." I keep the table between us when I stand, watching the doorway for Elora. It won't help me earn her forgiveness if she walks in to see me in a dark room with Agnes.

"I just want to talk to you, Finnian."

"There's nothing to fucking say!" I shout in a whisper. "I'm marrying Elora, Agnes. You need to leave me alone. Go talk to Beau if you're so fucking starved for attention."

She rounds the table. I backed away.

"Do you ever think about me?" She sighs longingly. "Do you remember how good we used to be together? It can be that way again. I would leave him for you."

I shake my head. "I don't think about you, Agnes. I stopped long ago."

I flinch when her hand touches my chest. "I think about you every day, Finn."

I grab her shoulders to prevent her from coming any closer. "You made your choice, Agnes. You chose Darius. I respected that. You owe me the same respect."

"I made a mistake," she whispers, her voice straining. "I need you. I want *you*."

Denial is at the tip of my tongue when my head snaps toward the door. Agnes takes the temporary distraction to lunge forward and throw her arms around my neck, pressing her lips to mine.

My eyes close instinctively but widen as I jerk my head away so quickly that it slams into the wall behind me. But through the pain and uncentered vision, I see her.

"Elora, this isn't what you think—"

She's gone before I can finish.

Irina blinks at me in surprise before chasing after her, and I try peeling Agnes off me. She grips my shirt to hold me still, trying to reason with me, bringing up memories I can't recall. It takes less than a minute to free myself before I run after Elora, taking the stairs two at a time to Irina's wing.

The door to Irina's quarters slams shut and locks right before I jiggle the doorknob. "Elora!" I shout, pounding on the door. "Irina, let me in. That wasn't.... I wasn't.... she just...."

Nothing I say will convince either of them right now. "I'm going to find a fucking key!" I yell.

That's a lie. I don't know who to ask for a key. I haven't even figured out how Irina procures keys to my quarters.

My forehead *thumps* against the door. "Elora, please. Please talk to me. I was waiting for you."

I'm met with silence.

"Irina," I try next, "Irina, you know me. I didn't ask her to follow me into the library. Irina, I'm asking you as your brother. Open the door."

I fall forward when the door flies open, but Irina shoves me back. I try to step inside, but she doesn't budge.

"Irina, let me talk to her."

"No."

"Hades, did you teach Elora that word?" I look over her head to try and spot Elora. "Irina, I don't want Agnes. You know that."

"It doesn't matter what I think, Finn."

"I know. I know I've fucked up." Anguish coats my voice. "I just want to speak with her."

She shakes her head.

I hit the wall. "What happened to you always being on my side?"

"I am on your side, but you're being an idiot!" Her voice carries and will give the maids something to talk about. "She needs time, Finn. You need to leave."

"We don't have time!" I turn away to pace. "We're getting married in two days, Irina. I won't wait until we meet at the altar to speak to her. Just let me *in.*"

Irina stepped into the hallway and closed the door behind her, doing the opposite of what I asked. "I don't know what's going on between you and Agnes—"

"Nothing," I whisper, falling against the wall. "You have to believe me, Irina."

Irina wholeheartedly believes she can tell when I'm lying, so I steadily hold her gaze.

Finally, she sighs. "I believe you, but gods, Finnian, she doesn't want to see you, and I won't force her. I'll see what I can smooth over, but I'm getting too old for your antics."

I scoff. "I'm chasing Elora like an infatuated boy would do when they have a crush on someone and want to stab them with wooden swords." I pause. "Would that work?"

Irina rolls her eyes but grins. "Come back in the morning. Saddle the horses and stop by after the ride. We'll be awake."

I hesitate and consider arguing more but relent with a nod. "Forget-Me-Not flowers and warmth help her sleep. Take her to the arboretum if she struggles with her nightmares."

Irina softens. "I will talk to her, Finn."

I feel the need to reassure her. "I'm not Jasper, Irina. I'll never do to her what he's done to Mother."

"Finn," she murmurs, palming my cheek. "I know that. Give her a little time, okay? She's learning more about us than she bargained for." She turned to leave me with a half-hearted smile and opened the door a sliver.

"Irina?"

She glances at me over her shoulder.

"Will you tell her how beautiful she looked tonight?"

She winks at me. "You just did."

Opening her door just enough to see inside, I lock eyes with

Elora as she waits for Irina to return. I don't move from the wall for fear of scaring her away, but I try to convey as much as I can in the shared look between us.

I optimistically wish for forgiveness, but her wistful stare holds nothing but regretful longing.

❧

After staying overnight in Major's stall and using one of his blankets as a pillow, I was discovered by more men than I anticipated. I ended up knocking on Irina's door twice overnight. She finally threatened to shove me off the balcony if I didn't allow them to sleep. The proximity between our wings was too tempting, so I slept near the only creature that could stand me.

We had just enough horses for the men sober enough to try their hand at winning the bottomless amount in the earnings pool. Richmond was the only one who gave Major a genuine challenge, but we pulled ahead in the end. I didn't spend months breaking and training Major to lose races. He was bred for speed.

But when I inquired where Gabriel was, he hemmed and hawed unconvincingly. At first, I thought maybe Beau had killed him while drunk, but then I remembered the way Elora had smiled at him during dinner.

Major was panting when we returned to his stall, huffing at me while waiting for me to refill his water trough. I didn't stick around any longer, immediately jogging back to the castle.

I'm sweating and smell of horse while banging on Irina's door until she opens, cursing at me.

"Where is she?"

Irina grimaces. "I didn't know. Neither did she."

I clench my fists. "Know *what*?"

She encouraged me to come inside and closed the door behind me. "At dinner, Gabriel asked Elora to give him a tour of Pumpkin Hollow. She declined since she doesn't know it well enough yet."

I follow her to the terrace, one step away from bolting out the door again to find them.

"This morning, before the ride, Jasper came to my door and demanded Elora accompany Gabriel to town."

If Irina's balcony wasn't so high off the ground, I would jump off to find Elora. "Why would he do that? Is he planning to negate our contract for her to marry Gabriel instead?"

Exasperated, Irina sighs at me. "That's a quick and overdramatic conclusion. No, Finn. Gods." She rolls her eyes. "Last night, Jasper learned that Richmond has access to shipments of cannabis since their kingdom has its own port. But thanks to *you*, he's only willing to trade with us for coal. Jasper doesn't want anyone to have access to the faeries."

"And Elora agreed to go." I finished for her. "What did he require her to give him in exchange?"

"Attention and nothing more. He won't run the risk of rumors spreading that Elora is unfaithful to you a day before your wedding. That would cause nothing short of mayhem. And if it helps, Elora did ask me how I thought you'd react."

I uselessly search the crowd. We're far too high to find her down below. "How long will she be gone?"

"Until the gathering this evening."

I bark a laugh. "No. She is not staying with him all fucking day."

Irina clicks her tongue with a sly grin. "I guess we need to find her."

With Jasper retiring to bed after drinking all night, men weren't given orders to follow Irina. Dressed in dark, hooded cloaks, we move swiftly through town to locate Elora. She isn't in any danger with Gabriel, but I'm uncomfortable with how freely my father gave her away to be used.

"How did she sleep?"

"She didn't," she mutters. "She woke up screaming and drenched in sweat twice. She said they're getting harder to wake up from."

I frown. "Maybe we should speak with the faeries."

"She did. Azrea told her the male she's dreaming about no longer exists, but I'm not entirely sure she was truthful."

Irina goes uncharacteristically quiet and furrows her brow.

I give her a sidelong glance. "Irina, what?"

"Something happened between them. I left her alone with them for only a few moments, but she came out upset. She hasn't asked to see them since. And she said something that afternoon before catching herself. She made it seem like something transpired to *make* these dreams happen, but she didn't want me to know."

I internalized what she said. It does seem abnormal for Elora to not ask to see the faeries after speaking about them so lovingly, but unless they somehow transferred magic to her, I don't know what could've happened to cause her nightmares. And as protective as she is over them, I doubt she'd tell me if I asked.

"How was Cedric around her?"

We exchange a knowing look, but Irina's is paired with a wide grin, while mine is tension-filled. "You can't admit it to yourself, can you?" she asks.

I fixate my gaze elsewhere to ignore her probing question. "Let's just find her."

"I already did. We've been following her."

I search the crowd before us, then locate Elora in the mix. She's laughing at something Gabriel is saying to her but shaking her head as he points to the flower shoppe.

"How sweet," Irina taunts, "he wants to buy flowers for her. Which do you think he'll choose?"

"He keeps glancing down at her legs," I growl, my jaw clicking with tension. "I need you to go over there."

Elora is wearing another dress that is too short for my liking. It's maroon, tight, and more than pleasing to the eye. Her hair is half up, the rest hanging freely over her shoulders and down her back. From where I'm standing, it looks as if Irina tried to put a red stain on her lips again, but it has faded from Elora trying to wipe it off. "Why must you insist on torturing me this way? Stop giving her those dresses."

"She's a doll," Irina retorts. "I want to dress her like one. Besides, if women see her wearing that style, they'll adopt it, too. I've grown bored of being the only scandalous one."

I roll my neck to loosen the stiffness and flex my hands. "You couldn't have fucking told me where she was?"

"Where's the fun in that?" Irina shoves her hood off and confidently approaches Elora, grandly gesturing toward the castle and motioning for Elora to follow her.

Gabriel doesn't hide his disappointment when Elora apologizes for shortening their outing. Irina takes her hand, and Elora barely has time to finish her sentence before being pulled away. I watch Gabriel stare after her, talk myself out of strangling him, and then turn away before Elora can see me.

Weaving through the crowd, I enter the bakery. Rhoadie agreed beforehand to let us speak with Elora privately in the backroom. And this way, she can't run away from me.

I remove my hood and walk straight through the front room until I'm standing in a space no bigger than a pantry with flour particles floating through the air and sticking to the dark cloak. I hear Irina's rowdy greetings and Elora's confused questions before she's shoved inside with me.

"Elora was being watched," Irina says from the doorway. "We'll need to return soon, and she can feign illness to explain why she left early. Be quick."

Irina leaves the door partially open to allow light to filter inside but gives us privacy, though I'm positive she'll remain close by to eavesdrop. My thoughts are erratic at best. I rub my neck, forgetting everything I wanted to say to Elora.

"You smell like Major," she mutters.

"I know. I won the race."

She lifts an unimpressed eyebrow.

I clear my throat. "I didn't want to kiss her, Elora. I didn't ask her to come to the library."

Her bravado wavers when her eyes lower to my chest. "You don't owe me an explanation."

I itch to touch her. "I do. I should've told you about Agnes yesterday, and that's why I returned before the others, but I became distracted. It's no excuse, Elora. And I shouldn't have come to you after drinking. It only made it worse. It always does."

I force a calm demeanor, but the vacancy of her stare adds to my hopelessness. "I meant what I said yesterday. There won't be anyone else. Please believe me."

She drags her fingertips back and forth across her forehead. "Finnian, I can't talk about this. Yesterday morning was,"—she blinks and covers the reddening of her cheeks with her hands—"I couldn't wait to see you again."

I try to contain my smile but fail miserably.

"But then, you told me I should've never come here." She wraps her arms around her waist. "And I was willing to move past that until I overheard Agnes in the arboretum."

"I did not try to kiss her," I add quickly. "Elora, I swear. I told her I didn't want her."

"But you let me walk in there, Finnian." She turns away slightly. "You didn't warn me. You didn't even try to find me yesterday afterward to explain. And that spoke for you."

My heart thuds dully in my chest.

"And then, I saw the kiss...." Her voice was raspy, and she grasped her throat. "And that felt...."

"Awful," I finished for her. "It felt like you couldn't breathe. It's how I felt when you told me not to call you Ellie, but you didn't flinch when Cedric did. That's how I felt, Elora."

Surprise lights her eyes, but she shakes her head. "I'm sorry about that, Finnian. Cedric has called me that for a very long time. Azrea uses it, too. But I didn't hide Cedric from you because nothing happened between us. Agnes was supposed to be your wife. There is a very intimate history between you."

"History," I repeat, giving in and reaching for her. With an arm around her waist, I pull her against me. "It's history, Elora. I don't have feelings for Agnes. I didn't invite her here."

Her touch is featherlight against my chest. She presses her forehead against my sternum and inhales a shaky breath. I use my other hand to tangle in her hair, gently tugging until she peers up at me. "I will be loyal to you," I promise her.

"Finnian—"

Every logical thought drowns from my need to taste her again, and I lean down before she can finish to capture her lips with mine. My memory of kissing her must've shielded me from how much I craved her again. I've tried so hard to numb the thoughts of her that holding her against me now makes every nerve ending stir and ache for her.

Before I can lose myself, I break the kiss but linger close. "Do you still hate me?"

"Yes," she breathes.

I use the grip on her hair to press her lips to mine again. This kiss isn't like our first—it's not purely from heat and tension, but the need I have to explore her.

I move slowly. Softly.

I stroke her bottom lip with the tip of my tongue, and the breathy whimper that leaves her has me backing her up until I can close the door and press her against it.

I won't pull away this time. I will not be the one to stop. Fighting my feelings for her has been like attempting to breathe underwater. I burn for her like the flames she described at breakfast mornings ago—unyielding.

Her lips part, and her tongue brushes against mine. Pleasure floods my body. I don't want to stop kissing her, but I want to show her how good I can make her feel.

My mouth leaves hers to travel down. I nip at her jaw and soothe the bite with my tongue. Her back bows in response, her gasp urging me to continue. I sweep the hair off her left shoulder and trail my lips down her throat until I can suck the skin where her shoulder meets.

She tilts her head to allow me more access, my name leaving her lips in a strained whisper. I won't be able to stop now; I've freed myself from the confines and will always want her as soon as I see her.

I bring her closer until she's molded against me, releasing her skin to drag my teeth across her bottom lip. My grip on her becomes more desperate and possessive every second that passes.

My cock pulses against her. I don't want the first time I taste her to be in the backroom of a bakery, but I also won't stop until she asks.

When I throb again, she lowers her chin to look between our bodies. And when she applies pressure between our hips, I groan her name. She does it again and gasps when I slide my tongue into her mouth, frenzied with need.

She lifts to her toes to slide her hands into my hair, breathless when she pulls away. "Finnian, I—"

"I know," I rasp.

She's never done this before, which adds to my desire to claim her. I want her to be mine—I want to take everything she's willing to give me, but not here.

When she presses against me again, my fingers bruise her waist when I shove her against the door to afford inches between us. "Stop," I warn gently. "My self-control is wavering with you."

She bites the corner of her lip with a slow-glowing grin. "Sorry," she whispers.

"Fuck, don't be."

"Can you kiss me?"

I touch my lips to hers but quickly pull away. "No," I reply with a frustrated sigh.

"Can I kiss *you*?"

I tip my head back with a genuine laugh, pinching her sides until she curses at me. "Gods, stop doing that," she snaps, but then slides her hands down my chest and stomach until she stops dangerously close to the point of no return. "I'm still upset with you."

I nod, caressing her sides. "I like the way you make me earn your forgiveness."

"So do I."

"Stay upset with me."

"You make it easy."

Irina shouts at us through the door to stop contaminating the flour and come out. Elora buries her head against my chest when I laugh and rub her back. "Believe me, Irina has done much worse. I'll tell you about the bell tower."

"Fuck you," Irina calls through the door.

I pull Elora off the door, but she lunges for me and kisses me again. I grab her chin and pry her off with a shake of my head. "Stop, little doe. I'm trying to be honorable."

"I'll stop," she says with squished cheeks.

But I can't stop and kiss her again until Irina busts inside with a dramatic sigh. "Get *out*," she demands.

The gentleman Rhoadie is, he knowingly smiles at me but says nothing about it. Irina, however, slaps my arm. "Gods, Finn, how old are you? Her dress won't cover that."

Elora looks down at her shoulder in horror and slaps her palm across it. "Finnian!"

A red patch of skin with bite marks shines boldly.

I slide my arm over Elora's shoulders. "Accompany another man alone and see what happens, Elora. That's only a warning."

She sighs in satisfaction. "Work on your threats."

Thirty

Irina passed her cloak to me before we left the bakery, and Finnian has continuously brooded about it. He's become more evident with his touching—sliding his hand underneath the cloak to graze my lower back until Irina shoved him away. He grumbled something before settling for holding my hand.

To the untrained eye, Finnian and Irina appear casual and confident while leading me back to the castle, but I recognize their cautious stares and darting looks as they search for the undercover men. Finnian explained that since Jasper hadn't yet chosen who would be assigned to me, Irina's bodyguards watched me this afternoon since Jasper didn't anticipate Irina ruining my outing with Gabriel.

Finnian and Irina's sighs of relief, when we stroll through the castle doors, are swallowed when the two guards we slipped into converge behind us. A man I haven't met rounds the corner to stand before us, blocking us from going further.

Dressed in a fine tunic, the sash across his chest boasts an embroidered family crest. He bows to Irina and Finnian before focusing solely on me. Finnian squeezes my hand before he drops it but pinches the cloak to drag me closer to him. The warmth from his hand in mine comforted me, but I'm slowly beginning to understand their fears of allowing someone to get too close.

My father might not've been a man of honor, but I never feared him.

I can count myself lucky for that.

"We have not been introduced, Miss Elora." He extends his hand to me. "I am Bartholomew, one of the kingdom's ambassadors, but you may call me Bart."

If being polite will save my head, I will be as sweet as.... Well, pumpkin pie.

I place both of my hands around his and smile brightly. "So wonderful to meet you, Bart."

Bart's recognition of me is given away when a soft smile appears. "You look just like your mother," he says.

My forced smile falters. "Did you meet her?"

Bart dips his head in a deep nod. "Oh, yes, years ago. I was in Ashbury after it fell to count the remaining residents and take their names. It was rather warm since the faeries had just arrived. Your mother invited me inside for fresh water."

The thought of my mother assisting any of the king's men because of my father's betrayal twists my stomach into knots. She should've been the queen instead of a traitor's wife.

"She wasn't with child yet but spoke fondly of wanting a daughter." He laughs lightly. "I suppose she got her wish."

"Not for long," I murmur. "I was six when she passed from an illness."

Bart's frown deepens to the point of his entire face falling. "I was sorry to hear about her passing."

The lustful and smoky haze that has lived within me since my first kiss with Finnian has overtaken the bitterness of why I came here, but now I've been reminded. "Yes, well, the physician explained that too much soot in her lungs prevented her from breathing correctly. She passed while choking." Those final moments are seared in my memories. "Blood mixed with soot looks like tar, but I doubt you knew that."

"Elora," Irina whispers sorrowfully, "I wasn't aware of how she died."

"No one was ever told the truth about her death by request of the king." I straighten my back when Bart seems to shrink. "Is there something you need from me, sir?"

Bart clears his throat. "King Jasper has sent for you. I will take you to his study."

"I'll accompany her," Finnian states.

Bart rubs his hands together, clearly discomforted by the powerful siblings behind me. "I apologize, Prince Finnian, but I am under strict orders by the king to only bring Miss Elora."

Finnian steps ahead of me, his shoulders rolled back, his expression stern. "No, no, it wasn't a question, Bart. Elora is *my* bride. We will join you in leading her there and remain in the hall while she speaks to my father."

Irina adds, "Lead the way."

We follow Bart up winding staircases and long corridors. Aside from leaving Gabriel in town, I can't think of any reason why the king would want to see me *alone*. Finnian is holding my cloak between his fingers, nearly making me stumble when he yanks me closer and places his mouth against my ear. "Don't volunteer information and *only* answer questions he asks, Elora."

On my other side, Irina's hand appears in front of my face with the jester card between her fingers. I take it, befuddled, until she whispers, "Always remember the true enemy. He's mastered manipulation." She gestures toward Bart. "He turns even the kindest of men upside down."

Was Bart sent to soften me up beforehand?

Can *any* of them be trusted?

We stop abruptly in front of a wide door with carvings of pumpkins etched into the wood. I'm already breathless from their warnings and too many godsdamn stairs. Bart disappears inside to alert the king of my arrival.

"Why didn't you tell us about your mother?"

I shrug at Irina's question. "Could you have changed it if I had?"

"No," Finnian replies, "but I would like to be aware of everything Jasper has done to you."

"Something to look forward to," I quip. "You really can't come in with me?"

Finnian exchanges a look with Irina before nodding at me. "I can try," he says.

"I'll wait out here for you." Irina readjusted my cloak to ensure the mark on my shoulder was well hidden before pinning another glare on her brother. "Trust nothing, Elora."

Finnian's posture is rigid.

Bart reopens the door and requests that I follow him inside, but Finnian stays behind me. Bart doesn't realize it until he turns, jerking his head back slightly. "Prince Finnian—"

"I need to speak with him about something," Finnian says.

Bart, unable to decline a prince's request, bows. "Of course. He'll be right in. Make yourself comfortable, Miss Elora."

That is highly unlikely.

Bart doesn't leave the way we came, disappearing behind a door on the opposite side of the expansive study. I snort, wondering if he did it to escape Finnian and Irina.

Wide yet strangely inviting, the king's study has a long desk covered in scattered papers and notes, sketches of the bridge and mountains pinned on the walls behind it, and bookcases that reach the ceiling on either side.

On the wall behind his desk, something pinned underneath a map catches my eye. I contemplate ignoring it, but my curiosity wins, and I step behind his desk to inspect it.

Nearly completely faded, a painted and detailed portrait of Finnian and Irina depicts them smiling widely, but the joy doesn't seem genuine compared to the downturn of their eyes—almost as if the smiles were painted on after they posed.

"I was ten," Finnian says, placing his hand on my waist, "Irina was six. And we were bribed to stand for it. It was a gift for him from our mother, but he instead asked why he wasn't given a box of his favorite desserts."

I cover the portrait with a frown. It's evident by the wall coverings that Jasper's priorities have never been his children, yet he requires me to give him a grandson to be placed under the same stress and demands as Finnian has been.

Taking Finnian's hand, I pull him with me as I continue touring the study. I study the books on the shelves, reading the spines, hoping to find the book on faerie history Irina mentioned, but I see nothing of interest.

I ask, "Do you have a study?"

"I do," he replies, bringing my hand to his lips. "You'll see it when you move into my quarters tomorrow evening."

My mouth dries. Since our brief discussion in Ashbury, I've not considered where I'll live. And we had agreed I would sleep in the guest room adjacent to his, but now.... will I sleep in the same bed as him?

His deep, throaty chuckle against my fingers draws me from my thoughts. "Don't be nervous, little doe."

"I'm not," I lied. "I just hope you're not a cuddler."

He brushes his lips with the tip of my middle finger. "That would require sleeping, Elora, which I do not plan to do much of if you're in my bed."

It is *solely* because of the enchantment that I bravely taunt him. "And if I'm not in your bed?"

Sliding his hand down to grasp my wrist, he pulls me close enough that our chests touch. "Then, you'll be bent over my desk, little doe, or I'll be on my knees for you while you're pressed against the wall. Do you need to hear more?"

His voice alone is enough to make me pant, but the visuals he's giving me have created a warm liquid between my legs. And when he catches me pressing my hips against his, he grins and lowers his voice into a gravelly whisper, "Are you wet for me, Elora?"

"I.... yes," I breathe, then bravely flaunt a grin, "and cannot wait to see you where you belong."

He cups my throat, leans in to kiss me, and whispers, "And where is that?"

I tilt my head back, allowing him to leave a stream of kisses down my throat where his hand was. "Bowing to me."

His eyes flare when he pulls up, his grip tightens, and he seems one breath away from forgoing this visit to take me somewhere, but the office door opens, and Irina peeks inside. "Finn," she says, ignoring his apparent murderous glare. "Mother needs us."

Finnian shakes his head, but I place my hand against his chest. "Finnian, go. I'm sure she needs assistance with all the preparations for tonight and tomorrow. I'll be all right."

Throwing caution aside, he squeezes my throat in his hand and returns to kiss me. It's wild and passionate, his lips moving quickly against mine but conveying so much more than words could. And when he pulls away, I'm aching *everywhere*.

"Remember my advice," he whispers against my lips. "And find me as soon as you're done."

"I promise," I reply.

The air in the room is suddenly tension-filled as he steps away from me, cursing when Irina snaps her fingers at him. I can't help but laugh, even more so when he throws a crumpled-up piece of paper at her that he swiped from the desk. Irina waves at me, he winks, and then...

I'm alone.

I idly kick my feet while exploring the king's inner sanctum, pausing to admire the realm's map hanging above his mantle. Pumpkin Hollow is substantial in size compared to the outline of Ashbury. The castle of Hogsfeet is drawn beneath the cliffside, but my assumptions of desolation beyond Ashbury are maddeningly confirmed. There is nowhere to escape.

Cracking pops of fire draw my attention to the fireplace. Dwindling flames of purple and orange ebb and flow, soothing me. The heat warms my legs and reminds me of our neglect—years of starvation and confinement.

I blink rapidly as visions of Ashbury morph into a single frame of pitch black. The harder I stare at the flames, the more in-focus the room in my mind becomes. Cries of agony echo through my mind, and I cover my ears, but the noises aren't happening around me.

They're unfolding *within* me.

The half-man, half-skeleton male comes into focus as he strolls to the center of my vision, his head tilting as he seems to stare directly at me. He doesn't speak, but the anguished screams increase.

"Stop," I whisper, squeezing my eyes shut to try and free myself from his grip.

Tormented shrieks claw at my chest until my breathing shorts. I stumble backward against a chair when black cracks shoot across the floor toward my feet. The male says something, asks something, but I can't hear him, I can't....

A strong hand touches my back, jerking me from the vision. My heart pounds in my chest, and my exhales are painful.

"Elora, are you all right?"

I whip my head toward the voice, sight clearing to refocus on the room around me, now *too* warm. "King Jasper," I breathe, "I apologize."

"Sit, sit." He guided me around the chair and assisted me in sitting before pulling another chair beside mine. "I've sent for some water. Deep breaths, Elora."

The screams become a distant memory, but my heart might erupt any second. I wanted to approach this meeting differently. "Thank you." I try to calm my trembling voice with a deep inhale. "I suddenly became very light-headed."

He pats my arm. "Do you often grow ill?"

The last thing I need is for him to believe I'm dying and rid me too soon. "No, only when I haven't eaten."

A servant enters the study with a tray, lowering it at my side. I wait for King Jasper's encouragement before I take the cold mug of water and silently curse my luck. Pumpkin tarts sit prettily on a doily. If I don't eat one, he'll know I lied.

I pop one into my mouth and pretend it's the tastiest treat, and only then does he dismiss the servant with a flick of his wrist. "All better?"

I drown the nauseating tart with a gulp of water. "Yes, thank you."

Standing, he waddles around his desk to sink into the more comfortable chair. Finnian could press a finger to his chest, and he would tumble over from the weight of his belly.

I wonder if prolonged silence is a tactic to force his opponents into speaking first, but I've mastered keeping quiet.

He pushes the papers on his desk into a pile to clear a space for his hands to rest and drums his fingers. "Do you believe I've called you here because of Gabriel?"

I relax my posture to appear comfortable in his presence. "I don't know why you've called me here, Your Majesty."

His full head of long white hair and crumb-filled beard don't hide the years of cruelty his skin portrays. Every line of his face is hardened, and no generosity peeks through. It would crack my chest if Finnian became the man sitting before me.

He's gauging how to interact with me, studying how to pummel through my wall. "The faeries haven't given my men a lick of trouble since your last visit with the princess."

Gods, this is a test.

It always comes down to the faeries.

I need to remain humble. He can't stand if someone believes themselves to be more important than him. "They will always follow orders set forth by their king. I am only useful for keeping them on task."

He wags a finger at me. "I don't believe that's true, Elora."

He is *highly* paranoid. "I don't understand."

He doesn't settle. He switches from waving his hands around to tapping the desk to leaning forward in his chair so far that it squeaks from the weight shift. "I believe you could order them to set fire to Pumpkin Hollow, and they'd obey you. They treat you as they should be treating me. I am their king!"

I place my mug on a small table between the chairs and clasp my hands in my lap. Console him as you would a child, Elora.

"If I may speak freely, Your Majesty?"

He huffs his acknowledgment.

"They would," I admit. "I have built a close relationship with the faeries, though most of them despise all humans. However, they want to survive and remain useful. And I believe we agree that their mining method is much faster than if you had hundreds of men at work. And cheaper."

Keep them alive.

Keep all of them alive.

"And maybe if I asked them, they'd set fire to the monarchy, but you're missing a significant detail, Your Majesty." I keep my tone steady and warm—a soft caress. "Me."

"You?" he grunts.

"Me," I confirm. "I don't want to set fire to our realm. Would I be overjoyed to work with you on giving my people a better chance at survival? Of course. But if not, this is still my home. I would not ask that of the faeries."

His fist thuds against the desk. "I don't know if I can believe you! You could be planning a revolt right underneath my nose." His arguments are entirely irrational. I can barely hold it together —planning a war would give me far too much credit.

"I won't," I assure.

"How can I be sure?"

Admission is the opposite of what Finnian would encourage me to do, but he *did* tell me to answer Jasper's questions.

So, when I shift attention back to the king, I lay the truth at his feet. "Because I am falling for your son, King Jasper. And he would fight for *you*. He is loyal to the crown."

And that is the part of Finnian that I tried to prevent myself from accepting—I don't want him to be faithful to an unjust king.

I want his dedication to be for the greater good. But I would never ask him to abandon his kingdom like my father betrayed mine.

Jasper searches for the lie that he will not find. I am falling for Finnian and becoming attached to Irina. I will help my people, but I plan to do so in a way that doesn't harm them or their mother.

"That is surprising," he finally says.

I want to verbalize my agreement, but less seems is more with him when arguing. He always needs the upper hand, which doesn't come naturally to me, but I'm more fond of my head than I give myself credit for.

"Would you sign your name to it?"

I blink. "Sir?"

"Your name," he emphasizes. "Would you sign your name as proof of your dedication to the Prince of Pumpkin Hollow?"

To protect him from harm? "I would."

A devious, chilling grin replaces his distrustful glare. "I'd like to show you something before you do."

I wasn't left with a choice. After the king called Bart back into the room, who seemed to be *right* behind the door he disappeared through earlier and demanded a contract be drawn immediately, I was instructed to follow Jasper.

A discreet knob beneath a picture frame reveals a hidden passageway into a dark and cold corridor. Holding a lit torch, he instructs me to take his arm. The risk of tripping over my own feet and falling into a pit of serpents sounds more appealing than touching the man who invited my stepsisters into his bed, but the reward would be coming out alive.

Or, so I hoped.

I steal a last glance behind me before the door closes, frowning at Bart's ominous stare. My cloak *whooshes* when the door slams shut, lifting the hem. I've suddenly become grateful for Finnian's mark on my shoulder that led to Irina lending this to me since my unease never sits well with chilly air—the air that doesn't seem to be funneling through; it seems trapped.

The tight corridor would be better suited for a child than two adults barreling through. My elbow or head scrapes against the wall every few steps, but I never make a sound. As terrified as I am, giving him the satisfaction of frightening me is the sliver of defiance I hold close.

"Why is it so cold here?"

Only his grin remains.

His profile appears satanic in the solitary flame. I briefly recap what I learned about the gods. Hades punished souls for trying to escape, similar to the fate bestowed upon anyone under the king's rule. And I willingly agreed to sign mine away for a man I hardly know. I've become the woman I swore I never would—swooning over a pair of hypnotizing blue eyes and a charming smile.

My decisions lately are highly questionable, yet I continue to round corners in a maze of my own making, trapped.

I already fell into the pit of snakes like a starved mouse, believing I could make a difference—*change* them, convince them not to eat me. And now, I'm clutching the King Cobra.

After descending so many steps that my lungs burned, we stopped moving, surrounded by nothing but pitch black. I wrinkle my nose at a foul odor mixing into the air and internally panic when the king steps out of my grasp.

He waves the torch before a door, but I stand deathly still when he opens it and steps inside. Lifting the torch above his head, the fire catches on a bundle of hay and spreads across a hollowed-out carving in the wall, revealing an octagonal room.

The foul stench becomes *unbearable*.

I grab the neckline of my cloak and cover my nose, trying to breathe as infrequently as possible and coughing.

"Follow my voice," he demands.

I look over my shoulder. I could run back, but I couldn't *see* without the torch. And there's the slight chance of him chasing me and burning me alive.

Pinching my nose with the cloak, I obey. I squint my eyes from the illuminating fire above, but it isn't the heat that is making my eyes water. The revolting smell seeped through the cloak as I stepped inside.

He slams the door closed, and I jump and tumble a step to the left.

Something on the ground *rolls*.

Oh, gods.

Oh, gods.

I squeeze my eyes shut.

Don't look down, don't look down.

His lingering presence does not comfort me. It brings a fresh level of doom to my already fragile psyche. "What do you think?" he asks with fucking *delight* in his tone.

He will make me stay here until I open my eyes to find what he has stowed away.

"Don't be shy." He pushes me forward. "I'm dying to hear your thoughts."

Every hair on my body stands.

I tremble uncontrollably.

But I open my eyes and look down.

Terror *shrouds* me. Horror shoves past every good feeling I've ever had and completely overcomes each one until it swallows me whole.

Because it's true.

It was all true.

The King's Collection isn't a rumor.

Because I'm standing in the center of it.

Thirty-One

Piles of skulls cover every square inch of the room except for the small space where my feet are frozen to the floor. Stacked waist-high, hundreds of decomposed heads stare at me—some with eyes, some without. Black sludge drips from those with the skin still intact, but dried black stains have soaked the floor. Clumps of hair hang from eyes and mouths. The top layers of each pile are held up by fully decomposed heads, the skulls entirely gray or black from the lack of blood flow.

I can't make a sound.

I can't even *breathe*.

The only reason I haven't fainted or gagged yet is a combination of shock and the very dim light from the fire above.

"I come down here when I need a reminder of what I've done to keep peace in my realm," he says.

I flinch at his voice and close my eyes. I did what he asked—I looked at his collection. I want out. I *need* out.

A warning like this wasn't required.

"Every member of my court and family has visited," he continues, ignoring my shivers. "Because I'll be damned if my own flesh and blood betray me."

I manage a whimper, chest aching from the idea that Finnian has been forced into this room.

"If someone I have extended graciousness and warmth lies to me..." His cruel and cold-hearted laugh sounds nothing like Finnian's. "Well, this is evidence of what happens. I prefer to keep heads, but I wouldn't mind a set of wings to hang."

Tears run down my cheeks, my words nearly inaudible through a stuttering cry. "I already said I wouldn't lead a revolt!" I turn, but he grabs my shoulder and spins me back.

"Good, that's good." His condescending tone forces a sob to sputter from my lips. "And maybe you believe this is my weapon." I assume he motioned to the piles at my feet when one arm left me. "But, it's not. *Love* is."

What could he possibly know about love? Love isn't shoving your family inside a self-made coffin of skulls. It's not mentally tormenting your son with the beheading of his friend. It isn't locking your daughter away because she wants to live her life outside of this wretched place. And it certainly isn't betraying someone as kind as Honora.

But then, I realized what he meant.

I gave him something to hold over me.

Finnian.

Irina's warning. *Fuck.*

'He doesn't allow anyone to get close to him,' she had said about Finnian because of this—because of the king.

His father threatened him with his sister and mother, the two people in his life he held dearest. And I fell for the same trap. I had no one worth bargaining for until I came here. He must've seen how I stared at Finnian and realized I meant something to him. Oh, gods, what have we done?

The king views the faeries as weapons. He believes if he harms me, they will fight him. And if they fight, my people would follow. But if I care for Finnian...

I would behave.

I cut my strings with Regina only to find a new master. Naively, I thought telling him I cared for his son would be enough

—that he would be satisfied knowing I wouldn't do anything to hurt Finnian.

But Jasper is not a father.

He is a vengeful king who holds all the power—the king who forced his son to watch the beheading of his friend. A king who's kept his daughter locked away.

'Always remember the real enemy.'

'He's mastered manipulation.'

He cares nothing for Finnian's happiness.

And he will dangle his life over me.

"I do hope you understand," he says.

I lower my head in a defeated nod. "Yes," I whisper, "I understand."

My hollow stare remains on the parchment King Jasper is signing with my declaration of allegiance. I'd already signed the marriage certificate a day early, but giving my freedom away wasn't enough for him. He understands better than anyone that marriage won't keep someone loyal.

He wants his threats signed in blood.

I don't even feel the pointed end of a disguised letter opener when Bart slices the tip of my thumb and presses it against the parchment next to the king's signature.

He reads it aloud as I sign, but it doesn't matter.

I lost before I began.

"To sum up," Jasper says. "Any digression against the Kingdom of Pumpkin Hollow or the monarchy is treasonous, and the cost is your life. If I hear even a whisper of a revolt, you will be torn from your bed and sent to the gallows, whether there is a child or not."

A solitary tear rolls down my cheek.

I take the quill and sign my name above my thumbprint. Bart lifts the parchment and waves it in the air for the ink to dry.

"Would you like to discuss your conditions again before you're dismissed?" Jasper asks. "They must be followed."

I shake my head. "No."

"Now, this evening is a celebration!" He comes around the desk to sit on the edge and pulls a cloth from his pocket to press against my bleeding thumb. It isn't an act of care. He doesn't want Finnian alerted of what transpired, which he reminded me of twice.

"After the wedding, you will be given two days alone with Finnian before the time starts." He taps the bottom of my chin. "Chin up, Elora. You're about to become a princess."

At what cost?

"Would you really do it?" I murmur.

He crosses his arms. "Do what?"

"Harm your own son?"

His belly bounces with a laugh. "My preferred way of handling the prince is with mental punishments." He taps his forehead. "I tried physical punishment once, but it is the mind, Elora, the mind that lives with ceaseless, permanent scars long after physical memory fades."

Bart helps me up from the chair. "I will escort you to Prince Finnian and Princess Irina."

"Their mother found a need for them," Jasper replied with a haughty grin, "They will be in her private quarters."

Their mother, not his wife.

The prince, not his son.

I look again at the inked paper on his desk, blotted with my shaky signature, confident that the queen was forced to sign a similar one to protect her children.

"I'll see you this evening, Elora."

I nod before Bart leads me out, but he doesn't take me to Finnian and Irina. Instead, he looks both ways down the corridor before pulling me into a room across the hall.

He closes the door, and I break.

My face, my back, my legs.

Everything gives out as I fall to the floor with desperate, silent screams. Bart lowers and allows me to tumble against him, my tears soaking his shirt. He muffles my noises by turning my head to his chest and holding the back of my head, not encouraging me to stop but shushing me when he worries someone might hear.

"I shouldn't have mentioned Finnian," I cry, stuttering.

"He would've killed you." His whisper is so tiny that my ears strain to hear him. "He needed a way to control you, Elora."

If he forced every member of his family into that morgue, what did he threaten them with?

What is Irina so terrified of losing?

I sniffle. "Why are you telling me this? He thinks it's treasonous to *breathe* near him, so I don't think he'd be okay with you consoling me."

He dabs my eyes with his sleeves. "I promised your mother I would repay her kindness someday, but I never tried. I wasn't supposed to be here today. My original assignment was to serve a visiting royal family, but another adviser took ill. I think your mother was demanding I follow through with my oath."

The thought seems so absurd and wonderful that I laugh through my tears. "If you speak with her, can you request that she get me out of this?"

He nods with a tight smile. We both understand there is no way once the king collects your sworn oath. "I need to get you to the prince, Miss Elora."

I frown. "When was he taken down there, Bart?"

Bart's brow furrows, a pained memory I want no part of giving him pause. "He's forced down there every year." He swallows and lowers his eyes. "He was locked in there once for disobeying an order. The queen stayed outside the door and talked to him until he was released."

I clutch my throat. "How old was he?"

His voice cracks on a broken whisper when he says, "Not old enough."

After providing a cold cloth to calm the blotching on my cheeks and eyes, I follow Bart to the queen's quarters.

Bart knocks on the door and gives me an encouraging smile before dismissing himself with a bow. I inhale deeply and exhale slowly, relaxing my posture and plastering on a carefree smile.

Irina opens the door and lunges for me, pulling me inside to inspect me head-to-toe. "Elora! He kept you for so long. Why?"

Finnian leans against a wall, his head tilted while studying me. I fidget from nerves, convincing myself he can't know me *that* well yet.

Irina snaps her fingers in front of me. "I refuse to become a third in this,"—she gestures between Finnian and me—"whatever this is."

With a fake and breathy laugh, I casually shrug. "He wanted to know how my morning was with Gabriel and went into detail about what will be expected of me with the faeries after I become a princess."

Finnian prowls closer. "Is that all?"

I'm unable to dissect his tone. "That's all."

Irina crosses her arms. "That was a long meeting to discuss something relatively simple."

I lick my lips. "I kept asking questions."

Finnian lifts my chin, and I swallow but hold his gaze. "Are you being honest with me, little doe?"

Admitting the truth will bring you more pain, Finnian. "Yes," I breathe. The lie tastes like ink on my tongue.

"Irina," Queen Honora says, appearing behind Finnian. "Will you fetch Elora's dress for this evening? She can bathe and dress here."

"Can't Finnian do it?" she asks.

"Finnian is busy," he replies with a grin, sliding an arm around me.

Honora sighs. *Deeply*.

"Fine," Irina snaps. "But just so you know, Elora said she'll sleep in my wing every night instead of yours."

I shove a hand through my curls. "Irina!"

She flips her hair over her shoulder and leaves. Finnian pulls me against him with a frown. "Is that true?"

I grimace. "I was upset with you."

His voice deepens into a toe-curling octave. "I think you underestimate how persuasive I can be." He brushes his lips across mine. "And I'd drag you right back. Preferably screaming."

It takes effort to remember we're not alone, but my lack of breathing spurs him to speak more. "Oh, Elora, if it's this easy to bring this reaction out of you by words alone, I'm looking forward..."

"Finnian," his mother interrupts.

I cover my face with both hands while he chuckles and loosens his hold on me. "I'm going, I'm going." He presses his lips against the top of my head but leaves me with a husky promise in my ear, "You won't leave my bed."

I suck in a tight breath when he winks before leaving. But my thoughts of him and the lack of his warmth take me back to the cold room beneath me.

"That wasn't all, was it?" the queen inquires.

I shake my head slightly.

"Oh, Elora." She approaches me like I'm a wounded animal. "What did he say to you?"

I close my eyes. "Horrible things."

"What did you tell him you care about?"

Tearfully, I look at her, unable to say it or tell her the details of what I signed my name to. "I'm so sorry. I'm so sorry."

She embraces me and holds me tightly to her chest, shushing me. "You are not the first to sacrifice yourself for love, nor will you be the last."

I gradually lift my eyes to hers. Something she said caught me off-guard. "Love?"

Cupping my face, she warmly smiles. "Why else?"

I try to shake my head, but I can't move. When... how? My

breathing shallows, my heart palpitates, and my palms sweat because *fuck me* if she's correct.

That wasn't why I came here.

Sacrificing myself for Ashbury and the faeries I was prepared for. I accepted that my life could be a penance for those.

Falling for Finnian deeply enough to fall in line... No, it can't be.

Sacrificing my heart wasn't part of my plan.

And if he's fallen for me, I've risked his heart, too. What would he do if something happened to me? What have I caused?

"I don't know what to do," I whisper.

"You do what I've always done, Elora."

I wait for a way out—a quick solution.

"You bide your time and fight."

❧

After bathing, I insist Irina sit for her hair first and dilly-dally on the queen's terrace, blankly focusing on the crowd moving through town—living their days peacefully, unknowing the truth about the king they served.

Or maybe they do.

Maybe he has something on everyone.

Maybe we're all puppets.

Leaning forward, I notice Finnian in the courtyard, standing patiently while another carriage rolls along. He has dressed for the evening quickly, boasting his required colors of navy, silver, and gold; only the ivory shirt underneath his embellished coattails matches my gown.

Before the guests leave the carriage, which is not a pumpkin, Finnian stills and slowly tilts his head toward where I stand.

I pull the borrowed silky red robe tighter, but the slight shake of his head halts me.

Gods. Here?

He wants me to tease him from multiple stories up in front of complete strangers with my hair wet and skin flushed from a hot bath.

With a glance over my shoulder to ensure Irina is still sitting at the vanity, I bite my lip and return focus to Finnian. I blow out a nervous breath and part the robe just enough to keep my breasts covered but the space between displayed.

If Finnian could be credited for anything, it would be for how distracting he is from the imploding chaos surrounding me.

He tracks the slow exposure. As inexperienced as I am compared to how ravenous he seems to be, each encounter between us will either lead to pleasure or me curled in a ball in the corner of a room.

I jump when Irina calls my name from inside, readjusting the robe so as to not give away the game I'm brazenly playing with the prince.

Finnian mutters something, most likely something negative about us being interrupted, and waves me off.

Offended, my jaw drops. He grins until Irina bounds outside and scowls at him. He returns it with a crude gesture. She drags me inside and sits me down, smiling.

"Forgave him, did you?"

I roll my eyes. "Hardly."

She begins work on a bundle of knotted curls. "Agnes will be there this evening, but tomorrow morning will be the end of it. She won't pursue him any further."

I sigh. "But tonight?"

"Tonight, well, it's a game." She winces. "You will dance with Finnian last. He'll dance with each lady; you'll dance with every man."

My eyes widened. "*Every* man?"

"Every man who asks. It's supposed to be romantic, standing at the end with the one you want to marry, but in my opinion, Jasper invented it to openly touch other women."

I slump my shoulders, envy already building at the thought of

Finnian dancing with Agnes. "Irina, why do you refer to your father by his name? Finnian does it, too."

"Because he's never been a father to us," she states simply. "And that title is a reward. That is the one thing he can't take from me."

I tilt my head slightly.

"My respect," she explains, "He will never have the respect a father should. And one day, most likely when he takes his final breath, I hope he rests eternally with that realization. He didn't die with everything he wanted."

❧

Instead of arriving early to the mingling, it's reversed. We will be the last to enter, but I dread it. After the prior dinner, the heads I turned proved I could hold their attention, even as the last person they expected Finnian to marry.

This will be no different.

Finnian's choice of dress for me is perfect. Instead of keeping my hair down as usual, Honora pinned it up to display the line of tiny buttons down my spine, leaving it and my ribcage exposed underneath the sheer fabric.

Before the doors open for us, Irina smacks her forehead. "Gods, I forgot a few buttons on Elora's dress. Mother, can you walk in without us? We'll be right behind you."

Honora studies her daughter with mirth. "Tell Finnian to be quick," she says. "We're only a few moments early."

Irina tosses a hand up. "Well, Elora, you can go to him alone." She points down an unlit hallway. "He's waiting for you."

I hesitate until Honora touches my shoulder gently, encouraging me. Between her keen eye and Irina's ability to lurk in hallways unseen, I will never be able to hide *anything*.

Delaying the evening made me nervous. If Jasper discovers us, the repercussions of bending the rules even a little could end in catastrophe. But that doesn't dull my smile when I see Finnian against a wall, his arms crossed, his long legs kicked out to the side.

The newly shaded boundary between us heightens my nerves each time we're close. I never know what to say since my mouth always dries.

"I had to choose between two options," he greets me. "The first was standing in that room with people I don't like and seeing you for the first time in that,"—his eyes lowered down my body and back up—"*Weapon*."

I spin in a slow circle for him.

"Or," he continues gruffly, "I could wait for you and be the first and last man to touch you."

But instead of touching me, he raises his fist and opens his hand. The pearl necklace dangles from his fingers.

"I lied when I gave this to you, Elora." He unclasps it and instructs me to spin around with a flick of his finger.

"Your mother *wouldn't* want me wearing it?"

He laughs as he secures it around my neck. "No, little doe. It isn't my mother's. It's yours."

I gently touch the strand. "Finnian, why? I mean, thank you, but you shouldn't have."

He drags a knuckle down my spine. "I wanted to, Elora. I wanted to because you wouldn't want it." He chuckles while both hands roam my ribs. "And I like being the one to frazzle you. Frustrate you."

The uncaged energy between us seems almost too good to be true, but if it's too late to save myself, I might as well play with him before it all ends. "You like doing the opposite of what I ask?"

He hums his approval.

"Don't kiss me then."

Still behind me, he takes a falling curl to twist around his finger and tugs my head to one side. His warm breath tickles my neck when he whispers, "Don't kiss you where? Here?"

The kiss he leaves behind my ear makes me sigh. "Or here?" He travels lower to kiss a delicate spot between my shoulder and neck. "Be more specific, little doe."

"Everywhere," I choke, spinning. "But start here."

And for the first time, I initiated a kiss.

Throwing my arms around his neck takes every spare inch I can find to raise up and press my lips against his.

I still can't accept what Honora said—this intense, stomach-clenching rawness in my chest every time we touch, dizzying, all-consuming need for *more* is love.

But if I need to kiss him a few more times to figure it out, I won't complain.

He snakes a hand into my hair to pull me so close that I feel him everywhere. The height difference seems awkward and unmatched until moments like these when he can command me however he wants.

And gods, I love fighting with him.

I still hate him for being so ignorant.

But I always want to remember what kissing Finnian feels like. Every stolen moment, every shy touch, all of it has built up to this. And how can someone so wrong for me feel so *good*?

Passionately kissing him feels natural. I'm not nervously wondering if he thinks I'm horrible at it without practice because we move together so effortlessly.

"I need to leave," he mutters, kissing me again and again.

"Oh," is all I manage to fit in.

A laugh in his throat, while he kisses me, causes me to pull away, but he twists us around until my back is against the wall—his favored position for keeping me controlled, I've learned. "I didn't finish what I wanted to say," he says. "I need to leave with *you*."

"Oh," I say again with relief. "But we can't leave." My lips are raw and swollen, but I want to kiss him again.

"Fuck them." He looks down the hallway, where Irina will pop up soon to tell us to stop contaminating the air. "I don't want to watch another man dance with you, Elora."

I want to leave. I would if I hadn't exchanged my blood for his safety. "I don't want to dance with anyone else, but—"

"Let's go."

"We can't."

He grins. "I do have some leverage as the prince, you know. They'll all be drunk soon enough that they won't notice we're not there."

I have to get him in that room.

Lie, lie.

"I need to see that you don't have feelings for her."

Something changes in the way he stares at me. Desire doesn't entirely dissipate, but disbelief joins it. "Do you not believe me?"

Even if I didn't believe him, subjecting myself to watching them dance is the worst form of self-torture. And I might be setting us up for disaster because on the off-chance that he still feels something for Agnes, marrying him tomorrow won't be as joyous.

"I just need to see it."

Irina appears, but he isn't surprised and doesn't even look her way. "We're coming," he says, eyes searching mine. "Elora doubts my loyalty to her."

I lower my head when he untangles himself from me, the hurt in his voice nearly pulling the truth out of me. "Finnian...."

Already halfway down the hall, his confident and determined strides make me yearn to be the one he's walking toward. Irina touches my shoulder gently.

"I don't doubt him," I whisper.

"Trust is important to him." She takes my hand. "I hope he tells you why someday."

Thirty-Two

Upon entering the banquet hall, Jasper immediately handed me a mug of ale and encouraged me to loosen up. My frustration is held in the way I can't seem to relax my jaw while I wait impatiently for my doubting bride.

I thought we turned a corner at the bakery and started fresh, but if she needs physical proof that I feel nothing for Agnes, I'll give it to her, though the way my body is still reeling from holding Elora in my arms should already be enough for her.

"Did Elora inform you of our meeting?"

Jasper's question jars me, temporarily forgetting the time she spent with him this afternoon. "Yes, though I would prefer you not use my wife for a beneficial rendezvous with another man again."

Foam from his ale bubbles on his beard. "Don't tell me you've fallen for the girl."

My grip around the mug tightens. My desire for Elora is clouding my carefully constructed responses. "I haven't."

He looks pleased. "Good. Keep making her believe you have."

I try to analyze what that means silently, but concerned curiosity wins. "What do you mean? How do you know she thinks I care for her?"

He slaps my back. "She told me she's falling for you." Raising his mug, he tips it toward my mother as she enters the hall, followed closely by Irina and Elora. "She promised to keep the faeries in line because she cares about you."

My heart pounds in my chest.

Hearing that should bring nothing short of joy, but it doesn't. I was already suspicious of Elora's honesty about the contents of their meeting. Speaking about Gabriel and the faeries wouldn't have led to her voluntarily offering that information to him. That would've only come from Jasper frightening her into admission. And if he wanted a confession for her, it was for a reason, but I can't approach her about it here.

If my fears are confirmed, and she has agreed to something, every move she makes will be analyzed. He'll try and find reasons to harm her—mentally or physically.

I have to find a way to stop him before that begins.

The evening is supposed to start with the king and queen's dance, but I fabricate one of my biggest smiles and step between Jasper and my mother. "I think the eve of my wedding is the perfect time to start a new tradition." My voice carries through the room. "I will be the first to dance with the queen if she'll have me."

Annoyed by the attention stolen from him, Jasper huffs, but outward appearances are far too important to him to reprimand me here. Instead, he extends an arm toward my mother with a tight nod. "All yours, boy."

I'll pay for this later.

Leading my mother to the center of the room, I extend our arms and place a hand on her waist but remain silent until the musicians drown our voices with song. I ask, "Elora lied to me, didn't she?"

Honora keeps a placated smile, but her eyes give her away.

"Fuck," I mutter. "What did she sign?"

"I don't know." She speaks through her smile, pretending nothing is astray. "She wouldn't say. We haven't been able to retrieve the contract yet. Whatever it is, he's hidden it somewhere."

"If he took her down there,"—my nostrils flare—"I'll fucking kill him."

"Finnian, look at me."

I tear my eyes away from Elora as she dances with an older gentleman. He isn't handsy and respects his wife, so I feel comfortable focusing on my mother. "Do not tell her you know yet," she says.

"I have to save her," I argue.

"Not *yet*," she emphasizes. "You have to make it through the wedding. He won't harm her before then. Take her to Hogsfeet afterward for your holiday."

I jerk my head back. "Hogsfeet? The abandoned kingdom? Why the fuck would I take her there?"

"To allow me time to learn what he has demanded of her." She pretends to laugh at something I said. "Reacting without a plan has never worked in our favor, Finnian, and now we have another life we're responsible for. Hogsfeet is close enough that you can return quickly if needed, but give yourself time with her. Do not inform your father of where you're going. Lie, if needed."

Admittedly, I want nothing more than Elora alone for two days, but constantly wondering which trap she's fallen into will sully my time with her. "Hogsfeet is impossible to reach."

"You bred Major for treacherous terrain, did you not?"

"I did, but there won't be food—"

"Bring your bow," she interjects. "Honestly, Finnian, must I tell you how to survive?" Her forced smile softens. "When was the last time you truly enjoyed yourself?"

In the hallway just before this, touching Elora, kissing her, caressing her, but sharing that with my mother would horrify Elora.

"It is time to stop running," she whispers, touching my cheek with all the tenderness she can allow in front of Jasper. "She isn't one of us. If you leave now, he won't hesitate to dispose of her when finished."

I watch Jasper dance with a visiting queen, grin when Irina denies a dance with a prince, sigh when Elora genuinely laughs at a story her partner tells her, and finally nod to my mother's request.

I've always left to prevent him from harming Irina and my mother, to stop myself from bucking against an order and giving him a reason to torture them, but for Elora, I will stand still. I will swallow my fears.

It is time to stop running from him.

I will save them from him.

"He won't fucking touch her," I promise. "I'm not going anywhere. We're going to end this once and for all, Mother."

❧

Apparently, I can't touch Elora, either.

The night has dragged by slowly. Each visitor wants to dance with one of us, though any time Agnes moves toward me, Irina prevents it by shoving someone else at me. She and Elora exchange mischievous little grins each time. I'm worried about the trouble the two of them will cause together in the future if they're already scheming together this quickly after being introduced. At one point, Agnes said something to Irina that had her rearing back to throw a drink at her, but my mother intervened before she could.

But when the song begins to die, the queen telling me facts about her granddaughter leaves me with a peck on the cheek and doesn't take two steps away before Agnes appears before me. Irina pops up at my side like a spring flower—if flowers can even grow in the underworld since hers would be poisonous to touch.

"Diseases spread, Finnian, and Agnes is known for carrying a toxic fungus that spawns from pathetic obsession."

Elora watches from afar with a smirk she valiantly tries to hide. I know Irina is doing this for Elora, but I need to get this over with to show Elora that my only desire is her.

"Don't you have a prince to dance with, Irina?" Agnes looks around. "Oh, wait, I forgot. You scare all of them away."

Irina rolls her eyes, unbothered. "I suppose when a woman doesn't reek of desperation, a man realizes she won't be an easy lay.

You don't have that problem, so I understand how confusing it is for you when I don't beg for attention."

Agnes steps toward Irina. All five feet of Irina would happily take the challenge, but I partially stepped to the side to block her from trying. "As much as eyeball gouging and hair pulling would liven the evening, this isn't the place," I say. I glance down at Irina, who would do much more than pull hair. "Irina, it's fine. I need to finish this so I can dance with Elora."

"Did you hear that, Irina?" Agnes grabs my hand to place it on her waist. "Finnian can take care of himself."

Irina narrows her feline eyes. "I've been looking for the opportunity to spit in your drink all night, so that's where I'll be." She flashes me a bright smile before sauntering away. "Remember to wash your hands afterward, Finn!" she calls loud enough for heads to turn.

I don't try to control *my* grin.

Agnes places my other hand on her waist, but I swiftly deny that and take her hand to extend our arms in a proper stance. She sighs deeply. "Finnian, we have never danced like this together."

Elora has successfully avoided Gabriel all night, but he has taken her hand and is pulling her close for a dance—his final dance if his hands wander in any direction I don't like.

Agnes squeezes my hand. "Are you going to ignore me again?"

"Preferably," I mutter.

She turns her head to follow my gaze, her lips pursing at the blatantly apparent direct line of sight at Elora. "She brings nothing of value to the crown, Finnian."

"I don't give a fuck about the crown," I reply.

She moves her hand from my shoulder to my face, and I jerk away. "Agnes, you need to stop."

I always receive Elora's glares, but the scowl on her face is pinned to Agnes. I enjoy seeing jealousy in her. It's unnecessary but refreshing to know I'm not the only protective one. Once we return to Ashbury, I won't feel guilty when mine resurfaces if Cedric bravely touches her again.

"I don't understand how you can see me and not feel *anything*," Agnes snaps. "After what we went through together and after we nearly married, spoke about children—"

"Stop," I snarl, finally lowering my gaze to her. "Do you honestly believe bringing this up will make me fall for you again?"

"Finnian, I made a mistake—"

"No, you did me a favor." I don't have a single ounce of remorse when hurt crosses her eyes. "You showed me that love shouldn't be conditional, Agnes. I will credit you for that."

"Finnian, I can change, I will be better...."

In the middle of her empty promises, I look for Elora, but my gaze snags on someone standing in the doorway and glaring at me. "Oh, for fuck's sake," I mutter.

Darius charges toward us, still dressed in his traveling clothes and looking like he hasn't slept in days. I release Agnes with a sigh, grateful that Gabriel notices him quickly and drags Elora away.

"You bastard!" Darius yells, drawing the attention of everyone —even the drunks.

At the sound of his voice, Agnes spins and gasps. "Darius, what are you doing here?"

"I could ask you the same fucking question," he shouts, shoving my chest.

I whip my head toward Irina before she can reach me and shake my head. "Stay back, Irina."

Ever since she admitted to seeing my lashings, I realized part of the reason she always stayed so close to me when I returned home was to protect me from ever being hurt again, but if anyone ever touched her, I would kill them with my bare hands, and Darius' blood on one of the only jackets I don't mind wearing isn't how I want this night to end.

"Darius," I say calmly. The last time I saw him, his face was battered from a rightful beating. I walked away with the threat of finishing what I started if he ever set foot in my kingdom.

But again, I've matured since that incident.

"You waited until I was away on business to try and get her

back, didn't you?" He paces in short spurts, panting. "Fucking coward."

I sigh when Irina shouts, "She sought him out, you fool!"

Elora leaves the safety of Gabriel's side to grab Irina's hand, her eyes darting between us. Evidenced by her bewilderment, Irina didn't share *why* I ended the engagement.

Guards surround us to drag him away, but I hold them back.

I lower my voice to say, "Darius, this is not the place. We can speak about this outside."

I silently plead with him to take the offer. Agnes' betrayal hurt, but his shocked me. Being the same age, we became best mates as young men and often traveled back and forth for visits. While Pumpkin Hollow was close to Fracas, the Merchet Kingdom neighbored hers.

We crossed paths often, sometimes even shared Agnes at night, but he never touched her without my permission.

Or, that was what I was led to believe.

I never asked how long they had a relationship before I found out, but I didn't want to know. It was painful enough already.

"Did you use some woman to entice Agnes to come?" His voice is the only sound in the room. Everyone has gone dead silent to watch an aged conflict repeat. "I found the invitation personally addressed to her."

My brow furrows. "What?"

He scoffs. "Don't feign obliviousness. You learned we were engaged and took the chance when you could."

What he believes doesn't matter to me nearly as much as the doubtful hurt in Elora's eyes. "That's not true. I didn't invite her here," I assure her.

"Your *beloved* has been begging Finnian to take her back," Irina says. "Agnes is not worth the trouble of faking a wedding."

Agnes scowls. "Darius, please, let's go. I shouldn't have come here—"

"Is it true?" he asks her. "Have you spoken with him about leaving me?"

"Yes," Irina answers.

Jasper encroaches slowly. If I don't get a hold of this quickly, Darius will pay the ultimate price for interrupting our evening.

"All can be forgiven," I say. "It was a misunderstanding. Take Agnes and leave."

But Darius, he rolls his neck.

There was always competition between us, but it didn't differ from how young men acted around one another. It was healthy, always friendly, and never crossed boundaries.

But Agnes, she changed that.

After I left her, he learned of her coming to Pumpkin Hollow to try and apologize. He sent threats, he pounded on our door once, and it wasn't until he made an offhand remark about seeking revenge with my sister that I found him in Merchet and left him with painful reminders to stay away from my family.

And seeing me with Agnes was a perfect opportunity for him to even the score again—to prove I wasn't any better than him.

I tense, prepared for a fight.

But he turns toward Elora, lunges for her, and kisses her. Agnes screams his name, but all the rage from his betrayal returns in a breath, and I react.

Elora stumbles backward as I rip him off her and throw him to the ground. Irina shouts my name as my fists fly, blood spills, and bone cracks. That totals two women he tried to take from me—two brides he wanted to steal to prove he could. I gave him the first one without looking back, but the thought of losing Elora has suffocated my logic and fed my fury.

It isn't until he stops fighting back that I wipe a bloody hand across my forehead and stand, demanding the guards retrieve him.

The lack of movement or aid coming to assist Darius by any other royal is a prime example of how much we genuinely dislike one another.

Everything is always for fucking show.

"Bart!" I call out next. "Remove Elora and my sister immediately."

"Finnian," Elora says, reaching for me.

I jerk away from her touch. "Leave, Elora."

I can't look at her as Irina whispers for her to follow Bart, and I can't reconcile the anger I feel that someone else has kissed her, unashamed that I harbor no guilt when Darius has to be carried out because he can't stand alone.

I called for another adviser. "Remove Agnes from this kingdom and issue a permanent banishment."

Agnes sobs beside me, her mother comforting her while her father yells at mine. He threatens war between kingdoms and promises Merchet will fight with them, but I am the one to respond. "If you so much as think of Pumpkin Hollow,"—my tone is a low, lethal growl—"If I hear a whisper of armies approaching, you will be the first to witness the power of our numbers."

I remain steadfast, my gaze not wavering from his for even a second. "I prevented your death once before despite your daughter's betrayal. I will not hesitate to be the one who personally escorts you to the afterlife if you decide to enter my kingdom again."

I roll my shoulders back. "Leave now, or Darius will become a permanent reminder of what happens when you touch what's mine."

His jaw clicks, his fists clenching and releasing, but he concedes and leaves his wife and daughter to follow behind him as he storms out of the room. I demand the advisers escort everyone out, listen as Jasper orders someone to wipe the blood off the floor, and flinch when he slaps my back.

"You handled that well, boy."

I start coming down from the high—the rare compliment sitting uncomfortably.

"Violence is always the quickest way to gain control of someone," he continues with a chuckle, "And fear for the long game."

I followed his gaze to my mother. She's the last person left—always the one to stay to assure my safety. But she isn't looking at me as her son. No, the disappointment usually only reserved for my father belongs to me.

What she just saw in me frightened her.

The bloody rags, the way I spoke to Elora, the bridge I just burned with an allied kingdom—it's all too familiar.

He shoves a mug of ale against my chest. "You've earned it."

Staring at the mug in my hand, yielding to the temptation to take the edge off what just transpired by drinking until the anger lessens, sounds appealing. Jasper is aware of my addiction, encourages lethal vices, and knows Irina and my mother disapprove.

He doesn't wait to see if I drink it. He waits until my mother walks out the door before pulling one of the maids off the floor and leaving with her.

And I stand alone.

I came here to prove my loyalty to Elora and planned to whisk her away afterward. But instead, I sent her away without thinking twice. I will never hesitate to protect her, but my overreaction bred cruelty toward her.

I've fought too hard to not be the monster Jasper continuously tries to create.

I place the mug on a table and jog down each corridor, taking the stairs two at a time, shed my jacket, and knock on Irina's door to beg for Elora's forgiveness. Again.

But there is no reply, even when I try to pull the brother card with Irina again.

I search for them, enter Elora's unlocked door, look over the balcony, and then sigh.

I want to be wrong as I run to the bottom level and jog to the back of the small library where Irina always stashes her disguise.

I growl at the lack of clothing on the bottom shelf.

Irina has taken Elora to the outskirts.

Thirty-Three

"Irina," I whisper, watching for any sign of anyone coming to retrieve us. "Irina, we shouldn't do this. What if someone sees us?"

Irina grunts while lifting a saddle over Major. "No one is going to see us, Elora. We're wearing all black, and it's nightfall."

"If Finnian learns we stole Major—"

"We're not *stealing* him," she interrupts. "We're borrowing him. He's the fastest. Plus, he likes me better."

After securing the saddle, she hops up and throws her leg over. "Listen, I'm not going to force you to come with me, but I can assure you that we'll be safe. Finnian will come looking for us, so if you want to wait for him here, it shouldn't be long until he realizes I've stolen his bride."

I gnaw on my bottom lip. If I tell Irina what happened today with Jasper, she will understand my hesitancy. But I'm also curious to meet her lovers and trust she is as excellent at sneaking around as she claims.

And after Finnian's dismissal, I'm not in any hurry to face him yet. His unleashing on Darius was terrifying; that reaction was over just one kiss. What was he capable of if truly threatened?

I take Irina's hand and jump up, wrapping my arms around her waist from behind. Unsurprisingly, she knows all of Major's commands, and he obeys her as he would Finnian. Their relationship makes me envious—I would've loved to have a close sibling instead of stepsisters who enjoyed making me miserable. Irina and Finnian's closeness is endearing. As often as they argue, they wouldn't hesitate to defend one another.

Dolly and Daffodil would give the other up instantly if anything could be gained from it.

Major races in the opposite direction of Ashbury and through a part of Pumpkin Hollow I haven't explored yet. We pass a carriage I don't recognize, but Irina shouts over the howling wind that it belongs to Agnes' father. I look behind us to see if Darius is with them, but I can't see anyone in the darkness.

"Did their engagement end because of Darius?" I ask, having to repeat myself when she couldn't hear me the first time.

"Sort of," she replies.

I blow out a frustrated sigh. Her short answers always mean she won't give me further details because she wants Finnian to tell me, but I can't spend more than a few moments with him before we're interrupted or upset with each other again.

"Hold on!" she yells.

I tighten my arms around her waist when Major leaps over an iron barrier, signifying the crossing of Pumpkin Hollow's border. Irina tugs on Major's reins to slow into a trot, pointing ahead to bright bonfires. "We're here!" she exclaims excitedly.

I grin. "How do you know when they'll be here instead of Ashbury?"

"We exchange notes," she replies. "There's a hollowed-out trunk in the woods. Massimo leaves me a note when they plan to move."

"Massimo," I repeat. "Your lover?"

"One of them. Leif is the other. They've been together for years, but I met them one evening two years ago, and when they invited me to join them, I accepted without hesitation."

"You've been doing this for *two* years?" I recall all the nights the wanderers stayed in Ashbury. Most of the time, I wasn't allowed to leave the manor until morning, but on the rare occasions I did, I would exchange pleasantries with them, but I never learned their names.

She shrugs a shoulder. "They'll move on when needed, but they have solid relationships with peddlers and some merchants."

"And what will you do?"

My chest tightens at how her face falls, her frown evident from where I sit behind her.

"Stay behind," she whispers.

She doesn't tie Major to anything, but he doesn't go far to graze. I follow behind her, smiling as she lunges into Massimo's arms. It's only been a few days since she disappeared mid-afternoon, but without knowing when she'd see them again, a few days could seem like forever.

Their passionate kiss is soon interrupted by a woman who takes Massimo's place, her hands roaming over Irina's body without shame. Irina is free to be herself here, surrounded by love and people who don't force her to hide her relationships.

Massimo approaches with a wide smile. He looks much older than Irina, but his youthful edge in carrying himself reminds me of her. His black hair and dark eyes aren't nearly as divine as his tanned skin under an open vest and loose brown trousers.

His chest is bare except for the fresh claw marks, which must be from Irina's greeting.

I feel entirely overdressed.

"Elora," he says, kissing each cheek, "I have seen you often in Ashbury."

My lack of personal space makes me unsure how to react to his greeting, my hands flailing awkwardly at my sides. "Yes, hello. Massimo?"

He nods and slides an arm around my shoulders to bring me to Irina and Leif, still heavily locked in their embrace. Gods, I can hardly let Finnian touch me in dark hallways, and they're openly touching one another in front of a large group.

But as I study my surroundings, I notice at least half of them are doing the same. It varies between kissing, singing, or drinking.

And I can *feel* their joy.

There isn't an ounce of fear or sorrow.

Leif notices me first and shouts her greeting to me, her arm remaining wrapped around Irina. Irina's cold, bored demeanor in the castle is completely gone. Her genuine smile and rosy cheeks signify the love she feels around these people. She can deny it all she wants, but it's apparent that Irina is in love with Leif. *And* Massimo—her lustful gaze turning shy when she glances at him.

And they seem to feel the same about her.

Leif's beauty intimidates me. Lean and tall like Azrea, her height matches Massimo's, and her full lips almost make *me* want to kiss her just to feel them. "Elora," she says confidently.

Maybe I should feel guilty for never asking their names since they all seem to know mine.

Another beautiful man stands on my other side and greets Irina before he turns to me. He places his hand on my waist, but Irina frees herself from Leif to push it away. "No." She wags her finger at him. "No one touches her."

"Eh!" he shouts, pulling at the cloak I borrowed from her. "Why would you bring her? She is like a gift to unwrap!"

Irina rolls her eyes. "She belongs to my brother, so unless you want me to give *you* to *him* as a head to cave in, you don't touch her."

"She is so vicious," he responds, pulling Irina to him by pinching her black dress and pecking her on the lips. "Why do you continue to tease me by not letting me have you, hm? And then you bring her here."

I can't differentiate if the sweat pouring off me is from warmth or the smell of sex wafting off every person surrounding me.

Irina throws her arms around his neck and kisses him again. "B, my fantasy of you puts me to sleep. Why ruin our dreams?"

The openness doesn't make me uncomfortable, but it's shocking. Looking at Massimo and Leif, I expect jealousy, but they laugh at Irina, and *B*. Irina catches my bewildered stare and breaks into laughter, releasing him to come to me. "Leif, what do you say we help eliminate temptation and change Elora into something more fitting for this evening?"

I start to shake my head, but Leif takes my hands and pulls me to her. "Come, come, Elora. We only bite if you ask."

Oh, *gods*.

❧

Multi-colored, covered wagons rest in a circle around their camp. Watchers are set up between each one for unwanted visitors, but most have fallen asleep with their heads propped against the wheels. Leif guides me to her wagon, using a small wooden ladder to step inside.

Irina lingers behind me but continuously has to stop when someone else either kisses her or embraces her. Everyone here loves her, and she's the most comfortable I've ever seen her.

I step inside the wagon, which seems deceivingly tiny from the outside. Inside, it's wide open and lit with multiple candles. Colorful blankets and pillows create a cozy bed on the floor, but it's the clothing hanging from the roof that I touch and admire.

Irina finally arrived inside and lay on the bed, her flirtatious grin soon pinned to Leif. I avert my eyes and pull in my top lip with my teeth while I finger through the dress choices. "What color do you like?"

Leif's inquiry gives me pause. I haven't been asked that before. I have always gravitated toward blue since it was my mother's favorite, but I have never given it much thought.

Lighter colors and pastels are always chosen for me, but I keep touching a deep purple dress. "This one?" I ask Irina.

Irina smiles softly—the first one I've ever seen on her. "Elora, *you* choose."

I lick my lips. "This one."

Leif unclasps it from the hook it dangles from and hands it to me. "Change here." She unhooks a rolling curtain, and it falls to cover the open door. Then, she hurls insults at the men who groan in protest outside.

Irina snorts. "Ignore them, Elora."

I wrinkle my nose. "All of you are so open with one another. Is there no jealousy?"

"Sure," Leif replies, lowering to lay beside Irina. "But there is also respect. My heart belongs to Massimo and Irina, but my body is mine. I decide who brings me pleasure."

"I've only been with Leif and Massimo," Irina adds. "But I'll kiss any of them. They'll tell me if it bothers one of them, and I'll stop. She wouldn't if Leif wanted to kiss you, but I didn't feel comfortable about it. We respect each other, but also understand that we might have needs that others can satisfy."

I nod. "Has Finnian... um, does he believe the same?"

Irina raises to rest on her elbows. "If you're asking me if he's shared, then yes. He has. But not anymore. Not for a long time." She kisses Leif once before she stands. "Elora, Finnian has a past. He'll tell you if you genuinely want to know, but you must keep an open mind. He didn't lie to you. He will be loyal to only you."

I gnaw on my cheek before whispering, "I've never.... And what if...." I awkwardly stumble my way through. "Well, with someone like him...."

"He won't care," she assures gently. "Massimo was my first. He was caring and gentle and never pushed me. Finnian is a man, Elora. All he wants is you. And I know him well enough to guarantee that you being completely his is an honor. You are enough, Elora."

In the fifteen years since losing my mother, rarely having a conversation with my father, and retreating into silence to avoid degradations from Regina and her daughters, not once have I heard those words.

I will not take one second with Irina for granted.

I press my forehead against hers. "I am delighted you'll be my sister, Irina."

She kisses the tip of my nose. "Now, get dressed, and I'll show you how to dance."

❧

The dress I chose is off-the-shoulder with cutouts on both sides, wholly exposing my ribcage. I fidget as Leif smears red lip stain across my lips and orange on my eyelids. Irina braids my hair and places purple and orange flowers throughout. And I was instructed to remain barefoot. But I kept the pearl necklace around my neck.

Irina insists Leif leave the wagon first, but I gasp when she hollers my name, humiliation painting my entire body when Irina *unveils* me to the waiting group. I cover my face with both hands, smiling through the embarrassment, and laugh when Massimo's arms curl around me. "Bellissima," he says.

I lower my hands. "What?"

"Beautiful!" he exclaims, taking my hand and spinning me around.

Someone hands him a tin cup, and he tips it against my lips, laughing at my sour face. Irina taps my hip with hers with a wink. "It'll help you loosen up, Elora."

I smack my lips. "What *is* it?"

"I don't know," she replies with a laugh. "But they make it, and merchants pay in gold for a jug." She parts her lips for Massimo to pour some into her mouth. "I hate it, but it helps loosen tension. Drink a couple more."

Massimo takes her suggestion seriously and pours another cupful into my mouth.

Soft-stringed instruments, bells, and taps of sticks against anything nearby surround us. Massimo takes my hands and bends at the waist. "You will dance with me," he says.

Better him than B.

"I must touch you to teach," he explains. "If I make you uncomfortable, you will tell me, yes?"

Irina trusts him, and I trust her.

I nod my confirmation, feeling the sour liquid mingle with my bloodstream. Irina dances independently, yet they all seem to move in the perfect rhythm.

My hips cannot move like theirs, but Massimo moves behind me and tries to force them. I feel every bit the newborn fawn Finnian calls me, unsure how to move my limbs harmoniously.

Massimo presses me against his chest while Leif stands in front of me. He keeps his hands on my waist, she takes my hands, and they work together to help me *feel* the rhythm.

Or, try.

Irina pours more liquid into my mouth. "No one here is looking at you, doe. Relax. Close your eyes and taste the music, grasp the freedom you feel, touch it."

I close my eyes, but I don't imagine freedom. No, I've started to crave something more than freedom. I think of Finnian—the way *he* tastes and touches me. I move my body in a way I never had before, breathe in the sounds of laughter around me, and grasp for the sensuality I desperately want to discover.

Leif and Massimo switch places. His hands slide down my waist, hips, and thighs before returning. Leif raises my arms above my head and moves them to where they rest on her neck, grazing my ribs with her fingertips.

"Brava ragazza," an unfamiliar voice whispers in my ear.

I have no idea what it means, but I love how it sounds.

Leif leaves me, but Massimo returns behind me. With another pour, I became used to the taste. He spins me out and laughs when I stumble into his chest from still learning how to use my own two feet.

Moments pass by in a blur, and I become more comfortable. Irina shoves B off me when he tries to replace Massimo, not allowing anyone but the three of them to help me. Irina kisses

Massimo behind me before taking my hands and encouraging me to use him, insisting he doesn't mind.

He confirms wholeheartedly.

So, I danced with him. I shove my insecurities aside and listen to his affirmations, trying to convince myself I can touch Finnian like this—that he wants me like this.

Maybe it's the liquor.

Maybe it's the beautiful man touching me.

But for the first time in my life, I'm not just Harry's daughter; I'm not the fae's pet or the unwanted stepchild—I'm Elora.

Jasper can't hurt me here.

And I start to move unrestrained, free of obligation, fearlessly and boldly. Irina cheers me on, throwing her arms around me and rejoining our coupling.

Until it's only us, holding hands and spinning, laughing so much that my sides hurt.

In this little spot, underneath a pitch-black sky, hidden on the outskirts of the kingdom that I was raised to hate with people I never believed I could have anything in common with, I experience genuine bliss with my sister.

Eventually, the drinks stop coming.

But we keep dancing.

Thirty-Four

When I told Elora she could borrow Major, I didn't anticipate her taking him to get away from me. Irina always borrowed him without hesitancy, but I half-expected Elora to wait for me in the stables. I was met with Major's trail of hoofprints instead. It has faded in the dark, but I know where I'm going. I've traveled to the outskirts many times to retrieve my sister. With Elora, Irina would've gone to Ashbury if they were there, but I checked the note in the hollow trunk before heading for the outskirts.

I spot the bonfires when I cross the barrier but find Major first. Sliding off the horse I settled for, I pat Major's backside.

"Traitor," I say.

He huffs while continuing to graze.

I changed into riding clothes before leaving, cleaned Darius' blood from my hands, and hopefully washed away any evidence of my earlier outburst. The night sky hides me well while I search the jovial crowd for Elora or my sister.

Massimo notices me first, not giving me away by quietly approaching instead of shouting my name as he usually would. "Come for Irina already?" he asks.

I grin. "You know why I'm here."

He drags his fingers down his chin in a contemplative manner. "Surely you will not take our gemstone."

I arch an eyebrow but follow his finger to the center of the crowd, where my sister dances and spins around with a gorgeous blonde. Dressed in a flowy, barely-there deep-purple dress, Elora's lips are red, her eyes painted the color of flames, and her hips sway in a way that makes me thirsty.

And as if he knew, Massimo passes me a tin cup full of their sour liquor.

I hesitate but don't pour it in my mouth. One swallow never does anything to me, but I have a feeling that Elora will soon become my new addiction. I can't take my eyes off of her.

"I don't recognize her," I murmur, handing the cup back to him.

He squeezes my shoulder. "If I show you how good she is, will you swear not to kill me?"

Speechless, I nod.

He jogs to the center and leans down to whisper something in Irina's ear. Her head turned toward me, and she shouted something to Elora before leaving her alone with Massimo.

Massimo taps Elora's chin, and her head tilts back, her lips parting just enough for him to pour the liquor into her mouth.

Hades, it's the most erotic thing I've ever seen. Her body is lit only by the bonfire, the flames licking up her legs and illuminating her silhouette. Her thick braid is falling apart, curls wrapping around her face and cascading down her shoulders in waves.

Massimo slips one of the flowers from her hair and puts it between his teeth, smiling at Elora's laughter. And then, he spins her and wraps his hands around her waist, pulling her close and moving her body with his.

Irina stands beside me, smelling like sweat and liquor but breathily laughing at what's unfolding. "She's exquisite," she breathes. "She just needed permission to let herself go, and gods. I'm proud of her."

I'm a combination of so many things.

Jealous, impressed, aching.

With her back against his chest, Elora raises her arms to hang from Massimo's shoulders and rocks her hips side to side while his hands drag down her stomach and rest on her hips. The knowledge that Massimo is in love with my sister is the only reason I allow another man to touch her this way.

And I love seeing her smile.

I love how her face lights up each time he nuzzles his cheek against her hair, the leisurely movements of her body, the flames reflecting against her hazy brown eyes and turning them gold.

I want her in my arms. I need to feel her smooth skin against mine while she laughs at something absurd I've said.

"Fuck," I whisper, doubling over into a crouch, unable to look anywhere but at her.

Irina lowers to rub my back. "What is it?"

I rake my fingers through my hair.

Euphoria seizes me. Floods me.

"I fucking love her." I shake my head and run a hand down my face. "I love her. Hades, Irina. I fucking fell in love with her."

Irina looks from me to her and back again, speechless. I stand and back away, turn around and look up, close my eyes, curse more times than I can count, and sigh.

"Finnian." Irina gently pats my back. "Finnian, it'll be okay. We won't let Jasper hurt her. We'll speak with Mother...."

"He already got to her, Irina." I turn toward Elora again, unable to tolerate not staring at her. "She told him she was falling for me. He did something to her today. We don't know what it is yet."

Irina threads both hands in her hair, her mouth falling open. "The faeries?"

"No, he wouldn't have used something against her that could turn on him." I rub my temples. "I should've known. I knew better than to believe he only wanted her for the faeries—that marrying her would be his only demand. And if he finds out how I feel...."

"Don't, Finn. Don't blame yourself."

"Mother is convinced we'll find a way out, but how?" I listen as Leif shouts for B to get away from Elora, who is approaching her with lustful eyes. "I'll fucking kill B, Irina. Get your friend. Now."

Irina grabs my arm. "Stop. I've already threatened him. Massimo won't let him touch her." She grins at my envy, and then it flips into a concerned frown. "Finn, we'll figure this out. He won't do anything before the wedding."

"Mother wants me to take Elora to Hogsfeet afterward." I shrug at her bewilderment. "I felt the same, but she said it was to keep us close. It'll only be for two days."

"Good," she says. "Good. You two need a chance to get to know one another."

"Does that mean you won't interrupt us?"

She mocks, then shoves me forward. "Take her back to the castle. I'll follow shortly." She rolls her eyes at my uncertainty. "Massimo will ensure I return safely, Finn."

I muss her hair, stare a moment longer at Elora, and allow myself to feel it for a moment—the swelling in my chest.

Then, I stroll into the center and nod at Massimo to release her, catching Elora as he spins her to me. Her eyes flutter open, glazed and hooded, but then widen. "Finnian!"

"Have we met?" I find her waist underneath the fabric where the holes in her dress lead, my thumbs brushing over her ribs.

She leans back and crosses her arms. "I don't know. Which version of you is this?"

Even while wasted from consuming her weight in strong liquor, she still manages to remember her anger with me.

"Right now?" I draw her closer. "I'm the one who just watched you dance with another man. Didn't I tell you there would be consequences?"

She blows an exasperated breath, throwing her arms out to the side. "Aren't there always with anything regarding *you*?"

"Let's find out." I remove my hands from her dress and wrap an arm around her thighs, lifting her over my shoulder.

Her new friends yell in protest at me for removing their *gemstone*. Elora pounds on my back, slurring something about putting her down, but Massimo salutes me with an arm around Irina. "Be nice to her," Irina says, "Be *gentle*."

"We'll see," I mutter.

I place Elora on the saddle of the borrowed horse, instruct Major to get Irina home safely, and then shove Elora forward to sit behind her.

Raising her arms, she feels for my face with her hands and yelps when I bite her fingers. "Gods, why do you always have to hurt?" she whines.

I chuckle. "If you think that hurts..."

Elora weaved halfway through the forest before I grew impatient and cradled her against my chest, not even trying to make sense of the words she strung together. I used the basement tunnel to avoid being seen, deposited Elora in my quarters, and then sought out a servant to ask that water and bread be left at my door.

She's exploring my quarters when I find her, asking nonsensical questions about scraps of broken trinkets on my floor before settling on the terrace. I leave her briefly to carry in the tray waiting at my door, grinning when she responds to my request that she not fall off the balcony with an annoyed sigh.

I offer water to her as a peace offering. "Please hydrate, Elora."

She lifts an eyebrow. "Or else what? You'll have someone come to take me away again?"

Sighing, I balance the glass on the iron rail. I owe her explanations for so many things, but I only want to kiss her. "I did that for your protection. I needed you away from that." I tap the glass rim with my finger and extend it again.

Her thirst trumps her stubbornness, and she drinks until the glass empties.

"You're kind of a hypocrite," I say.

She scowls. "Excuse me?"

Before I replied, I left the terrace to refill her glass and returned to find her staring at the stars. Fucking *mesmerizing*.

I ask, "Weren't you upset with me for drinking?"

She lowers her chin. "I was upset because you said unkind things to me, and you drank instead of warning me about your former lover."

"That's fair," I responded softly, handing her the glass. "But why did *you* drink?"

She circles the rim with the tip of her finger, shrugging slightly and avoiding eye contact at all costs. "I was envious of how happy they were. And I wanted to...." trailing off, she takes a sip instead of finishing her thought.

"Elora, we need to be honest, right?"

Placing the glass on the ground, she turns away from me and faces the drawbridge below. "I wanted to impress you." Her voice is so quiet that I must step closer to hear her. "I've never left Ashbury, but you are.... well-traveled."

I grin at the implication. "I don't know how else to show you that I desire you, little doe."

"It's not about desire, Finnian." She groans as she tips her head back. "It's about *want*. Lust doesn't last. What if we give in, hm?" She looks at me over her shoulder. "Desire fades. You would have to *want* me, Finnian. What if we give in, and I start to bore you? Since Agnes, have you not been bored with someone?"

"I was bored with her," I reply honestly, leaning against the far wall of the terrace, "I haven't ever wanted *more* from anyone, Elora. I wanted to possess someone and failed horribly. You could never bore me."

She falls to her elbows on the rail and rests her forehead in her palms.

"What are you so afraid of, darling?"

"You," she whispers. "All of this. I am risking.... so much to be here."

She has granted me a sliver of truth. I want to pry further, but only after I can be sure something happened between her and Jasper. I don't see the need to frighten her if our assumptions are incorrect. "I know you are, but I'm afraid of you, too."

Her head tips to the side, her temple resting against her palm. Her wavy hair partially covers her face, allowing her to keep a shield between us. "Why are you afraid of me?"

I push off the wall to approach her, waiting until she turns to face me before I place my hands on either side of her. She lifts her chin to search my eyes. I'm not ready to admit the whole truth—that I've fallen in love with her—but I do want to soothe her fears.

"I'm afraid of how you make me feel." I kiss her forehead. "I spent years not feeling anything for anyone, but one glare from you was all it took, Elora. Something rattled in my chest that night at the ball, and I couldn't stand the thought of wanting someone as.... *charming* as you, but I couldn't stop thinking about you. Chasing you."

She frowns. "Why did you try to apologize for kissing me?"

"I wasn't going to apologize, Elora. I wanted to promise it wouldn't happen again, but I nearly did it again right then."

"*Why*?" she repeats desperately.

I dip my forehead to rest against hers and close my eyes. "I can't allow anyone to get close to me, but I can't push you away anymore, Elora. I don't have the strength."

She touches my chest. "You always say everything right, but you're unpredictable."

"No," I murmur. "I'm not. I was stable until you barreled into my life like an angry, uncaged, miniature beast."

Hesitation to let anyone in is strangled by the way her eyes penetrate mine—as if she can see right through me. With her, I am unstable. Unhinged. She has chipped away at my hardened exterior, seeping in like an incurable virus.

"We hardly know one another," she murmurs. "All I know about you is what I've heard. Tell me a secret."

I love you, I nearly say. *I can't stand you, but I'm so fucking mad about you that being near you without touching you suffocates me.* But I don't share any of that. Instead, I respond with, "I don't have many secrets since Irina stalks me, but there is something I'd like to do someday that I don't believe she knows."

"Tell me," she says with a bright smile.

I twist one of her curls around my finger. "We have many stables, but we also have untouched land. I've thought about building another set of stables, an arena, and raising horses."

Her replying, warm smile ignites something in my chest that flickered out long ago. "For what reason?"

I could lie and say something frivolous like money, but she wants vulnerability from me, and I need to let my guard down with her a little. "Lessons, maybe. For children." I swallow. "Maybe therapy. Major has helped me."

I just bared a part of myself that I never planned on sharing with anyone, but she doesn't look at me with anything other than sincerity. "I think that's a wonderful idea, Finnian."

I blink, unsure if I'm still breathing from nerves and her approval swallowing me whole. "Your turn," I manage to rasp.

She traces my jaw with her finger. One single touch from her increases my pulse. "I love writing poetry. It was the one lesson I didn't mind as a girl."

I barely brush my thumbs across her ribs. "I love reading poetry."

She lifts a doubtful eyebrow, and I grin. "I know *how* to read poetry," I corrected. "I would read yours. And now, we know one another better."

The lingering, undeniable tension between us causes her smile to fade."Just physical, right?" she whispers.

I nod my lie. "Just physical."

Slowly, sweetly, she presses her lips against mine.

I dig my fingers into the rail and break away just an inch. "Elora, you've been drinking."

"I know what I'm doing," she murmurs. "I can recite a poem if you'd like."

"Do it." I kiss her again, breaking every few seconds to let her say a word. It's something about blue skies or cries, but it's convincing enough for me to wrap my arms around her and pull her inside.

She doesn't hold back. Her tongue twists with mine, every inch of her body pressing against mine. And I swear to Hades, if anyone knocks on my door, I will light them on fire.

My hands roam freely across her ribs, placing pressure against every dip and grove of her spine. I want to take my time and have her in every way all at once, and I can't choose between the two.

Until she says, "More. I need more."

More could cover many steps, but I'm not prepared for that with her. Kissing her is overwhelming enough—giving her everything might lead to secluding her here until I've had my fill.

I break away from her with tender kisses. "I can give you more. Do you trust me?"

She bites her lip as she nods.

"Go lay down in my bed."

She crawls onto my bed with trembling hands and slips beneath the blankets. I exhale slowly and remove my shirt. I want her so desperately that stopping myself from burying my cock inside her will be painful, but I need to be gentle with her before unleashing on her.

She watches my every move with burning intensity, reaching for me as soon as I crawl beside her. I grab her waist and drag her closer, kissing her softly. "You're so beautiful, little doe." I slowly bunch her skirt in my hand, eliminate obstacles between us, and flex my hand from how soft her skin is.

Fuck, I'm in trouble, and I soon decide to keep the blanket covering her lower half to prevent myself from tongue-fucking her right away.

"I want you to tell me how good it feels," I say.

She flinches when two of my fingers tease her navel, then releases a shaky breath. "You feel good," she whispers.

I haven't even *started* yet.

"Fuck, you're not going to make this easy on me, are you?" I trail my fingers lower. "Tell me what you thought when you first saw me."

"I thought..."—she sucks in a breath when I inch closer to her pussy—"I thought about how much I hated you."

Grinning, I stroke her clit with my middle finger. She gasps and claws at my chest, failing to realize I removed my shirt for this very reason—I want her to leave scratches.

"You're so wet for the man you claim to hate," I whisper, beginning teasing flicks on her clit.

Her back arches off the bed, her hips trying to chase my finger each time I pull away. "Finnian," she whines.

I nip at her ear. "Do you hate me still?"

"Yes," she breathes, moaning when I start a steady rhythm against her, "so much."

I groan, nuzzling her neck while I watch the blanket move from my hand teasing her beneath. "Fuck, Elora." My finger travels low enough to needle her entrance. "Hate me all you want."

She wiggles lower, whimpering.

"Have you ever touched yourself, Elora?"

Her cheeks reddened when she slightly nodded.

Envious hope pounds in my chest. "Did you come?"

I can tell by now when she wants to be stubborn and cruel, but she is too desperate for me right now to dare it. Instead of testing me, she bites her lip and shakes her head.

Fuck me, I will provide her first climax.

I will own her in every single way.

I tug her earlobe with my teeth. "Deep breath, little doe."

On her inhale, I slide my middle finger inside her, crying her name when she clenches around me. Her nails drag down my chest, her chest rising and falling in short, quick pants.

I want to give her body time to adjust, and I'm content to stay here. "You're so fucking tight, darling. Talk to me."

"It's sore," she rasps but quickly prevents me from pulling out of her by closing her hand over mine. "Don't stop. Give me more."

"Breathe for me, sweet girl." I take my time before adding a second finger, allowing time for her to relax before I push in and out, groaning from the way she reacts by thrusting against my fingers. "Are you okay?"

"Stop asking me that."

She takes my face between her hands and pulls me down. While kissing me wildly, her upper body twists toward me while I keep her bottom half pinned against the mattress with my hand.

I'm swollen against her hip, desperate to feel her pussy squeezing my cock instead of my fingers. She reaches for me, but I shake my head and capture her wrist with my other hand. "Not tonight, Elora."

Her eyes flutter open, but she keeps rocking against my hand. "I want you. *You*."

She's so close. Her eyes are rolling back, her lips forming the perfect pout.

"You'll have me," I promise her. "But I don't want to break you until you're legally bound to me. Now, come for me."

I roll the tips of my fingers over the spot that makes her react the strongest, catching each of her gasps with a searing kiss.

"You're doing so well, little doe," I whisper against her lips. "I want you to come on my fingers."

She clenches the sheets between her fingers, stubbornly trying to drag this out by slowing the rocking of her hips, but I want to hear what she sounds like during her climax.

I place my lips against her ear and murmur, "Say my name, little doe."

"Finnian," she breathlessly obeys, then throws her head back. "Finnian, oh gods, oh…."

"I bet you taste so fucking good," I growl in her ear, then nearly come when she pours onto my fingers, her cry of pleasure a strained attempt at saying my name.

Fuck, she's coming in waves, still going even as her body loosens. The fluttering around my fingers is dizzying, the smell of her the absolute worst kind of temptation.

"So good, Elora, you did so good." I don't pull out completely, slowing until her body is limp against mine. "You came all over me like such a good girl, darling."

Every breath she takes is a whimper, and she quivers against me. I shouldn't—I'll only be torturing myself—but I remove my fingers from her to slide into my mouth and squeeze her hips from the way she tastes. Fuck me, I need my tongue inside her.

She watches me with wide yet intrigued eyes. "I want you," she whispers. "I don't want to wait."

I remove my fingers from my mouth to touch her again with a grin. I don't know if her thrust against my hand is involuntary, but I chuckle. "Tempting, but you just experienced your first orgasm, Elora. I'm not going to push you tonight. I'm going to take care of you."

Her eyelids flutter when I brush over her clit. "But I want to make you feel good, too."

"Even though you despise me?"

"Especially because I despise you." She trails her lips across my collarbone. "Tell me how, Finnian."

I might've awakened something in her. She seems ready and willing for anything I can give her.

I can provide a *little* more.

I flatten on my back and tap her hip. "Come here."

She doesn't hesitate to climb on me, straddling my stomach. I hook an arm behind my head and shove the blanket off us. "Remove your dress, but only your dress."

Her cheeks flush.

I grab her arm and yank her down, kissing her for a full minute. "I want to see you, Elora, but only if you're comfortable. If there is any infuriating thought in your mind that is doubting how much I want you, I'm about to prove you wrong."

Determination crosses her face. Straightening, she doesn't give herself time to think about it before she pulls her dress off and drops it.

And I can't form a thought.

I stare before allowing myself to touch, frightened I might snap her in half. And I sigh when she shakes her hair from the braid and lets it fall naturally over her shoulders and chest.

Spending so much time not allowing myself to fantasize about her was worth it for this moment—my imagination wouldn't have been able to paint a picture this breathtaking.

Her porcelain skin, untouched and flawless, contrasts against mine—rough and scarred from years of work in the army. Her full, round breasts have been deceitful in the dresses she's worn since arriving. I've spent so much time focusing on her bare shoulders and imagining what she tastes like that I didn't consider how perfectly sized they are for my hands.

"This will be a problem," I say, fingering the pearl necklace around her neck.

She leans forward, her breasts bouncing from the slight movement. "What will?"

I cup her breasts in my hands, whispering her name. My cock is throbbing for her, but I want more time—I *need* more time to explore her before I can fuck her. Once I do, I'll be useless for much else.

Her head rolls forward when I brush her nipples with my thumbs.

"How perfect you are," I finished, but then I remembered how Massimo's hands explored her and clenched my jaw. "Tell me you're mine, Elora. Tell me that no one else will touch you."

She bites her lip when I massage her breasts with my palms. "Stop telling me to do things before distracting me." She's so wet that I can feel her cum on my stomach. "I'm yours, Finnian."

My cock twitches. "Again."

"No one else will touch me."

I raise up and wrap my lips around her breast, flicking her nipple with my tongue. She places her hand on my head and pulls me closer, whimpering my name when I take more of her in my mouth. "Finnian, please."

I use my teeth to pull at her skin, then switch to her other breast, sucking. She rolls her hips against my stomach, pouting. Seeing her puckered lower lip, I wrap my hands around her waist and scoot her down.

Her eyes meet mine when she settles right against my cock, dragging herself down my entire length. Even with layers still between us, the feel of her against me is unbearable.

I release her breast. "Roll your hips, Elora. Use me to make yourself come."

But she looks down between us with hesitation. "Finnian, that's not going to fit."

I move her against me with a grin. "I'll fucking make it fit."

"Finn—"

"Elora," I cut in, my self-control gone. "Brace yourself against my chest and *move*."

Hearing the desperation in my voice, she obeyed and leaned forward to place her palms against my chest, her nails digging into me. I guide her against me, dragging her back and forth in quick, smooth motions.

My gaze darts from her grinding against me to the soft bounce of her breasts until I lock eyes with her. And we stay that way through each moan, each thrust, every plea for more. I never look anywhere else.

I don't need to.

As delicious as I find her body, I enjoy watching her reactions more. That isn't something I've ever experienced with anyone else.

Her nails cut so deep that I bleed.

And when she whispers, "Kiss me," I sit up and obey, holding her head against mine while we come together.

I climax with her name muttered against her lips, my entire body shaking as it rocks through me so firmly that the blood rushing to my head makes me collapse to the pillow. But I bring her with me and keep her pressed against me.

And I kiss her until her body relaxes into mine and until she finally accepts that she needs to sleep, and I stop only when she rests her head against my chest and closes her eyes.

And I hold her with the terrifying realization that I will stop at nothing to keep her safe—that the loyalty beat into me for this kingdom, for my father, was all for nothing.

I belong to Elora now.

Thirty-Five

I wake up smiling.

I immediately recognize where I am, his smell encompassing me underneath the heavy blankets. Sore between my legs but aching for him again.

Irina was right—Finnian proved he wanted me, took his time, and made me feel safe. It was *me* who begged *him* for more. I awakened overnight once to him hard beneath me. I woke him with a kiss, and we came together again. But no matter how hard I pressed, how much I begged, he wouldn't give me *everything*.

Shoving my arms out from underneath the blankets, I bend and bow, stretching. I roll over and search for him, frowning at his absence. Holding the blanket over my chest, I sit up and sigh in relief when I spot him sitting at his table, staring.

Still bare-chested and mouthwatering.

And I'm marrying him today.

All of him will be mine.

His legs are stretched out, his elbow on the table, but he doesn't look satisfied. He seems exhausted; the circles under his eyes are black.

"I thought you left," I say quietly.

"I wouldn't do that to you, Elora."

"Why do you seem upset?"

"Because I am."

I tuck a stray curl behind my ear. "Did I do something? Talk in my sleep?"

"Do you remember waking up?"

I bite my bottom lip with a slight grin.

He nods slowly. "Do you remember what happened when you fell back asleep?"

I try to recall if I woke up again throughout the night, but his satisfied groans in my ear remain my only memory. "I don't. Why?"

"You screamed all night and not in the way I can make you scream." He sits up and brings his legs in, resting his elbows on his knees. "And I couldn't wake you."

I try my hand at attempting to distract him. "You can make me scream?"

For a second, I thought he'd take the bait when his eyes darkened, but he blinked it away. "You're a clever little doe. Now, talk."

I fall back to the pillow with a sigh. "It's just nightmares, Finnian."

"No, no." He stands and leans against the bedpost. "Nightmares aren't real. You screamed like you were in pain. Do you know how terrifying it is to want to help someone, but you cannot reach them? Elora, I couldn't *do* anything. That is more than a nightmare."

I cover my eyes with my arm. "I don't know what you want me to say. I'm sorry I woke you up. I can sleep elsewhere."

"The fuck you can." He hits me with a pillow. "I don't care that I was woken up. I need to know what these are and how to help you."

Helping me is impossible.

If he's being truthful and developing feelings for me, then the spell I drank wouldn't ever break. I wished for the confidence to ensnare him but didn't make it conditional, which meant that these nightmares might last forever.

"Does it have to do with the faeries?"

My breath catches. "What?"

The bed shifts from the weight change when he climbs onto it and crawls over me. Removing my arm from my face, he searches my eyes for honesty. "The faeries," he repeats slowly, knowing I heard him the first time. "Irina said you haven't asked to see them."

"I've been busy," I lied.

"Elora, I couldn't have bribed you to stop talking about them when you first arrived."

Truthfully, I miss them.

I miss Azrea. I want to tell her everything—share with her that I might be falling in love for the first time. And if anyone might understand why I keep seeing a man in a dark room with shadowy magic, it would be her.

But I resent how she asked me to walk away from all of this.

From him. From trying to help Ashbury.

I offer him a partial truth. "I haven't asked to see them because of you. And Irina. Something happened when we visited." I hurriedly add when his nostrils flare, "Nothing with Cedric. I mean, he touched me, but it wasn't—"

He moves to get off the bed, but I wrap both hands around his wrist. "Stop. Let me finish, please. You make me very nervous."

"I don't want to make you nervous," he sighs. "But I don't share, and hearing about it gives me visuals I do not wish to see. It's taking everything in me not to have him removed from this realm altogether."

"I've noticed," I mutter. "But you did share."

"Fucking Irina. What did she tell you?"

"Nothing," I reply honestly. And frustratingly. "She's annoyingly loyal to you."

A breathy laugh comes from his nose, but his jaw remains tight. "We've been through a lot together," he explains. "Before we proceed with this, Elora, I need to know. Do you have feelings for Cedric? Or Massimo?"

I jerk my head to the side. "*Massimo*? No. Gods, because I danced with him? I was imagining you. No, he is all for Irina." I tug at his wrist. "I'll be honest if you come here."

He stares at my partially uncovered chest before compromising by laying beside me on *top* of the blankets. I don't hide my disappointment, sighing heavily when he laces his fingers through mine. I struggle to understand how, at twenty-one years old, I only now crave anything physical. It might've crossed my mind sometimes, but I covet the pleasure Finnian provides.

"Elora," he says with a knowing grin.

I stop staring at his hand, only slightly mortified. "At one time, I did have feelings for Cedric. It was hard not to when he was one of the only males that showed me kindness, but nothing ever happened." I bring his hand to my lips, kissing each finger. "I didn't even want to tolerate you, Finnian, but I'm in your bed."

He nods but frowns. "Some of them are cruel toward you?"

I lick my lips, then gnaw on my top one. I trust Finnian. I understand turning into his father is *his* worst nightmare, but I've also witnessed firsthand how protective he can be. And I don't want to say something that ends with him storming the mountainside. "They're prideful, that's all it is."

He sighs through his nose before *slightly* relaxing. "So, you're mine."

The corner of my mouth quirks up. "You're awfully possessive for this being only physical between us."

He says nothing, but I lightly trace his brow. "I should go. I'm getting married today. I'd invite you, but the man I'm marrying is slightly predatory."

He flashes me a lazy grin. "Is he?" Loosening his fingers from mine, he slides his hand into the blanket and squeezes one of my breasts. "You're right. You should go. But I would be a rude host if I didn't leave my guest satisfied."

I am wholly satisfied, yet also starved.

He peels the blanket back and lowers his head to my chest, taking my breast into his mouth. I lace my fingers through his hair and hold him there, gasping when he clamps his teeth around my nipple right as one finger slides into me—only this time, he keeps his palm pressed against my clit. The friction from my hips rolling against his hand causes my eyes to roll back, but this isn't what I want. "Finnian, I want you. Please. *Please.*"

He releases my breast with a dissatisfied sigh, removing his hand and sliding his finger into his mouth. Wordlessly, he throws the blankets off me and to the floor and remains silent when he crawls between my legs and spreads my knees apart. And only when he sees me wholly bare before him does he whisper my name while he rubs his cock over his pants, which he *refuses* to remove.

I thought I'd be embarrassed to be naked in front of him, but his arousal was obvious. Yet, it bothers me that he continues to refuse my request. I didn't expect *him* to be the traditional one.

With his eyes remaining locked on mine, he lowers to his stomach between my legs. I rise to my elbows to watch him, stomach tightening in anticipation when he brushes his tongue across my clit.

"What are you—" I start to say, but it turns into a garbled cry when he flicks his tongue repetitively. How, how, *how* does he have so many ways to make me feel like this?

He groans when his tongue teases my entrance, shudders when it slides in, and balls the sheets in his hands to drag me closer until his face is completely buried in my pussy.

I don't know what to do with my hands, body, or head, constantly jerking or twitching, unable to comprehend sounds or feelings, because everything feels so wonderful that I cease to remember evil has ever existed.

I cry his name over and over.

I beg him not to stop.

I beg him to let me come.

I beg him to never leave this bed.

And he only continues to groan, yanking me closer, never coming up for air, just *devouring*.

I ignore the knocking on his door. I don't care if someone comes in and sees us. If the end is near for me, I'd rather this be my last moment. But that's only because of the desire to dismiss any logic. Fuck, reason no longer exists when I'm near him.

But the knocking doesn't cease, and he growls against me before he stands, leaving me to curse at him, breathless and empty. I hear him speaking; I contemplate using my hand to finish but doubt it would feel half as good.

He returns with the same heated stare, reaches over, grabs my ankles, and pulls me to the edge of the bed. "Irina can't cover for you much longer, little doe." He sinks to his knees and rests my legs over his shoulders. "Be a good girl for me, and come really fucking fast."

He resumes with toe-curling determination.

And I obey.

❧

Too many women are in this room.

I can't stop thinking about Finnian pressed against me, the way he said my name and caressed every inch of me. I avoid conversation, allow Irina to answer their questions for me, and exist purely on memories.

I haven't been prepped much for the wedding since it isn't my choice. Queen Honora plans events quickly and could throw a soiree together in a day, leaving me to wonder just how big this wedding would be if it only took seven days to prepare.

I wasn't given choices for wedding attire or colors. I didn't get to choose the ring Finnian would wear, nor was I told if he would even wear one—though I have a surprise for him. I wasn't sure if *I'd* even have a ring. Everything about this life-changing event was chosen *for* me without my input. The only detail I'm aware of is the flavor of the cake. Irina and way too many cousins of theirs will join us on either side of the altar.

We'll take a carriage ride around Pumpkin Hollow afterward before joining every guest for food and dancing since the night ended so *joyfully* the last time we tried that.

I have women doing my hair, fussing over which color lip stain I should wear, making last-minute alterations on my dress, and pulling at me so roughly that Irina has to remind them that I'm not a doll and can feel the pricks of their needles. But if any part of this could bring a smile to my face, it's how relaxed she seems after spending a night with Massimo and Leif.

Dressed in all gold, Irina looks like a goddess. Gold and ivory ribbons weave through her double braids, her arms are adorned with gold bracelets, and her gold dress brings out the luminous shine of her irises.

And she doesn't leave my side.

Queen Honora's quarters include two balconies, and all four doors are open so as not to miss the unmistakable chimes of the warning bell, sending every woman scurrying around the room like mice looking for a block of cheese.

Irina rolled her eyes and clapped her hands once to get their attention. "Leave us!"

They scatter, shouting wishes of luck and happiness, and curtsy to the queen before leaving us alone. Irina released a deep breath and took my hands to help me stand. "Dozens of weddings, but I suppose it's different because no one believed Finnian would ever wed."

Just his name warms my cheeks.

Irina snorts. "Spare me the details."

I wrinkle my nose. "I would never subject you to hearing about your brother."

She disappears behind me to fix the buttons of my dress. "Oh, I've heard plenty about him, but it was only to collect stories on everyone else." She squeezes my waist. "Are you ready to see yourself as a bride, doe?"

Butterflies flutter in my stomach.

This was it—the entire reason I came here. But I never thought I'd go into it while falling for him. Risking him. Gods, risking his life if I did anything wrong. If anything was to happen to him because of me....

My chest aches—inhaling burned, and exhaling is making me

lightheaded. I clutch my stomach and bend against the vanity, sweat beading my brow.

"Elora, breathe." Irina calls for her mother. "Breathe, *breathe*."

Honora's hands are on my waist. "Irina, go get her some water and a cold rag."

Irina runs out the door while Honora helps me walk to the terrace for a sweep of chilly air on my skin. "What have I done?" I cry. "What have I done? Why would he hurt Finnian?"

Honora pulls me to her chest. "Elora, it will be all right. I need you to tell me what you offered in exchange for his safety. What were the terms?"

I don't want to relive those moments in the king's study. I've worked so hard to forget the smells of that room, the way the dead eyes stared at me, and the paper I signed in blood.

I want to forget.

Pretend it never happened.

Just another nightmare.

With tearful eyes, I lift my head from her chest, my own caving in. "He wanted my allegiance, he wanted a guarantee that I wouldn't ask the faeries to attack him, he was so paranoid, so *angry*...."—I close my eyes, his erratic movements and threatening tone still so vivid—"I promised him over and over that I wasn't planning that. I just wanted help with Ashbury."

She shushes me gently, rubbing my arms when they pimple from fear.

A tear slips down my cheek. "He took me into this.... skulls were everywhere." My voice breaks. "He said he'd sacrifice anyone to protect his realm. I told him I understood, I'd sign something promising my allegiance to him, I would have the child he wants so desperately, but then...." I wrap my fingers around my throat. "He said the consequences would be given to Finnian—that he'd hurt him. But I negotiated."

"Elora, no," she whispers. "Elora, what happens if you break your word?"

I can hardly say the words; I can barely believe I agreed so willingly to lose my head for a man I hardly know and how easily I'm prepared to sacrifice my life for him.

But I say the words, admit to what I've done, and whisper, "He adds me to his collection."

❧

Irina hasn't returned yet.

Honora paces the length of the room while I sit slumped over on her bed. Tears have stopped falling, but despair lingers. Death was always a risk when coming here—I knew what could happen, but I came here with *hope*.

If the prince fell in love with me, his father wouldn't harm me. We would annul the marriage, and they'd let me go. I could reason with him, use Jasper's love for my father in my favor.

But the endless pool of the king's wrath doesn't include forgiveness or second chances.

I signed my death certificate.

Not only for Finnian, but also for Irina.

For Honora.

After learning what they've had to endure after years of his abuse, I couldn't let them suffer because of me. My missteps would not bring their suffering. "I don't want Finnian to know."

"He must," she replies. "Elora, Finnian must be told. You will wed, we will pretend all is well, and when you arrive at Hogsfeet, you will tell him then."

I stand on shaky legs. "With all due respect, I have not been entirely honest with you." Clearing my throat, I try my best to speak steadily. "If I become pregnant, it does not negate our terms. I will be allowed to carry the child to term, but then I will be disposed of."

Honora sinks into a chair, staring at me with wide eyes and parted lips.

"And if I do not become pregnant within three months, my life will end." My bottom lip quivers. "It would be a kindness for that to happen, but I will not take away Finnian's chance to have a child. And I do not want him to spend the length of our marriage wondering when it will end."

I sit across from her, tasting the salt on my lips from my tears. "Finnian is young enough to find another bride after I go. You will have a grandchild and both of your children. I have no family left. My death will bring the least amount of heartache. And, maybe, before my time comes, we'll have found a way to help my people."

Honora, the Queen of Pumpkin Hollow, wife of the most powerful king in these lands, falls before me and takes my hands. "Elora, my heart breaks for you."

Tears fall down her cheeks as she stares at me. "I weep for you, sweet girl, because you have been led to believe that you do not matter in this world and that the beat of your heart does not matter as much as ours."

I press my tongue to the roof of my mouth as tears fall from my cheeks to my dress and her hands, unable to speak, unable to believe.

She moves a hand to my chest. "But it *does*, Elora. You are made of flesh and blood and goodness. You move selflessly to protect the ones you hold dear, so quick to exchange your life for theirs because of lies you've been told."

My chest caves in when a sob escapes.

"Did you truly believe yourself to be so unimportant that you couldn't come to me with this?" She palms my cheeks. "You are not here simply to exist for others, Elora. Whether you bear a child or not, you have a purpose."

She brings my forehead to her lips and lowers her voice in a whisper, "Put your trust in me, dear one. It is long past the day we escape him once and for all. You will outlive me." Wiping my tears away with her thumbs, she lifts my face to hold my gaze. "Leave it to me, Elora. All will be well."

Before I could respond, Irina opened the door with a frustrated cry, trying to squeeze it shut against a weight holding it open. "He won't leave the hallway, but we must go!"

She's balancing the cold rag and water in her hands while yelling at someone on the other side to *leave*. Honora dabs at her cheeks with her sleeves before standing and calmly motioning for Irina to walk away.

Irina huffs while coming to me, wiping my tears with the cold rag and soothing the swelling underneath my eyes. "He's gone mad. He believes you've changed your mind."

I jerk my head to the side, trying to dodge her hand. "That's Finnian?"

Honora closes the door and turns to flash us a bright, albeit an annoyed, grin. "He is still like the excitable boy I raised sometimes, yet with much more power now." She exhales a steadying breath. "He will return if we are not there before the final bell chimes."

"Final touch," Irina says, crawling over to the bed and pulling a small wooden box out from underneath. "He insisted."

From the box, she gently slides her hands underneath a crown made of Forget-Me-Not flowers and places it atop my head.

The flowers that keep my nightmares away.

My gaze lifts to Honora, a spark of hope renewed that her words will ring true—that I can happily live a long life with Finnian and find renewed purpose within.

Her answering smile holds so much promise.

Thirty-Six

Situated along the outer banks of the kingdom, past the shoppes and cottages, down a pumpkin-lined path made of stone, sits a cathedral older than the castle. The history of Pumpkin Hollow pounded into me by tutors could be recited in my sleep, but I find this place most interesting.

It stood erected long before we arrived.

Jasper and his brother discovered it as children. Abandoned even then, they spent their days inside the cathedral until they were old enough to help my grandfather with trivial tasks, like washing clothes in a small creek nearby or grilling rabbit or squirrel for every meal.

After losing his wife, my grandfather didn't want to stay in the town where they met and fell in love, instead choosing to seclude himself and his children so they could be left alone.

Not born into wealth or titles, they resided in a cabin within a forest near the outskirts. Manual labor frustrated Jasper as a boy, but not his brother.

As the oldest, his brother worked to show his father that he could readily handle the responsibilities of taking over someday, but Jasper.... he wanted *more*.

Avoiding his chores led him to discover the bridge at seventeen. After showing his father, who had grown tired of living off the land

and working until his hands gave out, he wanted his oldest son to erect a kingdom.

Irate, Jasper began to resent his brother for being favored, convinced that this land was his because he found the bridge. And after learning that the castle his brother planned to construct was rather plain and modest, he decided to take back what was his.

He lured his brother to the cathedral under the falsehood of restoration and used a sharpened, dull end of a wood plank to drive through his throat, partially severing his head from his body.

His father had a decision to make.

Stand with his youngest son or face his vengeful wrath. Choosing the former gave him a place as Jasper's head adviser, tasked with choosing his future queen. My mother.

As an established kingdom, men of Ashbury assisted my father in building the castle and cottages, sending word to nearby villages that an opportunity to move into a young domain might bring wealth and steady food sources to an otherwise desolate area.

Small in size, Ashbury couldn't take in any more residents, initially sending travelers to Hogsfeet. Believing my father to be a good man, they helped him grow the population of Pumpkin Hollow, assisted in procuring weapons for defenses, shared plans with him for our trebuchets, and dined with him on multiple occasions to celebrate the sister kingdoms. But there was just one small problem—the bridge.

Jasper became obsessed with wanting reasons why it existed and approached Elora's grandfather about shattering it to have the magic for themselves, but continuously being denied reminded him too much of his father. He didn't want to share the bridge, nor could he sleep at night while envious that Elora's grandfather believed the bridge to be his.

It didn't matter that he wasn't the one to discover it—Jasper wanted it.

He maintained his friendship with the neighboring king while he married my mother, sired an heir and a princess to secure his lineage, invited the royal family to our christenings, and built our army and weapons with the resources given to him by the kingdom he wanted to destroy. He pretended to be an ally.

Ashbury never saw it coming.

Elora's father was nowhere to be found in our history books, but it was well-known by the elders of each kingdom that Harry was the one who helped Jasper tear apart the monarchy.

No one ever knew why he turned on his father and tossed his inheritance aside to help my father take his kingdom.

And just as he killed his brother, Jasper took the king's head, thus beginning his collection.

And for good measure, he captured the King of Hogsfeet for the same demise.

The arrival of the faeries and Jasper's trust in Harry kept the people of Ashbury alive.

But the bridge was finally his.

He stopped trying to find why or how it existed because it served as a reminder to those who crossed it—he would stop at nothing to have precisely what he sought.

But it marked a new chapter in Pumpkin Hollow's history—displaying our riches while the kingdom we destroyed starved.

The palace was rebuilt to match the bridge, and the gallows were erected beneath his balcony to warn those who tried to take what he believed he rightfully earned.

And now, I stand in the cathedral where it all started, about to marry his newest procurement while he accepts bows and congratulatory sentiments upon his throne, everyone believing him to be gracious for allowing his son to marry the fallen Princess of Ashbury.

Unbeknownst to any of them, Elora is the one with the power. *He* needs *her*—unable to use fear against a strong species. His slipping control is driving him mad.

But Elora's story will not end as my uncle's did. Irina and my mother will finally live peacefully. And *I* will serve as a reminder as the man who brought the end to my father's unjust and unearned tyranny. No one alive is ever allowed to harm my wife.

Long live the king.

❧

Lined on either side of me are cousins I avoid as much as possible. Only one belongs to my uncle, who was unsurprisingly quick with his forgiveness for *my* father beheading *his* father when given a title and wealth. The rest belong to my mother's siblings, who followed her when she left her kingdom to become the queen of ours.

Jasper welcomed them by offering a group of manors in the corner of Pumpkin Hollow, hoping they'd stay away from the castle. My mother's kingdom isn't necessarily dying, but with her parents nearing death and all their children split between our kingdom and others, it will slowly deteriorate until it's just another abandoned castle to be ransacked.

My weapons are waiting in Major's stall to bring with us to Hogsfeet for the same reason. I'm not taking any chances with Elora's life.

The bell tower chimes.

In three rings, I will learn if she's here.

Three.

I maintain a calm composure while my thoughts race. Irina didn't know why Elora was so upset, but I wouldn't blame her if she accepted my drunken offer of letting her leave this place.

Two.

I wouldn't stop her, but I would chase her.

I'd never forget how she tasted.

One.

I silently plead for her to give me a chance, wordlessly promising to protect her.

Come on, little doe.

Heads turn toward the grand doors as they peel back, guests smiling at the line of more of my cousins walking down the aisle and coming to stand opposite of the men behind me. Too many fucking people were asked to be part of a moment that has nothing to do with them, but Jasper required my mother to not spare any expense to make our wedding the grandest ever held in Pumpkin Hollow.

The number of flowers and colorful drapes adorned across every chair and window gives me a headache, but none of that matters if Elora just walks through the doors.

Jasper studies me from his throne, watching for any reaction that will give away my feelings for her. Unfortunately for him, after he beheaded my friend, I mastered how to maintain an expression of boredom.

My mother appears next, but it doesn't make breathing any easier. It only makes me more anxious. Per our traditions, she comes to me first and extends her hand for me to kiss, but she takes it one step further.

My mother leans forward and places her lips against my cheek for a peck but hurriedly whispers against my skin, "We must speak after you return from Hogsfeet, my darling."

I force a smile when she pulls away to join my father at the thrones, remaining on her feet while Irina walks through the doors next.

Tears fill my eyes.

I've spent so many years away under the assumption it would keep her protected that I wasted spending time with her. It shouldn't have taken a sharp-tongued little beast to show me the error of my ways. I should've been here.

Irina's eyes glaze upon seeing mine.

So much together—we've endured so much.

There are so many things we can never speak about.

Even with Jasper analyzing every emotion and reaction, Irina walked faster toward me and slid her arms around my torso, pressing her cheek tightly against my chest.

My heart nearly combusts.

And I embrace my sister.

I want to apologize to her. In front of everyone, I want to tell her how sorry I am for leaving her to navigate life alone while I selfishly lived abroad to avoid our father.

But Irina and I, we are above apologies. We each made our own choices on how to live the life we were given—decided the best way to survive. If we fucked up, we were straight with one another. We never excused ourselves with a simple apology.

We forgive and move forward.

But not once have we ever been openly affectionate in front of our father. Irina winked at me with tearful eyes upon release before she turned toward him and lifted her chin.

She doesn't waver.

Irina has always been defiant and never hidden her hatred of him, but this is different.

And he knows it.

Instead of standing with the women, Irina angles herself right behind me. Jasper's chest rose and fell with tight breaths, his lips drawn in a line, his face growing red from the murmurs of Irina breaking protocol and staying with me.

His look conveys a silent order for me to do something. And part of me instinctively wants to obey and protect her, but I will no longer silence her anger. So, I step closer to her.

A first step.

His fist curls on the arm of his throne, but the corners of my mother's lips lift.

I don't have to remain curious as to why Irina decided my wedding was the best place to mark the beginning of our internal familial war. Instead of my bride coming through the doors next, three faces I despise step out.

Regina holds her chin high, followed closely by her disgraceful daughters. Every urge to order them out, banish them from Pumpkin Hollow for eternity, is swallowed by the fear of the wedding being called off if I react how he's expecting.

They walk down the aisle slowly, wanting every set of eyes on them and their horridly bright dresses.

Regina curtsies to me with an apparent smirk, remaining

lowered while she waits for her daughters to do the same. I don't acknowledge them, but Irina mutters, "Tarts."

Regina's head snaps up with a glare, but I fix her with one of my own. She whips her skirt around and leaves her daughters in a curtsy behind her, snapping at them to follow her after realizing they remained behind.

Irina snickers.

I ask in a whisper, "Were they cruel to Elora? What did they say?"

"Now isn't the time," she snaps back in a sharp mumble.

I sigh, flexing my hands at my sides. After unleashing on Darius, the itch to pummel every irritation has taken over my need to drink.

But then, the room falls away.

Bathed in setting sunlight, Elora steps forward to the nave. I thought I had found my favorite version of her when she awoke naked in my bed with her curls wild and mussed from a night of pleasure with me, her eyes wide and soft in the morning glow, but I was mistaken.

This. *This*.

Her ivory dress wraps around her tighter than I ever could, baring her shoulders, her sleeves draped and brushing the floor. Gold blends into patterns across her corset, cut low enough to tease what lies beneath.

Spilling down her back and over her shoulders, her silky curls spiral into golden ends from the sun's rays, bathing her perfectly through the apertures in the sanctuary.

Her crown, made of Forget-Me-Not flowers, makes my heart shove against my chest to try to reach her. Not only have I fallen in love with her, but I am consumed by her.

Not once have I ever experienced a feeling like this with anyone else—not once have I ever wished to make someone my wife *this* strongly.

I will never question fate again.

It brought me here to stand with her.

The gold in her eyes snags mine, and her breathing calms, remaining focused on me as she takes one step at a time, ignoring the soft gasps of guests. I hope every one of them regrets ever doubting her beauty and grace.

Irina nudges my arm with hers, her smile wide and bright from the corner of my eye, but I refuse to look at anyone else. I couldn't even if I wanted to. Ensnared in Elora's trap and at her mercy is precisely where I need to be.

I extend my hands, and hers tremble in mine, her eyes reflecting the emotion in mine, her inability to smile from struggling to breathe wholly understood by me. Every moment before this one ceases to exist. I've waited forever for her, yet didn't even realize I was looking.

Enduring it all again to end with her standing here would be a sacrifice I'd make.

I never drop her hands, she never lowers her eyes, and we recite words and promises back and forth that hold no actual meaning at all because our loyalty will not remain to the king, and we will not honor him above one another.

This is it. It's Elora.

She will be the one to free me.

Releasing one of her hands, I pull a ring from my pocket to slide onto her finger. It belonged to my grandmother and was one of the few heirlooms my mother brought from her kingdom. Simple and gold, but it means she's mine, and she smiles at it like it's everything.

Since Jasper doesn't wear a ring, I'm not surprised when one isn't offered to me, but Elora clears her throat and whispers, "Wait."

Irina rolled her eyes when the bishop continued, repeating Elora's request louder, "*Wait.*"

I chuckle, as do a few of our guests. Irina held her hand out to Elora, and Elora waited for Irina to slide a loose ring from her finger into her open hand. Licking her lips, Elora holds the ring in her palm.

"This was my father's," she murmurs softly, only loud enough for me to hear.

And Irina, as she hovers close enough to make it appear as if all three of us are in this together. She looks unamused when I raise an eyebrow in a silent command for her to move back, taking the tiniest step away.

Elora exchanges a knowing smile with me. "The one my mother gave him," she continues.

My brow furrows. I can't comprehend why she'd give this to me when it has to mean so much to her.

"You don't have to wear it." She pulls in her bottom lip for a moment before taking a deep breath. "But if you want...."

"I do," I whisper, "If you're sure I've earned the honor."

Remaining faithful to herself, she shrugs a shoulder. "Hardly, but,"—her grin grows wide—"I'd like to see you try."

The emotion I've tried to hide shows when she slides the ring on my finger. I want to admit to her how deeply I've fallen for her, how meeting her has made me see the light, but I can't form any of those words.

Our union might have been forced, but this band around my finger was her choice.

And she chose to give it to me.

And maybe the hope blooming in my chest means she feels for me what I feel for her.

I hear the word '*kiss*' and do not hesitate.

Tipping her chin up with my finger, my expression is solemn while I study every inch of her face and eyes before my gaze lowers to her mouth. I can count on two hands the number of times I've kissed her, but each one has become more passionate and meant *more*. And this one is no different.

Leaning in slowly, her bright smile fades into a longing simper when I hover inches above her lips, but before I kiss her, I whisper with a grin, "Still hate me?"

"So much it makes me sick."

The lie is in her voice.

And I kiss her.

❧

Elora clearly hasn't been given instructions for each step she must complete before we can celebrate. After officially announcing our union to the guests, the bishop leads us to the thrones. Unsure how he procured it during the ceremony, I click my jaw when my father raises a goblet of wine at us.

Elora's gaze darts between my mother and Jasper as if she's being led to her death and not her coronation. I squeeze her hand, hoping to alleviate her fears, but it doesn't. She looks profoundly terrified, which surprises me.

This is the reason she came here.

She wanted a title to have the power to heal her home, but each step she takes toward the king seems riddled with regret and fear.

Instead of looking at her, I switched to my mother. She isn't watching Elora with the same confusion—she's staring at me.

As if to say *we were right*.

And then, I look at him.

His arrogant satisfaction is pinned to the trembling doe beside me. And I realize it doesn't matter how *I* feel about her—whatever she promised him is between them. She is his to control. And that terrifies me more than anything could. I know firsthand the lengths he *wouldn't* hesitate to reach for his benefit.

Elora's crown is brought out from behind the throne, and she is instructed to step forward. She sways, unsteady from her trepidation, freezing completely when my father stands.

I arch a brow. He has never crowned anyone. That honor is reserved for the bishop, but Jasper takes the crown from the bishop's hands. Irina appears behind Elora, her hand resting on the small of her back, and we exchange looks of bewilderment before my mother says gently, "Elora, come."

The tension in Elora's shoulders loosens slightly, and she inhales a deep, steady breath. Irina removes the delicate crown of flowers from Elora's hair—the one that flows better with the gentle nature of a doe.

Elora steps forward and tips her chin up. She keeps her gaze locked on my father's as he lowers the tiara of solid gold on her head.

The King of Pumpkin Hollow crowning the fallen Princess of Ashbury twenty-five years after he destroyed her kingdom and murdered her grandfather is a moment in history only few will ever witness.

And I watch with bated breath as the unwavering and challenging stare between them starts to crack the scale of power my father has kept over her kingdom for so long.

Then, Elora whispers, "Long live the king."

PART THREE

the penance

Thirty-Seven

After the carriage rides through town to officially introduce Elora as the princess to those who weren't invited to witness it, we have our first dance as husband and wife, Prince and Princess of Pumpkin Hollow.

Jasper and my mother watch from their thrones in the ballroom while Irina dodges princes.

Much to our relief, Regina and her daughters left after the wedding without a word to either of us, but I couldn't help feeling like there was a reason he invited them.

Elora is with me, yet distant. And frustrated that she wasn't allowed to remove the tiara after the ceremony for her Forget-Me-Not crown. I prevent her from pulling it off by placing her hands against my chest. "If you wear a flower crown, what will I wear?"

She pouts her bottom lip. "You look handsome in your crown. I look... strange."

I shake my head, laughing at her. "You're perfect, Elora. It suits you."

"Yours is silver," she mutters. "Mine is *gold*. They don't match."

I pinch her waist. "You're trying to find every excuse to remove that. I will have a godsdamn silver tiara made for you."

Her eyes widened slightly. "I won't have to wear this daily, will I?"

I must not be hearing her correctly. "Do you know how many women would love to take your place right now?"

"Gods," she snaps. "This isn't about how popular you are, Finnian. Yes, I know women want you, especially when I tell them how open to affairs you are."

I glare. "How long will you hold that against me? I can't fucking stand you sometimes."

"Your hands say otherwise."

I am failing horribly at not looking infatuated with her, having trouble keeping my hands from touching every part of her that would scandalize our guests. But despite her hatred for it, Elora looks radiant in the tiara.

"Keep it on your infuriating, perfect little head, Elora."

When my hand nearly slips over her backside, she yanks it back up to rest against her lower back. "Do I have to listen to your commands anymore? I'm the princess."

"Darling, I will always hold more power than you."

She rolls her eyes. "We'll see about that."

More couples join us to dance, but Irina stays to the side and pops strawberries in her mouth, ignoring anyone who tries to speak to her. I've danced with her once already, but when she noticed Beau walking toward my wife, she shoved me away and insisted I handle it immediately.

If keeping other men away from Elora means I must dance with her all night, I will.

We are currently on our third.

"Well, little doe." I nearly kissed her before I caught myself. "How does it feel having succeeded at your master plan of saddling the very handsome, mighty prince?"

She snorts but falters when her gaze moves to the thrones behind me. "When I tried talking myself into coming here, I promised myself I would only tolerate you."

I smile despite her sullenness. "Is that a confession of *more* than tolerating me?"

A watery glaze blankets her eyes, and without answering, she rests her cheek against my chest. I frown while holding her, rubbing her back. "Elora," I whisper, "Look at me."

But she doesn't.

Millions of thoughts cloud my mind.

Is she unhappy? Regretful?

Is it my father?

Is it me?

I just want to see her smile. "You know, I was warned many times by many men that while the beginning of marriage is full of passion and *need*,"—I drag my fingers down her spine—"that it's also full of fighting and misery. I guess you're getting started early?"

Her head pops up with a scowl. But upon seeing my smirk, she sighs. "I am not miserable with you, Finnian, as surprising as I might find that to be." The mischievous glint returns to her eyes. "As for the other two, I wouldn't know anything about those."

"No?" I press my lips to her ear. "You didn't wake me up last night from the *need* to feel me between your legs?"

She shakes her head slightly, but the pressure on my chest increases from her fingers pressing into it.

I move to her other ear. "The way you cried my name when you came on my tongue sounded passionate. Was I mistaken?"

"Maybe I can't remember," she whispers, sliding her hands up my chest and into my hair. "Maybe you should remind me."

Meanwhile, my hands have split apart. One wraps around her neck, the other lingers close to the base of her spine, tempted to inch lower and trace the curve of her backside.

"Maybe I want to fight first," I counter. I take her earlobe between my teeth and tug. "Maybe I want you to say wretched things to me so I can chase you again. Make me work for your taste. Because I hate you so endlessly."

"Infinitely," she whispers, turning her head against mine, our lips only inches apart. "But maybe, just this once, we can pretend otherwise." Her lips hover over mine, but she locks eyes with me. "Just for tonight, we can pretend I've let you catch me."

I drag my knuckles down her jaw, pretending to contemplate her offer. "Just for tonight, set aside our hatred and explore one another? Search for that pleasure and need?"

She nods slightly. "Just for tonight."

"And return to hatred tomorrow?"

She hums her approval, but I shake my head. "I don't think I can do that, little doe."

Her breath catches as hope springs to her eyes. "Why?"

Everyone else has faded around us, the song no more than notes, fear replaced by something more tangible and permanent.

Brushing her bottom lip with my thumb, I stare into her eyes. "Because once I stop hating you, Elora, I won't want to start again. I will be completely consumed by you. Addicted."

My confession seems to surprise her as her hands cease to move, her lips part, her eyes search.

But my calm demeanor stays. "So, tell me, little doe, do you still want it just for tonight?"

I wait, heart pounding and barely breathing, wishing to be alone with her and wanting to drag her out depending on her answer.

'No' means I have to continue chasing her.

But *'yes'* means we can hope for more.

I am prepared to hear the former. I understand I'm not her first choice, but when she whispers, "Yes," I toss caution to the side and kiss her. I kiss her in front of my father, in front of our guests, tenderly and honestly; I kiss her because she doesn't hate me. But when I break from her, smiling when she does, I wonder why hers holds such sorrow.

It doesn't matter how elated I make her this evening; something is holding her back from allowing joy.

I don't have time to find out why.

We are called over to cut the cake, splitting a piece between us. She smears icing across my cheek, laughing when I wipe it on hers. She smiles through conversations, accepts all the well wishes, and speaks of how excited she is to be the princess of our kingdom, but every so often, her stare turns vacant, and her joy evaporates. Irina notices it, too, but it isn't something we can approach with Elora yet.

Slowly, guests start to filter out. The afternoon drags into the evening, then the moon rises, and only our family remains. Servants clear dishes from the tables while Elora speaks with Irina while they share another piece of cake. So many presents await us, spread across multiple tables, but Elora shows no interest in them.

My mother joins them soon after, leaving me alone with Jasper. "Excellent," he says, watching Elora with fascination. "I almost believed you cared for her."

My mother laughs at something Irina says, causing Elora to join. If the man beside me wasn't so vile, their happiness would be a regular occurrence. I wouldn't need to pine for more seconds of this, longing for peace.

"Did you ever care for her?" I ask him. I don't need to elaborate on who I'm referring to as he continues looking between the three women he has treated horribly.

The women I love.

"Finnian, this role has no room for frivolous emotions." His attention moves to one of the maids I've seen in his wing often. "Plenty of time for pleasure. Get a son out of her, and you'll understand. The guilt will fade." He slaps my shoulder. "I expect to hear consummation coming from your wing tonight." He winks before calling for his favored maid to follow him.

My mother watches them leave, then looks at me. I don't care what it takes; I will find a way to make up for all her pain while being his queen.

I approach the table with bitterness. My wedding day shouldn't be veiled with uncertainty and unease. Elora shouldn't look sick with worry. And Irina should be with the ones she loves, not sitting alone and dodging men.

"I need my bride," I say.

Elora tries to genuinely smile, but she just... can't. My mother and Irina hug her goodbye, then come to say goodbye to me. Elora lingers to give me space, idly twisting the ribbon from a gift around her finger but conveying no other interest.

I place my hand on Irina's head. "You took a stand today, Irina."

She sighs. "I know, I'm sorry."

I shake my head. "No. No more apologies. I hope you're ready to do it more often."

She looked at our mother before slowly going back to me. "What are you talking about, Finnian?"

I chuckle. "You know better than anyone that these walls have ears, but you'll find out soon enough. Is the gift ready?"

"In your quarters," she says.

I look at my mother. "I'll find you when we return from Hogsfeet. We'll leave tonight."

She palms my cheek. "I am so very proud of you, my darling."

I've done nothing to earn her pride, but I plan to change that soon.

Irina shoves me away playfully. "Please remember that my wing is right beneath yours."

I roll my eyes. "Right, like you plan on staying in the castle tonight."

My mother covers her ears. "I am retiring to bed and want to know nothing further." She kisses us on our cheeks before taking her leave.

Irina sighs wistfully. "I hope you know what you're doing, Finnian. I fear Mother can't handle much more heartbreak."

I look at Elora, frowning at the empty way she stares at the thrones, her tiara between her hands. "None of us can," I murmur, squeezing her shoulder.

❧

I cradle Elora to my chest before we step into my quarters, requesting she close her eyes before we go further. She pulls in the corner of her bottom lip while smiling and closes her eyes, even covering them with a hand. "I've been in here, you know."

I grin. "I wondered who that was in my bed this morning, all wild curls and pink skin." I carry her into the sitting room since the gift I planned for her wouldn't fit on the table in the bedroom and lower her to her feet.

She keeps a tight hold on my jacket while slipping out of her shoes. "Can I open my eyes yet?"

I move her forward a few steps and stand behind her with my arms around her waist. "Three..." I kiss the left side of her neck. "Two..." The right side. "One," I whisper.

Her eyes flutter open, followed by a hand covering her mouth. Even from only seeing her profile, the shock is evident on her face.

Her dollhouse has been fully restored and painted its original color, but it contains every piece of furniture a dollhouse can hold. Irina found the velvet pouch of wooden dolls and placed them in different rooms, but two new ones sat in the center with a doll in a purple dress—the same color Elora wore when I found her sleeping in the gardens.

I've never wanted to be in doll form, but Irina insisted we be added to Elora's collection.

I guide Elora closer since she seems stuck to the floor, pointing out the newest additions. Her eyes search every corner, tears slipping down her cheeks. I wasn't expecting squeals of joy, but I wasn't counting on complete silence, either. Her face hasn't changed a bit.

I lean against the table, rubbing her back. "Elora, I know you don't like when I give you things, but I wanted to do this for you."

With her other hand, she touches the doll made to look like me, painted in a lot of blue.

I run a hand through my hair. "Does it bother you that we had these carved? You don't have to keep them. Irina just wanted to be part of something in your life that hasn't brought you sorrow." I keep speaking when her reaction remains the same. "Did I overstep?"

Finally, her head shakes slightly. She drops her hand to her stomach, but tears keep falling. I squeeze her waist gently. "Elora, say something, please. You don't have to keep this."

"I love it," she breathes.

I release a deep sigh of relief. "You do?"

She places one hand on my chest while her other picks up Irina's doll, the sweetest laugh following. "I can't believe you did this."

"I didn't," I say. "I mean, it was my idea, but we have a very talented carpenter..."

"Thank you," she interrupts.

I am feeling too many things. Too much warmth is spreading across me. The intensity of what I feel for her is agonizing.

"I just wanted you to feel at home here," I say softly. "With me." I look at the doll in her hand. "And Irina, I guess."

Her combination of a laugh and cry makes me pull her to me, wrapping my arms around her. "Elora, I know being here isn't what you wanted, but I promise I'll make it okay."

Her hands move to my cheeks, her head shaking as annoyance joins the jumble of emotions I can't decipher on her face. "You still can't see it, can you?" The pad of her thumb strokes my cheek. "*You* are exactly where I want to be."

My heart thunders in my chest, her words releasing something in me. My hands caress her ribs while I wait for her to tell me she's lying, that she would rather be anywhere else than in my arms, but I know she won't.

But the confession scares me more than if she were to walk away from me. Because it means that these feelings I have, I can't shove them down anymore. If I have even an ounce of hope that I can make this work with her, all the walls I've built for so long to protect this family will crumble.

And I want to be left standing.

With her.

But I've never been one with words.

So, I take her chin between my fingers and kiss her instead.

I don't rush it, I don't consume her as I want, I explore her. I hold onto the passion I feel, the need for her against me, and I replace hunger with tenderness.

She slowly pulls my jacket off while keeping me distracted with her tongue. Her breathy whimpers make me undo the buttons on her back while she starts on my shirt.

Until I stand shirtless, and she stands...

Hades, the *fuck*.

She takes my hands and pulls me with her, not looking the least bit insecure at what she had on underneath her dress all fucking day. "Elora," I say, her name breaking from my inability to breathe.

"I might've requested something from my new friends," she says coyly. "And Irina might've picked it up for me today."

I swallow pointlessly since my mouth is dry. "What friends?"

She wrinkles her nose. "I don't know all their names, but they call me their gemstone."

Ah. Irina's friends. "I don't think I want you sharing the company she keeps, Elora, especially if it comes with the risk of someone seeing what's mine."

"You just don't like sharing," she argues as she tugs me into the bedroom.

I can't stop staring at her body, momentarily forgetting the color of her eyes. Her name. "And *did* anyone else see you in this?"

"What if they did?"

My nostrils flare at the thought of anyone seeing her in lacy red stockings that reach her thighs, the rest of her body barely covered in black... it can't be classified as anything but torturous silk. It hugs her body the way I wish to be. It deeply contrasts her ivory skin and bright hair, making my innocent doe a little more sinful. "I'd be spilling a lot of blood."

"For me?" She twists us and places her hands on my chest to push me down on the edge of the bed. "Tempting, but only you."

I motion for her to spin.

She lifts to her toes and spins for me. My porcelain doll isn't as pristine as I initially thought. I lick my lips when her slip raises *just* high enough to reveal the tops of her thighs.

"Hades, Elora, you're bare."

She puts her hands on my shoulders. "I just..." Some of her unease returns, but she leans forward and kisses me instead of finishing her thought.

I reach forward and wrap my hands around her thighs, lifting her to curl around me. She settles right against my cock, rolling her hips while her mouth travels up my jaw until she takes my earlobe between her teeth, shooting a bite of pain down my spine.

"You're a fast learner," I say gruffly.

Her hands slide down my chest, slowing once they reach my stomach until the tips of her fingers push past my waistband.

I know what she wants.

I want it, too. I want her. All of her.

But I gently grab her wrists. "Elora, we can take it slow. We don't have to yet." I'm swollen and throbbing for her, groaning when she rolls her hips against me again, but something continuously holds me back from taking her the way I desperately want. "Elora..."

She retreats an inch to look at me. "Finnian, I want you. I don't understand why you keep denying me. Can't we try?"

I clench my jaw with a tight sigh.

"Oh," she whispers, hurt replacing lust. She removes my hands from her body and climbs off me. "You don't want to."

I knock on my forehead with a fist. "No, Elora, that's not it. I do. Believe me, I do."

The drawer opening makes me open my eyes to see her sliding one of my shirts on to cover her body. "I'm such a fool." Her voice shakes, her arms crossing over her stomach. "Can you show me to my room, please?"

"Your room? It's here. With me." I stand from the bed, frowning. Slightly panicking. "Elora, this isn't about you. I do want you. You know I do."

"Finnian, I'd really just like to sleep."

I step toward her, but she steps back, and my terror of losing her because of this tightens my chest. She needs me, I need her, but I can't give everything to her yet.

"Elora, please. Stay with me. I want you in my bed, asleep on my chest. We can do other things but don't need to rush anything."

"Why not this?" She pushes tears away with her palms. "Would I be that awful?"

My brow furrows. "What?"

She sniffles. "I know I'm not royalty, but do you really not want a child with me?"

I jerk my head back. "What are you talking about? Elora, titles don't mean anything to me. Of course, I'd want children with you."

"Then why? Why can't I have you?"

Her voice cracking sends my heart plummeting. She truly believes I don't want her because I give a damn about her position in life.

"You do have me," I whisper.

Tears won't stop falling down her cheeks, no matter how often she wipes them away. "Is it because of me? Is it because of someone else?"

I shake my head. "No. There's no one else."

She shoves a hand through her curls. "Would you please just answer me? Why, Finnian? Why can we do everything but this?"

I have to weigh my options.

I could continue to deny, ignore, remain silent, and risk losing her. Or, I could admit something I've held in for six years. A secret that only two other people know.

The other reason I've stayed away.

Why I haven't wed.

But admitting the truth to her could make her walk away for good.

Either way, I lose.

But she deserves to know everything.

I blow out a deep breath. "I think it's time you learn why my engagement ended."

Thirty-Eight

She looks disgusted with me. Irate. "Right now? You want to talk about Agnes right *now*? When you're...." she awkwardly gestures toward me. "And I'm...." She tugs on the shirt she's wearing. "I would rather not."

I end up chasing her when she backs away from me quickly, tugging her back to my chest. "Elora, I am like *this* because of you." I brush her hair from her neck and kiss it gently. "I want you. It pains me how much. I fucking love seeing you in my clothes, but I want to strip them off you. I want to remove every piece of clothing from your body and have you for my next few meals. I want to fuck you, Elora. I cannot make that any clearer to you, you irritatingly beautiful woman."

She twists in my arms and places her hands on my chest. "Then...." Her timidness returns, preventing her from repeating my vulgarness. "Have me. Please."

"I will," I promise. "If you still want me after I tell you this, I will have you all night." I kiss her softly, for far too long for my plan of denying her until then, and she groans when I pull away again. "Elora, please. Please let me share this with you."

I want to physically remove the doubt blanketing her, but I settle for taking her hand and placing it against my cock, and it pulses when she drags her palm down the length. "I swear to all the gods, Elora, I want you. I have wanted you since I saw you. But please trust me."

I remove her hand when she rubs me again, bringing her palm up to kiss. "I know you're new at this, but I can only handle so much of that before another version of me shoves down all my logic."

Sighing, she nods with heavy reluctance. "Fine, but if I'm going to have to talk you into this every time…"

I chuckle at the delirious notion of her needing to beg me for sex. "You won't." I pull a chair out for her from the table. "Sit, please."

She sits but watches me with heavy bewilderment when I remain standing, rubbing my hands together from nerves. "I'm about to tell you something that only two people know. This is… very difficult for me."

Her expression softens. "I'm listening."

I roll my neck, drumming my fingers against the chair I'm gripping. I don't even know where to start. "Six years ago, I asked Agnes to marry me. My union with her wasn't arranged as ours was, but it was heavily encouraged."

My palms are sweating. "She said yes. The wedding was going to take months to plan. Many pieces have to fall into place when royals from separate kingdoms wed. Events, meetings, dowries…" I wave my hand as if to say '*and more.*'

She nods in understanding.

Revisiting this memory still brings the pain of finding Agnes and Darius together. "What Irina told you was correct. I did share Agnes, but only sometimes and always with someone I trusted."

"Darius?"

I nod slowly, exhaling through my nose. "It wasn't like what Irina has with Massimo and Leif. Agnes was supposed to be only mine."

She shifts uncomfortably in her chair. I understand she's struggling to remain sympathetic, but that's difficult when envy pokes its ugly head out.

But I need to get this out. "I arrived at her castle one day and found them together. She was..." I clear my throat, trying to shake the memory free. "On top of him. And how they looked at me told me they knew what they were doing was wrong."

"But why did she do it? She seemed..."

"Obsessed?" I shrug. "She's not used to men not wanting her. But, she did it after..." I lock my jaw, my breaths shortening.

Elora furrows her brow. "Tell me."

I drag a hand down my face. "Before our wedding day, we were each checked by physicians. Heirs are important. Agnes was fine." I poke my tongue in my cheek. "But I wasn't."

She shakes her head slightly. "I don't understand. You're sick?"

"No." I nearly choke on the word, taking a moment to swallow and calm my raging heart. "No, I'm not sick. I am... unable to have children."

Elora pales. All the color drains from her. And she stands, tapping her mouth with her fingers while her eyes fill with water.

"That is why Agnes did it. And that is partially why I've stayed away from Pumpkin Hollow." I'm unsure what to do with my hands, settling with loosely hanging them from my waist. "I have met with countless physicians to find a way..." Emotion builds. "I haven't settled down because of this."

She turns from me when tears fall, remaining silent.

"The rumors about me are true. I did spend my time with women, but it's because I felt so..." I shake my head. "Angry, maybe. Lonely. I knew that if Jasper ever found out..."

"He doesn't know," she whispers.

"No," I confirm. "I feared if he learned, he'd see no use for us anymore. He can't stand my mother. My dedication to the crown has kept her and Irina alive."

I continue, "Irina threatened Agnes. I don't know what with, but Agnes never told anyone. And that is why I told you that you wouldn't need to worry about a child..."

"But you knew." She turns, her face covered in tears. "You

knew he wanted me to give you a child. And you..." she coughs a sob. "Oh, gods, you knew it would be impossible."

I lower my head. "We didn't set a timeline. I just wanted you away from Regina. And I thought I would have time to find a solution."

"A solution?" she cries. "What... What is the solution? Finnian, you knew he'd take my life if I didn't have a child!" She visibly trembles. "And you... you just..."

I step closer to her, my chest tightening when she backs away. "Elora, I'm not going to let him touch you. I will see more physicians and request more tests. We can find a way, but I will keep you safe, Elora. I will..."

"Oh, Finnian." She laughs through her tears, covering her face with her hands. "Oh, gods. It's over, it's all over."

My heart seizes. "No. Nothing is over. We have time, but we can be together until we find a solution. Elora, you're safe with me."

She tips her head back. She's weeping with so many tears that they drip from her cheeks to her neck and shirt.

I want to touch her, but she won't let me near her. "Elora, I'm sorry. Truly sorry. I should have told you sooner, but he still would've found a way to use you if I hadn't agreed to the union. I thought if I had some control and if I agreed, it would serve us both."

I haven't cried in a long time, but a tear slips past my eye. "Elora, please, say something. I needed you away from her; I wanted you to have what you needed..."

"Don't do that," she says, lowering her chin. "Don't try to rationalize your actions. Do not say you did any of this for me."

My jaw pops from the accusation. "I am not rationalizing anything. You came here for the same reason. You needed *me*. You wanted to use *me*. I gave you what you wanted, Elora, and it will be fine."

"What *I* wanted?" She goes deathly calm. "I'd like for you to leave. Either you do, or I will."

I shake my head. "No. We're going to talk this through, Elora. I am not..." I tap my fist against the tabletop. "I am not losing you over this. I am not letting you walk away from me."

"Finnian. Go."

I press my tongue against the roof of my mouth, shocked and angry. "Is that the only reason you wanted me, Elora? For a child?"

Her lips parted when genuine hurt crossed her face. "Get out," she whispers. "Get out!" Her voice raises when she repeats it. "I can't believe you just fucking asked me that!" She comes at me and shoves my chest. "Get out!"

I stumble backward when she keeps pushing me, trying to rationalize with her, trying to catch her wrists. Her hair mats to her tears, agony coating her voice. And I cry with her.

"Elora," I rasp, "Elora, I'm sorry."

"Get out!" she shouts, shoving her hair back and away from her face. "Go talk to your mother, and then come back here and ask me that question, you fucking bastard! Get out!"

She turns from me and crouches, her cries uncontrollable and tearing me apart. I don't know what my mother has to do with this, but I don't want to leave her, not like this.

"Elora..."

"Please." Her broken whisper strains with agony. "Please, just go."

I stand behind her, watching her cry but unable to say anything that can fix this—unable to accept that I could lose the first woman I've fallen in love with because of this.

"I'm sorry," I say again, knowing it makes no difference, and walk away.

I meant to find my mother but ended up standing in the gardens, staring at the flowers where Elora was sleeping the morning I returned. My thoughts race with a million things, unable to decide if she genuinely wants me or if she feels having a child with me would give her an advantage when asking for Ashbury's restoration.

Or if she does want me but feels betrayed that I've risked her life by agreeing to marry her under the pretense of a child, knowing I couldn't give her one.

It's me. It's all because of me.

Yes, Elora thought marrying me would secure comfort for her people, but I *know* her. She wouldn't have used me like that. I'm blinded by years of being used by my father, and I struggle to remember that not everyone is as callous as him. And she isn't him.

Elora is everything good.

And I might lose her.

I need to find my mother. Whatever she knows about Elora is why she wants me to see her after Hogsfeet.

"Tire of her already?"

I flinch, fists clenching on instinct at hearing the voice I loathe. Turning my head, I acknowledge my father with a tight nod. It helps that my chest is bare and my hair disheveled from how many times I've tried pulling it out.

He chuckles. "Well, you laid with her. With any luck, you won't have to do it often."

If I do lose Elora, I will kill him. The army be damned. I will get Irina and my mother out and take the consequences. It's what I should've done years ago. "Why are you out here?"

He rubs his belly. "Why else?"

He can't see how I roll my eyes in the dark. He's visiting his fucking pumpkins in the greenhouse. It's the only time he does anything physical that doesn't include sleeping with women who aren't his wife.

"Fairing, okay?"

He nods with pride. "After the smashed ones were removed." He points his finger angrily toward me but not *at* me. "Once I find out who did it, their heads will be painfully torn from their necks."

He will never learn it was us. I took significant steps to ensure that. If that's something I can promise Elora, it's that she won't lose her life because of godsdamn pumpkins.

"Come in for a drink," he says.

I nearly denied the offer. I almost lied and said I wanted another round with Elora.

I want to find my mother. I want to crawl on my knees while apologizing to my wife and beg for her forgiveness. I would share every test result with her, leave with her immediately, and find another physician.

I will fix this for us.

But if my mother knows a secret about Elora, it most likely concerns the tyrant inviting me inside to drink with him.

So, I fixed my face with a careless grin.

"Better than returning to her," I lied, forcing a laugh when he agreed. "Lead the way."

After turning the chairs to face the fireplace instead of his desk, I sit while he pours two mugfuls of whiskey. My gaze shifts between the fire and the door that leads to his crypt. The heat from the fire was suffocating me, but I added additional coal when the flames began to dwindle.

He hands me a mug before sitting in the chair beside mine, lazily gesturing to the fire. "How is Elora around the faeries?"

I pretend to take a sip, but the smell of the liquor pulls at my temptation to numb the pain. "Comfortable," I replied hoarsely, trying to avoid the overwhelming need for a taste, "very comfortable. She isn't afraid of them."

He seems displeased. "And the guards? Should we increase the number of men?"

I lift an eyebrow brow. "Why would we do that?"

He takes a long pull from his mug before answering. "Because of her, boy. If she asks them, they'll burn the castle to the ground."

I scoff. "Elora wouldn't do that."

His following chuckle causes my shoulders to tense. "I took steps to be sure, but I will add another man on shift."

I try to remain calm. Relaxed. "I don't recall you informing me of additional steps. Remind me?"

He stands for a refill already. "It didn't differ much from the one I made her father sign."

Hades, Elora did sign something.

My fingers tighten around the mug, my eyes searching the flames for memories, but I remember nothing about Harry signing his name to anything. But I was only a child when we took Ashbury.

I shake my head when muffled war cries fill my ears, shoving *that* memory back down. "I don't believe you ever spoke of that," I say, keeping my tone light. "Anything I need to be made aware of?"

He sits beside me again, propping one arm up on the armrest while using the other to balance his mug on his swollen belly. "Did you never learn of the reason for Harry's betrayal?"

"I never cared," I say. "I still don't, but humor me." Tell me, I plead silently.

He wipes whiskey from his beard with his sleeve. "He loved a woman. Elora's mother." The disgust in his tone is simply because he does not believe in any type of love unless it's made of pumpkin. "But his father didn't find her suitable for him. He ordered her death after learning Harry planned to run away with her."

I blink. Elora behaves like she's disgusted by her father's betrayal, which means she can't know Harry betrayed his father to save her mother.

"Stupid fool," he spits. "Came to me and begged to be spared if they crossed the bridge into Pumpkin Hollow, but I don't give anything for free."

I try to maintain a bored expression, but I itch to hear more. I need every detail to take back to Elora. "So, you offered to protect them in exchange for..."

"His allegiance," he finishes. "He gave me the number of men in Ashbury's army, where their weapons were stored, and when to invade."

I pretend to be as exasperated as him. "He gave all his power away for a woman?"

He finishes the second mugful. "He was going to bring her here to live, but then..." His malicious grin appears. "He learned I planned to kill all his people. He negotiated again."

I keep my breathing under control. "What else did he have worth those people?"

"I'll show you." He hands me his mug to refill while he stands and sifts through drawers on his desk. From what I know of the deals he makes, he negates the contracts upon death and burns them to prevent others from learning the torture he put them through while alive.

It's odd that he still has Harry's bargain in his possession.

I place his mug on the desk, pretending to drink from mine while anxiously awaiting. He pulls a yellowed parchment from a drawer with a chuckle. "Always interesting to see what men will settle for to clear their conscience."

I place my mug down and take the paper he offered, reading while he explains, "I owned his life already for allowing him to wed. When the faeries came, I saw no reason to keep the people of Ashbury alive. They brought nothing of value to us."

"Right," I say, acting disinterested while scanning the page.

"But Harry had one more card up his sleeve to negotiate away for the lives of everyone in Ashbury." He grabs his mug and tips it back while I search for what else he gave up in exchange for protection.

And then, I see it.

And the room starts to spin.

"His firstborn," he says.

My pulse pounds. I feel each pressure point as it throbs so quickly that I become dizzy.

I ask, "For what purpose?"

"Any purpose I deemed necessary." He begins searching his

desk again. "The only stipulation he requested was that I not take them until his death. I saw no need for the child of a peasant but agreed because a king can never have too many lives at his disposal."

I lick my lips, staring at the word.

Firstborn.

Harry sacrificed Elora before she was even born, ever thought of, to save the lives *he* put in jeopardy—to atone for choosing love over all.

"If he was a boy, I planned to kill him." He pulls out another paper. "When I learned the child was a girl, I let her live. What could a woman ever do to me? She was no threat." He offered the parchment to me.

Elora's name is scrawled on the bottom.

With her bloody thumbprint.

My inhales come in short spurts while I read what he made her sign.

"When Harry tried to quit on me, I killed him." He says it so dismissively that it tears my attention away from the parchment to look at him. "We had a bargain, and he thought he could walk away? So, I had him killed." He sighs deeply. "Such a disappointment. He said the job was getting too strenuous for him. He wanted to spend the time he had left with Elora, but Harry had forgotten he had given her to me."

Pieces start to come together in my mind.

"They were supposed to bring him here to kill, but those idiots in the fields stabbed him when he crossed the bridge instead." He motions to the paper in my hand with his mug. "I had the leader burn his body before anyone could discover what happened."

"The leader," I repeat, voice strained. "Of the faeries? Dolfe?"

"That's the one!" He says it with such pride. "But Regina knew Elora was my property. I didn't need her yet, so she was stuck with her."

His property.

His fucking *property*.

Elora was left to starve in Regina's care because he didn't see a fucking need for her.

I can't kill him here.

They aren't safe. I don't have a plan for them yet. I need them somewhere safe. But fuck me if I'm not tempted to strangle him where he stands, climb over the fucking desk and stab him with the letter opener.

I flick the paper in my hand with little care, needing *more*. More answers. "So... what? You brought her here for the faeries and made her pledge not to ask them to burn down the castle?"

He pats his stomach while he finishes the third mugful. "Regina assured me Elora would work with the faeries without being forced. I didn't need that on paper. I requested from Elora the same thing her father gave up so easily."

I couldn't *move*.

I couldn't *breathe*.

He points to the parchment. "Her firstborn. We need an heir; she was at my disposal. And you were taking far too long to choose."

I've been used the same as her.

I was roped into signing Elora's freedom away because Harry decided to give her life away to my father.

I'm positive my voice shakes when I ask, "That was already part of the agreement, wasn't it? An heir?"

"It was," he confirms with a nod. "But I'm growing impatient and would rather not provide Elora a life of luxury while waiting for her to fulfill her purpose. But, I am a man of my word. I agreed to take his firstborn, so I did. I found a way to make her useful. The faeries must be controlled, but I could've found a physical threat. Two birds, one stone."

I search the words for conditions.

There are always fucking conditions with him. Stripping her of her freedom wasn't enough—he needed something from her.

"She gives me a year and an heir. I keep the people in Ashbury alive until her death, and it gives me time to find a man to handle the faeries."

"A year," I repeat. "Which means...."

"Elora has three months to get pregnant. If not, she agreed to become part of my collection." He laughs while my despair chokes me. "All it took was me threatening to harm you if she didn't follow through. The stupid girl repeated her father's mistakes."

I bend over to press my palms against the desk while the bargain falls between them. That's why my confession upset her so greatly.

It wasn't because she wanted a child.

She gave up everything for me.

Her life. To save me.

And I only have three months before he would uphold his bargain.

And I fucking accused her.

I can't even stomach myself. I want to crawl out of my body and kill the man who said such hateful words to her.

I hope she'll never forgive me.

I don't deserve any part of her.

"Love," he sighs. "Such a waste."

I have to think quickly. "Foolish," I say, my eyes glossing over the words. "And after she has the baby..." I search for the answer on the paper between my hands.

"She dies either way."

My heart cracks. Tears sting my eyes.

I can't break here. "Good."

"I knew you'd understand." He retrieves both bargains and shoves them into his desk. "You're still young enough to try again if she fails. Enjoy her while you can."

I will enjoy tearing him apart.

Slowly. Limb from limb.

I will make him feel every ounce of terror and pain that he's given all of us.

I force a grin. "Oh, I will."

Thirty-Nine

I take the stairs two at a time, reaching my door quickly, then throwing it open and shouting Elora's name. I searched every room, every corner, the terrace, and below, but she was nowhere to be seen. I grab my discarded shirt and pull it on while descending to Irina's floor and banging on her door. She is most likely with Massimo, which only leaves me with my mother.

I run across the castle to her wing, skidding and nearly tripping twice, breathless as I knock on her door. Sweat coats my face and neck, but I have to find Elora. I won't give up until I do. Even if all she'll listen to is an apology, she needs to hear how sorry I am for ever doubting her.

My mother opens the door a moment later with heavy eyes, frantic as they widen from the state I'm in. "Did you know?" I pant through the question. "Elora told me to speak with you. You knew what she signed?"

"Come in," she says hurriedly, looking both ways down the hall while I step inside, but I stay right by the door after she closes it. "Yes, I knew. She told me this morning."

"That's why she was so upset," I guess. "Why didn't you fucking tell me?"

"I just wanted,"—she pauses and swallows—"I wanted you to

have a day together before it all changes. Finnian, it won't be simple if we try to break free."

"Break *free*?" I scoff. "You are leaving with Elora and Irina. I will find somewhere for you to go, then I will kill him and face the consequences."

"I will not," she says. "I will not leave my son to die. Neither will your sister."

"I don't give a fuck what you think you're going to do, Mother." I point toward the door. "If we do not end this, he will kill her! I am not going to sit by and let him. I have done nothing for far too long, and look where it's gotten us."

Her usual calm and understanding changes into something else entirely. "I did not stay by his side through years of torment for you to send me away and lose your life!"

I've been scolded by her before, but never like this. She rarely raises her voice at me.

"We don't have another choice." I try to calm my voice. "He killed Harry. Did you know that? He will not hesitate to kill her."

"I had my suspicions." She purses her lips and briefly lowers her gaze to the floor. "I need you to do as I say and go to Hogsfeet, Finnian."

I *need* to find my wife.

I throw my arms in the air. "I do not give a fuck about taking Elora to Hogsfeet!"

She rolls her shoulders back. "I have allowed you to travel. I remained quiet during the rumors that plagued you. I did not pry your secret from Irina. And I have given you the freedom you needed to heal from what he's done to us. I have allowed you to believe you were the only one protecting us."

"My.... My secret? You know?"

"You underestimate a mother's love, Finnian." She steps closer, every inch the queen she is instead of my loving mother. "I have been forming my own strategy. I have waited for you to grow up and take responsibility for this family as you should."

Her eyes water, but she doesn't back down. "I have listened for years that I raised the bastard child of the king and said nothing. I have held my place by his side for many years for my children, and now, it is time for them to do as I say and fight back."

I searched her face, somewhat surprised by her vigor. My mother is the calmest, gentlest person in all the realms. To learn that she has been planning something shocks me.

"Is she?" I grate my teeth. "Is Irina your daughter? Is she my sister?"

She lifts her chin. "Yes."

I exhale in relief. If I can take solace in anything today, it's that.

"She is my daughter but Jasper's biological daughter." A tear slips free. "I was sent away to wait for Irina's birth. I met her mother. Jasper promised a life of luxury in exchange for her child. But she lied about the sex of the babe."

I lean against the door in disbelief.

"She was murdered when Irina was born. He wanted a boy." She rubs her lips together like she doesn't want to say the words. "A spare."

I turn and press my palms against the door, staring at the floor, unable to form words.

"I begged Jasper to spare Irina's life, but it came with a condition. I could not leave him. I could not interfere with any affairs." She gently touches my back. "If I upset him, I risked her life. And if something happened to me, I risked him hurting you. So, I've taken my time. I waited long enough for him to believe I would obey the conditions."

"He tried to have more children," I rasp. "He wanted another boy. Why did he go to someone else? Why didn't he try it with you?"

"He did. We tried for two years after your birth, but I could not get pregnant. Eventually, I accepted that you were meant to be my only child, but he refused to stop."

My forehead thuds against the door. "He used all of us against one another. He punished Irina for not being a boy."

"You were too strong, too resilient." Her voice wavers. "He

continuously tried to break you down to control you. Irina made that easier for him. You two remained close as you grew, and that was all he needed."

I drag my hand down my face, convinced I'm stuck in a never-ending nightmare. "Does Irina know the truth?"

"Yes," she breathes. "I believe she has always known, but she doesn't want me to tell her the story. She is finally allowing me to get close to her, Finnian. And if you believe for one second that I am going to break her heart by leaving her best friend behind while we escape, then you are not the boy I raised."

I break.

I slide down the door and prop one knee up, hanging my head as tears fall. I've tried so long to do what I'm supposed to, protected my family by staying away, spoken with physicians, and it's all been for nothing. I turned into precisely who he wanted me to be by hardening myself against the ones I cared about.

Too scared to live.

"Please let me get you out," I whisper.

My mother lowers to sit on her knees before me, cupping my face between her palms, and lifts my eyes to hers. "Whether you want it or not, the throne will be yours. You owe it to our people to be the king they *need*. Do not run, Finnian. Do not yield to him."

"I'm sorry." I briefly close my eyes. "I'm sorry I didn't try hard enough to stop him. I just thought you'd be safer without me."

"My darling boy." She brushes a thumb across my cheek. "You just needed to find someone to stay and fight for. Go to her."

"And if she doesn't forgive me?"

She clicks her tongue. "A charmer like you?" Her gentle, motherly smile returns. "She never stood a chance."

❧

Unfortunately, while armed with my mother's confidence, I am not convinced there is anything I could ever say to Elora to fix what I accused her of, but it won't stop me from trying.

I find Major's saddle on the ground when I arrive at the stables. His blanket is thrown across his back, but if I had to guess, Elora isn't tall enough to get his saddle on.

Irina has more practice than Elora at saddling a horse Major's size. After searching the stables, I noticed one of our smaller horses missing from its stall. I finish saddling Major and ride to the hollowed-out tree, reading Massimo's note.

The wanderers are in Ashbury. I'm unsure how Irina crossed the bridge without the guards alerting Jasper, but she wasn't in her quarters. She had to have found a way.

Irina has become Elora's safe place, something I hoped to someday be. Finding Irina is my best chance of finding Elora.

I command Major into a gallop and race to the bridge, berating myself for ever giving the order that Elora be allowed to cross alone any time she wants. I would have found her much quicker if I hadn't done that.

The bridge comes into view, but neither lookout steps out from their hiding spots. Major slows, and I look around, calling for them. Calling for Irina. Elora.

But no one answers.

Sliding off Major, I trudge through the dead stalks, using a dagger from my waistband to cut them down as I walk. Two crumbled bodies come into view, and I jog toward them, relieved to see the bodies belong to the men on shift.

Their helmets are off and tossed to the side, but each man has red marks around their temples. I lean down to inspect them, touching the dried blood, and determine that they've been knocked out for a while.

Fearing an invasion, I stand to return to Pumpkin Hollow and alert one of our captains but freeze when the moonlight catches something on the ground. I want to believe I imagined it, but I sigh at the hoop earring in my palm when I lean down to grab it. Irina managed to get the men to remove their helmets and attacked them. That doesn't seem possible for her to do alone, but maybe I underestimated her, too.

I rub my forehead.

If I leave them here to wake, they'll tell my father what she did. He will find a way to punish her, and I can't handle anything else. I am only one thread away from unraveling.

"Hades, Irina."

She took my promise of fighting back seriously. And literally.

So, I go to work.

Major's saddlebags always contain weaponry or supplies needed for my travels. I move him off the path to graze behind the trees while I drag both men over to a tree. Retrieving a rope from one of the bags, I tie them to the trunk and secure their hands.

They remain asleep, slumped over. I slip their helmets back on, rip the bottom of my shirt to craft two gags and place them over their mouths. The helmets will prevent them from spitting them out. I step back to admire my work, then I chuckle.

Irina, as stubborn and infuriating as she is, was meant to be my little sister. After everything she has done for me, securing the men she knocked out to a tree seems fair.

❧

The Bohemians are right where I thought they'd be. Massimo spots me first and stands, disappearing into a covered wagon and coming out with my sister. I slide off Major and catch her when she runs toward me.

She stutters through apologies while I hold her, listening to her try to explain how it happened, but I don't care. Massimo stands by Major and greets him while giving me an apologetic grin.

"Irina." I set her down. "Irina, I'm not upset with you. I'm more surprised it took you twenty-four years to hurt one of them."

She laughs but looks frazzled. "I don't know what to do, Finnian. I can't go back."

"Oh, you have to." I squeeze her shoulder. "I have learned a lot tonight, Irina. And I will fix this for us, but I need you at my side just a little longer. You must return before the next man on shift discovers what happened."

"But the guards..."

"I handled them temporarily." I look behind her with a slight frown. "Elora isn't here, is she?"

She shoves my chest. "What did you do to her? Where is she? I'm away for one fucking night, Finnian! One night!"

"Hades," I snapped, rubbing my chest. "I am tired of both of you doing that. I will find her, but I need you to leave. Go say goodbye to Leif. Did you come here on horseback?"

She nods, hooking a thumb behind her, but I see no horse. "He's... somewhere. I can find him."

"Go, then. Quickly." I shake my head when she starts to pry for more information. "I need to find Elora before I do anything else. Oh, but wait." I raise a curious brow. "How did you talk them into removing their helmets?"

She winces. "You don't want to know."

I grimace. "Say nothing else." She's often informed me that soldiers want her, but she has never considered any of them.

But Irina knows when to use something to her advantage. I am grateful that *only* their helmets were removed.

Irina relents and jogs back to the wagon, calling for one of our more obtuse horses. Massimo stays, waiting until Irina is out of earshot before he asks, "What do you need from me?"

I contemplate answering. I know exactly what needs to happen to keep Irina safe and prevent my father from learning what she did.

And Massimo loves her. He has proved it time and time again by keeping her safe, always walking back to the castle with her to make sure of it. They all adore her. Irina has formed a family with them, and I will ensure it remains that way.

"The men are tied to a tree a quarter mile in. I need them to not be found. If you want me to do it, take them somewhere and wait for me."

"It will be handled," he says.

I nod, watching my sister hug Leif. "Massimo, I will sign off on it. I give you my word. I know you love her."

He turns his head to look at Irina with a slight grin. "She told you?"

"She did." I move to stand beside him. "Did she tell you what Jasper did to her?"

He slowly turns his head to look at me. "No. What did he do to her?"

I blow out a deep breath and tell him.

Months ago, Irina had excitedly come to my quarters and told me that Massimo proposed to her. He and Leif aren't married, but Massimo wants a wife and children. After asking Leif for permission, Massimo proposed marriage to Irina. I pleaded with her not to approach Jasper with the news until I returned from the trip I was about to take.

I knew how he'd react, and I wanted to be the one to receive the punishment for it instead.

She promised she wouldn't.

She said she'd wait.

I assured I would think of something to exchange for her freedom while I was away.

Just wait for me, I begged.

But my mistake was informing her of my idea to bargain with him for her. Irina didn't want me to sacrifice anything for her.

I was away when he took her to the crypt and threatened to kill them all if she accepted his proposal. Out of fear, Irina signed her name in blood, promising to stay in the castle and never speak of them again. It took weeks for her to bravely leave to find them, and she was caught and dragged back.

That was when the lock was placed on the tunnel door, which wasn't an addition she shared with me. She would sometimes find creative ways to leave, but visits became further apart. The longer she went without freedom, the more anxious she became.

And by the time I finished telling Massimo what happened, he was cursing and shouting in a language I didn't understand. "I thought she didn't love me!" he yells. "I thought she didn't want to be with me!"

"I know," I say, "but it wasn't her."

He motions in her direction with a dramatic wave. "Of course, it wasn't her! She gave her life for mine! For ours! I will kill him!"

"Massimo, you have every right to be angry." I hold up my hands to try and stop his pacing. "But, I don't need you to kill him. I will handle him, but I need you to do something for me. I need a few days, Massimo."

He mutters more obscenities in his language before he retreats into silence from the look of agony on my face while I listen to Irina laugh after wrangling her horse. "What do you need?" he asks.

Selfishly, I want to tell him never mind.

But my sister deserves to be with the ones she loves, as Elora tried to tell me once. I haven't ever been able to stomach the idea of losing my sister, but I love her. And she stayed this long because of her love for me.

She is not the spare.

She is exactly what I needed to survive our childhood. She kept me human. She gave me someone to protect while I waited for Elora.

She protected me as I protected her.

Irina tightened the saddle on her horse, giving me only a moment to decide if I was ready to tell her goodbye.

Swallowing the lump in my throat, I look at Massimo and say, "In a few days, I need you to get her out of this realm. For good."

Forty

I left Massimo with vague instructions to wait for me to find him. I do not know my plan yet, but Irina can't stay here. I need to focus on Elora, and Irina needs to be somewhere safe. She won't go easily, but with Massimo's help, we might be able to sway her.

If I can think of a way to save my mother and wife while also ridding us of my father, I will seek her out again immediately. I refuse to entertain the notion of never seeing my little sister again.

One of the men guarding the faeries is asleep when I calmly approach their station. The one awake punches the snoring one after noticing me, immediately standing and saluting. I wait for them to tell me Elora was here earlier, but like Irina, they don't mention seeing her.

Fuck.

She isn't here, either. She wouldn't have gone to her manor. Where else could she be?

I don't try to think of a reason for my visit. I greet them with a nod and head toward the dwelling where Azrea and Dolfe appeared out of nowhere the evening Elora brought me.

Unsurprisingly, it's empty again.

I pound the stone with my hand repeatedly. "Dolfe," I call, "I need to speak with you. Elora isn't with me." I don't know if that will help, but he didn't act like he liked her much the last time I was here.

I feel him before I see him.

A rush of heat overcomes me, making me step back. It feels as if he fanned me with his wings, but I still see no one within.

Until I do.

He comes out with arms crossed and jaw tight, either frustrated to be woken up or has this sunny disposition all the time.

"Is it true?" I don't care to lower my voice. "About Elora's father. Was it you?"

"Quiet," he growls.

I lurch forward. "I don't take orders from you. I asked you a fucking question, Dolfe." I look behind him into the empty cave, which only causes him to growl louder. "Does Azrea know? Does your mate know you burned Elora's father and hid the truth?"

He reveals the top row of his teeth, snarling at me. "You are a boy. Do not come here and speak to me like your hands are clean."

I seethe. Pain radiates through my skull from how tightly I clench my jaw. "You fucking helped him murder her father!"

"No." His wings flare. "I was woken and forced out of my dwelling to burn his body under the threat of losing my *mate*." The veins in his throat strain. "I respected Harry. He was dead when they brought him to me. But unlike you, prince, I *act* to save the female I love."

I am taken aback by his remark. "Just because I am not reacting with immediate violence does not mean that I will stand by and allow him to hurt her. You don't give a fuck about her anyway. You treat her horribly."

His fists clench at his sides. "Because the last mortal I showed kindness was murdered by your father! For wanting to help us!"

My brow pinches. "For helping you? Jasper said it was because Harry wanted to quit, that he wanted to spend time with Elora."

His chest rumbles with frustration. "Still so trusting of what your king says. This realm has no future with halfwitted rulers."

I've had enough of this arrogant prick. "I might have been careless before, but I am changing for her. You have remained an asshole while she has mourned the loss of her father, feeling as if she is at fault for his mistakes."

I stepped closer to him, aware he could snap my neck with a finger. "You might have respected Harry, but he *sold* her to my father before her birth. You might not have killed him, but you are no better than the king you claim to hate. We have both been used by him. We have both submitted to him to protect the ones we love." I don't look at Azrea when she slowly emerges from the dwelling. "As prideful as you act, you stopped fighting long before I did. And that girl you hate, that *pathetic* human, she signed herself to him to save us all. What have you done aside from accepting your fate?"

"What did she do?" Azrea whispers. "What did Elora agree to do for him?"

I don't answer her questions, but I do ask her mine. "Were you aware he burned her father's body and hid the truth from her?"

She wraps a hand around her throat with a slight nod. "Only recently. Does she know?"

"No." I shift my glare back to Dolfe. "But she will. I might be ignorant and careless, but unlike you, I will not hesitate to burn my father alive. Do not expect to see my wife any time soon."

Dolfe lowers his wings slightly. "Do not punish my mate for my decisions. Azrea has wanted to tell her, but Elora hasn't returned."

"Elora doesn't *want* to return." I turn from them to leave, ignoring Azrea's calls for me to wait. Everyone has used her. All of them.

"Her nightmares!" she calls out. "How are her nightmares? Please, you must tell me..."

But I don't. As far as I'm concerned, they've lost their privilege of knowing her at all.

I searched everywhere for Elora.

I revisit all the places she took me, scour the cliffside, and become more panicked each second that passes. She wouldn't have left the realm. She cares too much about... well, all of us.

I'm about to return to the wanderers to check if Irina safely made it back to the castle when I hear the *faintest* cries.

Major's hooves make no sound on the soil, allowing us to seek the noise without drawing attention. A dry field of dead flowers sits between two valleys, wholly hidden from view.

And my wife.

She changed out of my shirt and into a set of riding clothes, which she had to have swiped from Irina's quarters before she left.

How can they both break into my quarters while I struggle to keep them *out*? Irina has taught her too well.

Reaching into one of the saddlebags, I retrieve Elora's shawl, freshly washed and patched from the loose threads. It doesn't look exactly how it did when she arrived at Pumpkin Hollow, but my mother ensured that most of it remained intact.

I slide off Major, and he *huffs*, giving me away.

I glare at him, but Elora whips around to glare at *me* while standing. I hoped the wrap in my hands would entice her to hear me out, but that would've made things far too easy, and that just isn't Elora's style.

She starts to walk away, but I chase after her, my boots sticking to random spots of moistened soil from all the rainfall. "Elora, please," I beg, wiping my boot off on a dry area.

"Elora," I call out, chasing her. "Elora, stop. Stop, stop." I reach for her wrist, but she knows this land better than I do and easily dodges me. "Elora, godsdamnit, talk to me!"

"There is nothing to say!" she shouts, lunging for Major to try and steal him.

I don't have to rush, calmly standing next to her while she tries to swing her leg up and over. I look around for the horse she brought but can't spot it from where I stand.

Major looks at me. I shrug.

Finally, I wrap an arm around her waist and bring her down, tilting my head to the side when she swings for me. "*Stop*, you fucking wild turkey," I emphasize, keeping her hovering above the ground. "If I let you down, will you promise to stay put?"

"Why should I?!" she yells, flailing until I have to put her down or risk getting kicked somewhere that would render me useless.

"Because..."

I can't finish before she yanks the shawl out of my hand and wraps it around her. She pauses her anger to examine it, running the soft, *clean* fabric through her fingers.

"My mother told me why it's so important to you," I explained. "I'm sorry I was unkind about it before."

She crosses her arms. "Spoke with your mother, did you? And what.... you came here to apologize for being such an ass?"

I exhale deeply through my nose. "I talked to more than just my mother, Elora. I was pulled into Jasper's study and had a very enlightening chat with him. It seems like maybe *you* had a secret of your own."

Her pout thins. "I didn't want to tell you."

"But you told my mother? The morning of our wedding?" I throw my arms up. "Why, Elora? We promised to be honest with one another, and then you did something like that."

Her glower returns. "For you! I did it for you! Gods, does that even fucking matter to you? I did it because he threatened to hurt you!"

I rest my hands on my waist, loosely shaking my head. "He always fucking hurts me, Elora. You signing your life away to him wasn't going to stop that!"

Her restless stance has her walking away from me again. "If you came here just to yell at me, save it for your next wife, Finnian! You lied to me! You withheld crucial information! If I had known the truth, I never would have agreed to it!"

I follow her, cursing every time I nearly slip. "Oh, I'm sorry, I didn't realize that by me not telling you something very personal after just meeting you, it would result in you signing your fucking death certificate!"

She spins around and sticks a finger against my chest. "Do not fucking preach to me about being honest with one another when you *knew* we couldn't have children yet agreed to this union anyway!"

She's right.

I carve a hand through my hair. "I thought I had time, Elora. That's why I encouraged him to not put a timeline on how quickly it needed to happen! I thought I could come up with..."

"A solution," she finishes for me, widely spreading her arms. "And how did that work out, hm? Do you honestly think so highly of yourself that you can't allow anyone else to help you? I could've worked with you!"

"I didn't want to tell you!" I shout, my voice cracking. Turning, I tip my head up and will not allow emotion to build. "Elora, I told Agnes about it, and she fucking... I trusted them. I trusted both of them. But I told her, I told the woman I was supposed to marry, and she immediately went to Darius."

I hang my head. "I am the heir of a strong kingdom and should be able to guarantee the longevity of our line, but I can't. And the thought of telling you... I couldn't."

"Finnian, I don't care." Her own voice quivers. "I wouldn't have cared if you told me. I would've been upset that you agreed to the union without informing me beforehand, but I would've tried to think of a way to help you, but gods, you refuse to let anyone in."

"You're right." I face her again, allowing her to see the pain in my eyes. I've held this secret for so many years and avoided the heavy way it made my heart feel with the help of alcohol and convincing myself that I could rectify it. "I haven't let anyone in because the one time I did, she left me because of it."

I step closer. "And that was painful, Elora. I can't stand here and tell you that I wouldn't have married her because I would've. I loved her, but…" I stop just before her. "I never loved her the way I love you. And I was afraid you would hate me if I told you. You wouldn't see a future with us."

A tear falls down her cheek. "And why do you think I bargained with him? Gods, you are such an idiot sometimes." She wipes her cheek with her palm. "I needed to know that I could provide joy for you, Finnian. I wanted to be that person for you. After everything you've been through, *I* wanted to keep *you* safe."

My heart hammers in my chest, unable to fathom how someone like her could love me. I've hardened myself against everyone for so long, but she came at me swinging, chipping away at every barrier.

"You hurt me tonight," she whispers, twisting her hands together. "Me wanting you was just that. I wasn't trying…"

"I know," I interrupt. "Elora, I know. I never should've said that." I can't help but laugh from my nerves and the feelings I'm experiencing, unable to shove them down because she isn't going to let me. "You scare the fuck out of me, little doe. And I'm so terribly sorry for what I said to you."

She nods, then licks her lip with a small smile following. "You love me?"

I cough my half-laugh, half-cry, and take her face between my hands. "So unfathomably, Elora. You anger me, you drive me mad, but somewhere amid our arguing, I fell deeply in love with you. And no one is ever going to take you away from me."

She squeezes her eyes shut, so many tears falling that they pool against my thumbs. "I'm so scared," she cries, "but I'm not afraid of dying, Finnian." Her eyes flutter open to stare into mine. "I'm scared of losing this. Losing you. Us."

I shush her gently, leaning in to rest my forehead against hers. "We will fix this, Elora. Together. We will find a way."

"I love you," she breathes, sliding her arms around my neck. "I promised myself I never would, but I fell in love with you."

My smile is so broad that I worry my cheeks will split, but I don't care. I don't care about anything other than her at this moment. And I kissed her.

Amid this field full of death, Elora has brought me back to life.

❧

The treacherous trail down the cliffside to Hogsfeet nearly takes both our lives multiple times, but we make it to the ground safely, only to face the river between land and the castle. Elora almost slips into the water as Major crosses, but that's partially her fault. She hasn't seen a body of water up close, which fascinates her.

I promise her we'll return to the river when rain isn't pelting down on us, and I'll be able to accurately gauge the depth. Lack of water nearby means she won't know how to swim. The water in Ashbury used to come from underground, perhaps from the river. But Pumpkin Hollow has sporadic ponds and streams, giving my kingdom plenty of options for fresh water.

She pouts her agreement.

I am determined to have time alone with her, free of distractions and lurking siblings in dark corridors.

I want my wife.

But Elora is curious about anything and everything, and Hogsfeet is no different. We explored the outside of the abandoned castle in pitch black, but I couldn't stop touching her.

I push her against a wall and kiss her until she can't breathe. Finally, she agrees to explore with me in the sunlight and allows me to pull her inside. The castle contains enough windows to provide little light while we search for candles, stumbling over furniture and stairs from the inability to keep our hands off one another.

Someone could be living here; there could be skeletons in the corners, but I don't care. I can't focus on anything but her, finally feeling liberated to be myself with her—to let her in.

I eventually gave up on finding candles and scooped her up, running up the stairs with her laughing and clinging to me. We chose a room with a large window that faced the moon, soon learning it didn't include a bed.

I find a blanket strewn over a sofa to lay on the floor. And I can't stop fidgeting from nerves and an overwhelming euphoric need for her. All the other women I've been with have never made me feel like this.

I was numb with them. Bitter.

But with Elora, I feel everything.

I bring her to me and kiss her, trying to calm my hunger with tenderness, but I've held myself back so many times with her that I struggle to move slowly.

But my rotten little love wants to punish me for denying her so often. She kisses me passionately, then breaks away and forces me to follow her around the room, laughing when I trip over something to catch her.

Once running into a cobweb.

Then, I lunge, no longer patient.

I lift her, wrap her legs around my waist, and keep her pinned against the wall to keep her *still*, then nip along her jaw.

She shivers when I lick her throat from bottom to top, tracing my way to her ear and taking it with my teeth. Her hips press against my abdomen, her hands snake into my hair, and she yanks until I'm off her skin and kissing her again.

Soft drops of rain pitter-patter against the window, and we laugh at the irony of the constant push-and-shove moments between us during storms, now part of the moment when I'll make her mine.

With a grin, I lower to my knees on the blanket with her still tightly bound to me by my hand in her hair and the other tucked beneath her. "Can you be patient with me?" I ask.

She stares at me like I'm a mirage, positively mad. "You can't be serious."

I tug her bottom lip between my teeth and pinch. She yelps, digging her heels into my lower back. With a smirk, I release her.

"Elora, that's not even a hint of what I plan to do to you. We're going to ease into this."

"But it'll end with you..." she trails off with a shy little grin, "it'll end with me and you."

There are so many meanings to those words, and I nod to each of them. "Yes, my heart. This night and many others will end with us."

Forty-One

For tonight, I will believe Finnian.

We'll have many nights like this together and find a way out of Jasper's hold. Tonight, I want to hold on to everything he makes me feel. "Your heart," I repeat with a broad smile, my thumb tracing his brow.

He presses his lips to mine. "Yes, little doe. You have taken my heart, and I don't want it back." He remains on his knees after unraveling me from around him. "Everyone thought I didn't have one, but it was just waiting for an infuriating blonde to inject her venom into it."

I roll my eyes, but my own heart swells. As it turns out, I was just waiting for him, too.

I try lowering to rest on my knees, but he grabs my waist and shakes his head. "Remove your cloak, Elora, while I remove these." He hooks his fingers into my waistband and drags my pants down, waiting for me to step out of my boots.

Stripping bare for him doesn't make me anxious, but my nerves stand on end from where I hope this leads. But he still won't let me go to my knees even after removing my cloak. "You are right where I need you to be," he says, gently brushing his lips across my navel. "Put your hands on my shoulders."

I do as he demands, biting my lip at the way he keeps his eyes on mine while he pulls me closer. His fingers bruise my waist from the pressure, and I'm beginning to take his warning seriously. He has kept himself tethered, but I might learn the kind of lover Finnian truly is.

He drags his teeth across my hip bone, soothes it with his tongue, and repeats it on the other. His tongue circles my belly button, yanking me forward when I pull away instinctively. I gasp from the pressure from his fingers, but he just chuckles—a hoarse sound that vibrates against my stomach.

"Finnian," I whine, "too slow."

His hands slide up my waist to graze across my ribs, then around to slide down the slope of my back, all while he leaves light kisses across my abdomen. Torturing. Teasing.

"Finnian," I snapped.

All he does is grin.

His hands cup the back of my thighs before he bends to trail his lips from my knee to my inner thigh, using the tip of his tongue to slowly inch higher. Again, I try to move.

Again, I say his name.

He blows a hot breath against my clit, causing me to bend forward and squeeze his shoulders. He doesn't straighten but tips his head up to meet my eyes. "Do you hate me?" he asks.

I shake my head slowly. "Only sometimes."

A corner of his mouth lifts. "Do you love me? Are you mine?"

"Yes," I whisper, emotion rising from just how deeply I've fallen in love with him.

Maybe the admission of love had me believing he'll be gentle, but the second the word leaves my lips, he frees himself from the shackled chains and devours.

His fingers squeeze my thighs hard enough to surely leave fingerprints behind, ensuring that my body unquestionably belongs to him. He groans against me when I cry his name, my hands moving from his shoulders to slide into his hair. I search for more, I want less, and my mind and body can't agree because of every feeling I'm experiencing.

And this is just his tongue.

We're only just beginning.

I climb so high so quickly; he is so good, so, so good, but that thought also makes me irate. I pull his hair when I realize he's *this* good from being with so many others, and my envy flares.

He curses at me when he pulls away, digging his nails into my thighs. I didn't mean to hurt him, but I am also pleased that I did.

"*What*?" he growls.

"You," I respond with the so-called venom he despises as if he can decipher everything I'm feeling from that one word.

His eyes narrow. "How the fuck can you be upset with me right now?" He licks his lips and lowers his head to return, spitting my name like a curse when I pull his hair again.

"I swear to the gods, Elora, if you do that again, I will not let you come." He pulls me closer. "Whatever thought you have bouncing in your brain needs to wait until I am finished."

He doesn't give me another choice, removing my hands from his hair and wrapping them behind me to pin them against the back of my thighs while he punishes me with his tongue. He brings me almost to the edge, only to slow and remove his tongue altogether, repeating until I'm positive I've lost my mind from need.

I cry his name, claw at his hands binding mine, beg, and only when I promise that I love him does he relent and start a steady rhythm inside me, groaning when I clench around him. He releases my hands to hook a leg around his shoulder, staying right where he is after I come once, and brings me over again.

I'd believe he's generous if I didn't know him well. The rawness he leaves me with is retribution.

My legs shake, my body is limp, I'm breathless, but he keeps his head buried between my legs until he's had his fill of me. And when he finally releases me, I sink to the ground while he stands to remove his boots and shirt.

He is *glaring* at me.

"Want to tell me what the fuck that was about, Elora?" He returns to his knees and pushes on my shoulders for me to lay on my back while he hovers above me with palms on either side of my head.

It's hard to remember why I was so upset when I felt so satisfied and relaxed. "You," I repeat, pouting my bottom lip, "so good."

He raises an eyebrow. "And that *upsets* you?"

I nod and slide my hands down his chest. "I am wholly yours, but you're not mine."

"I am yours," he sighs, moving his hands to my knees to spread my legs apart, settling right between them. "Elora, you have part of me that no one else ever has."

I study his eyes. "You said you loved her."

He leans in to kiss me so tenderly.

I've never tasted myself before, but it's all over his lips and tongue, and I whimper. Something about me all over him makes me want to forget the conversation just to spend the night tasting him. But Finnian seems set on being honest with me to never cause doubt between us again.

"I did," he says, grabbing my chin when I scowl and try to turn away. "But I wasn't in love, Elora. I wish I could explain it better, but I don't know how. I thought she could fill a hole, but she didn't. She only created them. You are it for me, darling. You fill me up. You ignite me."

Liquid heat pours through me, either from his words or feeling like I'm in a perfect dream, and I whisper, "Will you show me?"

He smiles broadly before he kisses me again, moving one hand between our bodies and slipping one finger inside me. I grab his arms and squeeze, adjusting to the slight stretch, whimpering from the tenderness.

His length is against my thigh, and it terrifies me. I want him desperately, but the second finger he adds isn't half of what I feel against my leg. "Relax," he murmurs against my lips, lowering his forehead to rest against my neck, "you have to relax, Elora."

I chase his fingers with hip thrusts. "I'm trying, but the feelings,"— my eyes roll back—"so intense. Gods, Finnian, don't stop."

He lightly kisses my shoulder. "I need you to come again, little doe. You need to be very wet for me." He thrusts against my thigh. "I won't last much longer not being inside you."

I nod, unable to make noises other than tiny pants, and shove his head lower. He takes my cue and wraps his lips around my nipple, circling it with his tongue, tugging with his teeth. He thrusts against me once, twice, his cock sliding against the liquid on my thighs. Releasing my breast to look at our bodies moving together, his tone is gravelly when he says, "Come, Elora."

I throw my head back when I come from the desperation in his voice, arching off the floor and moaning his name.

My vision blurs and colors cease to exist. I can only focus on the tight fluttering in my lower stomach, the nerves he sends spiraling with his touch.

And I'm weakening. Exhausted.

He removes his fingers and slides them into my mouth. I flinch from surprise but suck when he demands it, clawing his arms from my taste all over his fingers.

His fingers leave me for him to move to his knees again, grinning when I stretch my arms above my head. "No, Elora, we're not done. You've begged for me. It's time to reward you."

I snort, my eyes fluttering closed. "*Reward* me? You're far too full of yourself..."

I hear him moving but don't have the energy to look until my fingers are wrapped around his pulsing cock. My eyes fly open, and I lift my head to see his head rolled back while he guides my hand on him.

A vein swells in my grip.

All of this, all of him, belongs to me.

I sit up, biting my lip, when he moans from my squeeze. He is as large as I thought he would be and throbbing. I had never seen a cock before but imagined what he looked like when I felt him between my legs last night. A solitary vein snakes around his length, thick in my hand but smooth. And the tip is moist, which makes me curious about how he might taste.

He removes his hand from mine when I find a steady rhythm, fisting him from the base to the tip.

His lips parted, and he whispered my name, lowering his chin to watch me.

"Tell me what to do," I say.

His hooded eyes turn mischievous. "Put your mouth on me," he replies huskily.

My eyes widen slightly as I return my gaze to his cock in my hand. "Um. *How*?"

Chuckling, he tips my chin with his finger and pulls my bottom lip down with his thumb. "Open," he instructs.

I obey, parting my lips and opening further when he shakes his head slightly. "Wider, darling," he says with a smug grin.

My jaw hangs open while he gently removes my hand and cups my head, guiding me closer.

I inch forward on my knees.

"Put your hands on my thighs for balance," he demands.

This will be the *only* time I listen.

I want to learn how to please him.

"I love you," he says, "but it might not feel like that when I'm choking you."

I can't question what *that* means before he slides the tip of his cock past my lips, immediately cursing when my tongue sweeps over it. The taste of him is salty, the swelling of the vein against my tongue makes me feel powerful from how desperately he wants me, and the look in his eyes is absolutely addicting.

Feral but soft.

But he only pushes an inch further before completely removing himself with a frustrated sigh. "I can't. I'm too desperate for you first. Lie on your back, little doe. I want to come inside you before you swallow me."

I'm suddenly nervous about this thing I've been begging him

for. My nails cut into my palms as I returned to my back, my entire body trembling.

He lowers on top of me but keeps his weight off. "Elora, we don't have to do this," he assures me upon noticing my trepidation. "I want you, but I want you to want this."

"I do want this," I whisper. "Can you kiss me first?"

He answers with his lips on mine, wrapping his arms around me and warming my body with his. His cock pulsates against my sex, but he doesn't pressure or rush me. He loves me through my nerves, kisses me until I stop shaking, and whispers nothing but affirmations in my ear, promising he'll make it pleasurable.

I never doubted he would.

He looks at me for permission, and I nod, holding his head against mine while one of his hands slips between us to align us.

When his cock nudges my entrance, I close my eyes but keep nodding. And slowly, inch by inch, he continues pushing inside. I'm so wet for him that he has to continually pause when he worries he's moving too fast, giving me time to adjust to his fullness.

"More," I breathe.

I adjust to the pain, but that isn't what makes tears fill my eyes. This is the last piece of myself that remains untouched. And I'm giving it to him willingly, but I will never get my heart back after this. It is now solidified that I will always be his no matter how this life ends. Even if my body ceases to breathe, my soul will linger here.

Always searching to reunite with him.

He pauses when a tear rolls down my cheek. "Do I need to stop? Talk to me, Elora."

"No, no." I shake my head, my eyes fluttering open. "Just tell me you love me."

"Oh, little doe." He kisses me softly. "I do. I have loved you since the first time you glared."

My breathy laugh is followed by a moan when he slips further inside. "Me and you?"

He nods against me. "Me and you." One twitch of his hips has him fully seated inside me, and he captures my moan with his mouth.

I wrap my legs around his waist, the movement revealing a new angle for him to thrust. His grin from my widened eyes hints at the idea that this is just a taste of the satisfaction he can provide. Gentle thrusts are all he gives, even when I beg him for more.

"Please, please," I whisper, trying to move my hips against his, but he has a hand pinning them down. "I'm *fine*, Finnian, please."

He raises up to rest on one palm to look between our bodies, watching himself move against me. "Hades, fuck," he murmurs, giving me a *slightly* harder thrust. "I want to tear you apart, but not yet. I need you to come, Elora." He groans my name, his pace quickening. "I waited too fucking long for you. Come, little doe, come."

His desperate pleas send satisfied jolts down my spine, pleased he needs me as much as I want him. I'm so sore, so full of him everywhere, but I will never not want this.

I fear I will want it often.

"Kiss me," I say.

He returns to me and kisses me, our moans of pleasure mixing, our limbs not leaving an inch spared between us. I cry from pain, from longing, from how right he feels inside me.

"Elora," he murmurs against my lips, repeating it with each thrust, his tone straining and growing louder every second.

Until he comes, shouting my name when his forehead falls against my shoulder. Vast warmth fills me, and I follow him over the edge, whimpering his name as we come together, sweat mixing, hearts raging.

I can't breathe; I can't think.

I ache everywhere; I'm slightly positive I might be bleeding from how sore I am from his fullness, but I don't mind. He wants all of me, and now, he has everything.

My heart, my body.

It's just him. All him.

I am consumed by him.

He remains inside me, trailing kisses down my throat, fisting my curls in his hand. "Fuck, you're mine," he murmurs, moving to drag his tongue across my jaw, "all of you is mine."

"Wholly," I reply, trembling in his hold, unable to reconcile how I can still want more after coming so many times.

"Rest," he whispers, but even he is unable to stop kissing parts of me that awaken from his touch. "I'll fuck you again when we wake. And again,"—he kisses the pulse in my throat—"and again. I'll be the one begging for you every moment."

These are puppet strings I don't mind being cast from. If anyone can use me however he wants, it's my husband.

"And fuck, you took me so well." He kisses my lips. "So well, little doe. You were made for me." Then, he sighs at himself. "Rest before I give in to my need for you again."

The last thing I remember is him rolling to his side and pulling me against his chest, asking how I feel, if I'm okay, and me whispering, "Wonderful," before my eyes close.

I stand outside with the shadowed male, watching gauzy strips of shadow circle him before they pause before me. They study me, size me up, and curl their black silhouettes to slither against the ground like serpents.

I should fear them, but I don't, even as they inch closer to stand erect, hovering near me.

The beautiful male speaks, but I can't understand him. He isn't speaking my language, but an entirely different one. It's lovely and melodic but heavy with sorrow.

I try to move, to step forward, but I can't. I try to touch my body, but it doesn't exist. I'm watching him as myself but *through* someone else. Are these dreams visions of the past? If the enchantment was made from ancient magic, perhaps I see his life before death.

Why is he so broken?

Thunder rolls, but the skies are clear above. The male continues to speak, but his voice lowers. And I panic, trying to communicate and ask what this is, but I can *feel* it this time, the tug between worlds, the glass barrier between us. I shouldn't be here; I'm not supposed to be seeing this.

And gods, the pressure, the weight pushing me away, causes my bones to bow and bend as my subconscious is ripped from his world and dropped back into mine.

I awake with a gasp as thunder shakes the walls of the dark room. Blinking to adjust, I sit up to look around, terrified by the unfamiliarity, until I realize that Finnian's hooded jacket is the fabric I'm clutching. But I'm alone.

"Finnian," I rasp, clearing my throat, scratchy from how many times he'd made me cry from pleasure. "Finnian!"

Howling wind pushes against the window, mixing with the heavy rainfall. I search in the dark for something to slip on, settling on the hooded cloak that falls to my thighs.

My legs tremble as I stand, my core biting from soreness, and I'm growing frustrated.

Did he leave me in this abandoned castle?

I tiptoe toward the door, wondering how long I've been asleep, though the sky still reflects night. "Finnian!" I whisper, peeking out into the hallway.

No signs of candlelight or life remain in the dark corridors, frames hanging crooked on the walls and covered in cobwebs. In our desperate state of need earlier, we didn't take time to explore what could be lurking in these forgotten rooms. Not that I was particularly interested in exploring them alone and bare.

Timidly, I step out of the room and grab the corner of a falling frame, tipping it up to study the portrait of strangers in crowns and odd garb, expressions serious yet relaxed.

The royal family of Hogsfeet, who might've heard the screams and cries of my people while Jasper tore apart my kingdom, gave them time to get as many of theirs out before he attacked.

Stairs behind me creak, and I whip around, about to scold Finnian for leaving me alone, when words catch in my throat.

A man leers at me, starting a distasteful trek at my feet and ending at my eyes. "And what do we have here? It looks like a midnight snack."

Forty-Two

I was semi-correct in assuming the castle was haunted, just not by ghosts.

I ran back into the room and tried to shut the heavy door before the stranger reached me, but he shoved against it and knocked me backward. I catch my footing before I fall, panicking while trying to find anything to defend myself.

But I haven't ever been taught *how*.

My weapon is my words, and Finnian isn't here to insult, so the best I can do is constantly back away from this man whose face I can't see in the dark. "Who are you?" I ask, hastily picking up the blanket to wrap around my waist. "Why are you here?" I have to give myself credit for the steadiness of my voice even as my body shakes.

Something shiny twists in his hand, and I can only assume it's a dagger. We were foolish to come here ill-prepared. Abandoned castles are known for becoming places for travelers to set up camp.

He prowls toward me slowly, knowing I have nowhere else to go. I've backed myself into a corner on the opposite side of where the door is. Even if I could get to it, I would have to run half-naked through a castle to try and escape.

"Finnian!" I shout, pulling the blanket around me tighter. "Finnian!" I scream.

Didn't Honora tell him to bring me here?

Oh gods, have we been fooled by her?

The man clicks his tongue. "Now, now, shouting for another man is impolite. We can make this easy, or..."—he rolls the dagger so it can be visible in the stream of moonlight through the window —"Hard."

I shake my head, too frightened to even cry. "Please, please, my husband will give you anything you want, just let me go..."

He makes a horribly cruel sound. "The one I left for dead outside? I don't believe he'll be able to offer me anything as pure as you."

Terror seizes me. Ice envelops my heart. Blood stops pumping. "No, no..." I whimper as my heart starts to shatter and crumble into millions of pieces. I didn't have only one night with him; I didn't waste so much time ignoring my feelings; this isn't true. I will see him smile again and hear his voice...

My shock gave the attacker ample time to come at me, giving me no time to process what he'd said, no time to react with anything other than cries of heartache. I brace however I can and fight him with strength I try to conjure, but if Finnian is gone, I am as good as dead, too.

He yanks me forward and tries to press his face against mine, shouting at me to stop fighting while my eyes squeeze shut and screams come out. Until it all stops.

Instead of words, garbled stutters leave his lips. My eyes open as his hands on me loosen, watching as he stumbles backward. Blood dribbles from his lips before he starts to sway, clutching his chest as he falls to his knees.

Then, forward to his face.

With an arrow protruding from his back.

It unfolds before me like a nightmare come to life, but when I look up, a breathless cry sputters past my lips at Finnian's silhouette in the doorway, soaked from rain, his arms still lifted in an archer stance.

He's running toward me before I can fully slide down the wall to the floor, lifting me up in his arms while I cry and touch any part of him I can reach to believe he's here, he's holding me, and he is *real*, alive, breathing.

He shushes me, cupping my head against his chest and pressing his lips against my hair. He's trying to catch his breath but keeps repeating my name, apologizing, thanking the gods.

And I don't know what else to do but kiss him. A messy, wet-with-tears kiss, but one of relief and fear, anger and shock. And he pours it all back, squeezing me so tightly that I stop breathing, but I don't care because he'll live for me. As long as we're together, he can have all my breaths.

"He said, he said..." My teeth chattered, and my hands clawed his neck and shoulders. "He said you were dead, and I couldn't, I just couldn't...."

He shushes me again, kisses me again, holds me tighter, and whispers my name. His heart thunders in his chest, beating so wildly that I feel it against my cheek when he pulls me *closer*.

"I'll tell you everything," he pants over my cries. "But I need to bury his body first."

I blink tears away. "What, why?"

He cleans my cheeks with his palms. "Because I just killed two men, Elora, and I don't think they were alone."

Finnian waits while I dress, standing by the door and staring into the hallway. He hands me his bow and quiver, slightly grinning at the look on my face. "You won't have to kill anyone, Elora. I need to carry him out."

I strap them to me, backward and somewhat upside down, watching as he yanks the arrow from the man's back and wipes it on the bottom of his jacket. It's the wrong time to find him attractive, but it isn't any less true.

He hauls the man over his shoulder and hands me the bloodied arrow, grinning further at my disgust from the still-bloodied arrow while I slide it into the quiver with the rest.

I ask, "Did you find this somewhere?"

He grunts while following me down the stairs, remaining silent until we make it outside. I hear his hooves before I see him, turning to find Major standing under a small archway of the inner curtain wall. I'm relieved to find him alive and still with us because a horse like him would be a beneficial steal for anyone.

Finnian calls for me when he notices I've been distracted by Major, slowing until I catch up. "Stay with me," he demands, with no softness or option to do the opposite.

"I don't understand," I say. "Your mother told us to come here, didn't she?"

I'm unsure if his jaw tensing is from the weight on his back or the curious accusation. "I don't believe she'd hurt us," I continue, "I suppose it's hard for me to trust anyone now."

The heavy rain has lightened into a drizzle, but the overgrown grass sticks to our pants, and the mud makes it more difficult to walk without slipping. I drop arrows twice and curse each time I have to pause to retrieve them, determined not to pry further until we stop.

A cluster of trees ahead is where Finnian nods, telling me to wait while he checks to see if it's safe. I *don't* listen to that demand, seeing as I'm the one with the weapon, and he's breathless from carrying a large man across a field.

"Godsdamnit, Elora," he mutters when I stick right to him and don't wait behind.

"You said to stay right with you," I say with a slight grin, side-eyeing him when he glares.

At the bottom of the middle tree, another body waits in a crumpled lump, the arrow through his throat instead of his back. Finnian hauls the body on his shoulder to the top of the other man, leaning against a tree with a deep breath and beckoning me over with his finger.

I drop the bow and quiver to the ground, staring down at the bodies when I pass by them to walk straight into his arms. He cups the back of my neck and brings my lips to his.

"I'm sorry I wasn't there," he whispers between kissing me and running his other hand down my ribs. "I planned to come right back, but Major had come out this way to graze."

I nod, frowning when he hisses from my fingers at his temple. Then, I noticed a bloodied patch, purple and red in color. "Finnian, you're hurt." I examine the rest of his face and head, but he doesn't grimace again until I reach the right side of his ribcage.

"Did he touch you?" he asks quietly. "More than what I saw? Did he hurt you?"

I'm too busy lifting his jacket and shirt to answer, gasping when I see the bruise forming on his ribcage—oversized, red, and hot beneath my touch. "Finnian, what happened? Tell me."

He grabs my chin. "You first."

He has prevented me from being able to shake my head. "No, he didn't hurt me. You came in when you needed to. He said something about me being pure...."

He nods with a slight sigh, his gaze shifting to the men behind us. "They knew who I was and might've hoped I hadn't... *unpurified* you yet. Once you fell asleep, I wanted to tie Major to something because he wanders."

"I couldn't tell," I mutter sarcastically.

He tucks a clump of matted curls behind my ear. "I found him and was walking back when they came out behind these trees. The first kill hit me with a rock." He points to his temple. "Must've thought he could knock me out."

I push the hair away from his forehead, worried that the deep cut will put him in a sleep he can't wake up from.

"But he didn't," he continues. "I fought back while that other fucking coward ran to the castle. He tried to take Major, but Major only listens to me and Irina." He gestures toward the bow on the ground. "I always bring weapons when I travel, but he had two daggers, so getting around him to retrieve mine was a struggle."

I wrap my arms around his neck and kiss him; the picture I'm painting in my mind is as terrifying as his story.

"But I had to get back to you." Cradling my neck, he tips my chin back with his thumb. "I *needed* to get back to you, so I killed him."

I search his eyes. "Was that your first?"

He nods tightly. "I've taken plenty of men to the edge but never over. I let them live." He brushes his thumbs over my cheeks. "But for you, I didn't think twice, Elora. And it fucking terrifies me what I'd do for you. I feel no guilt."

He's telling the truth—I see no guilt, but I do see apprehension. "You're not your father," I whisper, touching the tip of my nose to his nose. "You defending me is not the same as what he's done, Finnian. He kills for sport. You, for love."

He kisses my forehead and pats my hip. "We need to get out of the open. The cliffside trail will be too muddy to return to Pumpkin Hollow today. I must bury them and secure the castle until it's safe to leave."

I grab his hand before he can walk away. "Nothing you do could ever scare me away. I won't leave. You know that, right?"

He looks at the bodies with a distant stare and is barely audible as he says, "It scares me what I'd do to ever prevent you from trying."

It takes until sunrise to bury the bodies and cover them with enough grass to hide the eternal resting places from view. Unless someone stumbles upon them, no one should be able to tell what the freshly dug soil hides. Finnian allows me to help until light outweighs night, then instructs me to sit between tall blades of grass while he rolls the bodies into graves and covers them.

He holds my hand while we walk back to the castle, constantly checking our surroundings for any other unwanted visitors. "I don't know why my mother wanted us to come here," he says, breaking the longstanding silence. "But it wouldn't be to harm us. You shouldn't trust Jasper, but you can trust my mother."

"I know," I say softly, giving him my most assuring smile. "It's just strange, that's all. I've spent so many years watching this kingdom rot away that seeing anyone surprised me. And..." I squeeze his hand. "We have more to lose now. You're *okay*, but I really love Irina."

He huffed a laugh. "Funny."

"How would they have known about my...."

"Your purity?" he finishes. "There's an archaic belief that kings and princes only take brides that haven't been touched. And maybe that was true once, but it's not anymore. To my knowledge, there are no nearby realms or kingdoms. It makes me wonder how long those men and whoever they're with have been secluded."

"So, they've just been... watching?" I look toward the cliffside. "Unable to reach us?"

He follows my gaze. "Maybe. You've stood at that cliffside before, haven't you? Perhaps you had admirers."

I wrinkle my nose. "That's unsettling."

The castle comes into view, but I look at the river behind it, the water calmer than it was during the storm. He puts my hand against his lips for a kiss, drawing me back to him. "Elora, I can't risk you. I know you want to see it..."

I pucker my bottom lip. "Wouldn't it be better to see it in the daylight than tonight? I've never been this close before."

"We have ponds in Pumpkin Hollow," he says dryly. "I'll take you to one of those."

I tap the bow strapped across his chest. "You can protect me. I trust you. Please?"

His eyes soften, and a ghost of a smile appears before it's replaced with worry. He turns in a slow circle, not leaving an inch of our surroundings unseen. "We stay behind the castle, out of view. If I tell you to move, you move. Major will take you away from here."

"Wait, wait." I cross my arms. "You want me to run while you...

what? Sacrifice yourself?" I shake my head. "No. That's not a compromise. You're asking me to leave you."

"We're not compromising on this, Elora."

"I don't need to see the river." I turn away from it and walk toward the castle, shaking my head when he starts arguing. "No, Finnian. I can't agree to that and don't have to listen."

He grabs my wrist and yanks me back to him, pulling me against his chest. He has become rougher since revealing his darker side, but I won't complain.

"Actually...." He grins. "....You do have to listen to me. Lord Finnian, remember?"

I remain highly unimpressed with him. "Lord Finnian was on his knees for me last night, so there's a flaw in your demand."

His eyes darken. "And what will it take for Lady Elora to allow me to bow for her once more?"

I wonder how far I can take this while he lusts after me. "Bathe with me." I tip my head to the side. "In the river. Then, I will remain in the castle until told otherwise."

His gaze lowers to my mouth. "That's not a compromise, little doe."

"I suppose you're right." I press my hips against his. "It's more like a gift for you."

He's already pulling at my cloak, trying to hide his interest with a smirk, but his body betrays him. "You think rather highly of yourself, but I will agree as long as you promise to not make any sounds."

I feign innocence with my eyes. "And what sounds do you believe I'll make?"

A heady grin. "Let's find out."

❧

I need to remember how easily Finnian can be swayed when lust veils his logic.

I trail behind him to the backside of the castle, trying to

contain my excitement about stepping foot in a body of water. To him, it's ordinary and unexciting. I'm sure he's seen oceans before, but I haven't seen more than a muddy puddle in my lifetime.

He instructs me to stay put while he inspects the perimeter, but I see no harm in removing my boots and tiptoeing to the water's edge. Mud has settled on the bottom, keeping the top a bluish-gray and somewhat transparent.

Uneven and rounded curves span both directions as far as I can see, edging wet and dead grass. I curse from sharp pebbles as I hobble to the water's edge, bouncing from giddiness like a child. Soft chirps of bugs and frogs come from every direction, drafting a sense of security over me.

The river is peaceful.

Grimy and mucky but calming.

And godsdamn *cold.* Shivers race up my spine when I step into the shallowest edge. Though long, the river isn't wide. I could toss a rock to the other side if I wanted, but the mud from the rain doesn't make it simple to gauge how deep it is.

Mud encases my feet, making me laugh and wrinkle my nose from the clay, but at least I won't be bathing in pure dirt unless Finnian decides to kick all of it up.

The steep trail we took to get here has created a watery slide, producing a steady flow of mud and rock into the water. It might be bluer if we explore farther, but I won't push him.

This time.

I squeal when a strong arm wraps around my waist and carries me into the water, ducking us both under. Gasping as I come up, I slap Finnian's shoulder while trying to clear mud from my eyes. "You took your shirt off first!" I scold, flinging the dirt from my face onto his.

"You disobeyed," he retorts, wrapping my legs around his waist to wade. "Be still, and let's see how deep this goes."

I cling to him tightly. I do prefer to disobey, but I do not want to die from drowning. We stay tucked behind the castle, but he takes us farther south than where Major crossed last night.

"How did you know those men weren't alone?" I'm not fearful and meant it when I said I trust him to protect me, but his worldly knowledge is part of what makes him so attractive.

He stops when the water reaches his elbows, adjusting me higher around him. "From my experience, men travel in packs, and those men looked well-fed, meaning they'd lived off the land. If it was only them, they wouldn't have risked both their lives until they had a more solid plan than hitting me with a *rock*."

I grin at the cocky confidence in his disappointed judgment.

"I think we were spotted coming down the trail. Someone sent them as lookouts, but they believed they could take me down and get to you and had orders to return this evening." He bites my chin until I shove him off. "And you are rare. Men toss aside logic when something needs to be collected."

I frown. "What would they have done with me? To me?"

His jaw pops. "Raped you or held you for ransom, or waited until I came to find you and used me as bait, but they overestimate Jasper's loyalty to his son." He seems to want to say more, but he kisses me softly. "I haven't told you everything yet, Elora."

I nod with a sorrowful, knowing grin. "I know. Not yet. It's too late for me now, Finnian. I can't walk away from you, so let's wait."

Dimples. "You love me?"

I pinch my lips together in faux thought. "I tolerate *you* but love what you can do to my body. Is that fair?"

He pinches my sides, nearly causing me to flop into the water like a fish, and laughs when I curse at him. "Let's see how quiet you can be, little doe."

Forty-Three

As it turns out, Elora can't be quiet.

After discarding our clothing, we clean our bodies, but when Elora nearly drowns after I set her down, it results in dramatic flailing and squealing until I drag her over to show her that she can touch the bottom with the tips of her toes. She glares at me with only her eyes and forehead out of the water, the rest almost invisible beneath the surface.

She has to constantly hop around to be able to breathe, but I'm enjoying watching her struggle far too much to lift her up yet.

"Maybe I should refer to you as my little toad instead," I jest, grabbing her when she tries to insult me with her mouth partially underwater. "Easy, Elora. If anything is going to choke you, it'll be me."

She spits the water she's taken in my face. "I can assure you that I won't be choking on anything you have to offer." Her haughty little smirk is followed by her trying to wiggle free from me, but her exposed chest isn't for anyone's eyes but mine.

"Stop," I say, tightening my hold on her body. "Wrap your legs around my waist."

She shakes her head.

Sighing, I slide my hands down to cup her thighs and force

them around me. "You can defy me all you want except for this. I denied myself from you for far too long, and now I want what's mine."

Her scowl is natural, but the way her skin flushes is undeniable. Even after everything we've been through, after admitting that we annoyingly fell in love with one another, it still irritates her how much she wants me.

"Keep pretending if that's what you need." I keep one arm around her while my other lowers to fist my cock, aligning with her core. And when I push the tip in, her lips part. And fuck, the feeling of her tightening around me is incomparable to anything else I've ever experienced. "Ah, there's my girl."

I still have difficulty filling her because she has trouble relaxing unless I kiss her, and that's hard to do when she claws me and can't keep *still*. "Elora," I whisper, "Look at me, darling."

Her legs tighten around me, and her teeth grab her bottom lip, but she drops her gaze to mine. I stifle a groan from the feel of her stretching around me, nodding slowly instead. "It's just you and me. Relax for me."

She exhales tightly, then kisses me. She keeps herself distracted from the pain by exploring my mouth with her tongue, shoving her hands into my hair to try and give back what I'm giving her. Either that, or she's envious again over the plays she keeps writing in her mind about all the women she has imagined I loved at some point or another.

"I love you," I murmured against her lips.

Her eyes flutter open. I take the distraction to jerk my hips up, thoroughly filling her. She gasps as her eyes roll back but puts her best effort into being quiet, only releasing a breathy whimper.

"Good," I praise, "that's good, little doe." Wrapping my hands around her waist, I keep her pinned in place while I back up to find the wall, which is made of more mud than rock and is not the best for balancing without slipping.

"Put your hands on my shoulders," I say. "And talk to me.

Hades, you don't know how hard it is to be the one in control each time."

Instead, she cups her hands around my neck and presses her forehead against mine. "I know exactly how hard it is. I feel it."

I can't help but laugh, tipping my head up at the rain clouds rolling in above. "Fuck, this is about to get a lot more slippery. Move against me, darling." I use my hands to guide her, doing my best not to completely ravage her.

She finds a steady rhythm by anchoring her knees against the muddy wall. I need to get her inside the castle but also want to spend the rest of the day with her wrapped around me, and it's hard to remember our lives were just threatened when she's rolling her hips.

But she's also divine with her hooded eyes and parted lips, her breasts barely visible each time she bounces and teases me just enough to drive me mad with need. And the fucking rain falling on us dampens her hair, causing her wild strands to curl around her shoulders.

"I am apologizing in advance." I twist us quickly and pin her against the slick mud, bruising her waist with my fingers. "But shattering porcelain is just too fucking tempting."

I do not give her everything, but my thrusts are tight enough to cause her eyes to fill with tears, my name leaving her lips in raspy, uneven cries of pleasure.

She outstretches her arms and digs her fingers into the earth to attempt to keep still, but her arched back pushes her breasts out of the water.

The sight unleashes me.

I slam a hand against the ground and drive into her harder than I should this soon, but her mewling whimpers encourage me to keep going. And when she gets too loud, I slap my palm over her mouth and clamp it down.

Her nails claw my chest. I hiss from the sting, removing my hand to ply her mouth with my tongue. She bites my tongue, then my lip, tugging when she moans and tightens around me. I've only been inside her twice, but I've learned her body's cues for when she's coming. Explosive shivering always takes over her body, followed directly by my name on her lips. And she always sounds so fucking upset by it that it drives me mad with the need to hear it again because I know it angers her.

My lower stomach tightens when climax rushes through me forcefully enough that I have to collapse against her, panting her name. Her chest is heaving against mine, her body covered in mud all over again, and I could fuck her again right now if I wanted.

The more often I fuck her, the longer I'll last every time, meaning I could spend an hour hearing her cries for me—over and over, day and night. And what a godsdamn perfect life that would be. Gods, she became everything to me so quickly.

Goosebumps cover her, and she brings her arms into shelter under my chest, trembling. The raindrops turn chilly, but she looks and feels divine against me, every inch of her body slick. I lift my head to kiss her, concerned about the sluggish way her eyes open.

"Cold?"

She nods slightly. "And tired."

I blink from unease, studying her face while holding her nearly limp body around me. And for once, she doesn't tell me not to worry. Guilt strikes me like lightning, and I slide out of her gently and hop out to grab our clothing.

She rests her head against the ground, uncaring that mud is sticking to her curls and skin. Maybe I was too rough with her too soon. But I have never made someone look like they're about to take their last breath.

I dress quickly to assist her, shielding her body from view until her clothes cover her. She reaches for her boots, but I shake my head and scoop her up, cradling her against my chest while she holds them.

"Talk to me," I say.

She rests her head against me. "Tired."

Her creamy skin has paled, the inner part of her bottom lip showing the faintest hint of blue. I hoped it was purely from being cold, but that wouldn't have fatigued her.

"Stay awake," I murmur.

"I don't want them anymore," she whispers while water rimmed her eyes. "The nightmares. I don't want them anymore."

I frown. "Why do you have them?"

A tear rolls down her cheek. "Because I promised I wouldn't fall in love."

Elora is asleep on the floor, rolled up in as many blankets as I could find, and lying by the fireplace. She was too groggy for me to inquire what she meant by what she said, but I can't stop thinking about it. She has nightmares because she fell in love. Elora is human. Unless she's somehow tied to faerie magic, nothing in this world could punish her for falling in love.

While she slumbers, I secure the castle, going as far as bringing Major inside just so we're not spotted. If the group those men were part of spotted us coming down the trail, perhaps they'd believe we left if they couldn't see Major outside. I'll need to hunt for us soon, but I can't go until she wakes, and I refuse to leave her here alone again after nearly losing her.

I don't know the layout of this castle, but it's much smaller than mine, so finding the kitchens was relatively simple. The cabinets have been ransacked, of course, and since Hogsfeet was brought down over two decades ago, they have none of the newer inventions or instruments available for cooking.

But in one of the higher cabinets, most likely out of reach for most people, sits an untouched jar of honey in the shape of a bear. Since the family crest of Hogsfeet boasts two swords crossed underneath a bear's head, I imagine these were designed exclusively for them. And since Elora always smells like honey and vanilla, this will suffice until she regains enough energy to walk outside with me.

Then, I remembered something Azrea asked about last night before I left them—Elora's nightmares. And Irina mentioned something about their awkward conversation. I can't make it up the trail to ask the faeries why my wife is having terror-filled dreams, but I can ask the source.

And on cue, as if the demon possessing her heard my thoughts, blood-curdling screams come from upstairs.

With the honey bear in my hand, I take the steps two at a time and rush into the room. Elora's back is arched off the floor, her fingers clawing at the blankets, and sweat blankets her. But when I crouch and touch her, her skin is ice-cold.

"Elora!" I shout, crawling over her and cupping her face in my hands. "Elora, open your eyes. Darling, you're safe."

She gasps as her eyes fly open, and her heart pounds so wildly in her chest that I *see* the pulse in her throat. She covers her face with her hands, sobbing and rolling to her side. I go down with her, pulling her against my chest to try and calm her.

"I love you so much," I whisper, stroking her hair, "but it's your turn to be honest with me, Elora."

I don't rush her to calm down or force her to speak to me. I give her time to collect herself because if there's anything I've learned about my darling bride, she doesn't do anything unless she wants to do it. And she's admitted to me before that I make her nervous, so I soothe her by adding, "Nothing you say will scare me away, love. I promise."

Slowly, she tips her head back to look at me with tearful eyes, her cheeks stained and damp. "I did something awful," she rasps, squeezing her eyes shut again. "And I don't want to tell you because it means none of this is real."

I caress her waist, my eyes searching hers. "We are very real," I assure her. "You won't be able to change that."

I am not fully clothed, but far more than she is, and it seems to bother her now. Whatever she needs to tell me must be more significant than I realize, and I watch her as she rolls away from me to fetch one of the dresses I stashed away for her in one of Major's saddlebags. And I sigh when she covers her beautiful body, already planning to remove it from her again afterward.

She sits opposite me, inhales deep but quiet breaths, and tucks loose curls behind her ears. I might be more nervous if I wasn't staring at the most ravishing creature in all the realms. Elora could tell me she murdered thousands, and it still wouldn't tear me away from her.

"I lied to you," is not a great start to this conversation, but it's how she begins. "When you asked me if there's any truth to the rumors about a spring hidden within the mountains, I denied it, but that was a lie."

My curiosity is now fully functioning, and I slowly sit up.

She taps her fingers against her lips, her breathing unsteady and her chest rattling. "You figured out my plan far too early after we met—I did come to Pumpkin Hollow to persuade you into marriage." She pauses when a tear slips past her eye. "But, I knew I wouldn't be enough on my own to grab your attention, so.... I had help."

I tilt my head to the side. "What kind of help?"

She blows out a shaky breath. "I discovered the spring with Azrea a little over a year ago. She couldn't decipher the magic within, so we didn't touch it and agreed never to tell anyone because I didn't want your father to discover it. Fae magic is powerful, and imagining it in his hands was terrifying."

I nod slightly. "I can understand that."

She twists her hands together. "After Regina told me to beguile you, I became extremely nervous. I had... heard things about you, and Regina has spent years convincing me that being myself is comparable to having an incurable disease."

I rise to my knees and go to her, wiping away the tears on her cheeks with my thumbs. The fragile, delicate, kindhearted woman before me has been made to feel less important than everyone in her life when she is pure magic in human form.

I lower and pull her to sit between my legs, pressing my lips against her throat while she weeps in my arms. "Elora, listen to me.

If you only believe one thing I ever say, let it be this. You, as a person, as a human being, matter. You matter to me, you matter to Irina, and you matter to my mother. Do not let Regina and Jasper's words lie to you. You are more than just a mare to be bred and more than an inconvenience to her."

I tip her chin up with my finger. "I fell for you the second I saw you, little doe. I didn't know it yet. I didn't want to admit it, but I didn't want to let you go after we danced and you stormed out. I tried to follow you."

"But this isn't me," she rasps, removing my hand from her. "That's what I'm trying to tell you, Finnian."

I raise an eyebrow. "Is this when you tell me you're truly an ogre, hm? Will you change back into one during the next full moon?"

She rolls her eyes, sniffling. "No, Finn, this is when I admit to drinking from the spring and wishing for more confidence."

I wait for the horrible part, but she says nothing else. And all I ask is, "And?"

She blinks in confusion. "And? What do you mean by '*and*'? Finnian, I wished for enough confidence to ensnare you!"

"Elora, I was ensnared by you before you even opened your mouth."

She sighs, somehow annoyed at me. "You don't understand. The woman you fell for isn't how I am usually."

"You're not this irritating typically?"

She scowls. "I'm not so.... vocal about things I dislike so greatly."

Her pointed stare at me informs me that I am the thing she is referring to, and it's wildly offensive. "So, let me make sure I understand this. You drank from a spring containing faerie wishing magic?" I await her confirmation before continuing, "And wished to be confident enough to win me over, and now, you believe I fell for the venomous toad instead of the charming, kind creature in my arms?"

"Venomous *toad*?"

"A beautiful toad, but still a poisonous one."

She crosses her arms and turns her chin away from me.

I can't help but laugh. "Are you truly upset with me right now? You admitted to trying to persuade me with the use of magic and are boldly upset with me because I referred to your alter-ego as a toad."

Before she can reply, I wrap a hand around her throat and gently force her to lie down on her back. She's avoiding making eye contact with me, even as I hover over her on all fours. "Here's what I think," I say. "I think the thoughts you manifested into vocalizing are how you truly feel about Pumpkin Hollow and my father. I think the spell, or whatever the fuck it is, simply made you brave enough to say thoughts aloud."

I grin when she mutters something under her breath before I add, "And I think how you feel about me was hidden beneath the surface of each insult. You couldn't stand how much you wanted me when we met. And maybe you did despise me, but in your own twisted little mind, it made you fall harder."

I soften a *little.* "Elora, I fell for the girl beneath the bullshit. Fuck, I love fighting with you, but when you let your guard down with me and allow me to see the tender parts of you, I fall for you harder. I'll remind you of this any time you doubt which version of you I love, but you had my attention the moment I saw you on the drawbridge."

Her faux-hardened exterior cracks when she turns to meet my eyes. "What?"

I lower to lay on top of her, my elbows on either side of her head while I stroke her forehead with the tips of my fingers. "You're the reason we went to the ball. I was trying to talk Irina into staying and drinking instead of attending, but she dragged me downstairs to meet you. I would have fought harder, but I was too curious about who you were to not attend."

Her bottom lip quivers.

I brush a thumb across it. "Elora, you have always been

enough. Even if you hadn't braved telling me how you truly feel, I still would've wanted to touch you, talk to you, and learn who you are. You're mine, little doe, every part you can give."

"All of me," she whispers softly. "You have all of me."

I kiss the corner of her mouth. "That's all that matters."

Forty-Four

After making love very carefully, tenderly, and slowly, praising her body in every way it should be praised, I show her the jar of honey I found, which she has quickly fallen in love with. I've decided to inquire with Rhoadie how we can find and manufacture bottles like these because I'll be damned if I don't do everything in my power to bring a smile to Elora's face any chance I get.

I watch her with a broad smile as she pours honey on her fingers and licks it off. Honey has a long shelf life and can be safe for decades, though with how she's eating it, it won't last the night.

She's calmed since waking, even more so since divulging her secret to me, but anxiety still lingers in her tense shoulders. I'm giving her time to be less rattled before I press further about the nightmares and how they align with the faeries and the spell she drank.

We already have so many hills to climb with my father to try and bring peace back to Ashbury that the addition of defeating powerful nightmares is something I hope can be squashed quickly so her mind is free to help me plan for Jasper's demise.

After she's seemingly had her fill of honey, she hands me the bottle, but I'm not hungry for honey. I'm starved for her, long having tipped over the edge of obsession, and irritated that I've lived without her when she was only a bridge away from me for most of my life.

Her cheeks flush when she catches me staring at her, and I grin. "I've been inside you, yet I still make you nervous."

She confirms with a nod. "I don't believe you'll ever not make me fidget, Finn."

"Finn," I repeat, reaching forward to grab her wrists and pulling her back into my lap where she belongs. "It seems unfair for you to refer to me by my nickname when I can't use yours, little doe. Can you tell me why?"

"Because Regina uses it as a mockery," she whispers, resting her temple against my shoulder. "My mother used it lovingly, but once Regina and her daughters moved into the manor, they used it cruelly."

I bring her hand to my lips. "I am sorry for what you've endured with them, but allow me the honor of restoring what your mother called you, my love. I am not them. And maybe it seems small to you, but it's important to me that I belong in every part of your life, even something from your past."

I worry I overstepped when she didn't say anything, but after a moment, she lifted her head to look at me. "I think you love me too much," she whispers.

Her comment jars me until the words sink in, allowing me to listen to them from another perspective. "I think you haven't been loved enough, and the weight of my love smothers you." I leave a tender kiss on her forehead. "But I want you to feel choked by it, Elora, because only then will you learn how to breathe from the weight of it. It's an adjustment, I know, but abuse isn't only physical. I want to undo every pain you've been through."

Her eyes refilled with tears. "Jasper told me he's controlled you by instilling fear in you mentally."

I brush a tear off her cheek. "He has, but you're freeing me from those confines. You've woken me from years of ignorance. That is why it is so infuriating when you don't realize your importance. You changed me. You're still changing me."

She twists to straddle my lap and traces my face with her fingertip. "Does it bother you that you can't have children?"

The wall I've built around that topic instantly makes me want to change the subject, but she is my wife and deserves to know everything about me. "Yes and no," I reply honestly. "I never longed to be a father, even with Agnes. Everyone talked about our future children, but it wasn't something I was looking forward to achieving. But with you...." I have to pause to take a breath, spinning one of her curls around my finger. "With you, I would like to raise a child, and I'm deeply sorry that it's something you won't have."

"Don't apologize to me." She kisses me. "Don't apologize for something that can't be helped. I don't love you despite it, Finnian; I love you because you're you. I love you in the same way you love me. Wholly. And it breaks my heart that you were made to feel broken because someone couldn't love you through it. It makes me sick that instead of comforting you, she sought solace in someone else. I promise it doesn't bother me, and I promise I'll never think less of you."

It's incredible how much power words hold; hers releases something in me that I've been carrying for a long time. And the only response I have to her promises is to kiss her, holding her so tightly against me that we're no more than one body with two souls. "I can have more tests run—"

"Unnecessary," she interrupts. "If it happens, it happens. If it doesn't, then it doesn't. It's not going to change us."

"Fuck," I rasp, leaving a trail of kisses down her throat. "I'm never going to deserve you, Elora."

"Ellie," she whispers, leaning away so I'll stop and look at her. Then, with tearful eyes and a small, assuring smile, she says again, "Ellie. You can call me Ellie."

We don't stop touching and exploring one another until the sun begins to set, allowing us the freedom to hunt for food. Again, I've been too distracted with getting to know her inside and out to inquire about the nightmares. And now, I'm too concerned with keeping her fed to discuss them.

She's waiting with Major outside the castle's front doors while I search the perimeter, armed with a dagger. She doesn't know how to use it, but it makes me feel a little better about leaving her while I ensure no one is lingering close by to attack.

When I circle back to her, her head is nearly inside a saddlebag, and she's talking to Major while she searches. I lean against the stone wall, watching her with an amused grin. "My love, can I assist you with something?"

She pops her head out with a sigh. "He's hungry."

"Oh?" I lick my lips to keep from smiling. "Did he tell you this himself?"

She scowls at me and points the tip of the dagger in my direction. "Don't patronize me while I'm armed."

In two swift movements, before she could even take another breath, I disarmed her and slid the dagger into my waistband. "May I patronize you now?"

She stares at me in disbelief. "How did you do that?"

"Years of practice," I mutter, reaching around her to retrieve a handful of sugar cubes from the front pocket of the saddlebag. "Feed these to your talking horse."

She takes them, then wrinkles her nose. "Do I just..."

I drag my fingertips across my forehead, grinning at how differently we've lived. I've been exposed to so much life while she's been sheltered from.... well, everything. Something as simple as knowing how to feed a horse highlights a vast difference between our lifestyles.

Her cheeks reddened from embarrassment, but I quickly shook my head. "I find your lack of knowledge endearing, Ellie." My grin widens from using that name for the first time. "Trust me, there's a lot I'll be teaching you. It's better to start with something as simple as feeding Major."

Her eyes widened slightly. "What does that mean?"

Smirking, I put my hands on her waist and turned her around to face Major. Then, I lean in and tug her earlobe between my teeth. "If I tell you now, we'll never leave this castle."

She fucking *shivers*.

I adjust my hardening cock before guiding her hands toward Major's muzzle. "He's a spoiled bastard and knows what's in your hands, but he's going to sniff them because he's a snob. Lay your palms flat."

"Don't be cruel," she snaps, turning her head toward me.

"Ellie, this is the best-fed horse in every realm I've visited. He's rotten. I love him, but he's spoiled. He's not hungry. I doubt he even knows what it feels like to *be* hungry."

Major huffs in response and takes the sugar cubes from Elora's palms, causing her to squeal from his tongue grazing her. I chuckle, even when she turns to wipe her hands on my cloak. "He's even more slobbery than you," she taunts.

I gasp at her insult, then grab her face and lick her cheeks, holding her as she tries to shove me away. "Truce!" she shouts, putting all her strength into trying to turn my chin.

My chest warms as I recall the first time she shouted that word at me, and she smiles from how I longingly stare at her. "Was it the way I smashed pumpkins that made you so obsessed with me?" she asks, throwing her arms around my neck.

"It's the way you simply exist," I reply, kissing her.

❧

We ride farther away from the castle than we've been so far. She doesn't ask questions, too content with being free from her cage to care where I take her. I'm terrified of being in the open with her, in a place I've never been. But I know my mother well enough to understand that there has to be a reason she wanted us here so badly. But from right here, as we ride through tall blades of glass on nothing but land, the reasoning isn't clear as far as I can tell.

The river widened and cleared, and we rode alongside it, which was a mistake on my part. Elora keeps leaning over each time she sees a fish, slapping my thigh excitedly. I've seen nothing but bass and catfish so far, but to her, they're the most exciting specimens she's ever seen.

Never mind that she's friends with faeries—it's fish she wants to risk her life for each time she dips down to get a better look. Finally, after pulling her up for the dozenth time, I call for Major to stop and hop down before pulling her off.

"Go on," I say.

She excitedly claps her hands and runs to the water's edge, lowering to her knees to study the fish swimming past her. Having seen fish hundreds, if not thousands, of times, I watch her instead. She finds joy and bliss in things I've long stopped looking for. My life with Elora will include taking time to slow down and *live*.

Each time she points to a fish, I tell her the name. She was tutored, sure, but hearing and seeing are two completely different experiences. And I'm learning that Elora wants to experience everything. After spending so many years away while she suffered in a rotting kingdom, I owe her the time she needs to adjust to the world outside her heated chamber of faeries and coal.

I grin when an idea pops into my mind. "Take your boots off and roll your pant legs up," I instruct, ignoring her probing questions while I return to Major and pull a handful of sugar cubes from the pocket.

He follows me until I give him one, then settles for drinking fresh water from the stream. Elora raises an eyebrow at me when I kneel to dip the sugar cubes into the water, wetting them until they dissolve in my hand. I spread the sugary water across all ten of her toes. "See what happens."

Trusting me, she wades into the water until it reaches the back of her knees and stands completely still. I straighten and watch the fish timidly swim closer to her until a catfish takes the bait and latches onto her right foot.

Elora shrieks and slaps a palm across her mouth, and I break into a deep laugh. She could only stand it for a few seconds before hopping around until the catfish scattered, and she sloppily ran toward me. I grab her hands and pull her out, laughing harder at the red mark on her foot.

"Finnian!" she shrieks but laughs with me. "That hurt a little bit."

I nod with a knowing smile. "Irina and I used to dare one another to do that in the stream behind the castle. It used to be full of catfish, but now it's mostly bass."

"I've only seen fish in books," she admits. "They spoil too quickly, so they were never included in the deliveries."

My smile falters, and I wonder if I'll ever live free of guilt for all she's had to live without while I lived a life of luxury. "I can catch a couple if you'd like to try one. We can grill them over a fire before we return to the castle."

Her carefree, excited smile returns. "Yes, please."

Elora lounged by the river while I used a makeshift spear made of a stick and my dagger to catch our dinner. We didn't speak for a long time, but it wasn't uncomfortable. Being near her brings a sense of peace over me that I've long craved, and our silences don't need to be filled with idle chatter. I'm content to watch her while she watches the world around her.

But now, she keeps her head turned from me while I gut two fish on a rock and keep the pieces I think she'll eat. They won't taste as good without the seasonings I've become accustomed to, but I want to be part of every first experience with her—even the ones she finds repulsive.

She chooses a spot for us between tall blades of grass and only a stone's throw away from where Major continues to graze and drink from the river. I bring a small blanket from one of the saddlebags to allow us to sit on the ground—and perhaps lay on to enjoy dessert afterward.

Unsurprisingly, Elora knows how to build a fire, explaining that on cold nights in Ashbury, she used to help people in town keep warm by showing them how. I spare her from the remaining fish guts by sliding them back into the water, keeping only slices of meat to slide onto a pointed stick.

She sits between my legs and leans against my chest while I hold the fish over the fire, leaning over every few seconds to kiss her temple. "You must find this so dull," she says.

"Not at all," I reply. "I've spent so many days constantly moving that I've forgotten how much I like being outside."

"You are skilled at so many things." She idly rubs my thigh. "Yes, that, and this. Hunting. Fish *and* people."

I chuckle at the latter. "I assure you I don't make habits out of hunting people, only when they try to keep me from you."

She draws shapes with her fingertip. "Do you think, if we can eliminate the terrible men, we can build something that would allow the people of Ashbury to come down here?"

"It might take a while, but yes, it's something we can look into." I pull the stick out of the fire and bring it to her mouth to blow. "I am willing to look into any idea you have."

She raises for me to pull the meat off the stick, taking the first bite to ensure it's finished before holding the rest out to her. "All right, darling. Your very first taste of fish."

With a wrinkled nose at the texture of the meat, she takes it from my fingers and tears off a piece with her teeth. Her eyes flare before she pops the rest of it into her mouth.

I grin. "More?"

She nods and crawls away from me to grab another stick, waiting for me to slide meat on before she settles beside me to hold it over the fire. "What's your favorite?" she asks.

"Salmon," I answered quickly. "There might be some if we walk down farther, but it's getting too dark to explore much more tonight. We'll fill some jugs for water and return tomorrow. Maybe I can find a squirrel for us."

She blanches. "I'm okay with the fish."

I wrap an arm around her shoulders and kiss her head. "Tell me what you see in your nightmares, little doe."

She rests her head against my shoulder, staring silently into the fire until she whispers, "I don't know."

"Irina mentioned—"

"A male, yes," she finishes. "But I don't know who he is. Azrea said he died long ago, but he doesn't *feel* dead. It's almost like he can see me, but I don't understand his language. And he has shadows that chase me, and I'm afraid of what they'll do if they ever catch me."

I nod slowly but understand nothing about magic. I've never cared to learn anything about it. "What did you mean earlier about falling in love?"

She pulls the stick out of the fire, waits for me to retrieve the meat, and opens her mouth for me to drop it inside. And when I ask if she wants more, she encourages me to eat some instead. Then, she sighs and leans back on her palms, tipping her head back to stare at the stars rising. "When I consumed it, I was supposed to promise it something in return."

I look at her over my shoulder. "And did you?"

She licks her lips, and then sorrow floods her voice. "At first, I didn't think I did, but then.... I remembered something."

I swallow, anticipating the worst.

"I wished for enough confidence to succeed, then thought that if I didn't, it might as well take my heart."

"And since you succeeded...."

She conveys all the heartache I feel when she looks at me. "Yes, Finn, I believe it wants me to uphold my end of the bargain. I think the spell might be slowly killing me."

Forty-Five

I stare at her in disbelief, forgetting all about the fish until charred remains fill my nostrils, and I curse. Removing the stick from the fire, I blow on the seared fish to prevent the fire from spreading, then drop it to the ground to face her. "I don't understand, Elora. Why do you think that?"

"The nightmares are intensifying. As they do, my energy wanes. It's becoming nearly impossible for me to leave them. It's like...." she pauses while thinking how to explain this to me. "It's as if I'm stuck between realities. And I don't know if he's trying to pull me into his or trying to come into mine."

I hesitate to ask, "Have you tried speaking about this to Azrea since that day?"

She lowers her eyes to the ground. "You know I haven't."

I hook a finger for her to return to me, waiting until she's straddling my waist before I speak again. "What happened, Ellie? Irina said you left the faeries upset. You need to trust me."

"I don't want to tell you," she mutters.

"Hades," I sigh. "Did Cedric touch you?"

She refuses to make eye contact with me, focusing on my throat and hesitating for too long. "They...."—she nervously toys with the end of one of her curls—"They asked me to leave with them. Cedric said we could be together."

Too many questions flood my mind, but mostly, I only see red as jealousy combines with anger, coming out in short huffs through my nostrils. "He what?"

"You heard me. I'm not repeating it."

I untangle her from around me and stand, flexing my hands at my sides as I walk away, not from her—from this overwhelming need to pummel his face into the mountainside.

"Finn." She chases after me and grabs my hand, sighing when I yank it away. "Finnian, I denied them; denied him."

"I'm not upset with you," I growl, clenching my fists. "He saw you with me, he knew we were to be married, and he still fucking asked you to leave with him?" I turn around so quickly that she knocks into my chest, and I catch her by sliding an arm around her waist. "He knew you belonged to me."

She slides her hands up my chest, pleading with her eyes. "I know. I understand why you are upset, but please don't take it out on him..."

I release her. "Are you.... defending him?" That is the last thing she should've said to me. "After I've been inside you, *claimed* you, you're going to stand here and defend him?"

"No," she answers quickly, "I mean, yes, I guess, sort of, but it's not because I want him...."

I bare my teeth.

She rolls her eyes. "Stop! Gods. They want to leave! That's what I'm trying to tell you. You won't have to worry about him anymore—"

"Wait, what?"

She takes a moment to recollect herself by blowing out a steadying breath. "That is why I came to you to begin with. I want to help Ashbury, but the faeries plan to leave. I don't know how or when, but Azrea is pregnant, and she needs to be near healers. The conditions they're working in—"

"Jasper will never agree to that," I interrupt. "You have to know that, Elora. He will never allow them to leave the realm."

"It's not his choice," she snaps. "They might not be human,

but they do not deserve to be locked away to mine coal all day when men could do it instead!" She crosses her arms over her chest. "This is not something I will argue about. I needed you to love me so much that you'd stop him from killing my people once the faeries escape."

"Fuck me," I reply. "And I'm sure you've figured out by now that I have no true power regarding what Jasper wants? Aside from the pumpkins, the faeries are his most prized possessions. He has plans to double their workload."

"He already doubled their workload!" she shouts. "A year ago! They're strong, Finn, but he is working them to death."

I rest my hands loosely on my waist and tip my head back, trying to think of a way to fix this, but I can negotiate nothing with him in exchange for releasing the faeries.

"Azrea has to be near a healer," she reiterates. "They need to leave this place, my love. And I need your help."

I lower my chin to look at her. That's the first time she's called me that, and it soothes the icy burn from Cedric trying to steal her away from me. "Your what?"

Her own chilled exterior cracks. "My love," she whispers. "You are, aren't you?"

"Yes," I answered quickly, closing the space between us and cradling her face. "Yes, I am."

She lifts to her toes and weaves her arms around my neck. "I didn't want to leave you, Finnian, even then. But, please, help me help them. I need you. I can't do it without you."

How rapidly I agree internally is astounding, but I want to hear something from her first. "You stopped talking to them because they asked you to leave me?"

Her sheepish little nod in response makes me grab her thighs and lift her up to wrap around me. "Fuck, Elora, we wasted so much time. I could've had you sooner."

She presses her forehead against mine. "We found one another, Finn. I wouldn't have changed any of it."

I keep her balanced on one arm but snake my other into her

hair and tenderly kiss her. "I will help you, but this isn't simple. We'll need to involve Irina."

The fire behind us shows the shine in her eyes from relieved tears. "I know it goes against everything you've been taught—"

"Everything I've been taught is wrong," I assure her. "I promised you we'd find a way to live a long, happy life together, and I won't let you down. It won't be easy, but I love you. And my mother has taught me that love means sacrifice." I kiss the corner of her mouth. "If pushing past the discomfort of what's been drilled into me means I stand with you in the end, it's worth it."

"It means you'll have to speak to Cedric—"

I shush her. My last conversation with Dolfe floods my mind, and a new wave of guilt overcomes me. "There's something else I need to tell you...."

I stop when we both turn toward noises in the distance. Holding her tightly against me, I lower to my knees and remain utterly silent as we listen. The muffled noises soon change into voices, growing in volume.

"Listen to me carefully," I whisper. "I need you to remain out of sight while you walk through the blades to Major."

"I'm not leaving you—"

"I will be right behind you. I need to snuff the fire out."

She shakes her head wildly, curls bouncing. "Let's just go! We can run, I can't leave you—"

"Elora, I need you to trust me." I uncurl her from around me. "Remain lowered as you run. You've heard Major's commands. If I'm not there in three minutes, take him back to the castle."

"You have lost your fucking mind!" she shouts in a whisper. "I am not leaving you here!"

"For fuck's sake, Elora, just listen to me for once." I tap her hip. "Go, now. I need to put this out so they can't see us. The longer we stand here and fucking argue about it, the quicker they'll find us. *Go*."

She looks toward the river, then the voices coming from the

opposite direction, before sighing. And then, she kisses me. "If you die out here, I will kill you all over again."

I kiss her quickly. "Noted. Now, go."

She hesitates just long enough for me to smack her backside. Muttering something under her breath about me bossing her around, she takes off, remaining bent over and beneath the line of sight. I scramble over to the blanket and cover the fire, stomping on it to quickly suffocate the flames, then shove the dagger I discarded earlier into my waistband.

I can tell more than two men are heading toward us, and while I would stop at nothing to protect her, it was difficult enough to hold off two when she wasn't with me. With her more at risk of capture being by my side, I worry what I'll be capable of if someone tries to touch her. I've never been violent to the point of no return, but for her, I'm learning that a darker part of me does exist—one that would do anything to ensure she remains mine.

Not only do I have her heart, but her body. And I would rather die from protecting her than live while imagining someone else taking what belongs to me.

The cover of night keeps me cloaked while I run to the river, first spotting Major but not Elora. Panic seizes me as I call her name quietly, grabbing hold of Major's reins and keeping him steady while I twist and turn frantically, searching for any sign of her. It isn't until I hear the sound of grass blades breaking that I turn around, fists clenching as a man comes out—holding my wife against his chest, his hand covering her mouth, his other hand pinning her wrists behind her back.

Her wide eyes, full of fear, gripped me.

The man isn't dressed like the other two were—and he looks taken care of compared to the dirt marks the men wore across their faces and hands. And the two men that come out behind him, flanking on either side, appear the same.

I am severely outnumbered with Elora in their possession.

"We can do this the easy way," the man holding her calls, "or the hard way. I prefer the simple way if it's all right with you."

My bow is strapped to the saddlebag on the other side of Major, but I might be able to nock and loosen two arrows to take the two men on either side of her before driving my dagger through her captor. But they're also armed with weapons, and my reaction could bring injury to her.

Elora tries to say my name, her voice muffled against his hand, and attempts to free her arms. I have to weigh options quickly because the sight of another man's hands on her is blurring my vision into nothing but sharp shades of red.

I hold my hands out in front of me. "Easy way."

Elora screams my name, but he tightens his grip to keep her mouth beneath his palm. I roll my neck, trying to relax my shoulders to appear non-threatening, and put my wrists together when the man on the right pulls a shredded piece of fabric from his back pocket. Approaching me slowly, I remain utterly still, filling him with faux confidence and allowing him to loop the material around my wrists once.

Then, I headbutted him.

He stumbles to the ground while I retrieve the dagger from my waistband, aim it toward the second man now running toward me, and throw it. The blade pierces straight through his shoulder, knocking him down, and then I zero in on Elora.

The man holding her seems far too calm for my liking, dragging her backward hurriedly while I chase after him, her panicked shrieks terrorizing me. I promised her she would always be safe with me—that we'd find a way out of all the other problems we have, and now, she's being pulled away from me in a kingdom that was supposed to be dead long ago.

In the scuffle, he pulls out a rag from his pocket, places it against her mouth, and her eyes immediately fall shut.

I shout her name. I tell her to open her eyes, but her limp body in his arms does not move. I didn't lose her this quickly—I didn't waste time when I could've been with her.

I catch up to them, manage to get one swing in, and lunge for her when he stumbles back a step. But before I know what's happening, a rag is placed over my mouth from behind before I can get a grip on her to carry back to Major.

And her wilted body is the last thing I see.

Forty-Six

A pounding headache coils down my spine. I open my eyes to find myself in a room lit only by a single oil lamp. I am not in the castle, nor am I with Finnian. Though my head hurts, I don't recall being hit, but I also don't remember seeing what became of my husband after everything around me went black. However, I know I am groggy, and every thought is riddled with confusion.

"Finnian," I rasp, clutching my forehead as I sit up.

I know he's not here—I would feel him near me if he were, but I'm hoping he's right outside the closed door, ready to bust in, kiss me, and assure me everything's okay.

But my logical side, the one trying to shove past the disorientated, fatigued side, knows that everything is not okay.

I was almost to Major when a man lunged at me. He must've been kneeling beneath the blades, hidden from my view, and aware of my panic as I ran. The voices we heard must've been to distract us—trick us into believing we had time to get away. And Finnian tried—he tried to save me.

He took two down before a dirty rag was placed over my mouth. And now, he might be dead.

And that's when the terror sinks in, shoving past the murky

waters sloshing in my mind, and I cry his name. I stumble toward the door, jiggle the knob, and shout for him.

Forget saving Ashbury, forget everything I've worked toward if he's not breathing. I didn't fall in love with someone so smug and perfect only to have him for two days.

"My love!" I cry, slapping the door with my palms.

The thin wooden door rattles on the hinges, so I know whoever is out there can hear me. "Finnian!" I scream, my dry throat producing nothing more than raspy shrieks.

The gold door knob twists slightly, and I step back, ready to lunge if it's Finnian but looking around for where I can cower if it's not. The windowless room has only a small iron bed, big enough for only one, and a table for the lamp to sit on while it burns only brightly, sufficient for me to see a silhouette in the doorway—one that doesn't belong to Finn.

The stranger holds his palms up toward me when I slink back into a corner of the room, as wide-eyed as a doe. I don't want to be touched by someone else—I'll fight until I can't.

"Where is Finnian?" I ask, my voice shaking.

The man steps forward, his hands still raised. "I will answer your question if you sit on the bed, away from the lamp."

I recognize him as the one who captured me. He's an older man with gray hair and a full beard, most likely my father's age. He doesn't seem frightening at first glance, but he also poisoned me and probably harmed my husband.

I sigh at the oil lamp, ashamed that I didn't consider it a weapon. Finnian will need to teach me more about how to defend myself since this is the second time I've been at the mercy of another man.

"Tell me he's alive," I reply.

The man slowly lowers his hands. "He's alive. Please, sit."

I twist my fingers nervously. "Why should I believe you?"

"I have nothing to gain by lying to you."

I suppose that's true, though I don't seem to gain anything

from this unless it ends with Finnian and me reuniting. "I want to see him," I replied. "I don't care what you have to say. Let me see my husband. Let me see him, or I'll scream until you have to rip out my voice box."

To my surprise, the man grins. "You're just as fiery as she said you are."

I blink, taken aback. "Who?"

He motions for me to sit. "Care now, do you?"

I shake my head, braving a step forward. "Let me see Finn. Let me see he's alive, and I'll allow you to talk to me."

"I can't do that just yet, Miss Elora."

I'd be more surprised that he knows my name if it wasn't for Finnian shouting it while trying to save me. "Then, I suppose we have nothing to talk about."

He scratches his eyebrow, his expression the same as most's are when they look at me. Exasperated. But I've taken Irina's advice to heart. I decide how I'm spoken to and about. I've spent too long doing as others demand, and even though I don't want it, I am part of the crown now. I've earned respect.

He walks back into the hallway, whispers something to someone, and comes inside with a clear water bottle. "I imagine you're thirsty," he says, extending his arm toward me. "I didn't give you much, but you ingested a toxin that dehydrates you to keep you docile."

"I am not a rabid animal," I snapped. "Conversations can accomplish wonders instead of trapping people."

He shakes the jug. "That is what I am attempting to do with you. We were not fearful of you. We were fearful of him. We saw the graves by the tree; we know he handled those two renegades. And we know it was to protect *you*."

"And you expect a man to act differently when his wife is in the hands of another man?" I roll my eyes. "How did you expect him to react?"

He comes closer, and I step back, holding my breath as he sets the water jug on the table. Then, I see the red swelling around his eye and lick my lips with a grin. "Finnian did that to you," I say. "And do you believe that was unwarranted, too?"

He chuckles and lightly pokes at the swelling. "I suppose not." Tapping the lid of the jug, he tries to give me an assuring smile. "It's not poisoned, and it's clean. If you don't drink, the headache you have will worsen, and you won't be able to stand without falling. I won't return until you've finished the jug."

He approaches the door, ignoring me when I begin arguing with him again. Before I can speak, he adds, "Maybe when I return, you'll be ready to have that conversation. If not, I wouldn't count on seeing your husband soon."

I rush toward the door as he steps into the hallway, crying Finnian's name again as it closes. And behind the door, the man adds, "Scream all you like, Miss Elora. We're underground. Ain't nobody but us to hear you."

I don't know how much time has passed since he left me, but I don't drink the water, and my headache does indeed spread to my muscles, causing fatigue in every movement. I sink from the bed to the floor, pull the thin blanket with me, and curl into a ball in the corner. Without proof that Finnian is alive, I refuse to give these strangers the satisfaction of doing as they say.

I'm nearly asleep when the door quietly creaks open, and the man peeks his head inside, sighing at my state.

I can't lift my head but tighten the blanket around me. I will not be the damsel at the mercy of men anymore. I won't be touched by anyone else.

"Miss Elora," he whispers sullenly.

"I want to see him," I breathe, unsure if he can hear me. "I need to know he's alive."

He widens the door, rests his hand on the knob, and looks

between the untouched water on the table and me. Then, finally, he dips his chin in a single nod. "A sip for a step."

I don't take the first offer. "I won't take the first sip until I'm out of this room."

A combination of laughter and a sigh replies, but he approaches me and offers his hand. "You're going to need my help to walk."

I shake my head, pushing to rest on my palms on shaky arms. "I'm fine. I can do it." Every limb aches from my movements, but showing weakness won't help me.

I'm shivering from exhaustion, my mouth and throat dry from dehydration, but I make it to my feet with the blanket wrapped around me. I hold my hand up to stop him from grabbing me when I sway, determined to not be touched again unless it's by my husband's hands.

I look at the water jug with an anguished expression, imagining how heavy it'll be when I can hardly hold myself up. He doesn't offer to do it for me, and I refuse to ask.

I whisper, "Is Finnian drinking?"

The man slightly shakes his head with an amused and annoyed half-grin. "No. No, you're both too stubborn to help yourselves. He's refusing to behave, much like you."

I manage a small smile. "And you'll take me to him?"

"I won't break my word, Miss Elora."

My determination to see my husband alive outweighs my dread of carrying the jug, even when I nearly drop it after gripping the handle. "Neither do I," I say. "I'll take a sip when we step outside this room."

He stays beside me while we walk into the hallway, preparing to catch me if I faint. Holding true to my word, I twist the cap off and tip the jug to my lips.

And Hades, I despise how good it tastes. It takes effort to force myself to lower it again instead of guzzling the entire bottle.

I see no one nearby, but doors line the long corridor. Each one is closed, but they're all identical—wooden and thin. The low ceilings of stone confirm what he said earlier: we're underground. I can tell by the echo of our shoes against the ground. The sound is similar to when Finnian took me through the basement tunnel.

I look over my shoulder toward where my room is compared to how far I've managed to drag my feet, somewhat amused at how far apart they separated us. "You took precautions to ensure he couldn't find me," I say.

"He has tried," the man mumbles.

By his tone, I surmise that Finnian has been far more difficult than me. He tried warning me after killing those two men—he fears what he's capable of if we're ever apart.

I take continuous sips of water, each draw becoming a little longer, and feel the warm water combatting the poison almost immediately. My steps don't lug as heavily the more I consume. "Did he hurt anyone?" I look at each door as we pass by, impressed that so many people live here. "What's your name? Where are we?"

"Yes," he replies to my first question. "The man he pierced with his dagger survived, but we nearly lost him."

The sorrow in his tone does make a sliver of guilt spiral through my spine, but Finnian thought these men would harm me. "I won't apologize for Finnian protecting me. If you're truly not threatening to us, you should've chosen a different way to approach. Capturing me was not the way to handle it."

"The prince has a temper, Miss Elora."

I take a long drink of water. The dryness in my throat is soothed after half the bottle is gone. "Not with me, he doesn't. Your friends wanted me for...." I trail off, not wanting to verbalize their intentions aloud. "He had every right to fight."

"Those men were not our friends."

I could argue about that, pry *more*, but instead, I ask with a raised brow, "how do you know Finn is the prince? Hogsfeet isn't supposed to have people. He's never traveled here. How do you know him?"

Instead of answering me, we silently stop in front of a door. He knocks thrice and waits patiently for another man to answer. This man was not one of the men from our capture, nor did he look any older than Finn. And though we're underground, his sun-kissed skin and light blond hair tell me he spends plenty of time outside.

Without a word, I follow both men inside a small room, only to face another door with a rectangular foggy window above it. This door is not made of wood but steel and has an iron padlock hanging off the knob.

Surprise tilts my head. "Why isn't my room this.... dramatic?"

"Because your husband is a prick," the young one answers.

My eyes narrow into slits. "Excuse me? That's the prince you're speaking of."

"He is no prince of mine," he seethes.

"Reynold!" the older, kinder man scolds before looking at me. "He was in a room similar to yours, but we have children that didn't need to hear his.... colorful language."

I can't stop myself from grinning. "I hear nothing."

"Because it's the only soundproof room we have," the blond mutters. "It's encased in stone. He's still yelling."

The older one, whose name I still haven't learned, drags a stool to the door and motions for me to stand on it. I shake my head, remaining with my feet planted. "I am not going to look at him through a window. He needs to know I'm okay."

"I told you this was a stupid idea," Reynold replies, looking at him. "Neither one of them will listen. We're better off keeping them apart until they break."

I lunge for him, arms swinging and obscenities flying, but the man insistent on keeping me alive catches me right before I get a punch in. "Leave, Reynold!" he barks. "You ain't helping no one with your opinions."

I manage to kick his thigh as he walks past, and I'm quickly twisted away from him and held back by an arm across my stomach. "I can't wait until he's out!" I shout after him. "If I were you, I wouldn't be nearby!"

My captor shuts the door before Reynold can retort, locking it behind him. "Miss Elora, I really need you..." he trails off with a sigh, only now noticing that I had dropped and broken the water jug from my impromptu attack.

"I drank most of it," I mumble. "He's an ass!"

He nods slightly but also shrugs his shoulders. "He's been through a lot. We all have. I'll fetch you another jug after this, but only if you'll make another bargain with me."

I huff. "The last bargain I made with a man ended with me signing my death certificate, so pardon me for not jumping at the chance to swear any more oaths."

"Involving the heir that you're supposed to provide?"

Hearing it takes me back to that crypt beneath the castle, goosebumps rising on my skin from the memory. "Who *are* you?"

He tries another assuring smile. "I'm willing to tell you how I know that, but you have to work with me, not against me. I don't plan to keep the prince locked up, but allowing you in there now won't do me any good."

I tighten the blanket around me. "What do you *want* from us?"

He motions to the door. "First, I want you to climb up on that stool to see for yourself that he's alive. After that, I'll tell ya the rest."

The complete silence on the other side of Finnian's door causes my nerves to strain against my skin and my heart to thump in my chest. What if I step on that stool and see him lying on the ground inside? What if they're showing me his dead body?

I timidly approach the stool, my palms sweating and causing the blanket to loosen from my grasp. I balance my palms against the door to rise up on the seat, hesitating while debating if I want to see what's waiting for me on the other side. But if I'm not being lied to, I will regret missing the opportunity of seeing Finnian alive and breathing.

Lifting to the tips of my toes, I keep my eyes squeezed shut until I feel the chill of the window against my forehead.

"Please be okay," I whisper, "please be alive."

My eyes flutter open.

And my heart sinks into my stomach.

Finnian is pacing back and forth across the small room, his steps sluggish, but his anger is evident in his clenched fists. His mouth is moving, but I can't hear him.

"Finnian!" I shout, banging my hand against the window. "Finnian!" Tears fill my eyes at the sight of his bloodshot eyes.

"He can't hear you, Miss Elora."

"Finnian!" I scream, adding a second hand to the window. "Look up, my love! I'm right here!"

He pauses his pacing, slowly turns his head toward the window, and searches. It looks like he mouths my name, but I can't *hear* him. "Finnian!" I shout again and again, tears rolling down my cheeks.

He runs to the door, he shakes the bar holding the lock in place, and the veins in his neck strain as he yells.

"Please, please let me in to see him!" I cry, not looking anywhere but at Finn below me. "Please, just for a moment! I just want to touch him; I want him to know it's me...."

"I can't do that yet, Miss Elora."

"Please," I repeatedly whimper, smacking the window until my palms ache, until I can do nothing but claw at it while my tears blur my vision. "I love him, don't you understand?"

Finnian is feral inside the room, constantly shaking the bar across the door, hitting it with his shoulder.

I step off the stool and face the man. "His father kept him locked away in a crypt! You don't understand what you're doing to him! You have to let him out!"

Surprise lights his eyes, and he looks from me to the door containing my entire heart.

"I am not lying to you," I continue. "His father has made a mockery of his son by controlling him with fear. And part of that fear is locking him in a crypt full of skulls when Finnian does anything Jasper disapproves of!"

I don't wipe the tears falling nor allow my voice to be anything but steady. "You have a better chance of him cooperating if you show him compassion because I can promise you he's never been given that respect by his own father."

I clench my teeth and plead once more, "Let him *out* or lock me in there with him."

Forty-Seven

He pulls a key from a back pocket and spins it between his fingers, hesitation evident. I say nothing else, not wanting to push my luck, but hope sprouts in my stomach. I need Finnian to hydrate, I need him to know I'm okay, I need him to not be locked away.

"I will let you *in*," the man agrees. "You have thirty minutes to calm him down and get him to drink the water. When I open that door again, I will not be alone. If he attacks us again, I won't stop my men from defending themselves."

"I understand," I whisper.

He sighs, then waits for me to drag the stool away from the door before he slides the key into the lock. I gently place my hand on his wrist to stop him from unlocking it. "What's your name?"

"Gus," he replies.

I remove my hand. "Thank you, Gus."

He tilts his head to the left. "Come stand on this side of me so you're the first one he sees."

I obey immediately, practically hopping to his left side. I'm jittery and impatient, even though it only takes seconds for the lock to open and the bar to slide out.

Gus opens the door, Finnian rushes toward it, then stops and stares at me as if I'm a mirage. I run inside and leap, throwing my arms around his neck and kissing him. He stumbles back, either from dehydration or surprise, but responds by lifting me to wrap around him, shoving his hand into my hair. I barely hear the door shutting behind me, and he doesn't seem to care as he deepens the kiss.

"You're alive," he says before kissing me again. "Fuck, Elora, I imagined they had killed you. The last thing I saw—"

I kiss him again, stopping him from speaking.

I knew I loved him. I accepted that I fell for the man I wasn't supposed to like, but I hadn't yet admitted to myself how deeply entrenched he was inside me.

I unravel myself from around him, sliding my hands beneath his shirt, taking time to trace his stomach with my fingertips.

I need to feel his skin against mine.

Grabbing the collar of his shirt, he tugs it off, then repeats it with mine until our bare chests are touching. He doesn't inquire how long we have, and I don't stop kissing him to tell him. All that matters to either of us is that we're together.

We step out of our shoes and discard our pants, but instead of returning the blanket around me to obstruct me from whoever looks through the small window above the door, he drags me over to the solitary oil lamp and kicks it over, extinguishing the little light we have.

Somehow, one of us manages to cover the flickering flame with the blanket, but I don't believe either of us would care if we drowned in a fire as long as we burn together.

"Elora," he whispers against my lips, but it's not because he has something to say. "Elora," he repeats because I'm *here*.

He pressed me against a stone wall, sending icy chills across me from the cool rock, but he warms me up swiftly. His lips trail down my throat, his hands grazing my ribcage, and he groans when I tug his bottom lip between my teeth.

"I need you," I murmur, "I need you inside me."

His raspy groan is enough to make him sigh in pleasurable contentment. "Fuck, darling, say that again," he demands.

The lack of light inside this stone cell has made me brave, and I wrap my fingers around his cock. "I *want* you inside me, Finn."

He thrusts into my palm, curling his hand around my throat to pin me against the wall. "Again, Ellie."

I bite the corner of my lip, ignoring the way heat rises on my cheeks from timid mortification, before I whisper, "I want your cock inside me, my love."

He breathes my name and cups my backside in his hands, spinning us around until he's the one against the wall. "I need you to be a good girl for me, darling." He sinks to the floor and brings me with him. "I need you to ride my cock."

Liquid heat replaces my blood at his demand but also slightly terrifies me. I've done this once before we wed, *with* clothes on. Even then, I was unsure how he'd fit inside me.

"You can do it, little doe." He spreads my thighs apart, as desperate to feel me as I am for him, and drags the tip of his cock across my clit. "Hades, Ellie, you're so wet. Take me."

I want to desperately, but I don't know *how*.

"Put your hands on my shoulders," he instructs, as if reading my mind. "I'll help you, but I can't wait much longer. Do it before I do it for you."

I obey, placing my hands on his shoulders, then kiss him, unable to stand any space between us. He returns it passionately, steadying my nerves, and grabs my waist with one hand, using his other to line his cock at my entrance. And swiftly, in one sharp movement, he pushes my hips down until he fills me.

My cry of pleasure matches his groan, but he puts a finger against my lips. "I don't want them to hear you," he says.

"They can't," I rasp, tipping my head back from how full I feel with him seated so deeply. "They can't hear anything."

He wraps a hand around my throat, drags me closer, and growls, "Then I want you to fucking *scream*."

I am on the lap of a distinguished prince—one renowned for his charm—but this is the man in the center of every interesting rumor, every scandalous tale. And I hate him for it, but he's also mine now. These words, these sordid commands, will only be said to me.

And that knowledge instills power within me.

Guiding me with his hand still around my waist, he jerks my hips back and forth against him in unsteady waves. His tip rolls over a soft spot inside me that makes my eyes roll back, but the movements are so jerky that nothing but an abundance of frustrated bliss builds.

"You're doing so well," he assures me, breathless. "Hades, little doe, you were made to take my cock."

I moan his name, taking some control back by rolling my hips in a more subdued tempo and dragging my nails down his chest. He growls my name, releasing my waist to palm my breasts. "Tell me who you belong to me, Elora."

"You," I rasp, climbing, climbing.

He pinches my nipples between his fingers, causing me to cry his name. "Fuck, you're so good for letting me hurt you, darling." He squeezes my breasts. "Do you want more?"

I can't fathom all the ways Finnian knows how to give me pleasurable pain, but I find myself whispering confirmation.

Dropping his hands to palm my ass, he digs his fingers into my skin to raise me up to my knees and takes my nipple between his teeth. I clench around him; the discomfort is wholly gratifying, much to my surprise. But he doesn't ask if I like it, releasing one nipple to grab the other and sinking his teeth into my flesh.

I claw his chest, digging my nails into his skin until the slightest tinge of blood pools against my fingertips. He groans my name and grazes my collarbone next, nipping, biting, tugging. And I'm riding him, grinding against him so quickly that the sounds of our skin meeting fill the room.

"Finnian," I cry, my knees biting from rubbing against the stone floor, but all I feel is him. "Oh, gods, Finnian, oh—"

"There are no gods here," he replies, "only me worshipping you. Come for me, darling. Come on my cock."

I'm taken to the peak, tipping over to tumble, doing exactly as he demanded, and shattering. He palms my waist, squeezing until I have to bend backward, and continues to move me against him. "Fuck, I wish I could see your tits bouncing for me, Ellie. One more; give me one more."

I don't know how long we have until men bust in here, but I can only focus on him and how good he feels to care. So, I let him control me, allow him to lean forward and take my breast in his mouth, and I shout his name over and over.

And I come again, body slicked with sweat, breathless and dizzy, but trembling with nothing but relieved pleasure. He's always been so gentle with me, so patient, but now, I will be utterly craving this every moment we're together.

How can you stop when something is so satisfying? Even with our current predicament of being in the hands of strangers, being with him, coming on his lap, has turned me into mush. And I murmur into his ear, "I love you so endlessly."

He pulses twice, cries out my name, and explodes inside me, the warmth filling me so entirely that it drips down my thighs. And he does something so utterly depraved that I gasp: he pulls me off him to raise me up on my knees, slides his tongue inside me, and tastes our combined releases.

I fist his hair in my hands, jerking from how raw I am, but he takes everything he can get before shivers rock through me. Only then does he lower me into his lap, cups my throat in one hand, and kisses me, allowing me to share what he stole.

We're panting, pulses pounding, and I'm still half-convinced he's a dream—that I've died from dehydration and now live in the afterlife with him. But he's here, touching me, holding me. He's here, alive and desperately in need of water.

I start to laugh, dropping my forehead against his shoulder. "I was supposed to talk you into drinking the water, but I needed this more. I needed you more."

His arms encompass me. "Did they harm you?"

"No, not at all." I lift my head. "You?"

He kisses me before placing his forehead against mine and

slightly shaking his head. "Not physically. They refused to tell me if you were alive, Elora. I thought I was going mad. I've endured torture, my heart, but never like that."

Frowning, I trace his face with my fingers. "I'm here, and I love you."

He plants feathery kisses on my cheeks and eyelids and leaves a parting kiss on my lips. "Let's get you dressed before I have to kill anyone else."

I stand on trembling legs but don't try and search for my clothes in the dark just yet. "Not until you drink."

I only know he's rolling his neck by the slight pops of tension releasing. The sweet, gentle Finnian has been replaced by the one who craves control. "Elora. Dress. Now."

I cross my arms. "Finnian. Drink. Now."

I flinch when he grabs me, unable to see him in pitch black, and shove his face away when he tries to kiss me. "I will fuck you into submission, little doe. Don't tempt me."

I soften a little. "I dress while you drink?"

Sighing, he takes my wrists in one hand to remove them from his face. "And if it's poisoned?" he asks.

"Then I'll drink it, too," I whisper. "They won't separate us again, Finn. I promise."

Ever the one in need of dominance, he counters my offer with, "We dress, you sit in my lap, in my arms, where I know you're safe, then I'll drink."

He doesn't give an inch. Even when I dress faster than him, he still won't take a sip of water until we're on the ground, huddled in the corner, with his arms wrapped tightly around me. I tip the jug against his lips to force water into him since he refuses to release me. "See," I say, "It's not poisoned."

"There are poisons with slow releases, Ellie," he responds. "We don't know these men. One might've shown you kindness, so you're unsuspecting when they turn cruel."

I twist in his lap with too much effort since he won't loosen his hold, carrying the jug until I straddle him. I tip the bottle against his lips while my mind swims with thoughts. "How do you know all of this? Irina said you trained with the army, but you learned how to torture prisoners?"

"In a roundabout way," he replies sullenly. "I'm not going to detail everything to spare you the pain, Elora."

My sigh is chock-full of frustration. "You cannot continue living that way, Finn. You can't keep protecting all of us while you suffer from what you've endured."

"I know," he whispers, dodging the jug to leave a kiss on my throat. "But you must accept that some moments shouldn't be revisited. There are times I don't want to relive, Ellie."

As much as I want to know everything about Finnian, I can't push him to tell me all his experiences. If we succeed, we'll have plenty of days to learn the inside and outs of one another. Until then, I'm content with every next breath he takes. "Well, I assume you have a plan for getting us out?"

He takes the jug from me and swigs. "First, I want to know where my horse is. I'll be damned if I let them get away with harming him. I would be surprised if they even managed to bring him to wherever we're being held. He only follows me."

"And Irina," I add with a snort.

He sighs, annoyed. "She'll begin looking for us soon if we don't return. I don't know how long we've been here, but Jasper will expect us back in Pumpkin Hollow soon." He clears his throat after taking another drink, and his voice is already sounding better.

I would smugly remark about being right, but knowing him, he'd stop drinking just to be a bastard.

"Gus, the man who has been kind to me—"

His grip on me tightens, and I roll my eyes. "Relax, you beast. He's my father's age. He mentioned someone telling him I'm *fiery* but wouldn't disclose who."

I only know he relaxed his head against the wall by the soft thud. And when the silence draws out between us, I shift forward and kiss him to ensure he's still *alive*.

"I wonder if they know my mother," he says quietly. "She wanted us here for a reason. They haven't harmed you...."

I tilt my head. "Why would your mother know men in Hogsfeet? To our knowledge, this kingdom hasn't been touched in over two decades. That's a long time for her to know them and for Jasper never to find out."

Before he can say anything else, the sound of the key sliding into the lock causes him to lift me and stand. He places me behind him, keeping me squeezed between him and the wall. It's a tad dramatic, but I have a feeling he'd die trying to prevent anyone else from taking me away from him.

I squint my eyes when the door opens to an onslaught of lanterns, burning brightly as if lit only seconds ago. Finnian keeps a hand behind him, keeping my top tightly between his fingers. Gus, Reynold, and two other men enter the small cell.

"Gods, what did you do to them?" I mutter, noticing bruises on three of the four men.

"Fought for you," he replied, his tone short.

"Thank you," I whisper.

I place my hand over his tense fist, and his shoulders loosen *slightly*, but he keeps a hold on me. Gus lowers the lantern to search the floor, sighing when he realizes we broke the oil lamp and stashed the pieces under the blanket I brought.

"We can't easily acquire those, you know." Gus raises the lantern again. "Now that you have her, are you ready to behave rationally and have a calm discussion?"

"Tell your man to keep his eyes off her," Finnian growls.

I peek around him to notice Reynold staring at me. "He doesn't like me," I tell Finnian. "I tried to attack him."

Reynold's previously semi-permanent scowl is replaced by a somewhat amused one, but he averts his eyes away from me. Finnian looks at me over his shoulder, contemplation behind his eyes, nodding once at my slight shrug. "I want Elora fed," Finnian demands. "I want us to not be separated. And I want to know where my fucking horse is."

I have to laugh at his final request and how he sounded like a boy desperate to save his favorite pet.

Gus chuckles. "The horse was stubborn until we offered him food. He followed us here and is grazing above land."

"Fucking traitor," Finnian mutters.

"We have meat and potatoes for both ya," Gus continues, "we won't separate you unless you punch another one of our men. I won't be able to help you anymore."

"Keep your hands off my wife," Finnian replies, "And I won't fucking lay a hand on any of you."

If I was made of ice, I would've melted.

Gus approaches. Finnian backs me up until my spine is against the wall but takes the lantern Gus extends toward him. "Well," Gus says, "I 'spose you have questions. Follow me."

Forty-Eight

I keep Elora trapped in my arms as we follow Gus down a long corridor of closed doors. Elora doesn't seem misplaced, meaning she's seen this hallway before. Reynold and the two other men stay behind us, preventing me from lifting her and bolting in the opposite direction to find a way out. No, we're stuck here until Gus tells us why he felt the need to capture my wife and throw me into a stone cell.

I glance up at the ceiling, recalling his comment about Major being above land. We're underground, but why? Elora seems to be studying how the men dress, confusion knitting her brows. Since she's never left our realm, she's unaware that Jasper has kept too many styles from infiltrating Pumpkin Hollow. The men in loose vests and cotton pants behind us are more in harmony with what lives outside the only world she's ever known. It's a minor reason I stayed away as often as possible.

Time stands still in Pumpkin Hollow, whereas it flies by everywhere else. It's something I've always hoped to change when Jasper dies, but now, I want to spend my days traveling with Elora—taking her to all the places she never dreamed she'd be allowed to visit. I care nothing for the throne or the crown anymore. I live for the doe-eyed expressions she makes when she discovers something new.

And Irina deserves to see places, too. I often came home with gifts for her, though never the scandalous ones Massimo always finds for her—that she now uses to terrorize the somewhat innocent woman in my arms. As much as I desire to bring her pleasure in ways she didn't know possible, I hope to constantly surprise her with delights outside of the physical ones.

I want to always be why her eyes light up when she discovers something new to her—even if it's as simple as fish in a river. I'd live outside with her if necessary.

Elora tips her chin up when she feels me staring at her and raises an eyebrow. I ignore her silent challenge, lean in, and kiss her tenderly. Then, I whisper against her lips, "I love you so endlessly," repeating the heart-tugging words she said to me.

Her replying smile instills a fresh wave of hope in me.

We nearly bump into Gus when he abruptly stops in front of a door halfway down the corridor. I squeeze Elora against my chest, holding the lantern up when he opens the door and ushers us inside. Unlike my cell, this room is spacious and lined with wooden tables and benches. A woman around my mother's age is spooning stew into treen bowls, the wood showing signs of age through scuffs and scratches.

But what she's dishing smells incredible.

Gus leads us to the table and sets his lantern in the middle, motioning for Elora to sit first. I respect his kindness toward her, but I don't like how it makes me trust him. It's an ancient war tactic to trick your enemies into submission by earning their trust and then turning on them when their guards are down.

Elora, bright as sunshine and unwary, smiles at him and sits.

I place the lantern on the table, close enough to reach her quickly if needed, and kiss her temple before sitting beside her. Years of being well-mannered are tested as the smell of meat and potatoes fills my nostrils, and I become impatient while I wait for the others to sit. I don't want to appear too eager, but I've also become used to eating meals at certain times throughout the day, and we've been so busy getting to know one another that I haven't prioritized feeding my wife. Pieces of grilled fish did not last us long.

Elora, however, looks perfectly content to wait. And the realization that she's used to not eating stirs guilt in my chest. I owe the woman I love so much, and I fear I'll never be able to accurately make amends for the neglect she's suffered.

The woman who dished the stew returns with a plate of sliced bread and places it in the center of the table. Having seated, Gus looks at my wife with a kind smile. "Please, eat."

"It smells wonderful," Elora replies, scooping a spoonful and closing her eyes at the first taste.

My unrestrained grin is simply from watching the constant awe from her whenever she isn't glaring at me.

Before I realize what she's doing, she drops her spoon in her bowl and picks up mine, scooping stew out and sliding it into my mouth. I choke on a laugh and a swallow, tipping my head back slightly when some stew dribbles out the corner of my mouth. "It's so good!" she exclaims, retrieving slices of bread for us and dropping mine into my bowl.

She is correct; the stew is seasoned to perfection.

Gus, Reynold, and the other two men follow her lead and begin eating, and moments pass by while we dine in silence. Our meals are soon joined by mugs of ale, but Elora requests water for both of us, and my heart warms. Irina has always tried her best to care for me, but Elora.... Well, Elora won't allow me to slip. And for her, I won't.

After finishing my first helping of stew, I washed it down with water and cleared my throat. "Would you mind telling us how long we've been down here? My father will be expecting us to return to Pumpkin Hollow soon."

"Not as long as you'd think," Gus says. "Hours, maybe. Neither of you passed out too long."

I nod slowly, trying to recall what time it was when they found us. "So, it's... early morning?"

"*Early* morning," he confirms.

Elora places her hand on my thigh. "And can you tell us why we're here? You will let us leave, right?"

"You're not prisoners," Reynold answers, then smirks. "Well, not anymore."

I look at Elora when she turns to me, and we search each other's eyes, composing our own secret language. After a moment, I kissed the tip of her nose and nodded my confirmation. She wants to know who these men are and who informed Gus about her. She *is* fiery, but that's not information I want to be passed around to strangers.

I rest my hand on top of hers but place my other elbow on the table and focus on Gus. "Those men I killed—"

"Not ours," Gus interrupts. "They were once, but they left with some others after becoming impatient."

I raise an eyebrow. "Impatient with what?"

Gus exchanges a look with Reynold. "Change."

We wait until our bowls are refilled with stew before Elora scoots closer toward me. "Change with what?" she asks.

Before Gus could reply, I asked, "Do you know my mother?"

He stills, closes his mouth, and chews silently.

"She told us to come here," I continued, "And it didn't make sense until Elora conveyed your kindness toward her. I've never heard my mother mention Hogsfeet, even when discussing the history of our realm, and I'm assuming it's because of you."

Gus pushes his bowl forward, rests his forearms on the table, and looks between me and Elora. "Yes, I know your mother, but it's because of *her* father."

Elora leans forward, her eyebrows knitted. "*My* father?"

I tilt my head, remembering my conversation with Dolfe before searching for Elora. "Harry wanted to help the faeries," I say, squeezing Elora's hand. This is something I haven't shared with her yet. "And was killed for it."

Elora's head whips toward me, her lips parted.

I bring her hand to my lips, brushing my lips across her knuckles while gathering my thoughts. "I found out the night you left," I whisper, resting my cheek against her knuckles. "I was about to tell you everything when they found us. I don't know much, but my father admitted to having him killed because he wanted to resign as Keeper, but Dolfe said something entirely different. He said Harry wanted to help them. And I can only guess it was about the faeries wanting to leave the realm."

Tears rolled down her cheeks. "He was murdered? He was...." —her eyes fall closed—"It wasn't a heart attack. I knew it couldn't have been. He was too healthy. I didn't even get to say goodbye." She covers her eyes with her hand. "They burned his body and delivered his ashes to me."

"Darling, I'm so sorry." I turn to straddle the bench and pull her closer. "My family has caused you so much pain, Ellie, and I wish I could change all of it. I wasn't withholding this from you; I just wanted to give us time alone together to regain your trust." I kiss her temple. "My darling, please."

"I'm not upset with you," she rasps, lowering her hand to blink away tears. "But I don't understand. Why?"

That's a broad question but a fair one.

"Because he's despicable," I reply, slightly shrugging. "Your father wanted to help the faeries, but Jasper claims he wanted to resign as the Keeper to spend more time with you, but then...." I pause and drag my fingertips across my brow, unsure how to tell her this. "He showed me an oath your father signed long ago. In exchange for keeping the people of Ashbury alive, he agreed to give his firstborn to my father however he deemed fit. He sacrificed you, Elora."

So much agony fills her eyes that I nearly take it back—I almost tell her that I'm only lying, but I won't do that to her. She deserves to know the truth about all of it.

But before we can say more, the men I forgot were in the room shift in their seats, and Elora glances up with her tearful gaze, focusing on the man who seems most interested in her—Reynold.

Reynold drags a hand down his face, drums his fingers against the tabletop, then sighs. "Elora wasn't Harry's firstborn." He swallows before focusing on my wife. "I was."

❧

Elora has decided to pace the long room instead of coming to the table to listen to Reynold's pleas for her to listen. Gus has instructed him to allow her time to grieve and accept his admission. And I have given up on following her back and forth, resolving to lean against another table and watching her.

Her hands hang loosely from her hips, the confusion and anger evident in her features, and I wish she'd stop and allow me to kiss away the pain, but this is something I can't fix for her—as much as I wish I could. I'm just as curious about who the fuck Reynold is, but I can't force her to sit and listen to him. A lot of information was spilled onto her within minutes, and she might pace for days.

She often mutters something about men and secrets, but I refuse to inquire further about that. For once, I am not the one on the receiving end of her frustration. With my luck, anything I say could change that instantly.

Aside from their hair color, Reynold does not look like Elora. So, if I had to assume, they're half-siblings. And now, I don't have to worry about killing him because he's staring at my bride lustfully—he's interested in her because of their relation to one another. I'm sure he has as many questions about her as she does for him if she'd ever stop moving long enough to ask them.

I catch her by the wrist when she passes me again and pull her toward me, ignoring her protests. "Talk to me," I say, kissing her wrist. "Let me in, little doe."

She shoves a hand through her curls. "I don't even know what to fucking ask!" she snaps, glaring at my replying grin.

"I'm not used to hearing crude words from you."

"Fuck, fuck, fuck!" she shouts in a whisper, her words soon becoming raspy as emotion overcomes her, "fuck." She falls against my chest, her hands covering her face while her forehead rests against my shoulder.

I weave my arms around her, comforting her with soft kisses against her temple, caressing her back. "We're not prisoners here, Ellie. If you want to leave and never look back, just say the word. We will never speak of this again." My hands idly graze her ribcage. "But if you'd like to stay and find out why we're here and who the fuck he is, now is your chance."

She lifts her chin, sniffling. She's living too much life too soon. She only left her ashy, soot-covered terrace days ago, and her entire life has changed.

Sliding her arms around my neck, she remains pressed against me, placing her forehead against mine and taking each of my breaths as her own. At this moment, my stubborn little doe wants me to breathe for her, and I do. I hold her through multiple rises and falls of our chests, through each of her stuttering breaths, and allow her tears to fall without wiping them away. Elora has been alone for so long, unable to rely on anyone, that becoming that person for her is an honor that will never be replicated by anything else in our lives.

I will always breathe for her.

Wordlessly, she kisses me until she calms and until her tears stop falling. She still trembles in my arms, but her breathing steadies, and resolve lights the gold flecks in her eyes. I give her an encouraging smile and pat her backside, standing and holding her hand while we return to the table where the men patiently wait for her.

But she doesn't inquire about Reynold. Instead, she focuses on Gus. "My father was your way of gathering information inside the kingdom," she surmises.

Gus nods once.

Elora gnaws on her cheek. I have questions, but I want to hear what other assumptions she's pieced together. "Jasper discovered what he was doing and had him...." She clears her throat. "Jasper had him killed. Was the queen involved, too?"

I tense, instinctively shaking my head. In no universe would my mother ever involve herself in a takedown of Pumpkin Hollow if that's even what they're trying to accomplish? It would be too risky, and she wouldn't gamble our lives.

"Not until the end," Gus responds, shifting his gaze to me. "Harry trusted your mother. We were getting closer to a solution to our problem of getting into Pumpkin Hollow, but one of her maids overheard their conversation."

I wish I could be more shocked, but Irina has spent too much time warning me of the lurking servants in the hallway.

"As you can imagine," Gus continues, "your mother has wanted a way out. She alerted us of Harry's death shortly after it happened by dropping a bottle over the cliffside."

I blink. "My mother visited Ashbury?"

"We heard the glass shatter under the cover of darkness, so she visited when she wouldn't be seen."

I sit, unable to thoroughly process this information.

Elora rests her hand on my shoulder. "And she sent us here to pick up where my father left off? You need insiders."

Reynold shakes his head. "We need the Keeper and the prince. We've built ladders strong enough to withstand our men carrying weapons and accessing Ashbury from the cliffside for months. Harry's death slowed us down and instilled fear into many of us who remain, but Jasper has been withholding resources for too long."

I flinch at using his name without a title from a commoner, but I shrug it off. Jasper is no king.

One of the other men, who introduces himself as Grady, adds, "The faeries have been aware of our plan for a long time, but we haven't been able to contact them. They were willing to assist in overthrowing the king—"

"Not anymore," Elora interjects. "They want to leave. One of them is with child, and they need to be near the Fae healers. I will not ask them to risk their unborn child for this. They've already sacrificed too much for too long."

Reynold and Grady seem ready to argue with her, but Gus prevents them from trying. "That is understandable," he says, "And we will not force anyone to do anything, even faeries." He gives the men a warning glare. "That would make us no better than the man we're trying to overthrow."

I should feel guilty for listening to this. I should be trying to stop it as the son of the king they want to eliminate, but instead, I pull Elora into my lap and kiss her temple. The end of his reign would ensure the safety of my wife, and I promised to keep her alive. Breaking any oath to her would be breaking my heart—an idea I refuse to entertain.

I crave a long life with her, free from the control of my father, away from crypts and magic pumpkins.

I want her smiles, laughs, and moans. I want her venom, poison, and scowls. I want all of her, enchantment or not, crown or not. Nothing matters anymore if every night doesn't conclude with her in my arms.

"I have already sworn to assist my wife in freeing the faeries, but I am willing to offer my allegiance to your cause on one condition." I hold a steady gaze with Gus. "My sister and mother must safely be away from Pumpkin Hollow first."

Gus nods slowly. "If you can guarantee entry into Ashbury, we can guarantee passage for them."

"I'll do you one better," I reply, not doubting for a second the offer I'm about to extend to him. "Not only will I get you into Ashbury, but I'll fight with you."

Forty-Nine

After we finished eating, I held Elora's hand as Gus led us farther down the corridor, knocking on doors as we passed. Neither of us asks why, but he explains anyway. "Without natural light, we'd all sleep through the day and be up all night. I wake everyone each morning."

Much to Elora's relief, Reynold, Grady, and the man I never learned the name of left us alone with Gus while they went above ground to search the perimeter—their daily task, from my understanding while listening to Gus' instructions. With the murders I committed, the men remaining from that camp would suspect Gus' crew of the deaths. I offered to take the fall, but he wouldn't hear of it.

I'd take the act as generosity if I didn't know better. I am his best chance of getting into Pumpkin Hollow. And with Elora refusing to involve the faeries, I am also his *only* chance of defeating Jasper's army—men I trained with.

Elora looks over her shoulder at the long line of doors. She hasn't said a word about Reynold, and hasn't asked anything about him, but I believe that's for the best right now. Entering a war leads to lives lost, and I don't want her losing anyone else. She wears enough of her father's burdens on her own. She doesn't need to be weighed down with why he decided to keep her apart from her brother, too. I couldn't imagine what my life would've been without Irina. Through the muck Jasper dragged us through, it was comforting having someone to experience it with.

Elora wasn't given that chance.

"How many people do you have?" she inquires.

"Eight-hundred forty-four," Gus instantly replies, as if always having the count right at the tip of his tongue. "We had more, but after Jasper discovered us alive, some of his men stood at the cliff-side and waited. During a patrol, some of my men were unsuspecting and wandered too close to the old castle. They were taken down with arrows to the hearts."

Elora squeezes my hand. "I'm so sorry, Gus," she whispers.

Gus retrieves a key from his pocket and slides it into a lock at the end of the hallway, motioning for us to enter. The stone-walled study contains a desk and three chairs, papers scattered across the top and sporadically around the floor.

Elora lowers to gather them in her hands, but I pull her up and shake my head. "No, my darling. That is not your responsibility anymore." I brush her bottom lip with my thumb. "I know you do it from the kindness of your heart, but you are no one's servant."

"He's right," Gus adds, lazily gesturing at the strewn papers. "It's awful how Regina treated ya. We used to plead with Harry to do something, but I assume he didn't?"

"No," I confirm, my tone icy. "He didn't."

Elora collapses on a chair with a sigh. The skin beneath her eyes is black, her normally plump pout thinning from exhaustion. Her fears she has about the Fae male in her nightmares have inconveniently slipped my mind from the events that have happened since, but looking at her now, frail and fatigued, makes me want to leave here sooner rather than later so I can speak with Azrea about it.

"You knew?" she asks Gus, twisting her hands in her lap.

I've learned it's what she does often when Regina is mentioned, and I wonder if it's a coping mechanism—something to calm the anxiety that Regina's name seems to conjure.

Gus sits in the chair behind the desk and leans back. "We did.

Harry knew you were being mistreated, but he was too involved with all of this to listen to anyone. I don't know if he was trying to atone for Reynold or what, but Harry never seemed to want to talk about the choices he made."

I scoot the remaining chair closer to Elora's chair, sit, and take her hand. "Did he tell you about his bargain with my father? Did he tell you he offered his firstborn?"

Gus poked his tongue against his bottom lip, his nod tight. He seems just as displeased about it as I was when I thought it was Elora who was used as collateral for Harry's mistakes. "Harry didn't know your father planned to attack Hogsfeet. Reynold's mama was a maid in the palace manor. When Elora's grandfather learned of her pregnancy, he sent her to Hogsfeet."

Elora turns her head away, staring at the flickering flame in the lantern, but she doesn't ask Gus to stop talking about it.

"While she was away, Harry fell in love with Elora's mother, Edith. Harry continued to care for Reynold and his mama financially but wanted nothing to do with him once he met Edith. Reynold had been kept secret."

Gus glances at my silent wife, then at me.

I nod for him to continue.

"The boy was four when Harry bargained him away. He wanted Edith safe. She was his entire reason for going to Jasper to begin with, but I think when she died, the guilt of everything he had done didn't sit right with him." Gus leans his head back, staring at the ceiling while recalling memories long past. "The survivors of the attack on Hogsfeet were quick to believe his grand ideas of war and vengeance, but I had my reservations about working with him."

"Did my mother know?" Elora whispers, barely loud enough for either of us to hear her. "Did she know about the boy? Did she know I had a brother?"

"I don't believe she did," Gus assures her. "You were how old when she died? Six?"

Elora doesn't look away from the fire but nods.

Gus continues, "By then, Reynold was working to help build this underground corridor. He didn't know your father, just *of* him. He'd spend evenings staring at the cliffside 'til he realized ain't no-one was coming for him. His mama died of the flu not long after his tenth birthday. I've taken care of him ever since. I told him about you not long after Harry arrived. I thought he deserved to know the truth, but Harry refused to tell you about him."

"How did Harry get back and forth?" I ask, not wanting to interrupt Elora finally receiving answers, but irritated that Harry had been going back and forth secretly for nearly two decades without ever getting caught. While his daughter and people starved in Ashbury, he was playing games with another kingdom he destroyed, with the son he readily tried to hand to my father to atone for his traitorous choices.

Gus stood from the chair and shuffled to the back corner of the study, unlit from only two remaining lit lanterns. Something rattled in his hands as he picked it up and carried it over to me. I kiss Elora's hand before I stand, waiting for Gus to extend it and lay it across his desk.

Held together by thin rope, a makeshift ladder made of wooden steps gives away Harry's secret. Two wooden stakes show evidence of dried mud at one end, pieces dropping to the floor. "He'd jam those into the dirt," I surmise, twisting the rope between my fingers. "How did this support his weight?"

"He'd drop his boots to the ground first," Gus explains, "and his coat or whatever else he brought with him." He holds up the opposite end of the ladder. "It wasn't long enough to reach the ground, so he'd fall five feet or so each time."

Somehow, that only angers me further. If he had broken his leg from the fall, he would've left Elora alone much earlier to face Jasper's wrath for her father disappearing. It seems blasphemous to despise the dead, but I'm finding it challenging to harbor resentment for his murder.

I drop the rope and pound my fist against the desk. "He could've brought Elora here! She could've been with family instead of that abusive wench who made her the maid of the manor that is rightfully hers! Elora was supposed to be the godsdamn princess of that kingdom, and he took everything away from her!"

"Finnian," Elora says gently, standing and grabbing my arm. "Finnian, there's no reason to be angry—"

I turn to face her. "Of course, I'm fucking angry, Elora! You have been let down by every person in your life, then I come in and have been no better. Fuck, you deserve better than this, you deserve more than me and to share blood with that traitorous bastard. He fucking left you to rot for his mistakes."

Tears fall down her cheeks as she shakes her head. "Finn, you changed. You recognize your mistakes. *He* didn't."

"I would kill him again," I snarl, "if he were here and breathing, I'd fucking kill him for leaving you alone with Regina."

She places her hands on my chest, then slides one up to my cheek as the rapid rise and fall of my chest doesn't calm. Her soft skin against mine slows my heart a tick. "I know you would," she murmurs, skating her thumb across my cheekbone. "We have a chance to undo years of torment and abuse placed upon thousands of people by our fathers."

"Elora, you shouldn't have to do anything—"

She shushes me. "You do not need to avenge me, my love. I am right here. If I start feeling sorry for myself, that bitterness will poison the hope I have left. And they've spoiled enough of our dreams. Don't you agree?"

"I do, but...." I whisper, placing my hand over her heart and adding, "This is *too* good, Ellie. Too pure. Too kind."

She shrugs a shoulder with a sigh. "I have to see what *could* be, Finn, not what *is*. It's more charming that way."

I find myself grinning at her childish, innocent optimism, even after hearing what a bastard her father truly was. "What is, Elora?"

Her warm, comforting, beautiful smile returns—the one no one deserves from her. "Faeries and pumpkins and things. My father stole that joy from my mother. He kept it from me. Your father has honored magic above all—above you, Irina, and your mother. It's time to free us all, Finn."

She drops her hands to wrap her arms around my waist. "My father is gone, but I am still under the weight of him. Your father is alive, locking us in crypts and trying to control all of us because he doesn't want anyone touching his precious pumpkins."

I can't help but chuckle at the absurdity of it all.

"It's time to take it further than smashing pumpkins," she states, resting her chin against my chest. "It's time for us to live happily, free of fear and worries. The faeries might be locked behind a gate, but Jasper has held the key to our lives for far too long, my love."

I stare at the creature in my arms, my hand delicately stroking her curls, searching the eyes of someone years younger than me yet possesses more strength than I ever will.

"I will never stop trying to deserve you," I murmur to her.

The rotten tenacity I fell in love with returns when she smugly grins and winks. "I'll hold you to that."

I kissed her softly before wrapping my arm around her shoulders to keep her close to my chest and turned my head to look at Gus. "Well, we're yours. What do you need from us?"

Gus motions to the chairs. "Take a seat."

❧

Traitor Major is lazily resting underneath tree shade when we leave the bunker. We left Gus with next steps, which begin with us returning to Pumpkin Hollow. But first, we need to collect our things from the castle and stop by the mountains—a step I've yet to share with my bride. But before I begin my journey to treasonous affairs against my father, I need to speak with Azrea about my wife's ailing health and nightmares.

Reynold escorts us to Major, then awkwardly looks between us. Elora mimics the discomfort by staring intensely at my horse and nowhere else. I extend my hand to Reynold and give him a solid shake. "We'll be seeing you again soon," I say.

Like she is around most, Elora is much shorter than her brother, reminding me of the differences between Irina and me. Though both have golden strands, I see no similarities, even in the bright sunlight. Reynold's eyes are green, do not have any gold, and have none of the delicate features that make up every inch of Elora.

Elora timidly glances at Reynold. "What was your mother's name?" she inquires, placing her hands behind her back and rocking back and forth on her heels.

"Mabel," Reynold replies. "And yours was Edith."

"You have Harry's eyes," Elora says softly, "and we both have his hair color. Perhaps that's why I didn't like you when I saw you." Her following smile conveys lightheartedness.

Reynold huffs a laugh through his nose. "Likewise."

Elora's expression turns warm—tender, even. "I'm sorry your mother died," she says softly. "I would like to hear about her someday, if that's all right with you."

Reynold swallows, and if I didn't know any better, I'd confidently assume he's preventing himself from seeming too eager to get to know his little sister. "That would be fine," he responds with a slight nod. "And maybe you can tell me all about the Cinder Fae. I believe your stories about them would be far more interesting than Harry's ever were."

Elora beams, still fond of the faeries she's actively avoiding. "I would love that. After.... Well, you know.... We'll host you and everyone else in Pumpkin Hollow." She claps her hands together. "I must introduce you to Rhoadie! Oh, he's such a wonderful baker. He bakes the most delicious vanilla crème treats, and I've become quite fond of him...." Her cheeks redden as she trails off. "I'm sorry; I tend to ramble."

My smile is so vast from listening to her rattle that my cheeks burn, and I find that Reynold is grinning at her, too. "I've never had pastries," Reynold replies to her. "We hunt for our food. Sometimes, we'll send out scouts to scour towns, but those are weeks away by foot, and they only bring back food that won't expire too quickly."

Well, they have long-winded chattering in common.

"I can assist with that," I added to their conversation. "I'm working on supplying more food for the people in Ashbury. I'll see what I can do to deliver more food to you. You'll need it to take on the army of Pumpkin Hollow."

Reynold's jovial expression faltered as my comment reminded him of what was to come. I'd feel guilty if I didn't plan to keep both of them alive to have more conversations about pastries, faeries, and anything else Elora wants to know.

"That would be appreciated," he replies. "We have weapons. Hogsfeet didn't have what your father used that dark day, but we've spent years collecting what we could."

I nod, tapping my fingers against my chin in thought. "I might be able to pilfer some from our armory without question, but not many since we're short on time. We have to maintain normalcy for as long as possible, but I'll see what I can manage without suspicion. But for now, we need to return before he sends guards to search for us."

I nod my goodbyes and leave Elora's side to tighten Major's saddle. The awkward tension between them has returned, but Elora makes the first move and holds out her hand to him. Reynold doesn't hesitate to take it.

"Until then," Elora says.

"Until then," he repeats, then takes his leave.

Elora walks into my open arms, throwing her arms around my neck and sighing. "I didn't believe I could hate my father any more than I already did, but I would've liked to know Reynold. He isn't so bad when he isn't locking my husband away."

I chuckle and kiss her nose. "You'll have plenty of time to get to know him when this is done, little doe."

A frown replaces her smile. "Can you really do it, Finn? Can you really be the one to kill your father?"

I consider her question, mulling over how I want to reply to her. It frightens me how quickly the answer came to me, the lengths I would go to ensure she lives, but she already assured me once that nothing I do will ever scare her away.

My dedication to her overwhelms me, but as I stare into her eyes, calmed by how good it feels to hold her in my arms, I am suddenly no longer afraid to show her the man she's turned me into by giving me her heart—by gifting me her trust.

"For you, my darling, I would kill him with my bare hands."

Fifty

We don't speak while returning to the castle, and I know it's because he's allowing me to silently digest that I have a brother. But there's nothing for me to digest. I can no longer summon shock when it comes to learning things about my father—not even how he died. I've always had my suspicions surrounding his sudden demise but had no way of confirming it until Finnian.

Our paths that led to one another are riddled with bloodshed, most spilling by his father's hand. But for me, he wants to end his father's reign once and for all. For me, he's going to set aside years of tormented control to guarantee that Jasper does not separate us. And that knowledge makes the rest of it seem so irrelevant. Once this ends and we're standing together at the end, then I can face the rest.

Finnian still watches for the men who separated from Gus to seek revenge, but Gus assured us that they'd set up wide perimeters to ensure our safety up the steep pathway along the cliffside—logistics that they discussed in length.

Finnian slides off Major and guides him to a slender column to tie his lead rope. Finnian doesn't trust him not to wander off, now referring to him as Traitor Major. However, I know that Major would drop whatever he's munching on to come to Finnian's aid if needed.

Major whips his head around in protest as he's secured, and I grip the horn to keep from slipping off. Finnian argues with him while I try not to laugh, listening in amusement to Major's huffs and neighs of frustration. Finnian sticks a finger against his muzzle and ends the conversation with a frustrated, "I have spoiled you for far too long!" And wraps an arm around my waist to pull me down.

Major turns to nuzzle his head against my arm, pleading. I pat his neck and shake my head. "Don't put me in the middle of this," I say, "We won't be long, Major. And you don't have the greatest record of staying put. You're too important to lose."

Finnian takes my hand, drags me away from Major, mumbling something incoherent about horses, and closes the door after we enter the castle. "So much for time away from your father," I say lightly. "He seems to follow us everywhere."

"I don't believe he knows we came here," Finnian replies, pulling me upstairs. "I think he thinks we went to Ashbury for a few days. He wouldn't have allowed us to come here since he was aware that people who wanted him dead were building an army with Harry as their leader. That's why he's so fearful of you. It makes sense now. He thinks you're trying to take Harry's place, so he found a way to dispose of you quickly."

I tilt my head curiously. "If that's true, why would he allow you to marry me? Wouldn't he want you to stay as far away from me as possible?"

Finnian draws a lazy circle in the air with his finger. "That's why he's built traps for everyone. Imagine all of us as circles, and everything or everyone we hold dear overlaps with our circle. He knew you'd fall for me because I was bred to charm women, but just in case you were too stubborn, he told me I had to marry you for the longevity of our line, which he knows means nothing to me. Our line to me is Irina and my mother. It's all threats, Elora, and I wish I could say they're empty threats, but they're not."

"I didn't find you charming," I mutter, then laugh as he yanks me toward him and pinches my ribs on either side. "And I still don't!"

He bends and throws me over his shoulder, palming my ass before he smacks it hard enough to make me yelp and pound against his back with my fists. He does it again, and I kick his thighs. "Finn!" I shout, trying to wiggle free. "Put me down *immediately*."

He slides his hands to my waist and does the opposite. He lifts me higher instead of putting me down, extending his arms while I grasp at his shoulders, dangling helplessly in the air. "Finnian..." I trail off from my scolding. "Did your mother give you a second?"

He grins. "Did yours?"

I nod with an eye roll. "Only because I have royal blood. What is yours?"

He lowers me slowly, keeping my body pressed tightly against his. And that heat—that smothering, smoldering tension—returns.

"Alexander," he replies, beginning light traces of my ribs with his fingertips. "Finnian Alexander Grantham. And Irina's is Anne."

"Jane," I whisper, "Elora Jane."

"Elora Jane Grantham," he corrects. "You are Elora Jane Grantham, Keeper of the Faeries." He takes my chin between his fingers and tilts my head up, hovering his lips just inches above mine when he leans down. "It's such a pleasure to meet you, Elora Jane."

My gaze falls to his mouth. "Why weren't you this nice the first time?"

His grin widens. "If I had touched you like this the first night we met, I would've lost my hand instead of only my heart."

My eyes fall closed as he speaks, my hands threading through his hair. He presses his forehead against mine, pulling me tighter and *closer*. My breaths stutter, but his breaths are steady—his honesty stabilizing.

"I'll protect yours if you protect mine," I murmur, "even when I hate you."

I can *feel* his smile. "Endlessly, darling."

And he kisses me, long and slow.

These moments together will be our last before everything changes—before we risk our lives to bring an end to a cruel and terrifying reign and free everyone once and for all.

Without breaking the kiss, he slides out of his boots and waits for me to do the same. He slips one finger into the waistband of my pants and drags them down while it takes both hands for me to do the same to his. Our breathy laughter is swallowed by our need for one another as we discard the rest.

But I take a small step away before he can do what he wants with me. "I'd like to try again."

He's too busy staring at my body to understand my request, responding with a "hm?"

I lick my lips. "With my mouth."

His eyes darken when he lifts them to meet mine, but then they slowly fall back to my breasts, and he shakes his head slightly. "You can't say that when you're bare like this, Ellie." He steps closer, chasing me and catching me quickly when I try to move away again.

His arm around my lower back arches me backward, and he leans in to take my breast in his mouth. I whisper his name, trying to keep my eyes from fluttering closed at the sensation of his tongue flicking my nipple.

"I want to taste you," I say. "I want to know how to pleasure you, Finn. Teach me."

He drags his teeth across my flesh before releasing my breast to glance at me. The gentle, loving blue of his eyes now simmers with lust. "My cock deep in your pussy pleasures me, little doe. You coming on my tongue pleasures me. Those aren't just for you, but...."

He pinches my bottom lip with his fingers, and I feel his cock pulse against my thigh. The idea of my mouth around him is enticing him to give me control just this once. Tugging my lip down, he slips his tongue inside to tangle with mine. I use the tip of my tongue to circle around his tongue, giving him a taste of what I want to do to him on my knees.

His fingers bruise my waist as he jerks back with astonishment, then nods once. "I don't want to come inside your mouth," he says, "but I'll teach you how to prime my cock."

I pout, but he warns me with a look. "Ellie, tell me you understand that I'm only coming inside you."

I stroke his length with my hand, peering at him from beneath my lashes. "I understand, Finnian Alexander."

Smirking, his expression full of disbelief from my blatant lie, he removes my hand around him and pulls me to the corner of the room. He sits in a plush chair, clearing gathered dust with his hand, and dips his chin. "Kneel, Elora."

I slowly lower to my knees before him.

He fists the base of his cock, spreads his knees, and beckons me closer by hooking his finger. I inch closer until I'm settled right between his legs, sitting on my heels and resting my hands on his thighs. He strokes himself, causing my eyes to narrow.

But the smug prick grins. "I like seeing you on your knees for me, little doe. I've wanted to force you on them since the first time you opened your mouth to spew your lies about despising me."

I scowl, moving to lean back, but he anticipates it and catches my neck with his other hand, keeping me still. "Now, now," he patronizes with a smile he's failing to hide, "I thought you wanted to please your prince."

"I want to bite my prince."

His lazy half-grin pulling at the corner of his mouth is far too confident and mouthwatering. "I'd expect no less. Open."

I consider abandoning this venture altogether and forcing him to live without having me at all, but that would be punishing myself, too, and if there's one thing with Finnian I refuse to sacrifice, it's how good he can make me feel.

And despite how annoying he is, I want him to crave my tongue around him just as I desire his tongue—and cock—inside me.

I part my lips. He releases my neck to open my chin further, tenderly brushing my lip with his thumb. "I want to feel the back of your throat," he says, causing my eyes to widen, "but if it becomes too much, squeeze my thigh."

He waits for my confirmation, then takes my hand to replace his around his cock. His hand moves to my head to lower it gently, his cock pulsing in my hand before my lips even touch him. "Fuck, you're too beautiful," he mutters, seemingly annoyed by how attractive he finds me.

I laugh at the absurdity right before my lips close around him. He sucks in air through his teeth, fisting my curls in his hands and preventing me from going any further. I try to wiggle free, but he snaps at me to stop. "Give me a second," he bites. "You have no fucking idea how good you feel."

I don't move my head, but I do use my tongue to spiral around his tip. His fist in my hair tightens, sending a thick wave of painful pleasure down my spine. "Fuck, I can't even watch you," he growls, breaking his gaze with me to lean his head back against the chair. "Slow, little doe."

He loosens my curls but grips tightly enough to inch my head lower. I willingly take more of him in my mouth until my jaw stretches, then pause to pull a deep breath through my nose. He doesn't raise his head but whispers, "Hollow cheeks, Ellie," like that tells me *anything*.

I slacken my jaw and rise to my knees, ignoring the water pooling in my eyes. A thick vein quivers when my tongue slides against it, and he groans. The noise spurs me forward, even when my cheeks start to burn. Not once have I ever imagined what a cock tastes like, but Finn is smooth and salty, and the quickening of his breaths is an added delight.

A tear slips free, and his thumb brushes it away. I peered up at him, surprised to find him watching me with ignited intensity. Wordlessly, he guides me on him, using the grip on my hair to assist me at a steady pace. Neither of us looks away from the other while I take him until his tip hits the back of my throat.

I gag, choking on the sensation of him hitting my throat, and he moans my name. "Darling, look how well you take my cock," he praises, twisting one of my curls around his finger, "You're doing so well, Elora. I love how beautiful you look when you cry for me."

I inhale deeply through my nose and release the base of his cock to attempt to take more of him into my mouth. My vision blurs from tears. I'm positive I'm drooling, but he whispers my name like a goddess is kneeling before him.

Without warning, he tugs on my curls. "Off."

If I could smile, I would.

I graze my teeth up his length, snorting when he curses my name, then slide back down before he can yank me off.

"*Elora*," he emphasizes, his hips twitching, seemingly angering him. "Fuck, Elora, I'm about to come. *Off*."

I hold my breath and suck, using my tongue like a weapon as it drags around his length slowly. But I naively underestimated his strength and stubbornness against mine and yelped when he tore me off him and shoved me backward.

I wipe my mouth with the back of my hand, then widen my eyes when I notice his glare. Instinctively, I turn and begin crawling away, but he catches me quickly. With his hand around my ankle, he drags me backward and slips his head between my legs, sliding his tongue inside me. I cry out his name and attempt to pull away, but he keeps me pressed tightly against his face and moves his hands to my thighs to make me ride him like this. I don't know what to do with my hands or body, but I slide my fingers into his hair and anchor myself.

His groan against my clit sends shockwaves through my body, and it reacts before my mind can, my hips rolling against his face. It's depraved, and I feel like it's somehow sinful, but he's doing too many things with his tongue for me not to covet this all the time, and the risk of meeting Hades is worth it if Finnian can continue defiling me.

He sweeps the soft spot repeatedly with the tip of his tongue, groaning again when I flutter around his tongue. His hands on my thighs move to my waist, and he jerks me back and forth until I'm moving on my own, riding his tongue like I would his cock, screaming and crying his name over and over.

And when I come, he doesn't stay and drink as usual. He lifts me off his face, flips me to my back like I'm nothing more than a ragdoll, and slides his cock inside me. His mouth shines with my release, but I open my mouth wide when he shoves his tongue inside, moaning from the taste of me all over him. If this is punishment for disobeying him, I plan to do it much more often—even if my body feels like it's about to split into two from his thrusts.

My fingers claw down his back, his hand wraps around my throat, and he squeezes as I come around him. The lack of oxygen sprouts colors in my eyes, and my body seizes from the harrowing force of my climax, dizzying me. And he doesn't release my throat until I've finished, and I'm half-convinced I'm about to pass out, gasping for air when he lets go.

He comes inside me while fisting our discarded clothes behind my head, throwing his head back with my name leaving his lips in a frustrated, albeit pleased, shout. He pulls out and collapses beside me, his chest rising and falling in uneven breaths, sweat covering his forehead and dampening his hair. "You can't,"—he pauses to inhale deeply through his nose—"do that, Elora. I wanted to fucking break you."

Sore and raw, I'd do it all again for that result.

I crawl on top of him. "You can't break me."

He palms my breasts. "Little doe, you have no fucking idea what I can do to you. I can make you bleed for me. Your lack of experience is a fucking aphrodisiac for me."

I raise an eyebrow. "What makes you think that was my first—"

"Don't," he growls. "Don't tease about that. You're mine. Don't make me question that."

Guilt overcomes me enough to slide off him. "I'm sorry, Finnian, I was only playing. I didn't think...."

He sits up, wraps an arm around my waist, and drags me to rest between his legs. "Elora, I've never been an envious man. I've shared every woman I've been with. I can't stand the thought of sharing you. I can't imagine you with someone else, now or in the past. It does something dark to me."

He tucks a damp curl behind my ear. "I thought I had loved before, but I was wrong. What I felt isn't even an ounce of what I feel for you now. I'm mad about you, darling."

I twist to straddle his lap and slide my arms around his neck. "Finn, a day before I met you, I was convinced I'd never find anyone to love or want so passionately that I'd put aside everything just to be with him. But I have, and it's you."

I trace his brow with my fingertip. "I've never wanted anyone like this. All I can think about is how much I want you. There's never been anyone else. There never will be. And I apologize for my thoughtless remark."

"You don't need to apologize for my insecurities—"

"I'm not," I interrupt. "But I'm also not going to disrespect what you've been through. I love you too much. Plus...." I dip down and trail kisses down his throat. "I'm bewildered how a man who feels as good as you was ever betrayed."

He chuckles. "Was that.... A compliment?"

I scowl when I raise, sighing deeply. "Don't take me too seriously. I'm chock-full of lust and satisfaction right now. I'll say anything if it ends with your face between my legs again."

He faux-gasps. "Elora, that mouth of yours." But then, he lowers to his back and grabs my waist to drag me closer. "Can you be a good girl for me this time and do as I say?"

I bite my lip with a nod.

He licks his lips with a grin. "Fuck my tongue, little doe."

Fifty-One

I find it difficult to be irritated with Finnian when I'm this relaxed and satisfied. And I partially believe he did it on purpose, waiting until I was dressed and out the castle doors while snacking on more honey before informing me that we'll stop and speak with the faeries about my nightmares before returning to Pumpkin Hollow.

My protests were not heard. He barely entertained my reasoning for not wanting to see them because my life was apparently more important to him than my prior scuffle with Azrea.

And he won't drop the amused grin from my pouting, even when I try to scoot away from him on Major. He only pulls me back and kisses my temple. "You're behaving like a child," he informs me, clicking his tongue when Major hesitates while on the trail of imminent death.

"I am not," I mutter, though I know I am. If I was crueler, I'd remind him that visiting the faeries means we'll see Cedric, but I can't do that after I promised to not taunt him anymore.

Damn me.

From a distance, I look out toward where I think Gus discovered us and find the top of Reynold's head standing near the tree Major was resting beneath. Even though the land beneath the cliff is far and wide, I can see miles from our vantage point on the steep path back to Ashbury. But the higher we climb, the more cover the trees provide, eliminating Reynold from view. "You agreed so easily," I say, tilting my head back to peer up at Finn. "What made you trust them so quickly?"

Major's back left hoof slides, and I yelp as my heart plummets into my stomach. Finnian only grins and pats my hip. "Major was trained for this terrain, Elora. Ashbury isn't the only place that has rocky terrain like this. And that's partially why I trusted Gus easily. He didn't harm you, and he didn't keep Major. While you're decent to look at, Major would fetch a lot of notes."

I scowl but tilt my head. "Notes?"

Recognition crosses his face when he hears the confusion in my voice. "You've only seen coins, haven't you?" He doesn't wait for my confirmation before continuing, "Notes are for larger amounts. Major is worth many coins, but I would receive the amount in paper form and exchange it.... Well, through my father. Some institutions handle the exchange of notes for spendable bills."

"But I thought you didn't have to pay for anything...."

"In Pumpkin Hollow," he interrupts. "Did you believe I am awarded freedom everywhere?"

"I don't know," I reply, my eyes widening as I watch rocks tumble down the cliffside and shatter at the bottom. "I just saw fish for the first time, Finn. I haven't given your financial situation much thought. And no, I don't recall ever seeing any paper like that inside Harry's desk."

"That's interesting," he says, his voice distant and lost in thought. "My father pays salaries in notes, but maybe since Harry had no place to exchange them in Ashbury, he paid him in bills."

"Or maybe Harry sent them to Reynold's mother."

"They wouldn't have been able to exchange them. As Reynold said, there's not a kingdom close to them. Harry would've sent them spendable funds. And you said Regina spent everything, right?"

I wrap my mother's shawl tighter around me when the breeze picks up as we near the end of the pathway. It's mid-afternoon, but we're not close enough to the mountains yet to feel the heat radiating off the faeries. "If she hasn't, she's done an excellent job hiding what's left."

His silence makes me look at him again, but he kisses my forehead. "It doesn't matter. You'll be taken care of now. And after this is over, I'll take you somewhere and show you life outside our realm."

I have so many questions about the places he's visited, but when the mountains come into view as we level out on the dirt ground in Ashbury, I slide off Major and walk away. Finnian quickly follows me, calling my name when I won't slow down. "Elora," he tries again, jogging after me and grabbing my hand. "Darling, we must speak with them. I'll be with you the entire time—"

I whirl on him. "How can you be all right with them asking me to leave you?"

He stills and releases my hand.

I shake my head quickly, my tongue pinched between my lips. It's unfathomable how prominent my anger still is about the moment Cedric and Azrea demand I leave with them, and it has everything to do with the man standing before me. "They wanted me to leave everything behind. You, Ashbury, the scheme Regina lied about. Cedric wanted me to be with him, but that wasn't what.... *Hurt*."

I look toward the mountains. "Azrea was supposed to believe in me."

Finnian silently follows my gaze. His simmering agitation is always what frightens me the most. I'm not afraid of him, but I worry for the ones he believes will get in the way of us being together, and he didn't need the reminder when his primary focus for talking me into seeing them again is to save my life. And I realize it's most likely frustrating him that he's agreed to risk his own life to free them after learning that they wanted me to leave him.

He sighs and looks at me. "I'm not okay with it, Elora, but I understand their fear. Dolfe was the one who burned your father's body the night of his death. He was threatened with Azrea's life to do so. I imagine that's why they're desperate to leave. Jasper's hold has reached all of us."

I blink, though surprise doesn't overcome me. The faeries are always responsible for burning bodies in Ashbury. I don't know why I expected my father's death to be any different, though I wish they would've told me.

"Azrea didn't know," Finnian continues. "She didn't find out long before I did. Dolfe kept it hidden from her."

"He knew she'd be angry with him," I sigh. "I am the only one Azrea loves almost as much as her mate. Telling her would risk me finding out, and Dolfe knows me well enough to know I wouldn't have remained silent about it. And he's protecting their unborn child. I can't be upset with him about this."

"Mate," Finnian repeats curiously. "I read about that—"

"In the book that was stolen?"

Finnian tilts his head. "Stolen? That book wasn't stolen. I ripped it apart and burned it behind the greenhouse years ago."

My lips part. "What? Irina said it disappeared—"

"It did," he replies with a slight grin. "Irina liked reading it, but I was angry that Jasper's focus was always on magic. That's all he ever fucking talked about. And I thought maybe if he didn't have the book, he'd stop caring so much about it."

I try to force laughter away, but I burst into laughter anyway. Nothing about any of this is amusing, but it is astonishing. Everyone I've ever known has been held on puppet strings by one man obsessed with pumpkins trapped beneath a bridge. Blood has been spilled to protect it. Jasper's children have been tormented for years because of it.

My father withheld so many secrets because of his stupidity that I'm continuously paying for his mistakes daily. And creatures possessing more power than any of us will ever see have been trapped behind an iron gate for over two decades under the threat of arrows piercing their wings if they try to leave.

And I've fallen in love with the son of a despicable king and readily handed my life over to ensure his safety, unknowing that it wouldn't have even mattered. Jasper treats torturing Finnian as a delightful hobby, locking him away in a crypt to frighten him into submission.

"Gods, fear is a powerful weapon," I say when my laughter calms slightly, but disbelief and exhaustion have made me delirious. "We've spent our entire lives fearing his threats when we could've worked together to end this. We wasted so much time, Finn."

Finnian doesn't find any of this amusing, frowning when tears falling down my cheeks replace my laughter. "Ellie, come here."

I walk into his open arms and bury my face against his chest, allowing the last several days to overtake my emotions. He strokes my hair and sways with me beneath the hazy, blood-colored sky.

My enemy by birth—my heart by fate.

"I know you're frightened," he whispers, snaking his other arm around my waist, "I know you're overwhelmed. But I've always wondered why I was given this life if only to be anguished. The reasoning became clear the night I met you."

With my lower lip puckered, I peer up at him.

He clears the tears falling down my cheeks with his thumb. "It was always meant to be you, Elora. I was always meant to find you. I wouldn't have wanted to find you earlier. I needed to be ready to be a man you could rely on, darling. I would endure it all again to be with you."

"Finn," I blubber, shaking my head.

He catches my chin between his fingers. "All of it, Elora. If I had to undergo everything again to stand here and hold you, I wouldn't hesitate. I believe...."—a slight grin lifts the corner of his mouth, his eyes lined with tears—"I believe you'd be my mate if humans were awarded those. I feel for you what I imagine Dolfe feels for Azrea. I will stop at nothing to have you in my arms, darling. No feat is too great."

Throwing my arms around his neck, I pull myself up and kiss him with every ounce of what I feel for him. It's messy from our combined tears but passionate and true. Only days ago, I doubted I would ever love someone the way mates do, saddened by being a fragile human. But Finnian changed everything—he exchanged his heart for mine.

And now, he's going to win a war for me.

❧

After instructing the men at the gate to watch Major and catch him if he wanders off, Finnian holds my hand while we walk underneath hovering faeries to Azrea and Dolfe's dwelling. Many faeries murmur my name as we walk past, undoubtedly noticing my uncharacteristic absence lately. The whispers grow louder when Brig calls my name from above, and I look up to weakly wave at him. My nerves buzz from what we're about to discuss with Azrea—if she even wants to talk to me.

Finnian follows my wave, frowning.

"He's mated," I assure him. "That's Brig. He was willing to shake Irina's hand the day we came here, but Raul prevented it from happening. Otto overreacted and nearly shot him through the wing, but I stepped in front of the arrow—"

Finn tugs me toward him. "You *what*?"

I blow out a breath, wincing from his glare. "I couldn't let him shoot Raul, as annoying as he is. Faeries believe themselves to be better than humans, and Raul is no different. Brig nearly shaking Irina's hand was monumental. Azrea's love for me is the only reason the rest tolerate my coming here. Dolfe's respect for my father has kept me from being smashed to bits by them."

"It is Otto's job to protect Irina from harm—"

"Otto is an ass," I interrupt. "He wants to sleep with her, Finn. He's annoyed that he can't, and he despises me now. He was escorted away by the men at the gate. I haven't seen him since that day, but he promised to see me again."

His nostrils flare. "He threatened you?"

I shrug my shoulders. "I don't think our next visit will be friendly."

He bares his teeth as he glances backward at the gate. "Why didn't Irina inform me of this? I would've handled him upon my return."

"Because you were drunk upon your return," I mutter.

A vein in his neck twitches as his glower returns to me. "You could've told me the morning I found you sleeping in the gardens."

I throw my arms up. "The morning you tried seducing me? Are we truly having this argument? You know now."

He grinds his teeth and flexes his hands, then rolls his neck. I ignore the attention our raised voices have drawn and rock awkwardly on my heels. "I don't think anything needs to be done," I say.

"That's not up to you," he bites back. "He can't threaten my wife and disobey his superior, Elora. There are punishments in place for instances like that. Why didn't the guards at the gate inform my father? Otto should've been reprimanded for his behavior."

"We don't know that they didn't—"

Before I could finish my sentence, Finn left me and returned to the gate to speak with the men on shift that afternoon. I sigh but don't follow him. Reprimanding men who are compensated for watching our every move is not something I need to add to my plate right now. Plus, Finnian looks like he needs someone new to take his aggression out on, and Otto is the perfect candidate to be on the receiving end.

I spin around, then gasp when I'm greeted by Azrea waiting behind me. My hand flies up to cover my heart as it pounds in my chest from the adrenaline, and I curse under my breath. "Hades, Azrea, make a sound next time." My gaze lowers to the tiniest hint of a bump. "Az, look at you! You're showing. Oh, Az, how exciting!"

Her bottom lip quivers, and my eyes widen. I've never seen her upset over anything—especially not enough to shed tears.

Before my next breath, her arms are one move away from crushing my ribs entirely as she squeezes me against her. Her tears wet my already damp hair from sweat gathering across my forehead. I try to breathe or make a sound, but I simply can't because of her tight hold.

When the world begins to spin, Dolfe lands behind her to peel her arms off me. I stumble forward and draw deep breaths, catching myself against the mountainside. Squeaky sounds come from my chest as I try to steady myself and allow oxygen to flow back to my brain. Azrea shakes Dolfe free to rub my back, tucking hair behind my ear.

Brig lands with a thud beside Dolfe, sending a fresh wave of hot air my way, and I cough as dust infiltrates my already-starved lungs. "Gods, are you trying to kill me?" I shout, fanning the dust away with my hand.

I've only been away for a handful of days, yet I have already become spoiled by the clean air in Pumpkin Hollow and Hogsfeet.

When Cedric *thuds* on the other side of Dolfe, I groan and duck into Azrea's dwelling to try and separate myself from the dust clouds that follow their bulky arrivals on land. All of them follow me inside. "I don't remember being this popular during my previous visits," I mutter, shoving my hair away from my sticky face.

"That's because we saw you daily," Brig replies, leaning against the cave entrance with his arms crossed. "Where ya been, Ellie?"

My cheeks redden when the memories of Finn between my legs spring to mind first. "Busy."

Azrea's nostrils flare before a broad smile appears. "Indeed."

I wrinkle my nose. "I'm not Fae. How can you—" I shake my head. "Nevermind. I know why. It has everything to do with this spell I ingested, doesn't it? I'm connected to one of you. A dark, deadly one."

Azrea's smile falls. "How did you find out?"

I hang my hands off my hips. "Well, Az, once I started fainting from having no energy whatsoever and being discovered in my dreams by the same male each time, it wasn't difficult to piece together."

Dolfe pinches the bridge of his nose. "Has he touched you?"

"*Touched* me? No, but his shadows chase me. You lied to me. You said he's dead, but he's not."

Dolfe and Azrea exchange a look, but Cedric shoves through all of them to stand before me. I don't move until he tries to touch my cheek. "Ellie," he whispers, the hurt from my rejection evident on his face, "we've been so worried."

I retreat a step back. "I know, but I'm okay."

Cedric disagrees with a head shake. "Dreaming of Fae shadows chasing you isn't okay." He squeezes my shoulder. "I haven't been able to stop thinking—"

A deep, bone-chilling voice calls from the cave entrance, "I wouldn't finish that sentence if I were you." Finnian steps inside, his fists clenched at his sides and his darkened stare pinned to Cedric. "And I suggest you get your fucking hand off my wife."

Fifty-Two

Cedric doesn't immediately step away, but I push through Azrea and Dolfe to move to Elora's side. She gives me an apologetic grin, but it's not her fault this male refuses to abide by her wishes. Elora shakes her shoulder free from his grip and wraps her arms around my waist as mine slides around her shoulders. I kiss her head while Cedric's eyes narrow at me. "I need to speak with Azrea and Dolfe alone," I say. "Your input isn't required. And if you want my help in leaving Ashbury, keep your fucking hands to yourself."

"You have no power here," Cedric sneers.

"I have more power than you," I replied coolly. "One word from me, and your entire fate is decided. Others might fear you, Cedric, but I do not. Now, leave before I make you leave."

"Fucking human—"

"Cedric!" Dolfe barks.

The one Elora referred to as Brig mocks Cedric with laughter as he follows him out of the dwelling but calls over his shoulder, "It wasn't awful to see you again, Ellie!"

Elora snorts as she rolls her eyes.

I notice Azrea's stomach and dip my chin at Dolfe. "Congratulations. Elora informed me of your child. She is elated for you, and

I've agreed to help her succeed in freeing the faeries from my father, but I need questions answered first."

Dolfe looks at Azrea. Within seconds, the air in the cave tightens, and sweat gathers on my forehead as breathing becomes more difficult. Elora steps away from me and groans, shedding her mother's shawl to wrap around her waist.

"It's their version of a torture chamber," Elora mutters, wiping sweat off her forehead with the back of her hand. "Azrea can trap us here, and no one can see or hear us."

"Hades," I growl, turning around and pressing my forehead against the cool inner wall of the mountain. "How can I think straight?"

Azrea's amused grin is pinned to Elora. She is much calmer than me, but I suppose she's used to it. "Let's make this quick," I grumble, shoving my hair back. "Who is the male in Elora's nightmares? What does he want with her?"

Azrea motions for Dolfe to step forward, her jovial expression changing into frustration. Elora catches onto something quicker than me as she looks between them. "What did he do?" she asks, looking at Azrea.

"He understood the enchantment," Azrea replies, baring her teeth at her mate.

I'm slightly taken aback by how sharp her canines are, but hers are nothing compared to the ones Dolfe shows her in return.

"Wait," Elora says, stepping away from the cool wall. "The bells? He understood those?"

I raise an eyebrow. "Bells?"

Elora nods but doesn't look anywhere but at Dolfe. "The spring chimed until I drank it."

"He knew I couldn't understand the old language. He's much older than me," Azrea explains. "He didn't inform me of what the *bells* said until days after Elora consumed it. He was overcome with guilt, as he should've been. That's when he admitted to burning Harry's body for Jasper."

Elora crosses her arms. "What did I drink?"

Dolfe releases a deep breath through his nose. Unable to stand the distance between us, I stand behind Elora and wrap my arms around her waist. I'd rather suffocate than be away from her, especially if what we're about to learn means I'll lose her.

"The spell was not a wishing spell," Dolfe begins, sighing when Elora starts with her questions. He waits for her to quiet before he continues, "It was a looking-glass spell."

"A looking glass," Elora repeats slowly, "that's how he can find me. It's a reflection."

"He's searching for where you are," Dolfe says, dragging a hand down his face.

Azrea steps forward, clearly frustrated by how slowly he informs us of what he did. "The male you're seeing *is* alive but stuck. He was cursed long ago. He can only step outside his town every twenty-five years."

Elora tilts her head. "You've been here for twenty-five years. Do you want him to find you? You're using me to help him find you?"

Dolfe shakes his head with a sigh. "I knew he'd find you through the looking glass because it's one of his powers. His shadows can slip through the subconscious mind. I needed to know where he was and if he was close to us."

Spending the majority of my life being uninterested in magic is not helping me now while trying to understand why this spell is seemingly killing my wife. I ask, "Why? Why don't you want him to find you?"

Elora drums her fingers against her lips. "You said he had a lover. It was Azrea, wasn't it?"

"Long ago," Azrea replies, "before I was introduced to Dolfe. My bond with him snapped into place immediately. The male you're seeing didn't take it well. He tried to murder every one of us as revenge, but fate looked down upon murdering our own kind, and he was punished by a group of High Fae. That's why we relocate every twenty-five years. He's never been able to find us, but he's come close. And now...."—she touches her stomach—"... we can't risk it."

I roll my neck. “Let me make sure I understand this. You lied to Elora and told her the spring contained a wishing spell, but it didn’t. It was a way for this male to find her so you,”—I pointedly glare at Dolfe—“could know if he’s close to finding your mate.”

“Yes,” Azrea answers dryly. “He lied to me, too. It wasn’t until I expressed concern for how Elora reacted to drinking from the spring that he admitted everything he did.”

“That doesn’t explain why her energy is draining,” I say, “or why it’s becoming difficult for her to wake from these nightmares.”

“Magic takes to give,” Elora whispers. “Even if it wasn’t a wishing spell, it still needs something from me in return for consuming it. And I gave it my heart. That’s what’s happening, isn’t it?” Elora’s voice quivers. “He’s killing me.”

Azrea lowers her gaze.

“It rewards the caster with what the consumer was willing to give,” Dolfe replies, his tone sorrowful. “And you were willing to give your heart. Each time he finds you, he steals what you can give him while you sleep. That’s why you can’t wake up, Ellie. The more he takes from you, the less you have when you wake.”

“And if he or his shadows touch you,” Azrea adds with a frown, “He’ll see where you are.”

I blink in heavy disbelief. “How do we....”

But I don’t finish my question because it’s evident by the way they avoid looking at me that there isn’t a cure for this.

“You sentenced her to die,” I whisper, “You asked her to leave with you because of your guilt. You wanted to give her a peaceful death.”

“No,” Azrea denies, “We wanted to find a Healer. It wouldn’t be a guarantee, but only Healers can counteract spells, and it’s more complicated since she’s human.”

When Elora’s shoulders begin shaking, I turn her around and press her against my chest. “How long does she have?”

“There’s no way to know,” Dolfe replies. “As fragile as she is...” —he glances down at her, his eyes downturned—“I can’t imagine she has much longer before he completely drains her.”

"It's a risk she takes every time she sleeps," Azrea whispers, wiping tears from her eyes. "He needs hearts, and Elora's heart is pure. Kind."

I press my lips against the top of Elora's head, searching the ground for answers. I refuse to accept that a magical entity in her dreams will kill her after we finally have a plan to end Jasper's reign.

I lift my head and look at Dolfe. "Do you know where a Healer is?"

He nods.

I drum my fingers against Elora's lower back in thought. "I'll get Dolfe out of Ashbury tomorrow night, but he needs to return with a Healer."

"No." Elora lifts her head from my chest. "They all need to be freed, Finn. We don't negotiate like this. You have to trust that someone will return with a Healer."

I shake my head. "Elora, I am not bargaining your life away—"

"Finnian." She presses her palms against my chest. "We don't bargain with lives. Azrea will ensure a Healer returns."

"Elora, I can't trust them after what he did to you!" My voice raises and echoes off the cave walls. "If his mate is safely away from my father, why would he return here to save you?"

"I will if he doesn't," Azrea says, stepping in front of Dolfe and raising her chin. "I promise you, Finnian. I will return with a Healer."

Elora tenderly touches my cheek. "My love, we must be different. We cannot live in fear. We will not allow it to control our decisions."

I swallow, my mouth dry, but it isn't from the smothering heat. It's purely the thought of trusting someone with her life that chokes me. "Elora, I cannot lose you."

She tries her best at a lighthearted smile, but her glazed eyes shed light on her weariness. "I'm not going anywhere, Finnian Alexander."

Admittedly, I want to wrap my hands around Dolfe's throat for sacrificing Elora for his benefit of watching the mysterious male haunting her. I care nothing for who he is and why he's trying to take her from me—I only need her to remain breathing.

I inhale a deep, frustrated, but steadying breath, focusing on the gold in her irises to calm my heart from raging to resourceful. "What you did to her is unforgivable," I say with no guilt at the accusation. "Despicable. But as always, my wife is far too kind and generous with others, even when it comes at a cost to her, and ensuring her happiness is my only responsibility, which, unfortunately, includes sparing your life."

Elora might be quick to forgive, but I am not. "For her sake, I will initiate your escape tomorrow night, but if you do not return with a Healer to help save the woman you've sentenced to die, I hope the Fates bestow the same unkindness upon you that you've shown her. And I will find you, Dolfe. Mark my words. You will pay for your deceit."

For once, Dolfe doesn't look at me like he wants to kill me. Instead, he lowers his chin in shame for what he chose to do to the woman who has always shown them nothing but kindness. "I understand," he says.

Elora slowly turns to face Azrea and Dolfe. "I will not accompany Finnian tomorrow night. I understand why you did it, Dolfe. I understand love now more than ever, but I cannot...." She wraps her hand around her throat as her voice turns raspy. "I cannot forgive you for this. Not yet. It was cruel what you did to me. I considered you my family."

"Elora," Azrea whispers, but Elora turns her head away. "Ellie, I'm so sorry. I'm so sorry it has come to this."

"I know it wasn't your fault." Elora presses her palm to each eye before she glances up at me. "I'd like to return home now."

Cool air filters into the cave as Azrea releases her hold on the wall, trapping us within. I hold Elora's hand as we pass by Dolfe, but she pauses once we reach Azrea. Elora doesn't hug her closest friend goodbye, but she does peer up at her with tearful eyes. "I am overjoyed for you, Azrea, and I hope to someday meet your child."

So many tears fall down Azrea's cheeks that she can't wipe

them away and refuses to allow Dolfe to touch her when he tries clearing them. "I will return to help you, Elora. I promise. I will not let you die because of my mate."

Elora's deep sigh is followed by a glance over her shoulder at the male lingering behind me. "I am growing rather tiresome of men seeing me as nothing more than something to be used for their benefit. It doesn't matter whether he's human or Fae; I will always be seen as disposable to them. Why did it take me being loved by one to be respected?"

On our way back to Pumpkin Hollow, I rub Elora's arm, who has been silent since leaving the faeries.

"If you want a positive side to all of this...." I trail off, giving her the choice of whether she wants to hear.

She nods but doesn't tilt her head to look at me.

"Since it wasn't a wishing spell, the confidence you claimed to be why I fell for you never existed." I kiss her temple. "That was all you, little doe."

I'm awarded a slight grin, but it soon falls. "If I hadn't heard for years about how horrible I am, I never would've felt the need to drink the spell and wish for you. A bit paradoxical, no?" Her gaze lifts to the sky as it changes from red to blue, signifying the border between kingdoms. "How a jumble of letters can do so much harm to someone."

I listen silently.

"A declaration by a man many years ago decided everyone across this bridge was better than us in Ashbury—he decided their lives meant more. They were just words, Finn, but we believed him." She huffs a breathy yet unamused laugh. "Regina spent years degrading me. I was never taught I could question words. And because of that, I never stood a chance."

"I hear you, Elora," I call for Major to halt and dip the shoulder she's leaning against to force her to look at me, "I hear you. I'm listening. This isn't over for you, little doe. If I have to search every land to find a Healer for you, I will."

"I don't want to die before someone tells them," she whispers with tearful eyes. "I want my people to know how important they are. I need someone to tell them that they'll be heard." She raises and twists to look me directly in the eyes. "Promise me, Finn. If the worst happens, and I don't see this through to the end, promise me you'll tell them they matter."

"Elora—"

"I know you'll stop at nothing to save me," she interrupts. "I know. But please, Finn, please promise me."

Promising this to her feels like admitting that I will one day be forced to live without her—that I won't be able to fulfill my promise of finding a cure for her. But if making this promise to her brings her peace in the meantime, then I'd be an ass not to swear it.

So, I cup her throat, kiss her once, and nod. "I solemnly swear to tell them, Elora Jane Grantham."

Fifty-Three

We are welcomed back to Pumpkin Hollow with grandness. Townspeople litter the roads and wave as we stroll past them on Major, waving ribbons of blue and gray at us and cheering. Finnian doesn't respond with waves, but he doesn't discourage me.

I force a bright smile and wave at each person, accepting a pink flower from a little girl who ran up to us. Finnian plucks it from my fingers and slides the stem behind my ear before he kisses me so tenderly that the sounds of the crowd blur into just noise, and it's only us existing in this cruel yet sometimes beautiful world.

And as he kisses me warmly, his lips lush and full against mine, with the seconds of my life ticking away, I decide not to let the impending doom harden my heart against him. I won't allow it to darken my views on what the world could be once evil is eliminated from this kingdom. I have to plan for leaving this place better than what I was born into.

The king and queen wait for us on the drawbridge, the inches between them indicating how far apart they've grown in recent years. But Honora beams at the sight of us, covering her heart and blowing kisses as we approach. Jasper, however, looks upon us with a satisfied grin, still heavily under the impression that Finnian is only pretending to care for me in hopes of procuring an heir.

Finnian searches for Irina, his body tensing against mine.

"Your mother would've sent for you if something happened to Irina," I assure him, keeping a placated smile on my face.

"I haven't told you everything," he says under his breath. "Irina crossed the bridge the night we left only after subduing two guards by force. I tied them to a tree and Massimo.... Took care of them." He looks back and forth, searching the crowd for his sister. "She was supposed to return. He promised he'd get her here safely, but I didn't think to check—"

Irina strolls out from the castle doors, as bored as usual. I grin, but Finnian sighs in relief. "Hades, I can't stand her. She knows to be waiting for my arrival."

Even though two days isn't a long time to be away, I expected everything to have changed, but every inch of Pumpkin Hollow remains the same—every person naive to the battle brewing just beneath the cliffside.

Finnian slides off Major and assists me, keeping my hand in his as we walk across the drawbridge to greet his mother. Now that I'm a princess, I am unsure if I'm still supposed to greet the king and queen with a bow and curtsy, but when I try, Finnian tugs me back up and shakes his head.

"You're one of us now. You bow for no one, Elora," he says, then leans over and whispers in my ear, "but you can kneel for your prince any time you please."

I scowl and shove his head away.

He grips my chin and clicks his tongue. "Now, little doe, it's time to resume your doting wife act. Smile."

I pinch my lips with a raised eyebrow.

With his thumb, he shoves the corners of my mouth up with a smirk. "You can't make anything simple, can you?"

"Leave her be," Irina says, pushing past her parents to grab my hand. "I believe she's had enough of you."

"I truly have," I say, squeezing her hand.

The look I exchange with her requires no words, but Irina becomes anxious to steal me away so I can inform her of everything we learned during our time away. I leave Finnian's side with a subtle grin, bidding adieu to the king and queen as Irina tugs me away. I can't hear what he says to his parents, but he soon departs to return to Major. Our instructions from Gus were to begin immediately upon return, and Finn is supposed to collect any weaponry, food, or armor he can to stash in Massimo's wagon.

But first, that requires finding the wanderers.

My first task is to inform Irina of our plan, who can tell by the weariness in my expression that I have many heavy secrets to reveal.

Before we entered the castle doors, I cast one last look over my shoulder at my husband as he and Major took off toward the woods behind the castle to find the note Massimo always leaves behind for Irina.

But when I lower my gaze, my eyes catch on the king's. I try to disguise the look of desire and love for the prince I'm supposed to hate, but I know I've failed when he tips his chin at me with a haughty, calculated grin. He already believes he's won.

After loading a tray full of fruits and chocolate, Irina locked every door and threw a handful of blankets onto her terrace. We're lounging on the plush blankets and pillows while eating strawberries, her finger lazily twisting one of my curls around her finger.

She went into great detail about how she lured the lookouts close enough to her, which included her baring her shoulders with the promise of more to entice them into removing their helmets. And then, she knocked one out with a rock to the temple before the other grabbed her, managing to rip her earring out before she did the same to him.

Finnian found her shortly after, and Massimo escorted her back to the castle before he handled the men tied to the tree. She hasn't seen him since but knows he's all right from the letters he leaves her in the hollowed-out tree trunk.

After warming me up with her scandals, I inform her of ours, though I spare her the naughtiest details. True to herself, she doesn't give anything away while I detail how we were captured, dragged into an underground bunker, and tortured with dehydration and separation before learning we were sent there to find them by Honora. Her only emotion is from learning I have a half-brother who is somewhat of a jerk but seemingly has a gentle side when he warms up to you.

Much like *her* brother.

She only speaks to say, "Men," before gesturing for me to continue.

I dip a strawberry into the melted chocolate and pop it into my mouth. "So, now, Finnian has left to find Massimo. Gus doesn't need much from us, but Finn hasn't long to procure food and any weaponry he can spare without drawing questions. He will stash them in Massimo's wagon and drop them over the cliffside tonight."

Irina sighs. "I thought I'd be rid of you in my bed."

I roll my eyes. "I don't have to stay here."

She dips her finger in the chocolate and swipes it across my cheek. "You do. I can't leave you alone to scream and thrash."

My spirit dampens. "The nightmares are killing me, Irina. Finnian is freeing the faeries tomorrow night to locate a Healer to bring back to Ashbury. If the Healer can't fix the nightmares, then you'll never have to sleep with me again."

She raises slowly. "What do you mean?"

I lean my head against the wall and watch clouds pass above us. "I consumed a spell before I came here that I thought was a wishing spell, but it wasn't. It connected me to a Fae male who has been trapped somewhere for twenty-five years. He's trying to locate the Cinder Faeries but is using me as a catalyst. I sacrificed my heart for the spell, not realizing it would take it so literally. And now, each time I sleep, he finds me."

"He's.... Stealing your heart?"

I shrug. "The faeries aren't forthcoming with information, but that's what we took from it. And unless a Healer breaks the spell, I'll dream of him until I'm dead."

She switches from worry to anger in a breath. "And Finnian is just.... Gathering weapons? Why isn't he trying to find a Healer for you?"

"He will," I assure her, "but he doesn't want to leave my side right now. Dolfe doesn't think I have long. The attack on Pumpkin Hollow is happening in two days, Irina. He can't find a Healer that quick. Our best chance of ridding me of the spell is to free the faeries and trust they'll return with one."

She shakes her head. "No, there has to be another solution, Elora. What about your brother—"

"Hogsfeet is desolate," I interrupt. "It would take Reynold much longer to locate a Healer. And why would a Healer listen to them? I'm human, Irina. It'll take a faerie to talk one into coming here to save me." I wave a hand lazily through the air. "I deserve it for drinking from the spring. Azrea tried to warn me. It was Dolfe who assured me it was fine."

"That bastard!" she shouts angrily, throwing a pillow over the balcony. "Finnian should've taken his head!"

I peer over the balcony wall. Gardeners beneath us look up in confusion. The pillow landed on freshly planted flowers. Irina tugs me back down and stuffs a strawberry in my mouth. "If draining you is the asshole male's main objective, then we'll continue to re-energize you. I will wake you up every hour tonight. That won't give you enough time to dream."

I try to argue, but she shoves a piece of pineapple into my mouth before I swallow the strawberry.

"I don't want to hear it."

Morning turned into afternoon, then afternoon seeped into night. The moon rose and stars burned, but Finn never returned. I haven't seen him since this morning, and the longer I go without knowing if he's all right, the madder I become. Irina walked me through town, chose far too many dresses for me after making me try on dozens, fed me so many meals that my stomach hurt, and made me lie with her in the gardens because she believed sunlight would resupply enough energy in me to keep me alive for years to come.

And now, we stand in the kitchen, mixing ingredients to bake a pie. I'm trying to help, but every step I follow isn't good enough for her, and she ends up redoing it. I've resorted to taste-testing pie dough and filling while watching her work.

I hop onto the counter. "How did you meet Massimo?"

Irina snorts while kneading the dough. "Finnian was traveling. I needed something.... *Someone* to entertain me and had exhausted all the dull servant boys in the castle. I snuck out one evening and ended up in one of the seedier pubs that borders the outskirts. It's one of the places Jasper used to send his men to find a woman for him to fuck for the night."

She passes me a piece of dough. "I hadn't slept with a woman yet, but I was curious." She sighs. "But I was recognized quickly. I ducked behind the bar when one of my father's men came in. Massimo was at the back door, speaking with the owner, and saw me. He snapped his fingers at me and beckoned me over," she demonstrated by hooking her finger at me with a grin, "I thought he was the most gorgeous man I'd ever seen. He's only a few years older than me, but gods, I could just tell he was *experienced*."

I listen with a broad smile. Her face always lights up any time she talks about Massimo.

"He introduced me to Leif that night. I had already fooled around with him by then." Her laugh is akin to a girlish giggle. "We moved *very* fast. It was love at first sight." She rolls her eyes after she says it. "Gods, listen to me."

I throw a handful of flour at her. "Keep going."

"At first, I was envious of his relationship with her. I didn't understand how open they were, but Leif conveyed her interest in me. Since I was already curious and enamored by her beauty, I agreed to try, but I was too nervous to experience everything with her, so she left me alone with Massimo."

"But you fell in love with both?"

She loosely nods from side to side. "Sort of. I love them both, but with Leif, it's mostly physical. Leif is completely open. She doesn't dedicate herself to only us. Massimo, though…" Her timid grin returns. "Massimo proposed to me with Leif's permission. He wants more with me. He's willing to dedicate his loyalty to only me."

I nearly swooned *for* her. "I could tell how he felt about you the night I met him. He stares at you like you're a goddess."

"I am to him," she says. "And while I love being with women, Massimo satisfies me in ways no one else has. He's wild and passionate but so gentle and loving with me."

I declined another piece of dough. "But you've stayed here because of Finn? You declined the proposal?"

Her smile falters. "Yes and no. I stayed here for Finn but didn't decline Massimo's proposal. I mistakenly told Jasper about it, and he responded as you would expect. I went weeks without seeing Massimo. He thought I had left him. He believed I didn't love him."

Her eyes fill with water. "His notes were heartbreaking to read, but I was so terrified for him, Elora. I didn't want Jasper to choose him for his next beheading. It wasn't until Finn returned and promised to protect Massimo that I returned to him. It took a long time for him to trust me again, but he forgave me instantly. He proposes to me still, almost every time we're together. He promises me endless happiness."

I cover her hand with mine. "Irina, you need to accept."

A tear slips free, and she wipes it away. "Someday."

I slide off the counter and stand beside her, keeping my hand on hers. "Irina, I'm going to protect him."

"You idiot," she mutters, throwing flour in my face. "I'm not staying for only him anymore."

I cough from inhaling flour. "Are you trying to kill me quicker?" I grab a rag and wipe it from my face. "Irina, you cannot put your life on hold for me. I have Finn. I'll be okay."

"This is my life, Elora." She pours the filling into the pie dish. "Finn is my brother. You're my sister. It might not be the life I want, but it's still my life. I want to see this through."

I toss the rag at her. "You're both so godsdamn stubborn."

Her jaw drops when the rag falls into her pie filling.

"Oh gods, I'm sorry—"

She hurls a handful of apple filling at me. It drips from my face onto my dress while I stare at her in surprise. She raises an eyebrow in challenge, wagging her finger when I scoop two handfuls of flour. "Elora, I swear to the gods..."

She's unable to finish from the flour that lands in her mouth and chokes her. And then, she lunges, smearing more filling across my face and into my hair. I yelp in protest and grab a bowlful of sugar to pour over her head.

She slips and takes me down with her in the scuffle of ingredients flying and filling spilling to the floor. We cry out in pain and laughter, trying to clear our eyes of the sticky jelly we created, only to spread it.

We laugh so loudly from the chaos that we overlook Finnian in the doorway until he shouts our names, drawing our attention away from the mess. He leans against the doorframe, crosses his arms, and lifts an eyebrow. Irina uses the bottom of her dress to wipe her face clean, then lends it to me, our laughter dying out in spurts.

"I can't leave the two of you alone," he says.

"All fucking day," I snap, remembering how annoyed I am with him. "Did you forget you have a wife now?"

Irina clicks her tongue. "You're in trouble, big brother."

He scoffs. "What else is fucking new?"

Irina stands and pulls me up, winking at me as she tucks a stray curl behind my ear. She spins on her heels, nearly slips again, then pats Finn's chest on her way out. "Send her to my quarters when you're finished with her."

I remain where I am and cross my arms. He doesn't change his stance either, though he does study me with an amused smirk. "It doesn't seem like you missed me too much."

"I didn't," I lied, turning my head away from him.

I see him nearing from the corner of my eye, but I don't reward him with any attention. Instead, I turn my head further—to the point where if I try again, my neck might snap. He only chuckles and places his hands on my waist.

"Not at all?" he asks, dipping to remove some of the filling from my neck with his tongue.

I jerk my head away, ignoring the shivers that spiral around my spine. "That isn't how this works, Finn."

He bends, cups my thighs, and lifts me to sit on the counter. Bracketing his arms on either side of me, he leans in and tries to kiss me, but I lean back. His eyes darken from the rejection. "You know where I was, Elora. Let me kiss you."

"I don't know where you were," I replied with a scowl. "I know where you were *supposed* to be. You said you would come to me after you found Massimo, Finnian."

He sighs, brushing his thumb across my cheek to steal some filling and sucking it off. He's pretending to be doing it strictly for the taste, but I know it's because he can't stand not touching me when we're this close. "I'm not used to this, Ellie. Aside from Irina, I've never had to be somewhere for someone. I didn't think you'd mind, but you're upset."

"Of course, I'm upset. What you're doing is..." I look around and lower my voice. "Treasonous. I was worried you'd be caught and dragged to the gallows. I didn't want my next conversation with you to be with your severed head."

That makes him smile, which is the opposite of the reaction I want, but he catches me when I try to climb down. "Elora, stop. I'm sorry. I should've considered how you might feel, but I thought about you all day long."

"Yet you were fine being away from me all day," I mutter.

"Hades, you're more possessive than you let on."

I throw my arms up, flour flying through the air from the swift movement. “You want me to like you, then you complain about it. Forget I said anything.”

He narrows his eyes. “I don’t recall complaining about anything, Elora Jane. I was unaware of how bothered you’d be by a plan you were wholly aware of—”

“A plan you changed without telling me—”

“You wanted me to stop what I was doing to come tell you? I was a fucking bridge away from you, Elora.”

“Right, right,” I snap, “I forgot you don’t know how to cross those unless forced!”

“One day!” he shouts, “One fucking day, and you’re already back to being a venomous little—”

“*Toad*?” I try to shove him away. “You were going to call me a fucking toad again, weren’t you?”

“I wasn’t *not* going to call you a toad.” He opens his arms wide. “But if the fucking shoe fits....”

I glower and slide down, squeezing between him and the counter to walk away. “Excuse me for wanting to know you’re alive! Gods, you can be such a prick.”

His response is to chase after me and toss me over his shoulder. “You want my attention so badly, little doe? Let’s see how loud you can scream for me.”

Fifty-Four

I ignore her protests, growl at her constant pounding against my back with her fists, and nearly lock her inside a closet, but we eventually make it outside. It would've been easier if I had told her where I was all day, but fuck, her little scowls and insults constantly shove me to do the complete opposite. I want to frustrate her more than I already have, even if my day was spent with Massimo to ensure my life with her would be a long one once my father is eliminated.

I took a grand total of two water breaks throughout the day because I was so desperate to return to her, but am I going to tell her that just yet?

No fucking way.

Her fists weaken the farther I walk, her head popping up to try and figure out where I'm taking her, but she hasn't spent enough time here yet to learn every secret.

I have to constantly adjust her on my shoulder from the slick filling and sugary concoction she created with my sister, but if I let her down, she'll take off, and I'm not in the mood to chase her right now. I want to make her scream.

If she loses her voice, I'll tolerate her better.

"*Finnian*," she whines, trying to wiggle free.

"Be still," I demand.

She musters all her strength into pulling herself up, wrapping her legs around my waist, and weaving her arms around my neck. I lift an unamused eyebrow when she puckers her bottom lip, though it's killing me to see her dressed up as a delightfully tasty treat that I'm anxious to devour.

"I'm ready to talk," she says pleasantly.

I throw my head back with a dark laugh. "That offer has expired, darling. You wouldn't listen to reason."

Her infuriating, stubborn scowl returns in full force. "Why is your argument considered the reasonable one?"

I ignore her question, which only irritates her more. "Am I not supposed to miss you?" she asks in a sickly sweet voice.

"You're trying to soften me, Elora. It won't work."

"I think I'm beginning to hate you again," she snaps.

"I never stopped loathing you," I replied without jest.

"Then why even come back at all?"

"I was hungry. Don't flatter yourself."

We reach a ledge overlooking a transparent stream. It doesn't hover more than a handful of feet above the water, but it's enough for what I plan to do to her.

I set her down and grab her wrist when she tries to flee, dragging her back. "Undress, Elora."

She crosses her arms, refusing to obey.

I shrugged and began unbuttoning my shirt while sliding out of my boots. "You can stand there all night if you want, but I'm going for a swim. I figured you'd want to wash the apple filling out of your hair."

She eyes me suspiciously and then touches her hair, wrinkling her nose from the jelly that has matted her curls into clumps. Glancing at the water behind her, she holds onto her determination for only a moment before she mutters something inaudible and begins untying the laces of her corset.

I slow down, pretending to fidget with my pants while she discards her dress. The chilly air causes her to shiver, but she waits for me to finish undressing. Lust blankets her eyes when I stand bare before her, but I bracket her chin in my hand when she steps forward to touch me and walk her backward until she's standing on the edge of the shelf.

I lean in, my lips hovering above hers, and grin at the terror in her eyes. "Deep breath, little doe."

And then, I shove her off.

❧

She screams as she falls, the sound echoing off the stone walls enclosing the small stream on either side. I don't have to stand by idly to know she's okay. The water is deep enough to give me a few seconds to dive in after her, and I locate her quickly beneath the surface. I wrap an arm around her waist and swim with her to the top, dodging her hands when she tries to slap me.

She gasps for air dramatically, acting as if she nearly just experienced death.

I wade to the farthest wall, the smirk on my face making her scream again—only this time, from pure frustration. She shoves her hair from her face and curses at me, trying to garner any kind of reaction out of me that she can.

"I want out!" she shouts at me.

I drop her back into the water, then grab her again when she struggles. Her inability to swim means she has to solely rely on me to stay alive, which I love, but it fucking angers her. And her reactions only make me wish to torture her more. "Stop flopping like a fish and look around you, Elora."

We're in a moonlit paradise beneath the stars. The tall trees provide cover but not enough to block moonlight from pouring through the leaves. The area is untouched and private, tucked far behind the castle, and unreachable unless you're willing to brave the possibility of getting lost in the winding maze of trees.

A sliver of space between the stone walls calms her long enough for her to peer through the crack. On the other side of us, a small waterfall fills a pond beneath the stream.

"This is my favorite spot in Pumpkin Hollow," I explain. "I used to come here almost every night. That pond feeds into the well we used to clean ourselves after we smashed pumpkins. I came here the first night you stayed with Irina to clear my mind."

She side-eyes me. "I could've died."

I scoff. "I know how deep the water is, Elora." Placing a finger under her chin, I force her to look at me. "I missed you today. I didn't stop moving or take time to return because I wanted to finish quickly, but you fucking accused me otherwise before I had a chance to explain to you why I didn't come back."

"So you tried to drown me as retribution?"

"Yes," I reply with a grin. "And I wanted to bring you to the only place in Pumpkin Hollow that's mine. No one comes out here. Irina used to, but now she spends her free time with Massimo. I've never wanted to bring anyone else here."

She releases a deep sigh. "I was worried, Finn."

I nod in understanding. "And I won't make the same mistake of not informing you of where I am, but you have to give me a chance to rectify it before losing it on me."

With her elbows resting on my shoulders, she pins my hair back with her hands. "What if Jasper finds out what we're doing? What if you leave tonight and don't return to me?"

I loop her legs around my waist. "He won't. Massimo showed me how he moves back and forth between kingdoms unseen. I'll take his trail tonight, and he'll assist me in dropping the food and armor over the cliffside. I didn't gather much, but more than I thought I could in the first round. We'll drop the second load before I release the faeries tomorrow night."

She frowns, most likely anticipating my reply to her next question, "And how do you plan on doing *that* unseen?"

I graze her ribs with hesitation in my eyes. "Do you truly want to know, darling?"

My lack of a straight answer confirms her fears, and she presses her forehead against mine. "I know we have to keep pretending, Finn. I understand you want me to stay here—"

I interrupt before she can continue, "You're not coming with me, Ellie. I don't want you with me on the off-chance that I am caught. Jasper's accusations of why you're here will be confirmed if you are. It's not worth the risk."

"This entire thing is a risk!" she shouts. Her nature of wanting to build defensive walls around herself pushes her to try to loosen her hold on me. "If I'm with you, you can claim I manipulated you into it."

I slowly shake my head. "Without giving you too many details, Jasper ensured I couldn't be broken easily. He wouldn't believe you, even if I agreed to try to blame everything on you, which I would never do."

She searched my face in horror. "He tortured you?"

"*He* didn't," I said, leaving the implication open for her to figure out the rest. "I don't want to discuss it. What I want,"—I tighten her legs around me—"is to enjoy a night with my wife."

She kisses me softly. "I'm sorry I overreacted. I just..." She gnaws on her bottom lip sheepishly. "I more than tolerate you, I guess."

I chuckle. "You still can't stand it, can you?"

"I'm getting better," she argues.

I reach up, gripping the edge of the shelf. "Hold on tight, little doe." She's light as a feather, making lifting us out of the water and onto the ledge simple. I twist her around to my back and pat her thighs. "Deep breath."

"Wait... what are you..."—she peers over my shoulder and down into the pond—"Finnian, no!"

"It's not that far—"

She shakes her head so quick that curls whip me in the face. "What if I fly off?"

"Don't let go," I reply dryly, stepping forward to the edge.

Her arms tighten around my neck to the point of choking me. I pry her loose and turn my head to the side to see her squeezing her eyes shut. "Do you trust me, Elora Jane?"

"Hardly," she mutters, then ducks her head against me.

I don't give her time to try and talk me out of it again, instructing her to hold her breath before leaping off the ledge with her curled around me like a sloth.

My feet touch the floor of the pond, but she barely gives me time to frighten her before she's tugging the hair at the back of my neck. We resurface with me laughing and her gasping as she peels curls off her face. "I can teach you how to swim when we have more time," I offer her.

She tilts her cheek against my shoulder, and the annoyance in her expression dissipates. "I kind of like this."

The flutter in my chest when she kisses my cheek is comforting and jarring. I've never given myself to anyone like this, but Elora has my heart very much in her hands. With anyone else, I never would've apologized for not returning when they expected—I never would've cared.

With her, disappointment isn't an option.

I should be stronger than this. I should've been able to remain in Ashbury without returning at all, ensuring I dedicate all the time I can to removing my father from the throne, but being away from her for so long physically started to hurt.

"How long do we have?" she whispers as if reading my thoughts.

"I told Massimo I would return after the next shift change, so not long. I'll return you to my sister before I leave and kiss you goodnight, then I'll work as quickly as possible to return to you, little doe."

"You haven't slept much since we wed." The worry in her voice doesn't assist in me not falling more in love with her than I already have. "You need rest, my love."

"I will rest when I know you're safe," I murmur sorrowfully. "Until you're healed, I'll never truly relax."

She presses her lips against my shoulder, her silence sparking unease. "Finn, I need to know you'll be all right."

Wordlessly, I walked to the pond's edge and sat her down. Carving a hand through my hair, I have to take a moment to shove the agitated dismay down, only facing her when I'm positive I can speak to her rationally.

Her feet idly kick back and forth in the water, only stopping when I put an arm on either side of her and look at her with nothing but resolve. "I won't be," I admit honestly. "I had plenty of time to think about it today, Elora. But I cannot live without you. I won't. The idea of ever moving on...."

I can't even finish the thought aloud.

"Finn, I want you to live—"

"Elora, I waited too fucking long for you to live without you now. I will ensure Jasper is dead, Irina is safely away from this kingdom, and my mother is finally content before I leave Pumpkin Hollow to never return. I won't tell anyone, not even Irina—"

"Tell them what?"

My jaw pops, my tongue glossing the roof of my mouth. "I'm not living without you, Elora. I won't dishonor your memory by moving on. I can't stomach the idea. No. Did you know Fae mates die if the other does? I read about it before I burned that book. Their bond is that potent." My fingers dig into the moist earth. "I don't care if we're human, Elora, you are my mate. If heartbreak doesn't kill me, poison will."

Her eyes glaze as she wraps a hand around her throat, and her voice is raspy when she says my name. "You can't."

"I can. Do you think I want to go mad with guilt and grief like your father did? He loved your mother so much that he destroyed kingdoms, Elora. His guilt was so heavy that he bargained away the life of his firstborn child. He spent years ignoring you to relieve his own conscience in Hogsfeet."

"You're not him," she argues.

"I'm not, but I am in love. And you're ill because my father convinced everyone in Ashbury that someone like you would never belong with me. You drank from that spring because you didn't believe I could fall for you." I swallow the rising emotion. "No, I don't trust myself without you. You have made me good. You have changed me." I place a hand against her heart, my eyes watering. "If you're gone, if your light disappears.... Elora, I will be nothing but darkness."

She cradles my face in her hands, staring deeply into my eyes. "You won't be, Finn, because you fought through the darkness. You loved someone enough to search for the light." Her hands slide down to my neck as she pulls me closer. "You cannot give in after everything you've accomplished, and you cannot leave your mother. I need you to keep me alive by restoring Ashbury—by making our realm what it should've been. I am your light, but you are my dream realized."

I can no longer look at her; the thought of ever facing a day without her is too heavy. But when I press my forehead against her throat, she wraps her arms around me. "Finn, you've spent too long surviving not to live. I need you to *live*."

"Not without you," I whisper with backbreaking desperation. "I shouldn't be able to live while you had to give yourself away to be heard. To be *seen*."

"I will always be with you," she says gently, touching my heart. "You will feel me every single day."

I place my hand over hers and lift my head to stare into her eyes. "Stop speaking like it's already been decided, Elora."

She nods sympathetically. "I'm trying to be practical."

I shove a hand into her hair only to bring her face to mine, our foreheads pressed tightly together. "You will outlive me, Elora Jane. There is so much more I need to be reprimanded for. My power extends far and wide, little doe. I will find you a Healer. So, stop trying to leave me so soon."

She sniffles through a sweet laugh. "If it makes you feel better, Irina plans to wake me every hour tonight."

"It does. If there's anyone alive more stubborn than you, it's her." I can't tell Elora yet that I plan to help Irina escape before the war—not with everything else we already face.

She kisses me softly. "Let's get you fed. You said you came back because you were hungry."

I nod but grin. "I did. You're right." Using my grip on her hair,

I pull her backward. "But food isn't why I came back, Elora." I lean forward and trail kisses down her throat. "I desire something sweet." I nip her collarbone. "Something sustaining."

❧

Her responsive shivers unbound me from the sorrow, at least for a little while. For the next few moments, it was just me and her. Under a moonlit sky, hidden from politics, pumpkins, and glass castles, it was my wife writhing beneath me, her whimpers and pleas answered with pleasure and praise.

For one night, we weren't the enemies we were raised to be. We rose above the hatred instilled within us. For tonight, it was me and her—Ellie and Finn.

And in the very last moment, with her resting on my chest, I looked up at the sky at a star shooting past, but I realized I had nothing to wish for when my dream was in my arms.

Fifty-Five

When my eyes flutter open, it jars me to discover I'm in the arboretum, lying on a bench and hidden behind rows of plants and flowers—tucked farther back in a corner than when Irina dragged me in here. But the arm locked around my waist and the warm breath in my ear do not belong to Irina. No, my love sleeps soundly beside me under a thick wool blanket, though I do not remember him returning to the castle or how we ended up here. Morning sunlight pours through the windows and onto the leaves, but we're alone.

He remains undisturbed when I turn to stare at him, only twitching from a dream he must be having. I do not recall dreaming at all, and most of that credit is due to Irina. She followed through with her promise of waking me every hour, her eyes heavy with exhaustion the last I remember waking, and the book she began nearly finished, but the moon was still out. Finnian must've taken over shortly after and fallen asleep beside me from exhaustion.

My gods, the time I wasted not studying him after we met. I would never admit it to him, but he is a fallen god. Chiseled, strong, and rugged when he isn't bathed and in his princely attire, and far too striking to be walking about in public. I will insist he become a hermit if we make it out of this.

I frown then, remembering his wish to depart this life with me. And still, at this moment, even if the idea of him ever touching another could drive me to madness, I do not want him to follow me in death. I want to dwell in this place as spirit or soul, following him as he finally learns to breathe freely.

Only then would I be truly able to rest.

Far too melancholy this early in the morning, I decide to surprise him with breakfast, but when I twist to leave, his arm tightens, and a hum of disapproval comes from his chest.

"Where do you think you're going?" he asks, groggily and deliciously raspy.

I settle snugly against his chest. "To the kitchens."

"You would get lost," he responds, slowly opening his eyes and blinking away the sleep. "I do not have time to hunt you."

I rub the dark circle beneath his eye with my thumb. "Sleep more, my love. I didn't mean to wake you."

His lazy half-grin brings a broad smile to my face. "Why would I close my eyes when I can stare at the sun instead?"

I click my tongue. "I've heard the sun blinds."

He drags me closer. "Then visions of you will be the last I see, little doe. That will be well worth it."

Pressing my hand against my forehead, I pretend to swoon. "You are far too romantic in the mornings, Finn. You need to remember how much you dislike me."

"Love shares a border with hatred." He rolls to his back and brings me with him, gripping me tightly. "You can imagine how confused that leaves me each day."

"That is how I felt when I woke here."

He tucks an arm behind his head, looking purely sinfully handsome now. "I thought I'd be kind and relieve my sister of staying awake, as much as I despise sleeping with you."

I roll my eyes. "Sacrificial snuggling?"

He casts a rotten smirk. "I would appreciate it if you'd share how good I am at it when you convey to other women how open I am to affairs."

"Only after I compare you to—"

He pinches my side before I can finish. "Touché."

Victorious, I lay my arms across his chest and rest my chin upon them. "Continue."

He idly spirals a curl around his finger. "Irina was half-asleep when I returned, only opening her eyes after I removed her book from her hands. She said you didn't have any nightmares and also did not argue when I said I'd take over."

I pretend to be shocked. "Such dedication."

With a grin, he continues, "I thought about returning to our quarters, but I didn't want to risk it. You sleep well amongst the flowers, but it was too chilly to sleep in the gardens, and I did not want to wake to gawking gardeners."

"Is that their official title?"

He chuckles while rubbing my back. "Hardly anyone except my mother comes here during autumn and winter, so I knew we wouldn't be found. I carried you here, and you never opened your eyes, so I watched you sleep until, I suppose, *sleep* overcame *me*."

I brush my fingers through his hair. "I am pleased you rested. And I appreciate you returning to me."

"I will always return to you, darling." He leans up to kiss me softly before relaxing against his arm again. "Gus was right where he said he'd be. He and a handful of others were there to retrieve the bags of food and armor. I didn't see Reynold, but I assume he patrolled the perimeter for the others."

"And tonight?"

"Tonight, I will free the faeries and drop the second load with Massimo. Then, at dawn, it begins."

"And hopefully, it ends," I whisper.

"It will, little doe. And then, we will leave for the closest kingdom with a Healer. I know some places far away where faeries reside and are in power, but Healers could be anywhere. I've seen one a time or two, but they are likely employed by kings. I'll have to be resourceful."

I frown. "Finn, we can't keep him away. I will fall asleep one day, and you won't be near."

He lifts an eyebrow. "If you are sleeping somewhere other than with me or Irina, you will need more than a Healer."

I roll my eyes. "It is not unfathomable for you to have things to do outside of watching me sleep, Finn. If our plan is successful, you have a kingdom to run."

"My mother will have a kingdom, Elora. I don't give a fuck about the crown. I do, however, somewhat like your company, even if only to fuck."

"Gods, you say the sweetest things." I drag the tip of my finger down the bridge of his nose. "What will you do today?"

"Princely things," he responds with a lazy grin. "A meeting with advisers this morning was pushed, which gave me time to lie here with you. A specialty shoppe is opening in town this afternoon. Would you like to attend with me?"

I wrinkle my nose. "You want me to publicly pretend I like you? Women will be expecting me to relentlessly gawk at the playboy prince."

With a svelte, smooth motion, he grabs my thighs and pins them against his hips. "I will be the one staring," he replies, pressing my core against his cock. "I will be the one with my arm around you, preventing any other man from leering upon what's mine."

Instinctively, I roll my hips against him but then look around. "Finnian, someone could come in—"

He slips his hands beneath my gown. "Let them." Grazes my thighs. "I can fuck my wife wherever I please." Up my ribs, and a haughty smirk appeared. "Besides, it might be the last time before dawn. You wouldn't want to send your prince to war without a proper goodbye, would you?"

I lean forward, placing my hands on either side of his head and allowing him a tease of my breasts as my gown slips forward. It was a foolish idea. His eyes darken, one of his hands leaving my ribs to pull the shoulder of my dress down. He leans forward to trail his lips across my collarbone, his desperation to have me tearing the silky fabric.

"Finn!" I scolded in a whisper, "I liked this one!"

Annoyed to be pausing, he lifts his eyes. "I will order a hundred of these for you, then tear them from your body and order more. I will demand the fucking clouds come down from the sky and wrap around you like a blanket if you would do me the honor of riding my cock, *wife*."

How willing he is to deliver the sky to me just for sex is something I continuously forget but need to take advantage of more often. But I fix my face with faux disgust. "Must you remind me so often that I am bound to you?"

He fists the bottom of my gown to begin lifting it, and I can't help but laugh at how much he's changed since admitting his secret to me. No more hesitancy lingers between us. "And I thought I'd be begging you forever," I jest, raising my arms for him to remove it.

Lust has hardened his jaw and glazed his eyes, a feral untethering evident in the way his fingers apply enough pressure on my hips to leave prints. The more we're together, the more it seems he wants me. And the pleasure he brings me is without complaint, but the intensity with which he stares at my body causes my nerves to stand on end.

It is as if I am an addiction to him.

And then, I realize it.

Before I know what I'm saying, I ask, "I've replaced it for you, haven't I? The alcohol."

He stills. Stops moving altogether. And raises his eyes to mine almost shamefully. Understanding soon floods him, and he loosens his fingers around my hips. I did not ask him because I wanted his guilt, but I've conjured it anyway. But the thought that he could fall back into the comfort of whiskey and ale if we're unable to locate a Healer terrifies me more than dying.

I cradle his face. "I'm not complaining," I whisper.

His desperation for me turns soft as his arms curl around my waist, and his forehead rests against my shoulder. And I hold him. The strong prince, the unbreakable man, has become wholly dependent on me to feel something. Anything.

I brush my fingers through his hair. "Being that person for you is an honor, Finn. That's not why I asked."

He presses his lips against my collarbone momentarily before lifting his head and searching my eyes—something I've noticed he does often. "You steady me," he murmurs. "Liquor numbed pain and memories. Expectations."

I listen quietly, stroking his hair.

"I started too young," he admits sorrowfully. "And it became too easy to acquire because of who I am. Irina monitored me when I would pick it up again. Sometimes I'd stop for a while, but being here..." Sighing, he studies the arboretum. "It's been dark here for so long that the light you brought with you broke through the need for ignorance."

I tilt my head and brush my fingertips across his jaw. "I'm sorry you felt unheard for so long, Finn. You sought oxygen while drowning, but there was no one there to provide it."

"Until you." He returns to grazing my ribs, but the touch isn't primal—it's tender. Loving. It's the man behind the agitation and dominance. He's just my Finn like this—not the prince or treasonous heir to the crown. He's simply mine. "If I become too much for you, Elora... if my need for you becomes too heavy or overwhelming, you must tell me."

I relax against him but hold his stare with every ounce of what I feel for him, displayed in how tightly I hold him against me. "If there's one promise I can make to you, Finnian Alexander, it's this. The way you love me will never be too much. I will always be your anchor when you feel yourself sinking. I will always be the breath you need to take."

He dips his chin, but I catch the endearing dimples before he can hide them from me. They're rare to see and mostly only appear when he's being a nuisance, but these are from timidness, which is not something I ever thought I would make him.

I wiggle my hips. "What are you waiting for? Kiss me."

He doesn't unleash as I expect, instead leaving a gentle kiss between my breasts. His lips trailed up my chest, barely touching, but my eyes fluttered closed from the sensation. His teeth hardly skim my collarbone, causing chills to swell over my body. He's teetering me on the edge of consumption.

"Poetry," he demands huskily.

Unable to think of one to recite from the tortuously slow way he's dragging his tongue along my throat, I begin rhyming words in slurs of laden desire. "Finn is good," I whisper, dropping my head back, "Finn is fine..."

I feel him smile against me.

"Finn makes me feel.... Divine."

Chuckling, he pinches my chin between his fingers and lowers my head. "That was terrible, little doe."

I pull in the corner of my bottom lip. "Are you going to punish me for it?"

He nods slowly, adjusting to lean against the wall and straddling me around his waist. "I'm going to brand you, Elora."

I startle, my eyes widening. "What?"

He snakes a hand into my hair and fists it to tilt my head to the side. "We'll be in public this afternoon. I need every pair of eyes to know you're mine. I need it to be without question that I have stolen from you what others covet."

I swallow. "My heart?"

With a lazy smirk, he uses the grip on my hair to pull me lower. "Among other things." He seals his lips around a spot on my throat —one unable to be hidden with a cloak.

He sucks, using his tongue for suction. The friction from his tongue and cock throbbing against my core makes me whimper from need and a little pain. This mark will be unpleasantly large, but after what he conveyed to me in Hogsfeet about men wanting my purity for themselves, I suppose the evidence that he's taken it already will protect me.

When he releases me, he looks at it with pride and a little

amusement. It might be a little juvenile, but I don't see the harm if it brings him satisfaction and relaxes his fears.

Until I rise up on my knees to catch my reflection in the window, gasping at the raw, swollen red mark on my throat. "Finnian!" I shout, covering it with my palm. "I can't go anywhere looking like this!"

He pulls me down again, his rotten, lousy grin returning. "Oh, you will. You're a princess now, Elora. You have to make appearances in town. And I believe you have plenty of dresses to show everyone what I gave you."

I try to climb off him. "I will tell everyone you tried to choke me if they ask. My gods, this is horrifying."

He slips his hand between our bodies and unties his pants. Taking the distraction, I lean down quickly and choose a spot on his throat to leave him the same gift. But he doesn't pull me away or advise against it—the bastard lets me do it.

In fact, he seems to be *enjoying* it.

I release him, frowning in disappointment that the mark I left isn't nearly as significant as the one he gave me, but he taps the other side of his neck. Lifting an eyebrow, I switch to the other side and suck his skin between my lips, moaning when he slides his cock inside me. He doesn't let me move my hips, and he doesn't thrust; he stays completely still until I sit up.

Twin marks rest on either side of his throat, one red and the other purple, but both much smaller than mine. "I have plenty more skin if you'd like to keep practicing," he says.

I touch one of the marks. "We're not supposed to show our feelings, Finn. What if he sees? Won't this upset him?"

"It doesn't fucking matter anymore, Elora." He slides his hands up my back. "Loving my wife shouldn't be a risk I fear. I want to touch you in town. I want to kiss you. Hold your hand. I think we've learned life is too short to not live."

I nod, then sigh when he continues to prevent me from moving against him. "Finnian, please."

"Do you trust me, Ellie?" There is nothing but longing in how he looks at me. "Do you trust I'll take care of you?"

I want to list every reason why I don't think this will be as easy as he is making it seem, but strangely, shockingly, I do trust Finnian to see this through. I trust that if Jasper yanks us out of town for being too in love, Finnian will stand up for us.

He'll fight for me. For us.

Knowing him, he'd bring war sooner.

He might even be looking for a reason to end this now—baiting his father into a battle quicker.

"Yes," I whisper, "I trust you."

He releases my hips and tucks his hands behind his head, nodding for me to move. Balancing my hands on his shoulders, I grind my hips, my eyes rolling back each time the tip of his cock hits the spot inside me that tightens every limb.

"Fuck, darling."

His voice *unravels* me, and I pick up speed enough to make him groan. I can hardly focus on his face as my vision continuously blurs, one of my hands falling from his shoulder to lift my hair from my neck as sweat pools at the top of my spine. He curses under his breath and mutters something about not being able to stand me, but I feel too much in control to care. Finnian has freed every one of my insecurities.

And the louder his groans become, the faster I move until he's unable to live another moment without touching me.

He wraps his hands around my waist and holds me still while he begins bucking into me, his gaze moving from my breasts to our joined hips until he's staring into my eyes. We hold one another there through woven limbs, breathy cries, and sounds of pleasure. He holds me like he could lose me any second, sparing no inches between our bodies, melding us together as one—as if we never should've been split.

And in the pleasure, in the parting of his lips, and as my name flies off his tongue, I believe him.

I believe what he said about mates—that, maybe, in another

life, we weren't only human. We were eternal, boundless, meant for one another.

Because in no life could my soul attach to anyone's but his. Finnian, as maddening as he is, as arrogant as I find him, is also compassionate. And protective. Wild, yet tethered. And I desperately want to be the one to save him the way he plans to save me.

"Endlessly," I rasp between breaths, kissing him, "I love and hate so you endlessly."

"My love," he responds, the warmth of his release edging me until he thrusts once more, "Mine, all mine."

Fifty-Six

Before we could go into town, Finnian was called away to attend an impromptu meeting with advisers that had already been canceled once. He left me with Irina since I apparently needed to be watched at all times, and she smacked him on the chest when she saw the blatant mark on my throat, again scolding him for being such a child.

I made the mistake of leaving his twin marks too low, so they remained hidden beneath his shirt, but he swore to allow me more practice when he returned. He parted from us as I scowled at him, and Irina promised to find me something to wear with a high neckline, though it might take a fichu to cover his *branding* on me.

Irina was tearing through her drawers when voices from below her balcony drew our attention. I sit up from where I've been reading on her bed, only somewhat listening to how much she can't stand her brother, and toss the book down.

Irina frowns at the voices, seemingly hesitant to walk onto her terrace. I hop down from her bed and stroll outside, leaning my elbows against the railing to peer down at the crowd gathering around wooden scaffolding. And set upon the ledge, beneath nooses used for hanging, is a guillotine.

I noticed the gallows when strolling through town with Finn

and Irina but never witnessed the king's favorite tool for collecting his heads. I'm unable to look away but call for Irina.

I search the crowd but don't notice Finn or the king.

Irina breezes out as if reading my mind and stands beside me, saying, "He's right inside those doors." She points to a set of doors adjacent to the scaffolding. "Jasper forces Finn to attend every sacrifice, whether hanging or beheading."

If only I could, I would stare at the doors hard enough to set them on fire. I would burn this entire place down instantly. I've read about dragons in books, but none still exist. If Finnian is willing to give me the sky, I wonder if he'd supply a dragon for me to set fire to what lies beneath us.

Bart stands before the crowd, reading from a scroll. He doesn't mention a specific crime or a name but announces only one man will be executed for treason.

And as if that were a welcoming call, the doors opened for the king to stroll out, followed slowly by Finn in his crown. Knowing where to find her, he glances up and looks directly at Irina with a slight shake of his head. "He doesn't know who it is," she says, leaning so far over the edge that I grip her dress to keep her from falling. "He always knows. Why wouldn't Jasper tell him? Who is it?"

I hear the panic in her voice, but I can say nothing to calm her. Empty promises would be all I could say.

Two young men carry a throne out for Jasper to sit in while Finn lingers behind it, searching the crowd. Even as Irina tells me every thought he's thinking, I already know he's trying to find someone missing from the faces he recognizes.

"Finn was told he needed to attend a meeting—"

"He was told a lie," she interrupts, following his lead and searching the crowd below. "Jasper pulled him away from you for a reason." She seems to be piecing together a puzzle in her mind. "He knew Finn would bring you to me...."

As she speaks, a man is dragged through the doors. A brown bag is placed over his head, his muffled shouting unintelligible from what must be a gag in his mouth. He's pulled up the small set of stairs as Jasper watches, never once looking at us, but I have the damnedest feeling he knows we're here.

Finn tilts his head. Irina grips the railing so tightly that her knuckles whiten.

And I want to be anywhere but here.

The man is turned to face the crowd, held steady by the men holding him up, even as he struggles to try and flee. Finn steps forward when the bag is removed, his eyes widening as recognition crosses them, and then he looks at Irina.

Irina *screams.*

I wrap my arms around her body as she tries to lunge forward, stealing a glance at the man about to take his last breath, and water fills my eyes when I realize it's *B*.

Jasper stands from his throne. In a loud, deep, horrid voice, he calls, "This man killed two of the king's men and buried their bodies on the outskirts! We have not located his accomplices, but rest assured..." And then, he slowly turns his head toward his daughter. "We will."

B is forced to his knees as Irina shrieks, and Finn rushes toward the steps, only to be held back by a handful of guards, his crown tumbling to the ground. He fights forward, whaling on them, shouting for his father to *stop this.* But Jasper only sits back on his throne and watches in contentment as B is shoved forward on the bed, the lunette locking and securing him into place. Irina thrashes against me, screaming so loudly that people look up to find her, but I hold onto her with every ounce of strength I have.

B cries her name in return, trying to turn his head to search for her.

Jasper *grins.*

And time seems to slow as Finnian pushes through to get his boot on one step, as Irina shouts, cries, howls, and the blade is released, and I watch in horror and shock as the head is severed from the body quicker than a breath. Finnian falls to his knees, grief-stricken and pale, and Irina collapses in my arms.

❧

Irina's cries are so prominent that no one leaves, even as B's body is removed from the bed and his head carried in the basket to be added to the King's Collection. But then, a fresh wave of panic seems to overcome Irina as she rips free from my grasp and leans over the edge. "Finn!" she screams, the desperation of a little sister calling for her protector nearly knocking the wind out of me. "Go! Go!"

Without hesitation, Finnian leaves his crown on the ground, ignores Jasper's calls for him to stop, and takes off toward the gardens. Irina grabs my hand, says nothing about where we're going or what Finnian is about to do, and drags me behind her as we leave her wing and weave through the corridors to emerge in the underground tunnel.

I'm breathless from running, shocked by what I just witnessed, and confused about why we're not stopping. But I know better than to ask, and I'm already slowing her down by being unfamiliar with the corners we continuously turn, nearly knocking my head against one when she turns too fast.

Throwing open the tunnel door to the outside, we're met by Finnian—red-faced and teary-eyed as Irina throws her arms around him. He embraces her, cupping her head and trying to shush her cries. "We don't have time," he says, "I need to find Massimo, Irina. I need to get to the tree. Go find Mother."

He pulls her off him and gently places his hands on her shoulders, lowering to her eye level and holding her gaze. "Listen to me, Irina. This will end. I'm going to kill him for what he's done to us and our mother. But you can't break on me yet." From his pocket, he retrieves the unused padlock. "Take Elora to the arboretum after you locate Mother. Lock the door with this. I am the only one with a key, Irina. Stay there until I return."

"What if they've found him?" she blubbers, tears streaking her cheeks. "What if he's next? What if they find Leif?"

Finnian uses the sleeve of his shirt to wipe tears from her

cheeks. "They haven't. He would've thrown Massimo up there first. B was a warning, Irina. Jasper knows something is amiss, but I must go if you want me to find Massimo first."

She nods but weaves her arms around his middle. For the first time, I'm witnessing just how prominent the love is between Finnian and Irina. I'm witnessing the protective brother—the dependent sister; the woman who never lets her guard down with anyone and wholly relies on Finnian.

This is the version of him no one ever sees, and I'm overwhelmed with pride, desire, and unease. Dread.

A war is happening—spearheaded by my husband.

He holds Irina momentarily before pressing his lips to the top of her head. "Go," he whispers, "Keep her safe."

Reluctantly, Irina releases him with a nod, using her palm to clear tears away. Finnian comes to me, embracing me entirely, and kisses me. He cradles my face in his hands and holds my gaze. "Wait for me to return, Elora. Stay with Irina."

Panic seized me as I started to shake my head, tears slipping free. But Finnian kisses me again, fisting a clump of my curls in his hand and tugging my head backward. "I will return to you," he promises, his eyes searching for each gold fleck in my eyes, "But you have to remain in the arboretum. Understand?"

I squeeze my eyes shut as he kisses each of my tears away, ending with his lips against mine. "I love you," he murmurs, "and I will end this for you. For us."

"Please," I rasp, "please come back to me."

He rests his forehead against mine. "Always, Ellie."

❧

Honora was running through Irina's quarters when we finally located her, frantic to know where Finnian was. Irina explained that he was fine but instructed us to wait for him in the arboretum. Irina moved us quickly from the safety within the castle walls to hiding in cloaks while we trekked to the nursery with Zeb and

Georgie in tow. Blankets and pillows remained from my night with Finn, but Irina didn't use them. Instead, she laid on Georgie, her tears falling onto his lush coat. Honora sat behind her, stroking her hair.

I didn't know how to console her—I wasn't sure what to say. Instead, I braided pieces of her hair, keeping my hands busy while my mind imagined the worst. Any time Irina would blame herself, Honora would hear nothing of it.

The fault only rested with one man.

Hours passed since we last saw Finn, and we had hardly spoken since this morning. As always, Honora wasn't informed of the beheading and only realized something happened when she heard Irina's screams from her balcony. With the entrance locked, courtesy of the padlock meant to keep Irina inside the castle, I felt secure enough to climb on the settee beside her. Zeb jumped up to rest at our feet, Irina wrapped her arm around my waist, Honora laid her head on a pillow beside Georgie, and we all closed our eyes.

And we waited.

But I am not waiting alone.

Even in my subconscious, someone watches me.

Him, the male desperate to find where I am.

I run through an expansive mansion made of black everywhere —the walls, the chandeliers, the furniture. Everything is so dark that even the cool air coiling around me is discomforting, the complete opposite of the warmth of Finnian and the suffocating, smoldering heat of Ashbury.

This place wreaks havoc on my subconscious as it tries to claw its way free, but I can't find a way out. The farther I run from him, the deeper I lose myself in the hallways.

I don't make a sound, even my steps. I am barefoot in a long blue dress, the skirt nearly causing me to trip as I round corners to escape the shadows hunting me. But my pale skin stands out against the harsh, unlit corridors. And when I reach a dead end, he finds me.

He doesn't lunge as I expect. He doesn't even rush.

He stands before me, half-male, half-dead, his face contorted from skinless bones. He's beautiful. And broken. Terrifying. A black hole is where his eye should be on the skeletal side. But on the other side, his iris evokes visions of flames. The faeries he killed were Cinders, and I wish I knew if his nerves constantly burned from the lives he stole.

But he's young or *looks* young. Hardly older than Finn, the male before me looks lost but resentful. I imagine being locked away in a town for twenty-five years can do that to someone. Years of simmering rage are evident.

I can't understand what he's saying, but I've realized after so many of these nightmares that he isn't talking to me. He's talking to *them*—the shadows slithering closer.

"Coward," I whisper.

The shadows still when he cocks his head.

"You can understand me," I say, my voice steadier than my fingers grasping the wall behind me. "I know you're trying to steal my heart, but it's already been taken."

He slowly inches closer, one foot in front of the other. His voice is melodic and soothing, but his half-grin conveys something entirely different. And I'm entranced, watching his graceful movements.

As evil as he is, something about him is disarming. Instead of fleeing, I find myself frozen, from fear or curiosity.

"You cannot have it. You can keep trying, but he will find a way to stop you." I lift my chin. "He will find a way to save me from you."

He stops before me and lifts a hand, flexing his skeletal fingers before brushing them across my cheek. I can *feel* them—the cold, smooth surface. Bones aren't as chilling to the touch as one might imagine.

This close, I realize his voice mimics the bells from the spring.

He's speaking in the old language—the one Azrea couldn't understand. He's been locked away for so long as the world continues evolving that he cannot speak my language.

"You loved her," I continue, trying to appeal to the softness of his touch, "and she hurt you. She can't even understand you anymore, but you understand me. How?"

I stare into his lifeless, fire-filled eyes, wishing desperately to convince him to release the hold he has over me. And he seems to be studying me as intensely, his head tilting slowly, inch by inch.

"I wish I knew your name," I whisper, unsure why.

His response is a gravelly, deep ringing, but I imagine he just told me what his name is, even though he knows I can't understand him.

One bony finger drags down my jaw and grazes my throat until the tip touches my ribcage that protects my heart.

Finn's heart.

His voice rings.

"You learn from consuming other people's hearts," I say slowly, somehow understanding what he's trying to convey, and my eyes widen slightly. "I wasn't supposed to let you touch me."

His grin widens, pulling up the skeletal cheekbone. And his voice is deep, alluring, and eerie as he says, "Ashbury."

I don't even have time to scream as his finger pushes through my ribs, pushing past the layers of skin and bone, until unfathomable pain spreads across me from his touch on my heart.

He holds me still as I start to shrivel, as tears pour from my eyes, as suffering I never thought possible makes my knees buckle. Every good feeling, every flutter I've ever felt, the joy, the memories, he takes them. He devours and depletes. Steals everything.

It is not my actual heart he wants—it's what's inside.

I scream in agony, unable to conjure the energy to fight him. Instead, I use him for balance as my legs start giving out, my energy wanes, and my eyes start fluttering closed.

Only one name comes to mind to save me.

"Azrea," I rasp.

He jerks his arm away, his eyes widening in anger. He could feel her within me, the memories of her some of my best and most important, but hearing her name aloud distracts him long enough for me to fracture his hold on my mind.

❧

Sweat pours out of me as my eyes fly open, my gasps short and raspy. Zeb lifts his head but rolls over and falls back asleep. Sitting up takes far too much effort, and my chest *burns*.

I'm lightheaded and dizzy, reaching behind me to wake Irina, but my hand touches only plush. I turn my head to find Honora still sound asleep on the other side, her back toward me. Georgie is snoring, but Irina is missing.

With my body trembling from fright and exhaustion, I grab one of the blankets to wrap around me, swaying as I stand. "Irina," I whisper, using the rows of plants and trees to steady me as I amble through the arboretum.

"Finnian," I murmur, hoping to find them sitting somewhere, sharing what transpired since he left this morning.

But instead, I find nothing but an ajar padlock.

Fifty-Seven

I step outside and look around for her, too frightened to say her name and too weak to shout it. I see no traces of her or Finnian anywhere, but he wouldn't have returned without waking me.

No, this escape was all Irina.

Stumbling out the door, I tighten the blanket around me and walk around the perimeter of the arboretum. I naively hope to find her staring at the night sky while waiting for Finn, but I panic when I don't see her.

I wish I brought shoes with me as I step on sticks and rocks, padding barefoot through the trees. Every inch of me is sore, and my heart feels like it's on fire, but I can't leave her out here alone. And I can't allow Finn to return to her missing.

I pause to take a breath and lean against a tree trunk. I should've never closed my eyes. I should've fought to stay away, but sleep took all of us away from the day's events.

I close my eyes and listen to the soft sounds of leaves lifting off the ground; then terror seizes me as a scream cuts through the silence. I whip my head back and forth, unsure which direction it came from or where I *am*.

It's too dark outside to see the castle towers through the trees.

And the last time I ran through here was to escape Finnian. If only he could find me now.

But the scream echoes through the trees again, giving me a direction. My feet drag across the ground as I run toward it, breaths shortening. But the calls of panic grow louder the closer I get, and I breathe a sigh of relief when I recognize the stables ahead.

Of course, Irina tried to find a horse.

But that doesn't explain why she's screaming.

I shout her name, now fearing the worst and imagining she found my husband dead in Major's stall.

Jogging inside, I gasp when I see her pinned to the ground in Major's stall, kicking and screaming to try and free herself from someone I can't recognize in the dark. I drop to the ground and search for something I can grab quickly, cursing when I bump into multiple hay feeders. Locating something at the end of a short looped rope, I stumble to my feet and swing at the attacker's head. *Twice.*

Surprised to find me—too busy trying to subdue Irina to notice my entrance—he trips over his own feet as he grabs his head, blinking to focus on my silhouette in the doorway.

Irina cries my name as she crawls toward me, using my skirt to pull herself to her feet. But the man slowly lowers his hand and steps into the light, a smugly victorious grin on his mouth. "Well, it looks like I'll be finishing off both of you," Otto sneers, cracking his knuckles.

I'm woozy and swaying, barely able to keep my eyes open, but I'll be damned if our lives end by Otto's hands. Irina takes my hand with hers, her emotions from today bubbling over, and she can't seem to calm down—leaving me as the only levelheaded one to get us out of this.

Fuck.

"I promised I'd see you again," Otto says, glancing down at the weapon in my hand. "You couldn't find anything better than a salt block?"

"It worked," I mutter, tightening my hold on the rope. "Finnian will return any moment."

Otto tips his head back and chuckles a horridly egotistical sound. "Will he? Well, who was it I left for dead on the bridge? Your prince wasn't too—"

"You're a fucking *liar*," Irina interrupts. "You know Finnian well enough to understand that he wouldn't travel across the fucking *bridge*, especially since you were waiting here for him. Who sent you, Otto? Jasper?"

Otto raises his hands in faux innocence. "I was merely out for a stroll when I saw you wander in here."

"You were waiting in Major's godsdamn stall!" she shouts.

Ice coddles my bones. "You were sent to kill Finn?"

Instead of replying, Otto bends, grabs hold of something, and then pulls in one sharp movement. Irina and I fly backward, and I knock my head against the stall door. Otto tosses the blanket at Irina's face to impede her vision as she struggles to find her footing again, blood dripping from the crown of her head.

But his focus is on me now.

I thrash against him as he gathers my wrists in one hand, pinning my legs still by locking them between his. I shout for Irina to run, to free herself while she has the chance, but she doesn't. We're fighting him off within seconds, but we're too weak and tired to keep him down too long.

He grabs hold of our hair in each fist and drags us back inside the stall, away from the moonlight and any chance of being seen, cursing when I'm able to twist enough to bite his hand. Irina claws his face deeply enough to create a gash on his cheek, but that only angers him *more*.

He knocks her head against the wall, and I scream when she stills, trying to reach for her.... Grab her... if I could just...

He yanks me up to my knees and holds my head back with his grip on my hair, leaning his head so close to mine that I can see the whites of his eyes. "Where are your precious faeries now, Princess? Hm? There's no one left to save you."

I brace when he brackets my chin in his other hand, shoving me backward to crawl on top of me. And he's right—the faeries aren't here to fend him off this time. Finnian won't appear with a bow and arrow to shoot through his throat.

And again, I'm left at the mercy of a man.

With one last effort, I entwine my fingers into a solid fist and knock them against his temple. He rebounds as if I didn't touch him at all and instead starts untying the loop at his waist. "I think I need to experience the prince's wife—"

Growling fills the stall from the entrance.

Otto barely has time to glance up before he's attacked by two giant beasts. No, not beasts. *Mastiffs*.

Honora runs inside behind them, looking disheveled and unqueen-like in her panic, bending to peel my hair off my cheeks. I'm not sure when I started crying, but sobs ricochet through my chest, my hand shaking as I point to Irina in the corner. "She hasn't.... he threw her..." I stutter, unable to form words or look at Irina's still body. "She won't wake!"

With distressed eyes, Honora whips her head to where I'm pointing, immediately leaving me to crawl to Irina and pull her into her arms. Zeb and Georgie keep Otto subdued, growling and snapping their teeth whenever he tries to move.

I jump as a hand touches my shoulder from behind. Can barely register Finnian saying my name, my eyes searching the stall in grief-stricken terror at what just unfolded.

Finnian takes my face between his hands and repeats, "Elora, did he touch you?"

I can do nothing but nod and say, "And Irina."

Finnian rolls his neck.

He calls for Zeb and Georgie to come to me, then stands and flexes his hands. Otto crawls backward into a corner, trying to reason with Finnian—reminding him of all the times they spent together training in the army.

Finnian entertains him with slow nods as he approaches, a

breathy, unamused laugh leaving his nostrils. He grabs him by the collar and yanks him up, listening to his pleas to be spared but turning his head to stare at me on the ground.

Then, he looks at his sister passed out in the corner as his mother rocks her and begs her to open her eyes.

Finnian releases Otto's collar, cradles his head in his hands, and snaps his neck.

Otto's limp body falls to the ground.

Finnian barely blinks an eye.

I could write a poem about the charming prince hidden by moonlit shadows, the light in his eyes overcome by darkness with three lives now taken by him.

Beautiful and haunted, this prince of mine.

Massimo runs inside and bends to look at me before the limp body in Honora's arms catches his eye. He falls as he stumbles over to Irina, crying her name, saying words in the language I can't understand but with tears on his cheeks. I crawl toward them, my arms shaking, my body weak, and I use my skirt to dab the blood off her forehead.

Finnian kneels beside me but speaks to Irina when he says, "Open your eyes, Irina." He places his hand on her head, his voice betraying him as it quivers. "Open your eyes, you stubborn little free spirit."

Massimo has her hand pressed against his lips as Honora weeps so much that she's unable to speak. But Finnian doesn't give up, moving in front of me to lean over her. "Open your eyes," he repeats, ignoring the break in his voice, "You're not finished, Irina. Your life hasn't started yet."

"Irina," Massimo pleads, "Amore mio."

I wrap my hand around my throat when Finnian's tears slip free—as he grabs her other hand to hold. "I can't do this without you," he whispers, "I need my little sister. Irina—"

The tiniest groan slips from her lips.

The collective sigh of relief is followed by all of us crowding around her, repeating her name until her eyes open. Honora pulls Irina against her chest and kisses her head as Finnian falls backward to sit with her hand still in his. Massimo leans forward, kisses her cheek and temple, and holds her other hand against his heart.

Irina tries to wiggle free, overwhelmed. But as the memory of the last few moments returns to her, she finds her brother first. "He was waiting on you," she says, clearing her throat from screaming, "He knew you'd be here. Oh, gods, if Elora hadn't found me..."

I shush her and stroke her hair.

She slowly sits up with the assistance of Massimo and Honora, but she tries swatting their hands away to speak to Finn. "I planned to wait for your return,"—she sniffles, pausing to take a breath—"and he came at me. He didn't know I'd be here, Finn. He was going to kill you."

Finnian seems unsurprised. "I'm here, Irina. I'm alive." He props a knee up, exchanges a look with Massimo, then refocuses on her. "And it's time for you to leave."

That's when I realized that Finnian is trying to remain indifferent for this very reason. He knows Irina will not want to leave him, but he wants to free her.

Irina parts her lips. "What?"

Honora covers her eyes as her chest caves in, but she doesn't disagree with Finnian. She doesn't tell him to take back his suggestion because she knows. More than anyone, Honora knows it's unsafe for her daughter to remain when we're about to go to war. Until me, Irina was Jasper's weapon against Finn. For Irina's sake *and* Finnian's, she has to go.

"E' ora che andiamo," Massimo says.

Irina seems to understand him as she shakes her head, her eyes refilling with tears. "I'm not leaving, Finnian. Not now—not after...."—she swallows, continuously shaking her head—"No, I'm not leaving you here with him. We're supposed to protect one another!" Her voice raises. "I can't leave you now!"

"Irina," Finnian says softly, leaning forward, "I am still protecting you by sending you with Massimo. It is time for you to leave this place. It's past time. Leave with Massimo, then come back and visit me after this is over." He forces a half-hearted grin. "I'm all right, Irina. I have Elora. She's as stubborn and cruel to me as you are."

Irina throws her arms up, leaving her mother's hold to rise to her knees. "Are you not hearing me? He sent Otto here to kill you! I cannot leave you *now*."

Finnian steals a glance at the body in the corner of the stall and shrugs. "We knew the day would come eventually. And you were here to stop him, Irina. Jasper knew it'd be one of us. It's easier for him to win this if we're together. One of us has to go."

Honora touches Irina's shoulder. "He is right, my darling. It is safer for you to leave with Massimo."

My darling.

Finn's nickname for me came from his mother. And the warmth from that realization shoves through the fatigued chill in my limbs, threatening to soon send me back into slumber.

"I can't," Irina squeaks, looking at her mother. "I can't leave you here. I can't leave him or Elora...."

"You can," I interrupt gently, taking her hand. "Irina, you can. You've done all you're supposed to as Finn's sister and Honora's daughter. And now, you have to trust that Finnian will end this. And then, you can return to us."

Honora places a hand on her cheek. "Be free, Irina." She presses her forehead to hers. "For me and your brother."

Massimo gives her one of his brightest smiles, pressing her hand to his lips. "I will bring you here to see them whenever you'd like. Any time. But I want to marry you."

Irina blinks away her tears as she looks at Massimo, then Finnian. Finnian's grin pulls at his cheek. "I suppose that's all right. If you want to marry him, that is."

"We will officially recognize it when the time comes," Honora adds, using her thumbs to wipe tears off Irina's cheeks. "But for now, be away from here and marry for love."

Massimo clears his throat, which must've been a signal he and

Finnian thought of beforehand because Finnian leans back and hooks a finger for me to come to him. I leave Irina's side to crawl into his lap, closing my eyes when he kisses my temple and whispers in my ear, "I love you. Are you okay?"

Lie, I silently tell myself.

"Now that you're here," I respond, which isn't a complete fib. I feel better when Finnian is near me, though I'm desperately trying to talk myself into staying awake.

From his front pocket, Massimo produces a gold band. "It is not much—"

"Yes," Irina says.

"You did not let me ask..."

"You've asked plenty already," she responds with a breathy laugh, holding out her hand. "Yes, Massimo, I will marry you."

After asking her dozens of times, Massimo finally received the answer he craved, and his elation was so bright as he slid the ring onto her finger that I smiled with him. Finnian whistles through his teeth as they kiss then grins in contentment as Irina throws her arms around Massimo's neck.

Just stay awake for a little longer.

Sniffling, Irina scoots forward on her knees to us and embraces us, whispering unneeded gratitude to her brother. He responds by mussing her hair and motioning toward the door. "You need to go before Jasper realizes his plan failed. I need to hide Otto's body."

"Take it to the faeries," I say. "Dolfe will burn it before they leave. It'll leave no trace."

Irina looks at me in surprise. "Our doe isn't so innocent anymore, Finnian. What have you done to her?"

"Wicked things," Finn responds with a grin.

I force a smile and keep it plastered on my face as Finnian helps me stand, leaning against the wall as he hugs his sister fully before giving her to Honora for a tearful goodbye. Massimo kisses my head; Finnian pulls me over to him, unable to stand another man's hands on me, then laughs at the instinctive absurdity with Massimo.

Finnian shakes his hand. "Thank you for your help. Please protect my sister with your life."

"Always," Massimo responds with a dip of his chin. He takes Irina's hand. "They are waiting for us on the outskirts. We must go, Irina."

The reality hits Irina as she exchanges one last look of hesitancy with Finnian, but he waves for her to leave. "I will see you again, Irina. This isn't goodbye. Stay hidden until you're far away from here. Write to me when you're safe."

Irina nods, but before Massimo can pull her away, she comes to me and throws her arms around my neck. "You are everything he ever needed," she whispers in my ear, "Find a way to live, Elora. Not just for him, but for you."

I wrap my arms around her waist and squeeze her tightly. "The same goes for you, Irina. Live *well*."

Massimo tugs her hand. She walks backward toward the door, the moonlight making the tears in her eyes shine.

Finnian leaves me to watch them run into the forest, staying until he can no longer see them through the cover the trees and night sky provide them. He takes a moment to collect himself after they've gone before turning toward us again. "Return Elora to the arboretum," he instructs. "I will take Otto's body to Dolfe and free the faeries, and then...."

As he trails off, Honora nods and says, "And then, it begins."

I blink rapidly as my vision blurs, hardly able to hear what he's saying through the stinging torment in my chest. I clench and relax my fingers repeatedly, ignoring the cold sweat on my forehead. We're too close now to stop. If Finnian learns of my nightmare, he'll quit everything for me.

Too many lives would be risked without him.

This is why I came here—to bring freedom to my people. My fading heart can't stand in the way of that.

"Elora," Finnian says, noticing me swaying.

"I'm okay," I whisper, unsure if this is the last time I'll hear his voice. "You can go. Free them. Save them."

"Elora," he says again, panic rising in his tone.

"Did I ever tell you," I murmur, my eyes rolling back, "that your blue eyes felt like home the night we met?"

Finnian shouting my name in anguish is not the last sound I want to hear, but when darkness encompasses me, I fear it is.

Fifty-Eight

The second my eyes open, Honora calls Finnian's name. I can focus well enough to know we're in the arboretum, groaning as I try to lift my head from the soft, *breathing* pillow. The moon shines through the window above me, but Finnian is still here instead of where he should be.

Finnian stops pacing to rush toward me, ignoring my slurred protests. "I'm right where I need to be," he insists repeatedly, placing his hand against my forehead. "She's cooled down, but her eyes are still glazed. I need to fetch the physician—"

"No," I mutter, shivering beneath the blanket. "Azrea."

He nods. "You want me to bring her here?"

"No," I sigh, annoyed. "Go to them. You promised."

His eyes narrow, having the audacity to be upset with *me* right now. "I promised to keep you safe. *Alive.*"

Honora covers me with another blanket. "Kindness, Finn. Listen to her."

I press a palm to my temple to try and suppress the pounding headache. "Azrea is the only way to save me. You have to trust her." I pause to inhale a stuttering breath. "Tell her what's happened. She'll return as soon as she can."

"It won't be soon enough," he growls, the tone of his voice making me want to cower. "I can leave now and find one faster...."

"*No,*" I argue, using Honora's assistance to sit up. "You will complete your first promise to me, Finnian. You will help my people. You cannot do that by allowing Jasper's abuse to continue." My arm shakes from my weight resting on it to keep me upright. "Find Azrea, Finn. She promised to help."

He shakes his head as he backs away. "It is too much of a risk. What if I leave here and return to find you dead? None of this will matter then, Elora. Do you not understand that?"

I look at Honora. "Can you give us a moment?"

Honora stands and gives Finn a warning look before disappearing behind rows of trees. Finnian refuses to look at me, his head turned away, his hands hanging loosely from his waist.

"Finnian."

"I'm not fucking leaving you, Elora."

I will try to remain gentle with him, but he isn't making it easy. "Would you rather sit by my side and wait for me to die than free the ones who can give me a chance of surviving this?"

He scowls at me. "Don't twist my words. That isn't what I'm doing. I will load you into the back of a wagon if I have to and scour these godsdamn lands to find a Healer."

"Finn—"

"I am not leaving you!" he shouts.

"I have no more than a day!" I called back.

He pales, shaking his head in disbelief. "You can't know that."

"I do." I twist my fingers together. "I allowed him to touch me. He touched my heart, Finn. I thought if I could just talk to him.... Reason with him..." Sighing, I pinch the bridge of my nose. "It didn't work. He started taking everything. I barely got out before he could drain it completely."

I shakily throw my legs over the settee, but he falls to his knees before me, not allowing me to stand. "You have to free them," I say. "And you must tell Azrea what I've told you. I know you doubt them. I understand. But you can trust her."

He swallows. "Once I free them, I can't return here. It'll be too late. Too many people will see them leave...."

"I know," I whisper, placing my hands on his shoulders. "I know you can't return to me, but I promise I will fight to stay alive until you do. I won't close my eyes."

"I can't..." His throat bobs. "I can't leave you knowing I might not be returning to your smile." He kisses my hands. "Your scowls. Your laughter." He lays his head in my lap. "Elora, I can't. I'm not strong enough to be without you."

"Then, hurry back." I stroke his hair. "Hurry back to mc. Finnian, I believe in you. I believe in Azrea. It's not over yet. But Finn, you promised them. I need you to think of everyone relying on you—"

He lifts his head. "You are all that matters to me."

I nod. "I know, but their lives matter to me. Selfishly, I would leave here with you and spend all the time I have left in your arms, but none of the people under his rule deserve our abandonment, my love. Stop running from this."

He tucks a stray curl behind my ear, contemplating silently. I can't push him. The more I do, the more he'll argue. Like me, Finnian cannot be forced into something. But if he doesn't leave soon to uphold his promise, I will have to be the one to find a way into Ashbury unseen to free the faeries.

Instead of giving me an answer, he kisses me tenderly but passionately, his hand gently cupping my throat. The fluttering in my stomach from his touch will be what I miss the most, but I don't tell him that. Finnian must leave here in hopes of Azrea finding a Healer in time. I cannot make him feel otherwise.

When he pulls away, he doesn't go far. "Do you promise to remain here? I don't know how long this will take."

I pat Zeb behind me. "I will be here with my bodyguards."

He frowns. "You're being too lighthearted."

Sighing, I rub the tip of my nose against his. "Finn, I'm terrified, but I need you to go into this with a clear mind. Do you think I want to imagine this being the last time I see you? Irina needs a safe place to come home to, Finnian." I laugh lightly. "You know she won't stay away from here long."

He tries to laugh but fails. "You won't close your eyes?"

It wouldn't matter either way. The male took nearly everything; I'm unsure how I'm still breathing. It's unsettling to feel one's heart slipping away as seconds pass, but my life isn't worth thousands. Finnian staying by my side while I fade away will accomplish nothing but harm many.

"I won't close my eyes," I assure him. "Now, go."

He fists my hair in his hand, kisses me again, and whispers, "You felt like home, too."

❧

The moon lowers as we watch the sky together, searching for any sign that Finnian successfully freed the faeries. Honora sits beside me and holds my hand, squeezing any time we think we see something move in the clouds.

"He'll be all right," Honora whispers, pretending it's to assure me, but I hear the worry in her voice. "Finnian has always been strong. He tried so hard for so long to please his father. My cowardice allowed this to happen."

I blink in surprise as I look at her. "You are the reason we went to Hogsfeet. Because of you, he found the strength to finally do what needs to be done."

"It is not because of me." Her eyes light up when she points to the sky. "It is because of you."

I search the skies until my gaze snags on something in the sky—*someone*. Beautiful, solid, healthy wings glide through the sky, soon surrounded by multiple pairs. I raise to my knees and press my palms against the glass, joyfully crying out the names of the ones I can recognize from this far away.

My friends fly through the sky, merely specks of night aside from glimpses of red and orange hair. The comforting thought that my love is experiencing the same life-altering event anchors me when I feel like handing myself over to lingering death.

I trusted him with this, and he proved me right. I know I could close my eyes and leave the fate of my kingdom in his hands, but I made him a promise to try and stay awake.

Just a little longer.

"They're free," I squeak, tears rolling down my cheeks. "Twenty-five years later, they're finally free. He did it."

She rubs my back gently. "You did it together, Elora."

When the sun finally rose, I was nearly asleep on Honora's lap as she pleaded for me to stay awake. She continuously asks me questions about my parents, detailing how Harry approached her with the information about Hogsfeet. I found it too interesting to close my eyes, listening intently about how he admitted to her that he had been planning a years-long takeover of Pumpkin Hollow.

She explained that her friendship with him began over flowers, detailing Jasper's upset when my father gifted her a book on rare flowers from a nearby shoppe during her yearling celebration. My father wasn't invited back to any of her gatherings after that.

But she reiterated multiple times that nothing between them was ever romantic—it was purely companionship, which is why he trusted her enough to inform her of his plans.

He was murdered shortly after.

But when my stomach growls, she insists she leave to find us something to eat. "If Finnian has successfully helped the men of Hogsfeet into Ashbury, Jasper won't be paying attention to my whereabouts."

"You know that isn't true," I argue. "He'll use you to control Finnian. You are exactly who he'd want to find."

"Not anymore." Like Irina often does, she touches the tip of my nose. "You are who he'd want. Or Irina. I am far too old now, Elora. Finnian loves me, yes, but you are his wife. And try as he might, he has not been able to hide his feelings for you in front of his father. He would often stare at you like you hung the moon, even when he tried to do the opposite."

Warmth fills my cheeks as I smile.

"There is a small kitchen near the tea room." She fetched one of the cloaks we arrived in and slid it on. "Lock the door behind me. I will knock thrice. And stay awake."

I nod in confirmation, slowly rising and stretching my arms above my head. My ribs pop, my body aches, but I'm counting down the moments until Finnian returns to me.

I stand from the settee to lock the door, followed closely by Zeb and Georgie, but stumble backward when Bart busts inside, breathless. I consider running, but no tunnels are here to hide me. I quickly glance behind him for Honora but don't spot her. He must've passed her....

"You must come with me, Miss Elora!" he shouts, motioning for me to follow him as he steps outside. "It's Prince Finnian! He was discovered at dawn in Ashbury and dragged back! The king locked him in the crypt!"

What's left of my heart thunders in my chest, my ears ringing as adrenaline floods me. "The queen...."

"Told me you were here," he finishes, bouncing on his toes anxiously. "I have a key, but we must hurry!" He brandished a silver key from his coat pocket and handed it to me as proof. "The queen is already on her way there. Come, come!"

He gives me no time to deny as he takes off toward the castle, leaving me alone in confusion and alarm. Bart knew my mother; he comforted me after I bargained with Jasper.... I can trust him. I should trust him. Leaving Finnian locked in the crypt is a risk I'm unwilling to take.

So, I chase after him, wishing I had thought to grab one of the cloaks on the settee as my curls fly behind me. Every ounce of energy I have left goes toward keeping up with him as he enters through a back door of the castle, holding the door open for me to follow him up multiple sets of stairs to the king's study. "I don't understand," I say breathlessly, trying to keep my voice lowered, "How did he find Finnian?"

"The king was in the greenhouse when he noticed the faeries in the sky," Bart explains, ushering me inside the empty study. "He sent twenty men to Ashbury immediately and discovered the prince assisting men on ladders to enter Ashbury."

"No," I gasp, clutching my heart. "Did he harm him?"

"Not yet, but he has plans, Miss Elora." He opens the door to the dark corridor hiding the crypt below. Lighting one of the lanterns, he guides me through, constantly looking behind us. "The king plans to take Irina next—"

"She's gone," I interrupt. "Irina is safe away from here."

We come upon the door, and Bart takes the key from my hand, nodding as he slides it into the lock. The smell overwhelms me, and I pinch my nose closed, my eyes watering from the foul stench seeping through.

As he opens the door and gestures for me to enter, I blink as heat from the fire he lights burns my eyes as it fills the room. I start to tremble as the former memory of standing in this room jumps to the forefront of my mind, but I push it aside to search for Finnian. But the body lying on the ground doesn't belong to him. As I step inside and crouch, I realize it's Honora. I twist around to find Bart closing the door.

And locking us inside.

I pound on the door with my fists, screaming for Bart. The smell of rotting skulls makes me woozy, and pulling my dress over my nose doesn't help. I turn from the door and lower to my knees, inspecting the mark on Honora's temple. Someone knocked her out quickly after she left me, which meant Jasper knew where we were all along.

And he knows Finn freed the faeries. He knows of the men trying to get into Ashbury. How much of what Bart said was true? He knew too much about our plan. Jasper's army could be marching on Ashbury right now, and I have no way of warning Finn, and Finn won't know where to find me.

I fall backward as I glance up, screaming as B's dark eyes stare back at me, sitting atop a pile of gray heads. I squeeze my eyes shut and cover my ears, shoving the vision away.

He brought me in here to torture me while he tried to find my husband. Gods, he's going to bring me his head. I may as well die now, unable to stomach the thought of seeing Finn's head severed from his body.

The sound of the door slamming closed makes me turn around, naively hoping Bart has come to his senses, but someone far more terrifying than the cowardly ambassador stands before me. With her hands clasped at her waist, her chin held high, and her malicious grin too familiar, Regina stands tall.

I scramble to my feet and clench my fists at my sides. "I should've known it was you all along."

She looks me over from head to toe, her gaze snagging on the faded yet prominent mark on my throat. "My, my," she sneers, "You've certainly become comfortable in your role."

"It's not a role," I snapped, ignoring the urge to cover my nose. She fittingly seems entirely unbothered by the smell of rotting skulls. "You were wrong about Finnian. He loves me."

She unclasped her hands to reveal the silver key. "Does he? Hmm, perhaps that's true. Maybe that is why he fell into our trap so easily."

My mouth dries.

Her close-mouthed laugh makes me wish her skull was one of the ones decaying in this room. "Were you unaware? I worried he might've been too worldly to fall for such a simple scheme, but I have often overestimated men." She looks around the room, not even batting an eyelash at the death behind me. "Your father always thought he was so cunning, leaving every night and not returning until morning."

She spins the key around her finger. "For years, I wondered if he was having an affair. I didn't mind, of course, since I had the money, but one evening, I grew tired of allowing him to think he was stealthy." She sighs deeply. "So, I followed him. I watched him climb down that pathetic excuse for a ladder and drop into Hogsfeet. I watched him disappear into the night and not return until morning, smelling like sweat and dirt."

"You knew," I whisper, "You knew the entire time."

"Of course, I knew. Your father wasn't a bright man, Ellie, but he was resourceful." She rolls her eyes in annoyance. "Day in and out, he lived with the guilt of his decisions. He talked of your mother far too many years after her death. And I grew tired of looking after his daughter while he convinced himself he could make up for everything he did."

"Looking after?" I scoff. "You did nothing for me."

She ignores my accusation. "I knew if he somehow succeeded at bringing an invasion to Pumpkin Hollow, life as I knew it would be over. I had grown quite accustomed to purchasing what I wanted and having the largest manor in Ashbury. Little did I know, he was sending his money to some orphan in Hogsfeet and stealing from my daughters."

"From *me*," I interject. "*You* stole from *me*."

She tends to her tight bun, smoothing stray hairs. "As you can imagine, that was quite upsetting to learn. I couldn't take it anymore, so I went to the king. I told him I had information about the man he trusted so much but wanted something in exchange."

I tilt my head. "*You* bargained me away?"

Her replying scowl brings back all the feelings of shame I used to carry daily. "Please, Ellie, do not believe yourself so mighty that I would offer the king *you*. I offered him something far greater than an unloved child. I offered him an heir."

I jerk my head back in confusion. "An heir? You.... You laid with the king?"

"No, stupid girl." A victorious grin on her mouth spreads. "I offered him my beautiful, untouched daughters. In exchange for ridding me of your father, I promised to allow him to sleep with Dolly and Daffodil until a new heir is bred."

"*Bred*," I repeat in disgust.

"Of course, ridding himself of Finnian was a bit more complicated. That's where you came in." She steps closer, knowing I have nowhere to retreat. "He needed proof of treason before he could declare Finnian unable to take the crown someday. He had grown impatient with Finnian's unwillingness to wed."

I bite my tongue. Finnian had a reason for not wanting to wed, but not even a torturer could pull his secret out of me. I will carry it with me to the afterlife.

"You were raised decently. Harry had spoken about you to the king often." Her look of loathing I know well returns in full force. "He bragged about the motherless girl he rarely paid attention to, perhaps in hopes of Finnian bedding you."

Honora flinches behind me as she begins to wake, but it doesn't deter Regina from continuing, "Jasper hoped Finnian would fall for you and continue Harry's plan, especially once I told him that you were aware of it the entire time."

Tears spring to my eyes. "I had no knowledge—"

She waves me off. "It doesn't *matter*. Finnian did exactly as Jasper wanted. He fell for the fallen princess and followed her to Hogsfeet." Her eyes flicker to Honora on the ground behind me. "Of course, learning his wife was the one who sent the two of you there was disheartening, but he was comforted by your sisters."

"They are not my sisters!" I shout, my voice echoing off the walls in this chamber of injustice. "And you are not my family! You spent years punishing me because my father didn't love you."

She throws her head back in laughter. "You believe I did all of this because I wanted the love of a weak man? I wanted power, Elora. Security. I wanted a guarantee that I wouldn't become another beggar on the streets of Ashbury, so I took control. Unlike your weak mother who stayed with a traitor, *I* became one. How foolish of you to believe I would've allowed you to have the crown while we stayed behind in the manor. No, stupid girl, you were merely a pawn in a long chess game."

I refuse to break in front of her, but my voice quivers as I ask, "You used me for the king to find a reason to kill his son?" My head shakes. "I don't understand. I never did anything to you. I was kind to you; I did as you asked...."

"And that was your mistake. You were too eager to please." She doesn't look away from me as Honora sits up, clutching her forehead. "My only regret is waiting so long to throw the plan into motion. I could've saved myself the headache of dealing with you for so long. Oh, well. I will soon be the grandmother of the heir to one of the strongest kingdoms."

She finally looks down at the queen. "There, there. You will see your son again soon." With a parting evil grin, she turned to leave but looked at me over her shoulder. "Part of him, at least. Goodbye, Ellie. You were as disappointing as I knew you would be. Say hello to your mother for me."

Fifty-Nine

I lay curled in a ball on the crypt floor, waiting by the door like a dog longing for its owner. I've accepted that it's over—that we've lost. Irina was right—I trusted too easily. Because Bart knew my mother once, I willingly followed him here to be locked away while the king kills my husband in hopes of impregnating Dolly or Daffodil. He wants to start over, free of Finnian and Irina, away from a queen who has spent years protecting her children from him.

Instead of letting us all go, he wants to kill us, but not without torturing us first. We all fell into his trap, laid out by a woman I shared a roof with—a woman who has known me since I was young. She spent most of my life wondering how she could use me for her benefit and finally found one.

Again, because of my father.

I should've stayed in the manor, grateful for the rags I wore, living day to day visiting the faeries and never longing for more. Because I wanted to save my town, I ended up sacrificing everyone. Ashbury will be wiped off maps, forgotten it ever existed. No one will remain alive to try and build an army. The men of Hogsfeet, who have waited over two decades to seek revenge, will be eliminated. And Jasper will win, just as he knew he would. All this time, he was the puppet master, and we were all on strings.

"I'm sorry," I whisper, "I'm so sorry I failed."

Honora squeezes my hand, neither of us having the energy left to weep for the man we will soon lose—the man who holds the majority in our hearts. "He constructed this room when I was sent away for Irina's birth. I didn't know of its existence until he first brought Finnian here as punishment for something I can't remember."

I rest my head on her shoulder.

"After I returned with Irina, I planned on leaving him. After he brought Finnian here, I nearly did. Everything was packed. A carriage was loaded, but he chased me outside. He promised he'd always find me. It wouldn't matter how far I went. He would find me, kill me, and take my children."

She releases a weak breath. "I believed him. I didn't want to live with the constant fear of looking over my shoulder to see him standing there. I wanted Finnian and Irina to have a good life. Returning to my kingdom wasn't an option. It would've been the first place he looked. I have regretted that day ever since. I despise myself for being so weak."

"You couldn't know what he'd be like."

"He had the mother of my daughter killed and punished my son by locking him inside a crypt. I knew exactly the kind of man he was becoming, but leaving seemed harder." She pats my hand. "You fought for love, Elora. It doesn't matter what that horrid woman tries to tell you. You fought. You did not fail. You brought my son immense joy. You helped my daughter feel welcomed in her own home. You did not fail."

I roll my head against the door. "You didn't, either. You made a choice to keep your family safe. You thought what you were doing was what they needed." I smile despite our current predicament. "Finnian is the man he is because of you. You gave him someone to protect and honor long before I came along. You encouraged his closeness with his sister. You didn't let her feel unwelcome by her brother, even if they knew they were siblings by fate first and foremost."

I continue, "You raised two kind, decent humans. That is not a failure. They know what love is because of you."

She rests her head atop mine. "You have more kindness in you than anyone else I've ever known, Elora. I hope you know the power that holds."

I laugh breathily, trying to conjure some feeling of joy. "If I only I knew how to sweet-talk a door, this would be much more simple—"

I'm interrupted by a key sliding into the lock and the doorknob twisting. We stand and hold one another, watching the door in anticipation for the first life lost of someone we love, bracing as the door opens to reveal....

"Irina!" I gasp.

She rolls her eyes. "You didn't truly believe I'd leave, did you? Gods, Finnian is unbelievable. '*Write to me when you're safe*,'" she mocks in a deep voice. "Idiot. I didn't spend decades of my life keeping him alive for him to die now."

We both stare at her in shock and confusion.

Irina tosses a hand up. "We can stand here and talk about it, or we could perhaps leave this fucking creepy crypt and *do* something."

She holds the door open, annoyed by how long it takes us to get over our bewilderment and leave the crypt. "Ignore Bart's body," she instructs, motioning to him on the floor. "I tried to reason with him, but Massimo has no patience with men who deny me."

On cue, Massimo appears from the darkness. "It is clear. No one else remains in the castle. Everyone was ordered to take shelter. We must go if we want to help Finn." He jogs behind us and slides his hands under Bart's shoulders to drag him inside the crypt, closing the door behind him.

"Mother." Irina spins on her heel to face her. "Massimo is going to take you somewhere safe. I will escort Elora to Finnian. Seeing her will encourage him to continue."

Honora places her hands on her hips. "Explain. Now."

Irina blows wisps of hair from her face. "We went to the outskirts to wait until we saw the faeries. I knew Jasper sending Otto to the stables meant more than simply trying to kill one of us. Otto was a distraction. While we were all in the stables, the wanderers watched for any movement from the army. Sure enough, soldiers split into groups to march toward the bridge. While Finnian was freeing the faeries, Massimo climbed down one of the ladders on the cliffside to warn them of Jasper's plan to invade before they're ready."

I blink in confusion. "How did you know—"

"You were here? Jasper's forms of torture involve two methods. The guillotine or this fucking room." Irina took our hands and dragged us down the corridor as Massimo followed with a lantern. "I returned to the arboretum right after noticing you running into the castle behind Bart."

I look over my shoulder at Massimo, my mind reeling. I've been poked at by a skeleton in a nightmare, attacked in a horse stall, and locked in a crypt by my stepmother and the king's ambassador, all within a day's time. I'm wondering if *this* is the nightmare I'm trapped in instead.

"Regina informed me this has been planned for months," I say.

"Shocking," Irina mutters. "She's using her daughters. I thought I recognized those imbeciles at the ball but couldn't place how. It took seeing them at your wedding to remember why. I was strolling the castle late one night when I saw Jasper bringing them to his quarters. I thought it could be a coincidence until I learned you swore an oath to him." She side-eyes me in disapproval. "I told you not to do that, by the way."

I huff through my nose.

Irina continues, "While you kept my dear brother distracted and out of my hair, I started digging alone. As I've always said, maids have the best gossip. Wenches."

"Irina," Honora sighs.

"Apparently, the more annoying stepsister..."

"Daffodil," I mutter instantly.

"Sure, that one," Irina says. "Jasper favors her, but she is having trouble becoming pregnant. I thought that was an odd piece of information about one of his mistresses and wasn't sure why it mattered, but when Otto attacked me in Major's stall, it all came together."

Massimo steps ahead and opens the door leading into the king's study. "She was livid when Finnian wouldn't listen to her reasoning," he says.

I snort from imagining the earful Massimo must've received after Irina was sent away.

"Like always, I must do everything for him," she continues. "Finnian is beloved and too entertaining to locals to eliminate without cause. Jasper needed a random murder to take place. It would catapult our people into sympathetic condolences. Knowing my mother's age, they wouldn't discourage Jasper from taking a mistress for another heir."

"You speak as if I'm dead," Honora says.

With an apologetic grin, Irina sighs. "He wouldn't have killed you. He would've made you stay and show approval for his new child. For some reason, he will not let you go."

"Believe it or not," Honora says quietly, "I believe he loved me once. And once you love someone, you will always feel they belong to you, even if it's been years since that was true."

I haven't experienced that myself, but after seeing Agnes with Finnian, I believe her. Witnessing Finn moving on angered her, but I don't think Finn would react differently if I fell in love with someone else. He's repeatedly warned me that he would prevent that from happening.

But the difference is, while Finnian might be obsessively possessive over me, he honors me. He respects me. His mother hasn't been given that by her husband. Finnian wouldn't spend a lifetime making me miserable and refusing to allow me to leave him. His love isn't poisonous. It might be overprotective and domineering, but also lovely and enlightening.

In all the best ways.

While thinking of him, I ask, "Does Finnian know you're here?"

Irina snorts. "Of course not. I prefer to surprise him." She studies me with an amused grin. "I hope you're ready to fight a war, doe."

❧

Massimo escorted the queen from the castle, but I didn't inquire where he planned to take her. Before departing the castle, Irina managed to drag us to the stables unseen, if only because Jasper enlisted the help of his entire army to capture his son. Irina doesn't believe Jasper will kill Finn outright—he'll make him watch us perish first.

Unlike the pathway we typically take toward Ashbury, I can only assume Massimo taught Irina their hidden trails as we raced over overgrown grass and around trees on the outskirts of both kingdoms. It's treacherous and slippery, the mud moistened from rainfall. The faeries are gone, but decades' worth of ash still lingers in the air, sticking to the ground the horse is kicking onto our clothing. And as we near the bridge, I hear the sounds a person should never have to hear.

Cries of war.

Men grunting, weaponry clanking, and people screaming. But since the people of Pumpkin Hollow were warned to take shelter, I can only assume those are the shrieks of terror from my people as Finnian tries to hold off his father's army.

"I need you to get my people to safety!" I shout over the noise, whipping my head back and forth as I try to locate the chaos through the shelter of the trees. "Cross the bridge and find them! Escort them away from this!"

Instead of verbally replying, Irina nods.

As soon as the trees opened, we skidded to a stop, nearly falling off the jagged cliffside that encased the bridge. And my jaw drops open as what's unraveling beneath me. Men—some in armor, some without—are battling with swords while some of Jasper's men line the end of the bridge with artillery I've never seen before, loading them with powder.

I frantically search the bridge for Finnian, preventing myself from shouting his name, but Irina finds him first. She slaps my thigh repeatedly until I follow her finger, crying his name when I see him in the middle of a brawl. Covered in caked blood and wearing armor made of black, Finnian does not look like the gentle lover I've come to know. My husband is a weapon—a painting come to life of a warrior in battle.

But only half of his men are shielded and protected with steel plates against Jasper's fully armored army, and I cover my ears each time I hear a blade cutting through flesh. I will never be able to unsee the blood, the limbs cut from bodies, or the looks of sheer terror in the eyes of men as they're cut down.

We are losing.

On the opposite side of the bridge, Jasper awaits in an open carriage, his smugness sickening as death unfolds before us. He's watching his son fight his men with amusement, and I snap. I pry the reins from Irina's hand, shout for her to hold on, and kick the horse into a leap off the cliff.

I imagined landing smoother, though I don't know why. I've read about wars and chilling, heroic moments like the one I just attempted in fictional stories, and I suppose I thought I could have a story written about the time I leaped off a cliff on a horse *not* trained by my husband and landed on all fours.

That's not what happened.

Irina had chosen the first horse we found in a rush—one not as spoiled as Major and certainly not as strong. Instead of landing gracefully, the horse skidded before collapsing altogether, tossing us off his back and onto the glass bridge.

Already near death from faerie magic, rolling across a rigid bridge while partially bumping into multiple men was not helpful. My ribs ache, my head pounds, and the pain from landing has caused every limb to shake and quiver as I try to stand too quickly to avoid being stabbed. So much fighting was unraveling around me that no one appeared to notice me crawling toward Irina a few feet away, who was cursing at me in the language Massimo speaks while holding her head.

I would apologize, but I learned long ago that falling in love has made me not think clearly. Seeing Finnian fighting against men he was raised with, trained beside, and knew firsthand the repulsive behavior his father exhibited daily angered me.

I didn't, however, consider that landing in the middle of the battle would risk our lives.

The horse we arrived on is long gone, running off shortly after tossing us off. Irina looked around, put her fingers in her mouth, and whistled. I dodge a sword, tumbling backward into Irina's lap as she braces with her arms over our heads. But our savior doesn't come in the form of a charming prince—it's a white horse. He cuts through the crowd and kicks up on his hind legs, whinnying and knocking the man away from us.

Irina grabs my hand to pull me toward Major, but I yank free and shake my head. "Get Finn off the bridge!" I yell.

Irina widens her eyes, shaking her head and trying to reach for me again. I step away, ignoring the tears filling my eyes, and repeat, "Get him off the bridge, Irina! I'll see you on the other side!"

Irina hesitates, looking toward where we saw Finnian, then back to me. Wordlessly, she throws her arms around my neck, kisses my cheek, and tearfully releases me. "Live," she instructs me before backing away until she has to climb onto Major.

Before I bolted to the other side of the bridge to hide beneath brush and tumbling rock, I watched her ride away toward her brother. And then, hidden underneath my hood, I waited for someone else to fall.

After witnessing death so many times within moments, I started to become numb to it. I recognized no one from either side, grateful I hadn't seen Gus or Reynold yet but no longer naive enough to believe they'd come out of this unscathed. It's the second war in twenty-five years for three kingdoms. This one will undoubtedly scar many of us for years to come, just as the first did.

But hopefully, there will be one less king.

It doesn't take long for a sword near me to fall from the hand of one of Gus' men. I meet his eyes just before the light leaves him —seconds before his soul is carried into whatever afterlife we have after this place. And for a breath, I'm reminded why I'm doing this —why I'm risking everything.

Like so many others before him, this man gave his life to protect me. Even if I was only a thought, even if it was years before my birth, their families died trying to defend my kingdom—the one my father betrayed.

I could live my final moments with Finn as faerie magic encases my heart, or I could fight through to my last breath, saving the men hurt by my father's actions.

I take the seconds spared and leave my spot against the cliff, ducking and dodging swings, ignoring the glances of men on both sides as they notice me darting across to retrieve the fallen sword. Leaning down, I grab the grip and act as if it would be that easy to hold, but it humbles me quickly as I stumble backward. "Hades," I snap to myself, adding my second hand to lift the blade.

A man lunges toward me, but all I can do is stand here and hold the sword that's too heavy to swing, panicking as the sharpened point nears me. But before it reaches my ribcage, it's blocked by another. I whip around to see Reynold holding him off, yelling for me to *move*.

I have less than seconds to do what I came here for, but I can think of no parting words for the brother I was never allowed to know. Instead, I only nod and drag the sword with me through dozens of men, hopping over bodies and groaning as my energy wanes until numbness sets in.

Last breaths, Elora.

I have to make them count.

On one side of the bridge, Jasper leans forward in his carriage as he spots me, shouting something to the line of men waiting beside him—men he hasn't even needed to deploy yet because of the blood spilled by the men on the other end of the bridge. The men who just want to reclaim what belongs to them—fathers, sons, and brothers who wish to provide for their families. As I stand in the middle, looking between each side, sweat pouring off my body from the bodies and loss of lives at my feet, I realize in a split second that it was never us or them. This was never a battle between Ashbury and Pumpkin Hollow. Every person here was manipulated by two men.

That was all it took to enact decades of injustice—the words of two men. And if my life can be the answer to years of separation, then it's worth it....

"Elora!"

A horror-filled voice breaks through my thoughts. My hood has fallen down, revealing who lurks beneath. And as Finnian steps forward to come after me, Irina tries to hold him back. A tear slips down my cheek as I stare at the man I was told for so long was my enemy, now the reason I've held on as long as I have. But the faeries are gone, no Healer has come, and I can't live my last moments knowing I failed my people.

I love you, I mouth to him, tearing my eyes away from him when he breaks free from Irina's grip and runs toward me.

With all my might, I raise the sword above my head, time slowing around me as bodies fall and blood spills over my bare feet. Jasper's shouts for me to stop are only sounds muffled from the years of abuse at the forefront of my mind.

"I love you," I say again and again to Finn as he races toward me. I squeeze my eyes shut. "You were well worth the sacrifice, my love, but now I must smash the pumpkins."

I drive the point of the sword into the bridge.

And the glass fractures.

Blue eyes, Violet skies
Cradle me in slumber
Blue eyes, Violet skies
A dream to wish, so full of wonder

The fracture lengthens and widens into a crack, splitting the glass on either side of my feet. Fragmented webs split off multiple ruptures, causing me to stumble to the side. Finnian sways and extends his arms to steady himself on the opposite end of me, calling my name again, but it isn't enough to stop me from lifting the sword and stabbing the bridge again.

The sound that echoes through the valleys resembles rolling thunder, but the skies are clear of rain. The glass splits beneath my feet and sends men toppling over, ricocheting through the empty lands of dead crops and hollow rocks. Jasper climbs out of his carriage, his arms flailing as he tries to stop me from doing it again —but trying would be pointless. The fissure extends into the dirt pathway toward Pumpkin Hollow, stretching farther than I can see and sending the king falling to his knees as he loses his balance.

He crawls toward the bridge, even as the split in the ground is headed directly toward his kingdom. It's the godsdamn pumpkins he'd rather save—not his children, not his wife, not even his kingdom as the sound of ground splitting through town fills the air once filled with cries of terror.

The king is on his knees for the pumpkins trapped beneath. But the sound of glass breaking on our left has every head snapping toward the noise. Within seconds, the castle turrets that can be seen from the bridge teeter and fall, shattering so loudly against the ground that we cover our ears.

I drop the sword to the ground as I sway, the last of me simply slipping away. Reynold grabs my hand and tugs me with him toward Finnian, but my foot catches on the piece of broken glass, tearing the flesh enough that blood drips across the glass. Reynold twists to grab me as Finnian shouts my name repeatedly, hopping over bodies and shoving men aside.

Just hold on, I silently beg my heart.

One more touch, one more kiss.

As Reynold cradles me against his chest, running toward my husband while I slip in and out of consciousness, he stumbles backward when a thick vine sprouts from beneath the weakened glass. He trips on another that appears behind us, and I slip out of his grip and fall to the shards below.

I can hardly feel the sharp ends cutting my skin; I can scarcely tell the difference between the skies above anymore as they morph into twisted hues of purple through my glazed eyes.

As the bridge collapses, splitting in two, bodies drop into a chasm of pumpkins and darkness, and I fall with them.

My only regret is waiting so long to do it.

My last vision of this world, which was never meant for my survival, is a burst of orange flame in the magenta evening sky followed by frantic blue eyes, sending me into the deep, eternal abyss.

Sixty

I dodge growing vines and leaves longer than me as they sprout from the shattered bridge, skipping pieces that have not broken yet to get to her and reach her. Nothing matters now. Every moment of my life before this one just does not matter. All that I care about is finding her.

And when she tumbles down into the chasm of pumpkins and glass, I dive after her. Her eyes flutter closed, but I refuse to accept it's over. Even as vines wrap around her waist and arms, trying to claim her and take her away from me, I fall.

If she goes down, I will follow her into the afterlife.

We'll find the bottom of this pit together.

Extending my arms toward her as we tumble down, our bodies knocking against pumpkins and stems as they boldly rise from their glass tomb, I brush her dress with my fingertips. Her fragile, lifeless body hits a white pumpkin, and the sound of a snap within her causes a chest-splitting scream to leave me.

I land on a more prominent pumpkin beside hers and crawl off mine to land on the opposite side of where her body rests. "Elora!" I bellow, shakily rising to my feet to try and run, nearly losing my footing each time the pumpkin hits another as it grows.

The vine around her stomach starts to pull her farther away from me, but if she disappears below, there's a chance I won't be able to find her. The determination to touch her shoves through the panic and devastation of possibly never hearing her voice again.

I almost reached her when I stopped and shielded my eyes from the flames that intruded the chasm to begin burning the vines as they grew and wrapped around the cliffside on either side. Looking up, I find dozens of faeries flying above us, loosening more flames toward what remains of my father's army.

Elora was right—they came back for her.

Not just Azrea, but all of them.

Revitalized, I refocus on my wife and lunge, sweat building, nearly engulfed in flames, and grab her hand right before she slips. With my other hand, I try to untangle the vine around her stomach, shouting for it to release her, groaning and growling from its strength against mine. The solidity of the thick crawler compared to my weakened state is tugging me down with her instead of loosening.

"No!" I shout repeatedly, crying out in pain as my shoulder strains from trying to hold onto her while it pulls.

Landing on a stem opposite me, Cedric searches beneath Elora's body. "Hold on!" he shouts before diving under her.

I release the vine around her waist and hold onto her arm with both hands, digging my boots into one of the deep ridges of the outer shell, groaning as I try to *just hang on.*

"Open your eyes, darling," I rasp, using a hand to try and touch her cheek, "open your eyes, Ellie!"

Her body is bowed and stretched, her head tipped back, and her curls knotted and weighed down from moisture. Bruised purple and red from the fall, my delicate, porcelain doll is splintered.

I turn my head when fire erupts beneath her, then jerk back when the vine releases her and Cedric catches her from falling. An unnatural amount of relief and gratitude pulse in my chest, even as she's in the arms of the male who wanted to steal her from me. He looks at her limp body in his arms with heartache and disbelief. "We were too late," he croaks.

"Cedric!" I shout, refusing to believe that. "Healer! Take her!"

Tearfully, wordlessly, he nods and springs off the side of the pumpkin, carrying my wife away. I search above me for something to grab to ascend out of the chasm, but the more the pumpkins rise, the thicker the vines become, shielding the opening and cliffs from view.

I see Irina bending over and reaching for me from my inches-wide view. She's miles above me, but I grab the petiole of a leaf and use it to balance as I try going for a vine. My boot slips, and I nearly fall, wincing when Major's alarmed neigh cuts through the panicked, shocked shouting of men tumbling down into the chasm as they try to avoid being taken by one of the vines. Retribution for being trapped for so long, if I had to guess.

The inches of light slowly disappear, trapping me within. "Irina!" I call out, unsure if she can hear me, "I can't!"

I shove at pumpkins bigger than anything I've ever seen, wider and taller than they appeared beneath the glass, and I am met with nothing but unmovable shells. I knock into vines with my shoulder, try to rip away leaves with my hands, curse each time I find a piece of glass, and smear blood across my pants. "Irina!" I yell repeatedly, barely able to hear Major's whinnies in return.

As the pumpkins and vines grow, they push me farther down. The pit becomes engrossed in shadows and darkness, preventing me from seeing anything but the endless void beneath me. Exhaustion overcomes me as I fall to my knees, tipping my head back as breaths shorten from the oxygen unable to enter the entrapment. And all I can take solace in is that Elora wasn't taken by the poison these pumpkins brought to our lives.

I knock the shell with my fist.

These godsdamn pumpkins, my fucking father... is still alive. He's still alive. Elora may have shattered the bridge, but his reign isn't over. I didn't fulfill my promise to her.

No, this isn't over yet.

Shoving a hand through my hair, I pull myself up by gripping the stem. And then, I climb. I yank and pull away leaves, use my foot to break through thick, broad, stocky axils, and keep my wife at the forefront of my mind. Even as my muscles ache and I can hardly see through the darkness surrounding me, I hold that infuriating, stubborn, beautiful, kind creature with me and fight.

Each step is met with cursing, and each cut is met with a groan or a growl, but I don't stop moving, searching for the light. But it's not sunlight that greets me; it's bursts of orange.

I rear back when one nearly grazes my hand, shouting for whoever is trying to clear the vegetation away. Reaching up, I sigh in relief when someone wraps their hand around mine, smiling when Brig peeks through the small opening.

"Need some help?" he asks with a grin.

My smile is replaced by a smug nod. "I need you to take me to my father."

Brig matches my arrogance. "It would be my pleasure."

❧

Brig doesn't have to take me far.

Jasper is hobbling away, his leg seemingly hurt in the scuffle and intrusion of his precious pumpkins. Brig drops me to my feet to retrieve my sister from the other side, aware of my plan for my dear father. His men, now many, many less, do not come to his defense when they notice me stalking toward him. After losing over half the army to defend magical fruit, they have finally realized how twisted his priorities are.

Jasper looks over his shoulder at me and limps faster. Even if he could get away, there's nowhere left for him to hide. When Elora broke the bridge, the castle fell, too.

I consider taunting him with a slow catch, but returning to Elora quickly prevents that. Grabbing his collar, I kick his weak leg out from underneath him and hold tightly to his shirt when he falls backward. He knocks against my fist while I drag him with me toward the chasm, trying to remind me who I serve and where my allegiance lies.

I silently encourage him to keep talking, as it only propels my anger with him. Irina looks at me across the deep canyon when Brig lands beside her. Even over a mile away, I can see the amused smile that lifts her cheeks.

From behind her, another male appears, speaks with her, and flies overhead toward what remains of Pumpkin Hollow.

Reaching the edge of the ravine, I toss my father forward. He crawls backward until his hand slips off, looking behind him with a terrified shriek at the darkness beneath him.

"This is what you wanted, right?" I ask, motioning to the plump pumpkins. "Everything you've put us through since childhood was for these. I thought I'd reunite you."

He wobbles to his feet, trying to step away from the impending doom, and raises his hands defensively. "Listen to me, boy. Everything I did was to protect our family—"

I can't resist the urge to laugh darkly. "Our family? No, no." I wait for Brig to gently set Irina beside me on the ground. "She is my family. Our mother protected us." I step forward, flexing my hands at my sides. "Elora...." I swallow at the mention of her name, glancing at the mountains on the other side. "Elora is my family. And you hurt her."

He shakes his finger at me. "She chose to break the bridge on her own! I did not force her—"

"You gave her no other choice!" Irina shouts behind me. "Just as you never gave us any other choice but to listen and obey every order!"

He narrows his eyes at her. "I gave you a life of luxury! I could've had you killed, just as I had your harlot of a mother—"

"Enough!" I shout, lurching forward and shoving him backward a step. "*Enough*. Enough of your fucking manipulation, enough of your poison in our lives."

From behind him, carrying a vine in his hands, Brig appears. After a deep nod from me, he wrapped it around Jasper's throat, and then I took it from Brig as Jasper's eyes widened. His hands wrap around the vine and pull, trying to loosen it from around his throat.

"Son, son, listen to me—"

I shake my head. "I think I've done enough of that for a lifetime." Using every ounce of anger I feel toward him, I tighten the strand around his throat. "This is for my sister." I tie a knot at the base of his neck, tight enough for his face to turn purple. "This is for my mother."

I lean forward and hold his bloodshot gaze, grinning when he cowers. "And this, you fucking bastard, is for my wife." Taking one step away, I ram a boot into his stomach and kick him into the bottomless pit of pumpkins.

Brig dives after him with a grin, and seconds later, flames shoot out of the chasm as they burn through my father's body.

I tip my head toward the sky and release a breath so deep that my body shakes from the liberation of a lifetime of weight on my shoulders. But we don't have time to celebrate before another person is dropped to the ground from a few feet up.

Irina pops up beside me. "Thank you, Raul."

Raul lingers above with a scowl at the woman he dropped to the ground before soaring toward the mountains.

Regina stands shakily, looking every bit like the counterpart to Jasper's evil schemes. Her glower is pinned to my sister, but Irina doesn't even let her speak before she shoves her into the abyss.

Irina glances at me over her shoulder with a shrug. "Her voice has always grated my nerves. Wench."

I try to smile at her, but emotion overcomes me when the realization of freedom sinks in. When it hits her simultaneously, she falls into my arms, weaving her arms around my waist. We did it; we made it out of his clutches alive. Together.

Years of abuse and torment, days spent wondering when or if it'll ever end, finally happened. My little sister is alive and safe at the expense of hundreds of lives, and all because of Elora—the one who made the ultimate sacrifice for us.

"Go tell Mother," I breathe as the bittersweet moment with my sister changes into full-fledged dread and desperation, bringing me back to reality. "I need to find my wife."

I run through the mountain cave entrance, shoving through dozens of faeries to find Azrea kneeling over Elora's body by the spring and speaking with a faerie that looks nothing like the Cinders. She would look almost human with long black hair, pointed ears, and bright green eyes if not for the black fingertips. Instead of a Healer, she resembles death, and I nearly knock her away from my wife before Dolfe appears in front of me and grabs my shoulders.

"She's trying to heal her," he assures me.

"Is she…." I can hardly get the words out.

"Her spine is broken," he whispers, holding me upright when my knees give out. "The fall should've killed her, but Circe feels her holding on somehow."

I cover my eyes with my hand, relief pulsing at the hope that gives me. "She promised," I rasp through the swelling in my throat, "she promised to wait for me."

He squeezes my shoulders and allows me to pass him when my breathing steadies enough for me to walk toward her, but my body threatens to collapse all over again when I see my broken wife covered in purple bruises.

"Talk to her," Azrea encourages, taking my hand and pulling me to kneel beside her. "She'll hear you."

I gather my remaining courage and take one of Elora's hands between mine, wiping tears from my cheeks with my shoulders. "Ellie," I whisper, bringing her hand to my lips. "Darling, I'm here. I need you to hold on for me." I tap my forehead against her hand, unable to imagine living a day without seeing her eyes. "Little doe, please don't leave me."

Leaning forward, I press my forehead to hers and kiss her featherlight. "I love you endlessly, darling, don't you realize that? I cannot go on without you. I need your sweet, honeyed venom to remind me to breathe, Elora. You must remind me daily of how awful I am without you." I kiss her again and again. "Open your eyes, you stubborn, perfect creature. *Live*, Ellie, live with me. See the world with me, darling."

Her lack of movement adds to my despair. I glance at the Healer behind me. "What can you do for her?"

Circe exchanges a glance with Azrea before looking at me. "I can save her, but it will come at a deep cost."

That infuriates me. "She has already given *everything*."

Circe nods in understanding. "This will bring the end of her life as a human. I can heal her, but it is because of the Fae magic within her that she's held on this long. Once that slips away, once her heart stops beating, it will be too late."

I blink in confusion. "You want.... To kill her?"

"And bring her back as Fae," Azrea confirms.

Dolfe steps forward. "Our blood is powerful enough to do so, but we must act quickly. She has to consume it before the last beat of her heart. But she will not be as you've known her when she awakens. She will be...."

"Immortal," I finished.

"We are not immortal," Azrea corrects, "but she will live a very long, healthy life."

I swallow, unable to comprehend everything they're telling me. "But.... You have mates, don't you?" I rise but look at her nearly lifeless body. "What if...." I searched her face, shaking my head. "Can you make me Fae, too? I can't.... I can't make this decision for her unless I sacrifice myself, too."

Azrea grabs my arm. "Finnian, you would have to die. We cannot turn humans unless they're near death. Even then, there is no guarantee that you would be her mate. That is only decided by fate."

"I don't care," I replied quickly. "I don't care if I'm her mate. It won't stop me from loving her. I need to die with her. If it doesn't work, if she doesn't come back, allow me to follow her into the afterlife. But I cannot decide her fate without being willing to make the same choice. You must kill me."

And selfishly, I can't fathom living a lifetime with her as Fae while I remain human—knowing that when I die someday, she'll have hundreds of years to live without me and possibly in the comfort of someone else. At least if I die with her, we'll be together wherever awaits us next.

If we're both turned, I'll find a way to force fate to allow me to love her as endlessly as we promised one another.

Circe looks from Elora to me with apologetic eyes. "We cannot kill humans outright. We are bound by rules—"

"I'll do it," Dolfe interrupts, "I'll be the one."

Azrea whips her head toward her mate. "You cannot! You will be punished if the High Fae realizes what you've done."

Kneeling, Dolfe touches her cheek. It is the most tender I've witnessed him, and he gazes upon her like I look at Elora. "It is time I pay for what I did," he whispers to her before looking at my wife. "She gave her all for us despite the choice I made for her. It is the least I can do to make up for it."

Azrea leans into his touch, closing her eyes before she nods. And then, she looks at me with a tearful gaze. "We must act quickly for both of you. If you wouldn't mind retrieving that cup behind you...."

I twist and locate the cup, filling it with water before I pass it to her. Curiously and somewhat repulsively, I watch as she sinks a fang into her palm for a drop of blood to combine with water. Then, my curiosity morphs into awe as, one by one, every faerie in the cave forms a line behind Dolfe to contribute to healing the woman they claim to only tolerate.

Dolfe, Cedric, Brig.... The line seems to never end.

The last male to contribute is Raul—the one with a permanent scowl on his face suddenly replaced with a dip of his chin at my wife for all she's given.

I watch in equal interest when Circe cuts her palm, but her blood isn't red. It's silver, glowing, and reflective. "Mine combined with theirs will combat the Heart Dove's powers," she assures me, freely pouring her blood into the cup.

"The Heart Dove," I repeat. "The male from her nightmares?"

"Yes," Azrea confirms. "He was once High Fae with one-of-a-kind magic. He is frighteningly powerful, Finnian, but even he cannot combat a Healer's touch."

"Part her lips," Circe instructs.

Softly, tenderly, I lean forward and kiss my wife before obeying. "Stay with me, little doe," I murmur, waiting for Circe to pour the mixture of blood and magic through her lips before releasing her jaw. Perhaps too hopeful, I glance at Azrea. "How long?"

"Depends on Elora," she responds woefully.

Releasing a deep breath through my nose as adrenaline returns to full force, I look at Dolfe. "It's time. If I wait until she wakes, she'll try to talk me out of it."

Before I stand, Azrea grabs my hand. "Follow the light," she instructs. "Hold onto it. Death will try to guide you forward. You must hold on until Circe heals you. I will give my blood for you to be one of us..."

I furrow my brow. "Could I...." I glance at Circe. "Could I be a Healer instead?"

Dolfe cocks his head. "Elora will be a Cinder Faerie."

I nod with a sorrowful, knowing grin. "I understand, but I believe I've done enough harm. If possible, I would be honored to do some good if granted another chance in this life."

"Healers are bound to strict guidelines," Circe says. "You will be High Fae, but you will be expected to follow rules that cannot be changed. Are you positive that is what you want?"

A breathy chuckle leaves me as I look down at my wife. "She is what I want. She is all I want. But if I live a long life with her as Fae, she is all the fire I need." I look at Circe with all the strength I can muster through the anxious anticipation of soon taking my last breath. "It's what I want."

Circe looks at Dolfe. "Do not use fire or sever the spinal column. His healing will be quicker if it's strangulation."

"Hades," I breathe, tipping my head back while listening to them discuss how to kill me.

"The things you do for love," Azrea whispers.

I lower my chin, brush Elora's curls from her face, and sigh. "She is well worth the sacrifice. It wouldn't be true love if it was simple." Rising to my feet, I roll my neck and nod. "Let's get this over with."

All I feel is infernal fire in my veins,
All I see is orange and red, igniting,
Everything smolders as flames flood me.
But then, there is blue,
Cool, glacial water coils my spine.
Tethering and tugging,
Calming, Soothing,
Flooding the fire, wrapping around my heart,
Him, him. I feel him surrounding every part.
Deep, unyielding, desperate,
He flows through me.
Such a divine sensation, binding to his soul.
Ebbing and webbing and weaving.
My not-so charming prince,
Such a dream, such wonder,
His rinsing embrace rolling through me like
thunder.

Epilogue

Finnian

The face I awaken to isn't the one I long for, but at least I'm alive. Irina calls for our mother before I can take a waking breath, placing her hand on my forehead and keeping my eyes peeled open. "You idiot!" she screeches in greeting before calling for our mother again.

I try to sit up, but she shoves me back down.

Fatigued, yes, but I also feel so much strength spreading through me that I'm able to push her arms off me and rise.

"Finnian, I swear...." Irina says through clenched teeth, "Lie *down*."

"Elora," I breathe, dizziness rising. I clutch my forehead, then jerk back when I realize my fingertips are black. "It worked," I rasp, holding my hand out, then touching the tip of my ears and wincing from their rawness.

"Yes," Irina says, annoyance evident. "You're fucking Fae now, but you nearly died to become one." She pulls my hands away from my freshly-Fae ears. "Circe almost couldn't bring you back. Your soul apparently went rogue chasing Elora's."

I'm not sure why that surprised anyone.

"Elora—"

"Is alive," she finishes, "but not awake yet."

I move to stand from the cot I'm on, a pull in my chest yanking me toward my wife, taking a second to study my surroundings and recognize the stone walls. "Hogsfeet. We are in Hogsfeet."

Again, she confirms with a nod. "Dolfe brought you down here to heal privately. Elora is next door...."—she shoves me back when I try to stand—"let Mother see you first. Please."

I argue incoherently and try to stand again, but when the door opens and my mother rushes inside, the relief on her face knocks the breath out of me, and I fall back down. She clutches her heart with one hand, covering her mouth with the other as tears fall from her eyes. "My boy!" she cries, her voice muffled. "Oh, my dear boy." She rushes toward me, cradling my face in her hands.

For a second, I am the small boy who desperately wanted to be only a child, safe within my mother's hold.

She studies my ears and face, then looks at my throat with a satisfied nod. "Dolfe was truthful when he said his fingerprints would fade." She glances at me with a frown. "Do you remember anything, Finnian?"

My brow furrows. "Pain," I reply, blinking memories away. "None of it matters. I want to see her."

"You imbecile," Irina scolds. "What were you thinking?"

My eyes narrow on her. "I was thinking that I wanted to be with my wife in death or...." I graze the tip of my ear. "This life, whatever it may be. Tell me you wouldn't have done the same for Massimo, Irina."

With a sigh, she pinches my arm. "You could've waited for me! Did you not think of how terrifying it would be for me to return to both my brother and Elora *dead*?"

"Irina," my mother says gently, "Love makes us choose irrationally sometimes. You cannot fault him."

"I can fucking fault him," she snaps. "I came back here *for him*! For her!" She crosses her arms. "He does not have the power to decide when he dies without first consulting me."

I grimly rub my arm, partially annoyed with my sister for even returning here against my orders. "I told you to stay away until after Jasper was gone—"

She pinches my other arm, and I stand. "Do it again," I challenge, "I am almost positive I could—"

"Enough!" Our mother moves to stand between us. "The two of you have the oddest way of showing your love for one another." She faces me first. "Finnian, your sister is right. We are a family. If this is truly what you wanted, we wouldn't have tried to talk you out of it, but we are owed the respect of knowing when you're about to die by choice."

She turns to Irina next and tucks a piece of hair behind her ear. "You have every right to be upset with him, but you do not get to punish him for choosing his wife above us."

I sigh, loosening my shoulders. "I apologize for worrying you. Azrea said we needed to act quickly. I knew if Elora woke up, she wouldn't allow me to follow her in death or.... this."

Irina rolled her eyes, threw her arms around my neck, and buried her head against my throat. "Idiot," she whispers.

I embrace her with a chuckle before welcoming our mother into it, squeezing them both tightly just as the door opens for Dolfe to step inside. I release them in hopes he's come to tell me that Elora has opened her eyes, but the slight shake of his head deflates me. "Soon," he responds, "but there's something you need to know first."

❧

My mother and Irina stayed behind while Dolfe led me inside Elora's room. I stop, blinking upon seeing her, and remain in the doorway. Azrea sits beside her, Elora's hand in hers, and meets my confusion with an amused grin.

Elora looks... different.

Beautiful, enchanting, bright, and lovely, yet something about her makes me tilt my head.

Her champagne curls remain the same, but red strands have interweaved. Her skin emits a golden glow, warm and healthy, causing my shoulders to sag in relief. Like mine, her ears are pointed, but there's a quality about her that I can't quite place yet.

My heart lurches forward as if needing to be near her, my hands flexing at my sides from the need to touch her. And the itch to taste her overwhelms me.

A flare of warmth nearly consumes me, spreading through my black fingertips. I curl my hands into fists, my brows knitting from confusion. Dolfe steps closer to Elora, and I react by moving between them, baring my teeth at him. The tip of my tongue grazes a fresh fang, pricking deeply enough to draw blood.

His deep laugh echoes through the chamber as he looks behind me at Azrea. "It worked."

My nostrils flare as vanilla and honey flood my senses, causing my neck to roll from the proximity of another male near my....

My lips parted, and I slowly turned back toward Elora.

The pull in my chest upon waking, the instinct to protect her.

"Mate," I breathe, "she's my mate."

Dolfe retreats to the doorway, giving me the respect of not lingering near my wife, but Azrea beams. "It was Circe's idea," she begins. "You were given Circe's blood to be a Healer, but she suggested we add ours since we're mated in hopes of our bond creating one between you."

I crouch as emotion overcomes me. "She's my mate? She's mine?" Tears flood my eyes. "Fate gifted her to me?"

"She's your mate," Azrea murmurs, leaning forward to touch my shoulder. "And your mate is the Phoenix."

I blink. "The Phoenix?"

Dolfe chuckles, a hint of irony in his tone as he says, "Elora is the leader of the Cinder Faeries."

I fall backward to sit, unable to comprehend any of this. And all I can think to say is, "I don't remember reading about that in the book I burned."

Azrea laughs softly and looks at my slumbering wife. "Long

ago, there were leaders of each species of Fae. The Phoenix died many centuries ago, and another never replaced her. She ruled long before my time and lived to be a thousand years before her death. Dolfe knew her."

Dolfe nods his confirmation.

Azrea continues, "The Phoenix is High Fae. She will be awarded immense powers—powers we cannot imagine. Powers I have never seen, even in the Heart Dove."

A low snarl erupts from my throat at the mention of the male who tried draining her heart, almost permanently eliminating her from my life. "Where is he now? I will kill him for what he's done."

"Learn your powers first," Dolfe warns. "Elora's strength will be potent enough to handle any faerie who challenges her reign, but both of you will need time to adjust to them."

I glance at my hands before taking Elora's hand between mine, the tugging in my chest painful. "What is this called?" I whisper.

"A bond," Azrea replies. "It will only grow more intense after she awakens. Once you are connected by joining, nothing will ever be the same for you, Finnian. I know you love her now, but...."

"Let him learn for himself," Dolfe interrupts with a sly grin. "He will have no complaints."

I bring Elora's hands to my lips. "What are my powers? What are hers?"

"We will not know what Elora's are until her eyes open. You are a Healer." With her free hand, Azrea taps the tips of my black fingers. "All of your power resides here but lives in your blood. Circe will teach you and assist you in learning how to heal."

I loosen an impatient sigh. "Why is Ellie taking so long to open her eyes?"

Dolfe approaches behind me with a gravelly chuckle, squeezing my shoulder. "She is healing. Circe needed to mend her bones. Once you died, your souls tried to join together. Circe had difficulty prying you apart. We didn't realize she would become the Phoenix, but the mark appeared once Circe restored Elora."

I lift an eyebrow. "What kind of mark?"

Dolfe moves to my side, lifts his palms in the air, and slowly inches closer to Elora. I would peg him for being overdramatic, but it does take considerable self-control not to spring to my feet and restrain him. With a swift movement, he leans forward, turns her head slightly and very gently, and instructs me to move her hair.

Fisting her curls in my hand, I lift them and tilt my head. On the top of her spine, a silhouette of a bird in orange and red flame rests boldly on her skin.

I blink when it moves and twists its head toward me, the flames glowing brighter. "Is that... normal?"

Dolfe removes his hand from her. "The Phoenix is more than Fae. She is a symbol of change."

"And hope," Azrea adds.

My heart swells in my chest. Elora deserved nothing less than the highest honor, given the life she had lived and the outlook she always maintained.

Being mated to her is the highest privilege.

"We would like to stay," Azrea adds, her tone hesitant. "If it is all right with you and Elora, we want to stay. Circe has agreed to be with me until the babe is born and until you are comfortable as a Healer."

"Of course, you may stay." I scoot closer to Elora and kiss her forehead. "Unless Elora disagrees, which I don't imagine she will, you are always welcome here."

Azrea winces with a small smile. "Elora has no choice in sending us away or allowing us to go. She is our leader, Finnian. Where she goes, we follow. We are bound to her, just as you are as her mate."

I tip my head back in laughter. "Have you informed the others of this? I would've liked to see the looks on their faces."

"Raul was overjoyed," Dolfe mutters.

My laughter lightens into a chuckle as I peer over at my wife, sleeping soundly and beautifully.

Elora was perfect before the change, but now.... Well, I anticipate removing eyes from many males for staring at her. I am anxious for my first kill.

Leaning forward, I press my lips to her temple before whispering in her ear, “Wake soon, little doe. I need to see your smile. And other things.”

Elora’s response is a slow, deep breath.

“She can hear you,” Azrea assures me.

The tug in my chest tightens. “What now?”

Azrea broadly grins at my sleeping doe. “Now, we wait for her to rise.”

Acknowledgments

Dear Reader,

Wow! I can't believe we reached this point. Rise of the Cinder Fae was definitely a labor of love, but I am so happy I pushed through to the end. If you haven't followed my story, you might not be aware that this book almost didn't happen. I nearly gave in to an abuse of power, but it's because of readers like that you that I shoved that aside and continued writing Elora and Finn's story. And because of it, I am so much happier with how it ended.

Originally a standalone, the more I wrote and rewrote over the course of six weeks, the more I realized that Elora just wasn't finished telling her story yet. And because of her insistence, she will have a very prominent role in the next installment of The Dark Hearts Fairytale Retelling series.

If you're reading this, and if you've continuously supported me through this journey, I am so endlessly grateful for you. I would not be here writing this letter if it wasn't because of your constant encouragement.

Here is to many more stories with morally grey men obsessed with their women and women who learn just how worthy they are of the entire world.

Never underestimate your power.

Never fear your fire.

All my love,
Whitney

Milton Keynes UK
Ingram Content Group UK Ltd.
UKHW010016020324
438794UK00014B/133/J